OF HEXES AND *Hatred*

H. L. HAMILTON

Dedication

To those that are going through something,
This is your down payment to something amazing.
Better is coming and it will be so worth it. Hang in there.

"The light is brighter when we emerge from the darkness."
—Locke

Trigger Warning

Because your mental health matters!

This book touches on some darker themes and may not be appropriate for all readers. Besides the emotional damage H. L. Hamilton has in store for you, you can expect a little of the following themes; sexually explicit content, graphic violence, torture, allusions to knife play, mild bondage.

Contents

Map

Port Azure
Voidcall
The Dead Forest
Everwind
Bleak
The Water Court
The Air Court
Frostfall
Loc Valen
Scarlett Summit
Coldcross
Veinfall Mountains
Wayisle Pass
Poplar Hollow
Yemiran Vale
The Deep Wild
The Earth Court
The Fire Court
AKA Everday Isle
Puxaura
Infernum
Oakenshade
The Burnished Basin
Shield's Crossing
Meridian

Prologue

Scorpio

I should be dead. I thought I would be, based on all that I've researched. Once the black magic is too entrenched into your soul, aren't you supposed to die? Instead, it feels as if I've been split and both halves simply feel like they're perpetually dying but never actually finding the sweet release of death. Or perhaps the Grievling has found a way to toy with me from the Echo Isles, the rotten bastard that he is.

There have been two versions of me for five years: this version—the pained version who agonizes and regrets the curse, and the version who takes charge and works to end it, and the two are never in agreeance. At least in method. I'm well aware that when I lose blocks of time, I never want to know what I've done. I've learned the hard way not to ask questions. Not to look closely at the blood on my hands, whether metaphorical or literal. Both parts of me understand how cowardly it is.

I can't bring myself to care.

Nor can I seem to stop. Even when I'm aware. I'm terrified that even if I did try to stop what the other part of me is doing, it may fracture my mind further, which begs the question: what will be left of me in that case? So, I let it happen, I bury my head in the sand, and hope that I can make amends later. That I'll have decades, possibly even centuries to redeem myself. In my heart of hearts, I need this pain to stop. I can't breathe, can't think, without everything hurting.

I deserve it to stop.

The previous Scorpio's reign ended in bloodshed and suffering, and my entire reign has been nothing but more of the same. I'm beginning to think the title of Scorpio is cursed, not just me. But perhaps it's a silly fantasy I made up to ebb the steady undercurrent of guilt when my head comes above water. Lately, I try my best to stay under as long as possible. As much as it feels like drowning, it feels better than the alternative.

To face what I've done.

Chapter One

Lark

"**Y**ou will hear my voice again when the time comes and you need it most."

In my head all I could hear, all I could see, were the overlapping images of my death, of Scorpio's hands around my throat, and Amaya still drowning in the Vale. My mind saw both scenes clearly, distinctly. Her final message to me floating back in such a forceful way I almost looked around the room for her. Her final words to me were a tragic backdrop in my mind, mixing with Locke's confession yesterday: *I would suffer the curse to die once I loved him in return.* Scorpio laughing, punctuating each ominous word. But as I dug deeper into the fear, I found sprouts of hope I hadn't noticed before. Now, instead of images of death and dismay, I saw my body arch from lightning, my body bowing from the force. I felt, rather than see, my heart restarting, which meant only one thing.

I could survive this.

We could break all the curses and survive them.

"What are you talking about?" Locke's ocean and sunshine eyes searched mine for the answer my voice couldn't seem to say, his body falling eerily still. His breathing stuttered to a halt as he assessed me. The only movement and sound came from the sloshing suds of the tub, having been disturbed by my jolting awake and turning to face him. I didn't need his powers as Prince Cancer to see the guarded fragile hope building in his eyes like the first tentative blooms of spring, despite winters chill still clinging to the ground. I could feel that same hope rising in my own rapidly beating heart.

That was what Amaya had said that day in the Vale. And this—I felt it echoing in my bones—this is when our situation became most dire. Scorpio required my death to break her curse. And now that death was assured because of Locke's. This changes everything, I realized in this moment of clarity. No longer would we have to fight to capture an unkillable adversary and contain her long term. No longer would we have to search for a way to break a curse without my death.

A way that most likely didn't exist.

Frantic and scattered fragments of thought escaped my lips about what Amaya had sent me from beyond the grave. I rose from the tub, not caring for the bubbles and water making a slippery mess as I paced about. With a small flourish of my air magic, I dried my body before donning my earlier discarded robe. Locke followed me into the bedroom. I could see his desire to wrench my rampaging thoughts in my head from me, but he remained stoically silent. I could see the roiling tension controlling and stiffening each movement of his body as he donned a pair of pants. His eyes never left me as I paced erratically around the room in time with my thoughts when at last he caught my hand gently and bade me to stop before him.

"Lark, please." His voice was strained, and low, and desperate, and made my heart ache. His hands roamed my arms, his eyes searching mine. "I can read emotions, but not thoughts. I really need you to tell me what you just realized, love. Your emotions are too erratic to read."

"The lightning," I said, slowly coming out of my own head. I blinked up at him, and really saw him for the first time since I awoke, my thoughts and my reality finally melding together and coexisting. "The lightning is the loophole we've been needing!"

The vision rushed back to me in a flood of memory. I couldn't suppress a shudder as I recalled the eerie feeling of watching myself die in third person. The kind of horror that would haunt the edges of my nightmares for years to come. Of not being able to move while I watched Scorpio's hands around my throat, the savage triumph in her eyes as the light at last left my own. His grip tightened on my hand as if he could keep me on his plane if he held onto me hard enough. I told him about the cold feeling of death. And then as I watched myself die, my heart finally stopping, the lightning crashed down from the heavens, perhaps by the Goddess herself, and collide with my heart. How it burned. But how it made my heart beat once more. How I felt the curse shatter within me like glass fragments.

"The lightning will restart my heart." Conviction surged through my words, my only evidence being a dream, and yet I couldn't shake this feeling of absolute certainty that had found purchase. That calm resolution. Locke's hardened stare gave away his racing mind, doubt evident his posture. "Locke, we can't break the curse. But we can work around it! I have to die—" He flinched, and I placed my hand on his cheek, using my thumb to smooth away the crease forming near his eyes. "But nothing says I have to stay that way. Not only will your curse, our curse now, be ended, but we can finally take down Scorpio."

I could see the vague fragments of a plan falling into place. We could save the Water Court. Save everyone. And Locke and I could have a future. A real future as soulmates.

Locke's face turned from doubtful to bewildered, to angry and back again but underneath it lay something darker. More turbulent. His pained stare almost knocked the wind from me, the sheer gravity of it, before disappearing behind the curtain of raven hair. The periodic ticking of his jaw was the only movement for several long heartbeats, but in his eyes I could see ghosts of a past never fully forgotten catching up to him. Ghosts I knew nothing about.

"Speak to me," I whispered. He didn't answer right away. That anguished stare only deepened. The same one he'd first worn when I told him I loved him. Was that really only last night?

"You're asking me to watch you die," he said in a gravelly voice, accompanied by a slight rumble around me. The flickering of his magic cast tremors in the air, a sure sign that despite his relatively calm appearance his emotions were running haywire just beneath the surface. My heart wrenched for him. He tilted his head as if examining everything I'd said to him in his mind. "You're asking me not just to watch you die, but to allow it to happen. Something I swore I would protect you from. Under the mere *hope* that we can bring you back? You're asking me to stand by and let Scorpio, of all fae, murder the most important person in the world to me." His massive hands came up to cover mine near his face. "Am I hearing you correctly?"

I paused. When he said it like that, I could clearly hear how ridiculous it sounded. How very farfetched. But I held to the feeling of calm certainty I felt in the dream. In Amaya's vision. Of her voice from beyond the veil. Goosebumps erupted along my arms as I stared up at him in absolution.

"Yes."

"Why?" A simple question. A loaded question, paired with an equally loaded look. But it wasn't a simple, or uncomplicated answer. Feeling jittery, my legs moved in short, shuffling strides about the room, a reluctant pacing of their own accord. Locke stood still, eerily so by comparison, intently watching my every move as if I might disappear before him.

"It's our one and only chance to survive the curse and save the entire Water Court. You've looked for years to save them. This is that chance, Locke. Port Azure can be free. We can be free. Free of Scorpio, free of the curse, all of it. I refuse to be pushed to the side anymore." I stopped to stand before him again, raised my hands to cup his face gently. "I have a role to play here now. I can help. Or are soulmates not equal in relationships?"

"Of course you are, Lark. But—"

"This is a risk I'm willing to take. I *want* to take it. I believe that Amaya sent me that vision in good faith." I kept my voice gentle. I found myself standing directly in front of him again, wishing I could take the sorrow from him. I smoothed my thumb over his pinched expression again, hoping I was comforting him. He had that faraway look that told me he was scanning my emotions, seeing my resolve. "Locke, I'm going to die regardless of what we do here. This way, my death can save everyone and we stand a chance at bringing me back. We have a single chance at the future we want. But I can't do it without you."

"Tell me how." His gaze shifted then to showcase a hardened jawline, anger hinting there. "Tell me how I'm supposed to watch the most important Fae in the world to me die like it isn't going to rip my heart out. Like it isn't going to kill me too."

From a place I thought was buried yesterday, indignation flared. "I've only been the most important fae to you for a day, Locke." My voice was cooler than I'd expected. His eyes flared in response.

"You know that's not true." Locke's voice was somewhere between a whisper and a snarl. The volume didn't change, but the electricity between us surged as he spoke. "You've only known how important to me you are for a day. There's a very big difference, *soulmate*."

His words effectively stopped whatever argument was about to leave my lips. My breath stilled in my chest as Locke's gaze warred with mine. A battle of wills. Locke still didn't move. Not even a flicker in his eyes. The air shifted, getting thicker with each inhale.

"I will not yield on this, *soulmate*." I matched his tone. My eyes didn't waver from his. I didn't even blink. "This plan will work."

Eternity seemed to move by us when at last Locke let out a breath, though the anguish and skepticism on his face didn't falter.

"Let's call this plan B." His voice wasn't entirely calm. I could hear the cracks in his restraint. In his resolve. His anger was palpable at not having another option readily available, though I couldn't say I blamed him entirely.

"What's plan A?"

"I'll let you know when I come up with it." Grasping my forearm, he tugged me further into his embrace and I offered no resistance. I rested my head against his chest, listening to the rapid thump of his heart. My own heart responded in kind. I tasted blood. I let go of my lip, unaware I'd even bitten it. Even though I knew this was our best chance, a twinge of uncertainty formed in my gut, warring with the calm I had just moments before. In my heart of hearts, I knew that this was a long shot. That the future I was fighting for was like sand through my fingers. That the likelihood of my permanent death was high. That Scorpio would win. We had to orchestrate everything to the last detail.

"Oh, Crowned Assassin," I murmured, hoping to lighten both of our moods, "my plan will work. It can give us the happy ending we deserve. I just need you to believe in it." If he could believe, I knew I could too. I held to the certainty I'd felt only minutes ago as if it were my last lifeline, and I suppose in a way, it was exactly that.

"I'm trying," he whispered into my hair before placing a gentle kiss and tightening his arms around me, holding me as if I might disappear from him this very moment. "Until I do, I'll just believe in you. But believe me when I say this,; I will never let you go. If I lose you..." he cleared his throat, his voice losing all tones of doubt and indecision and in its wake was the quiet reverberation of certainty, "if I lose you, then the veil of death had best lock itself away. Because I'll pry it apart to bring you back. Mark my words, Lark."

My breath failed me. Because I knew without a doubt that he was telling the truth.

We stayed locked like that for a long time. It could have been minutes or hours, I wasn't sure. I melted into him as he rested his chin on my head. I closed my eyes, breathed him in, and loved him fiercely with my whole heart. I hoped he could see my emotions now. My resolve, but also my feelings for him.

"What else happened in your dream?" The quiet of his voice startled me, breaking me out of my reverie. It wasn't his usual quiet, like the soft kiss of a shadow. It was calculating, a hint of his mind whirring to come up with any other plan. "Can you give me any more details of your vision? We need to examine everything."

I told him every detail that I could remember. The rocky terrain which it took place. The iciness of Scorpio's hands, how powerless I'd been to stop her. The burning in my chest from the lightning.

"Where did the lightning come from?" That was the final piece of the puzzle that I couldn't seem to place, I thought. Water, earth, and fire magic had no claim over lightning. So I could only assume it was a gift of air magic, but doubt nagged me. Perhaps it was old magic. Or was it possible dark magic could summon such a thing? I wracked my brain, searching the memory of my vision for any sign of Locke's black magic, telltale black threads of wispy shadow. I found none. When I asked Locke, he shook his head.

"The shadows can't summon lightning. That I know of." His voice trailed off. When he spoke again, his voice had turned soft and thoughtful, matching the furrow of his brow. "Though, I'm forever finding more and more that its limits don't seem to exist the way I thought." I knew he was talking about Pisces. About Frostfall. About being under the other Water Prince's spell. That flash of wrath, and the quiet retribution brewing under his skin made the air crackle. "But lightning falls within Air Court's jurisdiction. And one fae in particular..."

"Let me guess. It's not just any fae, is it? You're talking about another Zodiac?" He nodded, his lips pursed a moment in consideration. I sighed. Of course it wasn't someone we could have easy access to.

"Aquarius is Princess of the Air court. She possesses an uncanny ability to control storms with terrifying accuracy. Including lightning. She's one of the few who can harness lightning the way she can. Many in air court never manifest that particular ability."

"She doesn't happen to owe you a big favor, does she?" I asked flicking my eyes up at him. Once again, his shaking head dismantled any illusions of this being straightforward. I wondered if the Goddess were laughing at us. Why was it that dire circumstances could not be resolved in a simple manner?

"No. We'll have to arrange an audience with her. Perhaps an arrangement can be made."

"You intend to bargain with her?" I felt my jaw drop. Fae bargains, much like promises, were laced in magic. One wrong word, one purposeful miscommunication, and you could find yourself on the receiving end of a lot of misfortune and pain. Fae had died from not thinking bargains through well enough. Or at the very least had been duped out of what they wanted, but the worst was when they gave you what you wanted, but so snared up in conditions, you'd wish you'd never bargained for it in the first place. Scorpio's situation was proof enough of that.

His eyes cut me and room for debate down with ease. "There is nothing I won't do if it secures her help, Lark. I'll pay any price."

"Locke, I—" He cut me off with his lips landing roughly over mine, his hands threading into my hair briefly.

"I'm going to speak very plainly: I will not rest until we find our plan A. But plan B is a failsafe, and in order for it to work, I will do what I can to ensure we have what we need. Including Aquarius." His tone gentled then. "I have loved you since the Yemerian Vale. I've not had enough time with you, and I'm not letting you go. I meant what I said before. The veil of death will not take you."

"Love at first sight isn't real. Don't flatter me with pretty words." I meant it to be teasing, but as the words left my mouth, I wanted to clamp my teeth on them and drag them back from whence they came. He scoffed at my words, a small, but sincere smile forming on his lips. He averted his gaze almost... shyly?

"It is with soulmates," he murmured. His voice never lost that gentle timbre as he continued. His hand reached for mine, threading our fingers together. "They recognize each other intrinsically. I knew immediately that day in the Vale who you'd be to me. I felt the realization physically anchor me to the ground and it felt like being struck by lightning all at once. I almost fell out of the tree I was in—that would've been quite the introduction." He chuckled, drawing a growing smile from me. I could feel my heart warming. A rush of love so potent even he glanced at me when he saw my aura. I didn't need his abilities to see the love shining in his eyes, a silent answer. He reached down, clasping one of my hands and squeezing it, and my heart right along with it. "Everything changed in that moment. I knew exactly what would happen if I got too close. That was why I pushed you away. And it's also why I couldn't stay away. I'm a selfish bastard. I loved you. From the moment I saw what you did for Amaya, I knew you were exactly the kind of faerie I would have wanted to fall in love with. I knew I needed just a little bit of time with you. Just a little before I made you hate me and I could let you go. And fate gave you the perfect reason. I could live with myself, with the decisions I've made, so long as you were safe."

I had to remember to breathe before I picked my jaw up off the floor. He gave me a halfhearted smile before pressing his lips to mine. I wrapped my arms around his neck, pulling him closer to me, pouring that overwhelming surge of love into it. He thread his fingers into my hair as his lips slid against mine. Never in my entire life had I felt more seen. More understood. More loved. It also made my own experience make sense. Why even when I despised him, I never fully could. I felt drawn to him, entranced by him, even when I didn't want to.

"Who knew" I said with a softly curling grin, "that you could be so romantic?" He chuckled before capturing my lips again, his tongue darting out along the seam of my mouth.

"Don't tell anyone. I have a reputation to uphold," he whispered with an edge of conspiracy. My smile widened in earnest, delight sparking in my veins. His eyes roamed me teasingly, mischief lighting his eyes before planting a kiss on the hollow of my throat. "I have to say though, your swooning has improved dramatically since Aramithia."

"Oh, I'm glad you noticed. I had some practice." He pinned me with a look of mock anger, raising an eyebrow at me. I winked at him, further provoking him. He stuck his face in the crook of my neck, making me shriek with laughter with his stubble across my ticklish flesh.

"Oh really? Who have you been swooning for?" he asked, unrelenting on his assault on my neck. I could barely answer through the fit of laughter.

"Some arrogant fae prince with a massive ego."

"Oh, so the worst kind. You have terrible taste in partners. Tell me what's so great about him," he said, finally granting me a reprieve and allowing my needy lungs a breath before I turned purple in the face, but he still didn't let me go.

"What can I say? I like the way he kisses me." His eyes darkened at that admission. "And you should see how strong he is. I couldn't imagine taking him on in a fight."

"He sounds fearsome. Handsome. He's probably hilarious too." He winked. "And quite the charmer."

"Yeah. Too bad his personality is a giant red flag." He cocked an eyebrow at me indignantly. "But apparently red-flag red is my favorite color." He grinned down at me in abject amusement. I traced the lines of his face with my eyes, the ridge of his nose, the exact placement of his dimple—only on the left, the high cheek bones, slightly crooked smile, strong jaw....

I took him in as if I could commit his face, this moment, to memory and stay here forever. I didn't want to forget a single detail.

"I love you," I told him. But that couldn't be all I said. Not with the way he poured his heart out just now. I stumbled, reaching awkwardly for the words. He watched me with a strange expression, caught somewhere between our previous teasing and our current emotional turn, which created a flicker of vulnerability.

A look I cherished. Because it was a look I knew he only wore for me. Prince Cancer, the Crowned Assassin, one of the most feared entities in all of Meridian, was vulnerable for me. It was time I returned that favor. Show him I was as here for him, as he was for me. That he wasn't alone in this moment.

"It was strange. Upon arriving here, I knew I should be weary of you. And I was at first." A small smile turned up the corners of my lips, ever so slightly. In my mind's eye, I vividly remembered meeting him in the Vale. And how I thought I was done for. I remembered the blade in his hand. Before I knew it, my mind flicked through all our moments of its own accord: fighting for my life and discovering my magic, his supposed betrayal, his magic lessons. The feel of lips on mine when he pinned me to the sparring mat. I remembered when he gave me Valor. I remembered when he told me he loved me in Frostfall. And how my heart stopped.

How very far we'd come in such a short period of time.

Locke's eyes sparkled at his own recollection but said nothing. "But after that moment in the clearing, after we discovered my magic, it was like something clicked into place. I can't really explain it. Even when I thought you'd—" I choked, unable to say the words. Locke's hand covered mine again; comforting, patient, and ever supportive, he waited for me to continue. But I didn't miss the remorse shadowing his face. "After what I thought I'd seen, I knew logically I shouldn't trust you. But some small part of me never fully believed it. Even with me seeing you standing over my father's body. After you pushed me away, after you gave me every reason to think you killed him.... It only made me hate both of us. I couldn't stop feeling drawn to you, which I'm now understanding was my soul connecting to yours." He nodded. "When Pisces told me he was the one... relief like I'd never known before hit me. Because it wasn't you. I could stop hating us both."

"I hated lying to you." Locke breathed, the crease in his brow deepening. "In the early days, your hatred and sorrow killed me. Every night you woke from a nightmare, I felt your fear, your pain, your panic. I sat outside your door. I wished I could be there for you. Comfort you. I knew my presence was the last thing you wanted... but I couldn't stand the thought of you being truly alone. You didn't know it, but I was there feeling your pain and suffering alongside you."

The selflessness of it all hit me not for the first time, squeezing my heart in its painful grip. He let me think the worst of him. For months. So I would hate him. So I wouldn't love him. He played with my emotions just enough that I would hate him more.

"I wouldn't say I played with your emotions, love." Seemingly reading my thoughts for the umpteenth time, he continued, "I actually couldn't stay away. Soulmates are naturally very drawn to one another and actively seek each other out once they find each other, even unconsciously. But it did kind of work in my favor, you thinking I was toying with you."

"I'm so glad it's over," I said. "There's nowhere else I'd rather be than here with you like this." Neither of us mentioned the ticking time bomb of the curse. The feeling of my life draining like grains of sand in an hourglass. We definitely didn't mention that Scorpio was catching up with us and held most of the advantages over everyone we loved.

Chapter Two

"Rise and shine Little Bird!" Aspen said by way of greeting and clapped me on the back, interrupting my yawn. I scowled at him as I tried to yawn again, stretching my arms over my head and blinking away the lingering sleepiness. Hell's Gate was full of warriors sparring; the clashing of metal and shouts made Aspen have to raise his voice slightly. "What? Your new boyfriend keep you up all night?" I shot him a warning glare that he ignored. "Rookie mistake." He poked my ribs near my underarm just at the climax of the yawn. I felt my eyebrow twitch in response. A few moments later, he was still staring expectantly at me. "Well? How was it?"

"Aspen!" I snapped, my temper flaring. Aspen's smile widened into his characteristic grin and his eyes promised mischief. A sure sign that he was going to be the utmost of pests. I mourned my luck.

"Yes?"

"Fuck off with your bullshit. It's way too early." I began yawning once more, tears now forming in my eyes, desperate for completion. I kept my eye on him, and refused to stretch in case I needed to fend off another unwanted poke.

Only for his finger to sneak up on my uvula. Interrupting my yawn for a third time.

A girl can only take so much this early in the morning. He chose his fate. Best friend or not.

My fist flew out and connected with his jawline before I even made the conscious decision to do it. Although, I probably would have made the conscious decision to do it. Knowing full well he would make me pay for it later on in the form of pushups. Why was it always pushups? He backed away just in time, my knuckles only dragging across his skin.

"What part about it being too early did you miss?" I folded my arms with a sigh. Aspen shrugged his response, the smile never disappearing from his face.

"Nothing. But you looked like you needed some help waking up." He waggled his eyebrows one at a time in such a goofy manner, I had to fight not to smirk. "I'd say mission accomplished."

"And you decided to wake me up by yawn edging me?"

Aspen looked at me with a bewildered expression before bursting out laughing. "Yawn edging!" he wheezed out, finally giving me the momentary reprieve it desperately craved. My jaw clicked and my chest expanded, stretching my ribs in the most glorious way. I finished my yawn loudly with my arms stretched above my head. I finally relaxed, limbs now hanging languidly to the side. "Feel better?" he asked, recovering from his amusement, though his eyes still twinkled.

"More or less." I huffed, trudging towards him now that my yawn was completed. I'd do better with a few more hours of sleep, but I knew I wouldn't be getting that. If anything, I got the distinct impression training was going to be longer and more intense. He tsked.

"You've got to have more energy than that, Lark!" he said as he sent me for my warmup routine I was in no mood for. His annoying morning person good mood grated on my nerves extra today. "I have something special set up just for you."

Sounding that ominous sounding this early in the morning should be illegal.

Aspen wasn't kidding.

Apparently, I'd impressed him so much that it was time to take everyone else on. Hand to hand sparring with everyone else. Some of them looked at me now as we approached the main sparring ring where everyone gathered around. I couldn't see through the throng of jeering fae, but the sounds of fists and feet impacting soft flesh and the resulting grunts of pain reached me. I felt some turn to eye me, some with curiosity, some with disdain. Some looked at me like an easy meal. I almost laughed at the way some of them sized me up, as if my small stature would stop me from competing with them. As if Aspen hadn't just trained me one on one for several weeks. I just hoped my confidence wasn't undeserved, but after the fight with Pisces, these fae felt less intimidating.

"I have someone special for you to spar with," Aspen said, becoming their general, our general, in a blink. His entire tone changed from that of my best friend to the hardness he needed to display. It was strange seeing him command attention like that. Bring all eyes to him. He gestured for me to enter the ring with one final pat on the shoulder. I moved on still limbs, hating the weight of every eye on me.

"I've been waiting for this," a voice said from the crowd, removing all gazes from me. My lips pressed together to see a hulking fae step forward. He was easily over a foot taller than me. I considered my training. His reach advantage was significant too. He grinned at me, showing canines as he stared at me. "Let's go Queen's Mark. That's what they call you, isn't it? Or would you prefer little girl?"

"Funny, I was just about to ask you the same thing." Chuckles and jeers sounded around us. Directly behind me I heard someone taking bets on whether Kirath would accidentally kill me. The fae in question glared at me before redirecting his attention to Aspen.

"When are you going to find me someone worth fighting?" He made a not-so-subtle show of ripping his shirt off and showing off his corded musculature. "This hardly even seems like a fair fight."

"If you underestimate her because of her gender, you'll be in for a rude awakening, Kirath. She took down a Zodiac, don't you forget." His tone or his words, possibly both, only served to fuel Kirath's chagrin.

"As if a female could take me down." He looked down his nose at me, smugness taking over his entire face, making it more than obvious what he thought of me. I stepped towards him onto the mat, keeping my gaze level with his.

"Sexism. How refreshing," I deadpanned.

Kirath grinned as he lazily walked up, as if he wasn't keeping me and Aspen waiting. Other fae filtered in, surrounding us. The crowd was growing and becoming louder. I couldn't help the nervous look I gave Aspen. He nodded his encouragement at me as we made final preparations for our match.

"You can take him, but don't get sloppy. He may be an ass, but he's one of our best. He can back up that attitude. He's a good fighter, but he's not terribly smart or imaginative. Use that to your advantage." Aspen's warning sounded in my ear as his final words of wisdom before he walked off the mat, allowing the fight to begin.

I raised my fists and dropped into my fighting stance, grounded and maneuverable, while he circled me like prey. I watched him intently, ready for him to make the first move.

"What's the matter, little girl? Are you scared to go up against someone who isn't going to go easy on you?" Chuckling sounded around the mat. Clearly, he wasn't alone in his opinions. I didn't allow him to goad me into a response. I just waited patiently for my opening.

Thankfully, a distinct lack of patience was a flaw we both suffered from. He didn't keep me waiting. He pressed forward, faster than I expected, his fist sailing straight towards my face. But I was fast too.

I ducked under his arm, my own flailing out and connecting with the soft flesh near his kidney, his grunt of irritation only fueling my smirk. His knee caught me straight in the chin, sending me flying backwards. Pain and irritation mixed to a strange combination, allowing me to focus on him. To zero in on his movements. I cracked my neck, alleviating some of the discomfort welling in my upper spine. He was saying something else asinine, but I couldn't hear it. I was watching. Waiting for his next move.

He had a size advantage over me, and a reach advantage. So, I'd need to remain quick and move in and out with strikes, otherwise one well-placed hit from him and it would be over. Stick close so he couldn't use his reach advantage with any degree of effectiveness or stay far away. And at this point, he reminded me so much of the fae back in Poplar Hollow, it was starting to feel a little too personal. And with all the stress I'd been under, it was time to let go.

I dove forward close to his body, catching him by surprise, darting in with a quick combo to his torso, and only just ducking out of his reach. His fist sailed by my face with sheer millimeters to spare.

"Good, Lark!" Aspen's voice reached me above the murmur of the crowd. Above my focus. "Keep that up."

"Yeah, little girl, I've got you pegged now. Do keep it up. Show us what you're made of. I dare you." He punched the air in warning, fists flying around the combination, bouncing on the balls of his feet. I saw that razor sharp edge to his focus. He was watching and analyzing every move I made. He was a lot bigger than me. I had to be smart about this. I dodged one attack and took another kick to the torso. My ribs screamed at the impact, my breath leaving me entirely. I launched a punch that was quickly blocked with ease. He smirked at me through a furrowed brow, the message clear: *you won't win*. His fists arced towards me in a graceful and deadly flurry, and even with my one-on-one sparring sessions with Aspen I wasn't fast enough to deflect them all. My cheekbone throbbed where his leather cuffed fists slammed into it, followed by one just off my chin. I fell back, my head dazed as I glared up at him. I had to change tactics. What I was doing isn't working.

"You know what? I've thought of a better nickname for her, guys," he addressed the crowd. "Cupcake. She's so small and smash-able, I don't think she even looks like she belongs here." He looked around, proud of himself before setting his sights back on me. "What are you going to do next, Cupcake?"

I saw red. I was about to launch into an onslaught of attacks when an idea came to me, blocking out the laughter of his friends. Aspen said he wasn't the smartest. Hopefully Kirath didn't know much about levers.

I hauled myself to my feet, wiping the blood from my mouth. I inwardly cringed at the tenderness and swelling that had already made themselves apparent. Then, without giving myself time to second guess, I launched. Darting for him again, I readied to deflect the hit I knew was coming. My forearms were acutely sore at the contact, but better than my face taking another direct hit. My face was in close proximity to his shoulder, my arms around his torso and one of his arms in a hold, praying he wasn't about to guess my game.

"Are we sparring or snuggling?" he asked before using his free dominant hand to deliver a massive blow to my side, making me cry out at last. The first sound I'd made this entire time as my abdomen spasmed around the pain. I nearly dropped—only by sheer will and the fact he only just missed my liver did I find the strength to stay on my feet. He laughed. I gripped his pinned wrist and he didn't object too much, unsure of my play. He launched another fist destined for the same spot, driving down with everything he had....

And I shrugged out from under him, knocking him off balance. One single well-timed leg sweep from me and he was on his knees. Before he could rise, I was already turning, my fist connecting with his now reachable chin with everything I had. And my next one, each one feeling like redemption and revenge all in one. I rounded on him while he was busy seeing stars, gaining his back while he was slowed. My elbow met his neck as I attached myself like an unwanted pest to his back and refused to let go, effectively choking him as he struggled. He rose with a hiss, hammer punched my legs—the only thing he could reach—but I held strong, taking everything he had to dish out until he started to fall back to his knees, his movements becoming close to nothing. When unconsciousness was close to greeting him, I allowed him the air he so desperately needed. I left him down on the mat and I hovered over him, ready to deliver the final blow in front of the now silent crowd: his ego.

"Come find me again when you learn how to fight, *Cupcake*," I said before walking off the mat towards Aspen, whose mouth hung slightly open. "How'd I do, General?"

Aspen smiled widely as he clapped me on the shoulder. I winced, his palm contacting a welt—a parting gift from Kirath, who was slowly gaining his wits about him again.

"You know what, Lark? I don't usually play favorites, but that was unforgettable to every fae in that arena. Just like I knew would happen." An energy I hadn't felt all morning zipped through me, electrifying my limbs.

"Was this a test?"

He shook his head.

"Consider it an initiation of sorts. Now everyone knows what you're made of. You'll be training with everyone from now on, not just me. You officially graduate from solely sparring poles and wooden weapons too."

"Are you saying what I think you're saying?" I asked, my words coming out breathy and disbelieving, my tone completely at odds with the energy lighting up my veins. My best friend smiled at me, the face of pure, unadulterated pride. For me. He crossed the sparring ring to the poles and grasped something hidden behind the rack. Something that glinted, something with a red ruby on the hilt. Something very familiar that made a lump form in my throat.

My father's sword.

I didn't understand why I was so emotional. I had fought with it only yesterday. Aspen presented it to me, beckoning me to take it. I grasped it, and drew the sword, the ringing out sounding louder than it should have in the surrounding chaos. But I found the world fading away. The blade had been thoroughly cleaned; I'm guessing I had Aspen to thank for that kindness. It gleamed in a way my father would have appreciated. But the fact that Aspen thought I was ready, that I was at last at a level of strength and control that he trusted me with a blade...

I couldn't quash the rising squeal in me even if I tried.

Aspen made a show of wincing and protecting his ears.

"Yes, yes, very exciting." He clapped me on the shoulder in congratulations with a wide smile and a surreptitious look back at Kirath, who glared at me from where his friend was healing his wounds. I fought my instinct to wave. Instead, I turned my back on him, which might have made him even more angry. "You did well, but you have a lot to learn. Once we heal those nasty looking welts you've got going on."

I grinned, determination and motivation running fresh through me as I followed his instructions with some fire in me. I grasped my father's sword, feeling not for the first time that he was with me.

Chapter Three

Aspen wasn't finished with me yet though. Not by a longshot. According to him, this was our last solo session, and he was going to make the most of it. Aspen ran me through sword drills, giving me what I wanted finally. A clash of steel on steel was as satisfying as it was exhausting, leaving my entire body feeling obliterated. I almost collapsed into a heap before Aspen released me and told me to go cool down and stretch.

I didn't need further invitation. I sank to the ground to stretch my exhausted and burning leg muscles.

"I hate you," I muttered as Aspen approached me with a cannister of water. He grinned at the lack of bite in my voice.

"No, you don't," he answered, his voice entirely unbothered as he handed it to me. He sat down next to me, his hands already glowing with that green healing energy I liked him for so much. Or so I kept telling him. "I'd rather see you sweat than see you bleed, Lark," he said as his magic soaked into my skin and I sighed at the offering of resplendent relief. "In here we train till we drop so we don't drop dead out there."

I nodded mutely. I didn't want to admit it, but his words struck a chord with me. Inadvertently, my mind saw the bodies of those laid out in Poplar Hollow. In Frostfall. The stillness of them, of their gazes. I remembered our collective terror when Pisces put that spell on Locke. I remember when there was a split second I thought he might win. I didn't want that to be me with the blank eyes. Or anyone else I loved. And with all that stood against us, Aspen was right. I shuddered as my muscles slowly began to unknot themselves from the tight cords they'd been strung in, not just from Aspen's rigorous training routine.

"What's on your mind?" His voice shook me from my wayward thoughts. I watched instead his steady hands and their green magic hovering over the tender muscles in my legs. He looked around for listening ears, but with all the training and commotion around us partnered with our distance, we had privacy I was grateful for. "I'm worried when you're this quiet." My empty smile did nothing to assuage his concern.

"I'm not sure," I admitted. "I guess…" I guess what? That I was scared? That I didn't know what I was doing? That we were talking about fighting Scorpio? Locke and I only had a quarter of a plan—get to her in time to kill me, and somehow be brought back. I had no idea how we would get to her. What war we would have to wage. Or would it be a stealth attack? And who would fight? The curse itched away inside me, slowly rotting me with every beat of my heart. How could I put any of this into words? Especially when I hadn't told Aspen, Lennox, or Lenore yet of Amaya's vision. To my knowledge, Locke hadn't either. "I'm just tired," I said at last. Aspen rolled his eyes. "It's just been a lot to process these last few days." Not a lie. A look of understanding dawned on him as he nodded.

"That's fair. How are you feeling with…" he trailed off, leaning closer so our shoulders touched, "the curse?" he whispered. I'd have laughed if he hadn't seemed so worried.

"I'm managing." I didn't mean for my tone to be so short. I gave him a terse smile as an apology. Concern sparked on his face again, his brows drawing close together and pinching in the middle in a deep furrow.

"Does it hurt?" He scanned me head to toe, looking for telltale signs of pain. Pain we both knew he couldn't just magic away. My heart warmed at Aspen's never-ending thoughtfulness.

"It's not painful per se," I mused, struggling to put the strange feeling into words. "It's like I can feel a tiny piece of myself die. All the time. And I know the time will come soon that there will just be no more left." It was the first time I'd verbalized this feeling, and I wished I could force the words back into my mouth. I specifically didn't tell Locke this, knowing he'd go further off the deep end than he already has. He didn't need more stress, and I just prayed that Aspen would keep this slip up between us.

"That won't happen." Aspen's voice was a mountainside, hard and unyielding, and it gave me pause. His conviction. His certainty. His face contained no doubt. No hesitation. Just steadfast loyalty and optimism. I could have hugged him. "We'll find a way, Lark. Trust me, Locke has done nothing but search since the moment he met you." His shoulders sagged, losing a touch of the seriousness, "Fuck, it feels so good to finally discuss this with you! You have no idea how hard it was for us to know how much Locke cared about you, and watch you despise him for something he didn't do. Something he willingly let you think. Don't get me wrong, I understand it. But it was crushing to see from this side of things. Because I could see your struggle not to fall. We all did. When he told us we couldn't tell you, when he told us you might fall under the curse... I had no idea what to do. How to help." I tensed as he spoke, my muscles coiling and tensing as if ready to run away. Or fight Aspen. I wasn't sure which.

"I know." I couldn't help the flash of irritation I felt. I didn't want to feel it, but there it sat inside me, buzzing away. I'd hoped that would be the end of the conversation, but Aspen turned so his whole body faced me.

"No." His eyes cut to me again, all traces of that humor gone. "You don't know. That day you were going to leave Port Azure... that would have broken Locke. Not that you would have gotten far. Locke would have tracked you down and brought you back kicking and screaming. But the Soulless..."

I shuddered, remembering that night. Especially when I think of how differently it could have gone if Aspen had not intervened. If I had gone. Would I have stood a chance against the Soulless? The terrifying spirits who roamed the confines of the trees? Or worse, the blood wraiths that also stalked the forest floor, just waiting for the right unsuspecting prey to stumble. I still heard their screams each night, and now that the foliage was nearly gone, sometimes I swore I could see their eyes staring, or perhaps daring me, from my window.

"Just do me a favor, Aspen."

He looked at me intently. "Anything." Uncertainty crested his features for the first time.

"I understand why you did," Aspen tensed at the anger in my voice, his face falling, "but don't ever lie to me again." It was a simple statement. A simple ask. But loaded with so much pain I thought until now was entirely behind me. But my best friend helping my soulmate lie to me, even for my own good, wasn't something I was entirely finished processing.

"Lark," his face opened up to show his sincerity, eyes shining with honesty, "I promise and swear on my own life that I will never lie to you again. Not for anything. I'm so sorry I did before, but I believed in my heart what we were doing—keeping you in the dark—was the right thing to do. We were keeping you alive, Lark. That matters to us above all else."

His words, the weight of the swear spell, the gravity of his sincerity, rendered me speechless. The anger that had just begun to sizzle under my skin cooled and vanished. My lips parted on a response, only to close again, the fire that had fueled me leaving me entirely.

"Thank you," I whispered finally, no other words coming to me. Aspen blew out a breath like he'd been holding it his whole life.

"I hate that you're cursed. I hate that this looms over you. But what I hated more than anything is you not having a choice. That you were kept in the dark. We will not fail to save you. But I could tell your heart was breaking and it was gut wrenching."

I couldn't tear my gaze away from Aspen. Probably the most words he'd spoken to me at once the entire time I'd been here, and each one had me so emotionally conflicted. He was right. He knew me well. I would rather die than not have a choice in my own fate. I would rather love for a short time, than be miserable for the rest of it.

I would choose Locke all over again, even if it meant my soul would decay in the process.

An hour later, after I'd bathed and donned fresh, warm clothes to fight the winter's chill, I found myself seated next to the hearth in Locke's office with a book ignored in my lap. I'd tried reading to take my mind off the incoming meeting, but I kept reading the same sentences over and over again. I stretched languidly, shamelessly getting closer to the fire as I resettled. Locke glanced over with a reassuring smile before brooding over his ledger again, leaving me basking in our companionable silence.

The silence was the calm before the storm.

My body tightened like an over plucked harp string when the clicking of the double doors announced the arrival of our friends, Lennox and Lenore piling in with Aspen only heartbeats behind them. My book fell from my lap, immediately forgotten. I watched as everyone exchanged pleasantries and greetings, and it struck me just how similar and yet different the twins were. Lennox with her braided hair woven with flowers, Lenore with her blonde hair loose in messy waves. Lennox with her flowy clothing, Lenore still in battle armor, and her axe strapped to her back. A questionable red stain on her sleeve matched the shade of red on her battle axe and left me questioning who had angered her.

How they were twins, I'd never understand. They were polar opposites. And yet they moved in sync to join me by the fire. Aspen came in looking casual, his hair more mussed than usual. Was that lip stain on his neck? I blinked, my head tilting to the side as if to get a better angle to examine. Aspen caught me, and he followed my eye line and winked at me. My jaw dropped in response.

"You sent for us," Lenore spoke first, dispelling the tenuous peace of the moment, her unblinking stare passing between Locke and me. Her expression cut through me in a way I couldn't describe. Friendly enough, but a weariness I hadn't seen in her before settled in her expression when she looked at me. "I understand it's something important?" Something in her tone made me fidgety to tell them about Amaya's vision.

To tell them about my death.

And my possible rebirth.

In my mind's eye I saw it. I saw Locke's gaze on me, though I ignored it. I saw it. Death. Destruction. Blood flowing in the streets. And for what? So I could remain alive?

No. I shook my head. Not just that. So we could at last break the curses that bound two of the Zodiac Kinship of the Water Court, and at last put a swift end to the Barbaric Queen's violent rule. A queen who had murdered entire towns of innocent fae for the majority of her rule. And I knew with certainty, she wouldn't stop until she got what she wanted. Me.

But would the twins accept it? Would Aspen? I coarsely swallowed the lump in my throat. Would Port Azure? Would they take up arms to get their Court back? Was that possible? Or would they rebel against Locke and deliver me to Scorpio in chains? Doubt clenched my heart as I realized, not for the first time, that it would be endlessly easier to give me over to Scorpio. And I wouldn't blame them. Abel took it too far, betraying Locke and all of Port Azure in his ambition, but his logic was plenty sound; give me to the Queen, and this would be over. I couldn't argue with that.

I wiped my sweaty palms on my pant leg, trying to be inconspicuous. The mounting dread was getting to me. Aspen spared me a glance that married confusion and concern as if he could read my thoughts. Or perhaps he could hear my heart thrashing in my chest.

At Locke's insistence, Aspen closed the doors to the office, leaving us completely alone and separate from the Court of Rebels. I knew that special spell work had been crafted into the very walls, keeping eavesdroppers wanting. Locke's expression was unreadable as he closed his ledger and stowed it neatly on the corner of his desk.

Stealing a glance around the room, I took in Lenore's weariness from earlier seeping into her posture. She avoided meeting my gaze, tightening the growing knot in my gut. Lennox blinked between us in confusion, nobody saying word. I had only witnessed Aspen looking so serious a handful of times, his green eyes normally so full of humor were sharp and assessing. He was looking for a threat where none existed in this room.

"Thank you all for coming so quickly," Locke began, eyes flashing to me. A silent question.

Are you ready?

Was I?

No.

Fuck no.

I was terrified.

Locke's expression turned soft—knowing—before standing. He reached me in three strides where I sat by the hearth, before turning to face the others. His hand reached down to clasp mine, a gentle squeeze. I felt like he was squeezing my heart. It was so gentle, so reassuring, it was enough to center me just a bit. His unwavering support. The tense knot in my stomach loosened a fraction and I nodded up at him.

"We have something to tell you," Locke said. Lenore sighed but said nothing. Locke shot her a warning glare. "We think we have a way to kill Scorpio."

There was an initial collective intake of breath. And then there was silence.

Total and complete silence for a few heartbeats.

"What?" Lennox's voice was scarcely above a whisper. As if speaking too loudly may dispel the news we'd just delivered.

"Why do you not look happy?" Aspen asked, astute eyes flickering back and forth between Locke and me, processing every detail. Locke sighed, getting to his feet and raking his hands through his hair, his feet striding back and forth across the room like a caged animal.

"It's not pretty. And it comes with a large sacrifice. And I don't-" His eyes cut to me before blinking back up to our friends "- we don't- ask this lightly." I'd never seen him stumble through his words before. It was clear to me how much emotion he was holding back and not for the first time I wondered how I'd ever thought him indifferent to me at all.

"I have to die," I blurted before I could stop myself. *Shit.* This was not the way I wanted to do this.

Their gazes snapped to me, expectantly waiting for information they didn't already know. That the whole court didn't already know. "But I don't have to stay that way." *That* got everyone's attention. Lenore's sharp inhale was audible even over the exclamations from Aspen and Lennox, who had begun pacing throughout the opulent room, her brow pinched together.

"Explain." Lenore's voice cut through the questions and confusion. Sharp as any blade, it cleaved through the heightened tensions. Locke and I took turns telling the whole story. Of the Vale. Of Amaya. And of her vision from beyond the veil that came to me in my dream. That I would die by Scorpio's hand, breaking Scorpio and Locke's curses. And of the lightning that brought me back. We could lay siege to Loc Valen, and I could play my part and come back to be with my soulmate and with them. Scorpio wouldn't just be captured—a future that by their own admission was unlikely and riddled with plot holes.

Scorpio would be dead.

The entire court would be saved.

No longer would the court be in peril. Because, I thought as grim satisfaction stoked the embers of vengeance within me, we'd get rid of Pisces too. And the land would once again know peace. Loved ones would at last be avenged, and finally laid to rest properly.

"I..." It was my turn to stumble over my words. I took a breath, steeling myself. "I understand if you'd rather send me to Loc Valen. I'm offering right now to send myself to Loc Valen. I can arrange this. You have an out."

Locke ceased his pacing, his head whipping around to face me, clearly disbelieving what I was saying. Lenore looked angry. Aspen and Lennox took turns looking torn between hurt and anger.

"Absolutely not." Locke snarled at the same time Lenore's voice raised, echoing about the room and startling me with its intensity.

"You're out of your fucking mind," Lenore spat, "if you think we'd let her hurt you. That we'd *negotiate* with her? Do you hear yourself? Maybe Scorpio will stop once she has you, sure. Doubtful, but sure." Lenore's voice turned steely as she looked at me. Her face revealed some memory playing that only she could see. One that haunted her. One that she couldn't escape. "But she needs to pay for her crimes. Everyone in this city has lost someone because of her. Including us. And let's be very serious about Pisces. Even if we kill Scorpio, he won't stop. Not ever." Her gaze turned to Locke. I followed her stare to see Locke's jaw tick as he cracked his knuckles, almost as if in anticipation. What Pisces had done to him, had done to all of us, was unforgiveable.

He needed to pay.

I would take sick satisfaction at making him pay dearly for what he did to my father. To Poplar Hollow. To my friends.

"She's right. Pisces is a bigger threat than we'd anticipated. Frostfall proved that," Locke said, shifting listlessly in his seat. "I don't know the depths of his treachery, but he's possibly even worse than Scorpio. He's always been ambitious, but when it comes to me, he'll never let us go. That includes all of Port Azure." At my disbelieving look he explained, "He's a petty, self-serving bastard. The fae here aren't safe as long as he's alive. He's an affliction I'm only too happy to remedy." Aspen and Locke shared a loaded look. One I intended to ask about later.

"Exactly," Aspen chimed in, settling in front of the chair at my feet and looking pointedly up at me. "You resigning yourself to death, while brave, ultimately would only stop some of the problem and create new ones. You're an asset, not a bargaining chip. Port Azure and the Water Court as a whole won't be safe until they are both dead. So whatever your plan is with negotiating this, get rid of it. We won't be giving you up."

"No, but this is an excellent time for launching the attack we've been planning," Lenore said, her voice steeped in chaos. "So, your quarter of a plan is die by Scorpio's hand, be revived by lightning and live happily ever after once we kill Scorpio and Pisces. Is that right?"

I nodded, exchanging a loaded look with Locke. His eyes burned with every single objection, but instead he sat quietly simmering. If Lenore noticed, she didn't acknowledge it.

"Great," . "How are we getting there? How are we getting the lightning? If we're doing this, and that's a big if, we have to make sure we can bring Lark back."

The emotion in Lenore was more than I'd seen in her previously. I felt a lump gathering in my throat for a whole other reason now. Locke kissed the top of my head.

"You may die." He growled the words like they tried to bite him on the way passed his lips, but the vow in his voice didn't waver. "But I will move the very veil of death to bring you back. Even if we have to force fate itself, we will not fail."

"As will I," said Aspen, placing his hand on Locke's and mine. Lennox, who had been quietly observing, also placed her hand on Aspen's.

"As will I." Lenore strode over to us, adding her hand to the pile. "To any end that awaits."

I couldn't believe my good fortune with these fae. How was I so lucky to have a soulmate and such amazing friends, when not too long ago, my entire town wanted me dead? Or at least gone? Knowing what I knew now, and how much I knew they care, those thoughts still tried to grasp me. But for the first time, I could at least try to shake them off.

We separated at last, the moment over. Lenore lounged sideways in one of the unoccupied chairs. She had borrowed a glass and a bottle of amber liquid from somewhere and began pouring herself a drink, flashing us all a grin.

"So, what's the rest of the plan?"

Chapter Four

We talked for hours. Of various scenarios. We discussed the extent of Port Azure's military force, whether it were possible to recruit or even liberate entire cities in time without sustaining casualties. Aspen and Lenore thought they were ready, but Locke didn't look convinced.

"We have the numbers to attack Loc Valen right now," Locke mused, looking at a map on his desk, moving several papers out of the way. His eyes ping-ponged all over the map, rapidly considering a scenario and quickly discarding it with a shake of his head and a deep sigh. "But I doubt it's enough if she calls for reinforcements, conscripts the court, calls for aid outside of the court..."

"So, what do we do? Recruit more to increase our numbers?" asked Lenore. I didn't know what that meant. "As it is, we're trying to free other towns and the hold Scorpio has on everyone is incredibly strong. They're terrified of her."

"We are already spread thin as it is," Locke agreed, running his hands through his raven hair again in exasperation. He pinched his lips together, clearly trying to make sense of too much information at once before letting out a breath. "We've had a few of our spies go missing from towns throughout the water court. Or come back compromised. Adding more is dangerous. Especially in the small towns where everyone knows one another and our fae will stand out more. Fae are scared, more so than ever." At my confused look he explained, "Scorpio is punishing anyone that is disloyal in blood. Even those rumored to be disloyal. Sources have told me she's getting more public with her demonstrations. More theatrical and more lethal. She's putting everything into finding us. It's making the whole court volatile and fearful. It's a breeding ground for anger and violence right now. She's afraid of us gathering numbers and she's doing everything to stop it. She's made orders to out anybody you don't know immediately. Whatever is about to happen, it's going to come to a head quickly."

Well, at least that played into our timeline. I sat back in my chair to absorb everything Locke had said. I tried to imagine the devastation at Frostfall, at Poplar Hollow. Tried to marry the images to the rumors I'd heard about these demonstrations.

"If the demonstrations are getting worse, that means she's desperate, right? She'll make a mistake," I asked.

"There is power in being hunted. We have what she wants, and yes, there is an advantage there. But for everyone else not in the safety of Port Azure, it's a liability. Time isn't on our side either." Locke's eyes met and held mine then. His aura flickered once more, making the air on my neck stand on ceremony. He had a look about him that didn't sit right with me.

"It's too dangerous to risk sending more fae out to towns," Lennox agreed, breaking the tension as well as my train of thought. "But I doubt we'd gain enough numbers that way anyway."

"No," Locke mused. "But an alliance with the Air Court might."

All movement stopped.

"Do you mean we're not just trying to get Aquarius on our side, but create an entire alliance?" Lennox nearly dropped the cup she was about to drink from. "Do we have favors to call in, or any leverage at all?"

"I know we need the lightning but..." Aspen pondered aloud while rubbing the back of his neck. "The Air court is..."

"Awful. They're awful," Lenore finished with a spiteful swallow of her drink. At my confused glance she elaborated, "They're cruel, selfish, and incredibly vain. Everyone thinks that because we're the Water Court we're ruled by our emotions. We get flack for it. But them?" Lenore sneered, evaluating her nails as she continued, "They have no emotion to speak of. They're callous and spiteful, the lot of them. The Scarlet Summit exists for a reason. It's basically a warning now."

If they were so awful, how were we supposed to create an alliance? I shuddered thinking about the Scarlet Summit. I don't think anyone remembers what started the war between Earth and Air, but the war raged for years. The final battle was won by Air when they slaughtered the Earth Court's forces at the Summit's peak. Their blood stained the rock and ice there, and was still frozen there to this day.

And we were to ally ourselves with them? Would they even agree to such terms? Before I could say anything back, Aspen enveloped me in a side hug.

"We're going to get Aquarius to help us. And with our combined forces, we'll have enough fire power to launch our attack. It's all going to work out. You'll see."

As comforting as Aspen's words were, why did they sound so forced?

"Then it's decided. I will begin preparations to contact Air immediately." Locke stood and turned to Aspen. "Aspen, I will give the order first thing in the morning that every fae willing and able to fight be ready as soon as possible. I trust you to oversee their training and arming. Call in any and all favors of Earth and Fire. I certainly will be doing the same." With a pointed look at the timekeeper on the desk he turned back to us. "Get some rest. We've been at this a long time and it's getting late."

Lenore and Aspen hugged me before they left, embracing me strongly. I returned it with equal fervor. But it was Lennox who tugged my heartstrings before she left Locke's offices.

"We won't ever abandon you, Lark. You're family. We fight for our family. You have a huge role in this to play yet, and we will be with you every step of the way. You're worth that and so much more. Please don't forget that." And with that, she slipped out of the room, leaving Locke and me together.

"I couldn't have said it better myself," Locke said, placing a kiss on my forehead.

"Thank you," I sighed as I numbly slumped into him. I didn't know how to express my gratitude. I didn't know how to fully assuage my guilt, or what to say. Words weren't enough to showcase the feelings I had towards Locke, towards our friends. If I'd known that I had to suffer through life the way I had to find them, I would have done over and over again. To find them, anything would have been worth it. I sank into Locke's embrace with another long sigh and let the calmness of the moment overtake everything. Overtake dread. Overtake uncertainty. And overtake guilt.

There would be plenty of time for those later.

Chapter Five

As I finished braiding my hair the following morning, a quick knock on the door had my spine straightening. Locke was meeting with Gemini today and he'd told me to wait until he'd summoned me. But it was an unfamiliar voice that floated from the other side of the door instead.

"My Lady," he began, his respectful tone was so endearing to me that I forced down my discomfort with the formality of his words. *Lark*, I wanted to say. *My name is Lark.* "Your presence has been requested in Prince Cancer's offices. I'm given to understand that this is an urgent matter and time may be of the essence."

What a nice way to say *hurry up.*

I opened the door to see an older fae in plain black clothing. He smiled—a cool, professional smile that made the corners of his eyes crinkle—before gesturing down the hall towards my destination. My feet moved quickly through the designated route as he politely escorted me. My heart panged in my chest. That smile and the crinkling eyes reminded me so much of Eldan in that moment, and despite everything, I couldn't ignore that pang of regret. I hoped beyond hope that he and my first equine love, Haven were okay wherever he was. Unbidden, the bodies in the street of Poplar Hollow grinned at me in all their painful, rotting glory. Gael and his family slaughtered in their home and left, along with countless others. The town had become a tomb. I cringed back from the memory. I refused to believe Eldan and Haven were there. I *refused*.

The heavy, dark wood double doors of Locke's office loomed ahead of me. My pulse began to race. I couldn't even press my ear to the door to gauge how many fae were inside, or the topic of their discussion with the spells in place. I had to go in blind. I took a deep breath, filling my lungs as my escort gave me a patient look. Using that to bolster myself, I grabbed the doorknobs and let myself in with my head held high.

Locke sat in his tall wing backed chair at his desk, where I would usually find him. A fae to the right of him was unfamiliar to me, and if his attire were to attest, I would say he wasn't from Port Azure either. Silver armor complete with white runes shone in the firelight. My own runes from my air magic came to mind immediately, telling me exactly who this was. If metal could look flowing, like metallic water, that's what this was with its curved lines and elegant angles. A flowing cape of steep green. Glints of emerald beckoned my notice—a silver crown with flicks of spectacular diamonds and emeralds. Two silver chips under them assessed me with a detached sort of interest as I walked in. I regarded him in kind.

"Hello Lark." Locke's unusually formal voice greeted me. I glanced over at him with a smile as he gestured to our guest standing with his back to the fire in the hearth. "Thank you for coming so quickly. Allow me to introduce to you Prince Gemini of the Air Court. He's here on King Libra's orders to verify the validity of our claims today to determine whether a meeting with us is justified." Gemini's eyes glittered at the introduction, but his face remained carefully blank as he appraised me, roaming from the bottom of my feet to the top of my braided head. I fought to keep my face indifferent at his unimpressed expression, but my spine straightened in response.

"I'm happy to hear my timing was favorable." I hesitated, unsure of what to make of this new arrival. I flipped my braid over my shoulder just to have something to do with my hands. "To what do I owe the pleasure?"

"A show of good faith," Locke said. Was there an undercurrent of tension in his voice? I couldn't tell. "With all that Scorpio has done against my reputation as Cancer, King Libra found it necessary to understand our claims. He wants Prince Gemini to see your powers firsthand. To verify our claims before hearing us out." I guess I couldn't blame him. Hearing about a fae with all four elements was a massive story, one that he'd undoubtedly have a keen interest in. Keeping a lock on my sudden nerves, I nodded before turning to address Gemini with the sincerest smile I could conjure.

"Prince Cancer speaks the truth. I've been gifted with multiple elements. I can demonstrate here if you'd like? Or would you prefer the arena where I can really stretch my legs?" Something flared on Gemini's face briefly. Something I had no name for before his features fell into vague shadow of boredom once more.

"Not necessary, Lady Lark, although I feel that I would enjoy such a performance." His voice was soft. Musical even, reminding me of the wind chimes in a lazy spring breeze. It was also overly formal, lending credibility to Lenore and Aspen's earlier assessment of Air Court. "Here is fine, as I simply need to verify the validity of your story."

It amused me on some level that his tone sounded so disbelieving. Keeping my smirk to myself, I nodded and summoned water into a ball between my hands. I allowed myself a moment to play, so I told myself. But in reality, I knew I was showing off a little. I played with the water, making it take the shape of a rippling flame, a conundrum of nature itself before I made the water take form of the Gemini symbol. His eyebrows raised. The first sign of curiosity he'd given me.

"Your control over your natural element is impressive. I'm to understand that you were unable to perform magic until recently?"

"Yes, Highness. I unknowingly had a block on my magic."

His gaze sharpened on me, like a hound catching a scent. "Why?"

"Some secrets I'd like to keep my own for the time being." I willed the water away, making strong eye contact with the Air Court Prince. "Your mission was to verify our claims are real. Not their origins. Is that not correct?" A single eyebrow twitch and a smirk raised to his face, but I didn't miss the irritation briefly flash in his eyes at my insolence. But I was right. They didn't need more information than necessary and getting into my past was both unnecessary and messy. Not to mention a time-consuming tale. I smiled at him with fake sweetness that soured my stomach. I felt like a flower that hid the venomous fangs of a serpent beneath, danger disguised as beauty.

Channeling that feeling I conjured flames to my skin, watching as the fire runes lit up across my arms and hands, loving the way they warmed but didn't burn me. Something I knew I'd never tire of. Flames coiled along my arms as familiar to me as old friends and wrapped alongside my torso in the fashion of a great snake, its eyes made of fire glaring at the Prince Gemini while I kept my face artfully serene.

"Have you enough proof yet?" Locke asked, his tone light and airy. As if there weren't a giant, fiery serpent in his office. I made it hiss, its tail rattling, the sound of spitting flames sounding behind me. Gemini's face remained impassive, though his eyes showed flickers of surprise. And I was certain I caught a glimmer of what could only be fear. My smile widened as I dismissed my flames, and they were gone as if they had never been there. I demonstrated my air magic by coiling air around myself, my hair floating on an invisible breeze, an admittedly tame showcase by comparison, but my air magic was temperamental at best, and I felt that wasn't the card to play at the moment. Earth was much the same, but I conjured a rose bud and made it bloom before offering it to him. He took it, examining it with great interest now, turning it over multiple times, though I was unsure what he was looking for.

"So, it's true," he spoke. "You have every element." He turned to Locke with a pointed expression. "And Cancer intends to use her as his secret weapon to overthrow Scorpio. To what end? Become King yourself?"

"No." Locke's response was as firm as it was quick. "Simply to end her reign. She is slaughtering her people in an effort to find a way to end her curse. This madness has gone on too long, too many fae have needlessly died. Many more are in the line of fire. My only ambition is to save my Court and its fae from utter destruction. Surely, you've noticed an influx of Water Fae in your borders. Surely, you must know why."

"And what do you want the Air Court's assistance for?" The Air Prince looked affronted before his face fell into skepticism. "We have no quarrel with Scorpio. Her Majesty is a close partner in trade. I don't wish to see her wrath inflicted upon my own court if you are unsuccessful."

Even I know the political translation to that: *what will you give us in return? She isn't hurting us.* My veins frosted over. Was our plan over before we'd even had a chance to pitch to Aquarius?

"We have a plan, but we wish to speak to Libra and Aquarius as well about it. In Air Court or here. Whatever you decide is best, we will follow. We simply request an audience as soon as possible."

"Thank you for your most impressive demonstrations, My Lady," he said to me after an incredibly long pause, before turning his attention back to Locke. "I'll pass on the information I have gathered here today. Libra, Aquarius and I will think on this matter and get back to you," he said in a tone much too dismissive for my liking. I saw movement in his hands and recognized the glimmer of a jump stone.

"Wait!" I called out before I even made the decision to speak. To his credit, he turned and gave me his full attention. "We're not yet asking you for your assistance. You don't even know what we'd ask. But time is of the essence. Your Highness, my very life is at stake. As are the many people of my Court. I watched the people in my town die. I saw their bodies left to rot in the sun. And my village is but a drop in the bucket of the death and terror Scorpio has unleashed upon us. And still nothing compared to what she could still do. She must be stopped, or you won't have a partner in trade. She'll destroy her own Court and be left with a corpse riddled husk of a once prosperous realm with nothing left to offer you." My voice was dangerously close to breaking but together by force of sheer will alone. I kept my eyes on his, I showed him the blazing fire behind my eyes. I let him see the passion in me. The fight.

"I will converse with my kin, and I will return to you tonight when the stars are brightest in the sky with our answer. Is that sufficient, Lady?" It would have to be. I nodded mutely. "Then it is settled. I will return tonight. And Lady Lark?"

"Yes?" My eyebrow quirked at the ominous tone his voice had taken.

"It was a pleasure meeting you. That fire inside you is astounding. I have a feeling that before all this is done, you're going to need it." Before I could ask him whether that was a threat or an observation, he travelled through the jumpstone and Locke and I were left alone. Locke immediately broke into a grin as he rushed me.

"You beautiful, clever, fierce girl!" he exclaimed as he hoisted me into his arms and swung me in a circle. I burst out laughing, spinning until we were both breathless. "You made him agree to that. Who knew you were so influential?"

"Why is everyone always surprised to find out I'm not just another pretty face?" I cracked. His face grew a bit more contemplative.

"I don't think anybody could mistake you for being only a pretty face, Lark."

I rolled my eyes, trying to ignore the anxious anticipation beginning to build in my gut.

"It's still just a maybe. We have the day to wait." I straightened as something occurred to me. "Hold on! How was he allowed to come to Port Azure? What if he told Scorpio?"

Locke snickered.

"Do you realize other fae get up before the afternoon?" he teased. "I portaled out to a neutral location this morning and met him. I brought him here via jumpstone. He has very little idea of where we are. He never left these offices, which are entirely underground, for this exact reason. He couldn't tell Scorpio anything specific even if he'd wanted to. Though, even if he could, I doubt he would. Scorpio isn't the only one who he's afraid of. And with good reason. My wrath is not to be taken lightly, even by other Court members."

"You're not very scary."

He blinked, incredulous. "What?"

"I might be a tainted juror here, but you're not nearly as scary as you think you are," I told him as I hoisted myself to sit on his desk. He barked a laugh.

"Well, I wouldn't be a very good romantic partner if you were afraid of me." He moved to stand directly in front of me, the warmth from his body seeping into my legs. Of all reactions I could have had, I blushed. His eyes tracked the growing redness on my face with a smirk. "What? You don't like being my romantic partner? It comes with so many benefits." He shot me a suggestive smile that was downright filthy. I shook my head, grinning up at him.

"I'm just remembering our first encounter when I *was* a little afraid of you."

"No. You weren't. You weren't exactly thrilled, but true fear is an emotion I've seen on many people firsthand. I was surprised to find some random girl in the Vale sassing me, not afraid of her Court's Crowned Assassin." He cut me with a look of mock exasperation. "Should I be offended that you didn't even recognize me?" I shrugged as innocently as I could, smiling as he shook his head at me. Our gazes met and held a breath before he continued. "The only time I felt fear on you in the Vale was when you thought you were going to die before getting your father that Aching Cress. You didn't necessarily feel fear for yourself, but for your father."

"I didn't sass you!" His eyebrow quirked in response.

"When I asked you if you really didn't know who I was you responded with '*you'd think a blank look and me asking would make that obvious.*'" I was about to object but he grinned and continued. "You told me I just enjoyed building suspense and that I was boring you. You accused me of having women give me my way all the time because of my fancy hair and nice muscles and called me a jackass."

"A jackass? Where could I have gotten that idea?" I mused. He lowered his face to mine and grinned against my lips.

"I haven't the slightest clue. As I recall—and I have perfect recollection—I was a gentleman that day."

"You were going to kill me!"

"Yes, and yet here you are. Against strict orders I might add. See? Gentleman." He grinned widely against my lips, still not kissing me.

Our breaths mingled in the limited space between us. His voice lowered then to that husky, primal tone that shot heat through my extremities. "I think the real question is, am I still boring you?" Losing my patience, I closed the distance between us, relishing the feel of his lips on mine.

"No. You've made me feel a lot of things, Locke. Bored has not once been one of them."

His grin changed against my lips, turning into something a bit more sensual. He kissed me slowly. Leisurely. He wrapped his arms around my waist and tugged me towards him on the edge of the desk. I snaked my arms around his neck, luxuriating in the feel of him. The musky, male scent of him. I broke away, a wicked grin on my face, even more wicked thoughts dancing in my head. "On second thought, I am bored. Terribly bored right now,

Locke." He raised an eyebrow, his expression descending into one that suggests. Explores. His eyes darkened, his thoughts clearly spiraling into sin. Where they met my own. I would always allow our sins to crash together. Would always crave it the same way my lungs craved air. I nearly crumbled under the depthless, scorching gaze he hit me with, eyes alighting with mischief.

"Well now, Lady, that simply won't do. Allow me to rectify that situation for you." He kissed me harder, his hands going to my knees. "These are in my way." My only warning before his hands parted my legs, freeing his hips to grind into mine, revealing his growing arousal. His tongue forced its way into my mouth, teasing mine that reminded me just how deftly talented he was with it. He swallowed the small, sound I made low in my throat and bit my lip lightly as he devoured me. His hands slid around the backs of my thighs, a promise. He wasted no time in pressing himself against me through my leggings. My hips bucked against him of their own will in direct response. His fingers toyed with my waistline, circling, dipping under the soft fabric. His touch travelled to the sensitive skin of my hips, but never lower where I was beginning to ache for his touch. I hissed at him to urge him on.

"Are you bored now, Lady?" he murmured against my lips, continuing to frustrate me, deny me.

"I will be if you don't start touching me," I panted at him, palming his considerable length through his black pants. He groaned before taking my hand away from him and pinning it to the desk next to me. He collected my other hand quickly and repeated the process.

"What's the magic word to get what you want?" he asked, nibbling my lip, my neck, my collarbone. My thoughts froze for a moment, unable to connect words together under his ministrations. His hands tightened on mine, a nonverbal warning—*Don't move*—before languidly dragging his fingers over to my thighs, tracing lines around my waistband of my leggings, dipping under the fabric far too briefly. They danced delicate lines over my clothing along the front of my hips, my thighs, continuously driving me towards madness. I lifted my hips, but he pushed them down again, tsking me, with his lips just a whisper over mine. "I want to see your pretty pink lips say it."

"Please," I whispered, tugging his bottom lip between my teeth, hearing the male satisfaction in his groan as I did so, sending every thought scattering into the heat building in my core. "I want you."

"Lift your hips for me." His voice was rife with the command as his lips hovered over mine. I bit my lip as I did so, watching lust darken his gaze at my obedience. "That's my good girl," he murmured, making my blood ignite in my veins. My leggings were inside out and across the room in the blink of an eye. He wasn't in the mood for patience.

He dropped to his knees before me, using his hands to keep me bared before him. Seeing him on his knees before me gave me a rush I never expected. Those blue eyes, darkening as he adjusted me to right where he wanted me. When his mouth caressed that very aching center of me, I was grateful his offices were sound-spelled. His tongue was slow, deft, and deliberate as my body arched off the desk, a low, strangled sound breaking from me. He was torturing me. And he reveled in it as my body writhed for him, quickened for him, completely under his command. "Am I boring you now, Lark?" he whispered against me, driving me wild. My hips kept moving on their own. I was panting. The feeling of his tongue in my most sensitive spot sending fireworks throughout my body. My moans were his only answer. I didn't miss his satisfied grin as he brought his fingers to work me too. He groaned as he felt how ready and wanting I was for him.

I tipped my head back and arched into him, feeling as if my spine might break. I didn't care if it did. I needed more of him to soothe the persistent, building ache. I felt the familiar rising pressure in my core, compounding with every swipe of his tongue, every punishing movement of his fingers. I cursed as my hands desperately clutched the edges of the desk, as if I'd fall off the planet if I let go. I panted his name. Or maybe I cursed it. He was driving me higher and higher to the edge of bliss. I felt the tingle of magic in the air and felt the coldness of his tongue at the apex of my thighs. A favorite trick I'd been sorely missing that had the pressure climbing to its peak. And I fell.

Loudly.

I wasn't sure I was even breathing as he continued to ride me through it. I was still in the throes of my undoing when he eased himself inside me to the hilt.

I groaned as I continued to spasm around him, his fingers still moving on my most sensitive spot. On some level I was aware of the growl of pleasure he elicited as he began moving his hips. I cursed and moved my hips in time with his, needing more, more, more of him. And I needed it now.

He kissed me then, ravenous, like he was drowning and I was oxygen. I gripped his hair and pulled him closer towards me trading passion for passion. Fire for fire. He kept up his punishing pace and my brain went fuzzy. I moaned his name as I felt the familiar signs of my oncoming release. I raked my nails down his back, not bothering to be gentle. I cursed as I begged him, urging him on. He bit my lip before kissing away the pain of it and I fell once again. My release barreled down my spine so fast, so intensely that I screamed as I spasmed around him again. I felt the telltale thickening of him as he too found his release with me. I heard some semblance of my name on his lips as he followed me into oblivion and he kissed me again. His forehead rested against mine as he caught his breath.

"Are you bored now, My Lady?"

I grimaced at the ridiculous title.

"You really don't need to call me that. Or anybody else for that matter. I'm just Lark."

"You're right. I think Your Highness suits you so much more." I gaped at him, incredulous. Of course, it only seemed to fuel him, the wicked glint in his eye daring me to challenge him.

"I'm just Lark," I said. "That's all I ever aspired to be. I don't need fancy titles or anything else. I just need you." His features softened at my words. I saw the vulnerability in his eyes then. Soft. Serious. Intense.

"You've never been 'just' Lark. Not to me. Not to our friends. Not to the people you've helped rescue and protect here. You're the love of my life. I'm the Prince of the Water Court. Being the object of my affection comes a specific amount of respect. And titles. When this is all over, I'm going to court you properly. The way you deserve." He smiled at me. His dimple on his left side showed, making him look boyishly handsome in that moment. I forgot to breathe for a moment. "Besides, I quite like the idea of calling you 'Your Highness' Or even—wait for it—'Your Majesty' one day. Now that," he punctuated his sentence with a kiss to my lips so sweet my insides melted, "I like the sound of."

This conversation quickly made my head spin. Your Majesty was how you addressed a Queen. I had zero qualifications for the role. Princess was bad enough. I wasn't a princess. Not by a longshot. I couldn't hold my own in politics. I knew nothing about being royalty. I hadn't been trained by the Zodiac Guild.

"You not being a zodiac can quickly be corrected," he said, as if reading my thoughts. I glared at him. "You're the most powerful Fae in existence. Zodiac Kinship status is within the realm of possibility for you."

I contemplated that for a moment. Me. A Zodiac. I didn't even know how to even begin to process that. Locke had told me about the process for becoming a part of the kinship once, and it wasn't something I'd ever aspire to. Rigorous magical and combat education. And the Rune Trials...

Locke never spoke about them. But that doesn't mean I don't see the ghosts in his eyes whenever I ask about them. Would I have to undergo Rune Trials? Goddess above. Locke's voice broke my train of thought once again, and for once I couldn't say I was upset about it.

"Assuming you keep me around, Lark, you're going to have to get used to some titles. Because Fae will respect you properly. Those who don't can either fall in line," his voice took on the hard edge of conviction, and something harsher, darker, "or leave."

"When my life ends, I will do everything I can to claw my way back through the veil to you." I didn't say the words to incite a promise, but it didn't matter. I didn't need the magic of a promise to bind me to that oath, I would see it through all the same. He loosed a breath.

The impact of my words hit home. What about when my life would end? I could feel the rot in my body even now. Even when I felt so alive, I felt small pieces of myself decaying. It felt strange, unnatural. And to know that a time would come very soon that there would be no more pieces left and I'd just be dead.

"How are you not afraid?" Locke asked in a voice that bordered on awe. "We're talking about you dying and shocking your heart and praying to the Goddess you come back to life while we finish off Scorpio. What are you thinking?"

"I'd be lying if I said I wasn't scared." I perused my brain for the right words, chewing them over before speaking. "Locke, I'm terrified. But the fact is that in order to save everyone here, and many more, it has to be done. And I have faith that I won't stay down. And you won't let me. You're too stubborn." I grinned at him. He gave me a half grin back, but I could see his heart wasn't in it. But I couldn't deny that my fear wasn't almost paralyzing. At times it was paralyzing. At times I felt my heart beat out of my chest and my breaths become shallow. I pictured the scene in my dream, or vision, or whatever it was. I felt her hands on my throat and the fear in me. I felt my lungs scream for breath....

I couldn't say I wasn't afraid. But I had to end the curse. I had to end Locke's too. And if it didn't work, if I didn't come back, I knew I could rest easier knowing that he was free to love whomever he wanted without consequence. And as a Zodiac, he had a long time to do so happily. And with Scorpio's curse ended, she could be killed. Would be, I reminded myself. Too many people had suffered at her hands for her not to pay for them in blood. And the Water Court would be safe once again. I could live with that. Or more accurately, die with that knowledge. He had that look on his face. Like he was reading me.

"What color am I?" I asked. His eyes unfocused, scouring the air around me with intent.

"Dark purple. Yellow. Green. Pink."

I felt my face scrunch into a grimace at his analysis. "That's an ugly color combination. It sounds like a bruise."

He chortled at my response. "Purple is resolve. I can tell you're doing this one way or another. Yellow is your fear." He wrapped his arms around me, as if his arms could truly banish those thoughts. I snuggled into his warmth. "Green is hope." I couldn't help but smile. "Pink is love."

"Really? Love is pink? Isn't that... I don't know. A bit cliché?" He laughed.

"Cliché, maybe," he agreed. "But I didn't assign the colors to emotions. Someone at some point must have found out the pink was the color of love and ran with it." I grimaced at how corny everything he said just sounded and fought to not roll my eyes. But I sank further into his embrace, the fear ebbing, though not fully dissipating. I focused hard on my hope and resolve. We'd get through this. Together. I would do that for this man. I'd do anything for this man. Including crawling my way back from beyond the veil of death.

Chapter Six

We had a whole day to kill.

Locke had made it his personal mission to combat my anxiety, and perhaps his own, by spoiling me. Courting me, he corrected, making my stomach flutter and flit. A beach ride with Valor and Aristocrat that was as cold as it was invigorating in the coming winter's chill. We whooped as our horse's hooves thundered over the sand, filling me to the brim with unrestrained joy.

Next, he told me to change into warm weather clothing. I made a show of glancing out the window over the hardened ground we'd just come in from. My face was still numb and windburned from the chilled wind. The frost addled terrain that no way indicated warm weather clothing was advisable. He smirked at me, that dimple peeking out.

"A little trust please, love?" he admonished with a teasing lilt, his hands playing with a few tendrils of my hair. "Wear your hair loose."

I now stood before him in a sweetly colored pink dress and sandals, and my hands rubbing warmth into my arms. He was dressed in a shirt of deep blue, making his eyes leap from his face. The fabric was soft and very fine under my fingers, more so than anything I'd seen him wear before.

He revealed a jumpstone from his pocket, piquing my interest. Upon activation, that small trill of magic echoed in the air, so soft you almost couldn't feel it. The portal beckoned with its warm amber glow, not allowing me a glimpse of our destination.

"Where are we going?" I asked him. He just gave me a small smile and took my hand with a gentle squeeze.

"You'll see," he said before tugging me after him into the portal.

I blinked, and not from being disconcerted from the jumpstone. Jumping was getting a bit less strange now that I've done it so much. It wasn't that I took one breath of icy air, and my next breath was warm like a summer evening. No, what stole the breath from my lungs was the incredible beauty of my new surroundings. I stood before a small, shimmering lake at the beginning phase of sunset.

But wasn't it only early afternoon?

At first, I thought the pastel hues of color in the water were painted there by the fading sun, but upon closer inspection, it actually was pink. The water was so still, so clear, the surface resembled a mirror. I glanced into the crystal-clear water, seeing pink sand lining the bed. A translucent mist hung close to the surface of the water, giving it an ethereal effect. Monolithic willow trees swayed in a surprisingly balmy breeze. A chorus of crickets sang for the fireflies dancing in the calmness of the evening. Locke took my hand and led me towards the water with a secret smile on his face—like he knew something I didn't. Which, knowing him, was likely the case.

"Where are we?" I asked, taking in the scene. I inhaled with appreciation, the scent of the water, the foliage, the assortment of colorful wildflowers out of season for this time of year, so we were clearly not in the Water Court. Winter had been nipping at our heels recently, even a few snowflakes had fallen. This place felt far removed from that with its temperate weather.

"Would you believe me if I told you we were in the Deep Wild?"

"Impossible! This place is so beautiful. I would have heard of it." I grew up so close to the Deep Wild. It was true that there were special or even secret destinations, not unlike the Yemerian Vale, but surely, I would have heard of this. Someone would have stumbled upon it.

"The Arim Aesor, or the Pink Mirror, is very far into the Deep Wild. A long way from Poplar Hollow. Or even the Vale..." he trailed off with a thoughtful expression. "The Arim Aesor is a secret place that the trees have to grant you access to. And they seldom do. There are very few who have ever set foot here." I could feel the strange magic of the place. Not elemental. Vast amounts of whole magic were woven into the very air, tasting like everything and nothing simultaneously.

"They say it's Goddess blessed. That this is the only place in Meridian that she ever touched down upon. Which is why even in winter it's frozen in this summer sunset state." I couldn't tear my gaze from the lake. I tried to take it all in—the way the sunlight shone on the water, diffused only slightly by the mist, the floral scented breeze, the way Locke's hand never left mine, the mirrored pinks in the sky married to oranges and pale yellow. It brought a wide smile to my face. To be here, with him. If only past Lark could see us now. I glanced up through the corner of my eye to see Locke gazing out at the water too.

Until I caught his eyes watching me sidelong, that secret smile of his still on his face. It was strange, seeing him so relaxed. So carefree. The weight of all he'd been dealing with seemed to burden his brow so often, that seeing him clear of that was still such a breathtaking sight.

"What are you smiling about?" I followed him to the edge of the water, his smile infecting me. His black hair hung ever so slightly in his face. I reached a hand out to smooth it away, so I could see all of the fae I fell in love with. His eyes sparked in response. His hands found my waist as he pulled me to him, his smile widening into a full, salacious grin. In that moment, I would have given anything to have his gift, to know what he was feeling. Because I could see thoughts whirling in his mind, but I couldn't grasp them.

"Just you," he said quietly, before pressing his lips sweetly to mine.

"Dare I even ask where your thoughts have gone?" I teased. His grin turned devilish.

"Just how much more of a pain in the ass you've become." At my undignified snort, he continued in a voice softer than velvet, "I'm thinking about how I'd love to court you properly the way I'd like to. To woo you. I'm fighting for the chance that we get that time when this is all over. I'm thinking about how you're simultaneously both my ruination and my salvation. And I wouldn't have it any other way."

I didn't know how to respond. I felt impossibly light. I crushed my lips to his, wrapping my arms around his neck. He pulled me up with him, my feet leaving the ground as he spun us. It was so easy to get lost here, in this entire little world that he shared with me. Just the two of us...

I pressed myself into him, every part of me craving every part of him. That devilish smirk came right back to roost on that sinfully perfect mouth of his.

"I know what you're thinking about," he whispered against my lips with mock admonishment and that devilish smirk rising to his lips. "Such immodest emotions." At my exasperated expression, he chuckled, placing a chaste kiss on my lips and one more forehead before speaking in that teasing tone again. "Try to control yourself a moment. I have something important to say."

"You think everything you say is important," I said as I wandered to the water's edge. Minnows scattered at my approach. The sunset had hit its golden hour, lighting everything in the most spectacular soft hue.

"Notice how nobody says otherwise?" His hands caressed smoothly up my arms, igniting little sparks where he touched me. His face turned soft. Serious. Assessing. His eyes searched my mine as his tone softened like the blanket of shadow enveloping us both.

"I will love you this side of the veil and the other," he said finally, his facing growing serious again. My heart beat triple time in response. His eyes dipped low between us and back up, that familiar glimmer of mischief there. "Take your shoes off."

My eyebrows met my hairline as I struggled to find a connection between his most recent sentence and the one prior, "I don't know where you're going with this, but I don't have a foot fetish."

He laughed as he shucked his shoes off and rolled his pants up. He walked only a few feet into the shallow water.

"Lark, for once in your life, do as you're told."

I mock scowled at him, but obeyed and joined him in the clear water. I dipped my toe in meekly, waiting for the cool water to drive the warmth from my bones. But the moment I felt the water slide over my foot, I felt its enveloping warmth. Not bathwater warm, but comfortable. Welcoming. The sand beneath my feet was incredibly fine and smooth and I couldn't resist burying them in it, relishing the feel. I reached for Locke's outstretched hand. Instead of taking it the way I'd expected, threading his fingers through mine, he gently steered me to face him and turned my palm over, so it faced up. His knowing glance met my quizzical expression.

"Watch." He closed his eyes, bowing his head in concentration. His hands began to glow. A smidge of pink colored my vision. Then red. Purple. Deep blue. It took me a long moment before I realized exactly what I was seeing. That I wasn't having a fit.

This was Locke's aura.

My eyes snapped to his to see the mirth there. Unfocusing my eyes, I saw it surrounding him, a kaleidoscope of emotion revealed just for me. My eyes flicked back and forth taking in each color, wanting to ask about several, but one prominent color made my heart ache in the sweetest way.

"I told you my aura would ," he whispered. For a moment I was brought back to the Inn. To the first time he murmured those words and couldn't even try to fight the elation rising in my chest. "I selfishly wanted one night with you. Just one night to be with who I knew was my soulmate. One night before I left her alone. Because having one night with you would keep me going for the rest of my days. Or at least until I found a way to break the curse. But one thing I now know I can't live with is you not knowing that I would lay everything at your feet just to see you smile. And the other is not having time."

My heart ached for him at his words. He knew. He loved me all the way back then, and I had no idea. And he was trying so hard to keep it that way, so selflessly. My heart throbbed painfully in my chest, at war with the bliss. That he'd tried so hard, even as I hated him, to keep me at bay. His hands gave mine a reassuring squeeze, reminding me that right now, we were exactly where we need to be.

Together.

I watched in awe as my own aura slowly became visible. Pinks, reds, vibrant yellows danced an inch from my skin. Interwoven into the layers of color, lay shadow tendrils threading themselves into each color. I gazed in wonderment at it, at us, where our hands joined.

"This is what you see all the time?" I wasn't even trying to hide the riotous excitement and wonderment. He nodded. I couldn't tear my eyes away as our aura danced as if aflame. "How is this possible?"

"I wasn't lying about this place being Goddess blessed. This place...this is where the Zodiac Kinship of the Water Court receive their gifts. So, this is the only place I can share it. But there's more." His voice dipping low. His eyes darted around in a movement I knew only too well. He looked...

Nervous?

The mighty Crowned Assassin, the Prince of the Water Court, Prince and leader of the Rebellion, wielder of black magic...

...Was *nervous?*

"I know others have tricked you in the past. Betrayed you. I wanted you to see with your own eyes how much you mean to me. That I would tear the world apart for you. The very cosmos if need be. Even the Veil of death itself," he grumbled that last bit with a bite of finality. His aura flashed an intense shade of red, pulsating and flickering, akin to a multicoloured flame. Closest to his skin, the shades of red yielded to that loving pink color. "This red is passion," he pointed to the bright crimson red that flashed as he spoke on the outermost layer. He pointed the middle color, which was a lighter red, indicating happiness. And a third color. The pink.

It was love.

I knew before he even had to say it.

"There's one more thing." His fingers at last threaded through mine, warmth spreading through my hand, and my heart. My aura blended with his where our skin mingled. I couldn't tear my eyes away. Where our skin touched, little sparks of golden energy erupted. I jumped, expecting a snap or a noise of some kind, but none did. Instead, our auras melted together into a beautiful pink and gold aura.

"The aura of soulmates," Locke whispered with reverence. "You are, and have always been, mine."

If my heart hadn't already belonged to him so thoroughly, it would have then. My heart screamed his name alone. I needed him. I had no doubt that even when it ceased to beat, it would cry out for him still.

Until our souls united once more.

His gaze was blazing. I didn't need his gifts to see the passion and the love burning in those sea and sunshine eyes.

"Only if you're mine too," I whispered. I saw his lips twist into that lopsided smile, his canine peeking out at me and his dimple making an appearance. A real smile that set the melted puddle of my heart on fire and made it hard to breathe.

"Oh, love. I've been yours since the moment you threatened me in the Vale." I chuckled, reflecting on how far we'd come. My laugh faded into a goading grin. His eyes lit up—something I should question—when my palm fingered the handle of the short blade at my thigh.

"I still have my daggers. And I've been practicing with Aspen. Don't make me angry." He shook his head, his hands going up in mock surrender.

"Oh, I wouldn't dare. Because I'm hoping that what comes next will give me a vastly different reaction from you then intense violence." At my questioning look, he took a step back, keeping my hand firmly in his, and knelt before me in the water. From somewhere—I had no idea where—he retrieved the most beautiful ring I'd ever seen.

Delicate diamonds clustered along the golden band framing the most stunning teal sapphire. Large enough to be fit for a Queen, it sparkled even in the muted sunset light. The air stopped moving in my lungs. My brain stopped being able to focus on any thought. Any thought except that Locke was kneeling before me with a ring. My other hand cupped my mouth and I closed my eyes, willing the tears to stop prickling behind them.

"Are you doing what I think you're doing?" My bewilderment and awe and breathlessness were evident even to me.

"That depends," he answered in a tone that made my knees weak and I threatened to join him there. "Are you going to open your eyes? I'm being incredibly endearing and you're missing it."

I burst out laughing, caught somewhere between a laugh and a sob.

"As much as I don't want to miss such a rarity, I can't see through my tears." I managed to open my eyes, letting the tears fall before quickly wiping my face clean.

"You know, when someone proposes, they don't usually expect sobbing." He grinned up at me. I chuckled in response, squeezing his hand.

"If you don't get on with it, the only remaining sobbing will come from you." But my tone had no bite to it, and the wide smile on my face removed any barb my words might have had.

"There she is." He laughed as he kissed my hand sweetly once more, and took a deep cleansing breath before continuing, "This side of the veil and the other, I will love you. I can't stand the thought of this ring not being on your hand for even a second of the time we have left." He breathed. His voice was calm and never wavered. His eyes never left mine. He laid his heart bare for me. And connecting the two of us, our hands still glowed that soft pink and gold, the proof of our entwined destinies. "Wed me, soulmate."

"This side of the veil and the other," I whispered back after a long moment. I felt the prickling behind my eyes then, the only warning for the hot tears spilling down my cheeks. "Yes. Yes, I'll wed you." He fluidly placed the ring on my finger. Before I even had a moment to admire it on my hand, he scooped me up into his arms, crushing me to him in his embrace. I whooped and laughed as he spun us, sending bursts of water all over us and in every which way. I pushed my lips to his, capturing them in a soul searing, heart melting, bone shaking kiss. A kiss that made me feel alive, with my nerves thrumming on high. A kiss that left me shattered and whole in the same moment.

"See? I was right," he chuckled against my lips. "Vastly different reaction than intense violence," I grabbed my knife from the top of my thigh and held it lightly to his neck.

"Too soon to rule that out yet." My breathy whisper came out so much more sensual than I'd expected as I caressed the blade ever so gently along his exposed throat between us. His eyes darkened in direct response, but I caught the glint of mischief I so loved.

"I knew you'd be into knife play," he answered in his husky voice, his hands rising from clutching my thighs to my rear. I bit my lip through a grin. "Hope you don't mind if I hold it against you." In the same moment, I felt two things: his length pushing into me, and his own knife dragging along my spine with the same gentleness I used on him. The knife didn't cut, but the whisper of what it could do tingled along my spine, making me shudder. Locke's lips landed on mine in a flash, making my blood sing, my blade precariously between us in a way that made my pulse race-for more than one reason. Locke noticed, wrenched my dagger from my grasp and tossed it to shore with our things, his own kissing at my neck in the space between us. I glanced up at him, watching his eyes heated like blue flames. "Careful, love. That dagger is giving me some wicked ideas."

"And if I'm not in the mood for careful?" I eyed the darkening red of his aura. It was a heady feeling, seeing his desire so openly before me. It was so intimate, I hated that this couldn't be more permanent.

"I was *so* hoping you'd say that." He dipped his head lower to devour me, the knife still between us. I felt tension and drag on the knife and I broke away in a panic, worried I'd hurt him. He towered over me, his hand coming to my wrist. "Your concern is cute. This is in my way."

In a heartbeat, Locke tossed his blade to the beach and was back on me in a flash of heat, his hands roaming me with reverence once again. And this time, I knew they'd never leave. My own hands explored as if for the first time, as I struggled to get enough of him, raking up his arms, his chest, the hardness of his abdomen.

And then we were moving.

His zodiac speed saw us the short distance across the beach to a cove where large rocks framed the water. Rocks large enough to support our current activities. A swipe of my hand along the rocks made them as smooth as the sand beneath our feet before my back met the cool stone wall. His hands grasped my rear, hauling me to him. My legs wound his torso, crossing my ankles behind his back and grinding myself on him, tipping my head back. His name, fueled with nothing but raw desire slipped from my lips.

"Fuck," he ground out as his lips worshipped a line from my lips to my collar bone. Pinning me against the stone with his hips, his hands were free to explore. One of which still held his gold hilted dagger. "I love when you wear dresses. It makes it so much easier for me to do this."

He didn't waste time. Pinning me against the stone his just his hips left his hands free. The coldness of the knife made me jump when I felt it whisper against my most sensitive flesh. It wasn't there long. It sheared my underwear off, leaving me bare beneath my dress. With another expletive, he wrenched my dress up with his other hand, exposing me to him.

"You're entirely too clothed, Crowned Assassin." I whispered before his lips crashed into mine once more, sending plumes of fire throughout my body and settle back into my core. I needed him. And he was wasting time. "Fuck me. Now."

"When did you get the impression you were the one in control?" His voice was a growl, rougher than raked coals. Hotter still. His dagger bearing hand came up to sit between us, making my breath still in my suddenly too tight chest. The blade glided across the skin of my collar bone with a feather-like lightness, making my skin tingle where the cool metal touched. My skin lit from within, turning pink, but not breaking under the dagger's kiss.

I'd never felt more alive.

Not even as the dagger's touch shifted lower, the drag on my skin never increasing. Never painful. The promise of pain hiding behind the pleasure and anticipation was making me high. Even as Locke had lowered his pants. Even as he growled, filling me inch by tantalizing inch. Even as I choked on his name. The cold steel of the dagger trailed lower, so close to where we were joined. I had no idea what his plan was. His next move. I didn't care as long as I could hold tight to this feeling for as long as possible.

Locke began to move then, his hips slamming into me. I cried out, my lips parting on a fractured rendition of his name. At some point the dagger was lost, his hands favoring instead to bury themselves in my hair, his teeth pressing into the flesh of my neck—not a bite but just as the dagger did before, leaving a small hurt that made the pleasure more intense. Opposing sensations left me feeling breathless and lightheaded while that familiar pressure began to build.

Locke's release sounded at the same time as my own, my name whispered between panted breaths that mingled with my own.

I was in no hurry to move. Even the thought was immediately off putting. I basked in the afterglow of Locke and the warm waters of the Arim Aesor with a bliss-filled sigh. No, I was perfectly happy right where I was. Locke reclined against the rocky backdrop and settled me against him. His muscular, runed arms enveloped me as I relaxed, my back against his chest. The comfortingly warm water level coming to my collar bone. I awkwardly stuffed my dress under my hips to keep it from floating around us, knowing I could dry it as soon as we rose. I sighed contentedly, his head propped up against his shoulder.

"I love you," I whispered before wrapping his much larger hand in mine and bringing it to my lips to punctuate my vow with a kiss. My left hand was suddenly out of the water, my new ring against his lips in turn, making me melt further into him.

"And I you," he murmured in that voice. That heartachingly sweet voice I knew was only meant for me. I glanced up at the stars wheeling overhead, simultaneously bursting with thanks for my current happiness, and horrible dread knowing it was going to come to a swift end.

And soon.

I knew that any moment we would have to get up and jumpstone back to Port Azure. Gemini and his answer would await us soon. But for now, I had everything I ever needed. And wanted. For once, everything was absolutely perfect.

Chapter Seven

Our quiet, comfortable peace had to come to an end. At some point, we had to head back to reality. I knew that. But turning towards the portal back to the bone penetrating chill of Port Azure made me feel like a prisoner forced to go back to their cell after a short recess outside. We slipped back home, but I couldn't stop myself from turning one last second at the glimmering pink pond and misty sunset.

Stepping back onto the frost addled cobblestone of the main square had me mourning the Arim Aesor fiercely, but I only had to look at my blank left hand to smile. Only he could see it for now. Locke shrouded it so we could tell our friends together later. Still, even though I couldn't see it, I could feel it. I couldn't stop myself from checking it was still there and I hadn't lost it every few seconds. It was still there. Still safe. Still real.

There was a strange pulse in the very core of my being that stopped my feet from following Locke towards the Citadel. It didn't hurt. Not exactly. It felt cold. Dead.

Gone.

Another piece of me had died. I suddenly felt as if I were standing in an hourglass, watching as the sands rose higher and higher until I was consumed. When my feet stopped, Locke turned to me, his face falling at my sharp intake of breath. Realization replaced his easy expression, hardening into that mask of worry I'd grown accustomed to of late.

What did it mean for me to be staring down death for me to fully appreciate all I had around me?

After all, the higher you rise, the sharper the blades that hunt you.

Electricity that had nothing to do with my magic thrummed along my body. I couldn't sit still waiting for Gemini to return, so I changed into sparring leathers, a gift from Lenore who hated seeing a regular shirt and leggings, and found Aspen, which based on the numbers of times he's knocked me to my now aching ass, was starting to seem like a shit idea on my part. My muscles strained as Aspen once again pinned me to the sparring mat with far too much ease for my ego. A whoosh of air forcefully left my lungs at the same time as Aspen sighed. He really was going easy on me before. A thought I shoved away, hauling myself to my feet and ignoring Aspen's outstretched hand.

"You're distracted, Lark. Focus. Show me your stance."

I sank into position, my leading leg ahead of me, my weight distributed the way he'd showed me a million times, trying not to huff. "Bring your elbows in. You're winging." I glanced down, sure enough, my stance was sloppy. A sure sign that fatigue was trying to get my attention. I studiously ignored it, bringing my elbows in, also ignoring the burning and heaviness in my shoulders and upper arms. A drop of sweat dripped down my check, tracked by Aspen's ever attentive gaze. "Maybe we should take a break."

"No. Hit me." The words came out harsher than I'd meant them. I couldn't stop though. Despite my body begging me to, I couldn't stop. I couldn't stew in my thoughts and anxieties about how everything depended on what answer Gemini would come back with. Assuming he deigned to return at all.

Aspen gave me a hard look, appraising before launching himself at me. I ducked under his first punch, using his momentum against him, I introduced his ribs to a sharp, needling elbow. Satisfaction filled me hearing his sharp intake of breath. I darted away, before his answering blow could make contact.

Aspen brandished his fists, regaining his breath before charging at me again, forcing me to move my feet around the sparring mat.

"Come on!" he bellowed, his voice echoing and drawing the eyes of everyone around us. "You wanted to hit me, let's go!"

I hesitated. He was goading me. His guard was tight, leaving me little room for opening. I had to be smart. Draw on my training. Open him up. Attack from everywhere. Force him back. I faked an attack from the right, watching him track it, and dart left. A move he was anticipating. He blocked my fist, and recanted with a quick one of his own, his punch landing in my ribs—retaliation from earlier. I ducked through the pain, hissing, as I slammed two weak hits to his body. His grunts once again brought me satisfaction. His stance lowered, his leg snaking out trying to topple me. I jumped, avoiding it, while going for the takedown.

He got a foot between us at the last moment, his foot embedding itself in my diaphragm and catapulting me away a few feet. I landed hard and flat on my back—my lungs spasming, refusing to draw breath. Using my air magic, I forced much needed oxygen into my angry lungs, alleviating the ache. I took a huge breath readying myself to go again—

When Aspen held his hands up and cut off my protests, effectively ending our session.

"You're spent, Lark. You need some energy for tonight. We don't know what we're walking into. Save your strength."

I loosed a sigh and nodded.

Aspen and I now sat together, his healing magic undoing untold damage to my muscles. Welts and bruises faded from view, and a particularly nasty one from my ribs vanished to such a degree I felt my ribcage spring open to take in more oxygen. The effect was immediate. My head stopped spinning on its axis and my thoughts became a bit clearer. Looking to my best friend, I was selfishly pleased to see him sweating. Not as much as I was, but I couldn't help the self-satisfied smirk that picked up my lips at the evidence of his exertion.

"Aspen," I said as his healing green glow faded from view. I stretched, allowing my freshly healed muscles to move languidly through their range of motion before settling next to him. "What's the Air Court like?"

"Don't tell me you're getting nervous?" He side eyed me. I bristled, my hackles going up on instinct before I saw his grin break through the stonefaced facade. "Relax Little Bird, you're going to love Everwind." His voice softened then, revealing a sense of awe. "It sits in the mountain range itself surrounded by mist. When you're there, it's easy to forget the rest of Meridian exists. The roofs of every building were made of a reflective material, which when viewed from above gives the illusion of lightning flashes. And then there's Windermere Castle. It's unlike anything else in Meridian. There was a time when everyone thought it floated above the city on a cloud."

He paused, I assume to be dramatic, and looked sidelong at me again, just to see if I were hanging on every word.

I was.

"And?" I probed. "Am I to conclude that it isn't, based on your ?"

"Damn, I need to work on that." He gulped down a drink of water, his throat bobbing three times before he continued. "You would conclude correctly. The castle is carved into the mountain. Is one with it. They're said to have the most terrifying dungeons. They used to train their dragons within the mountain's stronghold, but now that they're extinct, apparently they've gotten creative with the space. Getting on their bad side is a very bad idea. It's also perilously easy to do." He didn't say it as if he were recanting a myth or a secondhand tale. The faraway look his face took on made me think he might know firsthand. But as soon as I was about to press him about it, he smiled at me and continued, his silent tell. "It's an incredibly beautiful place."

"Is this whole thing even possible?" I asked him. He gave me a wry smile.

"The truth?" I nodded my assent, steeling myself for the blow I knew was coming. "I don't know. It could go either way for us tonight." I loosed a breath the same way I did when I received a punch to the ribs though it did nothing to quell the rising tightness in my chest. Anxiety was becoming an all too familiar, albeit unwelcome, tag along. "That being said, all of us have faced tough odds before. All of us. And we're still here, Lark. This will be no different. Locke isn't fucking around and that goes a long way with the Zodiac Kinship, even from other courts. There isn't much he isn't willing to do."

That was part of my concern, but I didn't voice it.

Aspen clapped his hands, stood, and hauled me to my own feet. "Now, go rest and get ready for tonight. If you're lucky, you'll have a few minutes of quiet alone time before the Terror Twins find you. I'm pretty sure Lennox has been looking for an excuse to doll you up for a while, so have fun with that." With a wink and a conspiratorial whisper, he continued, "If they're there when you open the door to your rooms, it's all over. You may as well just surrender."

He said that like it was a bad thing.

I remembered walking into my rooms. I remembered bathing, the heat of the water unknotting the muscles and the calming, sweet-scented soap washing away the grime and sweat. I remembered easing into the chair by the fire with the intention of reading a random book from my shelf for some time before Lenore and Lennox arrived. I remembered my weary body muscles sinking into the plush cushions. What I didn't remember was falling asleep.

Which was why it was so alarming to blink one moment safe in my rooms, cozy under a blanket by the crackling fire, and open my eyes to the lumbering throne room of Ari'inor. I hadn't seen it in real life, but with a deep certainty I knew. It was intrinsic. Sapphire and gold in all its extravagance, massive windows reaching the ceiling and towering columns of ice were irrefutable. I was in Loc Valen. I felt terror grip me all at once and I blinked against the vision, desperately willing myself to return to Port Azure. But my terror became all-encompassing when the vision before me didn't change. The throne of ice, the gleaming floors and the towering, opulent cathedral ceilings remained firmly in place. Ari'inor surrounded me, mocked me. And I wasn't alone.

Scorpio's grin turned taunting. Her eyes showed no hint of the green they used to be, and instead black voids stared at me. I shrieked, unable to move as Scorpio knocked me to the ground—the hard white marble floor. I couldn't lift my arms in my defense when Scorpio sealed her grip around my throat with a laugh. My heart thrashed in my chest, begging the Goddess, begging anyone to get me out.

"Locke!" I cried out as much as I was able before Scorpio's ever tightening grip silenced me. His name didn't echo the halls, didn't summon him.

My blood chilled.

A tear rolled down my cheek.

Where was he?

He swore he wouldn't let me do this alone. He swore...

Tears welled in earnest, blurring Scorpio's smug expression. This was worse than dying alone. I couldn't even use my hands to claw for my freedom. My magic had deserted me, as had the functionality of my body. I was finished.

"I told you I'd end this with my hands around your neck," Scorpio grunted the words while I felt my heartbeat stutter and slow. My lungs burned painfully, begging for oxygen. My limbs began to feel heavy and leaden—I suspected even if I could have struggled before, that time was up.

I opened my mouth in a silent scream. I shrieked my pain, knowing my last moment in this life was going to be Scorpio's mad, grinning face. I screamed with everything I had left, the one thing I could control.

I screamed my fear.

My anger.

My resentment.

The next moment reality snapped over me like whiplash. I heard my own shriek and my body moved once again, rolling itself into a protective ball. Arms gently came around my torso, instilling a fear so sharp and distinct my body acted of its own, throwing my elbows every which way until one made heavy contact.

A grunt responded, followed by my name, and the quick withdrawal of arms. I opened my eyes at last, blinking, head spinning, taking in the surroundings of my rooms. I dragged in several quick breaths, my lungs burning and my throat raw from screaming.

"Lark!" Locke's voice began to float down to me from the darkest reaches of my consciousness. Locke?

"Lark it's me. It's me. You're safe. You're safe, love. I promise."

I blinked. I swiveled my head, actually seeing my surroundings through the misty veil of panic. The soft cushions of my reading chair still cradled me. The cozy fire still roared in the hearth, though neither offered me the comfort they did before. Locke knelt before me, chest heaving and pinched eyes frantic. He kept murmuring my name and the one word that resonated with my very soul.

Safe.

I was safe.

I wasn't in Ari'inor.

I wasn't in Loc Valen.

Scorpio wasn't here and I didn't just die by strangulation. Locke didn't abandon me. I lifted my head and centered my vision on him at last, finally seeing him. The panic that had gripped me so tightly only heartbeats before finally loosened its grip, though didn't entirely relent. Just enough for shame for my outburst to mingle with it.

"I'm so sorry," I whispered, my voice opposite to my earlier screams. I touched my throat gingerly, wincing as I swallowed.

Locke's fingers brushed mine ever so slightly. So gentle I had to look down and make sure it had happened. When I brought my eyes back to his, they wore emotions so intertwined it wasn't possible to tell them apart. They flicked through so fast I couldn't read them.

"May I?" he asked in a voice like dark silk, holding out his other hand to me. I heard his real question; could he touch me? Could he comfort me? Could he help me? Would I let him? I nodded mutely.

That was all the encouragement he needed. He scooped me into his arms, carrying me to the bed where he sat reclined against the headboard, his arms tightly, protectively around me. As I listened to his steady heartbeat, they felt less of a cage now and more of a home. With protective walls around me to keep me safe. Each thump-thump of his heart reminded me that we were both still alive.

"You have nothing to be sorry for," he murmured against my forehead before placing a chaste kiss there. His arm smoothed lines along my upper arm. Light, rhythmic directions that helped focus my mind on the calm of the moment. "You're safe."

I felt the last of my terror ebb away, only to be replaced with a general sense of disquiet, like my mind and body would never fully settle again. He tipped my head to look up at him.

"No. Stop that. You have every right to feel how you feel." His voice was like the nearing evening calm. Gentle. Soft, with a growing darkness, bringing to mind the lengthening shadows dusk brings. "Fear is normal, especially given our circumstances. But never be ashamed that the fear took hold of you for a moment. It doesn't mean you're not the strongest fae I've ever met. Fear has a way of breaking even the strongest sometimes. Even me."

"The Crowned Assassin? Afraid? Of what?" My voice was so small, my attempt at a joke rang empty. He levelled me with a dark look.

"I was terrified when I felt how scared you were just now," he said. "I was never more afraid in my life than the moment I met you." My surprise must have been obvious. He gave me a pointed look before continuing. "I felt the curse snap into place. I knew that you were going to bring me to ruin or paradise. Not being in control of my own destiny scares the hell out of me. I'm terrified that I can't save the fae I love with everything I have. I'm one of the most powerful beings in Meridian, but I can do nothing but watch as you're ripped away from me. Because I would do anything to avoid this. All I can do is make sure you know you're not alone. All we can do is hope Aquarius agrees to help us." His voice cracked under the weight of his emotions, breaking something inside me too. I brought his palm up and kissed it before tightening my hold on him.

"I need you to know that no matter what happens, if our plan works or not, you should know that I'm so grateful for this time together. I will never regret loving you. Not for an instant," I said.

I heard his exhalation of breath. As if he couldn't believe that I cared as much as I did. That the sun rose and set with him. Which for the life of me, I'd never understand.

I curled into him further, relishing the way his arms encircled me tighter. I breathed in the scent of him, elation thawing my anxiety when his lips caressed the top of my head. I'd never needed anyone before, other than my father. I needed oxygen. I needed water. And I needed Prince Cancer, the Crowned Assassin. I needed Locke.

I don't know how long we stayed like that, arms encircling one another. My panic slowly ebbed away entirely as I focused on him. His musky pine scent enveloped me, leaving me in a lovely sense of calm. The daylight began to turn into warm late afternoon sun. I craned my neck up to him, a shy smile on my face. He smiled sleepily at me a pressed his lips to my forehead and then a sweet kiss to my lips that turned my insides into a puddle.

"I'm in no way ready to move," I stretched, reveling in the cracks my spine let out. "But I think Lennox and Lenore will be here shortly." I disentangled myself from him, strictly not noticing the way his eyes roamed by body as I slid from the bed. "What exactly does one wear to an audience with the Air Court?"

"They're formal," he said, taking to his feet. "I understand Lennox had a selection of dresses sent to your closets. Personally," his eyes raked over me one last time in a way that made my stomach flutter before bringing his eyes back to my face with a heart stopping smile, "I like you in blue."

I wasn't given an opportunity to answer. Two sharp, quick knocks and the twist of the door handle alerted me to the twins' presence before the door opened.

"Oh fuck, are we interrupting something?" Lenore asked, making a show of throwing her hands over her eyes. "You guys have clothes on, right?" Lennox rolled her eyes.

"Grow up," she hissed in a low tone I doubted she thought I could hear. I grinned, despite myself.

"I promise we're on our best behavior, Lenore." Locke mock saluted her before planting a chaste kiss on my lips. "I'll see you later. And I can't wait."

"Oh, vomit," Lenore gagged. "Just go. You guys are more insufferable now than when you didn't get along." Locke laughed as he made for the door. I looked at the twins expectantly.

"Now what?"

Lennox's excited grin should have been a warning.

Within the hour, Lennox had coaxed my unruly frizz tamed only by a braid, into freefalling waves, complete with an oil to increase its shimmer. I'd lined my green eyes with kohl under Lennox's watchful eye. She'd made me lovely. Lenore made me dangerous. Of course, she had gifted me a set of daggers. What else should I have expected?

I turned one of the daggers over in my hands, marveling at the light weight of it. It was entirely black, from blade to handle to hilt. The blade was impeccably shined and as sharp as they come. Well balanced, this blade was as much an art piece as it was deadly.

"You've used your old daggers," Lenore said to me in her straightforward, matter of fact tone. "It's time to retire them. I had these made for you. I have no idea what's going to happen while we're there, so you'll need these too." She revealed a thigh sheath from behind her back and handed it to me. I smiled widely. It was so in character for Lenore not to wrap or hide her gifts. "Rule number one: don't ever be unarmed in the Air Court. Or any other Court for that matter."

"Don't worry, Lenore, I'll keep your secret." I gushed over the thoughtfulness of the gift as I fingered the supple leather with admiration. She bristled.

"What secret?" She looked at me, expressionless.

"That you're not nearly as mean as you want others to think you are." I smiled at her with a wink. Her lips pressed together and folded her arms in lieu of a response while Lennox snorted from her place in the mirror where she was applying her face powder. "Thank you, Lenore. These are beautiful! I love them." She smiled. A rare, genuine smile, not her usual half smirk. I embraced her, much to her distaste.

"I'm glad you like them," she huffed, awkwardly patting my back. "We should get dressed."

I'm not sure what I was expecting their dresses to look like, but this wasn't it.

Lenore wore a show stopping red dress that fell to her feet with a daring slit up the sides of both thighs. At my gawking, she winked.

"I can move in this dress. My daggers are hidden on the backs of my legs. I'm set if anything happens. I'm not trapped under layers of tulle and pouf." She made a show of shuddering. "I can't even think of a worse way to go." I giggled. Because of course Lenore was worried about practicality in the face of death. At an audience with the Air Court Zodiac Kinship.

"Fuck. Lenore, do you always have to anticipate a fight?" Lennox glanced up at me from her place by the mirror. "It's most likely going to go down like this." She counted out the events on her hand, ignoring her twin's unamused look. "We show up, thickly lay on niceties, explain our case, bargain, and we'll be home before you know it. Who knows? Maybe there will be a party."

I hoped not. It's not that we weren't dressed for it. I wasn't ready to attend my first ever party with a myriad of fae I didn't know. It was hard enough being awkward around those I loved, let alone strangers. But all my thoughts stopped for a moment when Lennox turned around.

Lennox's dress was as lovely as she was, dark blue and flowing, with small tulle floral accents along the neck line. She too, had slits in her skirts, but these were so subtle you'd barely notice. Her skirts flowed like water in a brook, calm and pretty. But I watched her also place a dagger on her thigh, completely hidden. How merciless was the Air Court if both of the twins were arming themselves so covertly?

The dress Lennox helped me pick—blue as per Locke's request—was probably the most beautiful thing I'd ever seen. And also the most extravagant thing I'd ever put on my body. The sweetheart neckline was modest enough, the bodice clinging to my every curve without feeling restricting. The gold trim along it trailed regally down the front of the dress, where it hit my thigh and opened the skirt in a bold—though not so bold as Lenore's—front slit, revealing much of my legs to the world. It had small gold embellishments along the bodice that had the most subtle shimmer when I moved, like sunlight on rippling water. Like Locke's eyes. My shoulders were left bare, the lighter than air sleeves tight on my upper arms, loosened at my elbow and rippled and flowed elegantly to my knees. I looked as though I stepped from the sea. I looked like a proper Lady of the Water Court.

More than that, I looked like the embodiment of the Water Court.

I hated that I couldn't wear my boots. The fine leather ones that concealed my daggers, and would now conceal the beautiful black daggers Lenore had gifted me. I felt naked, exposed without them, as I shoved my feet into a pair of golden slippers. Lenore passed my two thigh sheaths, which were mostly concealed by my dress, especially when I oriented the daggers along the outside of my thigh. Lennox declared that it was finally time, making my breaths come shakily and my pulse skitter. I glanced out the window to see the stars brightly winking overhead, their reflection distorting in the soft waves of the sea beyond Port Azure.

We shouldn't keep Prince Gemini waiting.

Chapter Eight

We walked into Locke's offices without knocking. The first thing I'd noticed was that Gemini had not yet arrived, and I couldn't tell if that were a bad sign or not. The second thing was that I nearly didn't recognize Aspen. In place of the disheveled blond hair and training leathers, he wore a shirt of a fine material, possibly silk, and a gold overcoat with lovely blue embellishments and embroidery. Simple. Subtle. And completely unexpected. He raised an eyebrow at my surprise, grinning broadly as I eyed his slick backed hair into a neat bun. I couldn't help a sheepish smile as I was discovered gawking, but my surprise was so genuine.

A deep and familiar chuckle sounded from behind him and that was when my eyes first laid on Locke. My chest constricted at the sight. He was dressed in layers, each more intricate than the last. A blue shirt peeked out beneath a black and gold vest with stylistic buckles in the front rather than laces. A black formal overcoat with gold trim that reminded me on the piping on my own dress showcased a subtle pattern in the fine fabric. Embossments of a darker, shinier black along the coat that closely resembled the runes that decorated his arms and chest. As I stepped into the room, I realized my eyes couldn't move from him. As if also realizing this, and he most likely did, his eyes darkened, scanning me from top to bottom, somehow feeling more intimate than it should have.

"You look beautiful, Lark." Aspen smiled. A smile I returned. I opened my mouth to say thank you—

"Indeed, she does." Locke meandered forward, something shiny in his hand. "but she's missing something important." His steps towards me were deliberate, a ghost of a smirk on his lips. At my excited nod, he took my hand. With a small stirring of energy, he removed the shroud he'd had on my left hand, revealing my ring to our friends. Excited gasps resounded in the room, followed by a deafening squeal from Lennox, but Locke's eyes never left me. "Now she's perfect."

"When did this happen?" Aspen's voice was shrill, elation raising his usual pitch. As red as my face was, I couldn't help my shy smile as Lennox grabbed my left hand to examine the ring.

"It's beautiful!" Lennox squealed again as she embraced us both. Even Lenore smiled widely as she patted Locke on the back.

"It happened earlier today!" I couldn't help but gush. Surrounded by the fae I loved most in the world with such happy news, I'd never felt more loved in my entire life, I realized with warmth blooming in my chest. Locke's gaze met mine over the revel, making my heart melt. Making time stop. Making everything stop.

"You know what this means, right?" Lenore's voice brought me out of my reverie. She stepped back after exchanging a look with everyone and nodded. Lennox and her twin sank into a deep curtsy. Aspen followed suit, dipping into a low bow, all of them with their left fists over their hearts and pride written clearly on their faces. I glanced at each of them in turn and finally to Locke for answers.

"Scorpio can't do anything about my status as Prince of the Water Court. That power remains with the Zodiac Guild," he explained. "You're my equal. My betrothed, and as such you receive the title, respect, and power that goes with that." His eyebrows raised, as begging me to refute his next words, "Your Highness."

"Don't make that face," Lennox admonished me in a gentle tone, "We accepted you as Locke's soulmate long ago. This is the natural next step, *Your Highness*. And a role we're proud to see you take as your friends, and your knights." I stood there dumbfounded until Locke's hand found mine.

"We go to the Air Court together. As the rebel court. We are the prince and princess of the rebel court, and soon," He kissed the ring on my hand, "All the courts will know."

"Bunch of fucking gossips," Lenore muttered, making Aspen laugh. Tears prickled my eyes like tiny needles from the effort of holding my emotions in check.

"I couldn't be prouder to have you assume this role by my side, Lark. My soulmate. My princess. My match." His voice dropped into a voice meant only for me, "My equal." I looked over at our friends still beaming at me. I finally had it in me to return their excitement in equal measure, my face donning a cheek splitting grin. For the first time in my life, I knew peace. Happiness. Love. I had a place where I fit in and belonged. Fae I loved like family. A fae I loved with my entire soul.

If I knew I could feel like this, If I knew life could turn around this way, I'd go through it all again to have these fae before me in my life. A thousand times over if necessary.

The happy mood dimmed to something of a thrumming anxiety when we collectively heard a familiar of a jumpstone. Like air rushing by the opening of a cave. We'd all turned to the source of the noise when Gemini stepped through the portal, making my stomach buzz with angry hornets. His countenance gave me nothing, no hint at what his answer might be. Gone was his armor from earlier. In its place was the white and silver finery the set his hair alight, he resembled a storm cloud ready to sear us with lightning.

How ominous.

His eyes perused us each in turn, pausing on my left hand, widening with genuine surprise.

"It seems there have been developments since last we spoke, *Highness.*" He wasn't disrespectful exactly, but I bristled at his tone all the same. Maybe it was the way his eyes hardened. Maybe it was the way his voice grated over my newfound title. His eyes shifted back and forth between Aspen and Locke before settling back to me with a sneer. "I can see how quickly you worked your way up the ladder here. Is it just the Prince Cancer or is it the knight as well?"

"Bite your tongue, Gemini," Locke growled low in his throat. His warning was clear. His aura flickered out violently, making the air around us tremble and shadows recoil. "Unless you'd like to be relieved of your spine." His hand went to the sword he carried at his hip to accentuate his threat. Gemini's lips lifted into a haughty grin, his head inclining at the challenge. I didn't miss the way his eyes flickered to Locke's blade, still sheathed for now. I placed my hand on my betrothed's arm, doing little to cut the tension.

"Allow me," I whispered, my gaze not leaving the Prince of Air, even as he chuckled.

"Oh? Allow you to do what, exactly?" he taunted. Locke remained tightly wound next to me, as did the knights. I felt his challenge, his insult simmering between us. The gauntlet had been thrown.

And I would answer.

For the first time in my life, I would answer. I would not hide behind Locke, or anybody else. I fight my own battles. I would show him here and now that Locke wasn't the only one not to be trifled with. Locke grinned, with a gesture of *he's all yours,* and an almost sympathetic look at the arrogant Air Prince.

"If you wish to insult me, Gemini, be sure you can back it up." Bold words I spoke, especially considering his grasp over air will be significantly more powerful than mine, which would be concerning if I had only air magic to work with.

But I had three more elements.

I summoned the serpent of flames from earlier, this time wrapping it around his body. The snake hissed in warning as he struggled, trying to use his air magic to smother the fire. My flames sputtered, as I grappled for control. At his arrogant glance, I switched tactics. Thorny vines rose up to ensnare his ankles, not enough to draw blood. But held him there, with the promise of spilling blood if he moved an inch. I watched with satisfaction as my vines climbed him, wrapping and clinging to him.

And there was nothing he could do.

I watched the sweat gather on his brow as he considered his options. My final vines wrapped gently around his throat, which bobbed, betraying his nerves as he felt the tips of my thorns that were poised to strike at my whim.

He'd underestimated me. He wouldn't make that mistake again.

"I can make them sharper, or duller. Longer or shorter. The thorns, I mean." I said, imitating the way I'd seen Locke walk around those he'd considered prey. His body jerked for control, wincing when thorns dug crudely into his skin. "I have a question for you Gemini. A question a smart fae like yourself should know the correct answer to."

"You're attacking a member of the kinship whose help you desire so much." His sneer chilled me to the bone.

"Not an attack," I said, keeping my voice level. "A warning. That if you don't pay me the respect I'm owed, these thorns will find themselves in very uncomfortable places." I tightened my hold on him, just enough for him to squirm nervously. Lenore stood behind me, looking menacing as ever. Aspen grinned unabashedly from his place on Locke's desk. Locke himself looked—

—Locke looked enraptured, like he was waiting on every move I made. Like he was living for this performance.

"My question is simple," I drawled. "Will you pay me the respect I'm owed?"

At first, he didn't say anything. He held my stare with his own, the air rattling around him like the tail of the snake he was beginning to remind me of. I tightened my thorns, pressing them just into any exposed flesh. I watched his subtle intake of breath—I knew I was trying my luck here. His eyes quickly flashed as I refused to yield. This was a fae used to getting his way. In all things. I didn't need Locke's ability or anyone else's to see the simmering rage on his face. He was going to make me regret this. One day.

Possibly all too soon.

"Yes. *Highness*." He ground out at last in a tone that directly opposed his words. His lips pulled back in a sneer, exposing his canines, bringing to mind a rabid predator safely contained in a trap. From here, he posed no threat. But what happens when that same predator is no longer within the confines of that trap?

I dismissed my magic immediately. Gemini breathed a heaving sigh of relief, while looking at all of us with distrust. I smiled at him, having won that particular exchange. Locke snickered under his breath.

"Now, Prince Gemini, that that's out of the way, what is king Libra's decision?" Locke asked. The verbiage didn't escape me. King Libra's decision. Not the Air Court's decision, meaning Gemini wasn't necessarily as big a part of this as I'd feared.

Gemini straightened his coat. His face was a mask of practiced forced tranquility, but there was a seething rage behind his eyes. As elegant as I'd found him this morning, now I saw him as a roach— slimy and I didn't trust him. He seemed exceptionally two-faced, which might explain his Zodiac position. Gemini. The twins. Two faces. His glare was centered solely on me. I maintained eye contact, having already demonstrated I was clearly a match for him, I wasn't the least bit intimidated. Locke grinned, wrapping his arm around my shoulders.

"Beautiful and fierce. I'm so proud of you," Locke whispered so nobody else could hear. "And more than a little turned on." I fought a grin but pinched him on his leg to shut him up. I felt, rather than heard, his responding chuckle.

"Libra will see you now in the Throne room, if you're *quite* done." There was a pointed look at the two of us from Gemini over his shoulder. "You will arrive and disembark by jumpstone on my mark. Is everyone ready to leave?" He then glanced around the room without seeing any of us as we all joined hands. Locke joined hands with Gemini, who looked like he'd rather touch a three-week-old dead fish than Locke. Which, of course, only spurred on Locke's delight.

"No turning back now, Highness," he drawled. "You ready for this?" I glanced around us as the light from the Portal of the jumpstone deposited us in what could only be categorized as a throne room.

"Well, Locke, if I wasn't, it's a wee bit late to back out."

Chapter Nine

I took my first look at the Court of Air and forgot to breathe for a heartbeat. The beauty. The magnificence of it all. Windermere Castle was unlike anything I'd ever beheld. My head swiveled, my eyes not knowing what to settle on first. The Room was huge, airy, and grand, made up of clean, white stone. Archways ran along the length of the room on both sides, flanked by massive, billowing columns soaring to the domed ceiling. Runes of air magic swept their ways glittering and silver across the opulent marble floor contrasting the dark grey stone. When the firelight shone upon them, they flickered like diamonds.

No—not diamonds. Like flashes of lightning.

The Cathedral height room was colossal. Imposing. Full height windows on either side would allow scores of sunlight once dawn broke, and what was no doubt a breathtaking view of the city of Everwind below. As it was, I could see the stars glittering above. Hall would have been more appropriate given the length of the room. *The Hall of Kings*, the room itself seemed to declare.

There were massive archways every twenty feet apart or so rising high to the ceiling, each arch depicting a moment of the history of the Court, each one preserved beautifully etched into the stone itself. Most looked to be various coronations of Kings from olden times to current. The current King, Libra, sat upon his raised throne at the end of the room opposite us, eyes cool and assessing all of us. Dressed in resplendent red fabrics and dripping in jewels that matched his throne, it was obvious what Locke and Aspen meant about formal. Even his crown sitting elegantly on his dark hair, seemed unnecessarily decadent, silver, encased with rubies. Large ones. Looking around at the guards stationed every few feet along the back wall we were approaching, or the courtiers seated aloft above us, I saw more glittering runes and jewels, enough to end poverty in any realm. Material gain seemed to be a power in and of its own right here. I had to resist the urge to glance down at my own dress, knowing I'd defiantly under accessorized.

Instead, I swept my gaze across the throne. It was highly elevated, leaving no room for mistaking who the King was. Not elevated at all were two smaller, far less grand white marbled seats. Upon the right side sat what must have been Princess Aquarius in her flowing sky-blue gown. Prince Gemini forged ahead of us and took up his seat to the King's left with a look that made me feel like he was about to exact his revenge upon me. Our party's feet drew to a stop before the throne and the weight of everyone's gaze. It left me feeling unsettled. I fought the urge to palm my dagger against my leg, but knowing it was there was enough to take the edge off. It was then that I finally looked over at the fae we came to see.

Princess Aquarius had long hair, the color a rich chocolate that hinted of red undertones in the sunshine. Her blue grey eyes weren't unkind as they rested on me. Curious. Unsure. On her guard. The circlet on her head shimmered with diamonds every time she moved. Libra got to his feet and descended the stairs to stand between his kin, who remained seated. I glanced at Locke nervously. Do I bow? Curtsy? Locke then broke into a genuine smile then as he greeted Libra warmly. Libra's face also cracked into a more relaxed face, making him look like two entirely different people. They clasped forearms heartily with wide smiles.

"Welcome Prince Cancer of the Water Court! Welcome you, your knights!" His voice was exactly that of a King. Booming. Self-assured. Every courtier moved forward with anticipation. Libra moved down the line of our party, his footsteps joining the blood rushing in my ears as the only sounds. He reached me at last. "And you must be who I keep hearing so much about. Your reputation proceeds you, Queen's Mark." He extended his hand to me, and it took me a moment to realize what he wanted. I gifted him my left hand awkwardly, his cool palm lifting my fingers to his lips. His eyes focused immediately on my ring and I wondered if I'd made a mistake. "Prince Cancer. This is an interesting turn of events, friend. When were you planning on divulging this information?" he said, eyes appraising me, and my ring, with great interest.

"Admittedly, it has been such a recent development, Your Majesty," Locke said, stepping closer to me. "With such turbulent times, a proper announcement hasn't yet been made possible. But Lark is every bit the Princess now as she will be when it's official. But it's the turbulent times I wish to discuss with you."

"Ah. Meaning Scorpio doesn't yet know." Libra's gaze rested on me, as his words cut to the heart of the issue with a bluntness I couldn't help but respect. "Because you're both in hiding, is that not correct? And she cannot ascend as Princess of the Water Realm until such a time that you're no longer at war with her. Razor-sharp sharp attention missed nothing.

"Scorpio threatens my life, those I love, and my entire Court as a whole, Your Majesty," I said with an intentionally soft voice. I briefly lowered my head, paying him his respects as a King before continuing. "Which is why we've come. Not because of an issue of title or rank. But for a matter of life and death. For the future of the Water Realm."

"You come for aid in a war we want nothing to do with, Your Highness," he snapped, his voice turning cool. His dark eyes blazed as they assessed me anew.

"We don't come for reinforcements, Your Majesty. That is the tale I would like to tell you, if you'll allow me. Allow us." Libra's gaze remained unblinkingly on me looking like he was at war with himself over whether or not I was going to be a problem for him. With an exasperated look at Locke, he sighed.

"What trouble have you gotten yourselves into, Highnesses?"

"The usual sort," Locke shrugged, having the audacity to look innocent.

We told him the whole story. Beginning to End. About Scorpio destroying the Water Court. The horror she'd unleashed upon the citizens there. How Locke had found me in the Yemerian Vale, and what I'd witnessed in the Vale—the prophecy I was at the center of. About my four elements. We told them about how my father was using potions without my knowledge to suppress my abilities. How I'd never known I could do magic until fairly recently. I told them that I'd been training with the rebels now for months in an effort to bring myself up to speed so we could make a stand. Then we told them about Locke's curse. Locke had definitely kept details of his curse well hidden. Libra's gaze shot to Locke, appraising him with new and wide-eyed surprise, even Gemini lifted a confused brow. Aquarius took everything in stride, listening astutely to every single word. But even she couldn't hide her surprise.

We told them about Locke's curse and how it was now mine. How I'm destined to die. My magic's origins. We told them about our original plan of capturing Scorpio for her crimes and dethroning her for the good of the realm. But now with my death being unavoidable due to my being in love with Locke, I wanted my death to matter. To mean something. I want Scorpio to kill me. To break both curses.

"That's where someone from Air Court comes in," I said just as Libra was about to interject, glancing at Aquarius. Her eyes were assessing us, her sharp mind absorbing every detail. She straightened on her throne as my gaze landed on her. "I need to die, yes. But that doesn't mean I stay that way. I had a vision where a bolt of lightning shocked my heart back to life. Aquarius, I've been told you have the best control over lightning. I would ask that you bring me back from beyond the veil. That you try."

"Why?" Libra asked, bringing my attention back to him. There wasn't malice in his tone, just genuine curiosity. "Why should Air help in a conflict of the Water Court? You're talking about slaying a monarch—an invulnerable one, no less—and if you fail, Water will unleash its wrath upon my people. Scorpio won't discriminate bringing you back to life from sending reinforcements. Helping you, is hindering her. I don't need war on my doorstep, Highnesses." So it wasn't just Aquarius we had to convince. Libra needed convincing as well. I watched with a sinking heart as he turned his back to us and climbed back to his throne. He peered down his throne at us. His mind was made up.

This conversation was nearing its end. And not in our favor.

Locke spoke up first, his voice carefully schooled behind decades of playing Court. But I heard the undercurrent of desperation in his voice though, to anyone else he probably seemed cool, collected, and in control. "Do you think it stops at the Water Court? At the border? Because I've watched Scorpio tear her own Court apart looking for a way to break her curse. She's razed cities to the ground in retaliation when fae resisted giving her their seers. Do you really think that her cruelty will stop at the border when a seer inevitably tells her something about Air Court that's useful to her? Or when she's hunted seers entirely to extinction in our court looking for us, what makes you think she won't look beyond her own borders?"

It was in Libra's disparaging silence that I found my voice once more. "Scorpio is going to end up destroying her entire Court. A time will soon come where there won't be a Water Court. Just a wasteland where it used to be. A giant graveyard. Gemini told us that you're big partners in trade. How do you think that will go when there's nothing but death there?"

Gemini fumed in his seat.

"She's right," Locke said, giving me brief smile before returning his attention to the Air King. "Our biggest import to you is our fine silks, gems, and spices. These are luxuries in the Air Court that are coveted by all. How do you think it'll go if the Water Realm falls entirely to Scorpio's whims? Or when Scorpio decides that she requires something from Air. Or Fire. Or Earth. That time is coming."

"Who says?" snapped Gemini, his voice finding purchase on everyone's attention. He flashed me a dark look before turning to Libra, "Why don't we simply earn Scorpio's favor and give these pests to her?" Locke looked murderous as Gemini smirked at us. At me. This was his revenge for earlier. What horrified me most was that he was completely serious.

"No. I don't want blood on my hands. The idea is not to get involved. Besides, what if they win? The girl will die and end the curse regardless. If the rebels are successful and take the throne, do you really want Cancer as your enemy when he's crowned King?" Gemini paled, as if not thinking of that. Libra swung his head back to us. His eyes appraised each of us in turn, appraising for deceit in what we weren't saying. Hidden motives, perhaps. "Because that's what this is truly about, isn't it? Power?" Locke shook his head.

"No. I'm quite content being the Crowned Assassin. Being a Prince. I have no desire to become King. And Lark has even less interest. None of this is about power. Or ambition. It's about stopping a someone who has more than earned the moniker the Barbaric Queen. She's ravaged entire families over a rumor of disloyalty. She's killed children. And she's nowhere near finished. Make no mistake, Air Kinship." His voice turned grave, reminiscent of Scorpio's atrocities. And his own. "Her throne may be made of ice, but it's built on the blood and bone of those she's massacred."

A dark laugh rose above all else.

"It's too late." Gemini's voice, above of all of them, rang out. Gasps sounded across the hall. I didn't understand. I looked to the Air Prince, my heart understanding intrinsically that something was horribly wrong. The energy had turned fraught and turbulent. And I only had to follow his gaze behind us, to understand why.

I turned, glimpsing the red hair and penetrating stare that had haunted the edges of my nightmares for months. Green eyes veined with rivers of black, evidence of her excessive black magic usage. Pisces with his sickening, triumphant smile paced in behind her, his footsteps thudding loudly on the stone floor, echoing in the great hall. The second prince of the water Court was dressed for battle in his armor, his thick leather chest piece emblazoned with the Pisces constellation. One look behind me at Gemini's smug expression was enough for me to swear to the Goddess that his death would be painful. He would answer for this betrayal. Especially, I looked down the line at my friends as they took defensive stances, if any of them got hurt. We were vulnerable, not wearing any protective gear. I saw Lenore's malicious smile as she withdrew her knives.

Locke stepped towards me, standing protectively between Scorpio and I. A gesture that turned Scorpio's nose up in a sneer.

"Cancer." His title spat from her lips like it was poison. The air left the room as a hush fell over all who remained. "I see you've been busy." Her eyes scarcely left me, reminding me of the way a butcher eyed a prized cow. Just wondering how to slaughter it. "Betrayal is a bold and busy business, isn't it? Your friend Abel knew that."

"You accuse me of being bold when you yourself are in the Air Court uninvited." Locke's voice was downright predatory. Queen Scorpio facing off against Prince Cancer. The Crowned Assassin. Two giants standing off with nothing left but wrath and hatred and flickering magics between them that sent the courtiers scattering for every exit. "What do you want?"

Her eyes flicked to my hand, to the jewel resting on my on our engagement ring. "And what's this? You're attempting to make this peasant a princess? Cancer, really. She's not a Zodiac. She's... something. I'll give her that, but a Zodiac?" She scoffed, a laugh falling from her lips immediately after. "But I suppose as Cancer, you are the bleeding heart of all of the water signs." She shared a knowing look with Pisces, as if in on some inside joke. I wanted so fiercely to run her through then and there with my blade. "Pathetic."

I saw the rage in the set of his jaw. My temper flared in kind. "She's been more of a Zodiac than you've been since the day you were crowned, Scorpio," he pressed closer to me. I didn't miss his hand hovering close to the hilt of a sword he'd brought. He was expecting a fight. My stomach soured, feeling heavy at the thought. We weren't ready for this. Not by a long shot. I cursed. How was I supposed to fight while fitted so snuggly in this dress? "There was once a time you cared about those in your Court. Wanted to be the best Queen you could be for your people. Before your curse. That didn't last long did it, Barbaric Queen?" His voice hardened into a jab. She returned his glare with one of her own. Even though she looked at him, I felt the weight of it. Felt my ribs constrict, my lungs needing air.

"I guess you could say that I traded one curse for another then." Her voice was lighter than air, without a care. She made a show of inspecting her nails. "If I cared what others thought of me, I'd never get anything done. You can't do anything you want without hurting someone, Cancer. You of all fae should know that."

Locke flinched.

It was so subtle, I wasn't sure, but Scorpios lips turned upwards, satisfied her barb had hit its mark.

"Scorpio and company." Pisces scoffed at being so dismissed as King Libra finally found his voice. Or maybe he just got tired of watching. His voice boomed over all of us, sounding not unlike thunder. "Your presence here in uninvited" I had to admit, I liked

Libra. He had a way of seeing and cutting right to the quick. Straight through the bullshit. It was admirable. Scorpio smiled, slow and unbothered, reminding me of a sly fox.

"But Your Majesty," she started, feigning confusion, "we were invited. All of us." At her signal, Crownguards melted out of the shadows and from around corners, lining up behind her and Pisces. A small legion. A small, well-armed legion, I noted halberds and swords and archers. Not drawn. Not yet. She grinned. The look in her eyes was like the world was burning. Like she reveled in it. And when she spoke again, her words rang out clear and confident, growing in candor, "Didn't Gemini tell you? He's done well in uniting Air and Water. He gives me the heads of the rebel forces, and he earns my favor in the water court. He's united the courts through mutual trust. Is that not something you've strived for, for years, Libra?"

"I want no part in your civil war, Majesty!" Libra slammed his fists on the arm rests of his throne before taking to his feet at last. There must have been a command in there somewhere, because the Air Court forces—the Wind Guard with their silver armor flecked with the air court constellations—now flanked us, our numbers growing to match, even surpass, the Water Court. Scorpio flicked her gaze around, but didn't look concerned. With the odds clearly in our favor, it begged the question: what did she stand to gain here?

Was she so desperate to kill me she'd launch into a suicide mission?

No. She couldn't die. And there was a calmness on her face that bordered on triumph. A diversion?

No, that didn't fit. Scorpios eyes found mine, amusement turning her lips up.

They began to move in behind us, beside us. There were now two small armies gathered in this great hall. We stood on one side; my death appraised me from the other. "I believe you to be mistaken, Water Queen. Air territory is and will remain," he cut a sour look to Gemini that had him withering in his place, "neutral. We will have no part in your dispute. And I will not tolerate such intrusions. Leave now and you may leave unharmed. Consider your invitation rescinded."

For a moment, nobody moved. There wasn't a single sound. I scarcely drew breath. I glanced back to Scorpio for her reaction. I cursed my dress. My hand hovered close to where my dagger lay comfortingly against my thigh. My fingers itched to draw my blade, my nails digging painfully into my palms to quell the urge. I focused on it instead of my heart thundering in my chest. Instead of my fear.

Not yet.

Wait for the right moment.

Oh, fuck it.

Drawing my dagger, I sheared the skirt of my dress, allowing my legs room to move at their will.

"Oh, but King" Scorpio drawled, running her tongue across her teeth, her posture going eerily still. "I'll be going nowhere." As if a practiced cue, Pisces blinked, using his impossible Zodiac speed, he slipped by us all to stop next to Libra, sword drawn too fast for my eyes to really perceive the movement.

But Libra was no slouch. He was a member for the Zodiac Kinship too. A king at that. Matching Pisces's speed, he threw himself backwards, narrowly missing his own throne. He drew his own sword in a bellow of rage. A sword that was likely more ceremonial than war tested.

Locke and I had but a moment to share a glance. A moment where a look was all we had to convey how we felt. I drew my blades at last, as did every single fae there. I wouldn't have guessed the blades Lenore had gifted me would get baptized in blood so soon. The two lines of battle hungry fae appraised each other with palpable ferocity. Palms twitched over blades and arrows, ready for the command to strike.

It was the moment Libra screamed that I realized what Scorpio was doing. She was killing Libra. Possibly Aquarius too. And putting Gemini, her ally, on the throne of the Air Court. Gemini, the weasel who wanted power but couldn't take it by himself. Gemini who would absolutely aid in exterminating the court of rebels. With Everwind to the west of Port Azure, and Loc Valen to the East, we'd be decimated. Did they know our location? Was it possible?

We couldn't let them win this. We couldn't. Gemini had to die. He knew how to find us.

I didn't get a chance to say anything.

Because chaos erupted.

Chapter Ten

I'm not sure if a command were given, or if someone had just had enough of waiting. The two lines of warriors met with a resounding collective cry, both sides thirsty for blood. My knives were braced and ready in front of me before the sides collided with a thunderous echo of weapon on armor. They were comforting, solid, and familiar in my hand, gifting me some semblance of control amidst the mayhem. Or at least saving me from feeling helpless.

I caught glimpses of Lennox and Aspen as the battle exploded around us, robbing us of all sense and strategy. There was only cut. Locke fought at my back, snarling as he dispatched each assailant and moved on to the next. I was thankful for him keeping my back protected. Magic erupted overhead in the form of ice and wind. Ice I couldn't feel through the throng of bodies and blades.

I couldn't make sense of anything. Everywhere I looked were flailing bodies, brutality, and death. It was horrible. The screams of the injured permeated my ears, shattered glass, steel sluicing through the air, clanging against steel or slashing flesh. Violence. Pure, senseless, chaotic violence. Those who succumbed lay in heaps, some so disfigured you couldn't tell who they used to be. I barely saw the first several I killed. I hated that I lost count. They didn't expect me to be a threat. A fatal mistake. My mind railed against the feeling of their blood slickening my hands, warm and wet, but I shoved that thought to the corner of my mind. I'd worry about it later. My magic surged, humming in my veins, as if begging for my command.

Aspen had spoken before of war. Especially when motivating me.

Sweat in here so you don't bleed out there.

How many times had he said it to me? I understood it now. But what he never prepared me for, what I don't think anyone could ever prepare me for, was the horror of blood raining down on me. Arterial spray from a slashed throat spattered me in far too short a time to be considered sensible.

Energy hummed, thick with bloodlust. My surroundings came at me in fragments: a knife here, a halberd there, a shield threatening to crush me. Only instinct mattered. No time to think. No time for strategy. I lashed out, quick and light, Aspen's training guiding my blows.

I needed to thank him more.

Two of Scorpio's Crownguards charged at me, sneering at my small dagger. He flourished his sword a second before he struck. It was hard to move, to evade. Bodies flailed all around me. Locke was moving, keeping them off my back. I had to do my part to keep him safe. I knew they wouldn't kill me. Everyone here knew that my death belonged to Scorpio. That was my advantage. These guard's defenses were sloppy and uncoordinated. Easy to interpret. Easier still to predict. I dispatched them both quickly, unprepared for the fresh wave of blood that soaked me. Warm and sticky, I lost my grip on my blade and in the tight throng of fae, it was lost.

But who said I needed one?

Locke turned to me as I summoned my air magic, creating a shield around us for a moment. I needed to cut more of my dress. I sheared them above my knees for freedom of movement, Locke eyeing me with... hunger?

"If we live through this, I want you in nothing but those thigh sheaths and your new daggers."

"Locke, this is so not the time!" I released the air shield and to the terror of every Crownguard around me, I summoned fire.

A Wind Guard soldier sent air towards me, further fueling my flames, enlarging them. Making them hotter. I flashed a grin before charring a few oncoming assailants in a blast worthy of the underworld itself. The scent of burned and ruined flesh threatened to choke me in the aftermath, reaching down my throat and turning it to dust and ash.

An arrow narrowly missed me. It chinked the floor behind me. A second I ducked under just in time. That one embedded itself into the side of one of Locke's opponents. He didn't suffer. Locke ended him swiftly, cutting his screams short after that advantage.

I turned, searching for the source. Up where the courtiers had abandoned, above the mayhem of the battle raging below them, I spotted a row of archers taking down Air Court's Guard handily. Stealth was their element. From their positions swathed in shadows, they hid in the upper balconies picking the Wind Guard one by one. They would hide no more.

I thwarted their next volley of arrows next with an intense gust of wind, screaming, announcing their presence. Spears, arrows, and crossbow bolts answered from our side, several of which set aflame. I sent my own flames up, a fireball that ensured their demise by blocking their escape before spreading towards them. Sweat beaded on my brow, not from the heat, but exertion. My chest was heaving, but it worked. The archer's screams filled the top as they burned.

Soldiers from both sides had thinned out and I could take a moment to assess our situation. My friends were okay, thank the goddess. Blood covered, but alive.

Locke was still with me, carving through each Crownguard like it was personal. And maybe it was. Each swathing cut, deadly and precise, causing the blood and corpses to pile up around us, making the floor slick.

Libra's horrific scream brought my attention to him. My magic fizzled from my hands as I watched. Screamed when I saw Pisces's blade peeking through his chest. I watched in horrified fascination as time slowed to a near stop. I saw the blade wrench in Libra's chest and his agonized wails. I couldn't move. I was rooted to the spot. It was only when I watched the light fade from his eyes did my limbs suddenly remember how to move, albeit heavily. I ran with several Wind Guards towards Libra feeling like I was running through sand. Gemini couldn't take the throne. He couldn't.

Locke yelled out my name.

It all happened in a matter of seconds.

Pisces tugged his sword roughly from his slain opponent, crudely depositing him, the fallen king, to the blood slicked floor.

The room darkened. Everyone stopped moving as electricity hummed and snapped in the air. Aquarius screamed as she approached the throne that Pisces had now vacated with a horrible cackle. A clang of swords behind me briefly drew my attention. Pisces attacked Locke at my back. Locke bellowed in fury as he returned the assault in kind, each ripping at the other. The wrath in Locke's eyes was echoed in Pisces's. This was personal. Deep cuts between them that hadn't healed. Pisces was out for blood. And I saw it on his face even in the shadowed room. I recognized it because for months I saw it looking in the mirror back at me, white hot vengeance.

"I declare myself acting Queen of the Air Court!" Aquarius's voice echoed through the hall. Gemini laughed as he flourished his blade.

"And if I declare myself acting King?" he challenged with a sneer. Aquarius's laugh echoed through the throne room, humor not reaching her eyes. Lightning struck overhead, casting everyone in its stark glow. With a spared look at her fallen kin, whose blood had reached her on the dais, she appraised Gemini with rising rage, hands tightening on her Halberd.

"Then I get to do something I've wanted to do for so long, Gemini." She lunged herself at him. In that same moment, I heard my name being screamed. My only warning before a flash of red hair filled my vision.

"A fight to the death?" he scoffed, turning towards her with a flourish of his blood-soaked blade "I like my odds."

The two remaining Air Court kinship members, the opposing prince and princess, converged with the force of two opposing and equally mighty winds, wrecking destruction, lightning, and devastation upon all unfortunate enough to get too close. Windows shattered, screams erupted, violent winds whipped my hair into my face. I wrenched my hair out of my eyes to see a flash of red.

And green eyes.

Scorpio was making her move.

Scorpio had come for me at last. I wondered when she would. Had she been waiting in the shadows, studying me? Seeing what I could do?

I summoned my flames again, this time into the shape of a sword. In a perfect moment, I might have said something. Instead, it took everything in me to ignore my fear and steel myself. Lightning struck again, turning color to shades of black and white. A perfect dichotomy to the clash between good and evil that was taking place.

Scorpio wasted no time, flinging a flurry of at me. I threw up a shield of air only just in time. Some of them were too sharp and stabbed through, with another push from Scorpio's will. When they cut my skin, they almost didn't hurt. Not right away. Seconds ticked by before the slicing pain started. But the blood...

It poured from me, much to her satisfaction. A million super fine lacerations that had blood welling and pouring from me. Her nearly feline expression that warred between contempt and raw delight. A quick glance around me was all I could afford, but it was enough. Scorpio brought enough people to distract everyone. Keep them busy. Pisces's sole job was to keep Locke away from me. So Scorpio could take me on alone.

Shouts of attack, grunts of effort, and screams of the dying set the backdrop to this bloody affair. I narrowed my eyes.

"Is that all you've got?" I flourished my sword. "I'm disappointed, Scorpio. I expected more." I knew she couldn't die. But she could still hurt. The corners of my mouth ticked upwards. "How will you recover if my flames melt the skin from your bones, I wonder?" My flames flared in response, as if anticipating it. Savoring the thought.

With an enraged roar, she sent another barrage of ice at me, this time the size of hammers. She was lightning fast and I didn't get my shield up in time. I threw myself to the side, the hard impact thwarted by landing on a still bleeding corpse. I didn't have time to process the horror of my face next to his slashed throat. I had to keep moving. Keep dodging. I grit my teeth against the coppery taste in my mouth, but no more projectiles hit their mark. Who knew running for my life and dodging icy projectiles from those who'd hunted me for years would save my life in such a profound way? The thought tasted more bitter on my tongue than the blood did.

"You're like a pesky fly." Her slim hands conjured a whip constructed mainly of ice, not dissimilar to the one Pisces had fought with in Frostfall. Dark magic coiled around it in lieu of frost, a hiss emanating from it. I didn't know what would happen if that thing touched me, but I knew I didn't want to find out. Scorpio followed my gaze with a smug expression as she cracked her whip, demonstrating its lash, the sound tearing through me. "One hit. One hit in the right place will be all it takes. Are you ready, fly?"

A scream that sounded like Lennox snagged my attention just behind Scorpio, and I saw her get slashed across the ribs. Her name left my lips—

"Keep your attention on me, Lark!" Scorpio shrieked, raising her whip.

I jumped back, but not in time. Her whip was destined for my neck, but the extra distance I'd gained meant it attached itself to my ankle, hauling my legs out from under me. I fell immediately, feeling the searing pain of the whip. The dark magic burned like acid, eliciting a scream I couldn't keep within.

"Right where I want you, little fly," she crooned, tightening the hold. "You're about to be splattered!"

Real, genuine fear hit me like a wall. It was too soon. We were not prepared. Our plan wasn't in place yet. I glanced over at Locke, seeing nothing but death. He'd slain so many as they swarmed him, desperate to keep him from us. A pile of slain Crownguards lay at his feet with more pouring towards him with weapons held high. He cried out my name as his next sluice sprayed him in blood, giving credence to his other moniker. His darker one—the nightmare assassin—bathed in the blood of those who slighted him. Pisces was still alive, though thoroughly bloodied, still in the fray, stopping Locke from advancing to meet me.

Locke's frantic eyes met mine from across the hall, another cry mixing wrath and agony as he realized the same thing I did: he wouldn't reach me in time. Nobody could. It happened so fast. Locke's scream of my name in time with Scorpio's movements, almost too fast to watch. Scorpio conjured a spear of ice swathed in darkness and threw it directly at my heart. I was snared like a rabbit in a trap.

Luckily for me, her desperation made her predictable.

It hurt. It hurt so much more than I could ever imagine. I fought with the urge to vomit. Moving whilst the whip held my ankle was like moving through a vat of acid. The burn from her black magic infused whip in conjunction with the icy needles flaying my skin was its own form of torture. But I hurtled myself out of the way. I dove to the side, knowing I was successful when the ice shattered behind me. Too close for comfort, gauging by the spray of ice pelting my back, but I was intact. Scorpio bellowed her frustration at the same time Locke screamed my name again, eyes scarcely leaving me as he fought desperately to get to my aid. Where he escaped one weapon, another quickly replaced it, keeping him from reaching me, despite the valor with which he fought. Any other warrior would have perished long ago, but Locke still fought. Nonetheless, I was alone.

I backed up, crawling backwards, trying to get some space when something knocked my hand. I gripped it, the familiar weight the greatest comfort of all.

My dagger I'd dropped.

Scorpio lunged herself at me with her blade made of ice and that acidic magic. I let her.

I got the blade between us just in time. All too easily, the blade sank into her abdomen like it was going through butter. I didn't have much room to twist the knife, but what room I did have, I took. A sick satisfaction filled me at her scream, even has her blade pierced my shoulder. Hot, searing pain like nothing I'd ever known exploded where her ice blade ripped into me, causing me to cry out in tandem with her.

"You can't kill me, Lark." Her voice was pained, her breathing labored, and beneath it all, I heard her persistence. Her desperation. We grappled a long, heart stopping moment. I sent her ice dagger flying. Which gave her the moment she needed to rip the dagger from her gut and thrust it downwards. This felt eerily familiar. With both palms, I clasped the dagger's blade and pushed, flinching as it drew blood. I did the only thing I could do, delay the inevitable.

"Lark!" I heard Locke call my name just in time to see him send a strong wave of ice barreling into Scorpio, freeing me. It cost him when Pisces opened a deep wound on that shoulder. My stomach soured, but I couldn't see what happened to him. I had to focus in order to survive.

It was chaotic, but effective. It knocked her off of me, allowing me to rip the icy blade from my shoulder. I bit back a whimper as it bubbled and oozed, black tinting the blood. I paused. That couldn't be good. Thankfully the wound was relatively shallow, and I tested my shoulder by grabbing the dagger while Scorpio regained her feet. I found it wildly painful, but mostly functional. It would have to be a problem I dealt with later. Locke was quickly attacked by multiple guards, but I did notice a few less. I tossed a harsh wind at those attacking him, knocking them back enough that Locke could get to his feet. Have some breathing room. He was winning, but he was exhausted and bloody. This needed to end now. Scorpio turned her attention to Locke who was already engaging with Pisces, another ice blade at the ready. Locke didn't see her. Primal, protective rage stormed within me.

She should have never taken her eyes off of me.

I lunged, quicker than I thought I was capable of. I thought she'd move, ever aware of me, but she was so focused on stabbing Locke in the back, thinking I was too hurt, she couldn't stop me. What she didn't know was I'd go through any pain, any realms of Hell, to keep him safe.

"I can't kill you," I agreed, plunging my dagger into her back, narrowly missing her heart. She screamed dropping to her knees, black oozing from the wound in shadowy wisps. "But I'll bet this hurts like a bitch." I called forth my magic before she could respond, using my water magic the same way I did when those bandits kidnapped me. I was so much stronger now than I was then. I felt her grapple with me for control, but in her weakened state, she ceded the edge to me.

Her body was frozen, encased in ice.

And I had never fought harder in my life. I knew I wouldn't be able to hold her indefinitely. Probably not even very long. But if we could wipe out her forces, we could capture Scorpio. We could end the curse on our terms. She wouldn't have a choice. This would be the safest way. For that, I focused hard on my tentative hold, feeling her magic thrashing against mine, feeling much like a cat clawing its way through a sheet. It would hold for a time, but eventually she was going to rip it wide open, angrier than ever.

Sweat collected on my brow and the nape of my neck as I put everything I had into holding her there. I took a moment to take stock of our situation around me. Lenore had grabbed an axe from somewhere, likely one of the fallen on the ground, and was swinging her way through the last of the Crownguards. Lennox was on the ground, unmoving. The only thing that kept me from crying out her name was the next thing I saw was she was being healed by a desperate looking Aspen. He glanced at me with a solemn nod. She would live, but he couldn't leave her yet. From here, I spotted a deep gash on her ribs with a concerning amount of blood. A grunt of effort dragged me back to where my soulmate fought for our lives. I watched with my heart in my throat as Pisces rained assaults down over him.

I was thankful to see Aspen looked okay. Locke had finished off the other Crownguards and was keeping himself between Pisces and me, who fought like a rabid dog to get to where I stood in a morbidly fascinating turn of events. There was an immense sense of satisfaction to see Pisces's movements had slowed, and he looked to be bleeding heavily. Though to my horror, Locke looked a little worse for wear, cuts all over, and a gash on his forehead. Lenore made her way quickly over to me, brandishing her blood covered axe. A warning to any who approached.

"Lenore, I'm fine. Go help Locke!" I hated how strained my voice sounded. She stopped, glancing between Locke and me with heartbreaking indecision. "Please," I begged when she hesitated, caught between fighting to defend me, and defending Locke. I saw the rage surge in Scorpio's eyes under that ice. I felt her magic surge with it. I barely held on.

It was now just the traitorous Gemini, Pisces, and Scorpio that remained. In the corner of my eye, I saw the once stunning white marble floor running deep red and slick. Countless bodies from both sides spilled along the floor, being tripped over by those few still fighting. Aquarius was bleeding heavily from multiple wounds that didn't look like only flesh wounds but was still fighting what appeared to be a mortally wounded Gemini. Both of them had to be careful not to slip.

My resolve hardened to steel. I would not break. Even if it were the end of me, I would not break. Aspen had finished healing Lennox and both started towards me. I hated how pale and shaky Lennox looked. How rattled. I begged them to go help Locke and Lenore.

Returning my gaze to Scorpio I saw that same rage, that same hardened resolve in her, and I knew this was going to come to a battle of wills. Her magic warred violently for control with mine. I wondered if I could keep Scorpio incapacitated long enough that anything else she was planning would be thwarted.

But I felt my grip on the ice encasing Scorpio slipping as her magic slowly began to overtake me. Pieces of frosty ice were falling off her, and though she can't speak I could see the warning in her glare—that she would kill me. And it would be slow. Painful. Drawn out. It would be personal. I poured more magic into the ice, solidifying it again, buying more time. I wasn't sure how much longer I could hold on as the well of magic within me began to run low. I'd never used this much magic at once. Not even in my most grueling of lessons with Locke. Fighting Scorpio's ever insistent magic while also holding her frozen was quickly draining my resources. Hurry, I silently begged my friends.

A scream pierced the throne room and I flicked my gaze over to the events unfolding. The glance nearly cost me as my control over my magic sputtered, Scorpio making me pay for it. Still, I held on. But I was quickly losing ground.

Aquarius had a spear through her shoulder. She sunk to her knees, her consciousness drifting and ebbing. My gut roiled in response to the waning princess, whose help we so desperately needed. I couldn't even scream as Gemini moved in for the kill, head held high. He said something to her I couldn't hear. But her face contorted in such a way I knew it was awful. My scream of warning came out as a croak, too small, too weak for many to hear. Gemini glanced my way, his face smug with his victory. But then something happened he hadn't expected. Aquarius dug the spear from her body, and with the brutality I'd not expected, drove it into Gemini's. As if to say that if he were going to kill her, then she would drag him beyond the veil with her. I watched Gemini look down at his chest in disbelief at the spear striking him down through his chest. Blood soaked the front of him in mere seconds, draining to join the blood of those he'd conspired to kill. I watched on as he fell to the ground in defeat, life leaving his body. The spear remained lodged in his thorax. Aquarius swayed on her knees.

"Aspen!" I called, my voice straining, indicating Aquarius. If anybody could save her, it was him and his healing magic. Without hesitation, he abandoned Pisces to the aide of the failing Air Princess. The last remaining member of the Air Court Zodiac Kinship we could possibly trust. I hoped his magic was going to be enough. That spear had gone right through her shoulder. It likely had pierced a lung. There was so much blood under her, Aspen nearly slipped upon reaching her. From where I was standing, it looked as though she was fighting to hold on to consciousness.

And she was losing.

The sound of ice shattering at last filled my ears only a split second before the force of Scorpio breaking free of her prison sent me flying. I hit the carved stone wall I'd earlier admired, now coated in blood. My body shrieked and caved in on itself, my vision blurring for a moment or two.

Scorpio's roar of fury echoed around the hall, but to my failing ears, it sounded far away. My blurred vision saw Pisces looking like a faded shadow as he disengaged from Locke and Lenore to get to a severely injured Scorpio. They let him. Locke hurried to my side as I struggled to my feet. Relief unlike anything I'd known consumed every thought now that he was solid beneath my fingers. My hands caressed his arms, his chest, his face, just to prove to myself that he was okay. He was alive. He was with me. Thank fuck. With a shake to clear the last of the blurriness from my vision, the knights, combined with what remained of the Air Court Guard pressed in around them, caging them in. Locke and I pressed forward, breaking through a circle to join them, our blades drawn and ready.

Chapter Eleven

Scorpio and Pisces stood back to back, glaring at the surrounding Wind Guard and us. As I took my first shaky steps towards them, I eyed her injuries. She didn't bleed, but more of that black fume escaped her, as if she were made of smoke. She definitely felt the pain of each wound, more than one of them severe. Good. Her curse would be over soon enough. And with it, her life. She would pay for everything she's done.

I thought of my hometown, Poplar Hollow razed to the ground, only three survivors. For them, she would pay. And for all the lives she ruined. She would pay. For all she had done to Locke, she would pay dearly. Vengeance must have been twinkling in my eyes, because she huffed a laugh at me as the Wind Guard, my family, my soulmate and I closed in around them, blades all drawn.

"You think yourselves victorious, don't you?" Scorpio hissed through her teeth, while Pisces glowered. "So I didn't get the Air Throne under my thumb. I didn't need them. But a seer said you did. And I've made all the Air Zodiacs useless to you! So please, go ahead and celebrate your *victory*. It's a matter of time before I find your precious rebels. And they will all be found guilty of treason. They will all perish!" she said with venom. Black runes slithered across her skin and her hands disappeared into depthless, lethal shadow. Sweat ran down my spine. I may use ice magic, but the chill in the air left by heavy black magic was unprecedented. It drew every eye in the room.

"You haven't won. Not by a longshot." The Queen grinned as she continued. "Gemini learned the approximate location of the Court of Rebels. Between what he told me and what Abel did, it's only a matter of time before you're found."

"Your reign is as bloody as I am pretty," Locke said with a humor he clearly didn't feel. His back revealed how tense he was, like a tightly coiled spring. His voice was downright acidic as he addressed Scorpio, who inclined her head in disgust. Flames sparked around us all, swathing Scorpio in its stark orange glow, making her look all the more manic. "And really neither is justified, but only one is acceptable. Scorpio, you need to stop this. We can end your curse. But we do it our way."

"You should have thought of that before you betrayed me. Betrayed us all, Cancer," she spat back. "You call me the Barbaric Queen, but you're the traitor who turned on his monarch! On his Court! On his *friends*!"

"You gave me no choice! You're killing innocent fae!" Most didn't know him well enough to see it. The ghosts of his past swimming around him. But I saw the anguish in his eyes as he continued in a tone that broke my heart, "You forced me to kill innocent fae! You thought I would stand by you?"

"Yes. Dear old Mom and Dad do send their regards," Pisces probed. The hit landed. It was subtle, but I saw it in the way Locke's chest collapsed. The breath he forgot to exhale. The flicker of pain in his eyes. I've never hated Pisces more than I did in this moment. My hand tightened on my knife as I fought not to hurtle it at his eye.

"Innocence is a matter of perception." Scorpio spoke as if Pisces hadn't, drawing our notice. It was so tense, the air electric. Further chaos only one misstep away. "When they defy my orders, when they help you, when they keep secrets from me, that is betrayal. Betrayals are swiftly dealt with." The hostility in her voice was enough to make my pulse quicken. The warning in her eyes coupled with that mad grin was unnerving. Time stood still for moment. A brief moment in time in which my breath caught in my throat as she swept her gaze to me. "You will pay for what you've done. I'll lay waste to your so-called Court of Rebels. I'll make you watch. And when it's done, when it's erupted into flames and littered with the dead, you will join them too. All of you. There will be nothing left. You remember your precious Poplar Hollow, don't you?"

Pisces laughed, finally adding his voice to the fray as Locke came to stand beside me protectively. Pisces and Scorpio were now alone, standing back to back. Even with them wounded, they were still incredibly dangerous. "I destroyed Poplar Hollow just for you, Lark. Did you like my handiwork?" My eyes darted to him. "After speaking to some of the locals, it was clear how much they hated you. Not one fae went to look for you. In fact, I think they all hoped you were dead."

"You seem to think my town was precious to me," I began, bile rising in my throat. I don't know how my voice remained steady, but I thank the Goddess that it did. Steady and rising in candor as I found my voice. I found that tightly locked down wrath in the corner of my mind. I unleashed it. I let it burn. I hope Scorpio and Pisces could see the flames in my eyes as I spoke. I hoped they could see my vengeance. Their impending deaths. Even with all this emotion surging with me, my voice did not waver. "But those fae were cruel to me and I felt no attachment to them." a lie that tasted bitter on my tongue, "But they didn't deserve what you did to them to send a message to me. What was even the point? What is the point of all this needless suffering?" Scorpio cocked her head, as if the answer were obvious.

"Because I refuse to suffer anymore. And if I must suffer, I don't want to suffer alone."

I can admit that there was a moment, the span of a heartbeat where I felt pity for her. Her curse was abhorrent. Her mind had fled the restrictions of her body, finding precious respite in insanity. But that heartbeat passed and my anger returned in full force, drowning out any remaining empathy.

"What's a better motivation to do what you're told than fear?" Pisces spoke, culling the moment and bringing my attention back to him. "We can't control if we're liked. We can't control if we're respected. But I can control who fears us."

"Those who fear me will never disappoint me," Scorpio finished with her head high, sneering at us all down her nose.

"They fear you, yes. But you don't have their loyalty," Locke said. Scorpios and Pisces scoffed collectively.

"I don't require it," Scorpio argued in a voice that defied all reason. "Disloyalty is swiftly dealt with. Death has a funny way of keeping fae in line. As you will soon see for yourself."

Our forces had them fully surrounded now and we were ready to press our advantage. We blocked the what remained of the Wind Guard from escape, with Locke, the twins, and me cutting off their front. There was nowhere they could go. It was over.

"Surrender to us, and we won't harm you further," Locke said. "Abdicate the throne, Scorpio, and let this madness end."

Her eyes shifted between green and black before my very eyes, like a sunny day eclipsed in an instant by a storm. I'd seen them swirl between the colours before, green veined with darkness. But I'd never seen them change like this, leaving me feeling eerily chilled in a way I couldn't explain. A part of me wondered if that were the shattered pieces of her soul, what little good remained in her peeking out. I wondered if she saw the devastation she wrought. I wondered if she hid. If she cared. If she hated herself.

She should.

Fucking coward.

"End?" Her voice was barely above a whisper, her head slowly turning to meet him in the eye. "End? My madness doesn't get to end, Cancer. I endure the pain of every injury I'm dealt. I'm forced into a torturous existence and I cannot die." Her jaw clenched as she spat at us. "You want this madness to end? You know nothing. But you will." She smiled then, sending shivers down my spine. Her hands glowed black in earnest now. I heard the rushing air sound for a second before they blinked from existence. A jumpstone. They were buying time to charge the jumpstone. They were gone in a flash of light and laughter as we all rushed forward to try and land a last hit before they were gone. I sent ice daggers, as did Locke and a few others, into the portal. I hoped at least a few hit their mark, but I doubted we'd ever know.

Locke roared in frustration at not killing Pisces. I felt his pain. I also wished we could have seen his body littered and discarded on the ground. He deserves nothing less for all he'd done. Something recoiled in me, away from my retribution. Because at what point did justice become vengeance? The wails of the dying and injured permeated the air, separating me from my thoughts. There was so much carnage. So much to do. I looked at a very angry looking Locke, not knowing where to start, but seeing an exhausted Aspen hovering over Aquarius.

I was about to tell him I was going to help Aspen. The words died on my tongue when his hands grabbed my elbows and tugged me into him and a crushing embrace. One I held to. Because for a moment, I could be who I wanted to be. His. And I had been so *fucking* scared. For him. For our friends. For me. I allowed myself a moment to be that fae, clutching to him like he was my lifeline. And I was his.

"Fuck, Lark." His voice was rough. I heard the telltale growl behind it. The one that rumbled in his chest. The one most fae would run from. But I'd never felt safer. "I'd never known fear. Not like that. Not until today. Are you okay?" I nodded mutely. His chest expanded as he took a steadying breath. "When Scorpio had that knife made of ice..." His body spoke where his words ended. His love began where logic failed. Where words did. He clutched me tightly, as if the veil were still trying to take me. His hand touched my shoulder where I'd been stabbed. I flinched, a movement Locke didn't miss. His eyes cast down to where the fabric of my dress had now married my skin in a ceremony of blood that would be a bitch to remove later. He opened his mouth to speak but I beat him to it.

"I'm fine. We'll take care of it after we go help Aspen. I just needed to see you. Make sure you were still with me." I didn't give him time to respond. I turned to Aspen with haste. Because we had bigger things to worry about right now than my bleeding shoulder.

Lennox was power sharing with Aspen to keep Aquarius alive. Throughout the entire time we'd had the wayward Water Kinship surrounded, they'd been trying like hell to keep the only remaining Air Princess on this side of the veil. Healers had been called, and would be on scene any moment. But even as I assessed her condition when Locke and I looked at Aquarius, if they didn't hurry, this court would lose all three of its Kinship members.

I couldn't help but question how she was still holding onto life. Lennox and Aspen must have poured everything they had left into keeping her alive, but the rise and fall of her chest, however shallow, however unsteady, gave me hope that she could still be saved. Her shoulder had been skewered by Gemini whose body lay ruined mere feet away. She had a massive laceration up her thigh that was leaking blood, though it had reduced to a trickle. It was hard to tell whether that was Aspen's healing or if she had lost that much blood. Gauging from the amount under her, it could be either. I glanced at Aspen, perspiration collecting on his brow, his hands glowing green, but the brightness was dimmer than usual. It was then I knew he was quickly running out of magic, even with Lennox's help.

"Take our magic too!" I implored. Lennox sagged in relief.

"Put your hands on my shoulders. I need both hands for what I'm doing." We did as I was instructed, my palms contacting the tops of his shoulders. I felt his muscles tense and strain in congruency with his magic. The effect of his siphoning was immediate. Unnerving. Nauseating. Green tendrils of his magic rose up to meet with mine, teasing the edges of the well of magic within me. I could feel the siphon even now, like a suction on the most basic part of my soul. The well of my magic balked, as if resisting. I willed it outward to connect with Aspen, for it to join. And when it finally merged, the difference was instant.

The green light of his hands intensified, casting us in its emerald glow. I watched in fascination as the wound on her shoulder bubbled, but oh so slowly began to knit itself shut. Flesh and sinew began to reform, however delicate. Keeping a hand on Aspen's shoulder I checked her thigh. I was surprised to see the cut looked shallower than it had before. Aspen's breathing labored, but there was an intensity to him, a stubbornness that told me he wasn't giving up on saving her.

Other healers from Everwind had finally begun to filter in, tending to those injured, and those that needed comfort to ease their passing beyond the veil. Four filtered in to assist healing Aquarius with Aspen, lightening the load. Something I was grateful for, my magic beginning to wane to the point of a sharp pain deep within me. Finally, when Aspen was siphoning the very bottom of the barrel, an uncomfortable scraping sensation that had me jerking and uncomfortable, Aquarius took her first deep breath, her ribs expanding at last. She appeared to be relatively stable. Aspen sagged, I caught him, keeping him upright and off the floor. He murmured his thanks, patting my knee weakly, as if that were even the greatest of efforts.

"She needs a blood regeneration elixir!" he told the healers as they loaded her onto a stretcher. They nodded, thanking him for his help. Was it me, or were they a bit dismissive of the fae that just saved the final member of the Air Kinship?

Aquarius's eyes fluttered open for just a few moments as she was being loaded. I put my other hand on hers, squeezing gently. Her head lolled to the side, eyes dreadfully unfocused, uncomprehending.

"Hey." I murmured to her the same way I used to as Eldan's apprentice, giving me a twinge of pain in my chest that had nothing to do with my magic being on empty. "Try to stay awake. Stay with me. We've got you." Her blue grey eyes searched mine in a haze before falling closed again. Aspen's entire frame collapsed inward from exhaustion. His eyes were gaunt. I hadn't noticed he had a bloody gash on his forehead that thankfully looked superficial.

"Is she going to be okay? Did we do enough?" Locke asked. More healers had arrived as an army in and of itself. Soon we were surrounded by fae, green magic lighting the area in a strange glow, casting everyone in a sickly sallowness that made them look less healthy, rather than more.

"I think so. I hope so. It's up to her at this point," he said, grunting as someone put pressure on a wound on his leg before helping to heal it. She muttered a soft apology, so soft it was like a whisper disappearing on the wind. He looked at her with that charm he never could fail to conjure even at a time like this, "Thank you for your help, darling. I'm okay. I think that fae over there might need your help more." She blushed and walked in that direction, though I had no idea which fae he was referring to. Bloodshed was everywhere. The three of us settled on the steps of the throne silently watching.

Processing. I spied the massive holes in the once seamless marble. The fires were reduced to smoldering embers and countless corpses made the once astounding hall look like a pit of Hell. Rivers of blood ruined the once sparkling white floor. The glimmer of silver I had loved upon my arrival here was now indistinguishable. The spray had reached several feet up the historic columns, and the evidence of the carnage would be forever immortalized. A literal stain in the Air Court's history.

"What about you, Aspen? Lennox? Are you okay?" I asked him as Lenore padded over the carnage to us. Lennox had looked better, but it looked like Aspen had saved her life. There was a dullness to her I hadn't seen before, but she was relatively steady and solid on her feet and that was all I cared about. A blood-soaked Lenore settled next to us in a fit of exhaustion. I was happy to note that Lenore seemed to be covered in someone else's blood, not her own. Aspen gave me a weak smile before answering me.

"Yeah, I'm alright. Are you?" Unconvinced, his eyes looked me over the same way I'd seen him do with Aquarius. His magic probed me for injuries, frowning at the stab wound in my shoulder that I had forgotten about, though now that I remembered it, it hurt like a bitch.

"I'm alright. I'll make my way to the infirmary when everyone who desperately needs attention has had it." Aspen gave me a skeptical look and opened his mouth to protest, but I held my hand up, making a point to use the side that was injured. "I'm well enough. Honest."

"Let's not do that again any time soon," I mused. Locke laughed without a trace of humor.

"I think you'd better get used to it, love. I have a feeling this only the beginning."

Chapter Twelve

"I'm so fucking glad you're all okay," Lenore said capturing us both close in a devastating hug. Her hands clutched at us. Trembling. Lenore had been terrified. Of losing us. It made me clutch them both tighter, grateful they were alive.

I allowed myself a single moment to be relieved we'd survived an ambush attack from Scorpio herself. I'd even hurt her. I knew I couldn't kill her, but it gave me a bit of grim satisfaction to know I'd caused her pain. She could heal over and over and not die. I couldn't help the tiniest flicker of pity for her. What she must have gone through in the past. I knew there had been attempts on her life previously. Some were quite gruesome if the rumors were true. She never died. She would've suffered through the pain, healed, and gone on her way. It was easy to see how insanity had claimed her in a desperate bid for even a brief escape. Her mind could leave circumstances behind that her body couldn't. At least for a short time.

Screams brought me back to the present moment. Screams of friends finding friends dead in the fray. It made it impossible to remain even remotely objective. I now saw the tragedy, rather than just the carnage around me for what it was, the needless bloodshed and gore for what it was; horrific. My stomach roiled and I bit back the urge to throw up.

It was then that I began to shake. The moment the gravity of the situation hit me. The moment I realized how close we came to losing everything. How close I came to losing my soulmate and my friends. Losing everything good in my life all over again. How close we came to our plan being for nothing. If Scorpio killed me and we weren't ready...No tears came, but my body wouldn't stop shaking as the adrenaline refused to let go of my body despite the lack of current threats. The mayhem of the battle, my pulse still pounding in my ears drowning out the world, the fear of my friends, my soulmate, being taken from me, the blood... All the blood on the floor, and the bodies... their horrible wounds... My eyes wouldn't, or perhaps couldn't, stop staring into the wideset eyes of a fae, his throat crudely slashed. Blood no longer pulsing from the wound. His lifeless eyes stared at me and I felt a sob reach my throat.

"Lark?" Aspen asked with deep concern. Lenore was already scanning the room for a healer who wasn't elbow deep in their job, in some cases literally. Locke shook his head.

"The shock is wearing off. I have her." Locke's voice sounded so far away, so echoing. In my detachment I only sort of noticed as he grasped my shoulders, bracing me against the onslaught of my own mind and dragged me a short distance out onto a balcony, an alcove I hadn't even noticed was here. Help was flying in each direction, having finally arrived in full force. Stretchers, medicine kits, and bodies scurried everywhere, tracking bloody footprints. I looked down. I was also tracking bloody footprints. I felt something snap in my mind as panic welled inside me at the sight, only to be made worse when I realized how covered in blood I was.

Other fae's blood. So much blood...

How was it I was fine before? I reached for my previous sense of calm, feeling it escape me at each turn. Rationally I knew this was the shock wearing off. But I so badly wished I could bring that calm back to quash that panic quickly welling in me.

Locke held me to him as we sank to our knees on the balcony. The cold couldn't touch me, despair numbing me and making me sick all at once. He cradled me to him as he settled and brought me into his lap, rocking me gently. One hand combing through my hair, the other holding my body to his. He sat with his back against the banister of the balcony with my head tucked under his chin. My chest refused to open up, my ribs constricting my heart and lungs like an overzealous jailer. He turned my head away from the bloody footprints, angling us so I looked through the balcony railings to the sprawling glittering city below.

"Do you see that? Everwind?" he murmured to me. "That's the city you helped to protect. You saved them. And Port Azure."

I said nothing, content to listen to the timbre of his voice. His chest vibrated as he began to hum what sounded like a lullaby, soft and sweet and maybe a little haunting. I focused on that song, its rises and falls in crescendo, in pitch, until he finally eventually quieted, along with my panic at long last. "Take a breath with me, okay?" I nodded and took a deep, shuddering breath. And another.

"I'm sorry." Hot shame I couldn't explain washed over me for my outburst. Hot tears welled in my eyes as sobs threatened to take me. His one hand continued rubbing circles on my back whilst the other gently gripped my chin and turned my face towards his. He kissed my forehead sweetly before speaking to me, his eyes hard on mine.

"You have nothing to be sorry for. You have never been in a battle. Taking life, especially in that kind of a scenario is messy and isn't something that should ever be easy. It's going to come with some mixed emotions, love. Especially when the adrenaline wears off. It's natural. You have no need to feel shame. And your friends in there will say the same." His hand reached up and gently wiped away my tears on my cheeks.

"Thank you. Have I told you I appreciate you?" I asked with a shaky voice. His answering smirk was more a practiced one for my benefit. His eyes didn't spark to life.

"Not nearly enough," he teased, for my benefit. I punched him in the arm, but it had no bite to it.

"Come on, love," Locke woofed in my ear. He rose to his feet, holding a hand out to me. "Your Highness—" I glared at him. "Lark," he corrected with a much more sincere, yet still roguish, grin that made my stomach flip flop despite the circumstances. I took his hand, allowing me to haul me back to my feet. "Welcome to Everwind. And to Windermere Castle." He gestured to what lay beyond the balcony edge.

What lay beyond was like something out of a fantasy. The castle we were currently in existed on top of, or rather, built into, the highest mountain. I could almost imagine a dragon circling us, even though they were long extinct. We were high enough that I could see we were nearly in the clouds. From the ground it must have looked like the castle was floating in the heavens above.

But the city below was breathtaking. It looked like something conjured from a dream and given life. Aspen had mentioned the city and how their roofs seemed to spark to life, but it truly did resemble a lightning storm—perfect for identifying the Air Court— the magic of storms and air itself. From our vantage point, the city itself grew in the spaces between the mountains. Beyond the mountain was a thick wall of impenetrable mist. It felt like its own world here, like it was entirely separate not just from Meridian, but from the world itself.

My head was *fucking* killing me.

The Air Court had given us guest rooms in the west wing of the castle. Aspen got his own room on one side of us, and the twins got their own room across the hall. Locke and I were given a set of rooms so large I felt out of place. The foyer to our rooms was bigger than my entire cottage back home. The bathing room had a heated infinity pool that was open to the temperate outside. Or perhaps it was just spelled to stay warm as you bathed looking down over the shimmering city and the mountains surrounding.

The bedroom was exactly that—the bed took up the entire room, so big Locke and I could spread out entirely and not come close to touching if we didn't want to. An entire room of luxurious bed dressings, fabrics and the softest looking pillows. I was able to remove my once beautiful dress, now torn and covered in dried blood. New clothes were provided, a comfort I couldn't thank the Air Court enough for.

I felt hot and cold at the same time, my palms clammy as I tried to peel what was left of my dress off. Delicately, so as to not aggravate my shoulder, though when I felt the first painful snag of the fabric fused with dried blood over the wound, I knew it was inevitable. I felt Locke's attention snap to me, my skin prickling in recognition. I glanced up to see growing concern on his face. I followed his gaze to my shoulder. My mouth fell open at the sight of black veining around my wound.

"Lark!" Locke inspected my shoulder now with a look of grievous concern. His voice became low. Rumbling. Angry. I startled. "You said this was a shallow wound that was bloodier than anything. This is a black magic wound. Do you have any idea how serious this is?" He checked my forehead, confirming a fever.

He half-ran to the door. A fae ordered to attend us was startled by this abruptness, and paled when Locke ordered him to get a healer. And to bring a black magic kit. I hadn't the slightest idea what that was, but given the fact that my shoulder was slowly turning... dare I say necrotic, I was beginning to think the apple didn't fall far from the tree. An injury father hadn't told me about, hadn't gotten treated had put him on his death bed. Now, I had done the same thing.

I understood Locke's anger.

Locke came back in with a hardened expression on his face. He didn't look me in the eye. Not right away. I remembered feeling the same frustration when I discovered my father's injuries. Locke helped me drape a sheet around me, leaving only my wound exposed while we waited for help to come. Locke sat me back against the plush headboard, made sure I was pillowed and comfortable, all with a gruff look that I had to bite my lip to keep from giggling, despite my guilt. He shot me a glare to let me know he saw my amusement and he wasn't having it.

"I'm sorry, Loc—" The door burst open, drawing Locke's attention, hand on instinct going to his knife he now carried on his hip. The wide-eyed healer stood there looking somewhere between stunned and terrified, before bowing low.

"Good evening, Highnesses. I understand there is an injury involving black magic?" His voice wavered, especially when Locke's eyes refused to leave him.

"Your patient is here. Her shoulder. Thank you for getting here so fast." His last statement was absolutely an afterthought. He—there was no other way to describe it—escorted him to me. Completely unnecessary, he was taking care of me like a mother hen.

He was taking care of me.

It hit me. He'd taken care of me before, of course, but this was different. He was clearly worried about my injuries, eying me with great concern. Which led me to question myself. How dangerous were black magic injuries?

According to Melax, the healer, they were incredibly dangerous, especially this one with its proximity to the heart. Like Lenore in Frostfall. She only survived because she was treated quickly, drawing the black magic out of the wound as if it were a poison. And maybe it was.

It hurt. I swore, took the Goddess's name in vain, and I screamed as Melax apologetically used his instruments to draw out the foreign magic. I was suddenly thankful for Lenore that she was unconscious when this was done, acidic fire burning its way through my veins. I bit down on my lip, hard enough to draw blood. Locke offered me his hand, and to his credit didn't so much as flinch as I squeezed hard enough I was certain I could bend metal. As it was, I fought to check to see if my hand had indented his own.

Melax's hands glowed green like Aspen's as he used his tool to coax the infection from me. What I tried to focus on was the fact that it looked like a straw. Which I found absolutely hysterical.

Melax laughed.

"Not a straw, Highness," he said, drawing more out. He winced every time I did, which I found strangely endearing. Poor Melax was clearly in the right field, kind and empathetic, and seeing the nervous glances he kept stealing towards a very tense and brooding Locke, was clearly scared for his safety. "More like a spiel."

The spiel was inserted into the heart of the infection, and healing magic forced the black shadowy infection through the spiel and into the collection container. I learned very quickly not to look into the container. It was revolting, the mixture of blood, and an almost oily black substance that writhed like inky shadows within the confines of the jar. I was made queasy every time I looked at it. Despite that, the pounding headache that hammered away behind my eyes, the excessive heat in my body, was melting away. Despite the pain in my shoulder, despite the creepy spiel I hated, I felt myself relaxing.

When at long last it was over, Melax retrieved the spiel from my shoulder, his hands glowing green to bind what remained of the wound together, leaving only the faintest of pink lines in its wake. Upon inspection, there were no further hints of black magic. No black stain or veining blemished my skin. Locke's lines of tension in his face began to ease, and his eyes lost the hardness that went with his concern.

"Apologies for the scar, Highnesses. Some black magic wounds simply cannot be healed entirely, but this at least is entirely cosmetic. There is no lingering infection."

"I have many scars Melax. What's one more?" I smiled at him. "Thank you for your work."

He bowed low, something I don't think I'll ever get used to, and made his leave swiftly. Locke's intense gaze now focused on me, anxiety swirling in my gut.

"You could have died," Locke's voice rang out. It filled the room, filled me, and yet he didn't shout. "Do you realize that by morning it may have been too late?"

"I didn't realize, Locke." My voice tight with contrition. "I didn't know black magic could do that. I suppose I should've given what happened to Lenore, but in the face of everything, others needed healing more than me. I thought I was capable of stitching myself closed if need be. I didn't realize..." Locke sighed, enveloping me into a crushing embrace. He buried his face into my hair, and I in turn tucked my head under his chin, breathing deeply. "I'm sorry."

He took a deep, cleansing breath. The anger wasn't dissipating per se, but its sharp corners were rounding. And when he looked at me again, I saw all of his worry as clearly as if it were my own.

"Please, love, don't scare me like that again." His voice carried all the fear, all the anger, all the stress of the last hour.

"I promise." The first time those words had ever left my mouth. And almost greedily, he took that magic and sealed it between us.

"You're worth everything. I'll be damned to the echo Isles if I let that be your fate."

The words hung heavily between us. Would this really be the worst fate had in store?

Locke led me to the bathing room. I had never seen a tub take up the entire room before. It was basically a giant heated pool. A giant heated pool with no walls on two fronts, allowing us an unfettered view of the Veinfall mountains, and the shimmering city of Everwind under the night sky below. The hot water cleansed me and unknotted the incredibly sore muscles. The sound I made was nearly sexual as I sank my shoulders below the surface of the water, making Locke look at me with heat and amusement.

We talked for the next hour, Locke telling me stories of creatures long extinct. Hydra. Dragons. Wyvern. Who knew Locke had a penchant for storytelling?

I loved him for so many reasons. He gave me a place in this world, without judgement. He loved me even when I was weak and couldn't perform magic. He made me happy, yes, but that's not why I loved him. I loved him because he taught me how to be happy on my own. How to stand on my own two feet and thrive. And he was happy to let me stand on my own, supporting me any time I needed it. He showed me that it was okay to rely on another fae. And what it was like to love fiercely. I really didn't know what I did to deserve such an amazing faerie in my life, but I thanked the Goddess every day for him, and all the good he brought into my life.

"What are you thinking about? Your emotions are all over the place."

"What? You don't know?" I teased.

"I can't actually read minds. You're usually just easy to read. There's a difference, despite what you seem to think." He laughed, splashing a bit of water at me. I stuck my tongue out at him.

"I just can't get over how lucky I am to have you. And how lucky we were today that we didn't lose one another. Or our friends."

"I'm also incredibly happy you're okay," he said. His brow furrowed then. "When I lost sight of you not long after the battle began, I couldn't shake my panic. If anyone had taken you from me…" He trailed off, his lips pulling back in a soundless snarl. "If anyone had killed you, they would have joined you across the veil in pieces."

"Would it have been painful?" I grinned up at him. His answering malicious grin sent my entire body clenching.

"Very painful," he agreed before his face sobered. "But I saw you taking down opponent after opponent and I knew that we had trained you well. I was able to focus on the battle. I have never felt such pride in all my life. Then when Scorpio had you in her clutches, I thought my life ended. I was so desperate to get to you. We weren't ready to enact our plan. Aquarius was busy. Scorpio was going to kill you. But then you wounded her! I don't know anybody currently alive who can say that."

"Really?"

He nodded.

"Really. I'm not sure if she didn't take you seriously before but I'm more than certain she will now. You've come an incredibly long way, Lark. I am immensely proud of you."

When this is over, I want you in nothing more than those thigh sheaths and those daggers.

Heat flushed everywhere that had nothing to do with the water. Locke's eyes heated as he drank me in, his gaze that had previously been respectfully above the waterline, dipped low now. He drank me in like a man dying of thirst, and I was his only oasis. He took a step toward me, but I had other ideas.

"Hold that thought a moment," I said getting out of the warmth of the water. My skin mourned the loss of the heat and I forced myself to dry off quickly to stave off the cold. My air magic did the trick, thankfully as I rounded the corner and back into the bed chamber, out of Locke's sight. I put my leather holsters and daggers back on my legs but donned no other clothing or accessory. My heart was pounding an anxious rhythm, not sure I enjoyed being this exposed. I bit my lip and fought my blush before walking back into the bathroom, making sure to put a little extra sway to my hips. Locke's eyes found me immediately, tracking my movements. The devilish grin that grew on his face heated my very core, alighting each nerve. A grin that promised all manner of sin.

It felt good to be in control the way he normally was. I sashayed into the room with bolstered confidence, feeling the weight of his scorching gaze raking me head to toe.

"I didn't even know I wanted you like this until I saw you in the throne room holding your knife," he said, beckoning me to him with a crook of his fingers. "Lark, you're a fantasy." I shook my head at his arm outstretched to invite me into the tub.

"You come here," I demanded, reaching my hand to one of my daggers, beckoning him with it and loving the dark smile that dawned on his face. "You wanted me. Have me."

He wasted absolutely no time. He rose from the water, drying himself with his water magic in the same movement. My gaze flicked downwards, seeing the effect I had on him. Despite my knife being carefully placed against his throat, he captured me like a fae possessed, lifting me by my thighs against the first wall he found, pushing into me, the very tip of him coating in the essence of me. He groaned when I felt just how much I wanted him. Needed him. My toes curled at the sound. I ground my hips, my desperation to have him where I needed him growing. Desperation to feel alive, for us both to feel alive, grew like wildfire within me.

"You're not going to be a brat, are you?" he whispered against my lips. He moved his hips, teasing me horribly, leaving me horribly bereft of what I needed. "That knife of yours. Am I going to have to do something about that, love?"

"Where would the fun be if I weren't?" I was breathless even before his lips closed over mine, stoking the fire further in my core until I was purely just burning. For him. He wrenched my knife from me and tossed it, the clatter on the stone the only reason I knew where it ended up.

"I'll make you pay another time. I need you now," he growled in my ear, making everything in me clench in anticipation before impaling me on him, wrenching a strangled cry from my lips. His kiss swallowed each one and he filled me, over and over, using his Zodiac speed to send me into a quivering mess of nerves.

"Do you want to come, Lark?" His voice was like raked coals, with an air of desperation as he held off his own release. I nodded, words lost to me as that familiar pressure built within me. Just as that crescendo crept towards the peak, Locke slowed his pace, that crescendo falling away. I stifled a cry of frustration. "Use your words, love."

"Yes!" I almost screamed. "Make me come."

He slammed into me, my head falling back, my mouth parted on a moan. Again, building that pressure, right there. Right to where my legs began to shake and my vision started to blur...

And stopped.

"I think you're missing a magic word."

"Fuck. Me," I grated out as my hips searched for the release I was so close to. It began to fade as quickly as last time. His grip tightened on my thighs, removing my ability to move.

"Beg me, brat." He shoved inside me once again, just to tease me. To show me what I was missing. Keeping me so close to the brink, but pulling me from the edge each time. And I was missing it so much I could barely think. My nails raked his shoulders, his back, anything to spur him on. He stubbornly refused. That smirk undid me. My resolve shattered as desperation took control of my mind.

"Please," I whispered. "Please, Locke. Make me come."

"You're so pretty when you beg," he said, driving into me again. And thank the Goddess, this time he didn't stop. "I want to hear my name when you come this time."

I was already panting it, begging with that single word, a single reverent prayer to him. "Give it to me, Lark," he grunted as I began to shake, violently this time, just on the precipice. "Now," he commanded.

I couldn't stop it even if I tried. He gave me my release at last, a ruined version of his name falling loudly from my lips. Tiny dots of black and color speckled my vision as I clamped down on him, hard enough I worried it might hurt him. He kept going through every aftershock, drawing it out, before finally growling my name as he filled me. We both panted, our breaths mingling in the space between us. His hand came up to cup my cheek, his lips finding mine with a sweetness that was the complete opposite of the animal he had just unleashed.

My limbs were languid. When he pulled out of me and placed me on my feet, my knees still shook from the intensity of what we'd just done.

"Lark?" His voice came moments later as we both plopped onto the bed, exhausted. His arms came comfortingly around me, his impossibly warm body molding to my back.

"Yes?"

"Don't ever let me see you neglect an injury like that again."

Chapter Thirteen

We were both awoken from an exhausted slumber far too early. Groggily, I looked out the windows to see the earliest vestiges of sunlight hinting at an approaching dawn, meaning at best we'd only slept a few hours. Approaching dawn meant it was far too early for this. My sleepy eyes blinked open and I groaned against the idea of wakefulness. Locke laughed. Bastard. The knocking sounded again. I'd had my fill of violence, but I was starting to suspect I could make an exception for whoever was on the other side of that door. And I swore to the Goddess if it were Aspen, I would crush him where he stood. Locke put his pants and a shirt on and answered the door, making sure that whoever was on the other side couldn't see me at all in my current state of indecency.

"I apologize for the early hour, Prince Cancer," he said as if dawn weren't under way and we weren't about to drop from exhaustion. "It's the Queen. She summons you to her council rooms immediately."

"Thank you for letting us know. Will you be here to take us to Aquarius in a few moments?"

"Yes, Your Highness."

Locke thanked him and closed the door. He turned to me, smirking at my now wide-eyed expression. This worked better than all the energy elixirs in the world to get my heart pounding. "Get ready, Your Highness. We have an audience with Queen Aquarius. Right now."

I'd never dressed so fast in my entire life. Our clothing that they had allotted for us was supposed to be simple fare. Or maybe this just outlined the differences between the Air and Water Courts. And one massive difference I openly hated: corsets.

If another battle broke out, I wouldn't be able to defend myself. Because there's no way to breathe when my lungs could only hold half of my air capacity. But I wasn't ruling out that maybe I would wage war to free the fae of this entrapment.

I looked at it on the bed as if it might bite me. I donned it as best I could, Locke snickering to himself the entire time as he put on his shirt and overcoat. The raven waves on his head blended with the black coat with delicate silver trim. I sneered as he didn't even try to staunch his laugh at my expense.

Bastard.

He didn't have to wear a corset.

I took my last deep breath for a while and cinched myself up. I don't hate the figure it gives me at least, my eyes tracing the soft curve of my waist in the mirror. Locke pulled his boots on, looking at me with that telltale far away glance. "You look better without it."

I flushed, especially when just behind him was the wall where last night we…

I'd better not finish that thought. Locke barked a laugh at my expense once again, earning himself another steely glare from me. He held his hands up in surrender, biting his lip to douse his amusement. I'd never wanted to throw a shoe at him more than I did on this moment. Better yet, I should string *him* up in a corset. The thought brought me so much satisfaction, I wondered how I might make it happen.

I threw on the dove grey dress with long billowing sleeves that cuffed at the wrists and black slippers, leaving my freshly brushed hair in loose waves down my back. Simple. Clean. Pretty. But so *damned* uncomfortable. My rib cage strained against its new restraints, at war with the angry butterflies battling for my attention in my stomach. I usually had to have an anxiety attack to feel this uncomfortable, and yet these fae have made it part of their everyday wear.

Upon stepping into the towering hallway from our rooms, a duo of maids curtsied with a chorus of "Your Highnesses." They were so young. Younger than me. "Right this way. Queen Aquarius is expecting you."

They turned as one, guiding us down the impressive hallway. Or maybe I just thought it was impressive, as I'd never actually seen a castle before, other than peeks of Ari'inor's looming spires and walls from outside the castle grounds.

Castle was a stunning architectural marvel. One I hadn't been in the headspace to previously appreciate, but now I couldn't take my eyes off of the view. The halls were light, airy, and open to the outside, allowing the freshness of the high mountain air in. A deep breath here was cleansing, as if each exhale stole my troubles and garnered them away into the chasms between the mountains themselves. Every so often I'd get a sniff of pine and I wasn't sure if it were from outside or Locke. I almost asked to stop for a moment, to appreciate the sunrise that was in full unveiling before my very eyes. Hues of pinks and oranges softly canvassed the sky, putting every artist to shame.

Grey and white stonework crept up to impossibly tall ceilings which boasted stained glass, allowing the promise of beautifully colored light to rain down on anyone standing under it in full daylight, in direct contrast to the almost sterile starkness of the perfect white and silver that made up the rest of Windermere. I imagined it was a wonderful parallel for the Air Court as a whole, but perhaps Aquarius in particular. Hard, beautiful, and clean, followed by an unexpected vibrancy waiting to be discovered.

There was an electricity in the air. An alertness that had the hair on the nape of my neck standing erect. Our maids that escorted us said nothing, married to stoic silence. Soldiers lined the walls with stern expressions and eyes that followed my movements with rapt attention and skepticism, making every one of my steps feel heavy. Could I really blame them though? If their Prince Gemini could invite such violence into their Court so unexpectedly, what was to stop us from the outcasts of the Water Court from bringing more of the same?

Not for the first time I felt a stab of guilt that I hurriedly shoved to the little room in the back of my mind and shoved the door shut with a heave. My demons would break the door down eventually, but I had time before that happened. I took another big breath of that cool mountain air as we arrived at our destination.

A wide set of double doors stared impassively at us. A sleek dark grey in contrast to all the whites and silvers, though silver runes were threaded lovingly into the design. I fingered the engraving on the door moments before it was opened. Aquarius's likeness looked out at an enemy, lightning rods in hand. The artist had even captured the look of vengeance, the detail of her hair floating on the wind, and her vanquished foe smoldering in the ruin, all with such exquisite detail it was hard to believe it an etching. Even the folds of her clothing were done so delicately it was like I could touch them and feel the softness of the fabric. The doors opened and I hurriedly pulled my arms back to my sides, trying not to look as awkward as I felt.

"Her Majesty is expecting you. Please go inside." The young maid closest to me said without making the slightest bit of eye contact. I offered her a sincere smile of thanks that was destined to not be returned. With a polite curtsy, she gestured for us to enter. The doors creaked closed once our feet had traipsed the boundary of the room, sealing us in.

We weren't left to ponder our thoughts in thick silence long. Another door opened via a small, unassuming fae—another maid—and Aquarius stepped into view.

There were few signs of her harrowing brush with death, but the healer in me saw them. The lackluster, pale quality of her skin. Her silver dress shone and shimmered in the light somehow muting and enhancing her sallowness simultaneously. There was a slight dimness in her eyes, powder mostly hid the dark circles that come from exhaustion, but I saw the weariness that lay there holding her captive. It warred for my attention with the diamond encrusted crown she wore. To get her to this walking around state healers, and skilled ones at that, must have worked the entire time we'd been resting.

That wasn't to say I didn't also see the quiet, simmering rage there as she looked at us. A simmer I doubted would boil over until the timing was right. She was far too controlled for that. I wondered if that were just her, or if that were her Aquarius nature peeking through.

Locke bowed, low and respectful. I followed suit into what I hoped was a curtsy, though I wasn't entirely convinced I did it correctly.

"Your Majesty," Locke began, "we're both glad to see you well. I want to thank you for your accommodations and your medical aid. Your hospitality during this time has been exemplary."

She said nothing, giving absolutely nothing away. Her eyes traced us, studying us, and I suddenly felt like an insect in a jar to be observed. I willed myself not to squirm under her scrutiny. Locke's strong presence next to me bolstered me. His warmth calmed me. Once I nearly collapsed under the weight of his gaze and today I stood firm under the weight of a Queen's.

She moved to the fire that smoldered in the hearth, making me realize through my jittery nerves that the air was indeed chilled. A wind softly blew, stirring the embers, waking them, gently rousing them to warm us. But not enough. Her eyes hardened.

"If you would allow me." My voice was hesitant as I addressed her. She eyed me, but made no move to stop me. With a flourish of my fire magic, heat awakened now in earnest. I coaxed the flames higher in the hearth, driving warmth into the room. I resisted the urge to warm myself, to bask in the fire's glow. Instead, I fed it with air magic, giving it a stir.

Locke shot me a look. Real subtle.

"You really can use multiple elements," Aquarius mused. "Not that I thought you a liar. Your story is truly a unique one, is it not?"

"I can use all the elements, though admittedly, I'm still getting a handle on air and earth."

Aquarius stepped away from the hearth in favor of an easy wing-backed chair, looking every bit the Queen she'd become overnight. Her expression became wistful as she looked at Locke and me in turn.

"This isn't the coronation I ever wanted. The guild is coming today to assign a new Libra and Gemini." She shook her head, the very real sadness betraying her for the first time. I realized I was right earlier; she was strong and hardened and beautiful like the white marble of Windermere, but with such depth of vivid emotion as the outside ceiling seemed to hint at. "Tell me, Queen's Mark, have you the ability to wield the shadows as well?"

I bristled at her nickname for me. The Queen's Mark. What Libra had called me yesterday. A literal target. But that wasn't what snagged my attention. I wondered if I looked as bewildered as I felt. Locke looked over at me, his expression more contemplative than I would have expected.

"I can't say the question hasn't plagued me," he mused.

"Why do you think I can wield black magic?" I asked slowly with hesitation. I thought back to each of my elements. I called them forth one by one, the runes in question lighting my skin in turn. Black remained steadily absent. I eyed what little I could see of Locke's runes that I knew ran in swirls up his arms, across his shoulders and travelled his chest. Inky black and dark blue, black magic and water. Permanently etched into his skin. Aquarius's arms almost glowed with her silver runic marks. I had to will mine to the surface. No black showed itself, permanent or otherwise. "I've not been to the Echo Isles. Is that even possible?"

"Your mother used black magic to conceive you, did she not?" Aquarius's eyes narrowed on me, though not in anger. It was like she was trying to study me further. As if her thoughts were running away with her and she was trying the see the path they were taking. "If your mother had paid the price in childbirth, my curiosity is whether you were given the gift of shadows at birth. Curse free."

So my mother's death had been a down payment on this magic, then? That thought sat uncomfortably under my skin, making me feel itchy. I couldn't stop myself. My feet carried me across the room and back again, my thoughts and my feet in a flurry of emotion.

"How would I know?" I finally brought my feet to a stop between Aquarius and Cancer. My head swiveled between the two of them, assessing their reactions in turn.

Locke was quiet, his gaze focused, his head tilted to the left as if deep in thought. Aquarius looked vaguely impatient.

"Have you ever tried before, Lark?" Locke's velvet voice reached me. But of course, he already knew the answer. I shook my head.

"Try." The Queen took a sip from a silver chalice I hadn't even noticed was there. I glanced down at my arms, bringing my runes to the surface once again. And like before, the only runes were those of my elements. I searched within, going deeper inside my own mind than I normally dare trudge. I glanced at the rattling door of demons and pushed further, looking for anything the darkness within my mind may hide.

I found sorrow. Rage. Regret. Fear. Guilt. But no shadows sprang forth to my skin. Just the shadows across my heart.

"I'm not entirely sure what to try." I glanced at Locke. "What should I do?"

"While shrouding is an ability I have without black magic, it's also an ability easily granted to someone who uses the shadows," Locke explained, shadows beginning to shade his hands until darkness engulfed them entirely. Seeing him with his shadows so casually created a nervousness in me. At what point would it be too much for his soul to bear? In the same moment I thought of Pisces, who clearly used it considerably more than Locke. I found some degree of comfort in that. "Blend into the shadows. Melt into them. I picture it as fading from view. Imagine wrapping a blanket of shadow over yourself and becoming one with them." At first, it was just his hands I couldn't see through the darkness. Then his arms were invisible. His torso. His face. Until all I could see was the fire on the other side of where he'd once stood. And then he returned to my sight. "Easy peasy."

Easy peasy, my ass.

I closed my eyes, envisioning Locke's instructions. I pulled those awful emotions, picturing them as shadows. I tried to wield these emotions as I did for my elemental magic. It relied on strong emotions. Perhaps black magic was the same, relying on strong negative emotions. I coated my heart in an armor, to stop the damage the guilt alone could do to me if I let it. I imagined my body slowly fading from view as Locke had. I felt my magic whir in response. If my magic could express emotion, it would be just one, confusion. I opened my eyes.

To see them both staring directly at me.

"Did it work?" I dropped my focus. Locke's eye contact gave me the answer I needed. I don't know why I felt disappointed. Those negative emotions I dredged up swarmed like a nest of angry hornets, just waiting for the moment I got distracted. My own mind threatened to consume me. I couldn't even wrestle them back down the depths of myself. I almost wished I'd had black magic, if only so this wasn't for nothing. "I tried but I couldn't feel the shadows. Not like I do my elements. I'm sorry."

"No need for apologies. It was a theory. Thank you for assuaging my curiosity." She glanced at Locke with narrowing eyes. "Though I know you didn't come here to check in, or to dabble in magic and circumstances."

"We have much to discuss." Locke's eyes were hard on her. But she was a Queen. She backed down from nobody. She appraised him in turn.

"Indeed, we do." The fire sparked in the background; for a heartbeat the crackling fire was the only sound.

"We come to ask you once again for your assistance against Scorpio and her curse."

"Yes," she mused, looking at me with that same appraisal. Her tone was borderline dismissive, neither approving nor disapproving. She gave nothing away, yet we had shown her our hand just yesterday. "Though I'm unsure why I should be fighting your battles, Cancer. Are you not capable of fighting your own?"

Locke didn't take the bait. Ignoring the intentional barb, Locke began speaking as if she hadn't.

"We don't need to you to fight. Though I think we could all agree your strength in battle would be most welcome. We truly just require you to shock Lark's heart back to life. She has to die. That is our curse. But there's nothing that says she's to stay that way. We ask only for this assistance."

"What makes you think I can do this?" she asked. "What makes you think your plan will work?"

"It will work," I said finding my voice. Aquarius glanced at me with mild distaste, as if I were a child throwing a tantrum while she was trying to have a conversation. "I saved someone months ago. A seer named Amaya. I'm not sure how, but she granted me a vision that I would need in my most desperate time. In that vision, great bolts of lightning restarted my heart after Scorpio killed me." I hit her with a devastating look. "Lightning you yourself control better than any other fae in the Air Court, I'm led to believe."

She scoffed. "You're led to believe correctly."

"We saved your life yesterday." Locke's eyes glittered with resolve. "We saved your Windguard. We fought beside them. We bled with them. Lark suffered a black magic wound pushing Scorpio back. We spilled blood together. That cannot go unanswered. I call in a repayment of debt."

Aquarius didn't move.

"I'm not in your debt," she growled, her voice taking on a feral edge. "I owe you nothing." Locke smirked.

"Oh, but you are. You would've died if not for Aspen, Lennox, and Lark. It was their magic that saved you. All we ask is one favor. Revive. Lark" He bit out. "Her life was forfeit the moment she told me she loved me. You don't have to like me. But *she* doesn't deserve this. And neither do the innocent fae Scorpio kills. You do owe us. And I'm calling the favor in, right now."

"And what if I fail?" she asked, directing her attention to me. There was no uncertainty in her voice. No caring. Purely a question.

I shrugged. "Then you fail. Then I'm just dead. But please," I implored, "try."

Aquarius looked at me a long time, as if I were a complex riddle she was attempting to solve. For a moment, nobody spoke. Nobody moved. That deafening silence answer enough for me to glance at Locke. He kept his gaze fixed on the Queen of Air, willing her to come to the right decision.

"And if you fail? If you fail to bring back Scorpio's head, my court gets implicated. I have no need for a massive war."

"Your court was already attacked without warning or provocation," I said. Her eyes darkened as they flickered to me. I'd struck a nerve. Something she'd clearly not forgotten. "Scorpio is desperate. She's running out of seers in our court. After yesterday do you really believe she won't begin to take seers in your court? From Fire and Earth too?"

"I ask you one more time, would-be Princess of the Water Court. The Queen's Mark; what if *you* fail?" Each word punctuated as if its own powerful statement. I understood.

"I won't."

Her eyes lit. The reflection in the fire burned in her eyes and I saw the wrath and need for vengeance there. I recognized it in Locke too. In myself.

"The battle of Windermere Castle will be answered for. Libra will be avenged, as will the rest of those who fell. Their families, their legacies, deserve retribution." She skewered us with a look. "But I have stipulations."

It was Locke that answered. Thank the Goddess, I had no idea what to say. "Name them."

"I will repay my debt. I will fight. I will lend to you my armies to fight at the time of your choosing. I will use my lightning in effort to restart your beloved's heart. Air Court will have its vengeance. But," her gaze slid between us with a dramatic pause, "I get you, Crowned Assassin. I get your unique skillset. No questions asked."

"No," Locke answered. "I will not be your chess piece to start a war." Aquarius raised her eyebrow, with a smug expression.

"And yet you'd ask the same of me?"

"I'm calling in a favor, not making a bargain, Aquarius."

"Let me be clear, Cancer." She stood. Though she craned her neck to glare up at him, her confidence and resolve didn't waver. Neither did that smug look in her eye. "I will avenge the attack here yesterday. Make no mistake. You will have my army. That is my repayment of the debt. But reviving your soulmate? That's secondary business. I will help you..." She made a show of walking over to me, her fingers caressing my hair before I could stop her. "But how much is up to you."

"Locke, don't endanger the Water Court," I begged him. I saw his face waver. It was so subtle. So subtle I doubted Aquarius knew him well enough to see it. But I did.

"Don't make me start a war. Don't make me do something the Water Court can't survive. More innocent fae don't need to die."

"That won't be up to you. Does that not ease your conscience?" Her voice was lighter than air. Completely untroubled. A bird of prey circling just before the inevitable strike. She circled me now, scanning his reaction to her words. To her thinly veiled threat.

"I want access to your intel. Access to your spy network, where it concerns this. And anything else that may come up here," Locke said. Aquarius didn't even blink. She inspected her nails with scrutiny, not looking up.

"What makes you think I have spies in Water Court?"

"Because," he replied, his voice like lethal shadow, "we all have spies in every court."

"Your spies may not be as informative as they once were," she mused. Her entire posture changed when she zeroed in on Locke. "You're looking for something." Her eyes finally found his, searching for what I knew he wouldn't give. There was only one thing he could be looking for. I remembered back at Frostfall. How we never found his parents. He was looking for his family. "You won't tell me what it is?"

"I can tell you it poses no risk to you or your court. That, I can promise."

"Fine then. I can be magnanimous if I need to be. Let nobody say I don't make fair bargains. Keep your secrets. You have me, my army, my assistance, and my spies. All I'm asking for is one, teensy tiny favor." Her tone was a pretty package concealing something hideous within. Pretty, soft, but hidden malice was there, waiting for Aquarius's command. "Now choose. Do we have a deal?"

Locke glanced sidelong at me. And in that moment, I knew. I could see the torment there, weighing him down in the sag of his shoulders. That same torment I'd seen before when he thought Scorpio was going to kill me yesterday. The torment that I saw the moment he first told me he loved me in Frostfall. When I told him I loved him in turn. I saw that look of desperation hiding behind it. The resolve he displayed wasn't one of heat. It was stone cold, and as sure and prevailing as death itself. Aquarius's eyes brightened, sensing her victory. I opened my mouth, to stop what in my heavy heart I knew what he was about to say.

"Fine. I accept your terms of the bargain." Seven words. Seven words that simultaneously had me wanting to celebrate and deflate in defeat. Seven words so hilariously bittersweet it felt like the Goddess was laughing at us. My knees felt unstable in that moment under the weight of what he'd just done. It was a bargain that forced him to be the Air Court's Assassin one time. Just one...

It all hinged on who Aquarius targeted. And if she were willing to go to these lengths, I had to guess she had someone in mind. Someone high profile.

If anybody found out, Air Court wouldn't be implicated. The Water Court would. We were at her mercy entirely.

Locke just agreed to a deal to save my life, to save the Water Court from one evil...

To potentially damn it to another.

Locke and I walked back to our rooms, guided by our ever so helpful maids from earlier. They still pretended as if we weren't there, avoiding looking at us at all costs. I didn't care. The view, now fully spectacular in its late-stage sunrise no longer held the appeal it had before. My limbs felt heavy and awkward as I followed behind our guides. Locke didn't look at me, though I kept staring at him through the corner of my eye. I couldn't stop thinking about what he'd done. For me.

The air sat heavy between us once we closed the door to our rooms, sealing ourselves inside. The silence sat charged between us. Neither spoke. I didn't know what to say. What do you say to the person who made a deal with the very real possibility of condemning everything we were working so hard to save? To save me?

I wasn't worth that. I hated that this was put on my shoulders. I realized in that moment that the guilt and anger I felt had merged into a painful force that threatened to rip me apart. My heart thumped hollowly in my chest.

"I understand you're angry, Lark. But understand everything is under control. There's no reason to panic yet." Locke stood stock still, watching me with bated breath.

"How can you say that?" I asked him. "She could ask you to kill anyone and you have to do it." He pinned me with a dark look. Eyes with too many ghosts in them peered out at me. He crossed the room then, taking my face gently into his calloused hands, forcing me to look up at him.

"Do you have such little faith in me, love?" he murmured with a voice like silk. "I'm not called the Crowned Assassin for nothing. I have taken out high risk and high-ranking targets before. Many times. I've not been caught. As long as Aquarius doesn't sell us out—and I don't believe she will—we'll be fine. Furthermore," he said, his thumb softly caressing my cheek, "there is no deal I wouldn't make for you. There's nothing I wouldn't give. That being said, I'm still fighting with everything I have for our court and kin. I would not blindly abandon them. Here..." He took my hand, placing it over his chest. His heart. I felt the rhythmic thump-thump against my palm. Slow and steady. Unbothered. The exact opposite of my anxiety fueled heart pounding away in my chest. I blinked up at him. "Do you feel that? How calm I am right now? It's because there's nothing to worry about right now. We got what we came for. We have Aquarius's help, and we got a bonus. We got Air Court's armies. Scorpio fucked herself with the stunt she pulled yesterday. That or she has a secret we don't know about. But we have time, Lark. We have everything we need right now."

I wasn't sure if it were the steadiness of his heartbeat, the calmness of his voice, or the assuredness of his words, but I was finally able to breathe. The weight that had restricted my lungs in addition to my corset had eased.

"Of course I have faith in you," I replied in answer to his question. He smiled then. True. Gentle. Heart aching. My hand still on his chest, his hand still enveloping mine.

"Then trust me. I'm the best assassin in Meridian for a very good reason. Honest. The deal I made, while not ideal, is manageable. I can handle whatever, or whoever, Aquarius throws at me." He punctuated his point by pressing his lips to mine. His arms curled protectively around me, holding me close. I sank into him, his warmth, his comfort. "How did I get so lucky to have the most amazing soulmate?"

"You must have done something spectacular in a former life." I grinned up at him. I focused on his words, the calm beating of his heart driving away most of the adrenaline. He asked me to have faith, as if I'd ever had more faith in anyone or anything more than him. I took a cleansing breath, forcing the residual panic away.

There's a reason I'm called the Crowned Assassin.

I held to his words. My lifeline. I relaxed into him, a smile forming on his face as a direct result.

"There it is. That light red that's quickly becoming my favorite color. You're happy." He kissed my nose. His eyes followed a movement I couldn't follow. His eyes lightened as he looked down. "Oh, apparently you thought that was sweet, because that aura surged." He did it again, followed by another to my forehead, making my body tingle sweetly all over. This is what it must feel like, being head over heels in love. I grinned and looked away, heat fanning across my cheeks. I reached my arms around his neck, pulling him close. His lips were on mine breath later. Slow. Sweet. Unhurried. He kissed me like he was wooing me, without any expectations of more. Just to kiss me senseless.

"I love you," I whispered when we broke away.

"I love you!" called a familiar and altogether unwelcome voice given the circumstances. Aspen's snickering could even be heard through the door.

"Get lost. You're being a pest," Locke growled at the door. A voice behind it only laughed.

"If you guys could keep your hands to yourselves for a minute, that would be great." I heard his voice lower, as if talking to someone out there, "I swear they're worse than teenagers!" I heard a throat clearing, loudly and obviously from the other side, making Locke struggle to not laugh.

"If you two are quite finished, we've been summoned to the war council. Put your clothes back on and get out here." Indignation flared. I grasped my slipper before Locke could stop me and hurtled it at the door, clattering loudly against the wood and falling harmlessly to the ground. Aspen chortled on the other side, clearly not the least bit offended.

"Not too bad for aim, Little Bird."

I sighed. I thought we'd killed that nickname. I muttered about how much I hated him under my breath, Locke sighing his own agreement. "No, you don't!" came his singsong reply through the door. Locke and I shared a look of shared exasperation.

"Let's go, love. Lots of work yet to do." He opened the door and stepped aside to hold it open for me. Aspen's shit eating grin was the first to greet me.

"How nice of you to finally join us. Let's go. We have a war to plan."

Chapter Fourteen

Our guides brought us to yet another set of massive espresso colored double doors, towering high above me. As we were about to be ushered inside, Locke's head swiveled to see Aquarius striding down the hall, her diamond encrusted crown dazzling and spectacular on her head, larger than the one previously. It was hard to tell which was more stunning, the crown or the Queen wearing it. Abandoning the door, Locke met her, interrupting her path. Guards flared their weapons, but a hand from Aquarius was the silent command to stand down.

"You have something to say to me before the Council." A statement, I noticed. Not a question. Locke inclined his head in answer. She nodded, a silent wave of communication passing between them. "Come. We'll speak privately." She ushered us into a small room off the War room. She turned to the guards, "Make sure we are not interrupted." Their stoic nod their only response. She entered the room with a straight spine, steeled for whatever Locke has deigned to throw at her. And truthfully, I too had no idea what his play was. He was calm, collected, but steel underneath.

"By your countenance, I'm getting the sense there is something you need. Something else extraneous to our deal." Locke gave no response. "So am I correct in assuming this is a personal ask? A favor?" I saw Aquarius's eyes light with glee, and Locke shift his weight in discomfort. She had him with one deal already, we needed to be painfully careful. "It'll cost you. But I'm nothing if not fair. We'll just add to our original deal. Once more my assassin. At my discretion, of course."

"No," I said, finding my voice. I wouldn't let Locke do this alone. I stepped up, taking my place boldly by his side, despite his glare. "He will not. But I will. I have the four elements. I am the most powerful fae currently in existence. Take your favor from me. He's given enough."

"I see the Queen's Mark has finally found her edge. How exciting!" Aquarius's gaze flickered with amusement and appraisal between the two of us.

"Lark, what are you doing?" Locke hissed, his hand going to my forearm. I glared back in earnest.

"My part. I will not stand by while you risk everything. This is my fight too." Before he could even object further, I continued speaking to Aquarius. "You have a favor from me. To be decided at a later time. But I will not kill anyone, nor will the Water Court be in danger. Can we agree?" Aquarius made a show of examining her nails as if they were far more interesting than this bargain.

"How dreadfully boring. How about this? You won't kill anyone innocent. Can we agree to that?" my insides churned as I examined the weight of her words.

"Don't," Locke said at the same time I sealed my fate.

"Done."

Locke looked lost, like he was trying not to hang his head, but not in disappointment. In fear.

"Excellent," Aquarius clapped her hands. "The Queen's Mark shows her teeth at last. Don't be too upset with her, Prince. She's standing on her own two feet. Be glad that you've supported her well enough to do so." Locke was upset though. Flared nostrils, the clenched fists, the hardened stare. I swallowed, but I stood my ground. I wouldn't yield this. Not if it protected him. "Now, what was it you desired? You have my armies, you have my help in reviving Lark after her demise. What else does the Crowned Assassin require of me?" Her voice was all but a purr, enjoying every second of our pain as if it were put on solely for her own amusement. I cut my glare to her.

"I'm looking for my family." Locke's voice came out as calm as before, but he stood rigid next to me, his aura flickering, revealing how very not calm he was beneath the surface. Aquarius, I hoped, was far enough away so as not to notice. "Scorpio has them hidden from me as leverage, and I need them back before we launch our attack."

"I see." She snapped her fingers, the air shimmering a moment before a tall, hulking fae lumbered out of the shadows. They both grinned widely at my surprise. "You didn't think your Water Court Zodiacs were the only ones who'd received gifts from the Echo Isles, did you? Allow me to introduce the head of my own spy network, Wrought Iron Wren."

Wrought Iron Wren was massive. Towering over all of us, but covered in bulky muscle that made him appear lumbering and slow. But I had no doubt that his looks were deceiving, given his title. Eyes that were sharper than any blade appraised us all silently, but gave nothing away. Add to that a face full of scars, all black attire, a single unusually pale eye, and hands the size of hams he was downright terrifying. "He heard all you've said thus far. Is there anything else he may need to know before he continues to filter the information to the rest of the web?"

Locke provided him a detailed description of his family. I listened in, genuinely curious about those who'd raised him before the Zodiac Guild. It seems that Locke's black hair was a product of his mother. Her black hair and fine-boned features easily noticeable. Locke also apparently looked mostly like his father with his strong jaw, high cheek bones, blue eyes, and straight nose. Though Locke's father had light brown hair and pale skin that one could only acquire from chronic illness.

Wren nodded and strode to the door behind us, ready to cast his net.

"Wait!" I found my voice unexpectedly. Wren turned and regarded me with a blank expression. I thought the smile was terrifying. The blank expression was a whole other level.

"Was there something else?" Aquarius asked, looking surprised. I glanced at Locke, who looked just as confused as everyone else.

"Didn't you mention that your father needed an incredible healer? Someone capable of making the potion that keeps him alive?"

"Yes," he said in a tone that was neither approving nor disapproving.

"Do we have a healer currently that can do it?" I asked.

He shook his head. "Not even Aspen has been able to do it. Aspen's talents have always been with wounds and injuries. Alchemy was never his area of specialty." Alchemy. I knew someone who was a healer. An incredibly gifted one. One well versed in Alchemy.

"Wren. Can you add one more person to your list to find?"

He nodded.

"Search for Eldan ."

Locke's jaw dropped.

"The Eldan you told me about. The healer... He's Eldan Van Orhan?"

I blinked in surprise.

"You know Eldan?"

"He was the healer for the Zodiac Kinship in the Water Court for many years. But he was disgraced when a rumor began that one of his potions killed the late Pisces. It was never proven, but he'd lost the trust of the Zodiac Kinship and of the Guild and was under investigation. He not long after that. I think the whole city thought he was dead. I thought he was dead. He was in Poplar Hollow that whole time?" It was the first time I'd seen Locke truly dumbfounded. If the situation weren't so serious, I might've laughed. I shrugged, not sure how to find my voice with this new revelation. Eldan was healer to the Zodiacs?

"Do you remember him?"

"Vaguely. I was newly appointed as Prince Cancer at that time. But I suppose yes is the correct answer. I was aiding the investigation against him."

"Eldan wouldn't hurt anyone without cause. Could it have been a setup? Like the monster that had attacked and killed King Scorpio five years ago?"

"I suppose it's possible," Locke said, still not sounding wholly convinced.

I remembered asking Eldan once why he'd choose to live in a place like Poplar Hollow. It was small, business was hit or miss with a population so small, and even the outpost had closed down due to not having enough monster attacks to justify paid guards. He'd told me there was nothing for him in those big cities. He was happiest with small numbers of people around him. He said he liked knowing his neighbors. Now with everything I've learned, I think what he meant was that if he knew his neighbors, he knew who might betray him if they discovered his true identity. As the disgraced former healer of the Water Court Zodiac Kinship.

"If we find him, we find someone not in the Queen's employ. We find someone she might still believe to be dead. And we find someone who can keep your father alive."

Locke looked skeptical, but not unenthused.

"You trust him?" He asked me. My answer came without the drag of hesitation.

"With my life," I answered honestly. I grew up with him. He was practically family. The only fae other than my father who was kind to me despite my being magicless. I told myself that if Wren found him dead, I would find a way to accept it. But if he were alive, I owed it to both of us to find him.

"Alright then, if you're sure." He glanced up at Wren, who was waiting expectantly. "As she says, Wren." A single abrupt nod was his only response before he turned back towards the door, moving quicker this time. I bit back a smile. He didn't want anyone to add to his already heavy workload, without a doubt.

"Now what?" I looked at Aquarius and Locke.

"Now we plan our attack," said Aquarius. "I believe our audience is over." A simple, straightforward dismissal. I glimpsed Aquarius through the closing door as we entered into the hallway. She seemed relieved to be having a moment alone, at long last. She dragged a heavy sigh and began meandering to the large window looking down over her shining city.

One thing was bothering me as Locke as I disembarked for the war room. One thing that I dared not speak out loud.

Scorpio had Locke's family to keep him compliant. So why hadn't their heads shown up yet? Scorpio knew Locke was working against her, so what was she doing to them that would hurt Locke more than their execution?

Chapter Fifteen

Lennox, Aquarius, and a whole host of others I wasn't familiar with awaited us behind massive espresso colored doors. It was all too easy for fear to break into my mind as if with a battering ram. This wasn't my world. Wasn't my experience. What did I even have to offer a war council? Locke leaned down, sensing my discomfort, his fingers stroking over my engagement ring.

"You said yourself this is your fight too. This is part of that." He looked down at me, his fingers gently squeezing until I looked up at him too. "Let the flames fuel you."

That phrase. The one that instilled hope within me when I had none. Something that had become a reminder to me to keep fighting, keep believing, even when hope seemed lost.

"But don't let them consume you," I answered in response, feeling those flames bolster me from within. I didn't let go of Locke's hand as we moved together as a unit into the room. A unit not just of us, but with Aspen, Lennox, and Lenore trailing behind us. All of us united under the banner of rebellion in a foreign court. Every eye was on us as we took up our space in the War Room.

The space of the War Room itself was a marvel among marvels. More flawless white and sparkling silver was carried along, the stained glass windows spanned the entire ceiling, allowing flickers of color here and there. But what snared my attention so completely was the dragon.

It looked so lifelike, as if it could reach out and touch it. And that I might lose a limb—or worse—if I did. Golden marble eyes reflected the flames of the massive hearth across the room, further lending itself the appearance of a live dragon perched on a set of strategically placed columns. It was silver, much like everything else, but its scales gave it a shadowy texture that stood out in the room. It commanded attention. I supposed it was fitting for a war room. Nothing would have ever struck fear into the hearts of your enemies like seeing a dragon come after you.

"It's too bad they're extinct, eh?" Aspen's voice from behind me. I jumped, earning myself a sheepish grin from him. "Sorry. I guess we're all on edge." I glanced at him as he joined me in my admiration of the open-mawed beast. Its teeth were the size of my forearm. I shuddered to think the end that awaited you if something like that caught you. "Something like this big guy would be extremely powerful on the battlefield. Hell, I'd take a wyvern. Maybe a basilisk. Something big and mean." He flashed me a grin.

"Having something like that on our side, I'm pretty sure Scorpio would run screaming." As I laughed, Aquarius moved into the room towards the opulent glittering throne.

Her throne was at the head of the massive round table, surrounded by podiums, the head of which sat an elaborate throne made of crystal. Or diamond perhaps. Like everything else in this court, it flickered in the light, beckoning to the Queen of the Court. The silver swooping lines of the Air Court's emblem was visible on the middle of the table. Fae began entering the room in earnest, taking their place at the podiums. Whispers and stolen glances coming our way, hostility brewing hot. You could cut the tension with a knife.

"These fae are like Blood Wraiths, Lark," Locke's hushed tone was low, meant for my ears only. "Show no weakness. Nothing. Give them nothing." I nodded my response. I could do that. I always had to have my guard up in Poplar Hollow. I could never afford to show weakness. Even if my wounds opened up in the middle of class, or the market, I had to be discreet. These were the type of fae, I knew, to sniff out blood. I had to give them nothing. "Are you ready?"

I squared my shoulders and nodded. Locke and I took our place at our podium, wide enough for the two of us to stand comfortably. Lennox, Lenore, and Aspen stood behind us. Lenore kept her hand on her knife belted at her side, ready in the event of... honestly, I didn't know what. Did things usually get threatening at war councils? Even Aspen looked uncomfortable and on edge, his eyes scanning every single movement.

"Do these meetings usually get violent?" I whispered to Aspen over my shoulder, who grinned in response.

"You'd be surprised. Though usually it's more insults thrown back and forth. Royals tend to enjoy throwing their egos around, but sometimes an ego gets a little too hurt."

"Locke might be in trouble then," I whispered to Aspen. He chuckled as Locke turned towards us, that mischief I loved sparking in his eyes.

"I heard that," he mused, feigning outrage.

"You were meant to," I whispered back only a moment before Aquarius spoke, bringing the meeting to order at last. I watched intently the reactions of each of the councilfae as Aquarius explained the situation at hand, about joining forces with us. Our allyship. Some seemed accepting. Others glared at us in mistrust, a reaction I couldn't fault them for, given the circumstances.

"The attack on Windermere must not, and will not, go unpunished!" Aquarius stated in a firm voice that very much suited a Queen. A voice that silenced all others, a voice that brought every eye to her. "The Water Court will answer for their atrocities. Scorpio is our target, and we will reap payment for the blood shed here yesterday."

"But how?" One of the councilfae asked. "She's invulnerable. How are we supposed to kill her?"

"That's where our friends from the Water Court here come in." Aquarius gestured at us, bringing every eye back to us. The anger. The mistrust. The hostility. I saw it all.

"How do we know they weren't in on it?" one seethed.

"Did you not see them fighting for us? They even saved Queen Aquarius's life!" chimed in another. I was surprised to see one of them had our backs, but he didn't look over at me as he addressed his kinsmen.

"An act! To lure us into a false sense of security." Another slammed his fist on the table, hissing his words through a tense jaw. "My brother died in that fight. A fight that wouldn't have happened if they hadn't been here."

"We were here legally with an invite," Locke said calmly. I didn't miss his hand twitching next to his sword, as if aching to hold it. His eyes took in every perceivable threat, and without looking I knew the knights behind us did too. "It was Prince Gemini who betrayed you, not us. We didn't have anything to do with Scorpio entering Everwind." Hushed whispers broke out, heads turning, eyes wide at this revelation.

"What Prince Cancer speaks is truth, Mathias," Aquarius's voice rung out, cutting through all others.

"How can we trust them?" another spoke.

"Because they have even more at stake than we do. We go into this alliance freely and willingly for revenge. They do so for their very lives. Please enlighten us, Rebel Court. Please tell your story before the council."

Locke told the story once again. From his lips it sounded like a grim faerie tale. Magic, and curses, fated love, doomed to fail. Several faces softened as they regarded, us, some looked on at us in pity. But while it made my stomach churn, it did drastically weed out the hostility in the room towards us.

"Now that that's settled," Aquarius droned in a voice that betrayed her boredom, "can we move forward with the actual purpose of this war council? To plan a war? Or are you not done questioning my judgement?"

"Yes, your majesty." They all mumbled in unison, sounding like spoiled children who'd been scolded. Aspen wasn't kidding when he warned me about wounded egos before.

"What news from the Guild, Markham?" Aquarius asked. Markham produced a piece of parchment with a broken seal. The seal of the Guild. My tongue pressed to my teeth, a reaction I couldn't understand. After scanning the document for a moment, Markham cleared his throat.

"The Zodiac Guild has tried to wrestle Scorpio off her throne, but she and Pisces have become too strong. Her invulnerability means they can't kill her, and getting to her is near impossible, even for them. They support this alliance in hopes of breaking the curse and destroying her once and for all."

Aquarius rolled her eyes. "Of course, they're of no use. All powerful, my ass," she scoffed. She muttered something that sounded an awful lot like "useless bastards."

"What of their resources?" Aquarius turned to us with rapt attention. "Their numbers, their advantages, disadvantages, what are we up against, so called Rebel Court?"

"A few thousand, maybe more." Locke's voice matched the grave reality of his statement, sparking a tune of shocked whispers echoing around the room. I tried to hide my own shock at that reality. I knew Scorpio would be amassing forces to fend us off, but thousands? We stood no chance at all without the Air Court.

I thought back to what I knew of Port Azure. In Hell's Gate. Hundreds of strong, well-trained warriors ready to fight. One thousand strong at best. Fae with cause enough to despise Scorpio. But to take on thousands? Locke began speaking again and everyone, especially me, listened with rapt attention. "Scorpio is bolstering her forces through conscription. Every adult fae capable of fighting has been summoned to Loc Valen. Entire towns have been emptied. Those who resisted were subjugated or killed. She's training them in designated sectors within the city of Loc Valen itself so they're ready at a moment's notice. Even untrained."

Every time I heard something else that Scorpio had done, I felt more ill. She was forcing fae into a war, using as many bodies between us and her as she can. Despite not being able to die. And for what? A few rebels? The councilfae echoed my thoughts heavily.

"She's clearly afraid of a launched assault by the rebels," a councilfae said with robust confidence that bordered dangerously on arrogance. Crossing his arms he continued, "And she should be. If we strike at her with our combined forces she will fall."

"Don't be deceived." Locke's lips were thin as he spoke. "Scorpio and Pisces are master wielders of shadow magic—likeness before has never been witnessed. We're the only court in recorded history where all three of us bear curses. You cannot take that lightly. They will be more dangerous than you know."

"But we have you, Her Majesty Queen Aquarius, and the Queen's Mark," someone piped up, looking unabashedly right at me. Locke's fists tightened on the edge of his podium.

"She has a name, councilfae," he growled, all eyes drawn to him. "Lark. And I expect you to use it with respect."

"Lark, then," he said, waving a hand by way of an apology. "Between you three, do we not have an advantage?"

"Not necessarily. Scorpio cannot die, so her shadows do not threaten her life the way they do mine. I have used my shadows sparingly, whereas she hasn't. Shadow magic doesn't have limits the way elemental and whole magic do. There is, and I mean this quite literally, no limit to what she can do. We have reports that they have other black magic wielders as well, possibly even by force."

A hushed, horrified silence filled the room. Forcing fae to become cursed? That was outlandish. Cruelty in its highest form. It was essentially what she did to Locke, whose grim expression traded for my one of horror.

"She needs to be put down like the monster she is," a councilfae to my left spat. I was uplifted a bit to hear the outrage in her voice. In Air Court's acknowledgment of what was happening. We'd need all the help we could get.

"Whole magic never used to have limits," someone grumbled. Mathias again, probably. "We need access to that old magic."

"That magic has been largely lost, many of the old texts destroyed, much of it never being taught," someone else chimed in ominously. Her fingers drummed on her podium as she addressed us all. "And with good reason. We can try to find some spells of old whole magic, but most of us won't be powerful enough to use it, especially not safely. There is a very good reason why certain tomes and magics were lost to time. Fae lose themselves in power more often than they find themselves."

Fae lose themselves in power more often than they find themselves.

That phrase would never leave me. I thought about what whole magic can do. My ability to sense others around me, Locke's shrouding, Aspen's healing. What sort of spells caused this sort of a reaction? That they would allow such magic to fall into memory? And the thought nagged and pestered me, ensnaring my attention.

Were they right to do so?

Hours passed and I'd nearly had my fill of the never-ending squabbling. I pressed my tongue into my teeth as hard as I could to keep from shouting at them. This wasn't about planning a war; it was entirely about upping everyone else and impressing Aquarius, who didn't look like she cared whatsoever for the nonsense currently ensuing. There were collective discussions, strategies picked up, examined and discarded again, and each time one was, another argument erupted. I sighed my exasperation.

"Is this how these things usually go?" I asked Locke. He smirked, looking as if he were repressing a laugh.

"Far more often than not. Get used to it."

"Are we going to have a lot of these?" I asked him.

"You're going to be on a throne, one day. This will be part of your life," he said it so matter-of-factly. So casually. In any capacity, but I couldn't imagine seeing myself on a throne, let alone one carved from gemstones. Such extravagance, while my father and I scraped by, while other families did. I couldn't imagine. Aquarius finally had enough and stood drawing every eye her way and effectively silencing the room.

"It sounds to me like we have three strategies that show the most merit: take the fight to Loc Valen, Let Scorpio and her wretched curse come to the Court of Rebels through a myriad of traps in the dead forest to weaken them, or luring them to a grounds where we hold all the advantages. Or perhaps drive them there. Representatives of the Water Court, please state your positions on these strategies to the council."

The very idea of having Scorpio come to Port Azure made me sick. Of Scorpio, or any of her loyal followers, getting near someone like Elias, or anyone else there... My stomach sank under the weight of my horror. A single brief sidelong glance from Locke was all it took to reassure me he wouldn't let that happen. Not for anything.

"All of these strategies have merit, though I admit I'm loathe to allow Scorpio so close to the Court of Rebels. We've worked hard to keep it hidden from the Water Court for years now. There are scores of innocent fae who can't fight, including children. It's our only safe haven. To bring the fight to them would be disastrous, and it's not something I can allow." My heart swelled at my soulmate's compassion.

"There are sacrifices one must make in war," said a councilfae to my left. My head swung around to gape at him and his dismissive tone. He puffed his chest out, looking as pompous as he sounded, "War results in casualties. War also requires doing what's necessary to ensure the win. Scorpio and her forces would be weakened by the forest between the blood wraiths and the soulless, and any other traps we set in place." He scoffed, side eying Locke before continuing, "It is the height of stupidity not to use advantages in war because of the battlefield's proximity to home." He spat the word home as if it were a dirty, ugly thing. I was so angry, so disgusted with what he was saying. I turned away, killing insults on my tongue with great effort.

"How tall are you, council?" Locke asked, a smirk picking up the corners of his mouth. The sharpness of his eyes may not cut with blades, but they cut nonetheless. I blinked, wondering where he was going with this, almost in time with several others watching, waiting. Including the councilfae in question.

"What possible relevance does that have?" He clearly didn't know what to make of Locke, didn't know how to rein him in. Something he was clearly used to being able to do. He had a large presence, and I had no doubt he intimidated a lot of others. But Locke wasn't one of those others.

"Since we're discussing the height of stupidity," Locke's voice was calm, but his presence became bigger, more unrelenting. His eyes darkened as he spoke. "I can only assume you mean yourself with everything else that you're spouting."

A hush fell over the room for the first time, the only sound coming from the sputtering fae in question, and Locke let him. Locke let him look a fool in front of his fellow councilfae, in front of his Queen. Perhaps that was an even bigger slight in this kind of court than actually harming someone. I looked around at the fae snickering amongst themselves, the fae in question turning redder with each breath.

"I beg your pardon?" He slammed his fist on the table before him, several fae flinching back around him from the outburst. He puffed his already barreled chest out, as if that would make him look more imposing, more intimidating. Locke's lips pressed together, a sure sign of him stifling a laugh, before finally turning towards him, to address him fully.

"Then beg." Locke's power flickered through the room, startling several fae around us, showing everyone what a predator actually looked like. "We're all waiting." The fae looked to his Queen, as if to validate him, or perhaps save him. Aquarius regarded him frostily, bringing to mind the chilled northern winds on the coldest day of winter.

"Don't expect help from me, Mathias," she said, adjusting her crown. "You stoked that fire; you can put it out yourself." The fae—Mathias— glowered before returning to Locke.

"The point is, casualties happen. Homes can be rebuilt elsewhere." His voice lacked the conviction, the confidence of earlier. He looked like he wanted to crawl in a hole and stay there. But Locke didn't stop, but now addressed the council as a whole, leaving Mathias to wither in his place. Silent. Deflated. I wanted to laugh.

"Tell me, council, do you know what it's like losing your loved ones and your home in a single day? Because many who live in Port Azure do. They found a safe haven, somewhere they are free to live their lives in peace, hidden from Scorpio and her violence. And we're actually discussing the validity of bringing war there? There is no validity. The Rebel Court will not stand with this strategy. There are far too many innocent fae that would be at risk, for what could end up being far too little pay off. Port Azure is not a lure."

"Leaders must make tough decisions, Prince. Ugly ones even, to get the job done. Can they not be moved?" A councilfae said, across from us this time. An older woman. She didn't appear angry, or spiteful. Almost as if questioning his conviction. Mathias raised his head, a sneer forming on his face at her words before speaking up, cutting Locke off.

"Agreed, Cortina," he said, regaining his smug countenance, eyeing the room before pining us with a disdainful glare. "If you're not willing to concede anything while we fight your war for you, then—"

"I'm going to stop you right there, councilor." Locke abruptly cut him off in a low, frosty tone. A voice I'd only ever heard him use once—when Abel had threatened me. He said nothing violent, but the undercurrent was there for all to see. All motion stopped. A hush fell over the room for the second time. Not a single sound was uttered. Most didn't even dare breath as Locke geared up to put this fae in his place once and for all. He dropped the mask of careful indifference, and showed what lay beneath. The impatience. The anger. All directed at Mathias.

"As thrilling as it is to witness the thoughtlessness in you, we don't have the time for it today. This meeting's purpose is to narrow down a legitimate strategy to take Scorpio down, and I tell you now we are not endangering the Court of Rebels. And if you think that I haven't given everything in this fight, if my betrothed hasn't," Several eyes slipped to me, and I met their gaze with the same ferocity Locke showed. "and all fae within the

Water Court, then you clearly haven't been listening. We will all do what is necessary to get Scorpio permanently out of the picture. But I will not," Locke glared at Mathias, still seething and shrinking in on himself on his podium, "send fae away to their deaths and cause them to lose what home and safety they have accumulated once again. Have I made myself clear, Counselors?" There was a collective murmuring of agreeance, but Locke wasn't satisfied with that. He stared at Mathias, until he glanced up seeing the weight of the council pressing in on him.

"I said," Locke jeered, his shadows roaming the surface of his body, "have I made myself clear?"

"Abundantly, Highness" Mathias's utterance was almost too low to hear. Locke clapped his hands together, addressing the council as a whole once again, leaving Mathias to pout and wither.

"Excellent, then we are in agreement. That leaves two options we are open to. Bringing Scorpio to a third location, or bring the battle to Loc Valen."

"Scorpio will suspect a trap, regardless of lure," said a councilor to my right. Her hands were adorned with jewels, each more sparkly than the last. Their light refracted with every rhythmic drum of her fingers. "Why would she leave Loc Valen when she holds all of the advantages?"

"What advantages?" someone asked.

"The raised terrain surrounding it, the fact that there is only one portcullis entrance and it's surrounded by barracks, spelled to make intruders powerless, the list goes on," Locke murmured. "She does hold advantages there." That single sentence spelled trouble for both strategies. If we couldn't get her to leave the city, that forced us to launch an attack on Loc Valen, where she held all the cards. And all the hostages she could want.

"We have the numbers to raze Loc Valen to the ground," someone said. "Let's just be done with it."

"And what of the innocent fae we have no quarrel with?" I asked, drawing all eyes to me. I let them see my conviction. I thought of Lorelei from the inn. I couldn't not advocate for her, for everyone in that city. They deserved a chance as much as the rest of us. "Many of those in Loc Valen are as much victims of her as we are. Living in fear of her. Why should they die? Are we seriously discussing not demolishing one home, but then in the next breath bringing full scale slaughter to another? I do not think the only way is to turn the jewel of the Water Court into a tomb." I implored them to think of another way. There had to be an answer. Aquarius sat up, leaning towards the table.

"When we bring the fight to Loc Valen, the alarm will sound. Fae will shelter in their homes," Locke offered.

"Then we don't attack those who don't attack us," I finished.

"Agreed. There will be far too much bloodshed as it is. We don't harm the innocent."

"That's all lovely, but how do you plan to get in with only one, very heavily guarded entrance?" Cortina asked. "Do you have an answer for that as well?"

"If we go to Loc Valen, we need to level the playing field, yes? Between the terrain, and the high battlement walls." Nods and murmurs filled the room. They were following me. "We need inside those walls. We need to take those walls down, or draw her armies out of the wall, but what about doing both?" I beseeched the council with pleading eyes. "Blow up the battlements. Their armies will be forced to meet us head on, and we will win access to the city. To Ari'inor."

"How do we blow up the walls?" Cortina asked, intrigued. "We don't have incendiary magic. At least we don't. Do you, Queen's Mark, have a special magic we don't know about?"

"We send someone in ahead of time. In secret," Locke answered, where my own words failed. "Time bombs will be the perfect spell."

"What in the Echo Isles is a time bomb?" someone asked.

"A paused explosion, spelled with old magic inside a special container," Aquarius explained with a wide grin. "Frozen in time, until someone detonates it. Tricky and hard to do. Disastrous if made wrong and highly unstable." She smiled, holding a secret close to her as one might hold their winning cards. "But thankfully I know someone who is excellent at them." Wrought Iron Wren melted from the shadows next to her, shocking nobody, except me. I wondered if I'd ever get used to him blinking into existence. "Can you do this?"

"I can, Majesty." He bowed his head.

"Once the final battle between us is set, once Scorpio kills me, and the curse is broken, you'll have your shot at her," I said finally. Locke paled and grit his teeth but said nothing. Chatter opened up around the table, but all eyes were on me. I glanced at Mathias, and turned towards him, rage simmering at his earlier accusation. "Don't you ever say we haven't sacrificed, councilor," I said through clenched teeth. "I am going to die. I'm willingly laying down my life to secure our victory, so that the Water Court may be peaceful once more. What exactly are you doing?"

He said nothing, shaking his head and refusing to meet my eye. In turn, I made steady eye contact with each member of counsel and Aquarius in turn. "I will ensure that Scorpio's curse is broken so that she can at last answer for the crimes committed against you, and against the Water Court. The attack yesterday was unprovoked and must be answered. What say you, Queen and Council of Air?"

"Aye." Aquarius stood, supporting the motion.

"Aye," Cortina sounded her support. A chorus of "aye" repeating around the room. My gaze slid to the one council member who'd yet to speak. Mathias. With the weight of all the gazes on him, and him clearly not wanting to be on the wrong side, he finally uttered his agreement.

"I don't like this, Lark," Locke said. "You're throwing yourself into the fray. I can't protect you if you keep running into the thick of things like this."

"I'm going to die, Locke. Even you, Crowned Assassin, cannot stave off death." I touched his hand. "Though, I have no doubt that of anyone in Meridian, you'd come the closest if you tried. It's going to be okay. But I need your support in this."

"The manner with which you die matters! You can't be revived if you're dismembered, or you're blown up. If you're skewered by a weapon. We can't bring you back from everything." My mind stilled. It was something I'd tried like hell to not dwell on. Because I couldn't stand the thought of going through this only for my death to be too brutal to come back from.

It was like it was on cue, like the Goddess herself was laughing at me and my realization. That cold feeling, like a piece of ice dangled and broke from within me, dying immediately. I fought hard not to show it, for my breath not to falter, for the nausea not to rise up, but Locke's eyes flicked to me instantly, concern warring with a quiet sort of accusation. Like he knows I'm keeping something from him. How ironic.

"You and Aspen have worked hard to ensure that I'm strong enough to take care of myself." I murmured. "Did I not prove myself in Frostfall? The details of this may be decided later, but what is your answer, Highness?" He didn't move for a long moment. Didn't speak. His cheeks hollowed out as if trying to not speak rashly. But after several heart pounding moments, he at last spoke.

"Aye," he said without taking his eyes from mine. "I hope you know what you're doing, love." I knew that look. We were far from done discussing this. But I also knew he wouldn't undermine me here, in front of the counsel, or the Queen. I saw the hesitation there on his face. The questions. The concern. The fear. All of which echoed right down to my bones.

It was unanimous. That was to be our plan.

What had I just set in motion?

Chapter Sixteen

After what felt like an eternity, Queen and Court finally solidified our plan. Everything was in full motion now and there was no going back. The Court of Rebels and the Air Court were going to be at war with Water. Everything would begin once intel came back on Locke's family and Eldan. Orders had been sent to begin preparations; I could see the black smoke of the forges on the edge of the city from my place at the window overlooking Everwind. Aquarius's help was secured in my resurrection as well. So, why did I feel so unsettled?

Locke's mood matched my own as we entered our chambers. Outwardly, he wore the mask of the Crowned Assassin. The one of cool detachment. But there were signs. The tightness of his eyes, his lips pressed together, the stiffness of his gait, all gave me hints at the turbulence hiding underneath. And the moment those doors closed behind us, I felt my own walls and armor fall, finding myself too exhausted to keep them up any longer. The look on Locke's face was one familiar to me; dread. I could see in the hardness of his gaze that part of him was elsewhere, being haunted by ghosts of a traumatic past nowhere near behind him.

"Locke..." I started, I genuinely had no idea what to say. How could you possibly comfort your soulmate when you death might be just around the corner? Every day now, I felt the taint of the curse inside me, slowly spreading, an inch every day.

"I would do anything to save you from your fate." His voice was softer than I'd anticipated, stealing me from my own thoughts. He raked his hands through his hair with a sigh of deep discontentment. "I would give anything. *Anything*. I'd make any deal, any bargain." His voice shook with the weight of his words. I felt that same emotion crash into me. He finally looked at me, his blue eyes so bright they almost appeared to glow in the dim light of the sunset room. Tendrils of his black hair fell into his face. "I would bury myself alive, stab my own heart, I'd die a thousand deaths if it meant that you'd be spared this. If it meant you didn't have to do this." I reached for him, needing to do something.

I felt the curse within my body. Like black char that I couldn't cut from within me. The fact I could feel it felt like fate laughing at us.

"Don't do that. Any one of those thousand things." Gently, as if he might break, I placed my hands on his cheeks, forcing him to look at me. "I need you to know, if nothing else after all this is over, that this is real. That we're real." I hated more than anything else in that moment that couldn't promise him that it would be okay. I was going to die and Aquarius might not be successful. I had no idea how to make that okay. But I could see those weren't the only demons he struggled with. "I never needed or wanted anybody before you. Except for my father, and he'd trained me to be self-reliant. I needed food, oxygen, water. You're the first fae that came into my life and added value, rather than took it away. It's strange. Because it's not just that I need you in my life. It's that you're so incredibly wanted. Everything about you is desperately wanted and appreciated, Locke. The good and the bad."

For a moment, he didn't respond. But I felt his body shudder as he struggled to reconcile my version of him and his own, much darker version. I clutched him tighter still and returned my head to his chest, my head tucked under his chin. I lost myself in the moment, lost myself in loving Locke.

"How are you mine?" he murmured against my hair. Not an ounce of self-pity in his words. Just sheer wonderment. I remember he'd mused those words to me once before. I'd laughed him off, but I knew what he meant. He'd done deplorable things. Death, torture, exiling.

"You're an incredible leader, Locke. You give all of yourself for your charges. Look at how you stood your ground for the Court of Rebels earlier. I know you've done bad things in the past. But you're not Scorpio or Pisces. You didn't do those things because you wanted something from them or because you felt like it. You didn't revel in it. You did what you were forced to do. You saved all those you could. Otherwise, the Court of Rebels wouldn't exist. It's a testament to your kindness. Your worth. Don't you see that?"

"Nothing, and I mean nothing," his teeth ground on the word as if it had bitten him on the way out, "will stop me from bringing you back from beyond the veil. If such magic exists, it will be found. And if it doesn't..." His eyes bored into mine, the intensity robbing me of breath. "I'll pull you from death. Just as you have pulled me from my dark, colorless existence." The gravity of his words hit me in a way that rendered me speechless. Bereft of words, I responded the only way I knew how; I kissed him. I brought my lips to his, to show, rather than tell, how much I loved him. From this close, I could see the faint circles beginning under his eyes, piquing my concern.

"You look tired, Locke. We should both bathe and get some rest. When was the last time you slept the night through?" He gave me that halfhearted smile that I was pretty sure as for my benefit.

"I have a nap scheduled for next week, but I might have to reschedule it again." I rolled my eyes and fought the grin creeping onto my face. The joke was so stupid, but I couldn't help but huff a laugh. He grinned at me in earnest this time. "I love when you laugh."

I snorted, ruining the moment. "I love that you're vaguely funny."

"Oh? Only vaguely?"

"Yes!" I felt my smile widen. "Now I'm aching in places I scarcely knew existed. Please help me out of this Goddess awful corset so I can lay in the bath for some time. You, of course, are welcome to join." I added with a wink. Locke's gaze was scorching as he turned me around.

"You never have to ask twice for me to undress you, love," he whispered. He stepped up behind me, his warm breath teasing the skin of my neck as his hands undid the corset. Row by row, the strings slackened, making it so much easier to breathe. My skin buzzed with his proximity, fully aware of each movement he made. Every hair on the back of my neck stood on attention when he leaned in, pressing his lips to that little hollow below my ear. "I can make you ache in one or two other places if you'd like." Every muscle south of my stomach clenched together at the warmth starting there. His hands, now with access to some exposed skin, made me shiver. I toyed with my lip between my teeth as he planted a warm kiss in the crook my neck.

"There's not a star in the sky that can hold a candle to you, Lark."

"Not a bad pick-up line, Locke," I huffed to him. He chuckled, slowly releasing the last bonds of the corset. I wasn't sure who ripped it off me, me or him. With the corset discarded, hopefully to the pits of the Echo Isles, I took in my first full breath in hours. I melted into Locke, or I tried to, but the warm, muscular body had moved. Peeping over my shoulder, I saw him smirk at me as he discarded his shirt at the door to the bathing chamber and disappear into the bathing room.

I quickly shed my grey dress and slippers, remaining in my underthings for now. I walked quietly into the bathing room while tying my hair up top my head to avoid it getting wet. Locke, ever the gentleman, was waiting for me, the pants undone and his runed chest bare to me. The muted light highlighted his musculature flatteringly and I found my eyes tracing every inch of him. He looked like a god born of carnality. And that look in his eyes told me he knew it.

"Ladies first." His sultry voice invited me in. Desire swelled within me as I took him in, the bulge in his pants stoking my fires further. But this time, I thought, it would be me in control. Not him. I smirked at him as I entered the steaming water. Tonight, I'd be the one to make him beg. Gathering every bit of confidence I had, I removed what little clothing I wore, tossing it aside before entering the pool up to my breasts. Flames erupted in his eyes as he beheld me. I turned my back to him and wadded to the edge of the pool where the water dipped and fell over the city of Everwind, now lighting up in the coming dusk at our feet. I leaned on the edge of the pool, taking in the breathtaking scene.

I heard him enter the pool and wade to me. I felt him stand behind me, his erection pressing against me. I bit my lip harder as I fought not to grind against him. He would beg me. Not the other way around.

"Are you trying to play hard to get, love?" he murmured as his hands slid around my front and pulled me into him. He began tracing small patterns lightly over my stomach, and indecently lower, leaving scorching trails behind. I held to my earlier conviction. He would beg. Not me. "Because I so love a good chase."

I whispered my hands up his thighs in answer and bit back a smile when his hips jerked a bit. "It's not fair to tease when your ass looks this perfect," he said in that husky voice of his as his hands traced teasingly along my behind now. So close to where I was beginning to ache for him. I fought to keep my body from responding.

"Why, Locke," I said fluttering my eyelashes at him over my shoulder. "Are you flirting with me?"

"It's not flirting if it's true. It's not my fault that everything I say is suave."

"There's that massive ego. I can't believe we lost it for a second." His fingers found their way to my center then, stroking me beneath the water but not giving me what my body craved. With his other hand, he bent me over the wide edge of the pool and pinned me in place with his hips, while his other hand continued to torture me, making my breaths come in steady pants.

"I think you like my massive... ego," he said, his fingers now dipping into me. I moaned, pushing back against him. He tsked. "Now, now, love, this is the game you started. You'll have to finish it." I reached behind me to grasp his length, loving the hiss of pleasure that fell from his lips before moving out of my grasp. "Are you trying to hurry me along?"

"Yes." I whimpered. Two fingers sank into my heat finally, before withdrawing again. "Locke!" I cried out.

"Hmm?" he asked, repeating the process. In. Pause. Out. Stretching me, stroking me. Making me burn and crave. I struggled, but with him pinning me down there was nothing I could do but take it the torture. "I think there might be a word you're missing." Fuck. I wouldn't beg. I wouldn't do it. It was his turn. I reached for him again, to no avail.

"I don't know what you're talking about." My breathy tone turned into something carnal as he drove his fingers upwards, stealing my breath.

"Is that how it's going to be?" he growled.

"Until you beg," I panted. He chuckled darkly against the sensitive skin of my neck.

"Is that what this is about? How cute. I wonder how much longer you can hold off?" he cursed as he upped his ministrations, drawing more breathy, desperate sounds from me. "You're sopping wet, love. Beg me to fuck you and we both know I can make this ache go away."

"Fuck. You," I said, hoping to goad him into it.

"I'm trying to." I could hear the salacious grin in his voice as he drove me mad. He kept the same rhythm up, enough to stoke the fire within me, but not enough to build it further. I was so close to begging him, and he knew it. "Do you trust me, Lark?" It was a question I never needed to think about.

"Yes." A single word that spurred him on in a way I'd never seen. He withdrew his hand and rather than being bent over the pool's wide infinity ledge, I was now propped up on it, Locke's shadows, cold at odds with the hot of the pool, supporting me, but also restraining me. Ribbons of black magic coiled around each leg, each hand, baring me to him entirely above the water line. There was just enough space for my hips and lower back on the ledge, and below me was a several hundred, if not thousand, foot drop to the shimmering city below. If I could have held on to the shadows, to him, I would have, but they allowed for no movement. Heat and fear made for a heady combination, my heart racing in equal measure of both extremes, both emotions amping up the other, trying to outdo one another.

From his place between my legs, he looked up at me, humor and desire mixing in his gaze.

"Trust me," he implored. I nodded, trying to relax into his shadowy hold. "Eyes on me, love." My gaze snapped to his just in time to see his tongue meet that hypersensitive bud I was dying for. I cried out immediately, and again when he stopped. "You're going to have to keep your voice down. Can you do that?"

"No," I said honestly. He licked me once more.

"Let's put it this way, if you're not quiet, I'll stop," he said before resuming. I choked back a moan. I couldn't move, couldn't arch into him the way I wanted. Every time I tried, the shadows tightened their hold, forcing me to stay right where he wanted me. The glint in his eyes nearly had me undone. I moaned his name, followed by a string of curses as the pressure began to build in my core in earnest. His teeth raked across that sensitive bud, pain mixing with the pleasure. A warning. "Volume." He growled before soothing the small pain with the pleasure of his tongue. This time when his fingers stroked me, when they drove inside, it took everything I had to follow his order. I grit my teeth on his name, desperate to keep my volume down. As everything within began to quicken and my legs shook, I felt him pull away.

"No Locke. Please," I whimpered.

"There it is," he praised. "I want you coming on my cock though. Hold on, love." True to his word, as fast as he withdrew, he was lining himself up with my entrance that was begging for him. He slid home right where I needed him to be. When he began to move, slamming in and out of me, I didn't know if even his shadows could keep me on the earth. My insides quickened as curses spewed from my mouth.

"Fuck, I love how you take me." Locke growled, low and guttural, and feral.

His words were my undoing. Were all I needed to implode in a chaotic blend of desire and sin. When my release smacked into me, I knew I wouldn't be able to obey his order of keeping my volume down. The world fell away, leaving me breathless. He lifted me under my arms, his shadows disappearing in the same moment. I nearly screamed as I dove for him, wrapping my arms around him tight enough to strangle as he dragged me back over into the pool.

"You're not going anywhere. I'm not done with you yet," He growled low in his throat. He bent me back over the ledge, the way he had me before, my rear end just above the waterline. "Grip the ledge and don't let go," he ordered, my hands quickly coming up to comply. His hands came up to fondle it before driving into me once again. My lips parted on something between a gasp and a strangled cry as he upped his already punishing pace. I arched back into him, meeting him thrust for thrust. I wasn't sure if I whispered or shouted his name when I felt him swelling inside me, hitting just the right spot as I shattered around him falling headfirst into ruin. I heard him grunt my name in return as he followed me into the fall, holding me the whole way until reality came creeping back.

I turned around, wanting to hold him. He had the same idea. Locke sat on the bench in the pool, pulling me with him so I sat on his lap. In the warmth of the bathing pool, we basked in each other, enjoying the twinkling view of the city below as the last vestiges of sunset faded away entirely.

"I wish the water was just a bit warmer," he muttered, submerging us both up to our shoulders. I laughed, my head tipping back.

"Ask and you shall receive." I beamed at him. I pulled from my well of fire magic, heating the pool instantly. Locke winced while I luxuriated in his arms.

"Why is it one degree from boiling?" he griped, clearly resisting the urge to leap from the water. I giggled, but took pity on him, cooling it slightly until he sagged in exaggerated relief. As if he too couldn't have cooled it.

"I just like to practice burning in hell," I cracked, moving to lean against his solid form. He laughed before he kissed my temple and wrapping his arm around me and pulling me to him.

"That's not where someone as wonderful as you would go," he said in a way that had me thinking that the ghosts that haunted his mind were speaking to him. I kissed him, slow and tender, my hands coming up to cup his face.

"That's not where you're going either when you cross the veil," I murmured. I didn't give him a chance to rebut before leaning up and kissing him sweetly again, my hands twining in his raven strands. Not much. Just enough to bring him closer to me.

"Hey, Lark?" he whispered against my lips. I cocked my head at him.

"Yes?"

"You made fun of my pickup line, but I'd like to point out that it worked flawlessly." He grinned widely down at me. I splashed him, unable to fight my own smile. He looked at me adoringly, his hands caressing my shoulders. "There's my favorite color."

"That's because of you," I whispered.

I hoped his was too. Because all I could think about was how happy he made me. I hoped that I could make him feel one iota of this. Languid and spent in his arms, luxuriating in the heat of the pool, I found myself once again wishing I could pause time, so I could live in this moment forever.

After a small, pleasant eternity, it was clear we were spent and would fall asleep in the pool if we didn't move now. Locke dried both of us with his water magic, deftly returning the water from our bodies back to the pool. We both fell into the massive bed together, my head on his chest, his arms around me tightly. I could think of nothing more perfect than this moment.

The next day flew by in a blur, but time stopped when we met Aquarius in the Great Hall. I felt trepidation creep up at seeing the throne room again after all the devastation.

When last I saw the towering ceilings and historical archways, it resembled more a crypt than a great hall. Fire had raged. Bodies were strewn about, blood covering every surface, gore traumatizing every onlooker, marring the pristine white and glimmer of silver with the stark red.

I was relieved to see the flawless white gleamed once again with what was no doubt endless elbow grease, magic and hours of meticulous labor. But it still wasn't perfect. Far from it. I released a breath. I didn't know what I was expecting. Rotting corpses still owning the spots they'd died in, perhaps. My mind layered my last vision of the room with the current, as if to taunt me with ghosts of the fallen.

Pillars still bore battle scars, deep chasms cut into the marble that hadn't yet been repaired. I wondered if it would be filled with shimmering silver, so that the room could wear its battle scars proudly, like a badge of honor. And as a warning to others who entered. *Look what we've endured. We will endure you. And you will pay in blood.*

Aquarius stood by one of the cathedral height windows, glancing impassively over her city. Its usual glitter was lost to the grey, hazy fog drifting in over the mountains, even dulling the shimmer of the silver in the once proud halls, giving it a mournful look. She turned towards us as we entered, looking as somber as the room. And just as vengeful.

"Good luck to you, rebels," she said glancing at each of us in turn. "When next we see one another, it will be another blood bath."

"We have to stop meeting like that." I wanted to clamp my hand over my mouth to keep from speaking the words. I cringed. Aspen coughed to cover a laugh, despite my glare. Lenore took the liberty of smacking him for me, which, of course, did nothing but encourage him. Aquarius's smile was pinched and didn't reach her eyes.

"Indeed." She held her forearm out to me. I clasped her forearm cautiously, not sure if this was the correct response. Her wrist clasped mine, and I hers, locked in an unwitting camaraderie. "I look forward to avenging our fallen together Queen's Mark. May you prepare well. And may we not meet the Goddess in kindness anytime soon."

"May you prepare well," I echoed. It was strange. She wasn't the warmest of sorts, that was for certain. But she had a brash honesty about her. The kind that you wouldn't want to ask a question you weren't certain you wanted the answer to. I liked her. I respected her. I hoped she did prepare well. The last thing we—or the air Court—needed was to be without its third member of the kinship.

We turned to Locke, already holding the jumpstone in hand. Aspen, closest to me, held his hand out. I took it. I took one breath in the quiet of the air court, and my next in the briny center square of Port Azure. I felt my jaw slacken and my shoulders drop in response, the tension melting away a little, just for a second. Home. We were home. Not that we could enjoy it. There was much to do.

I felt the curse, that wretched char within me growing slowly.

We didn't have much time.

Chapter Seventeen

A week went by with no new information, meaning it was the longest, most anxiety ridden week of my life. Not on Locke's family, not on Eldan's whereabouts, nothing. I felt like a caged animal, pacing the citadel and pestering everyone for any scrap of information. But none came. Calan, who seemed to be for Locke whatever it was that Wren was for Aquarius and Wren himself both assured me with pinched expressions and tones schooled with practiced patience that this would take time. Weeks. Months normally. They were doing everything within their substantial capabilities to glean the information we needed in record time. What they were trying for would be a miracle. I knew I had to be patient. But still, my brain itched with the desire to do something—anything—of use. My fingers twitched. My mind refused to quiet, every possible scenario running through my mind, oftentimes too quickly for me to fully acknowledge or analyze them. But I felt them. The sinking feeling of dread making my chest feel heavy and tight, more so with each breath. I begged the Goddess to give me something to help. Anything that didn't make me feel so useless as I watched the worry grow on Locke's face with each passing day.

To the casual observer, Locke appeared calm and collected. But I knew better. Just there, underneath the surface was a turbulent, wrathful current. Locke's eyes had a darkness gleaming in them, his brow too furrowed. He didn't just undertake his duties; he attacked them. With a savagery with which I'd witnessed him take the blood of his enemies. He was relentless, never stopping. Never letting his mind quiet. And when we were alone, he was kind. Charming. Funny. The fae I fell in love with. My soulmate. I could almost believe everything was normal, except for the occasional faraway looks and the pinching in the corner of his eyes, giving away his secret anxiety.

I found myself in Locke's office, surrounded by books that either Calan or Wren had dropped off for me in the hopes that something may be useful. No detail was too small. I fingered the leather bindings, dusty and fragile, with utmost care. Books referencing old whole magic might be the key we were looking for. Or perhaps there were mentions of shadow magic and their curses. I sat stiffly in Locke's wingback chair with my feet up on his desk and one of the books carefully placed in my lap for perusal.

I was lost in ancient bound tomes, reading about the intricacies of whole magic of old when a sudden loud thud startled me from my reverie. My neck whipped to the left where I saw Wren waltzing in casually, his stern expression unchanged from any other time I'd ever seen him. I opened my mouth to casually ask if he knew what knocking was, but my eyes slid from him, to what he carried in his hands. Curiosity got the better of me as I crossed the room towards him voicing my question.

"I'm not entirely sure, with all honesty," he admitted in a low voice. He set the massive books down on the table. The table groaned as if in exertion from the added weight. I blew some of the dust off the tomes Wren had brought me, admiring his finds with appreciation.

These were old. Seriously old. Older than anything he'd brought me so far. My hand traced the runes embossed into the ancient, time worn grey leather, faded and cracked from years of loyal service. I opened one, eyeing the elegant script that lined the pages—worn with time and light exposure. The smell of dust, old parchment, and ink reached my nose, a bittersweet scent that was both calming and distressing. I felt excitement begin to bubble; these were the types of books that may have had the answers we were looking for.

"Scorpio had these in her personal library. They specifically mention black magic and curses. Maybe in the meantime, you can find something in here that'll help."

I didn't voice it, but I was extremely doubtful that we'd find anything of use that Scorpio hadn't already tried. If Wren had similar thoughts, he didn't show it.

"Thank you. Sincerely," I said, still gently leafing through some of the delicate pages, before turning my gaze to him. "This means so much." Wren shifted his weight uncomfortably.

"It's nothing, my lady." His penetrating gaze fell towards the window, where I'd been previously pacing, my anxiety quietly getting the better of me. "We're going to come out of this okay. Please don't wear a hole in the floor in the meantime."

"Thanks, Wow." I smiled ruefully, trying to force the humor I barely felt. But his attention, his unexpected caring, was touching and did lift my spirits a fraction. He was sweeter than first expected; he was rough around the edges, certainly, but only to hide what was no doubt a gem of a heart. His brows raised and his head cocked as he processed my nickname for him.

"Wow?"

"Wrought Iron Wren. It's a long name, so I shortened it." His arms folded across his chest as he huffed. His eyes rolled in time with the minute shake of his head. Even in my gloomy mood, I couldn't help a small grin at his discomfort. "I can't wait till it catches on."

He gave me a noncommittal grunt as an acknowledgment before awkwardly dismissing himself and closing the door quickly behind him. I giggled at how red his face had become. How his eye contact became nonexistent, how quickly he backed out of the room. Meeting him for the first time, I remembered being intimidated. Now I wanted to squeeze him. With the remnants of a soft smile Wow left me with, I turned my attention to the bound leather books he'd left for me. Dusty and worn with age, I couldn't even make out the titles, the words long faded. I opened the first one in earnest and leafed through the pages, eyes peeled for anything of interest when they snagged on a sentence.

The Zodiac Kinship are all granted special abilities with their titles. Cancer is given the ability to read emotions and emotional bonds. Pisces can manipulate emotions themselves. Scorpio is able to control beasts ruled by water magic.

That was odd. Pisces's and Cancer's powers were tied directly to emotions, and they also had water magic. Scorpio's power was the ability to control water monsters? I wracked my brain, putting myself into her shoes. What creature would be most abundant or most feared? Kelpies immediately came to mind. But it was hard to know what she would do. How she would fight. Could we even fight her?

But I did fight her. Successfully. I remembered the way my knife sank into her abdomen. I shuddered at the memory of the way it felt slicing into her skin. And the shadows that poured out instead of blood. The black veining around the wound. I knew that image would forever haunt me. I shook my head to clear my head and refocused my anxious energy on the book, before my thoughts redirected themselves.

I flipped through the delicate, water-stained pages, the writing getting less legible as I went on. There were some passages that mentioned dark magic and its seemingly nonexistent limitations, but just as I started reading on, the next page was ripped out.

Classic.

Whole magic made an appearance. Through the faded words, I could see that whole magic wasn't as powerful as it once was. I'd previously thought whole magic was simply magic not tied to an element, and that was true, but based on what I tried to discern from these pages, it was more than that. There were special spells, immensely powerful, possibly outlawed spells, some even with incantations and special, very complicated runes. Spells of communing with the dead, taking over another's body, and killing outright, but their runes were forever lost to time. Spells of old, laying forgotten in time on these pages. Age having laid them to rest in the form of warped and faded writing or torn pages leaving out massive details we'd need in order to execute these spells.

I worried that the answer to our prayers was here, answered in the cruelest way possible. I let out a long groan of anxious frustration. I focused hard on the words before me. Was that *M* or an *N*? The fading of the words made it incredibly difficult to fully understand the passages that were legible, making my frustration increase tenfold. Looking at the other book, I could see that much of it was written in the olde language. Something I was not proficient in, but maybe Locke was. I quickly returned my attention to the first book, scanning its pages for anything that mentioned curses, though I had a feeling that was the page that had been ripped out, making me huff.

Scorpio's disrespect for books and the written word was heinous of its own merit, if she were the one ripping these pages out for herself. Had she never heard of a bookmark?

I read as much as I could glean from the pages. While the information fascinated me, it got me no closer to anything remotely helpful.

That was how Locke eventually found me: bent over the book with a few pieces of parchment for taking notes, deeply focused on my task. When he said my name, I damn near jumped out of my skin. I turned around to glare at him, finding him grinning like a fiend behind me.

"What could possibly be keeping you from your magic lesson?" Locke's voice was soft. "Word on the street is your teacher is pissed."

"As it happens, I'm a bit of a teacher's pet, so I'm sure I can get back into his good graces," I told him, my heart not truly in it. His eyes sparked, but he didn't take the bait.

"What working on? Extra credit?" He began perusing through my notes, his expression unreadable.

"Wow brought these to me."

Locke blinked in confusion, his hands pausing in their task. "Wow?"

"Wrought Iron Wren. I call him Wow. I think it suits him." A riotous grin appeared, lopsided and dimples showing, making my own smile appear and my heart warm and light.

"Oh, I love that!" he snickered, looking every bit the mischief maker I knew him to be. "I'm making sure that catches on." He leaned on the table with his hip, perusing my notes, his face falling serious once more. "Have you learned anything interesting?"

"Interesting? Yes? Helpful to us? No. I've learned whole magic has outlawed extremely powerful spells, some of which Scorpio found interesting because some pages are missing. And I've learned a bit about black magic, but nothing that relates to curses." I flipped to the portion of the book that was the greatest source of my irritation. "The relevant pages were torn out." Locke fingered the frayed edges of the torn parchment.

"Doesn't that just figure?" Locke perused the pages just as I had. "That's just disrespectful to a book. She really is pure evil." I had never loved him more. I cracked a grin before returning my attention to the book. I showed him a few passages I couldn't decipher, hoping he might have better luck.

"There are some pages here in a different language. Are you able to make it out at all?" I gestured to the passages in question as Locke directed his attention to them.

"I haven't read the in a while, so give me a moment..." He trailed off as he concentrated on the pages before him. "This is an introduction to olde magic. Before the Courts, even. But of course, its specifics are the pages that were ripped out." He rolled his eyes. "It's possible Scorpio or Pisces ripped the pages out in the event the books were lost to them. Pisces misplaces stuff so often, he always carries the things he needs around in a satchel. Either he has it, or he assigns someone to it." At my astonished look, Locke laughed. "What? He's forgetful."

"I often forget that these were once your friends." I thought about what that must be like. I thought about what would possibly make me go against Lenore, Lennox, or Aspen. I came up empty. A surge of empathy for Locke made my heart squeeze painfully in my chest. He sighed wistfully, his face falling.

"That was a long time ago, especially Pisces." He kept perusing the pages. I saw a flicker of emotion there for me to read. Not pain, this was different. Something not so potent, like touching a raised scar. Not painful to touch, but full of memory best left resting.

"I have a question for you actually," I said finding that passage that had ensnared my attention before. "I knew you could see emotions. But Pisces can manipulate them? And Scorpio has power to commune with water beasts? Is that true?"

"Pisces can manipulate emotions, yes. But he doesn't manufacture them," he said, neatening my piles of paper and books. I almost smiled. I wondered how long he'd be able to tolerate the disorganization. "His power lies in manipulating the intensity of one's emotions. Scorpio's power has always beguiled me. I think it's strange how her power doesn't have to do with emotion, but I suppose with her reign, it makes more sense they relate directly to the court she resides over." At my horrified thoughts of an army of kelpies, Locke laughed. "Stop your thoughts right there. I don't think she can control an entire horde. Not last I'd seen anyway."

"Should we make plans for this? *Can* we plan for this?" Locke's dark look was his only response. And my answer. It was very likely that we'd fight more than just fae. Kelpies were the obvious choice I could think of, but they were more dangerous en-masse. My mind went to dragons, but they were extinct. Following that train of thought, my mind conjured images of the most fearsome beasts in all of Meridian. Wyvern were only in the Air Court and exceedingly rare. Basilisks were from the Fire Court so they wouldn't be an option for Scorpio. I wasn't sure what manner of creature had escaped extinction that could help her, so at least that was a relief. I flipped to another page, but of course the moment black magic was mentioned, the page was ripped out. I swear, I could kill Scorpio for her heinous mistreatment of these books. But I could sort of make something out.

"What's a black marked weapon?" I asked more to myself than to Locke. I'd never heard the term before. I perused the remaining pages, but whatever was there, Scorpio had taken. Of course. Locke's hands stilled, pausing in his tidying as he turned to look at me with a suspicious look.

"That's some of the darkest magic there is. And thankfully very rare." He came over to read over my shoulder, but he could only see what I saw. The frayed beginning of the sentence that should be continued on the following page. Correction, it was—we just didn't have it. Locke's eyes narrowed as he considered his thoughts before continuing, "Black magic that imbues a weapon with your will. Only the most bloodthirsty, cursed fae tend to do this. Basically, if you're wounded with one, it can't be healed. It's an almost certain death. You fracture a sliver of your soul and shadows, and combine it with the weapon. It's horrifically painful too."

"The fact that these pages are missing are not exactly a comfort," I mused. "Maybe we can see glimpses of Scorpio's plan based on clues of what she's removed. Though that'll only work if we have context from the previous page."

"It's worth a shot," Locke agreed. But I had one more question for him.

"How do you know you're dealing with a black marked weapon?"

His answer, his tone, the tension in his voice left me cold. "You don't."

Chapter Eighteen

I was finished with waiting.

There was absolutely no way I could sit here and continue to pour over these books and find nothing of use. Calan told me himself that he spent careful time looking over every inch of Eldan's home for clues to his whereabouts, and when he did, something clicked in my mind. An idea that was every bit as relentless as the curse that haunted me and hollowed me from the inside out. I knew what I needed to do, and it wasn't sit back and let someone else do everything. If there was a clue to Eldan's whereabouts, it wouldn't be coded in a way for anyone to read, but me.

It took an hour of convincing a very cautious and concerned Locke that we needed to go to Poplar Hollow. It was only when I told him I was going with or without him that he sighed into his hands. His eyes flashed to me as he sat up and appraised me. "You really think Eldan might have left you a message." It wasn't a question.

"If not a message, a clue, or something. If that possibility exists, than we need to explore it." I wasn't budging. I was immovable in my stance, and only for me would he yield.

"This is incredibly dangerous," Locke said as much to himself as me as he stood. I almost smiled as I moved towards him. "Stupid even. How am I letting you talk me into this? There is so much that can go wrong. Scorpio could be watching Poplar Hollow."

"This is better than doing nothing," I said as I took his hand. "And we've proven we can make a quick escape if the need arises. If Eldan left a message to where he is, Calan and Wren wouldn't find it. But maybe I can."

He didn't look convinced. "I hope you're right, Lark."

Five simple words. Why did they sound so foreboding?

Locke and I passed through the jumpstone, the bright flickering light plucking us from one location and dropping us into the frigid wasteland of another. I was surprised to see winter had hit Poplar Hollow hard, unusual given its proximity to the Fire Court. Port Azure hadn't even angered winter this much, despite its northern position. Everywhere you looked, frost coated the ground, leaving it hard and unforgiving, the trees barren and cold. And still. Everything was much too still.

"Stay hidden a moment," Locke said, taking a silent step forward.

"Wait!" I whispered. He halted, turning his head toward me, but didn't turn. As his eyes still scanned the forest, as his hearing did, I cast my awareness out, looking for signs of life. I almost jumped when I felt three separate presences only a short distance away, separated from us by a small hill. I doubted they were aware of us. Yet. "Three on your right. Just up ahead over the hill," I told him, keeping my whisper soft. He nodded once, an acknowledgment, before disappearing in a shroud of shadow. Following his order, I crept into the bushes. Bare as they were, the thick tangle of branches and my brown leather armor concealed me well enough.

I kept my awareness open, feeling now four entities brushing the edges of my consciousness. Then three. Two. Until only one remained. Locke returned moments later, unshrouding, my all clear signal. As I moved to him, the telltale scent of blood, tangy and coppery, hit my nose. My reaction was immediate, my eyes tracing every inch of him, anxiously hunting for injury. My chest tightened, seeing the spatter across his chest plate.

"The blood isn't mine," he said, quelling my concern immediately. "Are there others?" I checked once more. I didn't even feel birds in the trees. We were the only living beings in the immediate area. A fact that left me feeling more unsettled than not. We were close to town, not within the tangle of the Deep Wild. Wildlife wouldn't necessarily be abundant, but birds and other critters should be around. I couldn't even see any tracks from where we stood.

What had happened?

We crept toward the desolated town on silent feet. Well, mostly silent. I tripped over a root and would have splattered myself on the ground if Locke hadn't caught and steadied me with a shake of his head.

The sun was hidden behind a thick blanket of clouds, adding the greyness of the dead town at the bottom of the hill. Silence. Not even the wind moved to shake any remaining foliage still clinging despite winter's touch. My power confirmed that Locke and I were the only life around.

But why?

Where did the wildlife go? They should have flourished without Fae to hunt them. The hair on the back of my neck stood on end. One exchanged look with Locke told me he felt the same thing. We crept down the hill on high alert, eyes continually scanning for movement. It was taxing, keeping my power scanning for life, but ultimately worth it if anything did come.

At last I looked over the ruined landscape of my former home. As much as I hated my time here, as desolate as I had been, I still saw the town itself for what it once was with profound sadness. Dead was the scent of the bakery in the market. Gone were the flowers in the square where fae lounged about. Sometimes the roses were what made my own days. I saw my father picking one rose for me as a child in my mind eye.

Father...

From here, I couldn't see the cottage. I wasn't sure I wanted to. But I looked in its direction anyway, feeling the stab of grief that came with it. Locke's fingers twined through mine, a sweet effort to stave off the mixed feelings I was having. I gave him a smile I imagined looked more like a grimace.

"Where are the dead?" I asked. Last time we were here, the dead littered the ground like trash. They'd been everywhere. Now, you could see bloodstains, but no bodies.

"I don't know, but I don't like it," Locke said, his eyes continually scanning for danger. His hand toyed with the hilt of his sword at his side. "Don't drop your guard. Something is amiss, I can feel it. But I don't know what it is."

Crossing the brick bridge from the lower half of the town to the upper part where Eldan lived, we had only to turn the corner to see where the dead had gone. Tears sprung to my eyes. Even Locke loosed a breath.

Someone had painstakingly taken the time to dig graves for each of the dead that had laid here in the square. Each one with a marker. It would've been easier to burn them all, undoubtedly. All this work must have taken days. Names were inscribed on each one. Familiar handwriting. Eldan. Eldan had been here! My eyes passed several as I picked up the pace to Eldan's house, that didn't have names. Despite everything, my heart ached. Not to be remembered well enough in life to be left unknown in death was a tragedy unto itself.

As we got closer to Eldan's home, we made another discovery. One that froze me mid-step.

Graves had been brutally uprooted, only pieces of each corpse remained. A single head stared unseeing at me from within the grave nearest me, the flesh falling from the skull, its mouth open as if to scream a warning.

"Something came for an easy meal," Locke murmured, kneeling to inspect. Turning bones over in his hands, gauging the tooth marks on them. "This was recent. I don't know what did this, but we need to be careful. This just got more dangerous."

"What do you think did this?" I was almost afraid of the answer. Worse, I thought I knew.

"Blood wraiths," he said. "They must have scented the death and come down for an easy snack. It explains the lack of wildlife. They'd all been chased away." So Poplar Hollow was to be reclaimed by the wilderness. A literal haunted town. Frequented by monsters.

Seemed fitting, in a disturbing way.

As if on cue to make my blood chill, an all too familiar screech. Locke and I looked at each other.

"We should go," he said.

"No." I marched on towards Eldan's cottage. "We stay. We get what we came for and we get the fuck out of here."

Locke said nothing, but his lips pressed into a firm line. His eyes narrowed at the spot the scream came from, probably using his Zodiac hearing to assess if it were coming closer. His hand delved into his pocket. I had no doubt he was charging our jumpstone in the event we needed to run. And I also knew he wouldn't hesitate, so we needed to hurry before whatever prowled my former home found us.

Eldan's cottage was recognizable yet not at the same time. The shutters were intact, but with a layer of ash and dust muting their blue color. The stable had completely collapsed into a heap. If I hadn't known it was a stable before, I wouldn't have known better. I sighed, remembering the hours I used to spend here. My safe space. It wasn't uncommon for me to have Haven in her stall in the evening while I lay on her back with a book. One time, I remembered falling asleep there. I remembered jolting awake, and her sidestepping to catch me, saving me from one hell of a rude awakening.

The dilapidated house wasn't much better, a mere echo of what it once had been. I couldn't tell if it was haunted, or haunting in its now nearly grey monochrome. Even if this house weren't haunted by the ghost of a troubled soul, it was definitely haunted by the violent memories of what used to be. I didn't spy any footprints—fae or otherwise. It didn't appear to show any signs of life. Another scream, thankfully not necessarily any closer, sounded, reminding us that dawdling was ill advised.

It was unsettling walking up the front door. It dangled uselessly from a single hinge that squeaked deafeningly loud in the comparative silence. I flinched. Locke's hand rubbed my shoulder, a comforting gesture as we went. I hesitated a moment before stepping through the threshold. Looking around the entrance, not seeing a single thing out of place, but just as it had outside, a thick layer of dust had settled over everything. An umbrella still rested in its place by the door, even an old pair of boots sat next to them, as if waiting for the day they might get used again. A day that would never come.

The living room housed a few chairs and a decrepit couch, just as I remembered it, though the warmth had long left. Looking around it was as if the very soul had left the home, leaving it empty and gutted. Nothing seemed amiss, leaving my hope dwindling. Another screech, sounding closer this time. Time wasn't on our side. Locke looked out the window, jaw tensed, but once again said nothing. Though I didn't miss the way his hand grasped the handle of his knife, drawing in one smooth movement.

If Calan and Wren had seen signs of someone living here, they would have told us. I kept my feet pressing forward, fighting the feeling of trespassing as I crept silently through the house. Every shriek of the wood floors made me flinch.

"What is it you're looking for?" Locke asked me, a hint of concern in his voice. Even with his hushed tone, it sounded so loud compared to the permeating silence.

"I'm not sure," I answered, peeking into the kitchen. "I'm hoping I'll know it when I see it. Maybe he has something circled on one of his maps."

Eldan's second living space, which shared a wall with the bedroom, had a massive hole blown into it where a window used to be, left the house exposed to the outside and allowing the chill of early winter in. That explained the chill. No fire had blazed in the hearth recently. Its stone-cold face stared at me as I walked the rooms. The kitchen looked just as I remembered it, oddly similar to the one in my own cottage. The same dark cabinets, in the same layout. It was enough to make my heart squeeze. I began to search the cupboards, looking for any sign he'd been here. Opening one of the lower cabinets, a flash of grey and malicious red eyes filled my vision, it shrieked as it lunged at my face.

I threw myself backwards into the cabinet behind me, causing more shrieks to be heard. I reached for my knife when my eyes settled on a very angry, spitting rat. A large, likely well-fed rat. It stared at me, its creepy, beady little eyes boring into me. It screamed at me, angry for having its resting place disturbed. I hastily shoved the cabinet door closed with my foot as it hissed at me one final time

Locke's lips were twitching as he struggled and failed at hiding his grin at my discomfort. He coughed to disguise his laugh.

"Don't you dare laugh." I wasn't sure whether it was my words or my tone that finally did it, but he could no longer contain it. He burst into a fit of laughter, doubling over as I glowered at him from the floor. "Jackass."

"Sorry, love," he said, not sounding very sorry. He collected himself and extended his hand in offer to help me up. "You're..." He struggled to find the right word as he hauled me to my feet. "Cute."

"Cute?" I echoed in mild distaste. "You have an abundance of words from living as long as you have, and you call me cute?"

He shrugged, looking so un-prince-like as he grinned at me.

"Did you just call me old? That's just rude. I didn't deserve that."

"Yes, you did. You laughed at me." But now I was smiling widely too, taking the bite out of my insult. He laughed at me again. Jackass.

"It's just funny how you're probably the most powerful fae in Meridian with significant fighting skill and you're afraid of a *rat*." He wheezed through his laugher, his face growing red. I rolled my eyes, my own smile still not fading.

"I hate you."

"No, you don't."

I poked my head into the untouched bedroom, feeling like an invader. Leave, it seemed to hiss. Unwelcome. The ceiling had half caved in, making much of the room inaccessible. With a sigh of discontent and diminishing hope, I turned around, backtracking to the only room we'd yet to investigate—the dining room.

Eldan's dining room wasn't for eating. It was where most of his work was done. His modest cottage didn't have the space for a formal office, but the way he had this room set up kept it somewhat removed from the main living quarters. A small table and two chairs were mashed up against the wall in the corner out of the way. His desk took up the middle of the room, within eyeline of the front door. On the other side under the window was a long apothecary cabinet with all of his herbs and ingredients for his alchemy practice, neatly stored and tucked away. Eldan was meticulous. Never would a single thing be out of place. Not a chair ever not tucked in, never a paper left out. I couldn't help but wonder if he was always the way he was or a learned habit of working so closely to the Kinship. My mind raced, now ruminating on the fact that Eldan, the fae who had aided myself and my father, the fae who had been my father's close friend for my entire life, our town healer, had worked with the kinship. Had been in hiding. I couldn't deny it was a good place to hide, but it gives me pause about his motives for befriending us. A trickle of unease, of distrust slithered its way down my spine in a way most unpleasant, and for the first time I genuinely wondered if Eldan was exactly who I thought he was. If this was a mistake to find him.

No.

Locke needed him. His father needed him. And for that reason, I'd see this through.

I looked at the room, taking in every detail, my head swiveling. I'd spent many hours in this room, as both patient and assistant. It dawned on me then. If there were a message in this house, it would be here. A scream sounded outside, this one much closer. Locke looked at me, silently communicating our need to go.

The feeling I was missing something was maddening. Like my eyes were seeing something but my brain couldn't. Long seconds passed, maybe a minute. I didn't move. Another scream, closer still.

"Lark..." came his hissed warning.

"I know." I searched for any minute detail. Anything. But the longer I stared at the room, the more I began to realize there wasn't anything to notice. Not a damn thing. I resisted the urge to scream in frustration. To throw the vase next to me at the wall, just to watch it crack, like my patience. I opened his desk, seeing the maps of the area right on top. I withdrew them from their place and pored over them. Had he circled any locations? Left a message to me, perhaps? There was nothing. Not a single mark on the map that might've indicated where he'd gone. I dug deeper into the drawers, finding a bottle of whiskey, and a few letters and receipts, and finally a ledger. I flipped through the pages depicting monetary balances, thumbing through each one in search of a message. But once again, nothing of value to help us locate him. I looked over the room once again, seeing it for what it was—empty. I hung my head, close to admitting defeat. Locke continued to look at the maps, looking for the tiniest of details, though what he was looking for I wasn't certain.

But then I saw it. My brain finally processed what my eyes didn't and I felt like kicking myself. There was a drawer ajar in the apothecary cabinet. And not just any drawer. The one with Aching Cress written on it in Eldan's penmanship. It was dried, its scent no longer offensive. None of the other drawers held anything. Just this one. I grinned widely, opening it the rest of the way. There was no note. But Eldan was meticulous. He wouldn't have left it open. Not for anything. This was deliberate. A message. Locke didn't look so sure.

"You think he's in the Yemerian Vale?" The doubt on his face leaked into his voice. "One of the most dangerous places in Meridian?" At my sour expression, he added, "It's not you I doubt. I just don't understand why."

"Eldan never left a single thing out. He was obsessive. Once, he chewed me out for not labelling things neatly enough. He always said everything had to be in order, so if someone walked in and needed something, they'd know where to find it in an emergency."

"You think the drawer was left out purposely? You don't think someone opened it to search it?"

"Truthfully, I'm not sure." I chewed my lip, considering. "But he's like you. Everything he does is deliberate. Always. If he left the drawer like this, *this* drawer, it might be a message. One nobody else would notice but me. A scream sounded. This time, far too close for comfort. Casting out my awareness. I felt it. Right outside.

"We go. Now," Locke whispered urgently as wood splintered, and he retrieved the jumpstone as the hinges and floorboards creaked. We jumped into the portal just as I heard massive footfalls behind us and a shriek to freeze my blood.

The glimpse I'd seen of the blood wraith was just that: a glimpse. But it was enough. The sound alone was enough to call to mind the last time I'd heard it from such close range when Locke and I had first met. He'd kept my eyes closed, citing there were some things you didn't come back from after seeing. That lone glimpse was enough to tell me he was right.

Bone white skin. I hadn't expected that, but I understood it was their appetite and their blood red eyes that gave them their name; lidless, red, and glowing. Vaguely skeletal features held in a perpetual grin. It glided towards us, far smoother than I'd thought possible, as we disappeared into the void of the jumpstone. It screamed, that shrill shriek that had woken me from the deep of the forest so many times, I now knew the look of the monster that would now haunt my nightmares. The worst part was that it was significantly more terrifying than anything my mind could have conjured up. The descriptions others had given me had paled in comparison. Locke had been right.

That was one of the worst things I'd ever seen.

Chapter Nineteen

I remembered the strangeness of the Vale clearly. I so vividly remembered the strange scents to the air, sweet one moment, like rot the very next breath. The pale moon pond seemed to grin maliciously at me from the center of the clearing. I almost expected it to rise up in some form and greet me. Though now I knew what it was, I felt deeply disturbed wondering what—and who—was watching me from beneath that mirror-like silver surface. A non-fae scream sounded not too far from us to our right. Not far away from the clearing. Something close by was hunting. And hopefully whatever it had just caught satisfied it enough that it didn't come looking for seconds.

I glanced at Locke, who looked eerily calm. I felt the area around us, probing with my magic, feeling the tang of disappointment when I found nothing. No sign of Eldan, or anyone else. I wandered into the clearing, having spotted the Aching Cress near the water's edge. It was incredibly eerie how everything looked the same as it did that day. The pool, the waist high reeds, the flowering grasses, the incredibly thick treed canopy above me restricting the amount of daylight filtering down. Even with winter seated comfortably, pushing fall out without remorse, this place remained intact. Perhaps there was truth to the idea of this place being in another dimension after all. I half expected to see Amaya still laying peacefully with the flowers I'd placed on her chest in death. My eyes flickered unbidden to the spot where she'd lay that day. Of course she wasn't there. And I didn't want to think too long about why.

I looked long into the trees, looking for some sign Eldan had been here. But I'd found nothing. Nothing at all that seemed any different from my last trip here. Another scream sounded. It was accompanied by a low growl this time. From much closer. Locke and I shared an unsettled glance as total silence fell over us, our meaning clear; we had to hurry.

I moved around the Vale, keeping my steps light. I wasn't sure what it was I was looking for. Perhaps the Aching Cress itself?

There was the highly unexpected *clang* of metal on metal and the shout of alarm from behind me. Heart stopping, I whirled around, dagger drawn from my boot in the same motion, and froze mid stab. My thoughts halted entirely.

Eldan.

Eldan was dressed in his usual ensemble, the one I'd seen him wearing a thousand times. His salt and pepper facial hair sprouted a tiny bit more salt than the last time I'd seen him. His grasp on his sword was shaky as it crossed with Locke's, who looked bewildered.

"Eldan, I presume." Locke's voice was tense. Smooth. One just had to peak over the ledge to see the chasm of shadow his voice held. His blade held Eldan's still, waiting for his next attack. "I was wondering when we'd find you."

"Run, Lark!" Eldan growled as he regrouped and offered Locke another attack. "I'll hold him off!" Locke blocked it easily. He looked at me briefly, his smirk widening. I glared at him. Now was not the time for games.

"For the love of the Goddess, Eldan! What are you doing?" I exclaimed as Eldan brought his sword back down over Locke. Locke expelled almost no effort blocking it, their swords clashing in a sound of steel on steel.

"Saving your life!" he ground out as he doled out another array of angry sword strikes that Locke countered. "Run!"

"Run? Why? Eldan... we finally found you!" I felt the tears threaten to prickle the backs of my eyes as I approached on shaky feet. Emotion I hadn't expected to resurface welling in my eyes. Relief. Kinship. Love. "We found you...."

"We? *We?*" He looked from me to Locke with a growing horror I recognized. His eyes finally took me in, zeroing in on my armor with the Rebel Court seal with surprise and disdain. "You're working with the Crowned Assassin? Lark, are you out of your mind?" He flashed me a look so incredulous I could do nothing but stifle a surprised laugh.

"Working with him? I guess you could say that." I smiled at Locke briefly. Eldan didn't miss that look and gaped at me. "There is much to tell, Eldan. But Locke isn't our enemy" At his hostile stare directed at both of us, I threw my hands up in a gesture of peace. "Honestly. You can trust him." Eldan looked at him as if he were a very dangerous bug that needed squashing. The day I'd met Locke, I remembered comparing him to a venomous spider. I could see Eldan having a similar idea.

"Locke? We should get out of here before we end up with company we didn't hope to find."

"I couldn't agree more, love," he drawled. I think he was not-so-secretly enjoying Eldan's clear discomfort. He held out his hand to me and I took it without hesitation, to which Eldan's eyes nearly popped out of his head. This was getting old.

"You're on a first name basis with him?" Eldan looked like he couldn't decide between confusion, horror or grave concern as his gaze flicked back and forth between Locke and me.

"Eldan, I need you to answer a simple question, do you trust me?" I asked him. His eyes shifted between us in an almost accusing manner. "Locke isn't who you think he is. But let's leave the Vale and I'll prove it to you."

"I promise I mean no harm to you or to Lark," Locke said smoothly. The promise made Eldan do a double take between us. "I've never hurt Lark. Nor would I ever. But I need you to take Lark's hand because we've got company."

Something screamed in the trees ahead of us. But when I focused my eyes and cast my awareness out again, I felt two things there focusing in on us. They broke through the tree line then. The very sight of them was enough to make my heart pound out an anxious beat in my throat. My mouth dried as I beheld these... things. There wasn't another way to describe them. They were vaguely fae shaped in the body, if they'd been stretched impossibly tall. Its neck was too long for its body, and resulted in its head attaching to its body at a disturbing angle. So much so it was near impossible for it to stand up straight without leaning on the trees around it. It had black, matted hair on its head that was long enough to touch the ground. Glowing white eyes glared at us from within a sunken, thin-skinned face. An impossibly wide mouth with an array of sharp teeth situated into two rows. Dull grey skin hung off of it as if it were a rotting corpse. It outstretched a long arm, longer than its torso and legs, and used it to prop itself up while it staggered jerkily towards us with a sickening scream. Horribly long fingers crooked towards us, dried blood visible from even here.

The second one was even more terrifying. It looked much the same, though the way it moved was entirely more disturbing. It crab walked on its hands and heels, with its emaciated belly up towards the sky, though its head remained oriented in our direction. Its mouth took up the full width of its face in a grotesque smile as it roared that horrid scream in answer to its companion. This one was faster as it scuttled towards us, stopping my breathing in its tracks as I called for Locke to ready the jumpstone. The thing heaved a horrid version of a laugh at the panic in my voice as it neared.

I grabbed Eldan's hand, as Locke got the jumpstone out. The thing was mere feet away, faster than it should've been given its Goddess awful build. It reached out, close enough I could smell the rotten stench of it when Eldan led the way quickly through the waiting portal, away from the danger. Back into Poplar Hollow.

Or I thought it would be Poplar Hollow that we'd returned to.

Instead of the grave quiet meeting my ears, there was a gentle hum of voices and traffic. As I took in my surroundings, I realized we were in a small, dimly lit room. Dust invaded my nose, making me sneeze. A single dirty window allowed in the sunlight. Upon inspection, we were on the second story of some sort of establishment, though it felt like a cluttered and forgotten attic. Where had Eldan landed us?

I stumbled, tripping over some object in the room. Locke keeping hold of my hand ensured that I didn't fall inelegantly on my rear end. He steadied me as I blinked in our surroundings. Dust, wooden walls, and furniture that had seen better days examined me right back like an angry old woman with a nasty retort loaded and ready.

"Where are we?" I asked, looking out the window. I had to use my sleeve to wipe away some of the grime to view fae traipsing along outside.

"Listwyne," Eldan replied, eyeing both of us in a mixture of caution and concern. His watchful and expectant gaze seldom left Locke. Listwyne. Not very far from Poplar Hollow...

How odd to think when my father caught sick, I would've rode to Listwyne to get supplies here. Listwyne was a bit bigger and better equipped than my hometown, but was still just a small, quiet town. Quaint, though charmless in the unkind winter. In spring it was lovely, filled with trees and plentiful wildflowers.

"Where have you been, Lark?" Eldan's voice was hushed, though his tone levelled me as if he'd screamed. His stare was hard and unyielding, anger there. But relief too. "I looked *everywhere* for you. For weeks! I thought they'd actually succeeded in killing you..." At that, Locke growled, making Eldan's throat bob. "And then when I came back from a supply run, I saw Poplar Hollow razed to the ground... I thought it was you. I thought you exacted your revenge at last."

"You thought..." My chest constricted painfully. What happened to Poplar Hollow was despicable. I owed nothing to the fae there, true, but I would never have done such a thing. The fact he thought me capable... My heart teetered problematically between anger and knife-like hurt. And when I spoke next, I hardly recognized my own voice. "You thought I was capable of that level of destruction?"

"If you'd lost control of your magic. Of your anger. I could see it happening. And it wouldn't have been your fault. Many of those fae would've deserved any punishment you saw fit to dole out for what they'd done to you." A small part of me was fiercely satisfied by his comment. The rest of me felt nothing but dread. I remembered the blood running through the streets of my home. Cottages burned to the ground. Bodies littering the streets. Gael's horrid demise flashed through my mind. I could never have done something like that. I opened my mouth to say so when Eldan's untrusting eyes flicked to Locke as he appraised the Crowned Assassin, who inclined his head and assessed him in return, his face carefully blank. "He's the one who took you, isn't he?" I sighed, seeing the hatred and mistrust on his face for a fae he wouldn't even try to understand. I held up my engagement ring to him, watching his eyes widen and his mouth fall open. I fought not to roll my eyes at Locke for smirking over my shoulder at Eldan's reaction.

"I'm in full control of my magic, no thanks to you or my father," I said, trying to control the conflicting emotions in my voice. Anger I thought had died weeks ago resurfaced, hot and bright and consuming. How many times did Eldan patch me up? Found me broken, bleeding or unconscious? How many times had he brought me back from the brink of death? He sighed.

"I know, child." His voice full of age old regret. "You have every right to be angry. I hated dosing you each week. I told your father to tell you the truth. I begged him even."

"Why didn't you tell me?" I shot at him, anger sharpening my tongue.

"Because it wasn't my place to tell you. It wasn't my story to tell. But I can see how you've grown into yourself. I can see how powerful you've become. And I know I say this on behalf of myself and your father: I'm proud of you."

I'm proud of you. Words that my father would never get the chance to tell me again. Tears pricked the back of my eyes, threatening to spill over my cheeks. I launched myself in his direction, wrapping my arms around him, tears finally falling. Eldan clutched me tightly as I cried. He even told me he missed me. Eldan was a lot of things, but touchy feely was not one of them.

There was a long time where I considered him the only family outside of my household. The overwhelming relief of him being alive... of being here. That we'd found him. I didn't have words. After a long moment, I righted myself. Locke offered me a handkerchief from Goddess only knew where. He laughed at my incredulous and confused face. Eldan's own eyes looked a little less dry than they had previously, and I noticed the amount of mistrust Eldan had when he observed Locke had decreased a bit.

"Where is Haven?"

"I'm surprised you waited this long to ask about that damn horse," he said gruffly. Locke chuckled, disguising the sound as clearing his throat when I narrowed my eyes at him. "She's fine. Just north of town. My accommodations here don't have a place for her, so she's with a friend out of town. I assure you, she's enjoying her green pastures at the moment." His face and voice turned equally somber, losing that nostalgic twist. "When I left home that day and returned to a graveyard, I didn't know if you'd done this to get revenge or if the Kinship had finally found me. I knew I had to run."

"It was said that you successfully poisoned and killed the previous Prince Pisces. Was that true?" Locke asked. There was no hint of accusation in his tone, but I saw Eldan bristle at the question nonetheless.

"No!" he exclaimed, a maelstrom of long buried indignation rising to the surface, "My entire life has been devoted to helping and healing. Not killing. I'm no murderer." He gave Locke a loaded look that made clear what Eldan thought of him. Locke's face was still very neutral. I chafed at the unsaid accusation on Locke's behalf.

"Eldan, don't. Locke isn't a killer. I'll explain later, but you'd do well to be kind to him," I snapped in a sharp tone I'd never taken with Eldan before. But because of that, it made him pause. Look at me. I could see his eyes flit back and forth between us, that analytical mind assessing, trying to understand.

"How did you disappear so thoroughly? One doesn't just leave the Zodiac Kinship and leave behind no trace," Locke asked. Eldan looked at me, and I nodded.

"Lark's father, Vesper, was one of the Crownguards closest to the late King Scorpio, until the attack that killed him anyway. He and I had been something like friends in the palace in Loc Valen. He was the one who smuggled me out and found me a place with a weak patrol presence, Poplar Hollow. He kept an eye on me and was able to warn me of danger or patrols looking for me. Eventually, everyone assumed I was dead. I owed him my life. Everything." My earlier thoughts returned to me, sparking an iota of mistrust,

Is that why he'd been kind to me? Because he'd owed my father?

"Why the Vale?" I asked instead of what I wanted to ask, pushing any hurt down. Locke looked sidelong at me and I knew he was reading my emotions. "And I checked before entering the clearing. You weren't there. How did you hide from me?"

"The short answer is, I didn't. The long answer is, I spelled my house so that when you crossed the threshold, I would know. I knew then that it would only be a matter of time before you saw my message in the Aching Cress. I was able to use a friend's Short Port to get to the Vale. I arrived in time to see the Crowned Assassin at your back."

"What the hell is a Short Port?" I asked. Eldan laughed.

"It's like a jumpstone, but only one way and only relatively short distances as they cease to exist once used. Someone once trapped the essence of a portal in a small spell sphere, and it allows you to make a quick escape in tight situations. Though they're very expensive. Now, Goddess tell, what are you doing with the Crowned Assassin?" And this time when he said Locke's Water Court title, he didn't spit it out like it was poison.

I explained everything. It took a long time to get through, but Eldan never interrupted. He listened astutely as Locke and I took turns filling him in. We told him about the Vale and how we met, the discovering of my magic, Amaya and her prophecy, the curses, the circumstances of my father's death, and how Locke and I were soulmates. I breezed over the Court of Rebels. I wanted to make sure we could trust him and had secured his help before I gave him specifics. Locke told Eldan of how Scorpio forced him into the role of the Nightmare Assassin. How he saved all those he could, and continued to do so. I saw as Eldan flashed him the first look of sympathy.

"So let me get this straight," he said, looking winded. "You two met in the Yemerian Vale, he was supposed to kill you, which brought your fire magic to the surface, you somehow found out you're soulmates through a curse, you're going to die, and Locke, forgive me for addressing you so informally," Eldan turned to Locke before turning back to me, "Prince Locke and Queen Aquarius are going to attempt to revive you, you're essentially the princess of this Court of Rebels, of which I'd only heard hushed whispers about, your father was killed by Prince Pisces as an attempt to break Queen Scorpio's curse after there was a vision of your home, Prince Pisces also destroyed Poplar Hollow as a way to get back at you, and the Crowned Assassin here took you away from Poplar Hollow to harness your magic so you wouldn't hurt anyone or be hunted? Did I sum all of that up properly?" I looked at Locke, who grinned down at me. I shrugged at him, looking back to Eldan who still looked incredibly uneasy.

"Yes, I'd say that's about caught you up. But there's one more thing. We'd like to ask that you accompany us back to the Rebel Court. We have need of your skills," I said.

"And Lark has been missing you. It would be good for her to have someone she so clearly values among us," Locke said respectfully. "She's thought of you often since coming to stay with us."

"Since you so rudely kidnapped me, I think you mean," I said with a wide smile, to make it obvious I was kidding to Eldan.

"I don't see you complaining these days, love." His tone was light, but the smirk on his face and the look in his eyes wasn't. I blushed, of all things. Eldan cleared his throat.

"What exactly do you want me to do?" Eldan asked, thoughtfully stroking his chin.

It was Locke that spoke this time, all manner of humor gone. And he cut right to the chase. "Scorpio has my family. Which is why I've done the things I've done. I had no choice." I saw the surprise register in Eldan's eyes and something else that might have been sympathy. "But my father is sick. If we break him out, we need an incredibly skilled healer and alchemist to keep him alive."

"What kind of sick?"

"My father suffers from a disease called the red rage," Locke said with a sigh and a lowered gaze. Eldan's eyes widened. I looked over to Locke with similar surprise, lowering into sympathy. I'd heard of the red rage. I'd never seen it. Eldan showed it and other rare afflictions in one of his thick, practically ancient tomes one night. It starts out as red veining from the affected's eyes. Then the sickness, the vomiting. You knew it was too late to be treated when the blood flows through your eyes like tears. I always found it odd that it was called the red rage, given that it turned your blood to black poison in your very veins. And it didn't take long for it to happen. Treatments were frequent and expensive.

"That's extremely rare." Eldan mused. "Your father has it?"

Locke nodded. "He requires a potion that keeps his blood from turning. Can you make it?"

"Listen boy, there's nothing I can't accomplish." Locke didn't look pleased at being referred to as *boy*, but I was thankful that he let it go. "But the question is why would I?"

"Because you'd be safe from Pisces, Scorpio, and any of the Water Court who may continue to hunt you," I said. "We can offer you protection, a home, and an entire Court that can and will keep you busy and profitable. And because I'm asking you to. Please, Eldan. Please say you'll help us. Once we have Locke's family, the war can officially begin.

We're taking the Barbaric Queen down. But we need your help." Eldan turned to Locke and fixed him with a hard stare.

"You're truly going against your two Crownmates? You're truly planning to bring down Queen Scorpio?"

"Yes."

Eldan's voice was as grave as his gaze was penetrating, searching for lies and deception in Locke. "And you love Lark? And will never bring her to harm?"

"Yes. I'll kill anyone who harms her. And I have." I shuddered, remembering Abel. His betrayal. If that were how he handled someone he'd loved, I was almost fearful to think about what he'd do to someone he didn't care about who hurt me.

"I want your promise, Prince."

"Very well." Locke took my hand, despite my insistence that he shouldn't have to promise. He silenced my concerns with a chaste kiss. "I, Prince Cancer, Lachlan, the Crowned Assassin, do promise that I'm doing everything within my power to dethrone Scorpio. I promise that everything Lark and I have told you is the truth. I promise I'm doing everything within my power to prevent her from coming to harm. And when it's time for the curse to take her, I will do what I can to bring her back to me. I love her, Eldan. More than I can easily express into words. She is my soulmate."

Eldan stood there a long moment assessing Locke. I held his hand, giving him a grateful squeeze. One that he returned. Gone was that sarcastic smirk when he looked down at me. Instead, there was just a light smile, the kind of smile just for me. The kind of smile that made my breathing pause and restart at will. Eldan took the two of us in, watching our dynamic, looking for holes in our story—or red flags. Looking for traces of deception in Locke. He finally took a long breath before opening his mouth to answer.

Only to be cut off by a nearby scream. I jumped, the sound so out of place for the sleepy town I knew Listwyne to be. Locke's hand went to his sword, but didn't draw it as he came to the window. His brow furrowed—not good news. Another chorus of screams and the sounds of metal on metal—the drawing of weapons—alerted me to something being seriously wrong. Had we been discovered? But how?

I moved to the window then, despite Locke hissing at me to stay low. But I saw. Crownguards. Floods of Crownguards that were armed to the teeth. They bellowed orders, ranting about punishing the disloyal with blood. Bellowing about dissent. Sneering in satisfaction at the fear they sowed. I sucked in a breath through my teeth as reality closed in around me. Suffocated me. I knew what was happening. I'd heard how this started from the stories I'd heard. A demonstration. We were stuck in the middle of a demonstration.

"What do we do?" I asked as a Crownguard grabbed a fae girl not much older than me, wrenching her hands behind her back as she sobbed and pled innocence of whatever crime she'd supposedly committed. "There's no way we can leave them."

"We have to be careful," Locke said, narrowing his eyes. "Scorpio and Pisces are likely here. We can't risk them getting their hands on you or Eldan."

"Or you," I said with some force. He sighed.

"Or me," he relented.

"Let me charge the jumpstone," I said. "We need to get out of here. We can come back as soon as Eldan is safe, but they're going to search every building. Every room. They'll find us here."

"Shroud us." Locke nodded, already moving before I'd spoken, gesturing for us to sit in the far corner. He crouched next to us, his magic settling over us. I heard the telltale thump, thump, thump of heavy boots coming up the rickety stairs. Each stair shrieked in warning to us. When the door was finally booted in, I held my breath. Locke and Eldan did the same.

I watched as they evaluated the room. I prayed they didn't see the sections of disturbed dust.

"Someone's been here," one murmured, touching the areas where the dust was smeared from our footprints, killing that hope immediately. Thankfully they were all around the room, so none led directly to the corner where we currently sat. Fear and fury fought for purchase within me. Locke gave me a warning look. Stay put.

"Search the rest of the premises," the other one said, glaring at the room. At one point, his eyes slid right to our corner, and I swore we made direct eye contact. Locke's grip on my knee tightened, a silent warning not to move. My lungs burned for air. I needed to breathe....

Both fae spun on their heels and made for the door, satisfied that the room was empty. We let out a collective breath, smiling at each other, none of us yet daring to speak. My limbs went languid from relief. We were okay.

The next breath had that relief evaporating, smoke. On light feet I moved to the door and peeked out. I spied a hallway open to the foyer below. The dark wood reflected the firelight. Fire that had started downstairs and was licking its way up the banister.

"We need to run," I whispered.

"Eldan, you've been staying here. *Is* there another way out?" asked Locke. Eldan shook his head.

"There's only one staircase. The back door opens into a treed area though. If we can get to it, we might get away." The flames grew hotter, and the smoke was now greeting us in the room. I choked. Using my air magic, I forced the smoke out, keeping our lungs clear.

"We can't go around," I said. "We have to go through. We can't douse the fire, they'll know someone was here. Follow as close behind me as you can."

Locke nodded. Eldan looked surprised and unsure. As a unit, we crept forward, my control of the fire keeping the flames from reaching us. The second I stepped onto the first stair, it fell away from me. Locke caught me before I inadvertently followed. Three magics at once. I was going to have to use three magics at once now. I focused, sweat collecting on my brow.

"You can do this, Lark. We've trained for this," Locke murmured to me. I nodded. Using my earth magic, I solidified the wooden stairs beneath us. The flames staggered closer for a moment, taking advantage of my momentary lapse in concentration. Eldan gasped. I regained control of the flames and my earth magic, but my control of the air around us was fading. We had to hurry. We needed to get out now before I lost control.

Locke, sensing my distress, hustled Eldan along with him as we moved down the stairs, doubling our pace. Thick smoke was beginning to drift past my control, but I saw the open door. The trees beyond glowing orange in the fire. Escape was only feet away. And when we at last tumbled out the door and into fresher air, I let my magic go, feeling the strain in my body dissipate almost instantaneously. I took a huge breath, feeling my lungs expand almost painfully in my chest, still tight with anxiety. Eldan was gasping, his lungs weakened with his age, struggling at taking in breath. I went to Eldan, using my air magic to try and help him breathe. I took his hands, trying to help him stagger to his feet.

"Lark." Locke's voice was strained. Screams kept rising all too close to us. My head whipped around to see fae running for their lives, only to be bolted with an arrow. Tears filled my eyes. They weren't dying quickly. This was madness. The scent of blood rose over to mingle with the fire and smoke. Whatever Scorpio was after, she wasn't leaving until she got it. Images of what remained of Poplar Hollow flooded my mind and I prayed to the Goddess that wasn't what would happen here. It was then that I heard the Crownguards shouting. It was then I understood fully what was happening.

"By order of her majesty, all able bodied fae over the age of twenty-two must relocate to Loc Valen for training." Locke and I exchanged horrified looks. "Those who resist will be found guilty of treason."

This wasn't just a demonstration. This was forced recruitment. This was the most heinous type of conscription. Scorpio was amassing an army of everyone she could, and anyone who didn't fall into line was deemed disloyal. Tears picked at my eyes as I fought the rush of guilt.

I could just turn myself in and stop this.

Locke caught my eye at that, at seeing my regret, shaking his head at me. A silent reminder. So instead of regret, I turned to fury.

Anger seethed just under my skin, burning away every other emotion. Burning away everything. She would pay. She would pay dearly for what she was doing.

I caught a glimpse of a mother carrying her crying infant through the trees. Her eyes widened upon seeing us.

"You're—" Her face dawned in recognition.

"Run," I whispered, cutting her off. "Run *north*." I heavily emphasized. "As far as you can. Hurry." She nodded and fled. I had no idea if she'd end up at Port Azure. If she'd understand. But at least she'd be away from this.

"Let's go. We need to get you to safety," I said to Eldan who was getting his feet under him. The jumpstone wasn't done charging yet. Time wasn't on our side, so we needed distance. "We've wasted too much time."

"You're right about that," came a new voice from behind me, turning my veins to ice despite the oppressive heat. I whirled to see a Crownguard on us, his sword drawn. Locke melted from the shadows and dispatched him before he could take another step towards Eldan and me, using his Zodiac speed and his knife. The Crownguard crumpled inward, gurgling briefly on his own blood before dying.

"Let's go," Locke repeated, and this time we didn't hesitate. Eldan, Locke, and I fled through the trees as quickly as we dared. So many had the same idea as us. Crownguards spread out around us, leaving Locke to shroud us to ensure our safe passage.

A fae man, about Locke's age, stood shaking beneath a tree. Hands bound with cruel looking rope, his wrists looked angry and raw even from here. Tearfully, he begged for his life, beseeching two Crownguards with their hold over his fate. The one laughed, leaning into his face.

"You can't prove your loyalty to the crown unless you fight for your queen," he snickered. "Those who are disloyal, perish. It's simple."

"I am loyal!" he screamed as the second one drew his blades with a grin. A vicious looking red blade, glinting in the muted light. "Please, I'll do anything."

"Anything except what we've asked," the Crownguard sneered at the simpering prisoner.

"Please! I can't do what you ask. I have a family! They rely on me! I can't fight."

"We can't leave him," I whispered. Locke nodded, cringing as he did so. "What's the plan?"

"I'll take the one on the right. You take the left. Eldan, stay out of sight."

Eldan nodded, and crouched behind a wide tree. I pulled my knife and moved forward on silent feet. The faerie saw me, his eyes wide like saucers. The Crownguards didn't seem to notice. I put my finger to my lips, pleading with him to be quiet.

"Behind you!" he screamed. My stomach fell through my body. He'd given us up. A ploy to win his freedom. That dirty motherfucker. "The Crowned Assassin and the Queen's Mark are behind you!" Locke didn't hesitate, he launched an assault on his target. But I didn't reach mine in time. In the scuffle, the betrayer turned and fled, screaming the whole way.

He blew a horn, a warning to anyone who heard it, before my blade sank into the hollow of his throat. And my heart sank when I heard shouts of other nearby Crownguards rushing to our position. We needed to get Eldan and run. We wouldn't be able to help anyone if we were captured. The jumpstone had finally recharged, leaving my magic feeling drained. I tossed it to Locke, since he was closer to Eldan.

Locke took out the jump stone and we turned in unison to get back to Eldan. The place was flooding with Crownguards. Locke pulled me against him, shrouding us, rather than running. Just in time. Eldan nodded at us ever so slightly as Crownguards surrounded him. An understanding. Locke clamped his hand over my mouth before I cried out, weeping silently in Locke's arms. I sagged in his arms, his grip around my waist all that was holding me up as they punched Eldan in the face, knocking him to his knees. Leaving him dazed, they bound his hands behind his back and two guards carried him away.

"We have to save him," I whispered, sounding frightfully similar to earlier when we were betrayed. Locke nodded.

"We will. We're not going to leave him." He tugged me along, my numb legs barely obeying him. "But we can't help him if we don't get us to safety and have a plan."

I watched helplessly as they dragged the last remaining vestige of family back towards Listwyne. Flames piled high, smoke bloomed higher still, choking out sunlight, leaving us awash in a dark and amber contrasting glow. I had no idea how we were supposed to help Eldan now. Inside Listwyne, surrounded by Crownguards, Pisces, and Scorpio, I had no idea how I was supposed to save him.

Chapter Twenty

As soon as we were free of sight, Locke dropped his shrouding magic, but not his hold on me. I sobbed into his shoulder while he rubbed soothing circles over my back.

"Get it out, love," he crooned. "We're getting him back."

"How?" I sniffled. From our position, I could see the smoke pouring from Listwyne. Hear the screams of the resisting. And the sobs of the family member left behind. We were outnumbered. Outmatched. "How do we even try?"

"I have an idea." Locke moved away from the window, examining the room, listening into the hallway.

"Are you going to share that idea?"

"We need a distraction," he mused. "What's a better distraction than an explosion?"

"How are we going to make anything explode? We don't have anything combustible!"

He flourished the jumpstone.

"We have to run back to Port Azure. While I grab what we need, I need you to recharge this so we can portal right back here. Can you do that?" I nodded numbly. "That's my girl. Ready?" I croaked out a yes and a few heartbeats later we were back in Port Azure, standing on the veranda. Locke handed me the jumpstone and took off running.

I threw my magic into charging the jumpstone again, feeling incredibly sick with guilt. Eldan was caught because of me. I wanted to save that fae, and it bit us in the ass. We should have taken him back here right away and this would never have happened. The brutality of the demonstration was worse than I'd heard in the rumors. Scorpio was looking for bodies. Which meant one of two things; either she was getting ready for us to attack her, or she was amassing her forces to wipe us out. Which she could only do if she knew where we were.

That was a disturbing thought.

Seconds stretched into long minutes and I was sick with impatience. We needed to get back to Eldan now. Before something happened to him. I was pacing a hole in the courtyard when at last I spotted Locke speeding towards me with a few small glass spheres in his hands, but that wasn't what caught my attention. Aspen, Lenore, and Lennox trailed behind. Lenore twirled her battle axes with a vicious snarl on her lips.

"The cavalry has arrived." Aspen grinned down at me. At my sour mood, his eyes softened. "Don't worry, Bird. We're getting him back. And everyone else too. Hang in there."

I looked at what Locke was handing me, pausing at his nonverbal warning. I looked closer at this glass sphere outlined in shimmering white runes. It looked so delicate, which upon closer inspection was nerve wracking. Looking within, there was smoke and fire, frozen in time. I realized with a start what I was looking at. A spell sphere with something very specific inside.

"Time bombs," I whispered, Locke's plan clicking into place. Looks like Wren had been busy. The same thing we planned on using in Loc Valen. Explosions that were magically halted and stored at the moment of ignition.

"Very unstable time bombs. Borderline failures," he confirmed.

"Wren has been hard at work making them any chance he wasn't in Loc Valen." Aspen supplied for me as I struggled to figure out where these came from. "Turns out that's a stunningly helpful talent to have. No wonder Queen Aquarius keeps him around. It's too bad it's so rare."

Locke cleared his throat, "You won't need anything to set these off. Just throw them." He stepped forward before turning back to me with a grave expression, "Just don't jostle them needlessly. Is the jumpstone ready?" Oh right. Great segue. Thanks, Locke. I held the three in my possession as if they might bite me. At my stiff nod, Locke took my hand. He opened the portal, the smell of burning already wrenching my nose. "Let's go."

Stepping through, we must have only been gone fifteen minutes. In that time, flames and smoke threatened to choke us. There was still shouting and commotion going on, the first signs of real hope that we weren't too late. The occasional scream still pierced the air, making my blood chill. Locke lent his magic to me to help me charge the jumpstone once more, taking my focus off of my worry at least for the moment.

"For the purposes of this, simply throw it. When the glass shatters, it'll explode." He handed me three. I'd need to make them count.

"Let's go see what we're dealing with."

We crept silently through the streets towards the main square, Locke shrouding us all. To them, we looked like smoke and shadow drifting down the street. If even that. I could tell that maintaining this much magic was taxing, at least a bit. His step never faltered, but I noticed his look of sharp focus that always came with exertion.

We followed the sound of voices and scent of fear to the town's center where all the commotion was.

What struck me first was the stench. Blood. Death. Piss, and Goddess only knew what else made me want to gag on the air. It didn't take long to see why. The remainder of those in Listywne were forced to kneel on the uneven, frosty dirt below them. Scorpio stood above them, sneering down at the shivering mass of victims without remorse or pity. No shame. Just seething anger. And if that weren't enough, a pile of bodies off to the side, discarded like trash. But ever the flair for the dramatic, or maybe to further insight fear, a few heads rose up on pikes like balloons behind her for the most disturbing backdrop. Tongues hanging out, eyes still open on some. I only barely avoided retching then and there.

Everyone currently alive huddled together for warmth, comfort, and the illusion of safety, guarded and kept motionless by the Crownguards that paced the perimeter of the square, eyeing them with an eager bloodthirstiness that made my stomach sour. Whilst scouring the crowd for Eldan, I glimpsed several fae with significant wounds to their faces, arms, torsos. But I nearly lost my composure when I saw the children, crying, terrified, and huddling to their mothers.

She hurt *children*.

What a fucking monster.

Eldan was in the very back, shrinking into himself and trying to escape notice. If Scorpio saw him, would she recognize him? Would any of the guards?

Scorpio couldn't die. We knew that. But her guards could. We could outnumber her. Force her retreat. These bombs were big, meant to cause massive, destructive explosions. We may have to toss them to draw the guards away and toss a second bomb in to finish them off.

I stilled.

How was I so casually thinking about murdering so many fae? But I only needed to look at the helpless fae before me to know why. This madness had to end.

Lenore, Lennox, and Aspen split off just before the courtyard, ready to cause a distraction. That should give us time to get to the trapped villagers and get Eldan, and as many others as possible, to safety.

I grabbed Aspen's arm before he disappeared.

"Be safe," I told him. He smiled.

"Don't go all soft on me, Bird," he said with a wink. "Distractions are my specialty." He slipped away and was gone, but Scorpio brought my attention right back to her.

She stood on the , flames burning the dead further behind her. Every single fae before her cowered and avoided eye contact. Nobody wanted to draw her gaze.

"Bring me the next." The way she spoke made it sound like a spectacle. Like a grandstander. A guard picked from the group, eliciting screams and pleas from everyone in the vicinity. A fae man was wrenched from his screaming wife's arms. She was whipped by another guard when she tried to force her way between them, a selfless, protective act that was ultimately useless. I felt Locke tense next to me as we watched him be marched up the dais and forced to kneel to Scorpio. Scorpio's eyes grew dark, almost black like in Everwind.

"Do you accept the terms of conscription?" she asked him. He cowered, cringing away, but nodded. His wife sobbed loudly until another lashing quieted her. Crownguards severed his ties and led him around the corner. He was able to steal one last look behind him, where I could see fear and shame and revulsion mixing on his face, his head hanging under the weight of his decision before he was out of sight. The Crownguards wasted no time in dragging another one up at random. Forced to kneel, this fae glowered up at her. He didn't back down. He didn't stop staring her in the eye.

"Do you accept the terms of conscription?" she repeated the question. He spat at her.

"Fuck you." His tone was pure venom. Pure hatred. Scorpio smiled through her pinched expression.

"Fall in line, or fall into death. Those are your options. Do you care to rethink, friend?"

"I'd rather die than serve you, you fucking—"

His last sentence in this life would never finish. Scorpio created a sword made entirely of shadow and ran through her victim. The man's scream died—cut off by his own demise, before slumping lifelessly to the ground. A chorus of screams from the audience. His wife screamed, tears running unchecked.

"This is the price of disloyalty." Scorpio grinned wickedly as she peered down her nose at her subjects in what could only be described as gleeful triumph. She actually felt like she'd won something as the fae before her sobbed and cowered before her. Fae she was charged with protecting. Seeing it firsthand was a horror that did nothing but fuel my hatred for her. It forged my resolve to fix what she'd done. "Some of you have already betrayed me. Sold information. Helped rebels. Maybe even sought to join them." She leered over them, her face hardening. "This ends now. Or your lives do. Fight for me, and all will be forgiven. Or don't..." She knelt down to grab a fist full of hair from the dead fae at her feet. Horrified gasps sounded at the sight of his tongue lolling out in death. "And this will be your fate."

Not one fae moved.

"I'm tossing the bomb. Get to Eldan. Now." I blinked up at Locke. In the corner of my eyes, I saw a Crownguard go to drag another fae up to the dais—a sobbing girl about my age—while Locke wound up and threw the bomb with all his might. It landed on the other side of a row of buildings and exploded on impact.

The effect was immediate, the blast knocking everyone to their knees. Those already kneeling were forced to their stomachs from the blast. As hoped, the guards turned heel and ran in droves to the site, looking for the source. I heard Aspen's whoop of excitement as the fighting commenced loudly. I sent one more in a different direction, hoping to spread the guards thin and buy Aspen, Lennox, and Lenore a bit more time. The second blast wasn't as strong, but still violent in nature. Screams of terror sounded from the square. The few guards who remained shouted directives, but blended into the cacophony of screams. Eldan's face was white with panic.

"Insurgents!" a Crownguard cried. "The rebels are here!"

"Then they'll not leave here alive." Scorpio seethed as she strode towards where our knights waited near the first blast site. How I longed to throw a bomb at her. I wondered if she could piece herself back together after being ripped apart in an explosion. She certainly deserved it. But I couldn't focus on that. As soon as Scorpio left for the fight, Locke and I focused on the remaining guards around the fae of Listwyne.

Keeping us shrouded we approached, barely daring to breathe, lest we be heard. There were seven guards. Four for my Crowned Assassin on the left, three for me on the right. Locke struck with the precision and lethality of a basilisk, downing two with his knife before anybody could react with his enhanced speed. I sunk my dagger into the fleshy throat of one guard and moved to the next. I slashed his neck, but much too shallowly to cause any lethal harm. I ripped the air from the lungs of the two remaining guards under my watch, keeping them from shouting in alarm long enough to end them as well.

We had seconds, minutes at best. I began unbinding everyone I could. They looked at me with mistrust in their eyes. Some even with hatred. How could I blame them?

"I know what you must think of me," I quietly implored them. "But there isn't time for that. We need to run. We can take you someplace safe."

"Why should we trust you?" one spat. "The Traitor Prince and the Queen's Mark? You're the reason we're in this mess. She's looking for you!" Flashbacks of Eldan's capture came back. If they revolted against us, we'd be in trouble. They stared at me, some with open hostility and disdain, others with pure skepticism. One thing I saw building on precious few, was hope.

"Trust us or don't," Locke said in that tone that drew every wary eye to him. "Scorpio is returning. She will kill you all if you don't fight for her. Spare us the bullshit and follow Lark, or don't and die. It's your choice."

They didn't need more prompting than that. I took off running, trying to keep my feet from pounding loudly into the ground. I let out a heavy breath of relief hearing the collective steps behind me, rhythmic and thudding as they fell into step. I forged ahead, leading the way while Locke brought up the rear, making sure nobody was left behind.

We had to reach the checkpoint, where the twins would be waiting if all went according to plan. I spotted Eldan running close to Locke. The relief of seeing him nearly knocked the breath from my lungs.

It became obvious quickly all was not going according to plan. As soon as we left the town square onto the empty streets. I heard a strange bird call. Aspen's signal. Scorpio was on her way and we weren't far enough away yet.

"Hurry!" I said as loudly as I dared and urged others on ahead of me, pointing to our destination. I looked back to see a little girl struggling to keep up. No adults were helping her and she was quickly falling behind. I fell back a few rows to be beside her. "Get on my back," I urged her, kneeling down in front of her. After a moment of hesitation, she jumped on. I locked my elbows under her knees and surged back ahead. Her tiny arms held around my neck, just loose enough to allow me to breathe.

I heard yelling and commotion behind us. Our absence had been discovered and we were being tracked. I wasn't sure if Locke could shroud all of us, but I somehow doubted it. Not without help.

"Make for the trees. If we separate, Keep heading until you get to a meadow. That's your mark!" The little girl on my back whimpered. I brushed her knee in what I hoped was a comforting gesture.

"What's your name?" I asked her over my shoulder.

"Thyra." Her voice was as mousy as she was. What this little girl had endured at such a tender age was unforgivable.

"You're going to be okay, Thyra. Keep hanging on to me and don't let go, okay?" I felt her nod.

Fast footsteps were audible behind us now. We were still going too slow. I risked a glance behind us. A row of Crownguards had us in their sights, advancing on us.

"Okay, Thyra, you're going to hear a really big boom. Don't be scared," I said as I tossed a time bomb over my shoulder straight behind us. The following explosion and chorus of screams assured me that I'd been successful, but I'd also just revealed our location to Scorpio. A small part of me cried as Thyra flinched and tightened her hold on me. "We're okay, we're okay," I huffed repeatedly, even though my lungs were screaming and battering against my ribcage. Locke must have sent a follow up bomb because another earth-shattering blast echoed around us, this one so big it propelled me forward. No sound followed the bombs. No footfalls, no shouts. The dead quiet was almost like a victory in and of itself.

We were going to make it!

When we at last reached the clearing, the twins were there as hoped. Even Aspen showed up, looking winded, but he must have given them the slip, I realized with a wide smile. We now had the clearing filled with roughly fifty fae, including us. Fifty. Such a small number when you consider this morning, it was a full and vibrant town. This here was possibly only a single street's worth of families. I hoped that they weren't all killed. I had hopes that many, like the woman with her infant, made it out alive.

Unbidden, I saw all the blood, the arrows sticking out of the dying, and cringed away from the memory. I joined Locke and the others as we milled about. We had some time, but we couldn't waste it.

"How many can we bring in a trip?" I asked, looking at the jumpstone.

"If everyone is connected, all of them," Locke said to me, leaving me blinking in surprise. I wasn't sure why, but I'd thought there would definitely be a limit to how many we could move. Aspen began giving instructions for everyone to hold hands, and when the portal opened, not to let go. "Lark, you lead them first. If we're attacked, we can fend them off until you come back for us." I wanted to protest, but there wasn't time to argue. I kissed him, a silent bid for him to be careful, and traded my last bomb for his jumpstone.

"Everyone with me!" I called out. "No matter what happens, do not let go of the person you're holding onto." I activated the portal with a little push of magic. It tingled when the portal opened. I grabbed the hand of the fae closest to me. She held on with a death grip so tight I fought to not flinch. I jumped through, Thyra on my back and fifty fae behind me.

I jumped through, the crisp alpine and sea salt air refreshing my senses almost instantly and gifting me a sense of calm. Home. We'd made it home. I rushed away from the portal entrance to make room for those still coming through. Several fae from Port Azure stared in awe.

"Go alert medical that we have injured!" I pleaded. At first, they didn't move. "Quickly!"

They scattered, hustling around the corner to the citadel and disappearing behind the doors. More and more, fae came through the portal. They all drank in the first view of Port Azure like they were starving and Port Azure was a feast. Local fae saw what was happening and rushed forward to help, leading them into the main square, offering food and drink and blankets while the healers arrived. I've never been so proud of a group of fae in all my life.

"My lady, what would you have us do with the new arrivals?" An elderly fae woman approached me cautiously.

"Locke will be here any moment," I answered her. "But for now, ensure they're comfortable and their wounds are tended to."

"As you say, my lady," she said with a small, but genuine smile. I was going to correct her, tell her to just call me Lark, but she gathered her skirts and was gone faster than I would have thought possible. I watched as the flow of people coming through the portal trickled. My eyes scanned them all, my heart in my throat for the one fae I was desperate to see safe and sound. My heart stayed in knots as I let out a relieved breath to see Eldan pop through at last, the final fae before the portal closed. The relief of seeing him was almost too much. The smile on my face was wide as I saw him spot me. He stumbled through the portal, nearly falling to his knees. I rushed over to him, my hands going to his elbows to help him up.

"Lark, they found them." Those four words were all it took to drain the blood from my face. To ruin the moment of victory. Adrenaline lit me up from within. Grasping my knife, I took the jumpstone out of my pocket and began to charge it. But with the amount I'd been charging it today, my magic sputtered uncooperatively, and I hissed in desperation.

"Eldan, lend me your magic."

He placed his hand on my shoulder, giving me what magic he had. I took it greedily and funneled it into the jumpstone, every second feeling like minutes. When it was charged at last, I wasted no time. Leaving a wide-eyed Thyra in his care, I portaled right back to whatever hell had been unleashed on Locke and our friends.

Chapter Twenty-One

Turns out, the wreckage wasn't too far off from Hell. Flames had erupted in the trees around the meadow. Worse. They were spreading inward, constricting the battlefield considerably and blocking us in, while Crownguards surged towards us in waves. My lungs filled with smoke and my chest burned with the effort of expelling it in the oppressive heat. Scorpio and a team of remaining Crownguards fought hard against Locke, Aspen, and the twins. I was relieved to see my friends were looking relatively unscathed, and the meadow littered with the corpses of Scorpio's Crownguards. But more. There were always more Crownguards. How were their numbers so endless? My friends wouldn't remain unscathed for long if I didn't recharge the jumpstone.

"Locke!" I shouted over the fray. He glanced back at me before parrying Scorpio's attack at the last possible second, making me nearly shout with alarm.

"Lark, get the portal open!" he bellowed through another swing of his sword, effort evident in every breath.

"Hurry!" Lenore cried, swinging her battle axes, embedding one in someone's chest and countering an attack with the other in a feat of dexterity and precision. Her leg came up to the faerie's chest as she tugged it free, blood spraying grotesquely from the lethal wound as she did so. I held the jumpstone, so hot in my hands it took all my willpower not to drop it, despite the bite of it searing my palm. Instead of pain, I felt a flash of worry realizing the jumpstone had never felt hot before. I poured my magic into it, but I had company.

Two fae deviated from Aspen and approached me, thinking me the easier target. I grinned. My magic could use a minute to regenerate. Their stances were crisper than the last guards I'd fought, but they moved slow, not expecting me to be much of a threat, even now. They advanced on me with wide smirks. I let them think I was easy prey.

One swung his sword. I took a step back as it missed, and struck while he was off balance. It was countered by his friend at the last moment.

"No fair, saving his ass," I taunted. "It's already two against one. You can't take on one minimally trained girl?" He snarled in rage and attacked me again. A sweeping motion that was easily countered. My follow up attack hit its mark, slicing his sword bearing arm in the unprotected spot of his upper arm. He shrieked, the horror of his situation hitting him and going into shock. "And now it's one on one."

He didn't look impressed. Or angry. He glared at me impassively before striking. This one moved differently. I'd never seen movements like his before, making him hard to anticipate.

"What's the matter, little girl? Can't keep up?"

I grit my teeth, not taking the bait. I had to wait for him to come to me. I thankfully didn't have to wait long. He swung his sword with precision, enough that I had a hard time blocking. He kept coming, forcing me to back up. His sword nicked my arm; I wasn't fast enough and the pain from the slice made me gasp. This fight needed to end now. I needed to charge the jumpstone! A shadow weapon that could have only been from Locke whipped by my head and embedded itself within my opponent's eye, dropping him to the floor like a puppet whose strings had just been severed. I looked back at Locke, but he was too busy fighting Scorpio. My stomach heaved when I saw the blood accumulating on Locke. We needed to hurry. I needed to hurry.

"Keep them off me or we're not getting out of here!" I shouted as I spotted more opponents charging towards me. Aspen, Locke, and the twins made a protective circle around me, fighting off another wave of Crownguards. I'd never charged the stone so fast, and I'd never felt so sick doing it. As it began to glow, indicating it was ready, I felt the last tendrils of magic leave me empty, leaving room only for intense nausea. I opened the portal. I didn't need to give a single signal. All of us ran through.

A sole guard came through with us, but Locke dispatched him quickly enough. I could have cried. I could hardly believe it. We did it. I nearly slumped to my knees in exhaustion. Locke stepped up next to me, taking my hand in his.

"Valiant," he said, planting a kiss on my forehead. "You are simply valiant." My hands came up to his face of their own volition and brought his lips down to mine again. I wasn't ready to let go of him. Not after all of that. He smiled against me, his hands coming to rest around my waist.

"We made it," I whispered, before breaking into a face splitting grin. We got a win. For once! "I can't believe we pulled that off! I bet Scorpio is in a rage!" Locke boomed a laugh, resting his face in the crook of my neck. His warmth seeped into my skin, solidifying him for me. He was real. He was here. He was okay. I tightened my grip on him, letting him feel my earlier fear. My earlier panic. He rubbed soothing circles onto my back, bringing much needed relief.

"Of that I have no doubt," he said, straightening. I mourned the loss of contact and warmth. "Why don't you go take a hot bath and relax? I have to take care of matters here, and I'll join you." His voice dropped low, a voice only for me. "And I'll show you later just how proud of you I am."

I rolled my eyes, but my amusement prevailed and I grinned widely. "Keep it clean, Crowned Assassin."

"With you around? Impossible." He winked and sauntered away, immediately taking charge of the situation at hand. He wasn't one to bark orders. A natural leader and delegator, he doled them out calmly, creating a plan to house and feed all these additional fae. It was fascinating watching this facet of him. The Prince side I seldom truly saw.

Eldan came over to me, wide smile, arms outstretched, and joyous laughter on his lips. A laughter I returned before falling into his familiar arms.

"I don't know how to thank you," he said, embracing me. "You should have left me." Tears instantly stung my eyes, but he wiped them away with the pad of his thumb. It was strange seeing this side of Eldan. The kind and tender side I'd only seen a small handful of times. Usually when I was so injured I was near death.

"There was no possibility of that," I told him firmly before clearing my throat, gesturing to the vista that was Port Azure. The mountains, the intricacy of the city's architecture, the bits between where you could spot the sea. My home. "Welcome to the Court of Rebels, Eldan. Welcome to Port Azure."

It took until well into the early morning hours to tend to the wounded. Even more so to make sure everyone had housing. Locke had to open up the rooms under the Citadel, the rooms I was first in when I had arrived in Port Azure. Rooms that, since the wards had kept everyone safe from Scorpio's eyeline, had built their homes outside. Rooms that had been vacant a while, but were plentiful enough for the families that we just helped from Listwyne.

Eldan had a baptism of fire, being launched immediately to the infirmary to tend the wounded. I helped as I was able, tending to wounds that didn't need magical intervention, handing blankets and supplies to others. Locke assembled a team to get all the rooms in as good condition as possible, and assigning plots of land for future homes to be built, starting immediately.

It was well into the next day when Eldan was finally able to be given a tour of Port Azure. I couldn't stop my smile at Eldan's slackened jaw at the evening sunset kissing the sea and mountain tops goodnight. I couldn't stop my own joy as the fae fire lights turned on and lighting the place aglow in an amber hue, giving warmth to the square where the winter weather tried to take it.

"Any news of your father?" Eldan asked Locke while walking through the ice atrium out of the cold. "I'd like to know when to begin mixing the ingredients. They're a bit volatile so I can't make it too soon ahead of time." Locke plastered a fake smile on his face, though his eyes remained tight with stress.

"Nothing yet, I'm afraid. Though I'm tempted to run into Loc Valen after the success we had with finding you." Everything about his tone suggested he was joking. But everything about the hardness of his gaze, his lips, made me think he wasn't.

The three of us walked into Hell's Gate, greeted by the sounds of weapons clashing and leather against leather. I summoned my flames around my body, enjoying the warmth they ignited on my skin and driving away the chilliness I hadn't been able to drive away since leaving my bed this morning. Eldan's face was thoughtful as he appraised me, as if reconciling the helpless girl he remembered as his apprentice and the girl that stood before him now. I couldn't blame him. It was a struggle I grappled with on a regular basis. Locke and Aspen moved over to a weapons display, leaving Eldan and me for a moment in a move I wondered if weren't entirely deliberate.

"Your father isn't here to see this, so I'm honored to see it for him," Eldan said stroking his beard thoughtfully and looking around with great interest before swiveling his head to appraise me. I started, surprised at his forward words. His eyes crinkled with pride, making my heart squeeze almost painfully in my chest, while simultaneously warming me through. I missed my father; every day brought me closer to the day I avenged him. Every day brought me closer to joining him too.

Temporarily, I reminded myself. Only temporarily.

One second I was smiling and enjoying the moment, the next I felt the cold, rotten feeling of a piece of myself die. They were getting intense, this one was impossible to hide entirely, my breath leaving me for a moment. Eldan's eyes appraised me, the healer immediately coming out, looking for a cause. It was only a flicker of a second, but I felt rather than saw Locke's eyes gauging me.

"Sorry," I smiled sheepishly once the sharp discomfort wore off. They were always so brief. A fraction of a second, but painful enough that I wanted to fall to my knees. And then I said loud enough for Locke to hear as well as Eldan, "Leg cramp."

I stole a glance at Locke, who gave me a strange look, a concerned look. I smiled at him, showing him I'm fine. He appraised me, searching my aura as well as my body before finally relaxing, before finally regaining his smile with Aspen, looking so much more like themselves than they had in days. It thawed the anxiety that felt ever present in my chest, at least for the moment, lifting my own lips. Locke's gaze flicked to mine for a moment, smile widening when our eyes met, before turning back to Aspen.

"That's a sight to see," Eldan said softly. I turned to him, confused.

"What is?"

"You. Smiling." His voice was softer than I could ever remember hearing it before. "You seldom did in Poplar Hollow. Not that anyone can blame you. I can see how happy you are here. You finally found your place. You're thriving. And I can see how well Prince Cancer treats you. Admittedly, I'm still surprised given all I know of him, but," he dropped his voice an octave, just for me, "for what it's worth, I approve. Your father would too. You didn't need to tell me you're soulmates. You can see it in the way you look at one another."

My eyes filled to the brim with tears. I threw my arms around Eldan as he flailed, awkwardly patting my back. "I don't know how to thank you enough." Eldan shrugged it off, looking more like the fae I remembered. Awkward, but well meaning. I couldn't be happier to have a shred of my old family in my new life.

Chapter Twenty-Two

T he next day made me hate Aspen. At least in the moment. He came at me in our training session like a starved and unhinged beast, burning with an intensity I'd seldom seen from him before, and only in the most dire circumstances. Frostfall came to mind. Or when Abel held me captive and was discovered as a traitor. Maybe even Everwind. He looked at me with a similar look now—not anger per se, but something equally as volatile.

And he was beating the Goddess hating hell out of me.

Every hit he landed was with none of his usual respite. My ribs sang from his most recent connection—the soft spot just above my liver. My diaphragm spasmed as I struggled to breathe. I sank to one knee before him, spitting blood on the mat between us. His eyes followed the movement, flickering back to me as I grunted.

"We go again. Get up, Lark." His tone left no room for questioning. For hesitation. There was only obey. I had such little energy left to give that even the thought of rising to my feet was daunting.

"Aspen, I can't," I panted. "We've been at this for two hours straight. I need rest."

"We sweat here so we don't bleed out there." Previously, that mantra inspired me, pushed me to work harder. Now it felt like a mockery. I glared up at him trying to bite down anger.

"Aspen," I bit out. "Give me a moment."

"On your feet, soldier!" his voice boomed, becoming further removed from Aspen's usual sunny persona. His boots crunched on the mat, getting closer to me. Even other sparring groups posted nearby us were watching out of the corners of their gaze. Feeling the gravity of the moment, I lurched to my feet. "Again." I braced myself, setting my feet apart for a stronger stance, readying my wooden knife.

Aspen launched at me, my eyes tracking the movement. It was funny that there was a time that my being able to keep up with him would have felt like a victory. Aspen's fist was in my eyesight, and I dodged. Not fast enough. The leather of his gloves grazed my cheek, making it sing. I countered with a combination, successfully landing a weak blow to his ribs, mirroring my own welt I could feel there. He rushed me, looking for the takedown. I whirled with him, letting his momentum carry him past me and wrenching my arm around his neck from behind, my fake knife coming to graze his cheek.

"Yield," I commanded, my tone closer to that I would use for fae I hated rather than my closest friend. A tone I would've used against the fae in Poplar Hollow. A tone that hid the soft hurt behind a razor-sharp wall of hostility. The flashbacks began unbidden and consuming, fae I'd thought were my friends, suddenly turning on me. I bit the pain away with gritted teeth. Fuck, no not again. Not Aspen. What had I done wrong? "We're done here."

"I yield," he finally said, his words leaching the last strength from my body. I sagged in relief, melting to the ground in a heap. It was only when Aspen moved to heal me did he realize how covered in welts my body was. How completely depleted I was.

I saw the exact moment it dawned on him. His eyes widened, his jaw lost that tense edge that had been cutting us both all morning, and his own shoulders sagged, regret crossing his features. I moved to get up.

"No." Though my voice wavered, something Aspen noticed, I kept my voice quiet, so it was just the two of us hearing this conversation. A kindness I didn't need to give him, but I did nonetheless. "I don't need your healing, Aspen. I'm going to see Eldan. I don't know what the fuck that was, because that wasn't training. That was little more than a beating."

"Lark, I'm sorry," he said. I paid no heed. I lurched to my feet only for Aspen to gently grab my forearm, his hands funneling sweet relief into me and bringing my body back from the breaking point. It was only when I turned to look at him, when I was about to throw him backwards with my air magic that I saw the regret on his face—an emotion that looked so out of place on him—and I stayed my hand.

"A few years ago, my father pledged his undying loyalty to Scorpio," Aspen started, slowly, rubbing the back of his neck as he pondered what he was about to tell me. "When she first started trying to break the curse. Courtiers were desperate to appeal to her, hoping for scraps of power or favor. My father was no different. My mother was one of the first seers to go missing. I was forced to watch as my sister was dragged away, only to find out they were both killed in the Yemerian Vale in Scorpio's mad search for answers. And it, as you know, was only the beginning."

He looked at me briefly before his gaze flicked back down to the ground. In that brief moment, I saw a vulnerability, an old pain that lay there and I wondered how I'd never seen it through Aspen's cheery mask. I wondered if he would ever be able to hide from me fully again. His head hung now, his eyes hidden behind his golden hair. His voice was soft, subdued as he continued, "You're so like her, Lark. Fierce. Brave. Strong. Funny. Beautiful. And she would have loved you." He looked up at me then, eyes shining with ghosts he'd yet to outrun and a small, sad smile on his face. The look on his face reminded me of Locke seeing me and reading my aura; Aspen saw both the current and the past mixing together. He was both with me here in the moment, yet also seeing his sister in the past. "Yeah. She would have loved you."

"What was her name?" I whispered, tears springing to my own eyes, all my anger melting away.

"Asha," he whispered. "Her name was Asha." Asha and Aspen. My heart squeezed in my chest, my own loss of my father giving rise for me to understand this hurt.

"I'm so sorry, Aspen," I told him, his arms crossing, his shoulders folding inwards. His eyes cleared, as if grounded now. He looked at me with a sudden, sincere clarity I hadn't expected.

"I can't lose another sister, Lark. I won't. So I'll prepare you in every way I can to make sure you survive this. Your death is not an option. Fuck what the curse says. You will live to see this all end. We all will, because I'm not giving any of us any other option." The magnitude of what he'd just said floored me. Sister. He'd called me his sister. A lump formed in my throat as I spoke.

"When I was little, I begged my father for an older brother," I admitted, smiling sadly at the memory. I remembered my father laughing, rolling his eyes. I remembered him gently telling me that he'd get right on that for me. "I guess I finally got my wish. I'm not going anywhere to Aspen. But don't pull that nonsense again, or you might be." A small smile stole the bite out of my words. A smile he returned.

"I promise." The magic of the promise settled over us, fully restoring the equilibrium between us. "And to make it up to you, I'll personally make sure Eldan gets you some kind of energy enhancement drink. I can heal your muscles, but you do look dead on your feet."

This time when he offered an arm to haul me to my feet, I took it.

Eldan heaved an overly exaggerated sigh when Aspen and I asked him for the energy regeneration potion, as if it were the greatest inconvenience to him. There was the Eldan I remembered. Dry. Pragmatic. And most familiar of all, a little cold. As wonderful as the warmth Eldan had displayed towards me recently, it had been a bit unsettling. I supposed it was a sign he was acclimating. Instead of rolling my eyes, as I used to do, I found myself grinning at this unexpectedly pleasant familiarity.

Aspen handed over a few coins he'd grabbed on our way here, to where Eldan had set up temporarily in the infirmary while they figured out a more permanent location for him in the main business area of Port Azure.

Eldan handed me the warm, earthy smelling elixir that reminded me a bit of tea. Despite its name as energy regenerating, its scent was calming and comforting, and it made me wonder why I didn't use this to wake up every morning.

"Because you'd end up having heart problems," Eldan said. I waggled my eyebrows at him as I sipped my drink, relishing the feeling of my body deeply drinking in the much needed energy with a taste that matched its earthy scent. Not unpleasant, but it did have a bitter aftertaste. The effects were immediate. It felt like my body was waking up. My skin tingled, like numbness burning itself away, leaving me feeling more alert. "Don't look so innocent. You wear your thoughts on your face. This is for occasional use only. You can hate mornings all you want without the use of this. You're too much of a regular patient as it is. We don't need to add heart problems to the list of ailments I treat you for," he said with a scoff. I smiled, knowing I wouldn't be a patient anymore. At least not like I was, and certainly not for the same reasons.

Aspen and Eldan were talking, discussing alchemy with terms I didn't bother to try to interpret as I sipped my drink, relishing the feeling of strength warming my limbs again. I felt color coming back to my cheeks. I'd half finished my elixir when a rumble shook the room, making the floor vibrate. Glass jars filled with ingredients for Eldan chimed and chattered in their place. Eldan glanced around the room in confusion, catching on a glass bottle that had dislodged itself and found its way over the edge of the counter. I mirrored his movements, looking around until I saw the dark look Aspen donned. A knowing look that had an ominous tingle sent the hair on the back of my neck erect.

"What's wrong?" I asked him. Eldan huddled closer to hear Aspen's response when another hit, stronger this time. I had to hold the desk in order to keep my feet.

"Grab your sword, Lark," he turned to Eldan, his face full of dread. And one thing worse—fear. "Be ready for wounded. They'll be coming with certainty."

"Aye." Eldan bustled about immediately opening jars, and getting supplies set up.

"Aspen. What is going on?" I followed him out of the infirmary to Hell's Gate, where my sword still remained discarded. Aspen began shouting orders to those sparring still, sounding the alarm.

"I hope you had enough of the elixir, Little Bird," he said in a voice like the eye of a storm—eerily calm, but you could see the chaos rushing to meet you. "We're under attack. That rumbling? Those were some of the wards shattering. Scorpio might very well have found us."

His words stopped my entire world. Scorpio couldn't be allowed to find Port Azure. She couldn't. What would all those fae do? Would they have enough time to get people underground? Were there enough rooms for everyone? Did we seal the citadel shut? Fear held me in its deadly grasp, turning me cold.

"Where is Locke?" I asked, still in step with Aspen. Lenore, a face I was most welcome to see, joined us in the hall, falling in step with us and dozens of other soldiers as we made our way to the front line—the main gate.

"Locke is with Lennox. They were in town when the first blast happened," Lenore supplied for me. That's right, the memory came to me. He told me today he was going to try to run some errands in town, including checking on the progress of Eldan's space personally. He shouldn't be far, then. I should be able to get to him once I got outside. As if on cue, another rumble shook the ground. I barely kept my feet as I climbed the stairs with determination pushing aside my fear and doubt.

"Has this ever happened before?" I asked as we reached the ice atrium. Aspen shook his head—another sign of how dire this situation could become if it hadn't already. "What must I do?"

"Don't die," Lenore said, gripping her axes as we emptied out of the packed icy atrium and into the square. I scanned the area, looking for a flash of dark hair and sapphire eyes. Armored bodies had begun to assemble in earnest. Civilians unable to fight had either boarded up their homes, or were now being ushered inside the safety of the citadel. Downstairs where they would be undoubtedly safer. But for some it was clearly too late. They closed the shutters and barricaded themselves inside, hunkering down for the fight. Even the breeze held off, adding to the tension of the moment, as if awaiting to see the plans the Goddess had in store for us. Another shockwave—much stronger this time sent several fae to their knees, low screams sounding around me followed by a hush as we awaited our fate. With the gate closed, many were barricading it with whatever they could find. Wagons, haphazard pieces of wood or iron, even an old steel workbench was thrown into the mishmash. Aspen spoke, interrupting my desperate scan for Locke. Where was he?

I observed as orders were given, and a structured force began to take shape in a matter of mere moments. Companies of archers gathered into place, sword bearers gripping their weapons in front of them. Squad leaders took their places on rooftops, anywhere they could get a good vantage point. The number of fae running into the Citadel had dwindled but not stopped. I prayed that everyone would be safe. The square, usually so busy and cheery, was filled with a seas of soldiers, each taking turns between fear and ferocity.

"Have you heard of a mindspeak spell, Lark?" Aspen asked me, regaining my attention. I shook my head. I could guess its function by its name though. "Well, you're about to. Vanneck!" Aspen called to a fae nearby I'd not yet met. Vanneck, as Aspen had called him, shot over, his long, armor-clad legs eating up the distance in no time until he was next to us.

"Yes, Lord Aspen?" Vanneck's tone was so earnest, and I could clearly see the puff in his chest, his eagerness to prove himself. It would have been sweet if not for the precarious situation around us. I swept my gaze along each face again, still looking for Locke. Where could he even be?

"Please perform a mindspeak spell on Lark and me." Aspen looked at me beseechingly. "Locke is coming, but I need to know where you are. Locke will kill me if anything happens to you." I grimaced at him in response.

Vanneck nodded, gesturing us to join palms. "Are you ready, milady?"

I nodded as I brought my hands up to theirs, not sure what was about to happen. Vanneck traced delicate runic symbols on my hand, mirrored on Aspen's. A small, murmured incantation of the old language began as he traced. Whole magic. Old whole magic. That was interesting. So maybe whole magic wasn't as lost as I'd thought. The moment he completed the design, it lit up in bright white light. So bright I had to look away for the flash.

"Now we can communicate silently and over some distance as well. At least for a few hours," Aspen said. But his lips didn't move. It took me half a second to realize I'd heard his voice echo in my mind. Even stranger was the odd tickle, like an itch I couldn't scratch, not that it stopped me from trying.

Whoa, this is weird, I said mentally, checking it out. Aspen and Vanneck grinned.

Don't worry. You get used to it. Aspen's voice hushed over my mind. I felt his growing agitation, even without our mental connection. He shuffled around, unable to sit still. He blinked at me, as if finally realizing I had no idea what was going on. Is Locke going to be mad at my bonding to our best friend? *Don't worry, it's just a temporary spell.* His voice sounded almost amused, given the circumstances. *I just need to keep an eye on you until Locke gets here.*

And that was when the ice began forming along the gate, a hush falling over everyone. Aspen narrowed his eyes, drawing his sword. Lenore spun her axes over her wrists.

"Here they come."

Chapter Twenty-Three

That hush didn't last. Chaos erupted. Two captains shouted for a volley of arrows to be ready, and in unison they were fired over the wall in a storm of steel, wood, and even ice. I even saw a few light their arrows on fire. Screams from the other side of the wall sounded, making my blood course through my veins. I hadn't seen too many signs of the oncoming attack, just the earthquakes. Which now that I thought of it, had stopped. Did that mean they'd destroyed all of the wards? Did they even need to? Ice still continued to build up along the massive wooden door and I realized what they were doing.

And that I had the power to stop it.

Without thinking further, I left my place on the steps of the Citadel and sprinted, knocking into bodies as I went. I heard Aspen call my name, but I paid no heed, just watching as the ice kept growing, making the wood more and more brittle as it went.

I reached the door, unsure of which magic to use. I put my hands on it, using my earth magic first, to fortify our defenses. The wood of the door elongated under my command, digging deep into the ground and adding stability.

"What are you doing?" Aspen's voice called to me. "If anything happens to you, especially before Locke gets here, it's my ass he's going to shred."

"Kinky," came my distracted reply. I was careful using my fire magic. Its heat wanted to devour everything in its path, including the doors. That took an extreme amount of control to rein in and I knew I couldn't do it indefinitely. But the heat from my hands, the flames thawed the wood, rather than burned it. The effect was instant. The brittleness they were hoping for was gone. As soon as was safe, my earth magic refortied the wood, shedding its earlier brittleness from the cold and heat. The door was stronger than ever. Cheers sounded from immediately around me when they saw what I was doing.

Another volley, another round of screams. But this time the volley came from both sides. Fae on our side went down in heaps. An arrow landed not two feet from me, making me jump. Aspen suddenly appeared beside me. Lenore too, with matching grim expressions.

"When this door opens, all hell will break loose," Aspen exclaimed in warning. Sweat rolled down my neck. "And it will open. But you've bought enough time that everyone who elected to get into the Citadel has been able to safely do so. Well done, Lark."

A series of screams sounded then, but not from nearby. These came from further out and could only be one thing. The creatures of the forest have come to play. That meant two things; they would feast on the battalion sent to kill us, and it would further motivate them to get inside our walls. A screech, far too familiar sounded. Blood Wraiths. I smiled.

"Then I guess Hell's Gate is about to be living up to its name," I said.

A battering on the door bounced me, and the barricading items, off the door. Quickly, we struggled to put them back before the next great boom. My spine chilled, I heard the creaking of the wood, even with my earth magic fortifying it.

"Make ready!" I hollered. "They're coming!"

When the gates burst open, I felt it reverberate through my magic, like a sword being thwarted by stone. It was the strangest sensation, brute force overpowering magic, and it sent me stumbling back off balance. I had only a breath to steady myself before the gate crashed open and the first wave of Crownguards breached the city. The first row fell to arrows in a flurry of blood, steel, and death, but bows needed reloading. And in moments, blades clashed.

It was so much worse than Everwind. If I'd thought that was a little slice of Hell, this was the whole damned cake. I hacked and slashed, hot blood coating me in mere moments. Bodies piled by the gate as we surged forward, weapons drawn. But was it strange; the screams of my victims filled me with a sense of satisfaction rather than dread. An interesting turn of events, and one I was glad of, even if it were surprising. Gone was my guilt for spilling blood. They invaded my home. I would kill to defend it.

They. Would. Not. Win.

It was then, when I yanked my blade back through a Crownguard's throat and felled him instantly, that I heard my name, releasing my heart from a stranglehold of worry. He was safe. Safe enough anyway.

A black fog fell over the Crownguards just out of reach of the front line. Some fought despite it; others cast it a worried glance. They were right to. Because once those tendrils of shadows reached them, there was no escape. It painfully leeched their very life from them, horrid veins of black appearing from their now sunken in eyes. Some of them couldn't even scream through their seizure, though their jaws were opened almost too wide to the point of unhinging.

It was grotesque. But effective. And it gave us a moment to recoup.

Seeing Locke's black magic at work in such a way was like seeing a different side to him. The darker side. The Crowned Assassin, rather than Prince Cancer. Or given the state of the corpses after Locke finished with them, I saw where his other moniker, The Nightmare Assassin, came from.

"Why was it that from the moment I felt those wards shatter, I knew this is where I'd find you?" Locke asked, plunging his blade into the nearest Crownguard's skull. "Sorry I'm late to the party. What did I miss?"

"It's about time you pulled your weight around her, Crowned Assassin!" Lenore grunted, heaving her axes around. One embedded in someone's chest. Lennox, who'd' joined us, deflected a strike aimed at her twin before freezing over another assailant. "We were beginning to wonder if you'd up and left."

"That's a rude implication," Locke said, ramming his fist into someone's face before skewering them. "Unfortunately, traffic was a bit heavy given that everyone was running for their lives." So he'd been making sure his fae were safe. My heart swelled with pride. Of course he had.

He stopped, sniffing the air. His eyes widened. I smelled something floating on the air too. Something ashy, or burnt. I couldn't place it, but Locke could. He had time enough to scream one word of warning before the world erupted in flames.

"Hellfire!"

The word wrought panic to everyone. The first blast knocked me off my feet, my back meeting the brick and mortar and wood of the clock tower. Flames ravaged the stone and masonry. Hellfire. I'd heard of it. Originally from Everday Isle made specifically to fight the Water Court, it was a black, tar substance that once set aflame couldn't be extinguished, even when held under water. It would burn hot enough to melt flesh for up to an hour. I had no idea where Scorpio would have gotten some, or perhaps Ignatius of the Fire Court wasn't as far removed from this fight as he'd let on.

Fire had bloomed everywhere, screams of those afflicted scrambling my mind. My eyes scanned the battlefield. Lenore was up and fighting, but my gut sank to see her covered in blood. Lennox was down, being protected by Aspen while she regained her bearings. Locke sported a massive cut across his forehead, jutting harshly down across his orbital. His eyes flashed blue as his water magic, manifesting as ice, froze several Crownguards to their spot.

I can freeze the water within them.

No doubt he'd be interrogating them later, not that I had any remorse regarding that. Another blast hit, sending me, and several others, backwards several feet and belting us with shrapnel. It was then that I heard the creaking. Ominous in warning, the clock tower chimed out one final time before buckling. I saw Locke then struggling to get to his feet at its base, Aspen fighting not far away.

Aspen! I called to his mind. *Get you and Locke out of there!*

Aspen struggled to reach Locke, but the sheer number of enemies made it difficult. I ran.

I had no idea if I'd make it. I summoned flames to surround me, making fae run away from me rather than toward me. Anyone who dared challenge me joined those who'd already fell victim to the Hellfire. And I had a feeling my wrath burned hotter than even that.

I was running out of time.

The clocktower was crumbling. I dove as Locke tried to run, barricaded by corpses, Hellfire, and debris. I pushed out with all I had, a hurricane coming from my hands. Locke, and several others blew backwards, out of harm's reach just as the clocktower connected with the ground, crushing all who were unlucky enough to be in its wake and dividing the square into two halves. I myself came far too close for comfort, my screams being cut short by a rock colliding with my head.

For a moment, one blessed moment, there was silence.

But the screams of the dying punctured it with ease, stabbing at my mind like angry, gnashing teeth.

How did this happen? I asked myself over and over as the tears began mixing with the ash and blood on my cheeks. Massive amounts of debris from the clock tower made it impassable, walling me with my half of the soldiers from the rest of the fight. Fire burned everywhere, the Hellfire melting the very stone it had stuck to, new fires rapidly spilling from them. Black smoke poured into the air, choking out the sunlight and casting everything in a dreary, ominous glow, lit by the Hellfire. Worse, ash rained down, dusting the clearer cobblestone in fine black powder.

How did we get here?

My head spun, looking at but not processing the dead littered along the street with cloudy vision. Others ran by, magic and screams hurtled back and forth. Explosions sounded occasionally, spewing more debris and desecration.

I shook my head to rid the ringing in my ears. I would be dead on the ground before I allowed anyone the chance to break this place. Or its fae. It took longer than it should have, but I finally staggered to my feet, just in time for a Crownguard to finally notice me and rush me.

I smiled viciously. For the first time, I was not prey defending myself. I bared my teeth at my would-be assailant.

I had become the predator.

Port Azure would not fall. Not while I still drew breath defending it.

Lark! Aspen's panicked voice screamed into my mind, bringing me back from the void. *Are you okay?*

Yes. I answered him as my steel caught my opponent's. I used the same move on him that Aspen had most recently taught me, wrapping myself behind him and slitting his throat. *Are you and Locke okay?*

Thank fuck. His voice broke a bit. *I'd been calling and calling, and you didn't answer. Locke was about to have a meltdown, but I think he can feel you still.*

But he's okay? My heart felt like lead in my chest awaiting the exact words I needed to hear.

Yes. We both are. Thanks to you.

There are a lot fewer of these bastards, I seethed, dispatching one more. *What's going on over there?*

Locke and a large number of warriors we still have are fighting hard, but their numbers are beginning to dwindle. A scream sounded from behind me. What made my blood chill is that it was well beyond that battleground on the square.

Crownguards had gotten through.

I'm going to tie up some loose ends, I told Aspen. *Stay alive.* I could almost feel his pride at my tone.

You too, Little Bird.

I strode out to the center of our area. Our side was quickly destroying any remaining Crownguards from our side of the debris. But my stomach remained in knots hearing the chaos just beyond the clocktower's corpse. *Be safe, Locke.*

I found a large rock, stepping up to it to see everyone who still remained. Heaving my sword in the air I cried out, "Rally! Rally all!"

I didn't expect them to listen. Not to someone who wasn't their commander. Certainly not to me. But they did. They trudged over to me, looking dirty and exhausted. It was then that I finally saw Lenore and Lennox, both looking proud as they watched from their places to my right.

"We're not done yet." I divided them into two groups. One half to stay and kill anyone not from Port Azure who managed to climb over the heap, and the rest to comb the streets for stragglers. "We can save this city. Tonight, we wash the streets in the blood of those who thought they could keep us down."

It was a subtle thing, watching hope grow. It blossomed before me as fae looked to me, filtered in around me. I watched as apprehension and fear gave way to inspiration. Gave way to what could only be respect. Something I never in a million lifetimes thought I would be on the receiving end of, something that very nearly had me collapsing under the weight of my gratitude.

The most amazing thing happened then. They raised their weapons with mine, raising them to scream a war cry that I doubted the Goddess herself would have ignored. "To arms!" I finished, my voice finding every fae in the courtyard, sending the groups scattering with a mighty roar.

Lennox and Lenore approached me, ready to fight.

"Stay here," I said to Lenore. "If any unlucky bastard climbs that wall, you'll end them." She grinned, sickeningly malicious.

"Fine," she said. "I hope I get a little more action. Maybe I'll see if I can't climb that," I almost shook my head. My favorite little psycho.

"Lennox, you go down the other street. Between the two of us, and our backup we'll have the place fixed up in no time," I said, keeping my voice optimistic. She nodded her assent, leading her group down one road into town, while I headed for the other looking for a fight.

Running through the streets of Port Azure, I saw many things. One thing I wasn't prepared for was the sight of a small child, no older than seven years of age, breaking away from the relative safety of his home to rush to the still bleeding corpse of what could only have been his father. The pleas of his mother and siblings fell on deaf ears as he wailed for his father to wake up in a heart wrenching display of emotion that hit far too close to home.

I saw myself in his shoes, at such a tender age, no less. I knew that trauma all too well and my heart crawled up my throat as I approached on sprinting legs. He shouldn't be out here. It was too dangerous. My stomach soon followed my heart when I saw the glint of steel, a Crownguard come out of hiding, his bow trained on the little boy and another on his family behind him. What was worse was his mother had no idea, her sights solely trained on the sobbing little boy as she pled with him to come back to the cover of the house.

I screamed as the arrows were loosed, hurtling through the air towards their targets. In desperation, I used my water magic, forming a massive ice shield between the Crownguards and their targets with not a second to spare. The arrows each gave a *thwack!* sound as they embedded themselves harmlessly in the ice.

The little boy paid no mind, wailing pitifully over his father's corpse. I sucked in a breath, steeled myself and ran to him, ready to fend off any additional attacks. From the shouts, I gathered the fae fighting alongside me had taken care of the situation.

"Father!" the boy's tiny voice pierced my heart as he thrashed in my arms. His tear-stained cheeks wet my shoulder as I rushed him to his mother, who held the door opened for us.

"Thank you," she cried, enveloping both the boy and me, leaving me feeling unsure of what to do. "You saved us. Thank you, My Lady."

Drawing back, I set the boy in her waiting arms before slipping back through the front door.

"Close the door and barricade it. The fight isn't over. I'll fortify the door from my end." I started out the door before turning to glance from her to the small boy in her arms. "I'm so sorry." The boy nodded, fresh tears welling as I closed their door. I conjured my earth magic. Wood strengthened its hold, vines creeping over the door, making it entirely inaccessible. They would be safe. At least for the time being.

It felt like eons had passed by the time we had cleared the city. The sun was getting low and the lighting was getting dim. I was covered in dirt, blood, and Goddess only knew what else. We'd taken down far more Crownguards than I'd thought possible. How had this many escaped us? Guilt gnawed at me seeing the damage they'd done, the bodies they'd left behind. By the time Lennox's faction had met up with mine on the far side of town, the streets did indeed run with blood. Bodies from both sides littered the streets, the cause of immense sorrowful cries amidst the cries of victory. A bittersweet moment.

But Port Azure still stood. At last.

How is it going, Aspen? The city is clear on our end. I spoke from my mind to Aspen's. It was odd at first, hearing flashes of his thoughts as he fought, but it was a welcome relief. Him fighting meant he was alive.

Locke and the others are taking care of the last of the Crownguards. His immediate response brought further relief. Tangible relief. *I'm tracking a faction I saw sneaking around deeper into the Dead Forest toward the mountains. I think they were the ones tracking the wards, so I'll be taking them out. I'm not leaving even one of them alive.*

Be safe, I told him. *If something happens, bail. Come get reinforcements,* I whispered to Aspen's mind. I felt him laugh, rather than heard it, like something fuzzy tickling my brain.

This is your first battle and you're barking orders at me? You realize I give the orders, right? His exacerbated tone was far too pronounced to be real, taking away any sting his observation may have had.

Just be safe, idiot. I reached the main square—or what was left of it— with my lungs heaving for breath. It seemed that it was possible to cross the mountain of debris that once was the clocktower because there was a whole new wave of corpses that hadn't been there when I left. Unless they found an alternate way in. Lenore's smile was grim in the firelight, her blonde hair taking on a macabre orange glow as she twirled her axes.

"Looks like you've been kept busy," I said upon reaching her. I had to narrow my eyes against the heat of the Hellfire. Together we surveyed the death around us, careful not to look any one body in the face too long. Assuming they had one still. Stone had tumbled around us, melting under the flames, but thankfully it had largely been contained.

I marched over to the clock tower debris separating me from Locke, determined to find a way across when Lenore grasped my arm.

"What in the Goddess's name do you think you're doing?" She spun me around to face her. "You're safer over here. Locke made us all swear to look after you, and you want to run into the fray again?" I glowered at her.

"If Lennox was over there and you were here, would you let anything stop you from getting to your sister?"

Lenore looked away from my question. "That's not the point—"

I cut her off before I heard her point. "Locke is over there fighting and I'm not standing around waiting. Aspen might need backup too. You can join me, or you can stay here, but you will not stop me."

Lenore dropped her hand but the fire in her eyes stayed burning as brightly as ever. It reminded me of the first day I met her and I had punched her in the face. An absurd thought now.

"Lark?" her voice was chilled enough to make me shiver. I turned my head towards her. "Yes?"

"Don't try to be a fucking hero."

I didn't know how to respond, so I said nothing as I turned on my heel to climb the bones of my home.

Chapter Twenty-Four

Reaching the top of the massive pile of rubble was a struggle. More than once I stumbled upon what once was someone's limb, and I had to keep from retching. Especially when I'd seen some of the faces in the debris in Hell's Gate on multiple instances. I'd trained with them. Looking out over what could only be called a warzone, my heart sank.

There was nobody living. For several feet, the Dead Forest came alive with fire, as were several spots alighting the walk below. Screams sounded beyond, not all of them fae. I wondered if the flames would keep the creatures of the forest at bay. Corpses littered the area, most Crownguard, some heart wrenchingly not. Approaching the gate, the sounds of blades and spraying blood reached me, the coppery scent of blood and acrid scent of death mixing in the air with the thick smoke. I turned to follow the sounds to Locke, but the flames roared up to drive me back. Gritting my teeth in frustration I called my magic to me.

"Aspen?" I asked, driving the flames away from me. Driving them out from between me and the battle still raging beyond me. More abruptly than I'd expected, I broke through, my lungs grateful for the cleaner air. Ahead I saw what I'd sought; warriors surrounding Crownguards, maces and swords held high. While the battle continued to rage, it was clear the Crownguards were fighting their last. But then I saw Locke, fighting with all his grace and fury, carving his way through each opponent like it was child's play. He forged a path of destruction with a ferocity that even gave me pause. But the only thing I could think about was the immeasurable relief that nearly knocked me from my knees.

He's okay...

He's okay...

He's okay...

But why hadn't Aspen responded? I tried again, wondering if perhaps the spell had worn off, but the sparkly static feeling in my brain hadn't diminished. Indicating the link between us was still very much open. I felt my chest constrict as I weighed my options. Looking to my left, the rebels had everything in hand. I could go and get Lenore, but it had taken me nearly twenty minutes to climb that wall and Aspen might not have that kind of time if he were badly hurt.

Assuming he was only hurt...

I chided myself for such thoughts, even as my unease grew with every passing moment. Aspen didn't have time for me to get reinforcements. A distant scream rent the air. A plume of crows screeched anger into the sky as they burst forth from the trees. Not far into the Dead Forest. In the direction of the mountains.

The direction Aspen said he'd been going.

"Lark?" came a familiar voice I couldn't place. A small group of fae carried a tarp full of wounded. Vanneck helping to escort those who were unable to defend themselves.

"Vanneck! Perfect. Aspen is in trouble." I now had everyone's attention. "Listen, Vanneck, come with me. You," I pointed to the next fae in line behind Vanneck who glanced at me wide eyed, "tell Locke where we are when you get back over there. If we're not back soon, send reinforcements. Something else is going on and time is of the essence." Everyone nodded, not questioning me. Vanneck stepped towards me.

"What need do you have of me?" he asked, fist over his heart. Such a blatant show of respect I had no words for. I stuttered a moment from the direct impact his gesture had on my heart.

"I need you as my backup. I can't reach Aspen, we need to save him. But we also need to see what threat we've missed. Every set of eyes matters."

Three more fae joined in from escorting the wounded. Three more sets of eyes. Aramis, Daltan, and Lamir. Together, we turned and moved towards the mountains. One fae who volunteered, I bade to stay behind with a message to Locke. To let him know where we were going, knowing he'd catch up quickly.

We kept our pace quick as we dared, but moving along on silent feet. I kept using my magic to search for danger nearby. But with them taking out the wards, I had no doubt they had instruments to counter things like my talent. It meant we couldn't entirely rely on it. Something was deeply wrong. I could feel it in the tension of the air. There were no more birds. No signs of life. Nothing stirring anywhere around us. My mind went back to Poplar Hollow and I prayed there were no Blood Wraiths nearby. That was the absolute last thing we needed right now.

Periodically, I mentally called out for Aspen again. I never once got a response. The static of the mental bond still active and feeling like fizz on my brain, almost mocking me with how noticeable the silence was. We now stood on the edge of a large, muddy clearing that felt wrong in every way. The hair on my neck rose. It took a few moments, but I at last saw part of what had bothered me about this clearing. It was death.

The meadow had a slight incline away from us. My eyes found a smattering of blonde hair in the mud. A bun I would recognize anywhere. Fury and sorrow gripped my soul with equal measure, sending my heart into my throat.

Aspen.

He was just laying there, the rest of him concealed in the mud. From here I could make out shapes that could be additional bodies, but it was impossible to tell in the grey and green of mud and moss. Worse, I couldn't tell if he were bleeding. I couldn't see anything beyond the fallen fae, but it didn't matter. Discarding all sense of caution, I rushed forward—only for strong hands to pull me back by my forearms.

"Lady Lark, it's too dangerous. Let them go, instead," Vanneck whispered, signaling with his hands for the others to scout ahead. There was no yielding in his voice as he grasped his bow and notched an arrow. His eyes traced the perimeter, assessing for the smallest of movements.

"Wait!" I hissed. "Let me scan the area!" But my plea fell on deaf ears as they moved forward on quick and silent feet into the meadow. It was so quiet. Not even the air about us stirred, and the barren trees themselves stood on ceremony with watchful eyes. The sound of the blood rushing through me filled my ears as I opened my senses once again. Whoever was out there, whoever had hurt Aspen...

Their death would be slow and painful. I would personally see to it. Never mind the Nightmare Assassin. I would become so much more.

Wrath fueled me when I felt the presence of an entire battalion just on the other side of the meadow. I didn't know where they came from, only that they were there now and they would not be leaving this forest alive. I walked calmly into the meadow, my magic at the ready and a snarl on my lips.

"Come out, bastards," I shouted into the fray, bringing all eyes to me, seen and unseen. "Your fate is calling."

No sooner had the words left my lips did a volley of horrific looking arrows fire at us. Aramis, Daltan and Lemir used their water magic to form ice barriers, but it wasn't necessary. I knocked them all aside with a torrent of air.

"Is that all you've got, Wannabe Princess?" A dark voice taunted me only seconds before the group of particularly nasty Crownguards crested the hill. The one who spoke—the leader, I presumed—sneered at me in a mixture of revulsion and haughty amusement. "A little wind?"

They charged then as a unit, their yells mingling with ours as they rushed to meet us. All too soon, screams left me cold. I turned in time to watch serrated blades tear through Aramis, Daltan, and Lemir in the most particularly cruel and savage thrusts. I screamed in dismay, sending them all back several feet, but I was too late. Blood soaked the ground I stood on.

I had sent them to their deaths. All of them.

Vanneck still stood a bit further back from the fray, now screaming his own rage and ruin as he fired shot after shot, felling the enemies one by one. I alone now stood between them and Vanneck. We two now stood alone between them and Port Azure.

If they wanted a little wind, I'd give them a little wind. I called my magic to me throwing in my rage, my guilt, my sorrow for Aspen into it, unfettered for the first time ever. And the results terrified even me. I screamed as it ripped through me in a torrent, power flowing into every facet of my existence.

The sky darkened overhead, so much so it looked nearly dusk, though the hour remained early. I glared at the advancing Crownguards, now fewer in number, thanks to Vanneck. I screamed my fury, flames erupting between them and where I stood. I knocked aside another wave of arrows, my wind getting stronger with each beat.

A little wind, he'd said. I grinned wickedly at him. He didn't look so confident now. I'd show him a little wind. The Crownguards fired water at my flames, trying to thwart them. Instead, it turned to steam before raging once more. I'd never forget the look of pure panic in their eyes when they saw I would not be an easy target.

The wind picked up again, howling in my ears. I could barely stand against it. All other sounds faded into the background. I was vaguely aware that I wasn't in control of my magic anymore. It flowed out of me unchecked in a torrent unlike anything I'd ever done before. White hot magic. It poured out of me as I screamed into the void. Even Vanneck, who'd crept up beside me, gave me a look of trepidation.

I was unleashed.

The panic they saw when they looked at me faded in comparison to the utter terror they donned when they saw what my magic had wrought and the devastation that lay ahead. My grin widened. What I had summoned was straight out of Hell itself.

The earth quaked. The wind, now violent in its fury, screamed and tossed my hair around my face. I braced against it as I gazed upon the horrifying combination of wind and flame, the likes of which I'd never before seen. Flames spiraled from the ground, twisting violently to the sky. Trees were uprooted to the right of me and were sent flying in any which way. Those that weren't tossed precariously on the wind, caught flame. And those flames quickly spread. If nothing else, this was an unmissable signal for help a mile high. Barreling towards the battalion was a—there was no other way to describe it—a fire tornado.

Flames licked their way up the howling wind tunnel, though remained heavy at the base, carving a path of destruction in its wake. There was a moment of collected horror when all eyes watched as the fire twister came closer towards my enemies before me.

The screams of the damned echoed in my ears as I watched several of our oncoming attackers be ripped from their feet and violently sucked into the heart of the tornado. I wasn't sure what happened to them after that, but I did see a charred body part—an arm?—thrown not far away. The smell of burned flesh and melted armor was strong in the air and I fought a gag. I scented the heated blood from the fire, the very smell of it crawling across my tongue and threatening to choke me. Vanneck stayed loyally by my side ending all those who dared to get too close as I continued to add fuel to my hellish creation. And after it went through once I spun it around for another pass at the soldiers it missed the first time. This time my face held a sickening smile as I watched those who'd butchered my friends, my soldiers. I said I would be so much more.

And I was.

In this moment, I had become death.

In this moment, I doubted even the Grievling himself could stand against me as I watched enemy after enemy fall victim to my magic.

Chapter Twenty-Five

I saw Vanneck's eyes widen and his mouth part on a warning. A shout was all he'd managed when pain erupted in my stomach, hot and fiery. Unyielding. My breath left me as my knees threatened to buckle. I looked down in confusion, the shock beginning to find me. An arrow had embedded itself past my armor and secured itself tightly into my abdomen. *How*? I couldn't understand. Dragon scale armor was supposed to be impenetrable.

My diaphragm spasmed, unable to draw enough breath into me, though my lungs now begged, burned for air. I felt panic begin to take over my thoughts, my heart thrashing against my ribs on a quest for air. I sank to my knees, the soft mud welcoming me. In the corners of my vision, orange flame warred for dominance against the growing dim. My tornado had run its terrifying course and faded into the ether. Thick black smoke choked those who remained. A smug smile lifted the corner of my mouth at the death and destruction I'd wrought. They'd hurt Aspen. They'd hurt Port Azure. They'd spilled the blood of the Court of Rebels and for that, they paid with their lives.

Death and flame surrounded me, making me wonder if I had passed beyond the veil into Hell itself. Bodies in various states of dismemberment littered the meadow. Some charred to blackened coal. Some had been tossed and left to rot at odd, grotesque angles. I had no doubt that pieces of these Crownguards were all over the forest. When the calm returned, the Blood Wraiths and the soulless would feast well.

Vanneck grabbed my wrist, pulling me from my thoughts to my feet, dragging a weak scream from my throat as the arrow found new flesh to tear. He slung my arm around his neck, his arm supporting me under my shoulders, he half carried, half dragged me back the way we'd come as the flames and smoke moved in on us.

"We need to leave. Right now." Vanneck's voice was tinged in desperation he'd tried so hard to hide, but he couldn't conceal his widened eyes or the panic that kept growing on his face like a looming shadow. "Just hold onto me, Lady Lark. Don't let go of me." Using his water magic with his one free hand, he suppressed the flames around us to clear a path to hasten our passage out of here.

But the shouts of the damned chilled my blood despite the raging heat. I struggled not to scream as the arrow embedded itself further into my flesh, pain exploding at the site.

"Bring her to me!" I heard that same voice from before yell into the flames. Answering grunts and calls sounded. I didn't know how many had survived, nor how, but we needed to up our pace.

"I'm so sorry, milady" Vanneck said as he dragged me further, making my grit my teeth against the blinding pain. The flames began to cool. I didn't have to look to see why.

They'd begun dousing the flames around us, in a bid to cut us off. We'd start left to find our path blocked. Turn right, and someone else was there with a wicked grin. With a sinking feeling of dread, I began to realize I wasn't making it out of this meadow.

The one who'd spoken—the leader—appeared to our immediate left, only a few paces away, but it was the feral grin on his face made my spine tingle in warning. He sauntered as if he hadn't scarcely survived my magic. He was entirely charred on one side of his face, and that would scar horrifically. His eyes were as cold and menacing as a blade, completely at odds with the oppressive and unrelenting heat around us.

Vanneck changed course, scurrying to get us to safety. I pulled from my well of magic, summoning more fire to buy us some more time. But my magic hit a wall. A very familiar wall. Glancing from the arrow to the fae stalking us filled me with a growing awareness of what had happened. I tried again. And again, frustration making me want to scream. Powerless. I was entirely powerless. Something I swore I'd never be again. My panic became tangible now as I grappled with it for control.

Vanneck seemed to understand this new urgency and picked up the pace, making me cry out again. I could feel the blood pouring freely from my wound now, and I was getting dizzy. The end of the meadow was so close. But I knew with growing certainty that I wouldn't be making it out. My legs were already giving out.

I stopped my feet from moving further and I let go of Vanneck, pushing him weakly towards the exit. My message was clear: *run*.

"Go," I whispered. "Get Locke. Run. Please." My voice broke then as I looked to what remained of my fallen best friend in the mud. Or at least into the smoke in his direction. My voice shattered for him. "Get Aspen home after they take me. Don't leave him here to rot."

"Milady, I won't leave you!" He pulled me along, but I shrieked in agony, unable to move now. The arrow was digging and finding new places to shear to pieces. With tears in my eyes, I fell back to my knees. I was only slowing him down. We both knew it. He didn't need to die today. I had far too much blood on my hands with Aramis, Daltan, and Lemir. I couldn't watch Vanneck die too.

"Run!" I shouted at him, chords of panic and desperation coloring my voice. Grim understanding, cold and heavy in my gut, gave way to an overwhelming sense of dread. I looked at him with a smile. His silver eyes were conflicted, hesitating. "Run. Please don't die. Run! That's an order!" My words carried above the tension, above the death, above the flames. Above everything. Vanneck looked stricken as my words landed. I nodded one last time, the fae finally beginning to catch up to us, if the cooler air were anything to go by. He turned to flee. I heard the telltale whiz of an arrow I knew was directed at him. I refused to let him take it.

I launched myself upwards. The pain lanced through me now was all I knew as the second arrow pierced my shoulder as I let out a horrific wail. Vanneck looked back for only a moment, but I saw the promise that lay there. The visceral promise of help in his eyes. Of retribution. I didn't have the strength left in me to urge him on. I fell again to my knees and this time I knew I wouldn't move again. Vanneck placed his fist over his heart, a silent gesture of honor I didn't deserve before running. My eyes filled to the brim as he raced away, dodging arrows and magical assaults.

He escaped. Thank the Goddess.

Pain was all I knew. My shoulder. My stomach. Two arrows had me on my knees. I couldn't even collapse without making my precarious situation worse. Darkness threaded into my vision, shapes became less defined. My head went fuzzy. For a heartbeat or two, nothing made sense. I couldn't tell what was happening. Soft footfalls caught the edge of my attention and reattached my tethers firmly in the present moment. I saw a shadow looming over me, and I knew he was there. The fae with the awful, grotesque smile. I didn't have to wonder what they were going to do. I knew what was in store for me.

He was going to deliver me to Queen Scorpio.

Our planning would have been for nothing. There would be no coming back from beyond the Veil. My heart should have been pounding, but I feared I'd lost too much blood. It sputtered weakly in my chest. I coughed, the ground below me turning redder as I did so. I didn't even bother to wipe my mouth as blood dribbled down my chin. Maybe I'd get lucky and I won't make it long enough for Scorpio to kill me.

I heard the faerie responsible for the attacks barking orders. I heard the word "heal" somewhere in there, but I was too far gone to pay attention. It took all of my strength to remain on my knees and remain conscious. I smiled grimly. Vanneck had gotten away. My death would be avenged. I remembered the wrath in Locke's eyes, the severity in them when Abel betrayed us. Or when those bandits attacked me. Those deaths would be easy compared to what Locke would do to these Fae.

"Not sure why you're smiling, sweetheart. We won," he said, his breathing tickling my ear. I bit down on a retort he'd never hear as he ripped the first arrow out of me. Coppery blood welled in my mouth and overflowed down my chin. I spat at him. About the only thing I could do as I swayed on my knees. "And to think they revered you as some wannabe princess. Pathetic."

I raised my gaze to his, tipping my head back. I let him see my defiance. My rage. Though I was sure he also saw the exhaustion in my eyes.

"This pathetic wannabe princess created a fire tornado that took out most of your battalion single handedly. You look like shit. You were nearly bested by a girl. I bet that sits just splendidly with you." I meant for my tone to be mocking. The words were, but they came out with the breathlessness that came with blood loss. My head had begun to feel weird, like it was stuffed full of cotton. It was getting harder to string two thoughts together.

"The keyword you used is *nearly*." He grinned widely now.

"You'll all die. When Locke comes for you. Or when you lose control of me. I wonder how merciless I can be." The four fae that remained alive laughed. Only four… And not one of them looked in good condition. All of them had suffered severe burns and lacerations that no doubt hurt like a bitch. One, the hulking massive one, was burned on his face through to flashes of white under the charred flesh. His cheek bone. I shuddered.

I doubted he'd even feel it right now. I doubted he ever would again, even with magical help.

Good.

"By the time he gets here, we'll be long gone," the leader continued. "He doesn't know where we're going. And he won't know how to track us. And besides, dove, What's to stop us from doing the same thing to him that we did to you?" He nodded to someone behind me. I wasn't able to repress the scream as they tore out the second arrow from my shoulder. The sadistic madness in his eyes told me he loved seeing me in chains of agony.

"You were able to best someone with minimal training with her magic," I forced out. "Months. You've had centuries of training, so I'm glad you feel good about yourself for this supposed win. When Locke is done with you, you'll beg for death. For mercy. And you'll find none. But you'd better pray for mercy if you lose control of me."

He looked at me, but for the first time, I saw a tiny crack in his look of perfect self-assurance. "Shut the fuck up, wench." He made a sick show of grabbing the arrow still lodged in my stomach, of wrenching it around just to hear me scream, before pulling it out, savagely. Blood welled in my mouth. "Heal her," he said to his friend. "We can't have her dying on us just yet. But don't heal her too much."

"What's the matter?" I spat blood on the ground. "Did I strike a nerve? He'll be here any minute." He laughed. I tried not to lean into the sweet relief of the healing magic as someone funneled it into me.

"Have you not noticed we're no longer in that meadow?" His grin stretched wide as he took in my surprise. I hadn't. How had I not noticed? He presented what I could only assume was a shortport—a portal in a glass sphere. I swiveled my head around, taking in new but similar surroundings. We were now at the edge of the forest.

The other edge of the forest.

"All four of you will die," I said. "Locke isn't called the Crowned Assassin for no reason. He'll track us down. You'll see." My words and tone were brave, even if in my heart I had no idea how he could possibly find me.

"Can someone shut her the fuck up already?" a nasty tone came from behind me.

"Do you know his other moniker?" I asked, turning towards the one binding me. "The Nightmare Assassin. I'll give you one guess as to why."

"Gag the cunt," came the heated response of the leader, who was now the recipient of much needed healing.

"You're never not going to look like a melted candle," I snickered. "I may die, but you'll always repel everyone with how hideous you are. You didn't even have to be cursed." He glowered at me just as a piece of dirty, scratchy linen was in my mouth. It tasted awful. I refused to even contemplate what this rag had touched since its last wash. They weren't gentle when tying it, knotting my hair into it hard enough to make my eyes water on reflex.

They'd healed me exactly enough. I could move, but still in significant pain. I was in no danger of dying. Not yet anyway. But I still had several wounds that could, and likely would get infected. I was not in good shape.

Two of the four, whose names I'd gleaned from their conversation were Brashan and Eron, tightly gripped under my shoulders and hauled me to my feet.

"Walk," the massive one named Eron seethed, pushing me forward. I dug my feet in. He punched the arrow wound and I screamed through my gag, my body sagging. His eyes lit with delight. "Walk or be dragged. It's your choice. You can walk like a princess, or be dragged like a prisoner."

I seethed at them in response. I hoped my toxic stare gave me the message I wanted to convey: *Fuck you.*

"Suit yourself. It's going to feel like a long way to the carriage." He said it in such a way that the hair on the nape of my neck stood. I could clearly see the carriage, as they'd called it. It was a glorified flatbed pulled by two hulking oxen. Room for several to sit comfortably up front, but in the back...

Where I had no doubt I'd be going, lay mounds of thick chains.

I reared, digging my heels in in a feat of strength and resistance. My gut was met with another resounding fist, the impact reverberating through my entire body, driving the fight right back out of me.

"Stupid cunt," he said smugly.

I didn't have it in me left to fight. I had to bide my time. Wait for when the opportunity presented itself. Or Locke.

My father had always taught me never to expect to be saved. By anyone.

You should always expect to save yourself. Be your own hero, he used to say. Now all my hopes lay in my soulmate. The darkest hero of all. Locke, I knew, would slaughter everyone.

And for the first time, I knew I would cheer him on as he did so.

I bled the entire way to the cart. Their enjoyment of my pain made me bitter, but they'd successfully hollowed me out, removing all the fight I still had. Their demented enjoyment of my suffering may end up being their downfall, as they didn't seem to realize the trail of blood I was leaving for Locke. Or perhaps they didn't care for some reason I'd yet to discover, but that thought was every bit as bad of a blow as their punches were, leaving me tasting copper. I rejected it. Locke would come, and that thought was the only thing keeping me from caving in within myself.

Time and weather had worn the planks of wood that made up the wagon I was chained to. My restraints were heavy iron, and so short were the chains I was barely afforded any room to maneuver, forcing my broken body to suffer every punishing blow of the bumpy road beneath me. My bindings bit cruelly into my flesh with every slight movement, leaving swollen, chaffed paths in their wake along my ankles, wrists, and neck. If that weren't bad enough, it was open to the harsh elements and I was only given a small blanket to reduce my teeth chattering to a level that less annoyed them.

There was a moment I was able to retreat into the depths of my own mind, away from the pain in my body. It wasn't much better in there. Guilt and grief came at me in waves, battering my heart into submission until it drowned over and over again. Port Azure. Locke. Aspen.

Aspen...

"Lark..." A whisper across the edge of my mind reached me. So feather soft I could almost convince myself I'd imagined it. Almost. But that voice brought breath into my aching lungs. That soft voice of my best friend was deafening in the silence of my mind. I shuddered a relieved breath.

"Aspen...? You're alive...?"

"I mean, I don't feel very alive, but here we are." Even in my mind his voice took on a dry, weak edge to it. *"Where are you?"* Oh Goddess, it was so good to hear his voice in my head. He still sounded weak. I choked on a relieved sob, tears finally falling. I forced myself to remain quiet and not attract attention. *Aspen is alive!* I wasn't sure how to process that information.

"I'm not sure. Out of the forest in any case. I'm on a cart." I looked around me, with what limited range I had given the chain, and seeing nothing but open farmland around us. I relayed the information to Aspen.

"Locke is coming for you. He saw your fire and came running. He was held up by more Water Court fae. He finally ran into Vanneck who told him what happened. By the time he got there, you were already gone. He's back out and tracking you, however he does that. Are you okay?" I almost laughed in relief. Aspen was alive. And so was Vanneck. And Locke was coming.

"Not going to lie, Aspen, I've been better." I tried for a little humor in my tone, but found my voice dry and pitiful even in my own head. I could feel my best friend's dismay and guilt. *"This isn't your fault, Aspen. It's my own. I'm so sorry."*

"Don't be sorry. You were amazing. Vanneck told us all about what you did. I'm proud of you. We all are. Locke wanted me to give you a message," Aspen said, his pride clearly coming through in his voice. *"He says the bastards that took you will pay, and pay dearly. He says not to give up. And he says he'll see you soon."*

"Tell him I love him. Just in case."

"Shut up. You can tell him yourself when you get the fuck out of there." I could hear Aspen practically growling, his consciousness angry and desperate where it brushed mine. It felt less solid than it did before. Like a once vibrant paint faded by time and weather. His voice sounded thinner, like it was disappearing on the wind.

"The connection is fading. Stay strong, Lark. You'll be home soon."

"How much of home is left?" I was almost afraid to ask.

"Port Azure still stands with minimal losses. We did it, Lark. Locke even has a few people to interrogate when he returns with you."

"Bloody psycho." I couldn't help the grin, despite myself. *"Tell Locke to be careful. They have magic suppressant in their arrows!"*

"Well that seems a bit excessive." His voice was nearly gone, like listening to someone hollering while you're underwater.

"Tell me one more time that Port Azure is safe?"

I never received an answer.

A few minutes passed in silence. I felt the final fading of our link now, whether due to time or distance, I wasn't sure. Maybe it was both.

But I was alone. My mind was only my own once again. I wrapped my arms around myself and curled into a tight ball. The tears came unbidden. I was sure if my captors saw me, they would think I was weeping in despair. But they'd be wrong.

Tears of relief flowed over my cheeks silently. Tears of hope. Joy. All our friends were alive. Port Azure remained standing, Scorpio's forces were kept at bay. And while they had me, I knew in my heart that they wouldn't have me for long.

Another blanket was heaped onto me, something I'd never reveal my gratitude for. It was actually warm and would fend the cold off well enough that I might not freeze entirely.

"You know," Brashan's smug voice levelled my way, "the words 'thank you' would really suffice in this situation."

I felt my jaw drop. I grappled with my thoughts, trying to put a name to this feeling. Appalled. I was appalled. And outraged.

"Thank you?" I spat, my tone dripping in condescension and disbelief, matching the glare forming on my features. I opened my mouth to further my beratement, even with my still chattering teeth when he cut me off.

"Yes, like that. But this time try sounding more earnest and sweeter and less like you want to saw my head off with a bone cutter."

"I can think of a couple heads I'd saw off with a bone cutter," I said in a saccharine voice. "I'd start with the one lowest to the ground. I'd love to let the melted candle look go on a little longer."

He maneuvered himself into the cart with me. I side eyed him, my face still pressed into the wood. He punched me square in the jaw. White exploded behind my eyes. My jaw felt loose. I thought he broke it.

"Now then," he said as his fingers caressed my ruined cheek. "That's a good girl. Quiet and still. Just the way I like them." Revulsion levelled through me as I scooted back as far as I could. Which wasn't much. "Oh, don't worry. Before we deliver you to Pisces, we'll have our fun. But it's too cold out here for that nonsense." I knew the relief I felt would be short lived. He wouldn't force himself on me now, but would later.

Locke, please hurry.

When I opened my eyes, night had fallen.

I had no memory of falling asleep. Now my body ached so fiercely, I thought I could die just from this pain. In odd contrast, parts of me had become numb from prolonged compression. I was roughly grabbed and set down by the fire, chained to three different stakes, all in different directions to keep them all out of my reach. I laid on one blanket, which did nothing to repel the freezing cold or hardened winter ground, and the warm blanket was thrown on top of me. I faced the roaring fire, my limbs at last finding warmth.

It ached as my body came from its numbness, but it was a blessed feeling I would take any day. It made me miss my flames. I tried conjuring them again. Nothing. That wall of magic suppressant stayed stubbornly in my way.

I stared at the flames as the four of them chattered. Listening to their conversations, I now knew their names. Their leader with the melted face was Bashan. Eron, Cylix and Manson, were his little minions. Eron was the massive figure, whose face still dropped despite the healing. Cylix, the impulsive healer, and Manson, the psychopath who enjoyed torment the most. I often found his gaze sliding my way with sadistic glee. I knew rape wasn't on his mind. Whatever he wanted from me, it was definitely something even sicker. It was him that would 'give me my medicine.' Dosing me with magic suppressant was like a drug to him. He took great pleasure in the administering of it, stabbing me with another arrow.

I struggled vehemently against him, but it only seemed to fuel him more. Worse, it seemed to turn him on. I couldn't even gag at the thought over my screams as the knife edge of the arrow tip burrowed its way into my the tender flesh of my abdomen, a twin to the still healing one already. I felt like I'd lost so much blood, I didn't know how I could still be bleeding. If I looked, would my abdomen have a river of crimson? Or would so little be left that it ran nearly pink?

That was my first day with these monsters. I wasn't sure how they expected me to survive another. Frankly, I wasn't sure I wanted to.

Locke, my mind whispered into the void. *Where are you?*

It wasn't that I doubted he would find me. Quite the opposite. But I was beginning to doubt he would find me in time.

Chapter Twenty-Six

I lay bound to the wagon once again when my eyes opened. I blinked, trying to ascertain how I'd gotten back to the wagon. I remembered the fire. The hard ground. Had I been so exhausted they'd been forced to carry me to it? I was surprised, though what more likely happened was that they couldn't wake me, but it may not have been completely from exhaustion. My wounds fired to life and to the forefront of my awareness, refusing to calm or go to the background of my mind. They hadn't healed me much after my latest dose of medicine.

And I knew another was coming.

So with nothing better to do, I waited for an opportunity. Anything. I listened as they bickered. It was clear they knew I needed an alchemist. Magic alone wasn't healing me enough, and I needed to make this trip alive or they wouldn't be paid.

"Prince Pisces is waiting for us in Bleak, Brashan," said whichever one was driving with impatience. "This is the fastest way to Bleak. She won't make it if we turn south here."

"The map says this is the fastest route!" Eron's deep grumbling voice agreed. I was surprised that idiot could spell the world map let alone read one. Brashan heaved a frustrated sigh.

"The fastest route," he scoffed. "To where, the morgue? Do you want to die? Because that takes us through some dangerous territory. Fae disappear through Thousand Lakes. You want to be one of them?" He looked at each of them in turn, each of them shrinking away from him. "I have no desire to be overwhelmed and torn apart by kelpies, and Goddess knows what else is in there. They say something old escaped extinction, but nobody has ever survived checking," he said in a mock ghost-story voice. "So no, we turn south. We've gone through a lot of trouble and lost a lot of fae capturing that stupid bitch and keeping her alive for Prince Pisces."

"Turning south then," huffed Eron with a degree of indignation.

Bleak. Pisces was meeting us in Bleak. I wished I still had that mental connection to Aspen. He'd find a way to get the information to Locke. Wherever he was. I felt the pull of the cart once more accompanied by the rhythmic clopping of synchronized oxen hooves. The sound had become the only soothing thing and I held to it like a lifeline. My eyes closed again, despite the whisper of warning in my brain.

"Wakey, wakey, little wench." Manson's overly excited voice stage-whispered in my ear as he shook my shoulder. My red rimmed, exhausted eyes blinked open. Manson kneeled over me with a sadistic grin. Fear instantly prickled my spine as his smile widened. "It's time to take your medicine." His eyes lit up with relished malice as the arrow in his fist came into view. He laughed as he followed my gaze to it. It even looked like he'd sharpened it, the end narrowed to a sickening needlelike point. I felt around desperately for my magic, still running into the wall the suppressant had provided, as strong as ever. I had a feeling they were dosing me extra, whether as a precaution, or because they had fun with it, I wasn't sure. I strongly suspected it was a mix of the two. Even with their healing, I wasn't sure I could last with a third stab wound. I cringed back as much as my chains would allow me with a hiss.

"Fuck you," I spat through clenched teeth. I inwardly cringed at how weak and breathy my voice sounded. How dry. My lips were chapped and cracking from dehydration. My body was fighting an infection on multiple fronts. I'd be shocked to make it to Bleak alive. I coughed, blood once again coming up. The wounds in my abdomen clenched painfully and I gritted my teeth. I almost didn't see Manson's hand come up to sting the side of my face. It stole my breath with how much it hurt. My brain rattled inside my skull, but it remained intact enough that an idea began to form. Manson was psychotic, but he was also impulsive and volatile. And his friends were distracted for the moment.

"Amazing how a little thing like you still has spunk." He made a grand show of rising back to his feet and towering over me. "You're in chains, wounded, no magic, and you think you can say shit like that? Are you brave or just stupid?"

I spat blood at him, grinning as his eyes lit in fury at the insult.

"Because you could never have stood a chance against me otherwise," I said. "I destroyed your battalion on my own. You four got lucky. You'd never be able to take me in a fight, even without my magic and you know it. That's why you're keeping me like this. You're scared of me, and you're right to be." He laughed, the dark tone sending shivers down my spine. This fae had no compunction to keep me alive. I doubted he cared about getting me to Pisces. I wondered if he even cared about getting paid. The mad glint in his eyes told me all he lived for was blood.

"Those are bold words. Too bad you'll never know."

"Fuck you, you coward!"

He hit me again. I cried out as his fist connected with my festering wounds in my stomach. I curled inward on myself, my face into the wood to hide my silent scream. "You're only proving my point" I said as bitingly as I could manage.

"I'm going with stupid. Someone smarter would have realized that shutting up was better for you."

I smirked into the wood of the cart under me, knowing I was getting under his skin. The only distraction from the festering pain in my abdomen and shoulder.

"Cunt," I scathed, further baiting him. I turned to glare up at him. He came for me again, but this time I was ready. The chains didn't allow for much movement, but they did allow for enough. I caught his arm as it sailed towards my face, and with my other hand pushed his fingers straight back like Aspen had taught me. I felt the knuckles buckle, the snapping sounds like music to my ears as they shattered. He screamed in pain. In extreme, indignant anger.

I heard shouts from somewhere behind me and knew the other three were crawling out of whatever place they were relaxing in. I heard the thudding of heavy footsteps getting closer as Manson continued to scream obscenities and threats, mostly for my death. I smiled at him. But I couldn't block his heavy studded boot as it came and connected with my face. I didn't even have time to scream. Agony, hot and intense, brought bile to my throat. My vision went black, and then rainbow dots of vibrant color stormed the dark curtain of my vision. I'd felt something snap. I was afraid to even try to touch it, certain that my cheekbone had fractured.

"What happened?" Eron yelled as he approached, his boots stomping towards me, sounding like an ominous countdown.

"The cunt broke my hand!" Manson hissed through clenched teeth.

"You kiss your mother with that mouth?" I tried to say, but the left half of my face wouldn't move properly. My eye wouldn't even open. I didn't have to touch it or look at it to know my jaw was broken.

"You want me to kick your face in further?" he roared, towering over me and making a show of displaying his chunky boots. I smiled sweetly, at least on one side of my face. Which in all honesty, probably looked like a grimace.

"Pull yourself together, you fucking idiot. She's playing you like a fiddle," Eron said, turning his massive figure towards me. One kick from his boot and I was pretty sure the entire bone structure of my face would be rearranged. I didn't dare look down. I held his gaze as he approached me. His meaty hand wrapped itself messily in my hair, holding me where he wanted me. I didn't even bother to struggle, knowing full well nothing I did was going to help my cause.

"I think someone needs to take their medicine," he said to me, a slow grin rising to his lips.

"Get fucked," came my hoarse whisper. His grin widened. His eyes were the only hint of the dark thoughts swimming just below the surface. And I realized my mistake. My mouth really was going to be the end of me. Something Eldan and my father had warned me countless times.

"Oh, that could be arranged." He nodded to his friends who snickered. They utilized the chains on my wrists and repositioned me on my back as Eron got the arrow ready in his massive fist. I was too weak to struggle as much as I'd wanted, having had used everything in breaking Manson's hand. Eron stood over me with a sneer. "This is going to hurt, pet. Are you ready?" I kicked out as he approached further, my foot grazing a very sensitive area of his body. He swore and shoved my leaden legs aside, his knees between them. I wasn't even entirely sure what was going on, but all I knew was I wasn't sure I'd survive whatever it was he was about to do. Whatever punishment for my outbursts today might actually succeed in breaking me. I couldn't even try to hide the very real fear rising in my chest. He raised his fist. I closed my eyes, flinching away from the pain I couldn't even yet feel.

None came.

Instead, there was a guttural scream that raised in pitch followed by three more screams, scattering birds around us in a flurry. My eyes snapped open, my heart thundering in my chest, slamming hard against my ribs. My eyes fell upon a gruesome sight; Eron looked down at the blade playing a bloody game of peek-a-boo through the right side of his chest, his hands absently trying to dust the blade off as if it were a piece of lint. I watched as his eyes dimmed. The silver steel embedded in his chest winked at me through the crimson staining it. Blood pooled over me, but for once it wasn't my own.

From my vantage point directly below Eron and from the sheer broad size of him, I couldn't see *him*. But I knew he was here. He made it.

Locke.

My body sagged in relief at the thought. This would finally soon be over. I choked on a sob that pained my ruined cheek. He'd found me.

Eron fell to the ground, though he squirmed. He looked like a giant slug as he struggled to breathe and writhe away from his assailant, but to no avail. Locke stood over him as dark and inevitable as the dusk, watching him sputter and beg for mercy. He then turned his attention to Brashan, who screamed as he clashed blades with Locke.

It was then that I saw the Nightmare Assassin come out to play. Time stopped as I saw Locke for the first time since I'd left to save Aspen. My heart throbbed and my breathe felt stuck in my chest at the sight. Long ago, before I'd left Poplar Hollow, I might have felt a dash of pity for these monsters. But not now.

Locke's eyes, normally a piercing blue, had darkness rimming his irises, a strong indication of significant dark magic usage. I remembered how Pisces and Scorpio also had them, how Scorpio's eyes looked like jade and onyx mixed together. Flashes of burning blue meshed and collided with the black, warring for dominance. One thing they both agreed on: wrath. Wrath unlike anything I'd witnessed before, even in Locke. His black hair shone in the bright sunlight, giving him a halo effect. If ever there were such a thing as a guardian angel sent by the Goddess, this was it. Or perhaps Locke was more the avenging angel type.

Lennox and Lenore came from somewhere to my right screaming a war cry as they charged the two still holding me in place with a ferocity that had them backpedaling. They dropped the chains that bound me with a loud clatter next to either side of my face. They stumbled away from me, falling to their feet and regaining them several times as Lenox and Lenore fell on them.

"Sorry we're late to the party," said Lennox with a grin.

"Locke took off as soon as he scented your blood, and with his Zodiac speed, he got to the fun first," Lenore chimed in, her curved blades quickly disarming and carving up her opponent and making quick work of him. "Oh, chains. I love when they're kinky." She grabbed a chain from near my arm. I didn't miss the look of concern as she did so. She had him wrapped in chains before he could even beg for mercy. The other faerie had began inching towards the quiver of arrows as Lennox fought him, using ice spears as well her weapon.

"The arrows," I said weakly, my throat dry from dehydration. "Magic suppressant." Lennox nodded as she heard me, cutting him off from the arrows and any other weapons that may have been close to the cart. Lenore had secured the other prisoner before advancing on him with her sister, cutting off any escape well and truly.

"Oh, I'm going to enjoy this," said Lenore, licking her lips as she gripped her axes. She swirled them expertly in her hands before attacking. Manson was no lout though. He'd crafted a sword from ice, fended off their attacks, and even managed to get a few in of his own, even with his broken hand. Not that it seemed to faze the sisters. They used their small stature to their advantage, keeping just out of reach, using their speed to dance around him, wearing him out. Just like Aspen had taught me. Locke could do that. I'd seen him do it. I'd watched him pirouette paths of destruction before, the bodies piling up while he'd made it look like a dance.

He didn't bother with that this time. He instead seemed to be slowly carving his opponent, Brashan. Like a cat playing with a mouse, he let Brashan fight for his life, which he did valiantly, though ultimately in vain. Every time Locke got the chance for the killing blow, he didn't take it. Instead, he stabbed an arm, a leg, or between vital organs so his mark would bleed but not die. And every time he did so, he'd elicited a Goddess awful scream from him, but didn't down or kill him. He let him fight. He let him cower. Plead. Beg for his life. And then finally, Locke slowly slit his throat, smiling that dark, vicious smile as he watched the life slowly leave Brashan's eyes. His scream was cut off by the most horrible gurgling noise, blood bubbling out through his throat. It was awful. And he deserved it.

I should have felt something other than appeasement. Or satisfaction at his death. I tried to; I wanted to at least on some level, but I couldn't, and I didn't know what that said about me. But at the moment, I couldn't bring myself to care.

Lenore and Lennox had of course secured their final opponent, Cylix, who now lay sniveling and groveling at their feet. Locke strode quickly towards me, his long strides carrying him to me in short moments. His stoic and taciturn expression cracked a little as he took me in; for a moment, there was no anger, only crushing concern. He dropped to his knees before me, whispering my name in reverence. Tears formed then, of relief, and of pain. Now that I was safe, all the pain my body was in finally revealed itself in full blast.

I was in agony.

I choked on a sob, my whole body trembling with relief knowing Locke had saved me as he removed the remainder of my restraints, the key having been retrieved from Brashan's corpse.

"You made it. I was beginning to worry." I smiled on one side of my face, which turned into a pained grimace. One Locke noticed. I wasn't sure what I looked like, but if it were anything like what I felt like, it was absolute hell. I coughed, pain ricocheting through my jaw, and abdominal wounds. Blood dripped from my mouth again, but at least I wasn't choking on it this time. Locke's eyes flashed, his violent fury renewed in earnest as he took in my condition.

"I'm so sorry I took so long, love." He lowered his voice to that of a whispered vow. "Make no mistake, Lark, there is nowhere they could have taken you that I would not have found you." His voice was gruff with barely controlled rage as he pulled me gingerly into his arms and settled me against his chest. I groaned and winced as the movement irritated my injuries. "Before we make their lives a living hell, we need to get you healed. But we know that's not something anyone here is good at, but anything is better than your current state."

"What?" I tried to sound flippant. "You don't approve of my new look?"

"I'm relieved to see you haven't lost your sense of humor. But admittedly, seeing you half dead isn't my favorite."

"What is?" I felt the warmth of his hands as the tingle of magic flowed into my wounds. It was startling at first. Jarring. But with a little coaxing, I was able to relax into him. As he tended to my wounds to the best of his ability, his voice softened a bit, to a voice meant only for me. My body began to feel heavy, the exhaustion and trauma catching up with me now that I was safe.

"I love the you that's full of life. Vivacious. Your eyes light up when you see someone or something you love. Or the fire in them when you're challenged. The fully alive you. That's what we need to get you back to. Get back to feeling yourself. I need you with me, love. Always. When I'd heard about what happened from Vanneck, I nearly ripped the earth itself apart at the seams to get to you."

His words calmed me as his magic did its work. I breathed in the scent of him—the scent of male musk sliced by the sharp scent of pine—seeking and finding comfort in him. His voice picked up in candor as his magic seeped below the skin. I could feel the warmth knitting my skin back together from the inside, driving away infection and greatly reducing the pain. It was a slow process, one that took a lot of concentration on Locke's part. He perspired a little at the effort. He wasn't as good as Aspen—and especially not Eldan—but the pain was lessening. I was so grateful for a reprieve. I could finally expand my rib cage and draw in a full, deep breath into the depths of my lungs for the first time since I'd been captured. A time that had felt like eons.

"So if it's quite alright with you, I'm going to try to take at least some of the pain away. Because seeing your wounds, I can see how much you're hurt. I felt how afraid you were before I got to you. And it makes me want to rip those remaining bastards into fucking shreds. But I need them alive. I have some questions I'd love for them to answer."

"No objections on my part. To any of that." My voice came out a little breathless, despite the fact my lungs no longer burned for oxygen. No. I was breathless for an entirely different reason. He smiled against my good cheek before planting a kiss there. He planted another on my jaw before burying his face in the crook of my neck. Goddess, I had to smell horrible. I flushed, feeling embarrassment. "How did you find me?"

"Black magic has its uses," he said darkly. I realized I had bled the entire trip just about. And those oxen, for how hulking their stature, had proved they could pull a cart and long way at a decent pace for a long time. Locke having to find me and keep pace over such distance was impressive.

"Thank you for rescuing me. I'm sorry it was necessary," I told him, my voice sounding a bit more like myself. He held me tight a moment. Just a few heartbeats. The world fell away, and the only sound was our breathing.

"Lark, you saved Aspen's life. And so many others. But make no mistake," his voice hardened as he addressed me, his eyes glaring unwaveringly at me, "I'm furious you didn't wait for me. I would have gone with you!" He huffed a humorless laugh. "Lark, don't you understand that I will always come for you?" He kissed my neck once more. "I love you. And those that hurt you are going to suffer dearly in a moment."

"I've always wanted to watch you work."

"Well, today is your lucky day." He grinned into my skin, his breath tickling me. "Do you want to kill them yourself or do I get the honor?"

My answer didn't surprise me. The lack of remorse did. "They're mine."

We all jumpstoned back to Port Azure. Locke carried me, despite my protests. His hands clamped around my shoulders and knees any time I tried to stand on my own.

"I just lost you for a whole day," came his gravelly voice as he strode towards the infirmary. "That day felt like an eternity, so forgive me if I need to hold onto you and feel you near. Just don't move."

So I didn't move. I relaxed into him, my eyes falling closed. I didn't even remember coming home. I only meant to close my eyes for a moment, but my body had other ideas as my mind fell into the void of exhaustion and unconsciousness.

Chapter Twenty-Seven

I was floating.

I was absolutely aware that I was dreaming.

There were voices. Some were familiar. Some weren't. Some were panicking. Some weren't.

I couldn't figure out why there was panic. Everything felt so good and calm. My body was buzzing, like static given form.

Waves of euphoria continued crashing over me. I still felt the panic around me, but I was detached from it. Completely free.

I must look like hell.

I sure felt like death warmed over. Underneath the calm. I felt like I was on the edge of an abyss, looking over a ledge to disaster, but hadn't yet fallen.

But then I did.

I hadn't even opened my eyes yet, and my body was screaming. My joints were strung tight, my backside was stiff and sore from not moving, my face felt like it had been rudely rearranged by a hammer, and every muscle in my body, including those I only theoretically knew about, were voicing their displeasure.

Apparently, it wasn't my muscles that let out a groan, if the dry croak I felt in my throat were any indication. My eyes fluttered open, having to blink a few times to dispel the blurriness and the feeling of glue on my eyes. The smell of astringent and sterilizing agents dancing with the scent of medicinal herbs that told me Eldan had been here recently. The hospital wing. I was still in the infirmary.

My memories came crashing back to me in waves of horror and fear. A blink. The white of the infirmary disappeared, and instead of the soft cot I was laying in, I was back on the unforgiving wagon, chained like an animal. The excruciating pain of the arrows gouging and tearing into my skin, delivering the magic suppressant, a scream building in my lungs—

When a hand covered mine ever so gently. A voice in my ear. A girl.

"You're safe, Lark. You're home. I'm here. Listen to the sound of my voice. Come back to me. Breathe."

Breathe. I could do that. She bade me to breathe in time with her. I followed her instructions and all at once, the chains melted away, and the hospital returned to my vision. My heartbeat began to slow. Home. I was home.

"Lennox?" My voice sounded raspy even to my own ears. I heard Lennox say something to someone, and within moments had water with a straw ready for me. The water may as well had been from the Goddess's own hand with how it soothed the raging desert in my throat and revived my senses.

"Open your eyes again, Lark," Lennox's voice floated down to me. I wasn't even aware I'd closed my eyes. I followed her instructions to see her and Lenore staring at me with varying degrees of concern.

"There she is," Lenore's cat-like smile emerged, masking the concern I'd seen there only moments ago.

"Hey," I sat up, my own strength leeching back into my bones as my awareness crept back to me. I glanced around the busy infirmary. Healers were running around erratically trying desperately to keep up with the sheer number of beds, each with a patient. Several cots were on the floor, the room was so crowded. Everyone from my vantage point was alive, at least, I noticed with relief. The sounds of the injured began to fill my senses. "What happened? What's wrong? Where's Locke?"

It was so subtle. So subtle I almost missed it. The twins shared the briefest of glances before their smiles took over.

"I just sent someone to go get him." Lennox crooned as she smoothed my hair back in a comforting gesture. "He has a bunch of emergencies to deal with and he just left here about five minutes ago. He's going to be so upset he wasn't here when you woke up."

I opened my mouth to say something when Eldan peeked his head into my cubicle with a smile that was somewhere between relieved affection and sardonic exasperation.

"There's my favorite patient. How are you feeling?" His hands slid over where my most severe injuries had been with a practiced, feather-light touch, palpating for residual injuries. He frowned at my flinch when he examined my face.

"I feel fine." Mostly. "Drowsy. But I'm not in pain."

Eldan's frown deepened, bringing his brows down. "Are you sure?"

No.

"I've had better days, but honestly, I've had worse."

Eldan nodded as he rummaged in his kit for Goddess only knew what. His silence said it all; he remembered the days of patching me up. He absolutely knew I'd been in worse shape. He'd saved my life a handful of times. "I'd really like something to eat. And to stretch my legs." I hoped I wasn't pushing my luck. His sharp, assessing stare followed by a long pause deflated that hope.

"Lark." It's amazing how one word held so much connotation. So much warning. What I couldn't understand was why. Where was the danger?

"I'm fine. Honest. I just want to go find Locke, and survey the damage. Sleep in my own bed. That's all I have the energy for." I shot him my best placating smile, the one that often got me out of trouble and was rewarded when his face softened.

"Fine. But come back if anything changes. And don't overdo it." At my disgruntled expression, he continued in a slightly admonishing tone as he looked for something else in his kit, bottles clanking from the impact of him rifling through them. "Lark, whatever magic suppressant they gave you, it was awfully potent and they overdosed you. Your body is still suffering the aftereffects of it." He made a sour face as he turned, braced my shoulders in a firm , and bade me look at him. He sighed, his voice softening. "Your body is going to have a hard time with magic for a few days and it'll be unpredictable. No training, no magic. Nothing. You need to rest. Your body's injuries have been healed to the best of my magic's ability. But frankly, my dear, there are limits when your injuries were as severe as they were. You know this. You remember your father's wounds." I did. His leg had been in tatters and magic never was quite enough. "Your body needs to heal the rest of the way on its own."

"Okay."

"Okay, what?" He looked at me expectantly, one eyebrow quirked.

"Okay, I'll take it easy." I swiveled my head to look at Lennox and Lenore, who were doing their best to look anywhere but at us, but I saw Lenore biting down on a smirk at me being scolded. "No magic. No training."

"Fine. Go. We need the bed." Eldan tossed over his shoulder, presumably to get additional supplies to ready to bed I was about to vacate. Lennox took one shoulder while Lenore took the other, supporting me to my feet, despite my objections.

I tested my weight on the floor, happy to see my legs were shaky but functional. They held my weight, even if I weren't up to my usual routine. The twins released their hold on me, letting me stand on my own.

"Where is Aspen?" I couldn't believe I hadn't asked yet. "What happened to him?"

"It's about damned time you asked," said a heartachingly familiar voice behind me. I looked up to see Lennox and Lenore grinning at me, before parting to reveal Aspen approaching from behind them. He looked great, considering the last time I'd seen him. Clean, but the dark circles under his eyes spoke of the weariness that dragged at him. I noticed a slight limp that made me frown. "I'm fine," he said, following my gaze. "Thank you, Lark, for saving my life." Finding strength I wasn't aware of, I launched myself at my best friend, earning a heaved sigh of exaggeration from Eldan. My best friend was alive. He was really alive. I didn't dream his voice in my head. I ran the short distance to him, throwing my arms around him.

"I saw you in the mud," I whispered, the image flashing back into my mind. "I thought you were dead." His arms curled around me, much like the big brother he referred to himself as before answering.

"I know. But I'm alive and well because of you. I owe you my life."

"I'm sure I won't hold that over your head indefinitely," I teased. Eldan cleared his throat, drawing everyone's attention.

"If your reunion is quite done, Lark, I still have a lot of work to do on you before you can join Locke in his quest for information." He side eyed all of us. Lenore grinned in a way that I think was supposed to look innocent. I couldn't stop glancing between them all in a strange mix of relief and disbelief as we made our way to the exit. My family was all okay. We all made it out. Port Azure still stood proud.

We had won.

Chapter Twenty-Eight

Lennox pampered me while Lenore went to find Locke. She fed me until I was stuffed, sat me in a pile of pillows and blankets in a deep chair by the fire in my rooms, and generally fussed over me, even pouring me a bath. I told her I was fine so many times it felt like a mantra.

"I know but..." She paused, her nose wrinkled. My face heated with mortification as I all but dove into the bathing room.

"Don't even finish that sentence!" I said at the same time as she softly said,

"You stink." At least she looked contrite. So much so we both laughed. A little chuckle at first, but then we saw how hard we were both trying to hold it together and the laughter tumbled out of us unchecked until our abs and cheeks hurt.

Despite being in so much discomfort, despite everything, this small moment was precious to me. Eldan and my father had only ever been who cared for me. I doubted I would ever get over having an angel like Lennox by my side. We chatted animatedly through the dividing wall in my bathroom whilst I scrubbed blood, layers of grime, and Goddess only knew what else from my skin. I could feel the disinfectant on my skin, most likely everyone's best attempt to keep me hygienic while I was unconscious, but there was only so much they could do. The hot water felt heavenly, my sore muscles heaving a collective sigh of contentment. By the time I was done, I felt like I'd lost a few layers of skin and I was bright pink from scrubbing, but I looked and smelled clean. Comfortable.

Lennox filled me in on a few details that I missed as I dried myself off and dressed. Port Azure still stood. Some buildings and part of the wall were damaged, but there were more than a fair share of casualties on our end. We'd lost eighty-six fae. Not all of them soldiers. And with so many wounded, we could only pray that another attack didn't come. Because we might not be able to fight back a second wave.

That explained the panic I remembered feeling when I was dreaming.

And then Locke hurried through the door. His eyes flared wide as they finally landed on me. Took me in. He didn't even try to hide the relief on his face.

My heart hammered in my chest. I didn't think I breathed. I didn't even notice as Lennox discreetly exited the room. I stood in a jumbled mess of pillows and blankets that gathered around my feet. I took a step towards him, only for the blankets to bind my legs and send me sprawling messily towards the floor. It was only by the grace of Locke's enhanced speed that kept me from meeting the ground in a painful heap. His arms tightened around me, bringing warmth to my very soul. I didn't realize until that moment how frigid it'd felt. How scared and alone until I felt his warmth against me.

"There you are." He chuckled. "If you wanted to be in my arms, all you had to do was ask."

"Nah, this plan worked just fine, thanks."

He chuckled against my neck, and I wrapped myself around him. It was then that I broke down. My entire body shook like it was trying to summon an earthquake. My eyes filled with tears and a lump formed in my throat. Every terror I'd held at bay the last few days came crashing down on me in that moment.

"Lark." Locke tightened his hold on me, protecting me, before placing his arms under my shoulders and knees and lifting me as if I weighed nothing, and held me to him. I sobbed. I sobbed for myself. For what I'd endured. For what I'd done. For Port Azure, and those who didn't survive. I sobbed for that little boy, who was now without a father, a pain I knew only too well. I sobbed, because I was so afraid Locke wouldn't get to me in time. It was all going to be over.

"I was so scared, " I admitted out loud, surprising us both. He took a deep, shuddering breath before he spoke. And when the words came out, they came out a low growl. A sound that reminded me of the calm before the storm. Of standing on the edge of a cliff, watching the storm roll in.

"I know, love. I'm so sorry you were. I'm so sorry I wasn't there. I promise you here and now, anyone else who dares to touch you will be given an even worse end than those fae received."

I rejected the magic of his promise immediately.

"You can't make promises you can't keep." He glowered at me, his eyes sparking in the fire light. If I hadn't known any better, I'd say there was a hint of defiance in his eyes. "I have to die by Scorpio's hand," I reminded him. His eyes darkened.

"Plan B, remember?" he replied in a smooth voice. I didn't reply. I wouldn't let a false hope bloom in my chest for a plan B. For a saving grace. Our saving grace came at the end of a lightning strike and we both had to come to terms with that. "Stop that, Lark."

I blinked. "Stop what?"

"Stop trying to say goodbye. Don't you give up on me. Because I'm not giving up on you." He put me down and grasped my cheeks with both hands, staring intently into my eyes. I could almost see the depth of his soul, bared just for me. "I'm not letting you go," he growled. I narrowed my eyes as intuition danced with some kind of strange sense of awareness within me. The determined set of his jaw, the steely will in his eyes, the proud set of his shoulders...

"Don't be a hero, Locke. Please. If you're planning something, don't you dare leave me out of it." Locke remained quiet. His body tense under my fingers.

"A hero," he mused, mulling the word over on his tongue. The whole time his fingers busying themselves in my hair. "I've never claimed to be anything of the sort."

"That wasn't an answer."

"I'm continuing to look for a plan A." He held his hands up in innocence. "I have some possible leads I'm following up on, but that's it."

"Some leads?" I didn't know what to do with this information. Was he just not going to tell me? Curiosity and anticipation warred with something that felt an awful lot like anger and anxiety. "What kind of leads?"

He opened his mouth to speak just as a loud, urgent knocking sounded at the door. Locke crossed the room in sure, steady strides to peer out at whoever had intruded on our conversation.

"Forgive the intrusion," said the old fae with a withered face. He glanced at us both in kind before returning his attention to Locke. "The meeting is ready, Highness. All are in attendance. They've sent for you."

"Then let's not delay." Locke nodded before turning back to me. "I have some business to take care of. Rebuilding, planning, mass funeral pyre, that sort of thing." At my face his voice softened. "Why don't you relax? Perhaps spend some time with Valor? I'm told he missed you." At the mention of Valor's name, a pang of guilt and longing stabbed me. It had been some time since I had been out to see him. Lennox had informed me that during the attack the stable had remained completely unharmed and by some miracle, not a single horse was harmed. But it was increasingly hard to shake the feeling that he wasn't telling me something.

Again.

I chastised myself. No. I trusted Locke. I loved him. And he loved me. But suddenly the weight of my engagement ring was nearly too much for my hand. I forced a smile and a nod.

For now.

"I'll see you later?" I was surprised I kept my tone so light.

"Of course, love. Be safe. Relax. Enjoy yourself. You've more than earned it." He fixed me with one last unreadable expression before slipping through the door and closing it softly behind him.

"You too," I muttered to the empty room, hanging my head in what felt eerily similar to defeat.

He was hiding something from me. Again.

It took longer than I would have liked to get into clothes suitable for the barn. My body was slow going still, hampered by the stress of healing and the remnants of the magic suppressant. I had tried to put the fire in my hearth out before I left but I was left frowning. It was usually so simple, just a swift turn of my wrist. But my magic flowed and sputtered sporadically, and the fire swelled a moment before returning to its dim flickering flames. I sighed and doused the fire with water from a vase, trying not to feel powerless.

Like I used to be.

It was funny. I'd lived my whole life without magic, and now I was struggling to go a few days? It felt like a small, and now integral part of me was distanced, but not quite separated.

My walk to the stable consisted of me trying to summon each of my elements in kind, and having varying degree of success. My flames sputtered uselessly in my hand before fizzling out of existence altogether, I accidentally almost doused myself in water when I conjured a torrent from my palm, my air magic didn't respond at all, and my earth magic stirred, the grass rooting up from between the cobblestones of the walkway greening briefly, but stopped after I walked by.

Port Azure wasn't in one piece, I noticed as I took my first steps out of the Citadel. Not by a long shot.

A few buildings had been razed to the ground and lay in smoldering ruin, along with part of the wall, though the rebels had done well to erect a new wall quickly. They had also cleared much of the rubble away. But the scars of battle were impossible to erase.

Several buildings just on my route to the stable had been burned, some to the ground. Shattered holes had been punched into the cobblestones, making them difficult to pass in places. But the worst was seeing the stains of dark red that hadn't yet faded. I'd seen more than one family attempting to scrub the blood from their porches, walkways, and streets. Some wounds just wouldn't yet heal. Scores of fae were helping to rebuild the wall and their homes. My heart hurt for them.

"My lady!" A child's voice called to me. I spun to see the little boy I'd saved before. The one who'd lost his father in the battle. He ran towards me, his mother behind him struggling to keep up with her baby slumbering in her arms. "My lady!"

I smiled at him, relief flooding through me. They were okay.

"Hello. I'm so glad to see you're unharmed." I glanced up as his mother reached us. "I'm so incredibly sorry for your loss." The boy's smile faltered, while his mother's turned sad. Her red rimmed eyes were glassy with tears she'd yet to shed.

"It's because of you my son didn't have to follow my husband beyond the veil." She tugged me into a one-armed hug with the baby cooing between us, leaving me jerking in surprise. The boy joined in, his small arms wrapping around my legs. "Thank you, my Lady."

I didn't move. My heart thrashed in my chest for several long moments before I remembered to bring my arms up to them. So few others have ever put their arms around me, let alone a stranger, the feeling leaving my skin tingling and my cheeks heating.

"My name is Lark," I said at last, my voice wavering with a hint of emotion, the tip of the iceberg really. We broke apart, and I tried not to move as awkwardly as I felt. "Please just call me Lark. What are your names?"

"My name is Rilla," the young mother said. It was strange to think of her as a mother to these young ones, looking so young herself. My age, possibly even younger. But one look in those eyes told me she had seen many things in her short years. Many things to prove that wisdom comes at any age. "This is Isla...." She gestured to the infant who was now wide awake and smiling at us. "And this is Edwyn,"

"I'm so glad the three of you were unharmed, Rilla, Edwyn, and Isla," I said. "Dare I even ask, are you doing okay?"

Rilla shrugged. "Delran goes to the pyre soon." Her head hung low, and her shoulder sagged under the weight of her grief. My heart twisted in my chest for her. "May he meet the Goddess in kindness."

"May he meet the Goddess in kindness," I whispered.

"My Lady, if I may be so bold as to ask a question?"

"Of course. Speak freely with me, Rilla. What can I do for you?"

She glanced around nervously before leaning in. "I understand if you can't do anything, but do you know when we're getting more rations of food?" My blank stare must have surprised her.

"I'm sorry, could you elaborate? I just woke up from the infirmary wing this morning. If you could give me some more context, I might be able to help you."

"You mean you didn't know?"

A mounting sense of unease grew within me. "Know what?"

"The fields were destroyed in the raid. All of them. We have no incoming crops. We're relying on what animals and produce we have, hunting in the Dead Forest, and rations throughout Port Azure, but we're going to run out soon. We're going to starve if something isn't done."

I looked at Rilla in shock. My hands fisted at my sides, knowing what I needed to do. Sorry Eldan, I'd be breaking my word to him.

"Rilla, would you kindly take me to the fields? Right now,"

"My Lady, I'm so sorry if I've overstepped...."

I placed my hand comfortingly on her shoulder.

"No, Rilla. I'm glad you told me. Take me to the fields, please. And call me Lark."

It was every bit as Rilla had described.

I realized now that I'd never seen the fields that fed Port Azure. Not really. But as I stepped through the portcullis above, I saw them. It was a large, flattened area bordered directly by the Veinfall Mountains, the beach, and the Dead forest. Not massive, but enough to feed the town. Behind us, the wall loomed. Despite the winter season, crops had been growing here with considerable bounty. Locke had mentioned that the fields were just beyond the walls to ensure every fae had room within them. So everyone would be safe. As the population grew, sacrifices had to be made, and Locke refused to let anyone live outside the protection of the wall.

Had been growing, being the key phrase.

I saw immediately the issue that Rilla was concerned by.

Everything was destroyed.

Rows of corn completely flattened and singed. Carrots, potatoes, and other crops destroyed, their leaves nothing but muddy compost.

"How are the fields even growing crops this late in the season?" I asked, not understanding. This far north, this late in the season, the ground should be hard as ice. But I saw beneath the ruination of fire and footprints that fresh soil lay soft and fertile, in direct defiance of the season.

"Prince Cancer had called in some favors with the Earth Court when Port Azure first began. The ground is forever fertile, and crops will grow regardless of weather...." Her voiced trailed off as we assessed the extent of the damage. Plants had withered and wilted from the heat of the flame. Others had been trampled, barely peeking out of the dirt. but several still clung to life. I felt it, like its own aura. I wondered if this were like what Locke experienced when he read everyone's emotions all the time.

"Rilla, stay behind me. Just in case."

"Just in case, what?" she asked, following my orders with a nervous glance. "What are you going to do?"

"I'm going to fix these fields."

I knelt to the ground, burying my hands in the soft dirt. It was surprisingly warm, the soil soft and yielding to my hands, and strange considering winter was here. I tested the bounds of my magic, slowly waking it up. I felt it stir and sluggishly come to life. I also felt a kind of volatility. My magic felt different. Wild. Strong and weak at the same time. Unpredictable, as Eldan had warned. I pushed, sending my magic into the earth below me. *Grow.* I channeled my entire being.

When charging the jumpstone, it felt like I was slowly being siphoned. It felt like I was in control. I could kink the hose at any moment.

This was the opposite.

The ground quivered as I sent my magic into it, as it took hold. My magic sputtered with force violent enough to knock me upward, but the area immediately around me came alive. I grit my teeth and threw my will into it. If I ran out of magic but a lot of the field perked up, so be it. It'd buy Port Azure time to rest before I did it all again.

The earth responded to my call. To my command. Cracks formed in the blackened ground as if I were seeing the wounds of the earth crying out desperately for help. New life clawed its way from these scars and through the charred remains, like little green flames of hope. It was working. The soil shifted and churned beneath them, and the ruined crops began to revive row by row. My eyes widened; I hadn't expected this intensity.

My hands were heating up. I blinked. That was new. At first, the heat was warm and comfortable. But now it was getting incessantly warmer. Painful. I dug into the soft earth, my fingernails fracturing at the effort. My jaw clicked. Green popped up in my vision, and sure enough, row by row, the field came to life.

I could feel my magic swell and ebb within me, but I was no longer in control. It poured out of me unchecked, feeling very much like when I first discovered my magic. When fire poured from me and threatened to consume Locke and me.

Breathe, Locke had said. I had to control my emotions.

Except while my emotions were the ignition to my magic, they currently were not what was controlling it. Trying to grab control was like trying to grab the wind.

"Lark, you don't look so good. Maybe you should stop. I think you've done enough to buy us time...." Rilla's voice crooned from behind me. But I could barely hear her over the thrashing of my own heart. My magic turned even more turbulent, the blistering heat in my hands spreading throughout my entire body. Someone was screaming in my ears. What had I done? Had I hurt someone? Locke had warned me of magical outbursts, and Eldan had told me my magic would be unpredictable for a few days.

I couldn't find it in me to care. Port Azure wouldn't starve at least.

That was when the first cut opened up along my glowing forearm. Then a matching one on the other. Blood dripped down my arm into the soil. I gaped, unsure what to make of this new development.

"Lark!" boomed a familiar voice. A voice that rose above the carnage and the chaos. A voice that normally centered me, but now added to my panic. "Lark, stop! You're hurting yourself!"

"Can't. Stop," I ground out with more than a little effort. I tried desperately to rein it back in. To stop it. But it took off without me. The very magic I'd hoped to save this town may end up threatening it. And it would be my fault. Another tremor in the ground, this one violent. No. I wouldn't let this happen.

"Lark!" Locke was suddenly there. His body crouched next to mine. His hands on my hands. And the trembling stopped. "Take control. You can do this!"

Could I? I felt my body slacken, my mind go fuzzy, but the magic was still firm in its hold over me. I couldn't even move.

"Knock me out," I pleaded through gritted teeth. "I can't—control it"

"Yes, you can. Focus, Lark. Focus hard for me. Find that control and reel it in."

Find that control and reel it in. As if I hadn't tried.

But try again I did. Locke's hands rested on mine when I realized what he was doing. Jumpstones. He'd brought as many Jumpstones as he could carry, and my magic was being funneled off into them, charging them, but also depleting me. I reached out again to the stream of magic within me. Before it was like trying to grasp fog.

In my mind I toyed with it, finding it less like smoke and like something more tangible now. Something I could feel. I grasped it. It blew me backwards, but I held on with everything I had, towing it back in. It resisted, and for a heart-stopping moment, I thought it was going to run wildly out of control again. But this time, it settled and the chaos gave way to something that almost resembled order. Like a storm, the worst of it seemed to be over. It was slow going, reining it in, but my magic seemed to respond to my will once more. Even if it took its time doing it.

Then, without warning, there was a loud snap, and my magic stilled. I heard my name. I tried to respond, but my voice wouldn't work. Green. The last thing I saw was rows and rows of green.

For the second time in a row, I woke up in the infirmary.

I knew by the smell. I hadn't even opened my eyes yet. But when I did, Locke was there. Those were the second and third things I noticed. The first was my head was splitting open.

"Fuck the veil," Locke's voice was somewhere between a growl of discontentment and a breath of relief, "you're alright!" His voice wasn't loud, but my head throbbed nonetheless at the vocal intrusion.

"I'm fine." Even my ears didn't believe my own voice. I sounded like death.

"The fuck you are. Are you insane? Do you have any idea what you could have done? You could've died."

"But the fields are revived, right? Tell me Rilla and her children are okay. Please." Locke slammed his fists on my mattress. When he looked up at me, his eyes were wide with barely dissolved fear.

"Yes, Lark. They're revived. And yes, Rilla and the children are fine. But you didn't need to do that. To risk yourself. Between our rationing and the supplies I was trying to get Aquarius to send over, we were going to be okay until you were well enough to try the fields when your magic was stable. That was the meeting I had to get to earlier."

Shame filled my chest with lead. "It... it was for nothing?"

Locke's face softened. "Goddess, no. No, not by a longshot, love. Make no mistake, you saved Port Azure from starvation. And the whole town saw. If you were trying to ingratiate an entire town, you did it. And as angry as I am, as much as I would love to fucking throttle you," his voice softened further, "I'm so proud of you. And grateful that you saved us all." I hadn't expected that. The throttling part I did. The angry part I did. But the proud and grateful...

My eyes filled with tears, and a single blink sent them running down my cheeks.

"Oh, Lark. No..." Locke's hand stretched out to wipe my tears away. "You did so well. But you could have died. Do you get that?"

"I'm sorry," I whispered, my hands coming up to hold his forearms. "I'm sorry. But I'm also not sorry. This is my home. I had to protect it." My face hardened then. At him keeping this from me. "You should have told me."

"I didn't want you to worry. But you're right, I should have, and for that I'm sorry. But Lark, do I have to strap you to this cot in order for you to do what you're told?" He sighed, shoving his head into his hands in exasperation. "I tell the girl to relax and spend the day with her horse, and this is what she does," he murmured to nobody in particular in a voice that made me smile through the tears. until a new face showed up. One that was even angrier than Locke's, if that were even possible.

Eldan.

I thought Eldan was going to kill me. Locke too. They both took turns berating me until they eventually ran out of breath. Or maybe it was patience. Eldan threatened to flay me, strap me to the cot, and feed me only cold broth if I kept this behavior up. I glanced at Locke, whose eyebrows met his hairline.

"If you're looking for me to protect you, love, think again. Because one, I agree with him. And two, I'm a little afraid of him."

"Good lad." Eldan smiled, patting Locke on the shoulder like they were old friends.

I sighed. These two were going to be the death of me.

Chapter Twenty-Nine

Eldan was able to heal my new injuries quickly and with only a few unnecessary barbs at my expense. I was shaken. I still couldn't feel my magic where I usually left it. It felt like when you leave something important in the same spot for ages and come to find it one day misplaced. I didn't feel whole either, like a void in my chest, teaming up with the feeling of decay that was steadily growing. I swear, if you looked at me in the right light, really looked at me, did I seem paler? Armed with my daggers on my side, I was strong enough for what came next. Something I never thought I'd want to be a part of, but something I needed now.

I found myself at Locke's side a few hours later, finding out what the dungeon looked like. And it was exactly like what I'd imagined. A cold metal gate barred anyone from entering or exiting without Locke's knowledge, leading to a wide set of damp, mildew laden stone stairs. Each breath grew damper and fouler with rot, excrement, and death the further down we went. I tried to imagine Abel down here. His last moments. I almost couldn't.

Each cell was lined with stone, a sconce outside each one, a main chandelier made of what appeared to be bone lit the main space. The only sources of light. Prisoners were barred from even sunlight here. A rat hissed and scurried away at our approach, calling to mind Eldan's kitchen. I glanced at Locke, who smirked widely at the memory. I smiled in response, something I didn't think I could do in a dungeon.

At the very end of the hall, I could hear the faint rustle of chain scraping stone. There was a time that finding myself in a place like this as an interrogator would have been unfathomable. Especially with my aversion to blood. My aversion to witnessing the violence that wrought it. My inclination to help, not hinder.

And yet, here I was. They were content to take their pound of flesh with me, to carve me up before handing me off. They reveled in my powerlessness. But I strode forward, far from powerless now. Even if my magic still hadn't quite returned just yet.

Locke, Lenore, and I came to a stop at the end of the tunnel. Cylix and Manson were wrapped in chains, and from the wounds in their shoulders and the smirk on Lenore's face, I'd say she gave them a healthy dose of that very magic suppressant they'd given me. Though by the putrid smell of blood on the air, I'd say she administered it multiple times. Flies circled them from overhead, sensing the impending death. Manson glared silently at me from behind their filthy gags, and I couldn't help the smug smile I tossed them. Locke turned to me, his face unreadable.

"Are you ready? You don't have to do this, and you can leave at any time." I stepped forward in answer. Part of my gut was revolting, but some primal, angry part of me would not be denied the vengeance I sought.

"No, thank you," I said honestly, turning my head back to them. Their hardened gazes met mine in turn as retribution demanded fulfilling in my veins, hot and insistent. I swore I'd become worse than Locke when the time came for my revenge, and I could feel the steeling of myself. I glared back at them as I approached their cell. "It's my turn."

Locke nodded, emotions flickering across his face. Pride, mixing with concern. He and Lenore exchanged a loaded look I didn't care to understand before he unlocked the cell and stepped inside, allowing me room to enter as well. Lenore stayed outside the cell, content to watch and keep guard, I supposed.

"I told you before that one of his monikers is the Nightmare Assassin. You told me he'd never find us." I knelt down in front of Manson, stepping on his ruined hand. He thrashed against his restraints, chain links rattling in the dim, but fading in comparison to his screams. "I believe we won. And I do believe I owe you something." My saccharine voice was sickening, even to me. I drew the dagger Lenore had gifted me before; it was blacker than pitch, yet glinted in the orange sconce light before I plunged it into his abdomen.

His screams were like music to my ears, while at the same time I wanted to retch. The feeling of hot blood from someone wasn't a good feeling. But I wouldn't stop. Not after all they'd both done to me. Not for the moment I looked up and saw Aspen's hair in the mud. For his near death, I would make them pay. For Port Azure and all it had lost, they would pay.

His breaths came fast and labored. He hadn't yet begun to face my retribution. Let alone Locke's. I turned to look at my soulmate. There was pride there on his face. And if I weren't mistaken, arousal.

That was unexpected.

I smiled at him before ripping the knife from the wound and wiping the blood on my pant leg.

"Sorry, Locke, I didn't mean to get ahead of you. I just wanted to get that out of my system."

He grinned in response as I stepped back. "Truthfully, love, I've never been more thrilled to be interrupted." I could hear Lenore's gag from behind me as Locke turned to address the two on their knees in chains. "You haven't even begun to pay for what you did to my soulmate. But you will. You haven't yet paid for the atrocities you committed against Port Azure. But you will. Unless..." He trailed off for dramatic purposes. "Unless you answer my questions. I may be merciful."

Locke approached the first one, Cylix, and dragged his knife gently, tauntingly, over his face. Cylix flinched back, squeezing his eyes shut in fear, his breaths leaving him in panicked gasps. Locke's dark, humorless laugh permeated the air thick with the growing stench of sweat and body odor. He cut the gag from his face before stepping back. Cylix flinched before opening his eyes, to the knife primed at his eye, only inches away. Terror spread across his face. "Answer my questions honestly, and you won't discover what a dungeon lobotomy feels like." Locke twirled the knife. "But don't answer the question, or if you lie to me, you'll find out how slowly a person can stab. It takes patience and time, but I have both of those things. What say you?"

Terrified, Cylix nodded, careful to keep his head from getting too close to the blade. Manson, next to him, didn't move an inch, his gaze too, fixed on the weapon in Locke's hand.

"Perfect," Locke said with a growing smile that was colder than it was outside. "Let's start with something basic. How did you and your company find Port Azure? And does Scorpio know where it is?"

"I can't betray her," Cylix whimpered. "She'll kill me. She'll kill everyone. I get that you turned your back on her, on all of us, but my loyalty has to lie with the queen." Locke barked a laugh, the only warning before he plunged his knife into Cylix's hand. His screams were that of someone surprised and in true agony.

"Here's the thing you seem to be missing," Locke said, ripping his blade out. "*I'm* going to kill you if you don't talk."

"She's Scorpio," he whispered. I saw the exact moment something occurred to him, his face darkening as it did so. Perhaps he just came to understand he would, in fact, die. Perhaps he wanted to egg Locke on so it would be quicker. But I had no doubt Locke had seen that before. "Besides, the queen's curse is horrible. That bitch you have wetting your dick should die for her, and the realm would be better. Yet she sits here doing no good for anybody."

The sound that a kneecap makes when it pops sounds gruesomely like that of a champagne bottle. Locke plunged the dagger into his knee, severing the tendons there. The horrible wails and spurting blood made me sick, but not as much as his accusation.

"You'll do well never to speak of her again," Locke growled in warning. The fae before him writhed, the screaming never ending, a heavy sheen of sweat on him now. The air shimmered with something dark. Turbulent. I blinked. It wasn't my imagination, or even his aura flickering. He'd summoned the shadows to him. They coiled around him like an old friend, trails of darkness pulsing. I felt unnerved. Hadn't Locke mentioned that black magic usage corrupts the soul? At what point should I be concerned about that?

Locke's voice dripped with false pleasantry as he crafted a single blade, forged from shadow itself. The knife gave off a sinister presence that even I could feel. Its depthless black color absorbed every color around it, shadows writhing and dissipating off of it like mist. It was a particularly cruel looking blade, serrated edges resembling something closer to stacked arrowheads than a blade. Its point was clear; stabbing would be the easy part. Removing the blade would be an agony of its own bearing, tearing flesh and sinew and organ tenfold.

Locke wasted no time, his next question barreling into his victim, who was still grunting and writhing in his chains. Manson's face had paled considerably. He was so still I wasn't even sure he was breathing. Blood from Cylix had found its way towards me, redness creeping up and reminding me of a time I detested violence. I almost laughed, but I couldn't not mourn the girl who hated seeing others hurt. I couldn't tell if I had grown and matured, or if I had fallen into the depths of revenge.

Don't let the flames consume you.

That's what Locke had said. That revenge was a fine line. I wondered if this were what he'd meant. That losing yourself in the process of revenge was all too easy. I felt like I was walking the edge of a knife, and falling meant losing a piece of myself. That thought centered me, pulled me back from the darker side of my mind.

"Have you ever heard of death by a thousand cuts?" Locke's murmured question reached me. He eyed each of them in turn, Manson's eyes widening into saucers. Locke's voice turned contemplative. "How much worse do you think it'll be when I use this?"

He flourished the knife, showing it off. "I can't wait to see how much more damage this causes on the way out. Oh, and I have a few other fun surprises too."

Cylix whimpered, a soft sound following after that sounded suspiciously like an apology. Locke grinned. "Now let's try this one more time," he said, with exaggerated patience. "How did you find Port Azure?"

"I'm not telling you shit. Fuck you." Cylix's resigned whimper widened Locke's grin into something that bordered on maniacal.

"I do love it when they try to hold out." He glanced at me with softer expression. "I know you don't love blood. You may want to look away for a second." I smiled at him.

"I said I wanted to watch you work, Crowned Assassin. Do your worst." Was it me, or was the look he levelled me with significantly more heated than I'd expected?

"I love when you talk dirty to me," he crooned in a voice meant only for me before redirecting his attention to the trembling mass of information before him. "As for you, I'm excited to see how much this hurts."

The knife plunged deeply into the fleshy lower abdomen. I shut my eyes at the moment I would have seen blood spurt and weep from the wound, but his screams would stay with me forever. The screams of absolute, all-consuming agony. I shouldn't feel guilty. Not when they did this to me. Not when they laughed as I screamed.

When Locke ripped the blade out, blood sprayed everywhere behind him. Gore came away with the knife, and Mason's screams joined Cylix's.

"Whoops." Locke chuckled. "That might be too much blood. I'd better fix that, or this might be over a bit too soon. It's called a thousand cuts, not one and done, after all." Locke layered his limited healing magic into Cylix. It slowed the bleeding, but it didn't stop it. Locke's healing magic would stave off death, but not stop it entirely.

But they didn't necessarily know that.

"So I'm going to ask again. How did Scorpio find us?" His gaze flickered back and forth between the two of them. "Who else knows of our location?" When neither answered for a moment, I spoke up, stepping to stand behind Locke and looking down on them both.

"Did you know I can stab your liver in just the right spot so you don't die right away?" My voice was deliberately slow, allowing myself time to enjoy their reactions. "The pain is excruciating, and it takes hours to die that way. I can always cauterize a wound. No worries about you bleeding out that way." My time with Eldan as his apprentice had some obviously interesting applications. I imagine my mentor would be horrified by me right now. Locke, however, looked lit from within at my words.

"I'll tell you what you want to know," Cylix whined with tears falling down his face. "Just please stop. Stop hurting us."

"Like how you stopped hurting Lark?" His voice was as dark as the blade he carried. Cylix blanched, peering over Locke's shoulder at me.

"It wasn't me. I didn't do it!" he whined. My temper flared.

"Liar." The word fell from my lips before I made the conscious decision to speak. Locke turned towards me. "You held my chains while your friends tortured me. You laughed. You mocked me. You are every bit as complicit as Manson, Eron, and Brashan." The fury on Locke's face was terrifying—even to me.

"Well, Cylix, it's really not your day. You hurt Lark, you insulted her, and now I see you lied to me. I used to think there was nothing I hated more than lying, but it was nice to know I can still be proven wrong on occasion." Locke's blade came back up, the point only an inch from his eye, a warning. Or perhaps a preview of what was yet to come. My stomach roiled in response. I swallowed the lump in my throat hoping it would help keep my stomach contents where they were.

"I'll tell you everything," Cylix cried, his tears coming unchecked down his cheeks. The scent of urine added itself to the already horrific stench down here. One glance downward told the story of why.

"Tell you what, Cylix. If you lie again, Lark gets to decide how long your life lasts for. And how much pain you endure. And you should know she tends to be a bit on the vengeful side."

Cylix's throat bobbed, too scared to move. "Yes. Yes, I'll tell you. Please just move your knife." Locke did so and told him to speak. And speak he did.

"The Queen and Prince Pisces devised a plan to find you. They knew you must have been hidden with wards, so they found a special amulet of some kind that pulses when wards are near so they could be found and destroyed." The wards being shattered. That made sense. It explained how they found them. "A map of the water court was then divided into small grids, each grid with a number. Each team was sent in with this amulet. They tracked each team who went into each square. So if a squad never came back…"

"It would still be obvious which grid space the Court of Rebels was in." Locke finished for him. "So either Crownguards sacked Port Azure and told Scorpio the good news with Lark in tow, or if they were defeated and never returned, Scorpio would know where we were." Locke cursed. Scorpio likely already knew the location of Port Azure.

This situation has just went from bad to worse, with no end in sight. Just when Port Azure had weathered one storm, we found out a worse one was on the way.

Chapter Thirty

I t took another hour. Another scream filled, blood-soaked hour of carefully asking all the right questions—like where Locke's family was being held—but unfortunately it was clear they had no idea. I always wondered how you could tell the difference between not knowing and not telling. The palpable fear, the pleading, the begging, the screaming… they were all bone chillingly different. And I couldn't help but feel that I was too after that. And when Locke was finished with Cylix and Manson, their bodies were so bloody and mangled it was hard to imagine what they looked like before. Locke was covered in blood by the time he'd finished, and I saw the form that had inspired the moniker Nightmare Assassin. It chilled the blood even in my veins to see him like this. And yet, I couldn't help but find it thrilling that this dark assassin was mine.

The next afternoon saw me wandering aimlessly through the Citadel, my body passing between periods of numbness and exhaustion. Aspen couldn't train me, I couldn't use magic while I healed, and I felt useless. I pored over more books looking for any more clues, finding nothing. Wren and Calan had checked in with no new information. The last they'd been able to decipher was that Locke's family was being held somewhere in Ari'inor.

Now I sat on the steps of the Citadel leading the square with only my thoughts for company watching the comings and goings of the fae around me. Some waved at me. Others bowed respectfully when they saw me, but thankfully, nobody approached. I smiled in kind, waved when appropriate. Some fae were finishing the fixing of the wall that fell during the attack, the sounds of hammering nails and other carpentry floating down to me, a harsh sound in an otherwise serene place. I was surprised to see how much repair work had happened in such a short time. The homes that had been damaged, the buildings in the square had been patched up so quickly I could almost not believe it.

Some fae were milling about, chatting in easy chairs and enjoying the afternoon sunshine, despite the chill of the season, and turning cooler every day. I watched fae move around the square to different parts, some to the blacksmith, who seemed very busy since the attack. Others meandered around the merchants' tents, perusing wares and haggling for prices. It warmed my frosty heart to see the fae here bounce back as they have and carry on with their lives. I shouldered my blanket further around my torso and sank into the warmth it provided against the chilling sea wind.

I looked down at my clean hands but couldn't help but see the blood on them. In my mind's eye, they dripped torrents of blood. I shuddered, remembering my wrath as I wrung as much pain from Cylix before I finally killed him. His blood had run in rivers over my hands, and I swear I could still scent that coppery smell of it.

My blood felt cool in my veins thinking about it now. How I had actively participated in the torture of Cylix and allowed the others to be as well. To be interrogated. And we had gotten a lot of useful information out of them. I knew they were bad fae. An argument could be made that they deserved it. But did I deserve to dole out that punishment? What I'd done was horrible, plain and simple. I searched within myself of any remnant of the Lark I'd been before Port Azure. But I wonder if she'd died, leaving me in place. And I wonder what that meant for me. At what point was I too dark to be what the Court needed me to be?

It was the twins that found me. If I hadn't been so focused on looking at my hands, searching for the blood that was surely there, I would have noticed them sit next to me. Lennox took my hand and squeezed. I looked at her numbly and the weight of my thoughts had well and truly rendered me mute. Lenore sighed from her place next to me.

"What's on your mind?" she asked me.

"You look like a ghost," commented Lennox.

I took a deep, shuddering breath, dragging air into the very recesses of my lungs before I was able to voice my thoughts to the twins. I poured over how I didn't know how to reconcile who I once was, with the faerie I'd become. I hated that I wasn't completely repulsed by my actions yesterday. I wasn't sure what that made me.

"Simple," Lenore said, her eyes looking out but not focusing on anything in particular. Her knees propped her elbows up, her pretty face resting in her hands. "It makes you a fighter. It makes you strong. It makes you formidable. And it makes you fae. The fact that you're agonizing over the death of someone who wronged you... you haven't changed for the worse, Lark. You've changed, yes, but you're still you. Don't hold yourself to a standard you hold nobody else to."

As always, Lenore had cut straight to the heart of a delicate issue with all the subtlety of a brick, but the precision of the finest blade, leaving my breath hovering in my throat. I wasn't even aware I had been doing that. Locke, Lenore, Aspen, Lennox, I've witnessed them take life. I've witnessed some of them do far worse, and it had never occurred to me to be afraid of the darkness of their actions. Especially not Locke's. I'd not once balked at the shadows I see surging around in his soul, and yet guilt was lashing me from the inside out. "You don't have a desire to hurt fae for no reason," Lennox cut in before I could speak. "You hurt someone who'd gravely injured you. Tortured you. You thought at one point he'd killed Aspen. You take life when yours is in danger, or those you love are. You defended this city. You showed your considerable strength. That doesn't make you weak. Or bad. Or anything else. It makes you a loyal defender of those who can't protect themselves. To take life and not feel any remorse shows you've done it too many times. To be immune to death is a curse of its own."

"Vengeance and justice don't always have to be so different, Lark," said Lennox as she rested her head on my shoulder and looped her arm through mine. I mulled over their words. Lenore sat with me, her legs now stretched out in front of her as she reclined back on her hands, looking very like a cat stretching in the sun. They sat with me quietly while I contemplated. I gave Lennox's hand a squeeze, which she returned, and I gave Lenore a wistful smile. She smiled back.

"Thank you," I whispered when I finally found my voice. It wavered the slightest bit with emotion. They said nothing but remained quietly with me. Lennox's hand squeezed mine once more. Lenore said nothing but gave me a meaningful look. We sat there a long while, shadows becoming a bit longer in the late afternoon light. Fae came and went about their business as we sat on the steps, quietly observing them. I stole a glance at both twins, grateful for their intervention. With the twins bolstering me, I felt better. Lighter. I felt more myself again. And for the first time since I came home battered and broken, I didn't see blood on my hands.

"My lady." A gentle timbre stirred me from place on my chair in Locke's office where a book stilled in my lap. Locke himself was smiling to himself at his desk, which widened as Vanneck meekly peeked his head in the door.

"Seriously, Vanneck, Lark is fine. Come in." His stoic expression left my heartbeat picking up. "Is everything okay? What's wrong?"

"Prince Cancer. Lark." He glanced at us in turn before settling on me once again. "I wish to pledge myself to your service. If you would have me. It's so rare to see valiance like what you displayed during the battle of Port Azure. I will not forget that I'm only alive because of you."

"How do I formally accept, Vanneck?" I asked, rising to my feet, unsure what to do.

"Lady Lark," Vanneck's voice began, soft and sure. Unwavering as the dawn, he took a knee before me, his dagger clutched in his hand over his heart. "My sword is yours to command. My life is yours to command. From this day forth, your battles are mine. Whatever you and Prince Cancer face, my blade will be at your side. Even if the entire Court—nay, the entire realm—were to stand against you, Queen's Mark." For the first time, that title didn't feel like a barb, like a stain on me. I couldn't contain my elation, my gratitude, when he smiled. "I serve you."

"Do you accept his pledge, Lark?" Locke asked softly. I didn't hesitate, my smile of humble gratitude cracking my face into two.

"Yes, Vanneck. Rise as my knight. I will do my best to ensure I'm worthy of such a pledge. Thank you."

Vanneck rose with an awkward smile, turned, and left so abruptly, I felt my head spin. I looked to Locke, who looked like he was scarcely containing his amusement.

"What are you laughing at?"

"I'm not. I am forever amused by how awkward Vanneck can be. But you left quite an impression on him, and I felt how nervous he was to come in here. The poor guy was out there for ten minutes before he tapped on the door." He smiled. "You inspired him."

My heart swelled with the promise of my earlier words, a silent pledge to Vanneck. I would fight to be worthy of this servitude.

Chapter Thirty-One

I sat in the saddle of Valor's back at a comfortable walk with Locke and Aristocrat at my side. The sound of synchronized hooves slapping at the surf of the grey ocean to my right blended in with the sound of the branches and boughs on the other side of the sandy beach blowing in the wind. Dead leaves followed where the crisp wind took them, content to just be. I pulled my cloak closer around me to close any gaps that the wind had snuck into to steal my warmth. Valor tossed his head, ready to run once again. I scratched his withers affectionately. I looked to my left and saw Locke doing much the same thing for Ari, speaking to him in a low tone that the wind carried away from me. His ears swiveled as he listened to his rider's smooth voice.

"Locke?"

He looked over at me. The wind swept his hair to the side. Instead of looking wind burned, his hair blew in the briny breeze, giving him an effortlessly disheveled appearance that made my heart stutter a bit.

"Yes?"

"I want to ask you something. Something that's been on my mind recently." My hands tensed on the reins, something Valor stamped his feet at. I murmured a quick apology, and with a neck pat, I was forgiven.

"Well, that sounds all kinds of ominous." His tone was teasing, but there was a sharpness to his features that was all serious. "What's on your mind, love?"

"I guess I'm curious. Why does Pisces hate you so much? It's clear as day that he does." And just like that, his face turned to impenetrable stone. I softened my voice. "It's personal, isn't it? This level of hatred doesn't just pop up. What happened between you?" Locke looked alarmed for a moment. A heartbeat. But then he dragged a deep sigh as we continued walking along the beach. I knew I was in for a story when his face fell.

"It's a long story with a lot of gory details." He started slowly, as if searching for the right words. I could see how uncomfortable he looked. Vulnerable. And pained. I could also see guilt in his eyes. Whatever had happened, Locke felt guilty about it. He continued, "But I'll give you the short version. In the Zodiac Guild many years ago, we were the top candidates in everything. But I often bested him, much to his discontent. I was ranked higher in weapons, strategy, combat, everything. It's why I was appointed as Cancer long before he was at last appointed as Pisces. He took it personally. Very personally. But never more so than..." He sighed again looking down, radiating his discomfort. I almost asked him to stop telling me. But I couldn't. "Never more so than when it came to Wisty." At my confused look, he gave me a wry smile.

"Do you remember when you asked me if I thought knowing what happened to someone gave you closure? Made it better?" I thought back to our time together thus far, those words striking chords of memory in my mind.

I remembered. He told me he'd once loved someone and they'd died, but knowing what had happened hadn't made it any better. It had been along this very beach. The day I'd discovered my air magic, all those weeks ago. I nodded, urging him gently to continue.

"Her name was Wisteria. Wisty. Pisces loved her. Fiercely. And so did I. But she chose me," he said, his voice with a far-away lilt to it. His eyes stared out blankly, as if seeing a memory before him rather than the beachy horizon before us. Or perhaps he saw Wisty's ghost, still haunting him after all these years. He spoke calmly despite the rigid tension I could see in his shoulders, his jaw. I watched with dreaded mixed emotion as I watched various emotions dance across his features—hope. Love. Regret. Barely healed devastation. I tried not to let it hurt. "She chose me. She loved me. And Pisces never recovered from that blow. The jealousy ate at him. Until she died. She was killed. She and I were exploring the Fire Court, on a vacation of sorts. We'd gone looking for a hot spring we'd heard rumors of. What we'd happened upon was an ancient ruin—old even to the Kinship. As we explored it, we discovered it wasn't empty. It was guarded, or maybe it was haunted. By a basilisk."

My heart stuttered as I realized where this was going, giving a squeeze for Locke. Basilisks were extremely rare—nearly extinct, much like dragons. But they were huge, hard to kill through their tough as armor scales, and horribly deadly. Venomous. The kind of venom that there wasn't a cure for unless it was sucked out of you immediately, I knew. They were extremely territorial and temperamental. If it saw Locke and Wisty as trespassing, it was amazing that even one of them made it to safety. He gave me a pained smile as he continued.

"We'd unknowingly trespassed onto its domain. It wouldn't let us leave. We couldn't outrun it. It was a long and brutal fight, and to this day it was one of the hardest battles I've waged. Just when we thought we'd landed the killing blow through its heart, it struck one final time, biting Wisty in the shoulder. It could have attacked either of us, but it bit Wisty. It was dead before the bite was even complete, but it was too late. Even if the venom hadn't incapacitated her, it had nearly ripped her arm off from the socket, and she was losing so much blood. I didn't have much in the way of healing then, and we were miles from help of any sorts. It didn't stop me from trying. I hemorrhaged magic to try to heal her. I didn't even have black magic then. Nothing I did could stabilize her. There was... her blood... it was everywhere. It wasn't long before she... died." His head hung, and his hair shadowed his eyes. But I heard his voice waver with emotion. I banished the small bit of jealousy that reared its ugly head. My heart raced in an effort to go to him. In that moment, I hated being on horseback for once in my life. I just wanted to hold him close.

"She left for the Veil, taking her last breath in my arms. She told me one last time that she'd loved me, and then I was alone. Pisces has never forgotten. Has never let me forget that I'd failed her. That I was supposed to protect her. That he loved her. And that he'd do whatever it takes so that I would never recover. Then five years ago, I was cursed trying to stop Scorpio from turning to black magic and he laughed. He thought it was sweet justice at work. And maybe it was. There isn't a day that goes by where I wonder if my curse isn't retribution from the Goddess herself for failing Wisty that day." He looked at me then, eyes swimming his ghosts and guilt and shame. "Because you're going to be taken from me too. And I will never love anyone, nor have I loved anyone, the way I love you." He glanced at me again before averting his gaze. "That's why Pisces hunts you so fiercely. Why he's so cruel to you. Why he takes so much pleasure in all of this. Because he knows how much it hurts me. He can destroy me under the guise of patriotism. Long live the Queen and whatnot. But he's doing it to take a shot at me."

I wiped the tears that were blurring my vision and threatening to spill over my cheeks. I desperately wanted to hold him. To wrap my arms around him and never let go. So he could feel how much I loved him. The wounds on his heart were gaping. How could I have not known? Goddess, he'd suffered so much. So incredibly much. And so acutely. We rode along at a slow walk. My hips rocked rhymically to Valor's pace, though nothing about this ride now was leisurely. I paused as I absorbed what he'd said. Processed it. Jealousy once again making herself known, however stupid and childish, at not being the first fae he'd loved. He'd told me as such, but for the first time she had a name; Wisty. But ever more present was that my heart cracked for him. The devastation on his face was dark, and raw, and pain given form.

"I had no idea," I whispered at last, wiping a final tear. "That's why you tried so hard to make me hate you, and keep me from finding out about the curse."

He nodded sullenly. "I'd rather see you hate me than see you dead. I failed you too. If Pisces hadn't forced my hand that day, you'd still be in the dark about all of this."

"I'm glad your hand was forced," I said firmly. "You've never failed me. Not once. I loved you regardless, whether I wanted to, or whether I wanted to admit it or not. What you did when you told me you loved me was remove the guilt I had about loving someone I thought had killed my father. You took away my self-loathing. You've come through for me time and time again. And when I die, If I can't make it back, it will never be because you failed me. It's not on you, nor was Wisty's death. You've never let either of us down.." At Locke's silence I continued with vehemence, "Locke, none of it was your fault."

He let loose a shuddering breath, a dam breaking at last as he looked at me. "I love you, Lark. More than I realized was even possible," he said after a few beats. His voice was strained under the weight of his thoughts and his guilt he'd carried around with him. I waited, thinking he was going to continue, but more words didn't come. I saw them die on his lips, never to be surfaced again. But I felt those words regardless. I felt his guilt. The weight of it on his shoulders. He'd been carrying the weight of what had happened to Wisty all this time.

"I love you too, Locke. I'm so sorry about Wisty. I know you carry that guilt with you. The shame. The self-hate." I took his hand, reaching for it between the horses, the only form of contact we could have. I caressed over his knuckles. I made him make a fist, his hand over the surf we walked through. "It's time to let the guilt go. You don't need to let your memories of her go. But the guilt you feel over her death. It wasn't your fault. You said yourself it could've been you just as easily as it was her. And then I would never have met you."

I reached my hand out to him with a smile. He added his hand to mine with a look that looked like confusion, but heavier. A bit darker. Something more churned beneath the surface that I couldn't see, but I didn't need to. I opened his hand between us, symbolically dropping the chains that had bound and burdened him for so long. He took a deep, cleansing breath as he did so.

The look he gave me then. There were too many emotions to read. To sift through. Love. Pain. Guilt. Solace. Regret. Denial. I knew acceptance would come. One day. Locke needed support. And I hoped and prayed to the Goddess above that we both would make it through this. Because I couldn't bear becoming another hole in Locke's heart.

I hadn't realized in the exhaustion and chaos that it was Pyre Day. The beach behind Port Azure was full of pyres, evenly spaced and two or three levels high, with space between each body to afford each fallen fae as much dignity as possible. Wounds lovingly dressed, clothing and armor shined for the occasion, and each pyre surrounded by tear-stained cheeks, the occasional wailing sob and white knuckled torches. Eighty-one fae lost their lives—more having succumbed to their injuries—and more than three times that were injured. The sunset backdropped the entire settlement to say their final goodbyes to the heroes of Port Azure. To their loved ones. Families had painstakingly picked flowers to give their loved ones—a kind parting gift. My magic had largely returned to me, enough that I could cover the pyre with flowers. My own personal thanks. I heard sobs as the pyre exploded with color at my touch, a final thing I could do for the dead and those that remained.

"Today, we acknowledge the sacrifice each one of these fae made," Locke began, his throat thick with emotion. He stepped forward, commanding all eyes to him where he held his own torch at my side. The glint of gold ceremonial armor I'd not seen before reflecting in the late sun, and I knew it would become a beacon once the flames were lit. All the living came in the best clothing they still had. These were the final honor they could afford our fallen. "A sacrifice none of us will ever be able to repay. To honor them is to remember them. To fight in their name. To refuse to let their deaths be in vain." Locke brought the torch high above his head, all other torches following skyward. "May their light guide us, and may they meet the Goddess in kindness."

The answering echo was deafening in both volume and magnitude. I felt the weight of their prayers, the weight of the deaths on my shoulders like it was trying to drag me to my knees. Stepping forward, I placed my own torch on the pyre in front of us alongside my kin. Looking up, I expected to see anger at my being here. Reproach. Hostility even. Instead, all I saw was the raw sorrow that accompanied death so often. Peering over to the next pyre over, I saw Rilla and her children, tears streaking their faces. So badly, I wanted to give them comfort. As if she felt my eyes, she turned to me. She offered a half smile of acknowledgement at me through her tears, her son waving at me, before both returned their attention to the pyre.

As somber as the morning had been, the fae of Port Azure put on a party to celebrate the fallen, the victory they earned and the zest of life they still lived. The drinking began with toasts, so many toasts I doubted anyone could name them all, in honor of a fallen comrade. Everyone was drunk within the hour, smiles and melancholy stories giving way to happy memories shared through tears. Only a few drinks more, and smiles pushed sorrow out of the way, the celebration of life, of the life still had, had begun. Or at least that's what Lennox told me as I lined my eyes with kohl. I stood in the mirror in a simple, long green dress. Lennox was stunning in red, and Lenore was a vision in black with a flask of who knows what strapped to her leg. My hair had been curled to accentuate my natural blonde waves but kept loose and unbound. I couldn't help but remember the last time we all got dressed up and I kept sending prayer after prayer above to the Goddess that Scorpio wouldn't be featuring in tonight's festivities. Locke assured me that he had a few things in his offices to tidy up and he'd meet me in the square.

I'm not sure what hit me first the moment I was ushered out on through the doors of the Citadel—the smells, the sights, or the sounds. Drumbeats thumped heavily through me, the lively accompanying melody set fae around me dancing, some alone, others in pairs of swaying bodies. The warm glow of the magic lights and fires, and the warmth of many pressed in bodies was pushing out the worst of the cold. I was surprised, thinking I'd have needed a cloak, and while the air was cool, the party was just warming up. The smell of roasting meat from who knows where made my mouth water. There were few somber faces here. I spied several groups cheers whatever was in their cups with riotous laughs celebrating life.

My first ever party.

I wasn't sure why I was so nervous.

But my palms were sweating, clenching and unclenching, and my breaths came shallow. I had faced down members of the Zodiac Kinship, fought in battles, survived torture. And I was nervous to go to a party.

Lennox in her flower crown and flowy dress looked like a vision as she grabbed my hand with a wide smile. Lenore's smirking form in a tight-fitting black dress with a slit up each leg came up beside me. Her smirk widened at my expression.

"What are you nervous for? Never been to a party?"

"Of course I have!" I didn't mean to snap at her. I didn't mention that I made several casual appearances at parties in Poplar Hollow. The festival on solstice, the fall harvest, the midsummer festival for the Goddess... our town did their best to be festive for those events even if we weren't the best supplied. I was always forced to leave early by threat or others ignoring me to the point of being unable to partake in anything. Eventually, I stopped trying. Eventually, the thrumming of music had just been another day for my father and me.

"You're going to have the best time." Lennox squeezed my hand in a comforting gesture.

"Especially if you have some of this." Lenore shoved a bottle into my hands. Instead of the fruity smell of wine that I usually got from her, this smelled strongly of alcohol, leaving a slight burn in my eyes water, leaving me to wonder how anyone could drink this willingly?

"What in the Goddess's name is this?" I asked, genuinely both curious and horrified. But there was a small voice in the back of my head that was mildly concerned, especially when Lenore burst out laughing.

"The good stuff," she whispered conspiratorially, making a dramatic show of making sure nobody was watching before taking it from me to take a demonstrative swig before returning it to me with a deep exhale and scrunched face that did nothing to make me want to follow suit. At my look of hesitation, she smirked. "Just try it!"

I brought it hesitantly to my lips and tipped the bottle up, gagging for a moment. If the smell or the burn weren't bad enough, the taste sure was. I wasn't certain I was going to have taste buds after. At my grimace, Lenore heaved a laugh. I ignored the unpleasantness of whatever this was and took three large swallows that were little more than chokes before passing it back to Lenore, whose puffed chest left her looking almost proud. Which disappeared quickly when I fought a dry heave to keep it down.

"I promise you're going to have a great night," she said as the song swelled and came to its conclusion, resulting in riotous cheers and demands for more. The band obliged happily, launching straight into a lilting and merry tune that created even more resounding applause and cheers, and bodies were moving and twirling again, clapping and stomping in time with the music.

"I love this song!" Lennox pulled me towards the dance floor. I went, but in the back of my mind, I knew I was better prepared to take on the likes of Pisces and Scorpio than I was dancing.

"I don't know the steps!" I hissed in Lennox's ear. I glanced behind at Lenore, who was grinning at me from her place on the steps of the citadel. With a few flicks of her hand, she gestured for me to get out there with her twin. I noticed Aspen coming out to join her. His grin was wide when Lenore pointed us out and waved at me. Asshole.

"There are no steps! Just follow me! Move with the music. Have fun! You do know how to do that at least, right?" She winked as she pulled me into step with her. I gave a nervous glance at the Fae cavorting around me, pleasantly surprised that nobody was paying particular attention to us.

After a few minutes of fumbling and loosening up, I found that she was right. There were no steps. Just moving your hips and your feet in time with the music. The liquid warmth that had spread in my extremities, I suspected, didn't hurt either. I leaned into the heady feeling, letting the fun, the alcohol, and my senses take over for the first time in my life. My head felt light as it tipped up towards the sky, my thoughts scattering in the most pleasant way. My dress floated around me, the soft fabric caressing my skin, the feeling heightened with my mild inebriation. I moved my hips, my feet, to the music, faster and faster as the songs came, keeping up with Lennox while struggling to breathe. The party lights casting everything in a warm, happy glow. I glanced over to see Aspen and Lenore drinking on the steps still. But no Locke.

Where was he?

He was missing all the fun! As I looked around, I couldn't help but think that this might just be the most fun I'd ever had.

"I'm going to get another drink. You want to come with me?" Lennox asked, pulling me partly from my reverie. I nodded, thinking that a drink would be just the thing as my buzz was quickly wearing off. Lenore and Aspen met us at a long table filled to the brim with various refreshments and appetizers. Calan met us, his eyes set on Lenore and her coy smile. I watched him dare to approach the way I might approach a dragon, cautious and ready to run at the slightest provocation. But as he extended his hand, Lenore's smile changed. Not widened, more like lost a feral edge. To my surprise, Lenore and Calan disappeared into the dance space.

"Where's Locke?" I asked Aspen as I prepared myself a drink from the assortment available to me. A wine smelling sweet and vaguely like the color pink. Aspen shrugged.

"He said he had a few things to take care of before he joined us. So he's probably doing his hair or something." He grinned under his mug of ale before taking a swig. I laughed, knowing that was a very distinct possibility. I took a sip of wine, surprised when it fizzled on my tongue, before turning sweet. *Significantly* less awful than whatever Lenore had on her. I took another sip. And another before Aspen was in front of me. "Dance with me in the meantime?" Aspen held his hand out, and I took it without hesitation. He led me back to the dance floor for a partnered dance.

"I'm going to apologize right now." I was only half joking. "I have two left feet with this sort of thing." Aspen laughed as he easily took my waist.

"Little bird, how's that different from any other thing you do?" I smacked his arm playfully in response, his grin widening as he led me around in chaotic, frenzied circles, the alcohol and heavy concentration on where I was putting my feet keeping me from coming up with anything witty to say in retort. "Hey, my eyes are up here, you know."

I brought my head up, grinning. "I know, but I don't want to hurt you!" I said, unsure of where my feet should go when dancing with another person.

"You haven't hurt me yet even when we're sparring, I doubt you'll hurt me by stepping on me." He laughed. "And besides, you're doing it right now."

He was right. In our brief exchange, we'd gone halfway around the dance floor, bounding in frenzied circles alongside other pairs. My grin widened. I was doing it! Aspen's smile broadened with mine as we laughed. I spied Calan twirling Lenore around, though honestly I wasn't sure who was leading who. My wager was on Lenore.

Lennox was dancing with Vanneck, who I'd not noticed until now. He bowed his head to me briefly upon making eye contact and returned to the conversation he was so clearly engrossed in with Lennox. I couldn't imagine talking a lot while dancing like this. As it was, I was trying to school my breathing and hoping to the Goddess above that Aspen didn't notice how out of breath I was and decide I needed more cardio. The song came to an end at long last and I slumped in Aspen's arms. He even looked a bit tired.

"I'm grabbing another drink," I told him, separating myself from my best friend. "You want one?"

I hadn't even finished the question when a brown haired girl I'd not seen before slipped her hands over Aspen's impressive biceps. Her words, not mine. Aspen winked at me before extending a hand to her and asking to dance, only to be answered by a high pitched squeak of delight that made me wince and laugh simultaneously.

I returned to the refreshment station, getting a better look. Delicious appetizers invited me through smell. I picked at a few, savoring the treats before filling my cup to the brim with a sweet smelling wine. Upon tasting, peaches and strawberries floated over my tongue, masking the burn of the alcohol. I watched my friends with delight from my place near the steps of the Citadel, enjoying a moment to myself. It was cooler over here, but a fire light at my back drove the worst of the chill away. I focused on the point of this celebration. Being alive. And how alive I felt at this moment. I let myself take a deep breath, breathing in the smells, the excitement, the happiness and frivolity of the fae cavorting before me. I basked in the glow of it all, ecstatic to be able to openly enjoy such an occasion. I laughed as Calan dipped Lenore, and the face she made at the gesture—complete and utter confusion. Calan grinned wickedly, placing a slow, devious kiss on her throat. I didn't think Lenore had it in her to melt like butter, but here I was witnessing it. I gulped my drink down and poured another one. Locke should be along soon, I hoped looking at the clock tower on instinct, forgetting of course that it was no longer there. I turned, walking through the doors of the Citadel to see if I could find him in his offices, needing a moment from all the commotion.

"Are you enjoying yourself, my lady?" An unfamiliar voice needled me from behind after only a few steps out of view of the party, the title grated off his tongue, setting me on edge. I spun, eying him wearily, my earlier contentment vanishing. I glanced around, feigning interest in the high ceilinged atrium. We were out of sight of the party goers just beyond the door. A detail I had no doubt that he not only noticed, but was by his own design. He looked a bit younger than my father in age. His neatly groomed beard was more pepper than salt still, but the lines that had appeared on his face had spoken of a weary few years. Unbidden, my mind flew back to the days of Poplar Hollow. The days I was chased out of every festival and I prayed that wasn't about to happen now.

"Yes," I said, keeping my voice calm. His thin lips twisted into a sneer, his dark eyes taunting and humorless. "Are you having a good time?"

"No, I'm not." His voice slithered over me, making me feel gross and uncomfortable. I hid it with a shrug. The air between us was wrought with tension. The sharpness of his attention, the stillness of his presence, something I couldn't name stirred chaotically between us, fizzling and crackling, making the hair on the back of my neck rise.

"You should get a drink. Being the sober one around a bunch of drunks is a depressing thing, I'm given to understand." I held my cup in a mock salute and turned away, intending to get back in view of the party in the square and put some distance between this fae and myself.

"You being here is a fucking travesty," he ground out, stepping between me and my exit of choice. His hand jolted out to clutch my forearm, forcing me to face him entirely. My stomach plummeted and adrenaline hummed. Where was Locke?

"Take your hands off of me." I grit my teeth, keeping my voice low. A warning of my own. His grip tightened, crushing the delicate bones of my wrist. I couldn't help the wince at his predatory grin.

"If you were half the fae our dear prince thinks you are, you'd be dead by now," he spat, making my heart stop. When it pumped again, it pumped cold poison through my veins. Sluggish and freezing. Even my thoughts seemed to evaporate. Because he was right. I should be dead. He had every right to despise me. "And everything would be fine. You're incredibly selfish. *Living*." He spat, his grip tightening enough to make me wince while the other hand gesturing wildly, "While good fae, fae like my family, are slaughtered!"

And there it was. The reason for the hatred he now didn't bother hiding. I felt the weight of every word, the blow of each accusation leaving me in a wake of guilt and shame. How could I refute his claims? I could've scorched his hand off of me. And maybe I should've. Despite my heart pounding in my ears, despite it being all I could hear aside from his voice, there was a small inkling in the back of my mind that didn't wonder if he were right. That made me question the tenuous peace I'd found within myself.

"I fight for Port Azure, same as you," I said through tight lips, convincing myself as well as him. "I draw blood for Port Azure, same as you. We are not in opposition, sir. I will ask that you remove your hand and we go our separate ways." I hoped the *or else* was implied. He laughed as if I were a child throwing a tantrum.

"I've never agreed with Lark more than I do now," a familiar voice growled beside us, rising above the tension in the hall. "Unhand her. Immediately." My eyes snapped over to see Locke striding purposefully towards us. His eyes flicked over the fae who'd just threw my wrist away as if I'd burned him. Perhaps I should've. He squirmed under the weight of the Crowned Assassin's gaze. "And if you keep talking like that to her, you'll find yourself bereft of the ability to use your voice at all. And Tidas, before you speak your next words, understand that when it comes to her, I won't show mercy."

"Are you mad, boy?" Tidas exclaimed, his face turning red from fury. "She—"

His sentence would never finish.

One second he was standing two paces away from Locke. The next second saw a blur of motion so fast I couldn't track the movement, ending with Locke's hand encircling Tidas's throat and digging in. Tidas's hands were bound in shadow, leaving him unable to fight back, though he struggled valiantly.

"Call me *boy* again. Insult Lark again," Locke hissed, his tone dripping with dare, with warning. Fraught seconds came and waned in a war of wills, seething wrath on one side, unyielding and lethal power on the other. Every bit as unyielding as a shadow in the dim. "Well?"

Tidas blinked at last, breaking the spell between them. He shook his head, a subtle movement. Locke's grip loosened just enough for him to suck in a breath and stutter, "Apologies. Your highness." Locke's grip eased, enough that Tidas shrugged out and away from his Prince and fell into the wall behind him for support as he gasped for air. "But I will not follow her. She should be dead. How can you not see? She's the reason Port Azure isn't safe and you have her wetting your dick!"

Locke's voice turned grim. "I warned you."

Locke's hands became shrouded in shadow. His eyes blackened as they always did with his dark magic usage. Tidas shrank back at the sight, shaking his head. His eyes went wide and uncomprehending, his mouth opened to scream—

But no sound came.

Locke's magic wafted silently towards Tidas's struggling form. My breath showed on the air as a chill went down my spine. A chill not just from the sight before me. The magic glowed and writhed as if a living thing that delighted in torment as it forced its way down Tidas's throat. I watched as he thrashed, fat tears rolling unchecked down his ruddy face. Screams that should have been erupting from him went entirely unheard in a grotesque pantomime display of thrashing, despite his bonds. His hateful gaze stayed locked on me right up until his lungs finally gave up, until his face slackened in death. Tears ran unchecked down my face when Locke's hold on Tidas's corpse evaporated. The sound his body made when it crumpled to the floor would never leave me. Locke turned to me, his mouth twisted in a frown before turning me away from him.

"Was that really necessary?" I almost shouted. "He was in pain. I don't begrudge him his hatred. I understood it."

"I do. I begrudge everyone who has ill intent towards you." Locke's tone wasn't one of apology. It was of retribution. "If someone threatens you I cannot—I will not—stand idly by. If they harm you, they will suffer before their end. As Tidas did. If he were anyone else, his death wouldn't have upset you so much. You might have killed him yourself. So what happened?"

"Because he's right. His family is dead because I live. I might not have done the slaying, but that doesn't indemnify me. I bear that guilt."

"You haven't truly believed that in some time," he challenged. His jaw tensed, the muscles flickering out for me to see. "That's not the real reason, was it?" Locke pressed his forehead to mine, his eyes glittering as he looked at me, his eyes unfocused. The look he donned when reading auras. "You're upset because you flashed back to Poplar Hollow. You felt that same helplessness you used to. You thought for a moment you lost your home. That Port Azure was going to turn on you."

My breathing stopped. I felt my body go perfectly still, not moving an inch. Locke's lips met mine, his arms wrapping me tightly, as if he could squeeze my broken pieces back together.

"Port Azure will always be your home and I can promise nobody will ever hurt you again. Because if they do," his eyes blazed with quiet anger, "they answer to me. You think I'm always calm. You think I'm sweet, and to you I can be those things. But I'm still the Crowned Assassin. The Nightmare Assassin—a title I earned, Lark. A title that is mine in violence and bloodshed and darkness."

"Thank you," I whispered, unsure of what else to say.

"You're incredibly strong, Lark. Incredibly strong. Wield that. Because you don't need me to protect you. You have strength enough to protect yourself. But you'll never have to, if I have anything to say about it." I smiled weakly up at him as he wiped the last of my tears away with a mischievous wink. "Now love," he grasped my hand, entwining our fingers before placing a kiss on my knuckles, "what's this I hear that you haven't attended a party before?"

"Drink." Locke's voice settled over me. I glanced up to see him holding a cup to me, his own filled to the brim with the same sweet scented liquid. "You'll feel better."

I clinked my cup against his, resulting in a dull thud, and sipped the contents. The burn of the wine mingling with the sweetness in an intricate dance on my tongue that wasn't entirely unpleasant.

Vanneck's soft smile appeared next to us, holding his cup to mine as Aspen threw his arm around Locke's shoulders in a way I could only describe as giddy. "Cheers, my lady. Many of us are only alive because of you."

"I'm not sure that's true," shyness casting my eyes down. Vanneck waggled his eyebrows, Locke and Aspen grinning ear to ear.

"A toast!" Vanneck exclaimed in triumph, hoisting his cup over his head and drawing every eye to us. Color leached into my cheeks as even the music quieted to make room for him. "To Lady Lark, without whom many of us would not be here. To victory! To life! To sticking it to Scorpio!"

"To Lark!" Aspen joined in, excitedly.

Then Locke. Lenore. Lennox.

And all of Port Azure. Every single cup and goblet hoisted in the air with my name hailing from their lips in a moment I'd never before experienced. My heart stood still a beat or two before at least picking up. I raised my cup in earnest at last, much to the raucous cheers of the fae around me.

"To us all!"

It took a short while before the party seemed like fun again, but eventually I slipped out of the hold terror and guilt had bound me in, though Vanneck's cheeky little toast did manage to put a large smile on my face. I spied Lenore still in Calan's embrace with a knowing smirk. Lennox danced with Vanneck, large smiles on both of their faces. Tonight was the first time I remember seeing Vanneck so happy tonight. Every time I saw him, he was always so stoic and seemed so burdened with the weight of Port Azure's plight. It was nice to see a softer, happier side of him. He and Lennox danced and paraded around together, drinks in hand, blending right into the rest of the chaotic frivolity around them.

"Dance with me." Locke's voice, like the softness of shadows, reached me. I glanced over, seeing him offer his hand. His gaze didn't leave mine. Amusement. Joy. Slight inebriation. Locke's wobbly smile tugged straight to my heartstrings. I smiled as I placed my hand in his. I gave him the same warning about my dancing I'd given Aspen previously in the evening.

"I want you to still be attracted to me after this," I quipped. Locke's smile widened as he chuckled, showing his dimples.

"I assure you, that won't be a problem." He snorted. "Stop thinking. Just move with me."

The melody calmed. We went from a spirited tune that had fae moving their feet spritely around us to an almost haunting song. Locke's hand came to wrap around my waist and pull me close. I breathed in the familiar scent of him as I brought my right arm around his neck, my left hand finding his. The air stilled for just a moment before swirling gently around us, playing with our hair. It took me a moment to realize it was my magic responding to him that was the cause. Locke swayed us to the music, rotating us around the dance floor. Other couples danced similarly, but looking into Locke's eyes like this, the party slowly melted away until we were the only two. For only a moment, I swore I saw the pinkish aura surrounding us. I shook my head to dispel the illusion.

"What are you thinking about?" Locke asked me.

"Soulmates. We're really soulmates," I whispered. My eyes flickered to my ring. I couldn't help but marvel at how it glimmered in the fae lights. Locke followed my gaze, smiling that dimple smile that made my heart stop and pick up faster. The one that brought out his dimples. The one he gave only to me.

"You're just realizing this now?" He chuckled. "Here I thought our situation had been well established."

"I just keep waiting for the other shoe to drop, I guess," I said. "But that's not going to happen, is it?" He tugged me ever to slightly closer to him, my body pressed against his almost indecently.

"No, it won't. You're mine until the end of time. Just as I belong to you. Death may try to separate us, but it won't be successful." His voice dropped an octave. "If the veil tries to take you from me, I'll rip apart the very seams of reality and bring you back to me." My ability to breathe was taken from me. But I also listened to what he didn't say. Did that mean he has some sort of plan?

Before I could ask him, the song ended and we were greeted by Aspen holding an unusually large flask. Locke took a swig from it before offering it to me. My tongue sang with the sweetness. It may as well have been juice.

"Let's get this party really started." Aspen grinned and clapped Locke on the back. Locke laughed before returning the gesture and taking a big swig.

"I was beginning to think you'd never ask," Locke replied with an air of conspiracy. Very un-prince-like. Devious. I took another generous gulp from Aspen's flask, as if I could fully prepare for what the night had to offer.

Chapter Thirty-Two

Upon waking, I wasn't sure if my head had been kicked in and set on fire or not. The ever intrusive light was stabbing my eyes, making my already painful head throb. My throat was without moisture of any kind and should be renamed after something in the Fire Court, seeing as it felt as dry as the Burnished Basin was supposed to be. I groaned when my stomach heaved with the slightest movement. Oh, good. Today was going to be a blast.

A throaty chuckle sounded next to me and I didn't even have to turn. I recognized Locke. The dip in the bed moved and I felt warm lips graze my temple.

"Good morning, sleepy head." Locke's usually infectious grin was wide and massively amused, and I had the persistent needling feeling it was at my expense. I groaned in response, incapable yet of speech. "How do you feel?"

"*Likeiwannadie,*" I forced out unintelligibly after a moment, drawing a barking laugh from Locke. I blinked my eyes open with a hiss and curled under the covers. My stomach ached—more bloated than I'd ever been before, and this was one kind of fullness I wasn't fond of. I turned my thought over to last night and paused, coming up blank. I had so few memories. Including how I got to bed.

I peeked up at Locke, who still smirked and hadn't lost any of his amusement, with suspicion. Though I wasn't sure who I was more suspicious of, him, or me.

Though the sinking feeling in my stomach suggested me.

"What happened last night?"

"Wait, you don't remember?"

I grimaced at the implication in his tone, at his widening mischievous grin. I remember brief flashes but nothing consistent. Nothing that I could anchor to my brain and the longer I tried, the more fleeting the memory became and the more permanent my headache seemed to become.

"If I'm asking, would that not infer that I don't remember?" My voice came out as an exhausted groan even to my own ears. I pulled the pillow over my head.

"Someone is spicy this morning." Locke tsked, not looking remotely remiss. Bastard. I rolled my eyes, irritation warring with curiosity, both only just overshadowing the fact that I felt like death. "Where do we start? What's your last memory?"

I thought back, casting my mind to the events of the previous night. My brain felt like it was trying to hop up and down, pat its head, and rub its stomach at the same time, but I eventually made out some pictures in my mind.

"I remember dancing. With Lennox, with Aspen, and then with you. I remember drinking a lot of wine. I remember Aspen and me talking. But not much after that."

"Oof." Locke cringed for dramatic effect. "That's early in the night, love. Who knew you were such a lightweight?"

"Are you going to tell me what I did or not?"

"Spicy indeed." Locke laughed.

The more Locke spoke of the events of last night, the more I was glad I didn't remember them. But unfortunately, pesky bits of memory came running back like a dog who'd been summoned, despite my not wanting it. He described in far more detail than necessary with an ever widening grin at my mortification, the events of last night.

Apparently I had quite the night. I decided to go on an adventure and meet all the fae in Port Azure. Locke apparently had to step in at one point because while I thought I was making friends, I was actually being recruited for a threesome. My mortification was not finished there though. Goddess, no. Because Locke almost couldn't stop laughing long enough to tell me about how I'd gotten hungry and I stole all the mashed potatoes from the communal table, threatened anyone who tried to take them from me, and passed out holding the bowl. At some point, I had gathered other bowls of cheese and gravy and other fixings and made a mashed potato bar around myself in the foyer of the Citadel, using a rug as a blanket and claiming the ice cold floor was good for the soul.

My embarrassment reached new heights when my brain picked that moment to show me what Locke wasn't going to. The moment he found me there. With the bowls around me in a semi circle and the serving spoon still in my hand. Flashes of memory, the biting cold of the icy floor, the bowls around me, Locke chuckling as he found me.

Ugh.

I wasn't convinced the mortification would ever leave me.

As the snippet of memory faded I scrubbed my eyes to blur the memory, or better yet, rid myself of the humiliation altogether. If whole magic had fewer limits than we thought, I wondered if I could destroy that particular memory. I groaned in horror, which only served to make Locke laugh harder.

"Ugh, I hate you," I said digging my increasingly red face into the pillow as if I could stave off mortification. Locke laughed, pausing a moment for dramatic effect, as if considering something.

"No you don't!" His teasing voice came after a few short moments of silence. It was hard to miss that self assuredness in his tone. I felt the mattress dip further right next to me, making my stomach roil in protest. Those dips moved about as he positioned himself overtop me before flopping. The breath wheezed out of my lungs—partly from the sudden pressure and partly from a gasping laugh—as he went about settling his warm body over my back like a blanket and effectively pinning me in place. His stubbly chin tickled my neck, making me laugh and squirm despite my body's protests. He continued to drag his chin against the sensitive and ticklish skin there until I howled with laughter and tried in vein to buck him off. It was only when I was truly breathless from his onslaught that he at last showed mercy by removing his offending facial hair from my neck as I gasped for air. "The curse is still intact. You *love* me."

"False. Nope. Couldn't be," I said between dragging in breaths. "If I loved you, I wouldn't have the urge to stab you right now."

"You don't have anything to stab me with!" he reminded me ever so sweetly.

"Anything can stab anything if enough force is applied."

"Oh, love." His voice grated on that favored nickname. "I do enjoy when you talk dirty."

"Don't get any ideas, Locke. I'm about to die. Unless you're into things I'm not, keep your petty paws off of me."

Locke didn't look remotely remiss, but looked down at his hands in slight exaggerated confusion. "Petty paws?" His laugh rocketed around the room before he flopped to the bed next to me, pulling me close. His warmth was soothing and I melted like a puddle into him and closed my eyes.

"Can we just stay here like this?"

His arms tightened their hold on me in response.

"Sure. But what if I got Aspen to see if he can do anything for your hangover first so you at least feel better?"

My eyes snapped open. "That's an option?"

Locke grinned at my candor before beckoning me to follow him the short distance down the hall to Aspen's rooms. Knocking yielded no results. Maybe he wasn't up yet. Locke ducked his head in and quickly withdrew it with a hushed snicker. When I asked why we were leaving, he said Aspen already had 'lots of company to entertain.' My face split into equal parts amusement and repulsion. I would never get that horrendous image out of my head, as long as I lived.

"Thank the Goddess Eldan is an option," Locke said, steering me in the direction of his shop downstairs. I glanced at him in mock horror.

"Yes, but if he's in the same condition as Aspen, I'll need you to just go ahead and gouge my eyes out."

My magic slowly returned to normal. I began helping Locke with the project of carving out the earth under Port Azure further to accommodate all of the rebels in the event of another attack. When we left with our armies, these fae would still need some protection. Especially if we never came back. An entire day of using my Earth magic had wiped me out entirely, my forehead dripping in sweat from the exertion. So when I finally bathed and sat down to dinner at our usual table with Locke and our friends, I was almost too tired to eat, and too starving not to.

Aspen funneled healing magic into me, restoring life into my stretched-too-thin muscles. I sighed from the relief it brought, even if it were minimal. But it did nothing to quell the feeling of the curse still growing in me, something I'd not noticed with all the excitement. As I bit back and swallowed the now familiar pain I knew was coming, as I felt another piece of myself die, I knew I was nearing my death with every passing day. I could feel death, while not super close, stalking me at a distance as if gauging me.

"We need to take action soon," I said, after voicing my thoughts to the table. "We need to get into Loc Valen. And we need in there now."

"Agreed," Locke in a voice as tight as his clenched fists. The color had partially drained from his face. I wondered if he also could feel the time slipping away from us as I could. "We can't wait any longer for intel. We have no more time."

"How do we get in?" This was from Lenore. "It's warded against jumpstones and other means of portalling, the battlements are closely guarded, so I'm not sure how we're getting in. And with their wards, our magical signatures will be registered as soon as we use it for anything other than the simplest of spells. They'll know we're there."

"But not where we are exactly," Lennox mused. "But it does pose an issue."

"There are scouts along the perimeter and even as far out as the forest that surrounds," said Lenore.

"There is but one way in, the front door," said Lenore. I saw it in my mind's eye. The white walls of Loc Valen, accessible only by the narrow causeway, and the one and only portcullis. They had every advantage. We discussed briefly the option of going through the sewers, but truthfully, I thought I'd rather just die before resorting to that. A sentiment that everyone seemed in agreement in. But it was so far the only viable option, which left all of us desperate to find any other solution.

"Can we go over the wall somehow?" I mused more to myself than anything else. Going through the walls wasn't either. Wow and Calan had teased the stones of the walls, scouring for loose ones we could exploit, all to no avail. Even the seaside port was walled and warded, so going through the beach wasn't any better an option. Everyone turned to look at me with pinched expressions.

"Do you see anybody having wings, Lark?" Lenore snapped before apologizing in a hushed tone. She fingered her long blonde hair. An anxious tell I'd not seen her do before. She was really worried about this. If the violent one didn't feel confident about this mission, how much of a chance did we have of getting Locke's family out?

"Can black magic form wings?" I asked in a mousy voice. I wasn't even sure if it were possible or if I were being naïve. But Pisces seemed to be able to make his black magic do things that whole and elemental magic couldn't. All of the current Water Court Zodiacs routinely crafted weapons from their black magic. Would this be the same? If we could fly over while shrouded, that would solve a lot of issues. Locke froze as he considered.

"I can't really try here, but I'll try tomorrow in Hell's Gate," he said, taking a long sip of his wine. "I can't believe I've never thought to try that!" He grinned in a way that made me think that a few more glasses of wine and he'd be trying it before long.

"Okay, but you'll be sighted if you just fly in. You'll stick out like a sore thumb. It's the opposite of stealthy." This from furrowed-brow Lennox. Locke's idiotic grin remained in place.

"That's great and all, but now I really just want to know if I can fly."

I gave him a look of mock exasperation, widening his now toothy grin. "Glad to know your priorities are in line," I teased.

"You're just jealous," he replied. I couldn't deny that if he could form wings and fly, I would, in fact, be jealous.

"You don't even know if you can even do it!" I tossed back.

"But when I can, you'll be jealous."

"I hope you fall from an inconvenient height."

Locke burst out laughing. "Inconvenient?"

"Yes!" I bit back a laugh. "As in, I hope you fall and Aspen can heal your rolled ankle, not you fall and your head is caved in. Inconvenient." Lenore and Aspen snickered.

And then I had a very old fashioned idea. One that gave everyone pause. There was a lot of initial disagreement, but as I pled my case, and the lack of other options coming up, it was clear what we had to do. At first it seemed too obvious. Too on the nose. It was risky. But was likely the easiest way into Loc Valen unseen and undetected by the wards. And after some time debating, we finally had our plan of attack. We had the time bombs ready, tiny little magical explosions that had been paused at the time of detonation and sealed inside a strong containment spell. A very impressive magical skill one of Aquarius's councilfae possessed. When we removed the containment spell from close enough, the resulting continuing explosion would level the wall to the ground, gaining us access to the city and its Queen. Locke confirmed that he could shroud them from unfriendly eyes until the time was right. Wren and Calan would place them in hidden nooks and crannies so they were ready to the day we marched on Loc Valen. That was phase one. Phase two was getting Locke's family out of the city. Everything was in place. Tomorrow, we mobilized our small unit to place those bombs along the city's wall. Tomorrow, we bring back Locke's parents safe and sound.

Tomorrow we lay the final cobblestone on the road to war. Feeling how the curse writhed within me, it wasn't a day too soon.

Chapter Thirty-Three

Locke had clearly had too much to drink at dinner. I should've stopped him. I didn't want to see him hurt. But I could no more stop the riotous grin on my face as I laughed a cheer to him from my place on the stairs behind him. Aspen took up his spot on the arena floor of Hell's Gate, roaring in laughter and crude words of encouragement I'd scarcely heard from him before and had my eyebrows meeting my hairline.

It turned out Locke could, in fact, craft wings of shadow. A very interesting discovery. We'd all made the journey here after dinner when Locke couldn't stop thinking about it and wondering aloud how he hadn't thought to try this before.

He'd first tried to fly from on the ground. The air in Hell's Gate stirred with the movement of his shadowy wings, the black never fully still, always moving, swirling in the stillness. Tendrils of shadow writhed around him, as if with a mind of their own. The inky, black wings were massive. Much bigger than I would ever have thought they'd need to be. He'd tried an handful of times without any success. So Aspen and Locke decided that a running start into a glide was the answer. Lennox, Lenore, and I laughed as we began taking bets on whether or not he'd pull it off. But it was no fun, considering we all agreed this was going to end poorly. So now I watched him, peeking through my fingers at my grinning, tipsy soulmate as he assessed the drop from the edge of the stairs—a 30 foot drop to the arena floor. He flexed his wings with difficulty; I was sure the feeling was extremely alien to him, based on the look on his face. With the way Aspen egged him on, I felt badly for the Goddess attempting to keep him alive.

"He's going to die, isn't he?" I stage whispered to Lennox. Locke shot me a look over his shoulder and rolled his eyes skyward, muttering something under his breath about soulmates and their lack of confidence. Lennox shrugged, her smirk turning her lips upwards even as she shook her head at the male foolishness unfolding before us.

"Maybe not. He's one of the most powerful fae in Meridian. He might pull it off." Lennox didn't sound convinced, but at least someone was open minded. Lenore shot her a disbelieving look before winking at me.

"He's absolutely about to eat shit. And we get a front row view." The grin appearing on her face said she wished she had snacks. But alas, our glasses of wine, or in Lenore's case, a foul smelling concoction of her own invention will have to do.

"I heard that, Lenore!" shot Locke from where he was positioning himself at the top of the coliseum.

"Definitely about to eat shit," I whispered to the twins. Lenore flashed me a wide grin as Locke turned to glare at me.

"Lark! You're supposed to believe in me."

"You got this!" I gave him my most placating tone.

Locke muttered something about traitorous soulmates before returning his full attention to the task at hand. He once again flexed his shadowy wings, rolling his broad shoulders back with them. He took off at a run—the world's slowest run from the drag of the poorly positioned wings—and leapt from the ledge.

My breathing stopped as I listened for the telltale sounds of collision. When I heard nothing right away, we all rushed to the ledge, just in time to watch Locke's face meet the arena floor unceremoniously with a steady stream of curses. Aspen's booming laugh rose above everything as he stumbled over towards his best friend, his laughter rendering him too slow to run as he gasped for breath at Locke's expense.

My head fell into my hands as I laughed, shoulders shaking, stomach heaving. He'd fallen about half way before his wings caught the air, abruptly interrupting his freefall. He'd hovered a single moment in the air, a heartbeat at most, and then dropped like a stone when his wings couldn't hold their form any longer and damned near landed face first into the ground.

The twins and I were laughing so hard, none of us could get a breath. Lenore was shrieking and snorting, Lennox giving an odd sound somewhere between a screech and a laugh.

"Told you," Lenore griped as she slowly recovered. Her sobering face didn't last long, and neither did mine as we were sent tumbling into another fit at Locke's pout in our direction.

"I had it!" Locke exclaimed. "I can do it!"

"Maybe eventually," Lennox breathed out between a fit of giggles at Locke's expense. "But for now, you didn't fly. You straight up fell. On your face." Lenore was in stitches on my other side, the win having clearly taken a large effect on her sense of humor.

Locke hit her with a splash of water and moped. I couldn't breathe between my own laughing fit. At his fake mopey expression, still covered with dirt.

"Hey! Soulmate!" he grinned. "You're supposed to support me!"

"I told you this was a dumb idea. You didn't listen. Not my fault you have dumb ideas," I said. Though it just occurred to me that I could've helped him with a wee bit of Air Magic. A gust of wind to keep him aloft, or maybe even to cushion the landing. I'd save that tidbit of information for next time.

Chapter Thirty-Four

Hell's Gate lived up to its name. Scores of fae threw themselves into training around me, the sounds of mock battle, shouts, grunts, and clanging metal filling the room. Training had taken on a more serious edge around here after the battle. Fae were busy, committing themselves to their training now in a way that bordered on insanity the way the spent themselves in the arena. I spied Aspen running a small legion through a set of complicated swordplay drills, the likes of which he'd only just started to show me, while someone else I didn't recognize supervised a number of particularly intense hand to hand sparring sessions. Locke and I were in the middle of a quick magic lesson, and my fire gave both warmth and light to the arena. I bit back my fatigue as I threw myself into keeping up with Locke's demands.

"Lark, focus," he said with practiced patience. "Do it again."

Locke himself wore a pinched expression. The one he wore when he was studying me—looking for something. Of course, he never told me what. He gave me the order to summon flames and vines at the same time—something I was only sort of improving on. Sweat poured down my back from the effort of keeping my flames from catching on my vines after a time. Earth and Fire Magic really didn't mix. At least we'd given up on my summoning lightning like Aquarius. That entire idea was a bust.

My eyes wandered on their own, as they often did, to Locke. He was watching with narrowed eyes and his arms crossed over his broad shoulders. The shirt he wore showed off his muscular frame with just a hint of his runic tattoos I loved so much. And those arms. I knew so well how it felt to be wrapped up in those arms. The strength they possessed. His contemplative stare darkened as he watched me. Lost in the heat of flame and thought, I felt a whisper, a suggestion of tingling warmth throughout my body. A reaction I wasn't expecting, though I couldn't say it was unwelcome. Especially not when Locke's heating gaze snapped to mine, the blue and gold of his eyes contrasting and intensifying by the orange flames. His face changed then, to that faraway look told me he was reading my aura. And my thoughts had probably turned it a little burgundy. And then I got an idea. Flashing him a coy smile, I let that feeling fill me up. The searing heat my magic produced had nothing on the heat my mind was conjuring. My thighs pressed together and my teeth sank into my lip as I pictured his hands roughly grasping my hair, his length hitting that perfect spot. His hand—real this time—found my chin, tipping it up to look at him. His expression was impassive, but I saw the heat flare when I bit my lip. I saw his eyes divert to the action. I noticed the deliberately careful gap he left between us. The heat and electricity bringing every part of me to life at his proximity.

"I know what you're doing." His voice grated over the words, his reaction making me giddy. He hit me with a look of admonition over my shoulder. "Keep it up. I dare you. I have no qualms about putting you over my shoulder here and putting you over my knee behind closed doors shortly after."

My face flushed despite my riotous grin. Schooling my expression, I turned to Locke eyes with him over my shoulder with an innocent smile. I didn't stop. Even if I wanted to, my thoughts had run away with me. The thought of him putting me over his knee and then over his bedside was intoxicating. My finger nails bit into my palm. Flames sputtered and burned chaotically around us, the bonfire that both was and wasn't simultaneously. I couldn't care less about training right now. All I could think about was the few inches of distance there was between us. How there were far too many clothes between us, how there were too many fae here, and how liquid my core felt.

"Do you have any idea what you're doing to me?" His voice was strained in my ear. His teeth nipped the sensitive flesh of my earlobe, making my lungs lose control of my breath. "This is your final warning. Knock it off, or I drag you out of here in front of everyone." Did he honestly think that was going to dissuade me?

"Is that a threat, Crowned Assassin?" I teased. Feeling bold by the cover of my flames around us, I grasped him firmly and let out the smallest moan, one only his Zodiac hearing could detect. He growled low in my ear, widening my smile, and my body clenched in anticipation. "Or is it something of a promise?"

I pictured his cold tongue between my thighs, his hands roving over my breasts—and true to his word, paying no mind to the now gossiping fae around us, he hoisted and threw me over his shoulder. My squeak of amusement and delight as his large strides made for the exit. My flames dispersed, all my magic fell away as I giggled. Though my face flushed hot when I looked up to see Vanneck staring with a look somewhere between discomfort and amusement. Locke chuckled darkly as he walked through the doors of Hell's Gate and marched towards his office.

"It's too late for embarrassment, love," he growled again low in his throat, a hint of the beast I was certain I'd just unleashed. I grinned as we exited the arena and strode into the hallway. "You did this. Own it." He made sure nobody was looking before his hand came up to strike my rear, making me jump. I bit my lip as his hand caressed where it had collided, his fingers roving far towards my center. I squirmed, feeling desperate for his touch now that we were approaching his destination. He threw open the door to his office, striding through and hurrying to lock it. Though I doubted anyone would be looking for either of us for the time being. He deposited me on his desk.

"Oh? Not your knee? I must be getting off easy. Don't tell me the Crowned Assassin is all talk?"

His eyes darkened as he surveyed me hungrily. "Oh, you'll be getting off soon enough. But not before I've had my fun. You want over my knee so badly? It can be arranged." He sat down on his chair by the fire, the one I liked to read in, looking like a dark god upon his throne. He patted his knee, looking up at me with an expectant expression that turned me molten. "Come, Lark," he said, now crooking two fingers at me. When I was close enough, he grasped my arm and pulled me the rest of the way. I wasn't even fully settled yet when his hand smacked my behind, not painfully, but hard enough to take notice, his hand kneading the small stinging hurt immediately after. I found myself arching back into his hand, wanting more. So much more. His hand collided with me again, sending warmth cascading through me, his kneading palm making me squirm with need.

"Locke..." My voice was hoarse and simmering with desire. His hand every so slowly pulled down my pants to expose my behind, his fingers wasting no time burying themselves in my waiting warmth.

"You're so ready for me, already."

His growl of approval followed his fingers stoking me higher. I moaned his name, palming his now very hard length through the material that separated us, wanting, needing to give him pleasure too. I undid his pants, loving the way he cursed when he sprang free. Loving even more the next expletive when my hand ran along him. I could feel my pulse quickening as my body began to coil tightly, reaching higher and higher towards the waiting bliss—

When his hands stopped their ministrations.

I cried out, my hips grinding into where his hand resting on my rear, searching desperately for the release his hands were promising. Pleas on the tip of tongue that never came. That dark chuckle again told me I was in trouble. "Oh, love. Did you think I'd let you off the hook so easily?" I didn't answer. Because I knew better. But I could play his game. I went to slide off his lap, to get on my knees, but he held me firm. "You're not hijacking this game. You'll be taking that punishment." His hand smacked me again. And again. And it was all I could do not to cry out each time. But I lost control entirely when he gently swatted my core—not enough to hurt. But only just. It sent me feral. Gone was my dignity when we alternated between smacking my behind, my waiting warmth and his fingers sinking into me and driving me towards that high again. I begged, I pleaded with him until I was trembling.

"Do you want to come, Lark?" came his sultry voice. I nodded, another plea falling from my lips. A growl rumbled in his chest as his fingers sank into me again, stretching me. "You're soaking my hand. You don't come until I say."

I nodded as if I had a choice in the matter. His hands worked me in earnest now, driving deeper and harder. And faster. My hips pushed back against him, my cries filling the room. "That's it, love. You're so close." My insides quickened, and I was so close. He slowed his pace and I wanted to scream.

"It would be such a shame if I stopped, wouldn't it?"

"Please. Locke. I can't take much more." My breaths and words came in pants.

"You'll take everything I give you to take, Lark," he said in a rough voice I'd never heard before. A voice rife with authority. With command. Just when I thought I couldn't hold off any longer, I heard the words I was desperate to hear. "Come for me. Give it to me." My body coiled tightly around him, our connection becoming the center of my entire world before I spasmed around his hand, falling to pieces. My body sagged on his lap while I caught my breath. But I smiled. I knew what to do next.

This time when slid from his lap, he let me. He watched me with a scorching expression as I settled on my knees before him. My hands slid up and down his thighs, building the tension. His darkened gaze never left mine.

"Allow me to make it up to you. But first, I think you're overdressed." With a growl fueled by desire, he remedied that for me, presenting himself to me. I breathed before licking him base to tip and taking him into my mouth. My tongue swirled around his head, over the very sensitive top before taking him deep. Satisfaction rippled through me as he hissed a breath, followed by a grunted version of my name. His hands came up to fist themselves in my hair, forcing me to pick up the pace while also flexing his hips into me. His cock hit the back of my throat, making me gag while he released a sound of pure ecstasy. And I let him do it several more times, listening for the telltale sign of his breathing picking up before wrenching his hands from my hair and sitting back on my knees with a coy smile. "I can play your game too."

I'd never get used to his Zodiac speed. One moment I was on my knees smirking up at him, and the next I was bent over his desk and he was lining himself up with my entrance. I pushed back against him, impatiently impaling myself on his waiting length. We both hissed our satisfaction as he swiftly filled me and I was reminded how my imagination didn't do him any justice as he hit that aching spot in the very center of me. I cursed as he withdrew and quickly filled me again, his pace increasing to something that had me crying out—loudly enough I was grateful that his office was spelled to silence.

"Oh fuck, I love the way you take me." His praise had me nearly ready to combust. My legs began to shake from the tension building again in my core—though this time it threatened to tear me apart when it exploded. His one hand reached down found the sensitive bundle of nerves that staggered my breathing. His other gripped my scalp by my hair, gently enough not to hurt, but firm enough not to be able to move. To force me to take everything he gave me as he saw fit. "That's it, love. Nobody can hear you but me. So I want to hear you scream my name from your pretty pink lips."

A few more thrusts had me following his command. I arched my back into him further, moaning his name over and over. A beg either for mercy or for more, I wasn't sure. I felt myself clamp down hard on him as the tension finally detonated. He grunted, feeling how tight I held him as my orgasm swept through me, obliterating all thought and reason until there was only the two of us and nothing else. A few thrusts later had him slamming into me with almighty force before thickening still and spilling himself inside me.

I was spent. Exhausted, I sagged on the desk for a second before pulling my pants back up. In the heat and excitement of the moment, neither of us had fully removed a single item of clothing. As a result, his pants had my essence on them. I flushed, knowing everyone was going to know. Locke throwing me over his shoulder was one thing. This was another. He righted himself, following my gaze to the mess on his pants. He chuckled.

"If anyone sees before I change, I don't care. Let them all know you're mine. Let them know I belong to you body," his hands found my face, cupping gently before placing a kiss to my lips, "and soul." I melted in his arms, my hands coming up to wrap around his neck and pull him closer.

"Goddess, I love you. But your water magic could wash that out in an instant. Now you're just being sloppy." I whispered against his lips. He smiled in response. Not a grin. Not a smirk. A dimple bearing, heart wrenching, knees weakening smile.

"And I, you," he said. "And I'm going to ignore that statement about me being sloppy, because we're having an endearing moment I won't let you ruin." He chuckled against my lips when I used my own water magic to clean my essence off his pants. His hand came to rest on my cheek, tilting my face to look up at that brilliant smile. "No matter what happens in the coming days, no matter how much time we have, it will only ever be you. Forever. Soulmate."

Only hours later, Locke gave my attire a withering look, complete with thinly pinched lips and a furrowed brow, but remained stoically silent as I did up the last remaining laces of my leather armor. I could feel his disapproval from here. I knew why. Even though we'd both agreed that dragon scale armor was far too rare and therefore far too recognizable. We had to remain as inconspicuous as possible.

That required not putting anything on that might draw attention. I shoved my feet in my leather boots and dropped my knives in them as always, making me feel slightly more protected. I felt even more bolstered when I hoisted my father's sword—*my* sword, I corrected myself for the umpteenth time—to its resting place on my hip.

Gazing back at me in the mirror... I almost didn't know who this Lark was. She was certainly a far cry from the angry, wide eyed girl that landed here months ago. Now who stared impassively back at me through emerald eyes was a warrior. Strong legs clad in black pants and sheen-less black leather boots that were ideal for moving through shadows unnoticed. Black leather chest plate swallowing rays of light as they encountered it. Black leather gauntlets laced up my arms all the way to my wrists. The pale skin of my wrists and face were like drops of snow above a black chasm. I dragged a brush through my blonde tresses and wrangled my hair into a long braid that tumbled over my right shoulder where it draped over my chest. I crossed my arms, frowning at my reflection. I looked far more menacing than I'd ever looked previously. The blade at my waist hinted at danger and warned others away. Locke appeared in the mirror's reflection with me over my shoulder looking so much like the day were first me: dangerous. Dangerous and not to be trifled with.

Everything rested on us not being discovered or recognized. Locke, as if reading my thoughts, brought a hood up from his cloak over his head, and with a twist of his hand, enshrouded himself in shadow, leaving him completely indistinguishable. I saw my eyebrows raise in real time, surprised with just how well it worked. I pulled up my own hood and Locke's magic replicated the effects on me as well, casting both of us as completely anonymous. The only thing: we couldn't use his magic to get past the border of the city. Once within the city, Locke could use his magic sparingly, as could I. Shrouding our faces and the bombs would take little magic or effort on his part. Thankfully, Wrought Iron Wren, who I would forever refer to as Wow to his ever grumbling disapproval, was also gifted with shrouding abilities along with his black magic. He would share the load of hiding the bombs for the final battle.

Four of us would go in. And only two of us would come out. That was the plan. Wow and Calan would stay behind to gather intel and find out if Scorpio were regrouping for another attack on Port Azure, and when. They would attempt to figure out the size and scale of Scorpio's army. They would pull out in a couple days time and report back with anything they could glean. Information that may alter our plans. As it was, the smithies were working around the clock to get armor and blades made for all those who needed it. A tall order, information of this magnitude often took weeks, not hours or days, but they were confident they could pull it off. They each had a jumpstone, so even if they were separated, they could get out in the event of discovery. A thought that settled my heart a small amount. I didn't want to see anything happen to them.

Locke and I shared a loaded, somber expression. One that spoke in volumes enough that words were rendered useless. Locke's eyebrow twitched as he read my emotions, his eyes searching my face. For what, I wasn't sure. His lips parted as if to speak but I beat him to it.

"I love you," I blurted out. I stumbled over my tongue trying to find the words, but Locke spoke then.

"Don't you dare." He levelled me with a strange expression I couldn't understand. Several emotions registered on his face, too fast for me to pinpoint all of them. His sharp eyes missed nothing as he read my emotions. "Stop saying goodbye. We're going to do this. Our plan is solid."

"I know," I said, grabbing his hand and squeezing gently. A squeeze he returned. "And we'll get your parents too. After today, Scorpio won't have anything hanging over your head." Although, I thought to myself why had we not received word, or more, about their deaths considering his now being a confirmed traitor. He went against her. Why were they not showing up in pieces at our doorstep, now that she knew where we were?

I was certain we'd find his parents. I was certain we'd bring them home. What I wasn't certain was what their physical or mental condition would be when we found them. What I wasn't certain of was were we bringing home two fae? Or were we bringing home two tortured souls, two husks that Scorpio had let wither and wilt under pain of Goddess only knew what? But I schooled my worried expression back, lest he somehow track the course of my thoughts as he occasionally did.

We met Aspen, Lenore, and Lennox at the Gate of Port Azure, now fully reconstructed. Scouts now resided in place along the perimeter, a measure Locke had ordered immediately after the assault Scorpio had rained down upon us. I wondered what would happen if Scorpio's denizens returned. Would they all run to Hell's Gate to try to outlast them? Would it work? I didn't know. At this point, I wondered why they didn't just get on a big ship and sail to a distant land. But I knew the reason. This was their home. And they would rather die defending it, protecting the slice of freedom they'd found, than have it wrenched from them or be driven out.

While we waited for Wow and Calan to show up, I fortified the gate once again with my Earth Magic, thorns and vines making it impossible to open. I threw my magic into it further, the vines in turn pushing further outward along the entire wall. I gasped at the amount of magic I used, but I couldn't stop. Because I knew it would be incredibly difficult for anyone to get to Port Azure now. I heard a chilling shriek from not far into the trees.

Wren lumbered his hulking frame into view, Calan next to him looking chipper and excited. Or perhaps that was just in contrast to how grumpy Wow was all the time.

"Okay, let's get this show on the road," Wren grumbled by way of greeting. I smiled.

"I want snacks before we go," Calan said. Aspen laughed.

"Only if you share."

"For the love of the Goddess, can we please just go without everyone bitching about snacks?" Lenore simmered from her place against a tree sharpening one of her axes.

"Don't mind her," Aspen stage whispered to Calan, whose eyebrows met his hairline. "She's just cranky and wants snacks." Her axe met the tree next to his head a second later. When I glanced over, Lenore had drawn her other axe and proceeded to sharpen it, a whistled tune and a smirk on her lips.

Calan eyed Lenore with... appreciation? I cast my eye at Locke, who confirmed my thoughts with a wink. I remembered them dancing the other night, but this was different. Calan looked at her with a softness I'd not seen from him before. He had a crush on Lenore. I beamed. I wondered if she knew. Calan was certainly handsome enough for Lenore, a strong jaw line, and cheekbones you could slice yourself on. Tall, and clearly a capable spy, and very trusted by Locke. Oh, this could be so much fun later. Locke's rumbling chuckle from beside me told me he knew where my thoughts had taken me. Locke's expression sobered after a beat. He brought forth the jumpstone from the pocket of his cloak, eying all of us.

"Does everyone remember the plan?" he asked all of us. "Now is the time to say something." Everyone nodded, but no words were spoken. Everyone grew silent with a quiet restlessness between us.

"I love you all," I whispered, breaking that silence. "Please be careful." I grasped Lennox's hand when she gave mine a gentle squeeze.

"Love you too," she whispered. Lenore rolled her eyes as she grasped my other hand. In Lenore's language, I knew she was returning the sentiment. Aspen winked at me and crossed his arms, calm and confident. Wren shifted his weight and averted his gaze, looking incredibly uncomfortable. Calan and Vanneck smiled gently.

"Ready?" Locke asked. I nodded, the others following in sync. The familiar bright light reached out to meet me. And when it faded, I was surrounded by trees. The forest to the edge of Loc Valen. Deep into enemy territory.

I doubted it would ever not be disorienting to blink once and be in one setting, breathing in briny, yet alpine scented air, and to blink once more and be surrounded by a sleeping forest and the scent of frosted forest. I blinked a few times to right myself and as I observed the others, I seemed to be the only one who felt disoriented. Lenore palmed her own jumpstone in her pocket almost absentmindedly. Just to reassure herself of where it was.

We had agreed that each group get a jumpstone in case of emergency. Locke carried ours at my insistence. He'd tried to give it to me but of course the pockets of my clothing weren't deep enough for my to feel like it wouldn't get lost. Locke's face soured before pocketing it himself. I knew why. He wanted to do the hero thing and give me a way out if he felt the need to be self sacrificing again. I crossed my arms. As if..

Calan carried his and Wren's, and Lenore carried for Lennox, Vanneck, and Aspen. So many of the jumpstones in the Rebel Court possession, right here. It seemed unwise and yet a necessary risk in the event of detection or worse—capture. Dismissing the thought as soon as it occurred to me, I pressed my lips into a thin line as we pressed forward towards Loc Valen. Locke and Wren bade us to hide until they found what they were looking for: Loc Valen scouts. And our disguise.

I rubbed my hands together, bracing against the heavy and oppressive chill in the air. Winter had come, bringing with it frosty temperatures and a light dusting of snow. The ground was frozen here, hard and unforgiving under my leather clad feet. I summoned a tiny shred of fire magic over my skin to drive away the cold. Lennox looked over at me longingly.

"Hold on, I have an idea," I said brightly. I called the flames forth as close to my skin as possible, so that they ran just along the surface of my body, not burning my clothing thanks to my control. Just heat. And a bit more light than I would have liked. But that was quickly taken care of by my friends closely surrounding me, both to douse the light of the flames and to savor the heat I now radiated. Lennox, Lenore, Aspen, Vanneck, and Calan warmed their hands over me like I was their own personal bonfire.

"I have literally never wanted to hug you more than I do right now," said a less shivering Lennox in a quiet, breathy tone, making me huff a laugh. Calan chuckled as he too thawed his chilled fingers over my arms.

I shrugged.

"What can I say? I'm hot."

"I mean, most of us aren't usually so literal, but here we are," said Aspen with a riotous grin at his own joke. Even Calan gave him a sidelong look that told him he needed to try harder. I rolled my eyes in sync with Lenore and shook my head.

"I hope Locke and Wren get back soon," I said, trying to staunch the threads of anticipation in direct opposition to my current stagnation while also trying to stave off the electrical pulses of anxiety that attempted to fry my nerve endings. The more I sat here and waited, the stronger those pulses got.

Vanneck was quiet and contemplative, and barely spoke a word other than one of thanks. I imagined he was preparing himself mentally, however that was for him.

"They will. It won't be long now." This from Calan, his head on a swivel as if watching for oncoming issues. Or perhaps having an internal conversation with the Goddess.

"Hey Lark, can you turn the heat up at all?" I glanced at Lenore with a smile and obliged, watching as she nearly purred as she nestled herself a little bit closer to me in the most feline way. Calan gave her an adoring smile. The kind where the corners of his honey gold eyes crinkled and his face softened. One I didn't miss, but I didn't think anyone else noticed. He caught my eye and I raised my eyebrows at him. He quickly averted his gaze and found something extremely fascinating on the ground beneath our feet. I had to bite my lip to keep from smiling.

Just as Calan predicted, Locke and Wren were back shortly after. In their hands were the dark green robes the scouts wore with the swooping crest of the Water Court in silvery blue over the heart. Locke and Wren had put theirs on already and brought the deep hoods up. Even without shrouding magic, it was hard to see who it was underneath. But that was the thing about scouts. They weren't supposed to be spotted. They relied on moving stealthily and remaining undiscovered. This would hopefully be our ticket in. I donned mine, purposely not seeing the bloodstain on the shoulder. The hood was deep, perfect for enshrouding your identity in shadow. Perfect for being anonymous. A wolf in sheep's clothing. Vanneck, Lennox, and Lenore were our backup if all else failed. Vanneck would be connected to me through a mindspeak spell like Aspen and I did during the attack on Port Azure, as would Locke and Wren. Vanneck performed the spell quickly and efficiently.

Admittedly, I wasn't excited about having someone else in my brain again, even if it were Vanneck. Last time didn't exactly go splendidly. I glanced at Aspen without even thinking about it, and stopped myself. Everything was going to be fine. I needed to relax. If I didn't, I would be the definition of *suspicious* once we were inside the walls.

Everything is going to plan, Vanneck whispered to my mind. I jumped, causing him to frown.

Sorry, I said back to him in my mind. *It's such an odd thing to get used to.*

I understand. Vanneck's frown disappeared. It was odd feeling his thoughts, feeling his worry that he'd offended me. I offered as much of a smile as I could in an attempt at being reassuring. *I will do my best to stay out of your head unless we have need to communicate.*

You can block it off? I wasn't sure I was asking him or musing to myself.

A bit, he offered. *Picture a solid wall in your mind, shutting out communication. I always picture the walls of Port Azure.*

I did that. I pictured my mind as a fortress. I could feel Vanneck, a bright spot in the corner of my mind. I found myself not even wanting to wall off from him, finding it both too stuffed inside my own head, and enjoying the company of his easy presence at the same time.

Did I do it? I asked.

No response. I grinned up at him and he smiled widely in return. Now we wouldn't bother one another. This was excellent news.

Chapter Thirty-Five

W e hid in the tangled pine trees, the only coverage the forest offered in view of the jewel of the Water Court—Loc Valen. And waited. Waited for the changing of the scouts. As they filed in, we would enter the city in their place. I hoped to the Goddess that we weren't the only ones with hoods on so as not to be suspicious. Because if we were discovered at the gate, it was over.

So we waited. My eyes traced the towering white walls of Loc Valen, scouring for a weakness, anything that might have been missed. I still didn't love the risk associated with this plan. Frowning and with an increasing sense of dread, I admitted defeat in that errand.

Scorpio had done her job well.

I remembered when I first came here all those months ago, there were fae on the walls patrolling, but now it seemed like they had doubled their numbers, considerably strengthening their perimeter.

We had to do our job well now too.

Part of me felt confident in our plan. The simplicity of it. A much bigger part of me was glad for the number of blades I had strapped to me. But a small and unfortunately loud part of me, the part I was trying desperately to ignore, whimpered. Was our plan destined to be suicide?

I took in the shining backdrop of the sea. I took in the winter sunlight and surrounding dusting of snow that made the city almost glow. It was... I felt the breath catch in my throat for just a moment. It was an incredible city.

I wondered briefly where Lorelei was. I wondered if she were serving patrons at the Inn right now. Or perhaps it was her day off and she was shopping. Perhaps she milled about the market, or was floating on the water ways that made up the arteries of the city. I wished so fiercely that I could speak to her. To warn her about what would soon happen. Get her and her family out of the city. But I couldn't. Not without risking myself, the mission, and my court. It made my heart hurt.

Movement snagged my vision. I bumped Locke gently with my elbow to remain silent and pointed at the causeway where three figures identical to us walked up. When they reached the gate, they walked inside and three other hooded and cloaked figures walked out, down the causeway, and into the section of the trees that had just been vacated. The forest was never unpatrolled, it seemed. The thought was eerie and like ice water down my spine, forcing my back straight and rigid. I cast my awareness out, as I had several times in the last few minutes, feeling no other fae forms in our immediate vicinity. I knew paranoia was getting to me, but the whole mission relied on us being stealthy. Undiscovered. And right now, I felt so useless I couldn't stand it. We weren't close enough to the wards from here. Unless we shot magic at the walls of Loc Valen from here, we should be fine. It wouldn't register us. A moment later a few more cloaked fae, two this time, went up the causeway to relieve themselves of their post, two more striding in black clothing. Inconspicuous. Blending into the shadows, I would have never seen them. I wondered how Wren and Locke tracked them down. But I knew the answer. These fae were simple scouts. Locke was the Crowned Assassin. And Wrought Iron Wren was the head of intelligence for the Air Court. They were the best in the business.

Finally, it was our turn. Calan, Wren, Locke, and I stood. I brushed pine needles off of myself and pulled my head deep into my hood. Lennox, Lenore, Aspen, and Vanneck remained in cover.

"Be careful," Aspen said to us in a solemn tone that was painfully unlike his usually cheery disposition, turning my thoughts even more ominous. Calan gave Lenore a long look, a look Lenore returned, I noted, and walked away. I turned to look at my friends.

"You lot be careful. I'll see you on the other side." Lenore and Lennox gave me a synchronized mock salute, looking so twin-like it hurt. I smiled as I turned away with Locke at my side.

It was time.

And we would not fail.

I prayed to the Goddess I wouldn't trip over my shaky feet as they carried me out of the forest's cover and into the open area, viewable now to the guards of Loc Valen. Calan and Wren's large, domineering presences felt comforting and reassuring at my back, but even it did nothing to quell my racing heartbeat and unsteady breathing. Locke whispered to me, despite the distance yet to traverse.

"Easy, Lark. Keep it together."

I wanted to tell him that I knew. I wanted to be reassuring. But my voice was lost on the other side of my revving nervous system. I pressed my mouth into a firm line and chewed the inside of my cheek in lieu of my lip. I knew I was chewing too hard when I tasted copper, but I couldn't stop. Grass gave way to cobblestone and Wren's shadows enveloped all our faces, since the wards wouldn't know his magic like it would immediately know Locke's. We marched quickly up the causeway now, every step booming and loud and echoing in my ears. Locke's stride never faltered as he approached, his baleful and watchful eyes cast down and forward from deep within the hood of his cloak. I wished I could bury my face further into mine. Despite the hood shadowing my face effectively, I still felt naked, bared, and obvious. This plan was too obvious. There were four guards at the gate alone, with Goddess only knew however many more I couldn't see. Each one peered at the four of us walking in pairs of two. One guard, a large, brawny fellow with a square jaw and angry, deep set eyes under a giant ridge of a browbone, took in the sight of us with a look of suspicion. His eyes raked up and down each one of us with blatant skepticism.

He knew.

I didn't know what intelligence told me, but every nerve was standing up on edge screaming at me to run. But I kept my feet moving steadily forward, matching my step in time with Locke's next to me. *Don't falter. Don't show fear. They can't see your face,* I kept screaming inside my brain over the constant thrum of anxiety.

We were so close now. So close to them I could see each of their faces clearly now. I could see Loc Valen beyond just as I remembered it from the sliver I could glimpse through the gate checkpoint. Though, Scorpio must be expecting us to do something because I didn't remember there being this many guards when I came here alone. Nobody had given me a second thought, let alone stared me down like this. And I was dressed as one of them.

The other three seemed disinclined to care about our appearing. They each gave us a bored, cursory glance before going back to whatever else they were doing. But the big one with the large browbone continued to stare at us as if he were looking for a puzzle piece. Like his eyes knew the problem but his brain refused to process it. I sent a prayer up to the Goddess that his brain didn't make the connection.

We were at the checkpoint now. I barely dared to breathe. I kept my eye on the horizon where sidewalk met the walls ahead. Kept my eyes glued there. Down, but not at my feet.

"Stop," the large one said, causing my blood to freeze in my veins. The air left my lungs. Locke stiffened almost unperceptively next to me. But I felt it.

"What?" Locke grunted, disguising his voice slightly. Just enough, I hoped.

"Remove your hoods," he demanded. The other guards watched with mild interest, their hands on their weapons in a casual threat.

"I don't answer to you," Locke growled beneath his hood. "It's been a long day. I'll not be tolerating you this baseless interrogation. I'm leaving."

The captain's menacing stare didn't lessen. "I don't care who you answer to. This is my gate. If I tell you to stand on your head, you'll fucking do it, scout!"

Locke laughed, deep and low in his throat. "And yet, here I am. Not doing it. Fuck off," he said as he took a step forward to shrug him off. I stepped with him. He was wrenched backwards by the guard's hand on his shoulder.

"You dare disrespect your superior like that, retch?" His voice was low. Gritty. Almost excited. He was begging Locke to give him an excuse for a fight. Any excuse. Locke snarled low in his throat in return.

"You dare think that you're my superior? Get your hands off of me, or my real superior will do more than have words with you."

"Good. Bring the Cascade down here. I'd love to have a word with him. I'll see you flayed for you disobedience."

Locke shrugged out of the fae's grip and kept walking. Calan, Wren, and I continued on with Locke once his feet began moving. I fought to keep my steps confident and steady. Long, slow, unhurried strides rather than the short steps in rapid succession I was desperate to be taking.

"The Cascade sends his regards. But he'll be along once I speak to him. You can be sure of that." Locke finished smoothly, "I'd sleep with one eye open if I were you."

The guard captain snarled his rage. "I said hood off, scouts! And I won't tolerate your lack of respect." One of them grabbed my shoulder and spun me around as the captain advanced on Locke again, a grim, self-satisfied smirk in place. I panicked, unsure what to do. Play it cool? Scream? Fight? Even if these fae saw my face, did they know what I looked like?

The fae in front of me who'd looked incredibly bored previously now looked at me with an expression somewhere between hostility and curiosity. I held my ground.

"The hood, if you please," he ground out, reaching for it. I smacked his hand away as he did so. A flare of anger and outrage dilated his pupils as he wrenched me closer to him and his fingers closed on my hood.

And then I was blind. My body was thrown violently to the side. There was no sound other than the yelling of the Guards and the drawing of swords.

This is it, I thought with a sickening sinking feeling. My heart plummeted out my body and through the ground. A freefall to Hell itself. We'd been caught. This stupid plan didn't even get us in the door.

We'd failed.

Chapter Thirty-Six

I felt someone grasp my arm. I thrashed against it. As it tugged me along, I stopped struggling and I followed. The bright light had taken precedence over our rudeness and refusal to fall in line. The guard captain bellowed orders to his underlings, and they cast themselves into position in a flurry of magic and melee weapons and arrows. Movement was all around us, though my vision was still compromised. I saw only in extremes, in stark light and opposing shadows as they moved through it. When, above the chaos, I heard Locke's voice.

"Follow me, Lark! You're okay!" I held to his hand in answer as he, Calan, and Wren shouldered our way through the oncoming throng of weapon-bearing fae.

"Make way!" I heard Calan's voice over the throng of others. "We have injured!"

By the highest mercy of the Goddess, not one fae questioned it, letting us pass by as they rushed forward by us to the gate. Like water around rock. I even added a limp to sell the story.

My head spun as color began to leech back into my field of vision, blurry at first but regaining focus moments later. But then I heard a fae shout something that made my heart stop and give an anxious squeeze.

"...twins..."

My heart sank. How did they find the twins? We had no time to lose if Loc Valen were looking for them. At the same time, it meant they weren't necessarily looking for us.

The road opened up into a familiar sight: the square I'd visited before, and Lorelei's Inn on the corner, looking just the very same as it did those months ago. Before, I'd looked up at all the bustling fae in wonder. Now I looked around and saw a risk in every face. If they saw me, saw us. If they knew who we were... We needed to find cover. Now. I cleared my throat to grab the attention of my companions and gestured to the Inn.

"We're four scouts in need of a beer," I said. They nodded. Locke gave me a strange look I couldn't decipher. But he looked hesitant. I hoped against hope that Lorelei would help us. Or at least not hinder us.

Our boots thumped loudly on the wooden steps leading to the tavern. The door creaked as it swung on its rusted hinges and I was struck by the scent of it as it hit me—the same pale citrus cleaner, stale ale, and something homey wafting in from the kitchen. There were a few patrons chatting easily and paying us no mind as we entered, despite the hoods being drawn. Lorelei looked just as I remembered: tall, pretty, and with a rag in her hand, working so much harder than she ever should need. I walked to the bar, my heart pounding with the risk I was about to take. I could feel Locke bristling against what he now realized I was about to do, but he couldn't stop me without drawing suspicion to himself and our party. I could only pray. And hope.

"Hi!" Lorelei chimed as brightly as I remembered, before bringing her eyes up to look at me. "What can I do for you?" Her voice trailed off as I brought my face forward in the hood, but didn't remove it, showing her, and only her, my face. Her eyes widened, both with surprise and recognition. Locke stiffened next to me and I could only hope that we weren't making a mistake.

"Is it really you?" she whispered, side-eying the fae around us. The patrons of the Inn dutifully nursed their drinks, paying us no mind. I nodded, leaning onto the counter to keep my voice low between us.

"Can you get us a private room for just a few minutes? I can explain."

Lorelei hesitated but nodded. "Follow my lead." She winked. Her voice rose in candor at her next words. "Of course, sir. I'd be happy to accommodate you." I grinned. *Sir.* Great touch. "If you and your companions would accompany me this way." She gestured to my friends. Instead of leading us left towards the rising stairs taking us to the rooms for rent as I had expected, she steered us right, to what looked like a basement. A shiver of unease dripped down my spine. Was this a trap? Was she about to lock us down here and alert the guards? Did I just doom us? I exchanged tense, tight lipped looks with Calan and Wren, whose hands were slowly drifting near their weapons.

Lorelei entered first and beckoned us to follow suit. I walked in, followed closely by Locke, Calan, and Wren bringing up the rear, his massive, hulking figure having to fold significantly to avoid hitting his head on the door. With the door closed, I removed my hood, revealing my face fully to Lorelei. Her gasp hit me like a blast of ice water.

"It is you!" she exclaimed, enveloping me in a bear hug. I hugged her back. "What in the Goddess's name are you doing? You're in league with the traitor Prince?" I felt Locke stiffen behind me, but gave no other reaction to her choice of words.

"I can explain everything," I whispered to her. "I'm not sure what you know, or what you've been told, if anything, but I can explain."

Locke removed his hood and I almost smiled at Lorelei's dumbfounded, nervous expression. Calan and Wren looked hesitant as they too unveiled themselves. Lorelei looked torn between fear and shock. I wanted to take my time explaining. I truly did. But time wasn't on our side. I explained Locke's curse, and mine. I explained about my part of the prophecy. I touched on the rebels but didn't go into detail. I told her about looking for Locke's parents.

"This is... a lot to take in," she said. She looked at Locke with hesitancy. "So you're not a criminal? You're not killing fae in droves?"

He shook his head. "I did only what I was forced to do. We're rebels, not murderers. We're trying to dethrone Scorpio, not help her bring more chaos."

Lorelei looked torn as she took a long, loaded look at each of us in turn. I could see her thoughts spiraling through her head as she assessed whether or not she believed us. Whether she trusted us. She opened her mouth to speak after a gut wrenchingly long pause, when the door opened out front and voices filled the foyer around the corner. She pointed to a barrel of ale along the wall.

"If you need to run for any reason, there's a tunnel behind that barrel. Use it." Her whisper was so soft I almost didn't hear her even thought I was right in front of her. "And be safe, Lark. I've been so worried when I saw your face on those wanted posters."

I shouldn't be surprised that they had wanted posters for us, but I was all the same. I couldn't explain why, couldn't put it to words, but the entire court being fed the idea that we were common criminals set my blood aflame. Not rebels, *criminals*. Fae who hurt others. Fae who targeted others. She would want others to be terrified of us, it made sense. Anger and sadness mixed to form a deep chasm of irritation I couldn't explain, but perhaps it was a blessing. With it igniting along my nerves, it left little room for panic or anxiety, so I held to it like fire held to kindling.

Booted feet stomped into the bar area before falling silent. They were waiting. Lorelei gave us a pointed look, her finger raising to her lips. Her message obvious: keep quiet. She hoisted a keg from beside us like it was nothing and walked back around the corner to greet the new patrons. It was when we heard her use the word Crownguard that the tension in our party spiked, the four of us sharing loaded glances and nervous heartbeats. A stern voice from the front echoed around the corner to the store room where we shrank into the shadows. I glanced at the barrel hiding the passageway, gauging how fast the four of us could escape if the need arose.

"Ale for three?" Lorelei asked, her sunny tone giving nothing away. I could hug her. Three. There were three Crownguards out front. She was feeding us information covertly.

"We're looking for a few fae who might've come this way." There was the familiar and distinct sound of crinkling parchment. Our wanted posters, no doubt. I grit my teeth as I shrank further into the shadows on instinct. "The traitor, Prince Cancer, and the Queen's Mark. Have you seen them? We have reason to believe they, or some of their contacts, may be within the city."

"I haven't seen them," I heard Lorelei murmur thoughtfully. To her credit she continued, "Are we in danger? Should I lock the place up?"

"No ma'am, but may I check your rooms? Make sure they didn't sneak in?"

"You're welcome to check the rooms upstairs. I've been here the whole time and didn't see anyone, but of course, do what you need to do. Please just announce yourselves to our guests. I have to get some ingredients for dinner in the back, so if you need me and I'm not here, just holler."

I didn't hear a reaction from the Crownguards trailing us, save for the heavy thud of their black buckled boots as they meandered up the stairs above us. It must have only been a moment later, but my lungs burned from how little I was breathing and made the second stretch on before Lorelai was in the room with us again. I hugged her once more, thanking her for helping us. She wrenched the barrel aside, revealing the hidden trap door she'd told us about.

"It leads to a spot a few blocks from here. A gutter. Go, before they're crawling through this area. Be safe."

"I don't know how to thank you," I said as Wren shimmied open the door. Calan lowered the hinged door to the ground gently so as not to make noise.

"Thank me by succeeding." She urged us on. "Hurry."

Locke leaned in to whisper in her ear. Old habits dying hard, I guess. She looked him in the face and nodded. I assumed he told her about how to find the rebels. Two soft thuds sounded one by one as Wren and Calan dropped into a dusty, cobwebbed hole, and I was so glad I didn't have to be first. My skin itched thinking about what lay down there waiting to crawl all over me. I looked at Locke expectantly. He shook his head, gesturing for me to go before him.

"After you, love."

"One more thing," I whispered, kneeling down to drop into the hole in the ground. I looked up at Lorelei beseechingly. "Get out of the city. For as long a possible, as soon as possible. Run. And don't look back." At her hesitation, I urged her once more, "Promise me." Lorelei nodded, not saying the words. It was good enough. It had to be. "Be safe," were my final words to my friend before dropping down onto a ladder and disappearing into the blackness of the hole. The foulness that awaited me made me choke on the damp, mildew-laden scent. The passage was confining; I could stand almost to my full height, but the others had to be permanently crouched to avoid smacking their heads on the ceiling. Although, looking at all the hideous cobwebs up close, I crouched so my hair wouldn't cross paths with anything unsavory down here.

Locke's footfalls thudded behind me moments after I moved and the trapdoor closed over us, submerging us in rank darkness. The last sound I heard was the barrel being scraped over our heads again. I ignited the flames along my body, casting an amber glow along the narrow, cobwebbed tunnel. Wren led the way, followed by Calan and myself, with Locke bringing up the rear.

"We should split up after this," Wren said. We all agreed. It was too noticeable having the four of us together. We could move more unseen with two groups of two.

"What was the bright light earlier?" I asked finally. "How did we make it in the gate?"

Nobody answered at first. I knew they'd heard me. I was about to ask again when Locke sighed.

"It's the reason we need to hurry. Either Lennox or Lenore sent their magic at a ward. The ward recognized their magic and that's what sent everyone into such a frenzy."

"So they know we have backup. Or maybe they think we're with them."

"You don't understand," said Locke, upping his pace. "Lennox and Lenore had to fake their deaths in the eyes of the Water Court. Their father would never let them defect to Port Azure. He's the Zodiac Kinship's advisor, and the most loyal follower of Scorpio. He fully agrees with everything she's doing. Lennox and Lenore supposedly died in battle three years ago. The wards remember their magic. And now everyone knows they're alive. Scorpio may have seen them in Everwind, and hopefully was too distracted by you to really take notice of them, but for their father to know they're here?" His head dipped low before his lips parted on snarled words, "He'll want their heads. They will be hunted, and not just for today's events. They'll be hunted for being involved with us. I fear for them."

"As do I," said Calan, no doubt thinking of Lenore. Urgency tremored in his voice in a way that echoed my own mounting terror for the twins.

"They can take care of themselves." I said as much for myself as for them but my words were too breathy for them to sound as confident as I wanted to. We had to hurry. There was precious little room to deviate from our goals, and even less room for dawdling.

"Yes, Lark. The twins also aren't alone. They have Aspen and Vanneck. They'll be okay." Wren's soft voice was both logical and reassuring but did nothing to stifle my nerves entirely.

Stay safe, I willed them. I willed the Goddess to protect them all.

"Locke, give me your bombs. Wren and I will do all of that. We need to expedite this process in the worst way."

Locke considered a moment and paused, reaching for a satchel I hadn't even noticed, and handed it to him.

"Get your family out," said Calan. "Tell them hi for me. I want them to know I miss them too."

"You'll see them when we get back," I pointed out. Calan looked at me and shrugged.

"Doesn't matter. His family was amazing to me before Scorpio took over. They treated me like their own when Locke and I were little kids. I want them to know I never forgot about them either. Tell them I'll see them soon."

Locke nodded, a rueful smile on his face. A happy thought amidst the madness around us. Those are the moments we all clung to. Our light in the dark.

We continued forward. I wondered how long this tunnel went for when I reached out with my mind to Vanneck, unsure why I hadn't yet.

Hey. What's going on over there?

Nothing presently, My Lady. We've been pursued, but we've outmaneuvered them for the time being. Please, don't worry about us. Are you all okay?

That's a nice way of saying Lenore and Aspen are having fun, isn't it?

Feeling someone laugh inside your head is a strange feeling, like buzzing over your brain that left it somewhere between an itch and a tickle. It was a welcome distraction.

Yes, we all made it in. Thanks to the twins, from my understanding. Are they alright? The thought of the twins having to fake their deaths to get away from Scorpio and their father made my chest ache fiercely. I couldn't even imagine.

Yes, Lennox was beside herself when she thought you weren't going to make it in. She saw the one guard grab your hood and it would've been over.

It was Lennox? It seemed so rash, I was surprised to hear it was her.

Lenore was right behind her to do the same. We all were, she just happened to beat us to the punch. Once again, gratitude that knew absolutely no bounds threatened to sweep my feet out from under me.

Just stay safe, Vanneck. And make sure the others do too.

Yes, My Lady.

Lark, I corrected out of habit more than anything.

Silence.

"I just checked with Vanneck," I announced to the group. "Everyone is safe currently. Sounds like Lenore and Aspen are likely having fun leading the guards on a wild goose chase." Calan and Locke chuckled.

"Yeah, that sounds about right," Calan said as his feet drew to a stop in front of us.

We'd come to the end of the tunnel, a disgusting looking ladder at the end that I sincerely doubted would hold my weight, let alone someone the size of Wren. Using my Earth Magic, I quickly bolstered it so it was sturdy enough for all of us. Locke gave me a silent warning, a side-eye glance. I knew what he meant. Restrict my magic. I was already using my fire, and that was enough.

"This is where we part ways," Calan said. I looked up at him and Wren.

"Be careful. The both of you. If you die, I'll bring you both back to kill you myself."

I heard Wren's deep, throaty chuckle for the first time ever.

"Don't worry. You can't kill the Wow factor." All three of us looked at him in stunned silence. "What? I can't make a joke in the heart of enemy territory? That's where you need jokes the most. If you can't beat them, join them?"

I didn't mean to burst out laughing; I stifled it just in time, my mouth coming to silence myself. He shrugged with a grin that didn't quite reach his eyes. I doused my flames just as Locke opened the trap door above us, the sunlight rushing in and offending my eyes. He came up first with his hood drawn once again, looking around for signs of danger or even witnesses. Satisfied none were around, he hoisted me up, followed by Calan and Wren. I sent my consciousness around us, looking for signs we couldn't see that someone may be nearby. I found none.

Looking around, I could see why. We were in a dingy alleyway. The sunlight that had initially seemed blinding was actually very little back here. We settled the trap door back silently and covered it with trash bins. I marked the location in my mind in the event we needed a quick escape route.

We said no further goodbyes. Calan and Wren settled back into their hoods and disappeared around the corner, quickly doing what they did best, noticing while remaining unnoticed.

Locke indicated with his head the direction we needed to go. So out of the alley we travelled and into the steady pedestrian traffic of Loc Valen. Little did anyone know, the traitor Prince and Queen's Mark were walking among them, moving steadily towards Castle Ari'inor. With a heavy swallow, I steeled myself inside as I fell into step with Locke. We would free his family. And we would all escape.

Of that I was certain.

Chapter Thirty-Seven

We would get Locke's family out. We had to. The question was how were we to get into Ari'inor unseen. Truthfully, I didn't expect to get this far. But we had one thing Scorpio didn't; Locke was the Crowned Assassin. He could get anywhere with his skillset. I just hoped I wouldn't hold him back. We walked on silent feet by passersby who seemed oblivious to our presence. Other black clad Crownguards were intermittently spotted but the paid us little mind, at least for the time being. To them we looked like one of their numbers with our faces deep in our cloaks.

"What's the plan?" I whispered to Locke as we slowly approached the castle grounds, a place I'd only glimpsed before from the river last time I was here. Now from our place in the shadows on the cusp of the perimeter, I could glimpse massive archways of flawless, crystal ice and colossal towers of white and grey stone rising to meet the sky above us. Beyond, I knew there were sprawling grounds, the likes of which I'd not seen but only heard about. Ponds with never ending waves and pristine fountains complete with intricate bridges lit by sconces of Fire Magic.

Locke slipped us into another alley way that directly lined up with the white perimeter wall of Ari'inor. Our dress meant we didn't draw attention, at least not yet, but if we didn't hurry, we might. I kept my head down, fighting every urge to glance around us, both in wonder and to assess for rising suspicion. Locke's hushed voice broke through my foggy thoughts.

"The servants' quarters is through here." He opened a door that was hidden entirely into the stone. I had to pick my jaw up off the ground.

A secret entrance.

I felt a little giddy. I shouldn't, but I couldn't help it. Locke's eyes flicked to mine at my excitement and shook his head. I didn't miss the little smile on his lips before he turned away from me though, some sarcastic remark dying on his lips by the oppressive tension we were under.

If you didn't know it was there, you'd never find it. Only the smallest indentation of stone gave it away, and only because Locke pointed it out. I expected the stone to grind, to create noise, but it silently opened for us to my surprise. We moved inside, shutting it quickly. I blinked in the dim, looking around, the smell of cold, damp wood dominating my senses. It wasn't hard to see why. Stone with fresh condensation and damp wooden floors lined our pathway in either direction. With Ari'inor in such splendor, or I assumed it was, and the servants' halls looked this decrepit? Even the Citadel's lowest rooms were cleaner and dryer than this.

Locke held out one finger, a gesture to wait, before taking up his hushed tone. Safe for the time being. "They have a system of hallways all through the castle, and they're not terribly well guarded simply because the only fae who know them well are the fae who use them most. We just need to avoid being recognized. Once inside, we need to get to the tallest tower. That's where Scorpio keeps fae for long term."

"Not the dungeon?" I asked, remember Port Azure's dim, reeking dungeon. Locke shook his head with dismay as he led us on, down the hall on silent feet.

"She likes to taunt her victims with the freedom they can no longer have by forcing them to watch as others live their lives."

I blinked. That was... bleak. And unnecessarily brutal. To see others living carefree while you're stowed away on the brink of despair. It was a wonder fae didn't jump to their deaths.

"How much magic can we use?" I whispered as we took our first steps into Castle Ari'inor. A deep sense of foreboding accompanied a shudder that went through me and I just hoped it was the damp chill and not an omen of some kind.

"As little as possible. We resemble one of them. We won't draw suspicion. Not yet anyway. I can shroud us, but it's risky. You'll need to use your magic to scout ahead for us."

I flashed him a smile, despite the lingering sense of dread I was feeling. "It's kind of awesome that our powers complement one another," I whispered, my steps echoing his. A wry, twisted smirk flashed for a moment before returning to his expressionless mask.

"Yeah, we're a real pair for the history texts, aren't we?" His head swiveled to the corridor coming up on our left. "We head right. Don't look back."

And then I heard it. Two fae servant women chattering. Too indistinct yet to ascertain the topic of discussion, but close enough. And gaining. I didn't look. I followed beside Locke, moving forward with the purposeful strides of the Crownguard. Locke's confident swagger never changed—never slowed. Just kept walking. Their voices got louder, until I could hear distinctly, their conversation.

"They have a red alert, Junie, we can't leave the castle. Don't meet him tonight. The Crowned Assassin and the Queen's Mark are here somewhere."

Locke's fists clenched at my side, but otherwise neither of us responded. Just keep walking. But my heart flew into my throat at their proximity.

"If he's here, I doubt he's going to kill me," replied who must be Junie with a dismissive scoff. "I've met him. He's not that bad."

"It doesn't matter if you've met him." The one talking to Junie sounded exasperated and scared for her, "If someone sees you near him and reports you, you're as good as dead. Even if you didn't know. Scorpio isn't exactly known for her mercy."

There was no more talking after that. They'd spun off down another corridor, something I was glad for. I knew Scorpio was killing innocent people. I knew she was conscripting every able-bodied fae to deter us. It wouldn't ever be easy to hear. My hand went to my stomach, as if to quell the nausea.

We passed two more groups of fae, Locke shrouding our faces lightly. A flare of alarm raced through me until I was a walking anxiety addled mess at the sight of them. My breath left me, but their eyes didn't shift to us. Their gazes were downcast and I couldn't tell if it were a show of respect for their Crownguard or fear. But I had a pretty good guess.

I wasn't sure how long we crept. Long enough for my heart to leap into my throat at every small noise, certain we were about to be discovered, but the corridors were eerily empty. I didn't know if that were a blessing from the Goddess or a hint that something was amiss. At some point, we had exited the hidden servant's hallways and found ourselves in the colossal splendor that was Castle Ari'inor. Whitewashed stone was interspersed by hues of blue, and everything was rimmed in gold. Everwind reminded me of air—clean, cold and minimalistic. Somehow mixing beauty and sterility. This was something different. More extravagant. Windows with the finest filigree in the blue and gold of the Water Court. Archways and columns made of gold so pure it could feed a whole city for a year. The ceiling boasted more gold in intricate patterns playing over the white stone, with drops of sapphire to accent.

I felt disgusted.

My father and I had often gone without food if we hadn't been lucky in our hunting. And one item from this castle of excess would have fed us for our lifetime. I fought to keep my face neutral as we trod along. Crownguards, some of which were also hooded, passed us by and continued to pay us little mind, and I was beginning to find it odd. Given that they knew we were in the city, you'd think there would be more security. But how often do you look at your own forces when an outsider infiltrates? You look for the different, not what looks like you. And that would be their mistake.

The hallways began to get less ornate as we walked, the gold and blue all but winking out of existence as we travelled swiftly and quietly through the halls. We swept passed a beast of a wrought iron gate, for which Locke apparently had a key. Of course he did. He was a prince here, traitor or not, and beyond that, the Crowned Assassin. The dungeons, interrogation chambers, they would have been his domain. He would know these halls better than anyone.

Slipping passed the gate, Locke and I rounded the corner for the hallway to discard us into a stone atrium, lit by fire sconces. And with two guards, whose eyes widened to see us.

"Orders," the one on the left barked at us. "What business have you here?"

Locke stopped for a moment as a smile spread across his face, giving me pause.

Using his Zodiac speed, he knocked both of them out before they could even shout, neither of them expecting an attack. Beyond them had to be what we were after. Two monstrous winding stone staircases greeted us in muted light of the sconces. It was colder in here, the stone freezing to the touch. There was no trace of the earlier beauty and excess of earlier, rough grey stone instead was harsh and uninviting entirely. The complete opposite of earlier.

One stone staircase—with some perilously questionable looking steps, I noted—beckoned us upwards. Next to it, an even more ominous staircase curved downwards into deep darkness. Firelight lit this hallway and our ascent, but no light penetrated the abyss.

A clatter broke my reverie and I whirled to see Locke picking up the first of the Crownguards he'd knocked out.

"What are you doing?" I hissed. "We're wasting time."

"Two unconscious bodies will give us away, then we'll really have no time," Locke said before heaving him down the darkened stairs. I waited for the sound of steel armor meeting stone, but none came. I blinked. Locke didn't hesitate, turning to do the same to the remaining guard, and once again, silence clutched hard to any sound on those stairs, making the hair on the back of my neck stand in warning.

"Down we go, I guess." I stepped towards the blackened abyss, ignoring the foreboding warning in my stomach. The darkness was so deep, I couldn't gauge how far down we had to go. Not even the curve of the stairs was obvious. I glared at the sight, ashamed to admit to myself that no part of me wanted to go down there.

Locke's hand cupped my shoulder. I turned to face him as he shook his head and indicated the other staircase, the one spiraling upwards.

"Up is worse than down," he whispered. Eying the darkness like it might bite, I took my first steps upwards after Locke. How was that possible? What could possibly be awaiting us at the top of these stairs?

We climbed so long, my legs began to protest. The occasional narrow window, barely more than a slit in stone, told us how high we'd climbed. Too high for my liking. Not so high as Everwind where it felt like you were separate from the world, but high enough to see your death in your head should you fall.

If the height weren't enough, the increasingly frigid temperatures were. Each step made us both colder. I longed to use my Fire Magic to warm us, but it was too risky, so I settled for rubbing warmth back into my arms with frozen hands. But at least my palms weren't sweating from the view. But what truly bothered me was the screaming. Not from above us, but from outside. Peering through the tiny windows, I could just glimpse a piece of one of the training camps. So Scorpio had them on site. Close so they were ready at hand when the need arose. Good to know. I stashed that tidbit of information away for later.

Ice was forming now on the narrow stone steps. Unpleasant at the best of times, the stairs when icy were downright treacherous to navigate. My feet lost contact with stone on more than one occasion, forcing Locke to reach out and steady me with a sigh.

"You okay?" he asked me, his breath floating in white puffs. I nodded. He glanced back upwards, his hand not leaving mine for several steps. "We're almost there."

Chapter Thirty-Eight

Howling wind was my first indication that we'd made it. And when Locke hurled open the door that separated us from the stairs and our destination, when we truly reached the top, I understood why Locke said it was awful up here. The stairs opened up to the top of a tower. I didn't know what to call it. A room would mean there were walls and a ceiling. There was an icy floor only. And on that icy floor, were frozen statues of fae.

I could freeze the water in your body for as long as I needed.

The memory of our first magic lesson returned to me unbidden. Locke's face fell when he spied my horror. These weren't statues. These were fae. These were prisoners, captive in their own body. Frozen, unable to even breathe, but magically sustained. I could scarcely think of a crueler fate. The pain would be incredible. And if that weren't bad enough, I realized with a sinking heart, they were given the best vantage point to watch life go on without them. Previously, I'd wondered why they didn't jump to their deaths. I knew why now.

Locke hesitated, his emotionless mask slipping, before taking his first steps onto the top of the tower. We had to fight the wind, who with every step threatened to team up with the slick and solid ice to push us over the ledge. The frozen fae didn't have to worry about falling, but we certainly did. I clung to the nearest one, eying the ledge with trepidation and scrutiny.

"I'm sorry," I said to whoever I was holding onto, as Locke prowled the rows of fae, inspecting each one for his mother and father. Minutes passed, his countenance growing darker as he lost hope. "Did you do any of these?" I asked, looking around at the sheer number of prisoners. "These fae, I mean." I didn't mean to ask the question aloud, but the withered, guilt ridden look from his gaze to mine gave me my answer. *Yes.*

"Not the time," Locke said softly. His eyes that had held so much anticipation now sparked with panic as he searched the last section of fae, travelling from prisoner to prisoner, and finding no sign of his family. I stood useless, unable to help. I had no idea what his family looked like. I only watched on with numbing fingers as I felt our hope dwindle, becoming as much a prisoner of this place as these fae. At last, Locke looked up at me, rage and despair warring on his face. "They're not here," he breathed the words at last, after double checking everyone in attendance. "I can't pick up their scent at all either. I was so sure that they'd have been held here. Pisces gloated about it before to me."

"Where else would they be?" I asked. "A holding cell? An interrogation—"

I cut myself off when his face fell.

"The other staircase," he growled low in his throat, in a tone that would even give the Grievling pause. "The interrogation chambers" Fury unlike anything I'd ever known crept over Locke's face. "If Pieces has them there, I'll rip him to shreds." Of that I had no doubt. And I would help in any way possible.

"Where is that?"

Locke looked at me expectantly. I knew where it was. I was so hoping it wasn't there. The other staircase. As the realization hit me, a muffled scream sounded, so low I wasn't sure I'd heard it. Glancing up to the frozen fae I clung to, I heard it again. She was screaming incoherently behind the ice.

"Locke, we can't leave them here."

"These are some of the most dangerous fae to exist in the Water Court," he said, his smile picking up the corners of his face. His aura flickered, giving me pause. "They will make an excellent distraction in about an hour's time." He knelt the ground, palming the ice and closing his eyes in concentration. Ice shifted and melted. I almost flew backwards when the fae I was holding onto blinked.

"Don't hurt anyone innocent," I said to her, knowing she couldn't respond. To all of them. "Good luck." A series of moans and gasps of first breaths began to sound. It was eerie, hearing them cry out for the first breaths of oxygen they'd been given in however long.

"They'll be ready to move in about an hour," Locke said, returning to my side. "Let's go. We don't have time to waste."

We quickly descended the stairs, getting back to the much warmer atrium in record time. Rounding to the lower staircase, I stepped carefully over the two we set down here, eying them skeptically to make sure they didn't grab me. I rubbed my warmth into my fingers and relished the thawing out as we descended, but I didn't think Locke's heart would thaw until he saw his family alive. His shoulders and jaw were so rigid I thought he might shatter as we hustled to the bottom of the stairs. I hurried to grab and torchlight from the wall, gagging at the lingering spider webs coiling on my skin, before steeling myself and walking into the deep darkness that awaited us with a malevolent and oppressive glee.

"Wren just contacted me," Locke said suddenly, making me turn to him. "The plan is set. The bombs are in place and they're getting out of Loc Valen now. Calan says hi." A stitch of relief in a dire moment was welcome. I was so glad to hear all was well with them. But I couldn't focus on that. Right now, all that mattered was getting Locke's family.

I wasn't sure what I expected. Screams of agony, certainly. Pleas for mercy, yes. But even more unnerving was the thick and persistent silence reigning over us. Even our footsteps were swallowed greedily by the void. I could only see two or three steps ahead of us at any time in the firelight. And the light from the doorway had disappeared, leaving me feeling like we were descending into Hell.

Maybe we were.

There was no ice here at least; my feet had no problems finding purchase on the rough stone. We reached the bottom quickly enough, telling me we weren't more than a few levels below the ground floor. There wasn't enough mustiness in the air to give the idea of disuse. Instead, the coppery scent was strong enough to taste on the air, and I gagged. Locke took my torch and dunked it into what could only be fuel by the way fire spread throughout the room, illuminating it for us.

We were in a long, wide hallway. The stone floor was stained red, if the grey walls were any indication of what the color was supposed to be. Massive, heavy wooden doors lined each side of the hallway, and I just knew I didn't want to ever see the inside of any of them. I didn't know if each door held a different morbid surprise, or if they were all outfitted for every need, but I knew I wanted no part of it. Locke glided through the room, looking increasingly distressed as he peeked into each room.

I almost hoped his family wasn't here. I couldn't imagine how badly this place would break a person, but I couldn't imagine one would be whole again ever either. The sense of dread and hopelessness would be enough to quell the hope of even the strongest minded fae. Nerves of steel wouldn't help in a place like this, a place built for ruining them.

"Locke," I whispered into the silence, "I don't think anyone is here."

"Don't be so certain," he said as he continued to search the rooms with a hardened face. "The stones that make these walls are spelled so as not to echo the screams of the victims here. It will always be grave silent. It's done to make fae feel utterly alone."

That thought horrified me. Locke said earlier he thought up was worse. I thought he was wrong. I wasn't sure how, but feeling entirely alone during torment like this seemed so much worse than hearing the screams of another condemned. If your only retreat were your own mind, if you couldn't cast your mind to anything else, if you couldn't even be given clues to what you'd face and your mind wandered…The fact that Pisces might have brought me here if Locke hadn't saved me made my stomach sour and leap into my throat at the same time.

"If I used my magic, would it penetrate the stones?"

"It should." Locke's tone was a warning.

I tried. I sent out my consciousness. In our immediate vicinity, there was nothing. It was just… blank. I wasn't sure if the stones were thwarting me after all, or if truly nobody were here. Where the hell was Locke's family? Why were there no other prisoners? His pinched expression confirmed his similar thoughts as he paced the rooms and peering in every door. I thought of what I knew of Scorpio. Everything she did, right down to controlling others, was her way of furthering herself towards her goal. Of breaking her curse. I didn't think she would have killed them. Unless they gave her reason to.

Pisces, on the other hand, was a vindictive bastard. Petty and ruthless, and with a deep seated jealousy and hatred of Locke. So if I were him, what would I do with Locke's family?

I still didn't know. Because I would think here. But Pisces was showy. I wondered if they were his personal pets. His slaves, perhaps? When I asked Locke, his eyes sparked with war at the suggestion. But we were running out of time.

There was a flare on the edge of my awareness before I could finish the thought, a sense of alarm gripping me tight. Someone was coming. At my hiss of warning, Locke and I hurtled ourselves into one of the questioning rooms, closing over the door. Not latching the door completely so we could hear him despite the spelled masonry. I couldn't keep my eyes from taking in the space we'd entered and it was every bit as horrifying as I'd feared. An array of blunt weapons and particularly cruel, sharp ones lined the furthest wall. One glance was enough to tell none of it was cleaned often, if at all, and the smell of rancid blood and excrement threatened to choke me. Rusted chains on the walls were heavy and too thick to break. Magic blocking chains, undoubtedly, like what Abel had used on me.

But what really bothered me was the drain in the center of the slanted room. I knew why it was there. The drain being stained a dark shade of red was enough to make me want to empty my guts into it. My stomach lurched violently and I had to focus hard to not be sick.

"I'm so sorry, Lark," Locke whispered. I glanced at him.

"For what?"

"For everything. But especially for what you're about to see." If he still thought there was a chance I didn't also love his violent side, he had another thing coming. Every part of him was mine, including the Nightmare Assassin Scorpio had forced him to become. As if I hadn't seen his darker side in the dungeons of Port Azure. As if I wouldn't accept him. I smiled at him.

"Bring it on."

A whistled tune overshadowed the sinister look on Locke's face. The lone guard, doing his rounds and twirling his keys in his hand, absentmindedly walked into my limited view through the door crack. He didn't even have time to scream.

Locke surged through the door, and hauled the Crownguard into the soundproof room where I waited. I shut the door, using my Earth Magic to craft thorns the size of my thumb around the door. Even if he got away from Locke, he couldn't open the door to escape now. Locke flashed me an approving look.

Locke had put this fae on the ground and in the iron chains in mere seconds. It was impressive, if you thought about it. The Crownguard in question was currently sputtering and hurtling threats and insults at Locke, who smiled when he removed his cowl and hood, relishing in the recognition in the fae's eyes. His eyes flickered from Locke, to me, to the exit no longer available to him. And by the building perspiration on his face, he knew it.

"It's you. You've returned. The Crowned Assassin." The blood drained from the Crownguard's face. His bald head made me think he looked like an egg. He glared at me. "And the girl her majesty is looking for. The curse."

I inclined my head to him, staring him down through the bridge of my nose. "If you know who we are, then you know how this will go down, don't you?" I sneered. The fae gave no response. Not even when Locke casually, too casually, walked over to the wall of torture instruments. He glanced at them the same way one might glance over a selection of prized chickens for dinner. He made his selection—a particularly cruel looking mace—and sauntered back over.

"You're going to answer a few questions for us," he said, dragging the mace along the floor. The fae flinched at the sound of metal scraping stone. "Answer them, and I let you live. How does that sound?"

"Why should I trust a traitor?" he spat, wrenching his body against the chains. They held tight, as we all knew they would.

"Because I'm not the one killing innocent fae." Locke's hatred leaked into his tone now. A dark, pulsing tremor that hid within Locke had now been unleashed, shaking everything in the room. "Scorpio is. I'm not the one tearing our realm apart, Scorpio is."

"You dare speak her name!" the chained fae snarled.

Locke laughed.

"Oh, friend, you'll find I dare to do far much more than that. Don't forget, she was my friend too."

"Just kill me." He sagged in his chains. "I'm not telling you anything." Locke's eyebrow twitched. The only warning he received before the mace met his knee with a sickening crack. I sauntered over to him, kneeling at his side as he screamed.

"What's your name?" I asked in my most gentle voice, the one I reserved for the injured I treated. He looked up at me with a mix of surprise and hate.

"Ronan," he grunted, panting through the pain, while Locke twirled the mace, a movement I'd seen Lenore do often.

"Ronan. That's a nice name. Look, Ronan, we don't want to hurt you. We don't want to hurt anyone. If you can help us, you can trust no more harm will befall you. We may incapacitate you for a short time, but truly, we don't want to hurt you. Will you consider helping us? We're looking for someone. That's all."

His eyes flashed towards the door, eying the massive thorns covering it. I saw the resignation there. His screams would go unanswered down here. Ironic, given that he'd probably ensured this fate for so many others. I saw his shoulders slump in defeat.

"I appreciate what you're attempting to do, girl. Truly, I do." He flashed a withering look to Locke. "But I would rather die than betray my Queen." Locke's voice carried one word. My name. Before Ronan's face collided with mine. Pain exploded behind my eyes. Tears blurred my vision. Locke snarled as he shoved Ronan away from me, tightening his chains to force him to stand now on his one good leg. His ruined one bled heavier in response.

"You shouldn't have done that." Locke's growl echoed in the room. I heard screams. Horrid screams, but I couldn't see anything through my tears as I reset my broken nose. I managed not to scream, but I was covered in blood when my vision finally cleared. I now saw Ronan had several long cuts from a knife. Deep lacerations welling with dark blood that pooled beneath him. Locke had stripped him of the clothing and armor on his upper body, so nothing separated Locke's knife from Ronan's flesh.

"That was for Lark. Now, where is my family?" Locke's voice filled with malice. He really would kill him now.

"Fuck you." Ronan's words came out in panting gasps before he spat on Locke's boots, earning himself a jaw shattering punch. I saw blood and I noticed Locke had formed small, icy spears on his knuckles. A half-inch long each, but jagged and unforgiving, and coated in blood. Locke landed another bone crunching combination, bloodying his ribs, abdomen, and face once more. Ronan's grunts of pain were hard to bear witness to. "I'll never tell you shit. Waste your time with me. Or kill me. I won't help you."

Locke plunged his blade into Ronan's good knee hard enough the blade broke off in his hand. Locke frowned, unfazed by the shrieks, before glancing my way. "I hate when faulty equipment gets in the way of a good interrogation." He turned to me with a practiced carefree smile, "Lark, you wouldn't happen to have an extra dagger, would you? My sword might be a bit too much, and the ones on the wall are so brittle." I smiled, pulling one of my hidden daggers in my boot and presenting it to him, not looking at Ronan as he seethed at our interaction. Locke smirked.

"Always so prepared, love. I like that," he purred. I'm not sure if it was the adrenaline, if it was the high stakes, or the unexpected sultry tone that gave me a little rush. Color tinged my cheeks while Ronan made a show of gagging. Locke rounded on him, losing the softness he'd just donned for me, a sharp edge to his voice that was closer than ever to falling off the deep edge. To losing control. The wild in his eyes, his tightly clenched fists, the feral anger that stirred when they rested on Ronan told me one thing; he wouldn't leave here alive. "One last chance before I make this truly hell for you, Ronan. Where are my mother and father?"

"That's really why you're here?" Ronan spat blood onto the already drenched floor.

"That's what we've been trying to tell you," I said from my corner of the room. I fiddled with my other blade, just to have something to do other than watch. I may have become a bit desensitized to blood compared to what I used to be, but this was still a gruesome sight.

"I assumed you were stupid enough to kill Pisces or even the Queen. You can't kill her." He laughed with a chilling look at me. "Not unless you're planning on dying too." When he laughed, he choked on his own blood, punctuating his point in the most macabre way. Locke put his blade just behind Ronan's ear, a warning.

"You're avoiding the question." Locke wrenched his face away from me and back on him, careful not to hurt him more than needed right now. "I know better than anyone about Scorpio's condition. I'm not here for her. Tell me where my family is."

"Please, Ronan," I added.

Ronan tipped his head back and laughed. A deep, chortle mixed with gagging on blood. He spat more blood into the waiting pool beneath him. My blood ran cold. He knew where they were, but I had this growing dread within me that suggested we weren't going to like the answer. Locke's family meant everything to him. The reason Scorpio had been able to force him to kill at her behest for the last few years. I dared not say it out loud... but what if there were no saving them?

"Have you really not figured it out?" Locke glowered at Ronan, my hope diminishing every second. Locke's gaze flickered to me. Ronan followed his gaze to me too, a wicked smile forming on his face. His bloody smile was missing a few teeth, making it all the worse.

"She's figured it out, haven't you, Curse?" His words were crisp. Clear. Haunting. He laughed so hard, his chains clanked against the stone. He paid no heed to either of his ruined legs. "Scorpio needed a way to keep you in line. But did she really need them? Or just need you to think she had them?"

"No..." The breath left my lungs before I could clamp down on the word. Realization destroyed all semblance of hope now. There was a reason they weren't in Frostfall. Why they weren't on the Tower's top. Why they weren't here.

They wouldn't be found anywhere.

At least not alive.

"Yes!" Ronan sneered at us, the truth laid bare. Locke looked stricken, his mask cracking for the first time down here and Ronan knew it. Prince Cancer would see through his aura if he was being deceitful. I watched him search for the signs, the eyes widening in realization. I didn't need Locke's gifts to see the mounting glee on Ronan's face which drove the point home directly into my chest. "They've been dead for at least two years now. Maybe three. Your father was too much of a hassle to keep alive what with his condition. And your mother... she asked every day to see you. I do hope someone told her you were forbidden to see her, why you didn't come. I hope nobody told her about the monster you became. All those deaths. Do your hands ever come clean, Crowned Assassin?" He laughed, throwing his head back at the tortured look on Locke's face. He'd cracked wide open. Who knew Ronan had the ultimate weapon after all? "Do you think Mommy and Daddy would be proud of their traitor, fallen prince?"

Locke was right about one thing. Once Ronan talked, his suffering would end. I drew my knife to silence Ronan, jumping to my feet. But I was too late. Locke's scream of despair-fueled rage filled the room as his blade shot out, severing Ronan's laughing, sneering head from his shoulders in a single, fluid motion. The head landed with a wet, splattering thud in the red pool beneath him. His eyes remained open in death, his mouth open in a never-ending taunt, his final 'fuck you' to the Crowned Assassin.

I had never hated anyone more. Not like this.

I wanted to kill him myself all over again if it would bring Locke comfort.

The Crowned Assassin was looking very much like the fallen prince Ronan had described him as: covered in blood with a despondent expression on his face. He fell to his knees, a dry sob escaping him. I couldn't fathom what he must be feeling. What do you say to someone who just lost their entire family?

No, I corrected myself, hurrying over to him and dropping to my knees just to crush him to me as he broke for the first time since I'd known him. I cradled him to me, rocking silently as tears poured down both our faces. He lost his family years ago, he just had no idea. What do you say to that?

Worse than that, he'd gotten so much blood on his hands—innocent blood— all to save his family. All those ghosts that followed him every day, all for nothing. Words failed me often, but I'd never been so entirely clueless for what to say, what to do. There was always something, even if it were insane. But right here, right now, all I could do was be there with Locke and try to keep pieces of him together as he broke.

But we also couldn't stay here.

"Locke..." I whispered, we've got to get out of here."

He didn't move. Didn't acknowledge me in the slightest. I grabbed his hands, trying my hardest to get him to stand. "Locke, please, I'm so sorry. We've got to go." I begged through falling tears. I rejoined him on the floor, cupping his face and lifting his gaze to mine. "I'm not going to leave you. Please don't leave me." His eyes, normally so blue, so full of life, were dull and glassy as he looked at me. I saw the deep chasm within which he spiraled inside, reconciling all this new information. With who he was now. He needed to grieve, but that time wasn't now, and nobody understood that more than I did.

This city was on edge, and one missing guard was going to be noticed now more than ever. Not to mention the two in the void stairwell. They would search along his route and it would lead to us. We would never leave this hellish pit and then nothing we'd done would matter.

"Locke, please. I need you." My fear must have finally registered with him. I saw his vacant expression soften, his misty, faraway eyes finally meeting mine.

"Lark." He blinked as if seeing me for the first time. His voice softer than a raven's feathers as he tracked a tear spilling down my cheek. "You're crying." I'd never been more glad to hear someone speak in my entire life.

"Yes, my love. I am."

"Why?"

"Because when your heart breaks, mine does too." I cupped his cheeks in both of my hands, touching my forehead to his. "Because your pain is mine. Because I'm terrified. Because we need to go. Right now." I tenderly wiped his tears. He shakily gathered his strength and rose at last, bringing me with him.

"I lost my family today." His wavering voice prodded the frayed remains of my heart. "I'll be damned if I let anything happen to you, Lark." It scared me to see the resolve there, forged stronger than I'd ever seen it. Scorpio thought losing his family might break him, but it did the opposite. It created someone who would do anything for retribution. Who would go to the ends of the world if it meant breaking the curse. I was worried what he might do, how much of his own soul he'd sacrifice for mine. Because I couldn't lose him either. He gave me a long, appraising look, reading my emotions before loosing a heavy breath. "Let's go."

Chapter Thirty-Nine

A sickening, sucking sound filled my ears as I wrenched my dagger from Ronan's knee and sheathed it, willing myself not to feel the blood wetting the material of my boot. I picked up my other knife where I'd dropped it when I ran to Locke. I disintegrated the thorns on the door. We listened. I felt for signs of life on the other side of the red spattered door. Nothing.

Our luck needed to hold, I thought, as Locke and I carefully ascended the stairs back up to the hallway. The darkness hadn't become any less chilling going up. We had a long way to go: exiting the castle, getting across the city to the gate, and jumpstoning out of here, all unseen? Or at the very least, without getting caught?

That was a fucking miracle I was asking for. But I asked the Goddess nonetheless.

Damn Scorpio for warding against jumpstoning within the city. Between that and an army within the city itself, we were looking at some pretty shit odds. But if we could make it to Lorelei's tunnel, we could stand a chance. My foot snagged on something, nearly smashing my face into the nearest stair, but I managed to catch myself. The two men we'd hidden earlier.

"Locke, change our over clothes. We're covered in blood. We can't sneak around like this." We switched with the guards on the stairs in record time, which I think was even more impressive, given the fact we were doing this in pitch black and a single torch. Sorry to the fae who were going to wake up very confused.

We made it back the way we came, through the servants' corridors, to the alley with no issues. We saw no one. No resistance. No witnesses. Nothing. I wanted to thank the Goddess, but I held off because deep in my bones, I knew something had to be wrong. A guard has been missing for a significant length of time, and yet we'd seen no patrols?

Outside the alley, the street was quiet. Some small groups moved quickly about their business, but it was nowhere near as busy as it should've been.

We were walking into a trap.

"Locke, you have to shroud us."

"Way ahead of you." Focusing on a task—like keeping us alive—seemed to breathe a bit of life into him. I used to say he looked so haunted. Now he looked tortured, like his ghosts finally caught up to him. But at least it was something, like day old embers stirring once again. "I can hear them. Not just their voices, their heartbeats too, if I listen enough. They're waiting to ambush us around the corner."

"How much danger are we in?" I asked. Locke looked down at me, his hand going to his blade and partially drawing it.

"I won't let anything happen to you." While his words were hopeful, the tone wasn't. His eyes drifted back to where they lay ahead of us, narrowing. Wrath and violence stirred within him, an aura of its very own. I wondered if bloodlust had a color that he could see.

"Locke. How much?" I grit my teeth when he paused, looking towards our goal. He loosed a sigh.

"A lot."

"Where are they?" I couldn't feel anyone. Locke gave me a loaded look.

"Around the corner. The fact you can't feel them is concerning. They must be using an enchantment or spell of some kind to avoid detection." Well, that would be something I could kill for right about now. I raked my hands through my hair, glancing up between the buildings to see the dusk just beginning to color the sky.

Between the buildings.

That's it!

The thought was so loud I could have sworn I felt Vanneck bristle against my consciousness, the way one reacts to a sharp, sudden gust of wind outside a window.

"What if we went upwards?" I asked, a smile coming to my face. I used my Earth Magic, not caring anymore, since they knew where we were. Sort of. No alarms sounded, no lights lit up the sky. There was no indication that my magic had registered with anything, though Locke cast it a dark look. I crafted strong vines for Locke and me to climb. My muscles, especially in my upper body, screamed in protest, burning with effort only seconds in. Not that I would ever tell Aspen, or he'd make me do this constantly.

Locke reached the top before me, offering me his hand and hauling me up with him to the roof of the building. From here, I could see Ari'inor and I had to force myself not to gawk. It was every bit as beautiful as I thought it would be. Gold columns continued out here, sapphire blue ponds with gold fountains, and creamy walkways beneath that light dusting of frost. Gardens with blue rivers running through them, a gardener's dream. I spied the top of the tower. I wondered if those fae had left yet.

I crept to the roof's edge, knowing I was shrouded and peered over the ledge. To my eye, I'd say twenty Crownguards awaited us around the corner, blades drawn. They didn't look particularly engaged though, as if they'd tracked our way here and decided to camp out to ambush us, but had no idea when we would arrive, and more importantly, they had no idea we were straight above them. I loosed a long sigh of relief.

Thank the goddess.

We stayed close to the center of the rooftops as best we could to avoid detection from the pedestrians or the massive Crownguard presence below, and shrouding when needed. They knew we were here. It didn't matter now if we used our magic. We needed to do whatever possible to get the fuck out of here. Now.

Screams sounded periodically in the distance, followed by the faraway thumping of running feet. I only needed to see Locke's demeanor to know that our distraction was working in full force. I knew that was good. That it would buy our safety. But guilt gnawed at me endlessly, souring my stomach. Would those prisoners hurt the innocent? I felt sick at the thought. I glanced toward our goal, forcing everything else out of my mind. The fewer Crownguards that were between us and freedom, the better, I thought to myself, but I'd be lying if the thought didn't turn to ash on my tongue and threaten to choke me.

Buildings in this part of the city were close together and easily jumpable. Only once did I have to create a bridge of vines from one end to the other, dissolving them once the gap was behind me. I refused to look down, knowing I'd be paralyzed by fear if I did. I kept my eyes on Locke ahead of me. Every building, he took my hand, leading me to the next gap to cross.

"That's it, love. Keep going." His soft voice reached past the fear in my mind, sounding so much like his normal self my heart ached. But when I checked, his eyes still held that dullness of grief. Of guilt. And I realized that I was the only reason he was trying this hard right now. Because he couldn't bear to lose anyone else. I didn't think the pieces of my heart could shatter further, but they did for him. If they were fragments of glass before, they were nothing but dust now, waiting for the wind the separate and scatter them.

Vanneck's unexpected voice in my head just about made me scream. Locke looked at me in alarm as I caught my breath. Vanneck's voice was thin and hollow, the connection beginning to weaken. He'd been separated from the twins but was on his way back to the meeting spot where he and Aspen would await all of us, a grove a safe distance away from Loc Valen.

We're on our way out of the city now, I told him. I was so glad to see the massive walls only about a block away from us.

What news of Locke's family? I could feel the hope in his words. I felt it decline when he felt my despair.

Dead. Apparently killed some time ago.

How's Locke?

How would you be?

Understood, he said sadly. *Are you sure you don't need our help? This doesn't feel right.*

It's okay. Just go. I'll feel better knowing you are both safe, I cajoled, feeling his resistance flare before subsiding. *Try to find the twins, if you can. We'll see you at the grove.*

The crummy things about being a block from our goal was the fact that these buildings were further apart, and this close to the wards, Locke couldn't shroud us without a beacon going off signaling our proximity. There was no way to be stealthy, so Locke and I were forced to the streets, forced to make a run for it. In our Crownguard ensemble, we blended in, just as we did before. The only thing, we were now the only ones wearing hoods. I prayed we didn't stand out too much as we moved among the fray.

"Stop," someone called to us as we walked by. A familiar voice that shouldn't have surprised me this close to the main gate. The captain with a power trip from earlier. Both of our feet stopped moving. We turned to face them, in sync with one another. Fuck. We were so close. The wall was right there. I could throw a stone and touch it!

"Hoods down. Show your face."

"Why?" I asked.

"Because something is afoot in this city and hoods are awfully suspicious. Especially if someone refuses to remove them. Did you not see the wards earlier? The fucking twins are apparently here and launched an attack."

Neither of us moved. I didn't even dare to breathe. I knew he couldn't see my face, but I felt his stare searching for and somehow finding my eyes under the canopy of my shadowed hood. I saw the suspicion on his face change to realization and at last evolve to feral hostility. He knew. Locke and I turned and fled towards the main gate, the Captain's voice screaming behind us.

An arrow whizzed past me. Another over Locke's head. I pushed my air magic out around me in a sort of force field. Just in time. I felt an arrow hit the wind at my back and fall to the ground with a harmless clatter. Another followed suit that likely would have struck me in the leg. Locke picked me up the way he did the Frostfall that day. We just had to get across the wall and we could jumpstone to safety. He picked me up, one arm under my knees and the other under my shoulders, and he ran with the full speed of the Zodiac towards the gate.

"Stop them!" someone screamed. Shouts were coming from everywhere. We were mere feet from the open gate. One moment, Locke and I were running frantically for our lives; the next, there was nothing but agony. Pain crumpled me as we rammed into something hard, sending both of us loudly sprawling to the ground. Locke took the brunt of the fall, shielding me from the worst of it with his body. I didn't understand, my eyes immediately searching for the cause, finding the gate. It *was* open....

I looked up at it now with my head beginning to clear. Swirling, screaming, black miasma coiled and slithered along the gap where it hadn't been mere seconds ago. The gate remained open on the other side of a screaming, shadowed wall, and my blood turned to oil in my veins. I heard a slow, throaty laugh that made my teeth grind and my hands clench around my dagger hilts. Fear and all consuming rage at war with one another, two unstoppable forces battling for dominance. One of the only fae who could truly capture us. A fae whose name turned to bile on my tongue when I spat his name.

Pisces.

His form was half veiled by the long reaching shadows of the approaching dusk. It was hard to make out most details other than that sick, insidious grin spreading over his face like oil over stone and his distinctive moonlight colored hair, a beacon in the growing darkness. I narrowed my eyes at him before looking around us. The guard captain and his team were advancing on where we got to our feet, weapons drawn, their sharpened edges glinting in the fae and firelight around us. Beyond them, the city was abandoned. Its citizens evacuated quickly, doors closed, windows shuttered against the threat—us.

Bile burned the back of my throat. We weren't the enemy. We weren't the ones burning cities for rumors of disloyalty, weren't the ones forcing fae into the Crownguardianship. We didn't hurt innocent fae.

"Do you trust me?" Locke whispered above the chatter, his shoulder brushing mine. I didn't dare look away from the nearest guard, knowing that doing so would cost me dearly.

"Without question."

"Good." The edges of his lips picked up in a sinister sneer at Pisces as he advanced step by step closer to the middle of the fray, the Crownguards parting at his command. That bloodlust I saw earlier had expanded, wrath taking up an entirely new control over him. "Because you're going to need that trust."

"You have a plan to go with all that anger?"

"It's a shit plan. But it's all we've got," he admitted.

"I'm with you." I meant it. If we lived. If we died. This side of the veil or the other, I was by his side.

"Traitor Prince and the Queen's Mark. What a treat. And totally unexpected. Truly." Pisces' tone dripped with condescension, which only served to heighten my revulsion of him. His eyes flashed with giddy excitement as his boots thumped over the cobblestone to stand in front of us, leading the charge. "How do you plan on getting out of this one? You're surrounded, you can't jumpstone out, and your only exit is blocked."

My grip tightened on my daggers, a snarl dripping from my lips--

"When I say run, head for the stairs behind you as fast as you can, and do not stop until you're at the top," Locke's whisper broke through my haze of anger, ignoring his former kinship brother entirely. "I'll be right behind you."

"I'm not leaving you, you self-sacrificing, stubborn ass," I whispered back. Out of the corner of my eye, I saw the dry smile.

"Trust me. Right behind you."

"You and me. Together. We both get out, or neither does." I was adamant.

"You and me. Together," he placated. "Now run." He spun, sending ice in a flurry of razor sharp daggers at our opponents who'd now gotten too close. They hissed and returned with a volley of magic of their own. Colder still the air got, as Locke summoned his shadows, "Run, Lark!"

Chapter Forty

I turned and ran as fast as my feet would carry me, blind faith the only thing that I was going on that I wasn't leaving a very outnumbered and out-weaponed Locke to his death. I shook my head as I panted my way to white stone steps, dodging ice, black magic, and arrows. I had to trust him. I *did* trust him.

Right behind me.

He said he'd be right behind me. I made it to the stairs, hearing shouts of pain and clashing steel behind me. It took all my will power not to look back. Air cleaved a horrendous path through my lungs as I breathed heavily, taking the steep stairs two at a time. I got to the top and my mind was emptied of rational thought.

The strong winds up here were what I noticed first. My hair whipped around me. The second thing was that I found myself on the very top of the white stone wall that separated the city from the rest of the Water court. The very wall we were going to blast apart when the time came. Two Crownguards rushed me from each side. I wasn't sure if I'd surprised them, or if they'd intercepted me somehow. I drew my sword, the ring of it leaving its sheath, or perhaps the sight of it, causing their step to falter momentarily. Long enough for me to make the first move. I dove at the first one, too quick for him, and knocked him off-balance. A strong gush from my Wind Magic and he fell over the ledge. I tried not to flinch at the scream. At his body hitting the ground far too long later. I'd forgotten that the ground dipped down significantly at the wall, adding to the length of his descent. The final one regarded me warily and with extreme disgust.

"Back down now, and no harm will come to you," I said, emotion thickly leeching into my voice. He acknowledged my words with a condescending sneer. He brandished his weapon. A flail. Its sharp points poked out, boasting dried blood from its last victim. In the long, narrow space around me, it would be extremely hard to dodge, let alone launch a counterattack. I made my feet reverse, all the while searching for a way out. Where was Locke?

"Do you feel that, Curse?"

I bristled at the title. "What?"

"Your impending death," he said, swinging his flail in graceful, swooping arcs over his shoulder. "Not that you'll die here. But it's not like you need your legs to be functional when Her Majesty takes your life from you." His hand raised to strike. I called upon every kind of magic I had. Fire, Air, it didn't matter. The rush of air with the strength of a tornado blasted him backwards, forcing him to land hard on his behind. I felt my feet leave the ground and my body move through the air without my consent. I shrieked when I looked down, seeing the ground terrifyingly far below me. My body froze, but paralysis did nothing to quell the scream that was ripped from my throat.

"Fuck the veil, Lark, you've got a set of lungs on you. I might be deaf," Locke said over the wind screaming in my ear. Locke had his arms under my shoulders and knees once again, and we were flying. The rushing wind sputtered problematically and we dropped a few feet, making my heart lurch in my chest. I looked up, seeing his black magic wings erupting from his back. I saw him struggle to flap them. The momentum he'd gained from pushing off the wall was wearing off. We didn't have enough wind now to keep going. My stomach sank when I remembered how his previous attempt at flying went. If we fell, we were far too high to try to land.

"Where's the jumpstone?" I hollered into the wind.

"It's in my pocket. I'm not sure if you can get it." His answer had my palms sweating. "We might have to wait until we land." With the number of arrows flying at us, that might be a tall order.

"Keep your wings out steady!" I hollered. Locke nodded, the strain evident on his face.

An arrow whizzed by. And another. I summoned my Air Magic, Locke's shadow wings tenting over the strong gust I provided in a last-ditch effort to get us to safety near the trees. Ground was coming steadily closer at a significantly less harrowing speed as we glided to safety. Locke's feet hit the ground hard, running into the stop as I clung to him. He grunted with what must have been relief and exhaustion from holding those wings open, because by the time I looked back, they had already dissipated into the night. I could have kissed the ground for how happy I was to be back on it safely. Our relief was short-lived. Furious roars erupted from behind us as we ran for the safety of the forest, now dark in the waning twilight, and I heard the gate open. I heard the clatter of hooves, followed by war cries. They were coming.

We were being hunted. I just hoped the others were okay.

"Where's the jumpstone?" I asked Locke again as the sounds of the hunt moved swiftly closer. Angry shouts came closer, faster than I'd thought possible. Locke was already pulling it from his pocket and hastily palmed it, watching the dim magical glow of it as it lit to life. I took his hand to follow him into the portal back to the meeting place. I told Vanneck through the waning spell bond that were on our way to the grove. I only hoped he could hear me, because I felt no response, no stirring in that corner of my mind that said he had.

The sound of shattered glass reached my ears only a fraction of a second before a bright light exploded in front of my eyes and I was thrown backwards. I flew an impossibly long way, gauging by the amount of time I spent without any part of me touching the ground until I collided with something scratchy and solid, causing my body to crumble and my head to explode. My body caved to it, succumbing to the pain. Had I hit a tree? My eyes crossed and all I saw was a buzzing, static-fueled white light, but my ears heard nothing but humming. Disoriented, I looked around, fighting the urge to be sick. I fought hard, rallying against the violent throb that cut like a knife behind my eyes.

As I struggled to regain my senses, terror gripped me. All I could do was wait for my vision or hearing to return to me, all too slowly. After what felt like a lifetime, I could make out vague shapes and colors. I saw two figures fighting. A figure of black hair and one of white hair. Black magic clashed with Water Magic, sending resounding shockwaves all around, making my head further throb behind my eyes. Trees bowed away from the force, creating a small, open glade. Steel collided with steel, the sounds now somewhat audible to me. Mouths were moving, though for the life of me I couldn't hear anything over the ringing in my ears and the clash of blades.

I tried to get my legs under me, but my injured body refused to cooperate. My head spun as my body retreated back to the ground, trying to take in air. I looked down at myself at last, taking inventory of myself. I could wiggle my fingers and toes. But there was a worrying slash along my shoulder, leaking blood everywhere. Touching my head, I noticed a massive swelling where I'd indeed struck a tree. My hand brushed up against something impossibly hot and smooth and out of place on the frosty forest floor.

My hand closed around it, only just cool enough to touch. Smooth, opaque glass...

Smooth glass...

The explosion...

The reality of what I was seeing hit me.

The jumpstone. Our escape route. It'd exploded. Realization slowly came to me as I picked up and examined a tiny piece the size of my thumb. Looking up, I saw moonlight hair and I knew. Pisces somehow had shattered the jumpstone. We had no way out. Locke was fighting like hell to protect me in my weakened state, but if I didn't help, I feared Locke would get hurt. I surged forward, desperate to keep Locke from coming to harm.

But my balance wasn't cooperating. I struggled to find my equilibrium and rise to my feet, but I could do little more than sit and try desperately not to fight the ever-consuming waves of nausea. I needed Aspen's healing magic. I was in bad shape. Of that, there was little doubt. But I couldn't sit here and do nothing. Locke needed my help. Although now that my vision was clearing further, I could see the relentless rage and determination in Locke's steely eyes. The pent-up kind that echoed in Pisces's icy glare.

They battled strike for vicious strike. Both were bleeding. We desperately needed to get out of here, and we couldn't do that while Pisces stood. I forced myself to my feet, gripping the tree as I did so. I palmed my dagger's hilt, unsure what I planned to do. Perhaps a distraction?

Before I had a moment to come up with even the thinnest of plans, Pisces jumped backwards, creating space between himself and Locke before glancing at me.

"There you are, darling," he drawled languidly, as if he didn't have blood coloring his hair. "Have you missed me? Because I've so looked forward to seeing you." Pisces's eyes levelled into my own. I saw the weight of his hate. His anger. His eyes were like two voids, completely without any scrape of hope or decency. A shudder trickled over me with the onset of a horrid thought; Scorpio did what she did because on some level she believed it was necessary. Previously, I'd thought no fae could possibly be worse than that, but Pisces was proof that I was wrong. He was so much worse. He did evil things because he reveled in chaos and torment.

He reveled in causing it.

His hand twitched, his sword moving incrementally. The most inconsequential of movements. Enough to jolt my body and send an aftershock reverberating through the earth below me. My body bolted before I could stop myself. My hand gripped my blade in a white knuckled grasp and a slight tremble I didn't think was entirely fear, but adrenaline. From the widening grin on his face and the grim concern I saw on Locke's, I knew that if Pisces launched an attack, my broken body wouldn't be able to fight him off.

"You want something from us," Locke growled. He'd placed himself directly between us, recapturing Pisces's attention. Locke fixed him with what was no doubt a terrifying glare that would have sent lesser fae running for their lives. "Spit it out and run back to Scorpio like the good pet you are."

"Cancer, ever so astute. I do want something." His gaze slithered back to me. Something wicked lay there, just waiting to be discovered. I felt hot and cold all over, and I prayed my head would stop feeling like it was stuffed full of cotton. "And I think the terms of my proposal are beyond fair. So relax and enjoy the party, Cancer." I fought to keep my face neutral. What he was saying was riddled with untruths given that he'd shattered our only escape route. "I want to strike a deal. A peace deal."

"A peace deal?" I couldn't keep the surprise out of my voice. I hated how small and faraway my voice still sounded to my own ears. I shook my head, trying to clear it, but only succeeded in making the buzzing noise in the back of my brain louder for a moment. I winced.

"The right answer belonging to the little curse that could." He winked in a way that I thought was supposed to be charming before his face settled into something more serious. "Will you hear me out?"

I glanced at Locke, who shook his head no. Imploring me.

"What do you want, Pisces?" I chewed the words over as I spoke them. Was I walking into a trap? He was all about killing us ten minutes ago, and now he just wanted to chit chat?

"If you come with me right now, if you surrender yourself willingly, your entire Court of Rebels," he mentioned my entire home in quotation marks as if it were a joke, "will be given leniency. You will save the entire Water Court—especially your new home—a grim fate. Scorpio would only be the beginning." I froze, silently turning the offer over in my head and examining it.

"Lark, you know this is a trap" Locke warned, pressing closer to me.

"How is it a trap?" Pisces feigned outrage before sighing. "I offer a genuine olive branch. Look, clearly the fighting is getting us nowhere. Why not try a way of peace? Something that helps everybody? Scorpio and Locke get their curses removed, and everybody else lives. Except for you, Lark, I'm afraid. I apologize for the touchy subject."

I couldn't move. Couldn't breathe. Every hateful thought I had about myself, every selfish impulse that haunted me since I found out about my curse, every thought I dared not examine was hanging right there, raw for all of us to see: fae were dying because I was still alive. But I could end it. Right now.

"Lark." Locke's gravelly voice reached me through my bleak thoughts. "Run." I could hear his plea. His voice still contained that hard edge for Pisces, but I saw it for what it was. He was begging me not to consider this. But he knew. He knew I was.

"Not without you," I whispered.

"So you won't leave your soulmate to fight me alone. Interesting. You do have a sense of nobility." His words hit me like a punch to the gut. "So you must see that the only course of action that will save everyone is to come with me now."

"Do a swear spell." At my utterance, Pisces's grin sharpened. Locke spun around, exposing his back to Pisces for the first time, to look at me with a horrid, tormented expression. Real, Goddess-damned torment. It made me feel wretched and like I wanted to hurl my guts up. But if I could guarantee his safety, didn't I have to try? A deal with the devil. For him, for Aspen, for Eldan, for my friends, I would at least hear him out.

I would take it if they would be safe.

"I solemnly swear on my own life that when Lark gives herself to me with the voluntary intention of dying by Scorpio's hand, leniency will be granted to her Court of Rebels and her rebel Prince Cancer."

My heart thudded almost painfully in my chest. Seconds passed as I turned the deal over in my head. I scarcely breathed.

"No," Locke said for me. Pisces tsked.

"Now, now," he admonished with a derisive snort, "you're not the one I'm making the deal with. You know you can't answer on her behalf."

Time stood still for me. Long seconds passed while I looked Locke in the eye, pleading for him to understand. That I couldn't let anyone else get hurt because of me. Horrifying images of Listwyne and Poplar Hollow both flashed through my head, taunting me. I felt that silent conversation between us. Almost hear it. I could hear his very soul screaming at me to say no. To ask what changed between the last time I'd offered myself and now. To choose our original plan. Pisces waited with bated breath and a now sincere looking smile. Well, as sincere as a sociopathic, narcissistic, violence-craving lunatic could be. I took a step forward towards Pisces's outstretched hand. I opened my mouth to speak—

"Ask him what he means by leniency, Lark." Locke's voice became quick, menacing punctures to the thick silence around us. At this, Pisces's eyes darkened, though his sickening smile remained intact. Locke's brow ticked, focusing in on the wording. My caution rose and I hesitated. "Go ahead, Pisces. Tell her." Pisces grit his teeth, his anger now apparent. My stomach fell through my body and continued to freefall straight through the earth.

"You were never going to grant real leniency," I murmured as I realized the intentional wording of his vow. How he disguised brutality as mercy. "Everyone you deemed a traitor would still die even after I upheld my terms of the deal."

"Ah, but at least I'd ensure quick deaths. They wouldn't be tortured, starved, or enslaved." Pisces shrugged as if this failure didn't bother him. "I didn't lie about one thing. And here's one more truth for you, Little Curse: you decided the fate of all you hold dear tonight."

I hated how prophetic it sounded, resonating in the silent night around us. Even the surrounding silence seemed to punctuate his threat. I squared up, my head feeling less foggy at last.

"Let me give you my formal answer then, Pisces." I spat as much venom into my voice as I could manage. "The answer is no. And when we at last meet on the battlefield, we will not be the ones who perish. I will die, but it will be on my terms. And you will not live to see peace renewed."

Pisces snarled in response. Locke's gaze stuck on me a moment, before returning to Pisces, but I saw that look. One of immense relief and pride.

"You're right about one thing, Lark. You will die. But it won't be on your terms." He hurtled himself at me. There was a thunderous bang as Locke propelled himself into his path, and body-blocked him with a swing of his sword. Pisces diverted course with a curse and a flow of icy magic at both of us. I summoned my air magic, mitigating the worst of it for Locke and me.

Pisces was a schemer. A true master in the art of manipulation. But there was one thing he never expected.

Me.

That I would fight back.

And that would be his undoing.

I knelt to the cold, rigid, unyielding ground with a smile. Pisces had the good sense to look unnerved as he watched me, confounded before sending a maelstrom of blackness at us. Just as before in Frostfall, the whispers began—some quiet, some sounding like muffled screams. And just like before, I couldn't hear what they were saying. Locke countered with silent shadows, a dark light flaring where they met. A thin white light glowed where their powers collided.

"Remember what happened last time we did this dance, Cancer." Pisces sneered his taunt. "You won't win. I'm far more adept at the darkness than you are."

"Your soul is close to breaking, Pisces!" Locke snarled. "Don't you see that? Your power grows the most when your soul has the most cracks!"

Pisces's laughter boomed, sounding so close to mania. His eyes had blackened, delicate black veins running slightly around them. I startled. Is this what would happen to Locke if he weren't careful?

"As long as you break before me, I don't care," he roared back before his voice tumbled into a whisper devoid of anything but pain. Glaring at Locke through his brow, he continued, "For Wisty, you will break."

The stricken look in Locke's eyes did it for me. This was over. Right now. Pisces kept his eyes on Locke, taunting and loud. But it meant he paid me no mind. My hands felt frozen on the frosty earth. I didn't care. I poured my magic into the earth, begging it to bend to my will. It responded like an old friend in its eagerness. Thick vines with long, sharp thorns erupted from the ground, the fractured earth splintering beneath Pisces's feet, before ensnaring his feet, his legs. He screamed as he bled, the thorns biting hungrily into his flesh. The black glow of shadow magic sputtered as his focus disrupted, his gaze now fixed on me.

I smiled grimly.

"Tell the Grievling we say hello," I snarled, pouring more magic into the ground. The thorns rose higher, devouring as they went until the only thing free was his neck.

"I'll fucking gut you for this!" he shrieked, fighting the thorns. Freezing them, hacking them. Nothing availed. Every vine he destroyed with his own magic, I replaced with three. I had become like that of a hydra of Water realm myth, replacing the dead with live, new vines, stronger than ever. Locke's magic came in to aid my own, freezing Pisces in place so my vines could wrap him more securely. "I'll make sure Scorpio kills you slowly. You and your friends will die in agony!"

I rose to my feet, continuing to funnel my magic, but this time, below his feet I opened a chasm below him. And just like that, my vines pulled him in, faster than I ever expected, dragging him down as he screamed and vowed his vengeance. I laughed.

"Not if you are dead," I said in my most saccharine voice.

Wind howled in the yawning chasm below my feet as I watched Pisces struggle to get out of what will be his grave. The panic in his wide eyes betrayed his fear. I couldn't even try to feel remorse as I began to close it over his head, entombing him forever.

"No!" He pled, before the ground shuddered once more and swallowed him at last. His fate was sealed.

My breath left me as I collapsed, my head swimming. Gingerly, I touched the back of my head, not surprised to find it wet with what was certainly blood. Despite this, I grinned weakly up at Locke, who knelt down to me and pulled me into the fiercest embrace that embodied every emotion from today. A day of triumph and despair in equal measure.

With Pisces in the ground where he belonged, I felt a strange sense of comfort wash over me. I knew we weren't done, not by a longshot, but killing Prince Pisces was a massive victory. Not only was Scorpio weakened, but my father was avenged at last. I let out a shaky breath. I glanced up to see Locke looking at me with pure, jaw slackened awe.

"Are you alright?" His hands gently roamed every square inch of my body, eyes perusing for signs of injury. I saw the rage whenever he found one, especially as he eyed my shoulder.

"Yes, I normally bleed from the back of my head," I said, my breathy tone making my joke fall flat. We were here. We made it out. We were really alive.

"Well, your sense of humor is intact, which is a good sign." His relief was palpable, the tenderness with which he helped me to my feet made my heart ache.

"I'm okay," I said, wrapping my arms around him. Letting those words sink in, I couldn't believe them. His face turned then, his relief falling away, leaving space for only wrath. His eyes barreled into me, hitting stronger than any physical hit anyone had yet to land on me. I braced myself for what I knew was coming.

"Lark," His growl punctuated the tension, the crackling shadows around us, "what the fuck were you thinking? You were actually considering Pisces' offer." It wasn't a question, but a statement in roiling anger. His jaw ground so sharply I could hear it.

"I saw a way to save everyone." I said, "I couldn't not at least examine it."

I watched him loosen a frustrated laugh, his hands raking through his raven hair, coming back to settle on my shoulders. I could feel them shaking. His eyes flared with a recognizable glisten as he shattered before me, pieces of his soul laid bare and bloody.

"I'm not someone who will ever tell you what to do. I don't own you. We are equals in every way, Lark," his voice was smooth. Rather than the softness the darkness of twilight, of a lover's embrace, his voice embodied a stormy night, tempestuous and unwavering. "But if you continue to attempt to throw your life away, I don't think either of us will like who I become in order to keep you safe. To keep you with me. Because I've lost too much to lose you now and know that I've reached my limit. I know plan B may have to be our only chance and I'm fighting like hell to make certain all the variables are in place to make certain you have the best chance at surviving this. Don't throw your life away. Not for anyone. Stay with me." He implored, his face inches from mine, "I don't care how selfish that is. You can blame me. I can be the selfish one, not you. I will gladly shoulder that blame if it keeps you from ever doing something like that again. You're the furthest thing from selfish, do you truly not get that?"

Tears blurred my vision. For the very first time in my life, I genuinely had no words. Nothing. Understanding finally closing in on me with a finality that robbed me of breath. For my entire existence, my life meant precious little. Even to me. I'd learned to value other before myself. But in his eyes, that wasn't the case and I'd almost lost him the last thing he held dear aside from his friends. My hands reached up to caress his where they sat on my shoulders, his fingers fisting the ruined material of my cloak.

"I'm sorry." I whispered, never feeling more so than in this moment, seeing Locke break before me. Seeing him hurt because of me. "I'm so sorry."

"I know." He said, straightening his spine, and clearly seeing the contrition in my aura. "I know."

One look at Locke was all I needed to see the thinly veiled pain there. The weight of his grief was only just light enough for him to bear. I opened my mouth to speak, to ask him if he was okay, but Locke beat me to it, his eyes sharpening like steel.

"Don't say it, Lark. Not yet. When we get home, I can grieve. If you ask me right now, if I feel it right now, I might be crushed under the weight of it." I wish I didn't understand exactly how he felt. When Pisces killed my father, I remember how the grief had threatened to consume me. The only difference was that I would make sure Locke knew he wasn't alone. Now or ever. I took his hand softly instead, reaching up on my toes to kiss him.

His arms encircled me, and the kiss was no longer sweet. It was desperate. It was celebration that the other was still here. Still together. That we had made it. Our mouths clashed, and warred over and over again, slanting against each other. My hands tangled in his hair, pulling him ever closer, just as his arms snaked around me until I wasn't sure where I ended and he began.

With one last kiss, as soft as feathered wings, he pulled away. But not before kissing my nose gently, making my grin and bringing heat to my face.

"As much as I'd like to continue this little tryst, we have to get to the glade. We need to find everyone else. Before someone, or something, finds us." His eyes darkened over me. "The sooner I see our friends, the better I'll feel."

Chapter Forty-One

The moment my eyes laid on Aspen and Vanneck hunching stiffly over the small fire they'd built in the clearing, I could have cried from relief of seeing them okay. I moved from Locke's arms where he supported me, my feet moving as fast as I my limping would allow to get to them, my arms reaching around them both.

"You blocked me out," Vanneck's voice was thick as his gaze flicked from Locke to me with concern. "I could feel what you were feeling, but not your thoughts. It made me realize how it must be for Locke."

"I think what Vanneck is saying," Aspen chimed in, clapping Locke on the back as he approached, "is we were starting to worry about you both. Goddess above, at one point, Vanneck just felt fear and despair and we didn't know what to do. We just had to trust you were okay, but that didn't mean we weren't this close from storming Ari'inor ourselves." Aspen pinched his thumb and forefinger almost together, just as Locke and I exchanged loaded looks that didn't go unnoticed.

"Lark, you don't look so good." I didn't want to say how not good I felt. I knew how I looked though. Blood was smeared all down my left side, my hair was matted in it. I was covered in too many cuts to count. I was limping enough that Locke had to carry me part of the way.

"She needs help, Aspen. She's lost a fair bit of blood." Locke answered for me, spurring him on.

"Hold on," I said, looking around and noticing too few fae around the fire. "Where are Lennox and Lenore?" I knew Wow and Calan were going straight back to Port Azure and weren't going to meet us here, but how was it possible that the twins hadn't returned yet? Aspen and Vanneck exchanged deeply concerned looks, their eyes tight.

"They haven't made it here yet," Vanneck said hesitantly.

"Heal Lark enough so she can fight," Locke said again with determination. "Then we go find them."

"Do we have time for that?" I asked while Aspen's hands glowed green over my head, soothing the throbbing behind my eyes and the ringing in my ears. I almost dropped in relief.

"You're no good to us half dead, Little Bird." Aspen said. "Two minutes and we're out."

"Fine, two minutes. "I guffawed, trying to deter this ominous feeling in the pit of my stomach. The twins were fine. We were late getting back. It's realistic to think they might have needed more time too.

"Yikes," Aspen smoothed my hair and pulled what was revealed to be a large chunk of glass—a piece of jumpstone. I fought the urge to be sick at the feeling of it unsticking to my scalp. "You may only have a small bald spot," he said, rearranging my hair just so. My hands bolted to my hair, feeling the damage stitching itself together inch by inch. Nervous laughter sounded from Vanneck and Aspen, even Locke laughed a little. I glared at each one in turn.

"I hate you," I said. Aspen grinned widely as he ruffled my hair as if I were an adolescent male. I swatted his hands away, to which I was met with a resounding cackle from him.

"No, you don't." He was right, not that I'd tell him.

Turns out, two minutes was exactly long enough to finish healing me and for Locke to recant what was revealed in Loc Valen. His tone was clipped, his eyes staring at the flames Aspen and Vanneck had started while waiting for us. I stretched as Aspen finished healing me, grateful for my head to feel some semblance of normal.

"They should be here by now," Vanneck repeated with urgency.

"We're done waiting." I said. More than well enough now to pose a threat to any who crossed me now. "Let's go get them."

A lone figure began walking towards us in the shadows, ensnaring everyone's attention. Aspen tensed, Vanneck's hand went to his sword, the sound of it sliding from its sheath echoing behind my head. My hands slid to my boots to grasp my daggers. Until the firelight revealed their identity.

Lenore.

She was covered in blood. Her hair, usually the color of spun gold, was red and smattered to her scalp and forehead. The massive battle axe strapped to her back was a mess of red with bits of fleshy gore I'd rather not look at too long. And when the fire light hit her, she looked like a deity of war. Releasing my daggers, I shot to my feet when I saw her limping on her left side, Aspen coming to her aid as well.

"Lenore, are you alright? What happened?" Aspen got right to work healing her. Locke was by our side in a heartbeat, helping me settle her by the fire. Lenore flinched as we half carried her, and the fact she wasn't biting my head off for helping her told me how much pain she was in. Her head swiveled around, taking each of us in. She uttered only two words. Two words that made my stomach heave.

"Where's Lennox?" Lenore looked to each of us individually, her eye contact strong and pleading. She flinched once again as Aspen healed her. Vanneck ripped a piece of cloth from his own shirt, soaking it in conjured water and began to clean Lenore's face of the blood she was covered in.

"Only some of it is mine," she said with a voice full of spite. "You should see the others." I had no doubt that whoever attacked Lenore lay in the puddle of their own blood somewhere. Assuming it didn't all get on Lenore. "Now seriously, where is Lennox?"

"We haven't seen her," Aspen said gently. "We thought she was with you."

Lenore's face transitioned from deep concern to wrath in a matter of moments.

"We got separated," she explained as Aspen set to work healing a massive wound on her thigh. She shoved him off of her with urgency that echoed in my very being. My stomach jolted into my throat at the amount of blood leaking from it. Her eyes met Aspen's. "I'm okay. But we need to find Lennox! Now."

"We'll find her. She's going to be just fine," I said to Lenore, ignoring the racing of my heart. I held to my own words as a shield against fear for Lennox. "And just in case someone hurt her, think of how much fun you get to have together when you both kill them." Lenore's eyes shone with the promise of a slow death to anyone who dared touch her twin sister, and for a moment I almost felt bad for anyone on the receiving end of that look.

Almost.

Chapter Forty-Two

The site of the ambush was nothing short of a massacre.

Lenore being covered in blood made so much more sense now. What I couldn't figure out was how she wasn't hurt worse. How she lived through this and still managed to make it back to the glade. Bodies littered the area, blood already freezing to the ground.

We weren't too far off from what I imagined the Scarlet Summit to look like.

My foot met something round and solid. Bending down to examine it, I saw it was a jumpstone. It hit me then—Lenore didn't jumpstone into the glade. She walked the whole way, while trying to catch up with her sister. She thought she was behind Lennox and hurried to catch up. This also meant Lennox didn't jumpstone out of this.

I hoped that was a good thing. That Locke could track her. I tried to ignore the rising panic, the voice in my head telling me that Lennox was in serious danger, but I couldn't. Not entirely. Instead, I watched helplessly as Locke scoured the area with his black magic, sniffing the air, searching for any sign of Lennox.

"What does his black magic do here?" I asked Lenore.

"It acts as a kind of detector. Whoever he was looking for, his magic will react to. It'll be like a beacon for him to follow, all the way to his target. The stronger his connection to the fae in question, the easier it is to find them. But he has to know them personally, I believe," she said as she paced, running her hands over the back of her neck or crossing her arms over her chest. I wanted to say something. Do something.

But one thing Lenore wouldn't appreciate was a lie. Comforting or not.

So I kept my mouth shut.

I'd seen the exact moment Locke picked up on Lennox's trail. His eyes narrowed, and his jaw tightened in a grimace which only deepened when his gaze flicked to Lenore. His posture was far too stiff for there to be good news. A silent exchange between them had her grabbing her smaller axe and twirling it in her hand and spinning it over her wrist.

Locke led the way into the trees, following where his shadows led. His nostrils flared as we moved further away from the makeshift gravesite.

"Dare I ask?" I asked in a voice tighter even than Locke's posture. Locke hesitated only a moment before speaking.

"I smell Lennox's blood."

Lenore's eyes filled with war and despair and the promise of ruin and wrath. I felt the very aura around her vibrating with the need for vengeance for her sister being injured. My heart squeezed tighter, and I felt like I couldn't breathe. Lennox...

I wanted to scream to the Goddess above. Please let Lennox be alright. She was strong, I reminded myself. She'd make it through this.

"We have to hurry," I said.

"Be prepared," Locke's voice leveled me. "It could be another ambush."

Lenore brandished her weapon, fingering the incredibly lethal, very bloody, axe blade. She looked at Locke from through her brow-bone, intense eyes biting into him with a terrifying smile.

"So ambush me. I'm in the mood for murder," Lenore said before turning on her heel and striding away in the direction Locke indicated.

It didn't take us long to find Lennox. Turns out she wasn't far. But that was the end of the good news. They weren't even trying to hide her, giving credibility to the idea of this being a trap. We started into a run—as quietly as we could manage, our steps nimble, short and quick. It was hard staying light on my feet to reduce the amount of noise the steps made along the forest floor. But then it wasn't just Locke that could locate Lennox. We all could hear her screams echoing through the trees. My blood chilled in my veins and the desperate need to take off at a full run was almost unbearable. I wanted to shout to her. Tell her we were coming. I remembered when Aspen's voice was in my head telling me help was on the way, the hope I'd felt. I wished so badly I could give that hope to Lennox in this moment.

It was a fight to keep Lenore in check. She was ready to charge in blazing. No plan, no assessment of the situation, blind. We needed her with as clear a head as possible.

I saw a fire flickering through the bushes. We crouched into the foliage, looking for the signs of our threats. I pushed my consciousness out, feeling only a few bodies. My eyes found Lennox immediately. Her hands her bound behind her back, and she was lying on her side near the fire. They had stripped her of her weapons and armor, leaving her in just pants, boots, and her leather and buckle shirt. From my vantage point, I could see the gashes along her face, still oozing blood. I could almost see the hopelessness in her eyes.

But I saw two fae in attendance, one of which made my heart stop and my hands fly to my mouth to keep from screaming. One with filthy, moonlight colored hair. Locke and I exchanged confused looks. How was Pisces alive? I killed him! Only an hour ago. Locke's wide eyes showcased his shock to me.

The other was Scorpio, dressed in her golden armor. Her green and black eyes scanning the perimeter with intent.

I decided it didn't matter. I would face Pisces, I would face Scorpio, together. I would face a hundred enemies for Lennox. As she would for me. I didn't hide the clang of metal on metal as I drew my sword. Their gazes drew to my general direction. I stepped out from the trees, a nasty glare on my face. My friends filtered out behind me and fanned out, each locking on to a Crownguard that seemed to melt from the shadows. Where the hell had they come from?

Vanneck clutched his sword, where Aspen smugly called on his opponent. Lenore was murder incarnate as she beheld her sister's bound and weakened state. Locke and Pisces eyed each other up with silent reproach, the stark glow from the massive bonfire the backdrop between the two sides.

One thing was for certain: someone would die tonight before this was over. I'd thought that would be Pisces, but I supposed I could take the pleasure of killing him again.

"You don't stay dead, do you?" I asked him as he dragged his eyes from Locke to me. "Tell me, do you often keep showing up where you're not wanted? No wonder you don't have any friends."

Pisces grinned that unsettling grin of his, characterized by that too wide smile with a touch of mania in his eyes. As often as I've seen it, I still felt that nervous energy it instilled into my bones.

"Did you really think you could dig a chasm deep enough to bury me?" he seethed. "You said to say hello to the Grievling," he said, stepping closer to us. "He sends his regards."

"Let Lennox go." I skewered Scorpio with a look that I hoped appeared formidable. "You've gotten what you wanted, right? I'm here. Unbind her."

Scorpio laughed then. Throwing her head to the stars.

"Funny that," she chortled, turning to an equally amused Pisces. "You didn't tell me she was funny. Ordering around a Queen. No, my curse. You will all die tonight. And before the morning, the Court of Rebels will be nothing more than a smoldering pile of ash and rubble. Gone will be your pesky rebel influence, and my curse with it."

"What good is ruling if you're ruling over nothing but a mountain of corpses?" Locke asked her. There was tension there in his voice, hiding some form of plea for this to end. For her to see reason. "Because that's what you're going to be left with."

Scorpio hissed her response. "You overestimate your numbers, Cancer. And you underestimate the fear they will have of crossing me. It's amazing how much control you have when the whole realm is afraid of you. When they're right to be. The only corpses I rule over will be those who are disloyal to me. I will make an entire monument of their bones so nobody will turn on me again." Scorpio's head tilted to the right when she smiled, adding to the insane look. The pain she endured must truly be unbearable for her mind to have truly fled. But it had. And now we were forced to face the emotionless, guiltless shell that was Scorpio, whose only motivation was ending the curse.

Pisces pounced on Locke with a shout. The Crownguards fell mercilessly on Aspen and Vanneck. Lenore shot to her sister. Scorpio shot ice at her to divert her. I used my wind to cast them aside and offer Lenore protection. Scorpio's eyes narrowed on me as her body turned to take me on.

"You've gotten in my way for the last time, retch." She summoned her whip into existence, too lightning fast for me to have seen coming. It wound around my neck in a shock of cold and splicing pain. I felt the blood drip and ooze and I gave a shout of alarm before I conjured my flames around me. My neck didn't free up as expected. It should've melted the ice. Why was it still holding tight?

When I looked again, I saw it wasn't only ice and water magic. The whip was imbued with shadows, making it resistant to my flames. I felt the whip tighten again around my neck, now cutting off my air supply effectively, and the tiny, razor sharp ice crystals stabbing into the delicate flesh of my throat with vigor. With my vision beginning to blur, I heard my name called. I couldn't tell who called for me. I grasped my sword and swung. It bounced harmlessly off the whip. I fell to my knees, my body demanding oxygen. I sent my flames up the whip to the one holding it—a smirking Scorpio, looking confident in her victory.

Her grin faltered while she leapt aside, out of the flames' path, dragging me forward with her momentum. I wanted to cry out. My mouth hung open, but no sound came. I felt like it was merciful that my head was even still attached. I couldn't even look around from where I was. My sword fell to the ground. My hands, desperate in their quest to find air for my lungs, clutched uselessly at the ice and shadow whip, never once finding purchase. Panic flared through me now. Aquarius wasn't here. My heart wouldn't restart without her. We have no chance of my coming back from the dead if I died now.

There was a scream. Of fury or of pain I couldn't tell. Maybe both? Another scream, someone else this time. The whip slackened then. My mottled brain cleared as I dragged in two deep, painful breaths. I unwound the spiked object from my neck, wincing when I saw it was stained red—it was slick, coated with my blood. I felt it now, pouring down my body in that perfect, gory halo around my neck.

I saw now who screamed. Lenore had untied Lennox and they had slashed Scorpio across the back with her axe, denting her armor. A distraction enough to free me. I coughed, the pain of my neck nearly dropping me back to my knees. I spit, the wad of blood landing in Scorpio's direction. She seethed at me as I met her gaze head on.

"Die! Why won't you die?" she screamed at me.

"Because you haven't asked very nicely," I said, my sarcasm negated by my voice being little more than a whisper. But I gathered my magic around myself and picked up my fallen sword.

"Get to Lark!" Locke's voice boomed over the battleground. "Rally!" Everyone exploded into motion. My friends were suddenly everywhere, gathered around me in a semi-circle, with Locke next to me. Lenore and a weakened but fierce Lennox next to me. Aspen and Vanneck were on the other side of them, helping to protect Lennox.

"Scorpio. Your name is currently synonymous with death and destruction," said Locke. "You've become the very worst of what Scorpio is supposed to represent. Hatred. Manipulation. Rage. Jealousy. You should be ashamed of yourself."

"And you? Have you not betrayed your very oath as well? The Zodiac Guild should regret ever bringing you into the power of the Kinship. If I have skewed the ideals of Scorpio, then you have perverted the ideals of Cancer!"

"Look around you." Locke's voice bellowed about the clearing. "Your Crownguard is dead. It's just you and Pisces. Against all of us. You can't win this fight."

Scorpio bared her teeth in a silent snarl while Pisces cast a venomous look at all of us. I could see his eyes searching for a weakness among us, waiting for an opportunity.

"You can't kill me." The Queen seethed. "So neither can you."

"We don't have to," said Lenore with a terrible, cruel smile slowly creeping across her face in a way that made the hair on the back of my neck stand in end. "You can pay for your atrocities in blood. Who says death needs to be a reprieve for you? You can acutely pay for all the deaths you caused, one by one. You'll never be done suffering if I have anything to say about it."

"Good thing you have nothing to say about it, little girl." Scorpio smiled ominously, her attention slithering over to settle on me. She flourished her whip, the crack making my spine tingle as I fought a cringe.

Pisces rested his head back in a laugh as they clasped their hands together. They each raised the opposite hand, and a pillar of raging shadow appeared on either side of us. This didn't look like the shadow magic I'd seen so far. I'd always been able to gauge outlines of objects through it. This looked like a wall, vibrating with dark energy. A pulsing, writhing black dome had closed in around us. We'd fallen into a trap. Scorpio and Pisces were laughing as they realized too that there was nowhere to go. "Pisces mentioned you were down a jumpstone," Scorpio sneered. "How unfortunate for you."

Goddess above, I hoped our current jumpstone would work through the shadows.

Scorpio sent a massive onslaught of black tinted shards of ice at us. Wave after wave of them. Razor sharp and pulsing with a black aura. I wasn't sure if she blended the shadows into her magic on purpose, or if she were losing control. Either way, it wouldn't make a difference. These were deadly. My Air Magic shoved into them, just as Locke shoved out with shadows of his own, our combined forces diverting course and slowing them. It didn't stop some of them. I heard shouts and hisses, and I knew some had been struck regardless.

I felt the familiar tingle of the jumpstone and I grinned at Scorpio. We'd retrieved Lennox. We were going to escape from under her thumb once again. Her face registered the indignation of our escape, and her scream of defiance and rage echoed off the shadowy walls that contained us all, reverberating my very bones as we fell into my portal. I flipped them off as we began to disappear, Locke and I keeping our shields up as much as possible while everyone got out.

It was then a moment of chaos. Magic was flung from both sides in the seconds before the portal transported all of us. Pisces threw wave and wave of ice daggers at us, and I deflected them all with my waning Air Magic. I saw Scorpio launch two black viciously curved daggers. They sailed end over end at me in a final bid to end my life before the portal wrenched us from her view. They were coming too fast. They tore through my magic shield as if it weren't even there. I couldn't stop them. I flinched, waiting for the bite of pain I knew was waiting.

I heard my name, and I was shoved hard. Hard into Locke, the center of the circle. I heard a scream. I thought it was me. I blinked. My eyes opened into a familiar sight Port Azure. The sea air mixed with alpine spruce and baking bread from the market welcomed us back.

I turned and realized it wasn't me who'd screamed.

Chapter Forty-Three

L ennox...

There was blood everywhere. Lennox was laying on her back with the daggers lodged in her abdomen and chest—the vulnerable places her armor should have been to protect her. My brain wasn't processing.

Lenore was crouched, holding her sister's hand, begging Lennox to stay with her. Aspen had retrieved the daggers, shrieking about the black magic spewing from them as he struggled to heal the black stained wounds that resisted his magic, the flesh stubbornly refusing to knot itself together.

"Locke, are these what I think they are?" Aspen nodded towards the discarded blades to the side of him, his hands too occupied trying to slow the bleeding. Lennox whimpered in response. The blades in question were solid black from handle to the very tip of the curved blade. Writhing shadows frothed off of them, almost like they were alive.

Locke's eyes widened as he threw himself into ripping the shadows out of Lennox's body, grappling for control over their lethal will.

"Black marked blades." Locke's jaw clenched over the words, like if he beat them into submission, they'd no longer be true. I remembered when the healer from Everwind told me that black magic injuries were difficult to heal. I remembered Locke's words to me from a previous conversation days prior. Black marked weapons were the darkest, deadliest magic ever to crawl this realm. And it was ravaging one of my best friends alive. "I'm going to try to draw the shadows out."

"Can you?"

He didn't answer me.

I gave Aspen my hand and told him to empty my power. Make Lennox better. Maybe we could still fight to save her. Maybe if Locke pulled the shadows out while Aspen healed her, she'll be okay. *She's going to be okay.* He didn't hesitate, scraping into the reserves of my magic, his healing magic brightening and making the area around us glow green.

I screamed for someone to get Eldan. And fast. Vanneck turned and ran as fast as he could, screaming for Eldan before disappearing, taking a piece of my hope with him. But I saw Lennox's head fall to the side, her eyes barely open. Dread filled me from the inside.

She wasn't going to make it.

Tears poured from my eyes as my mind finally processed what I had witnessed. Scorpio had thrown her cursed daggers at me while I fended off Pisces's attacks. The shove. The scream.

Lennox had sacrificed herself. To save me. A sob wracked my body.

"Why!" I demanded Lennox. "Why did you do that? You shouldn't have done it!" Lennox opened her eyes, now full of pain, to look at me. And smiled.

"You're my best friend. I couldn't... I love you." Her voice dropped to that of a whisper.

"I love you too, damn it!" I shouted, tapping her face with my palm to keep her with us. To keep the veil at bay. "Don't go. I don't know what the Court looks like without you!"

"Stay with us! Please, Lennox!" cried Lenore, echoed by us all. Tears falling unchecked down Lennox's twin's panicked face. "Don't leave me!"

"I'll never leave you, sister." She smiled at her twin.

I pressed the wound, ignoring the sickening feeling of my friend's hot blood pouring over my hands, trying to close the wound. Put pressure on it. Why wouldn't the wound close? I could feel Aspen still using my magic to close the wound. I could still see Locke trying to draw the black magic out. Why wasn't it working? What if I sewed the wound shut? Would that work?

I didn't get to make a decision to try. Eldan showed up, with his potions and kits. And I saw the hope leave his eyes. He knew. He knew what I was trying not to know. Lennox was dying. And it was too late.

"Lennox..." I started to say. But what could I say? "I love you. This will not be in vain," I told her, pressing my forehead to hers and clutching her hand. She squeezed mine softly, so soft I wondered if I'd imagined it.

"Make it hurt," she said, her eyes, normally so bright, looked dim. I nodded, tears falling down.

Lenore pled with her sister not to give up.

"I'm already gone, sister. Just don't let me be alone."

Lennox's body rapidly lost warmth, and her body was horribly pale and blotchy.

"I'm so sorry," I whispered as a sob broke from me. Not just to Lennox. To everyone. Locke's arm came around my shoulder when a thought struck me. "I have an idea. Give me the jumpstone."

Aspen gave me a questioning glance and handed it to me. I charged it with what little remained of my magic, emptying me entirely. But it was charged and I bade everyone to hold onto Lennox.

We didn't go far. Just the beach with the final whisper of sunset on the horizon with a smattering of bright stars dotting the sky. Even the moon came out to witness the death of a hero. Lennox loved two things: flowers and sunsets. I could give her at least one of those things. If my magic weren't tapped out, I could give her flowers.

I brought her close to the water, so she could fall into rest to the sounds of the shores and the gulls overhead, having one last soar before turning in. The sand that had been dry upon our arrival was already wet and slick and sticky with Lennox's blood.

"Thank...you..." Lennox's voice was barely discernible now. We all sat around her, softly telling her how much we loved her. Sobs broke from each of us at least once.

There was a pause. A moment where I knew she was seeing the light of the veil. And then her breath left her, never to come again. She passed beyond the veil with the dying of the last vestiges of daylight. I sobbed in earnest now, my body wracked by grief. Aspen and Locke also cried, the tears streaking dirt and blood down their mottled faces. The latter punched the nearest thing to him—a massive rock—crumbling it beneath his fist. Vanneck and Eldan misty eyed behind them. Lenore screamed. Her knees digging into the soft sand as her head whipped up to glare at the clouds above us.

"Take me!" I could hear Lenore's sorrow, grief, anger, and pleading in her voice in equal measure. The ground shook from her violent aura. "Take me!" she screamed again, her voice catching on a desperate wail.

There was no answer for her. Just as it wasn't clear if she meant for the Goddess to take her with Lennox or instead of her. My heart gave a painful squeeze as if it were trying to rip itself to pieces. More than it already was.

"TAKE ME PLEASE. DON'T LEAVE ME ALONE HERE," Lenore screamed at the sky. I took her hand and pulled her to me in a crushing hug. She dissolved into me and we collided in a mass of tears and grief. Aspen and Locke sat side by side, close enough for their shoulders to touch, their heads in their hands. Between us, lay the broken body of Lennox, her soul now beyond the Veil.

Lenore made the sign of the funeral rite on her twin sister's forehead, a crossing rune that required four swipes of her thumb, and said the words. It wasn't fair. We needed something better for Lennox. The words of a warrior. Of a friend. Of someone who sacrificed herself to save me. What words were there for that? For the injustice that Scorpio killed sweet, kind Lennox? She was the best of all of us.

She was dead because of me.

How was I ever to live with that?

Self-hatred fill me in a way it never had before.

"I'm so sorry," I whispered again. Lenore clutched me tighter, words failing her. But I knew their meaning.

She didn't blame me. She should. But she didn't.

"Scorpio will pay," Lenore seethed. "We'll make it hurt. For Lennox."

"Yes," I said, feeling grounded by the idea of revenge for our fallen comrade. More solid under my feet. The very idea of Scorpio's end coming even if it meant my own bolstering me where I'd just be free falling. She wouldn't hurt another fae the way she hurt us. The way she killed Lennox. The end was coming. Tomorrow, we make the arrangements for the final battle. The Air Court would join our ranks.

It was a strange feeling. In the wake of everything that had happened, I still felt like myself. But as I looked over the body of one of my closest friends, her blood still wetting my hands, my clothing, I saw nothing but red. I needed only one thing before I crossed the veil—vengeance, paid with interest. Lennox's death would be paid for in blood. Even if I had to destroy the entire army myself to ensure it.

Chapter Forty-Four

At sunrise we held a funeral for Lennox. Even with no sleep, even as we all sat on the steps of the Citadel under a blanket of stars, even as we listened to Lenore sob over her sister, my magic had restored enough. Enough that I could do for Lennox now what I wanted to do for her last night. Hero Hill was a quiet hill just off the beachy shores of Port Azure. It was where the heroes of the Rebel Court were laid to rest. A large, sloping hill overlooking the sea covered with what had to be hundreds of crosses, each marking the place of a fallen fae and their ashes. Some were new, erected after the most recent battle. Some had flowers on them, lovingly showcasing how missed those fae were. Others wore marks of time like battle scars. Lennox would love it here. She'd see every sunset over the water without obstruction.

Lennox was brought to the pyre by those of us who loved her the most. Locke and Lenore carried the front of the platform, Aspen and myself in the middle, with Vanneck bringing up the rear. Lennox herself was dressed in a blue gown that floated on the breeze and hid her wounds. Her hair was braided into a crown with fresh flowers woven in, as she so loved in life. I tried not to be disturbed by the fact her skin was almost the color of ivory. Far too pale for the lively Lennox. As she looked now, she looked so heartbreakingly beautiful. Like she was sleeping. I felt sorrow mix with rage for a moment as we ascended the steps to the pyre.

Scorpio would not win.

And I would not rest until Port Azure was avenged.

Until my father was.

Until Locke's family was.

Until Lennox was.

Before the burning, everyone was welcome to say their goodbyes, beginning with us. Locke leaned over Lennox, his hand falling to her shoulder as he whispered something to her. Her hands were clasped over her torso, where he slipped a letter. Words to be given to Lennox, and nobody else. They say those letters that get burned go with them beyond the veil. I hoped they were right.

There wasn't a dry eye in attendance as Lenore kissed her twin sister's forehead for the final time, sobbing uncontrollably, her wails feeling like knife blows to my chest. It was the most undone I'd ever seen Lenore. Aspen made his way up next, planting a kiss on her forehead as well. He took her hand and whispered a few things to her, his words for her, and her alone. I prayed that she heard them wherever she was. I hope she could see, could understand, how loved she was. I glanced around, looking for Calan and Wren, surprised they were missing this. But it was entirely possible they didn't yet know.

Vanneck was next, bestowing upon her his lucky knife. A knife whose sheath was embedded in enough jewels to make a king envious. I was close enough to hear his words of departure.

"Just in case anyone gives you any flack in the afterlife. I wouldn't want you to be unprepared. Rest well, my lady. It's been an-an honor." Tears blurred my vision the second his voice wavered.

At last, it was my turn, a moment that surged ahead almost without me. Woefully unprepared to say goodbye to Lennox, I walked on numb legs, feeling every eye on Port Azure on me. A lump formed in my throat as I focused on one foot in front of the other. I saw Lennox's face, now surrounded by fresh blossoms, roses and even lilies. I waved my hand, filling in the gaps, so she was blanketed now with a colorful array of flowers. Her face looked serene, despite the trauma of death, as if she'd left it behind entirely right before her crossing over. I kissed her forehead as the others had done, a tear escaping down my cheek onto hers as I did so.

"Rest well, Lennox." I choked on my words. "May we meet again." I looked down, unable to stop the flood of tears now. Checking my wavering voice, I continued, gripping the sides of the platform she lay on, "I promise this will never be in vain. I will make Scorpio pay." I closed my eyes a moment, taking a deep breath to center myself. A knot formed in my stomach as I waited for the magic of the promise to drift over me, but none came. It didn't occur to me that you couldn't keep a promise to someone no longer breathing. I still couldn't believe she'd saved me. How was I supposed to live with the weight of that? I pictured her laughing. In my mind, I could see her telling me it was okay. Or maybe she'd tell me she was honored to be my first friend. But when I opened my eyes, no response came, of course. "I love you. You're one of my best friends. Would you believe me if I said you were the first friend I ever made? And now you're gone. You should be here, Lennox. But I hope wherever you are is better than here because you deserve nothing less."

I stepped down from her, going to stand between Locke and Lenore, allowing the next person in line to pay their respects. But what filled my heart was just how long that line was. The entire town of Port Azure showed up to pay their respects to a knight that had fought valiantly for them. Had been a Lady of the Rebel Court. Many brought flowers. Now dozens of arrangements lay around her, sweetly going with her to meet the Goddess. Many more brought letters. It seemed like hundreds of letters appeared, many wanting to gift Lennox their last words to her.

Locke stepped up to address all of us as one when the final person had given their solemn respects.

"My mother once said to me that there any many types of beauty," he began, taking me by surprise. But I supposed for him, he was saying goodbye to his mother and father as well. "Sunsets. Mountain ranges. Flower gardens. A clear night sky, filled with stars. But I think we can all agree there are some things paramount in their beauty. Lennox was a shining example of that. Not for just her outer beauty. It was who she was that made her beautiful. I have the gift of seeing others' emotions, and Lennox was one of the few fae I've been privileged to know that didn't harbor a negative thought about anyone without grave cause. She was kind. Brave. Her fierceness knew no bounds. Her loyalty. Her capacity to love was unparalleled, something we could all learn from. These qualities are all what made her so beautiful, from the inside out. Losing her... The whole of Meridian is poorer for us waking up in a world where she isn't any longer." It was only then that his voice wavered. He held his hand out to me, beckoning me to his side. "May she meet the Goddess in kindness."

"May she meet the Goddess in kindness," the crowd and I echoed solemnly. My hands fisted at my sides, yearning for the strength to keep my tears behind my eyes. But how did that honor Lennox? So I let go. I let my tears flow freely, hiccupping sobs attacking my chest as I summoned my flames.

It was time.

As soon as my flames caught on the wood near her feet, I backed away, surprised with how fast it attacked the pyre. I resumed my place between Lenore and Locke. I felt hollow as I watched the flames lick towards where Lennox lay so peacefully. So serene in death, flowers now pillowing her head like a halo. A hole had been wrenched open in my chest, like a piece of myself I'd only just discovered had been shorn away, leaving me feeling raw and breathless. But one look at Lenore showed me that no matter what I felt, it didn't hold a candle to the devastation that was on her face.

Lenore's tears were like the dragons of old—impossible. But as the flames rose to engulf her twin, I saw them streaming unchecked down her face. There were those that would see tears as a sign of weakness, but I'd never look at Lenore and think that. Instead, her tears were a dam breaking, water rushing towards you with lethal force and no chance to escape. One only had to look to see under that current of sorrow, lay a ravaged land of wrath and ferocity that wouldn't be quelled until Scorpio lay dead and bloodied at her feet.

"Lennox will not go unavenged," I offered quietly. She side-eyed me, her thoughts her own. "I'm so sorry, Lenore. I'm so fucking sorry."

I waited for the anger. The judgement. The blaming. Even if just in her eyes for now. Her face didn't change, but her hand found mine with a squeeze.

"The flames that carry her to the Goddess," she whispered tersely through her tears, "are but a fraction of the hell we will unleash upon Scorpio, Pisces, and their sycophant followers."

"Let the flames fuel you." I offered the words that wrought hope from me in my darkest, and most vengeful time. Her face fell into a glare, her eyes sharper than any blade.

"No. The flames will not consume me. I will consume them until nothing is left of Scorpio but ashes. She will burn for what she's done to us all, to you, to Locke, Aspen, me, and—" her voice dropped off suddenly, and for a moment I saw the sorrow and hatred merge into something terrifying, "Lennox."

I clung to Lenore, as she did to me. Locke and I shared a loaded look, that spoke that he felt similarly to Lenore. To me. The fires of vengeance stirred in my heart too, not for the first time, but I didn't think they'd ever burned so brightly. Looking to the pyre, Lenore, Aspen, Locke, Vanneck, and I stood with our Court of Rebels at our backs looking onward, united.

United we'd fight. United we'd mourn.

United, we'd burn.

Chapter Forty-Five

Lenore, Vanneck, Aspen, Locke, and I sat under a heavy blanket of grief together as a group. Nobody spoke. Aspen simply began pouring liquor and we began drinking, the burning of the alcohol pairing perfectly with my frayed nerves.

The door burst open, unusual given the reverence most fae paid to Locke and his privacy. Locke's brows raised in surprise as a lone fae stood at the threshold, looking stricken. I could see it there. More bad news. I emptied the remainder of my drink.

What else could be wrong?

Lenore was quick to respond by grabbing her axe, making the fae at the door swallow thickly.

"Forgive the intrusion Highness, knights, and Lady." He bowed hastily, mulling over his words as if he were afraid to speak. "I understand this is a trying time, but there's a new development you need to see."

Locke stood, easing into the mask of the Prince of the Rebel Court. "What's happened, Kassik?"

"Before I tell you, I must warn you that it's...morbid. And upsetting."

"Out with it, Kassik!" Lenore's voice was higher than usual. I turned to look at her, but she'd decided to down her drink instead with a choke.

"We... found Wren and Calan." Those were the words I'd been hoping for, but the tone...

Oh no. They said they'd gotten out. They said they'd made it...

No. They said they were on their way out. Not that they'd made it. My stomach heaved.

"What's wrong?" I asked, almost afraid to know the answer. I couldn't bear it. Not Calan and not Wren. Not them. They didn't deserve any of this. Locke's eyes flashed with anger. He and Calan, I knew, had been friends, and this too would be a big loss for him.

The Crowned Assassin just kept taking punches. How long before he shattered? Perhaps that's exactly what Scorpio was banking on.

"Do we send for Eldan?" Aspen asked, his real question underneath it, the question we were all afraid to ask: were they alive?

The grim set of Kassik's mouth answered louder than his voice ever could.

We followed him, each step resonating on the walls. Our footsteps the only sounds. I barely dared to breathe. When the inside gave way to outside, I noticed the stillness of everyone around. Even the breeze seemed to pause. All eyes were on us as we were led forward. There was horror in their gazes. They weren't just dead, I realized. Something was terribly wrong. Fae were crying. Some were puking, the sounds like a pickaxe at my brain. What the hell were we about to witness?

The guard turned around to address us as we approached a crowd close to the gate.

"I'm sorry. All of you. This will be... distressing." The anticipation and dread knitted my stomach in random knots. I didn't have butterflies. I had wasps cramping and stinging within me.

The guard announced our arrival, and the crowd parted for us. Bitterness and copper scented the air, affirming my suspicions, but nothing would ever prepare me for what we saw. My feet stayed rooted to the spot and a scream was trapped in my throat. Not another loss. No. Please. Not them.

But my prayers would come too late. Calan and Wren's dismembered heads stared blankly at me from their places on the ground, a burlap sack soaked with their blood on the ground only a small distance away. The bloody, frayed edges of the skin still leaked.

This was done recently—the realization kicked me in the stomach, and the wasps buzzed. While we mourned Lennox, Wren and Calan suffered. Wren's tongue hung out of his mouth in the most grotesque fashion. Calan's eyes were wide open in death, a frozen scream immortalized on his face. I lost the contents of my stomach then.

"Calan!" Lenore wailed as she dropped to her knees. She choked on a sob before crying his name once more, before dissolving into a puddle of despair. "*Calan!*"

"Calan," I murmured numbly. It was like someone else was feeling this loss. I watched on with a strange sense of detachment, not unlike how when my magic was sealed off. But this time when the dam broke, it might break me with it. "Wren..."

Neither of them deserved this. Hatred unlike anything I'd ever known boiled and bubbled in the very core of my being. This was nothing more than retaliation. Nothing more than a warning. They died for Scorpio's and Pisces's egos, and I would never let that lie. All I could think about was Calan telling Locke to say hello to his mother for him. Of Wren awkwardly bumbling into every room and blushing anytime anyone called him Wow. The only time he'd ever called himself the Wow Factor. I joined Lenore in her heartbreaking sobs.

"There was a message..." I heard someone say to Locke, whose stiff posture and fists balled tightly at his side gave him away. He was furious. He was grief-stricken. Calan was his friend. And Wren had become a welcome presence as well among us. I was horrified on a new level when someone said the message was written on a piece of parchment and shoved into Wren's gaping mouth.

"What was the message?" Locke was visibly pale and shaken, and when he responded, his graveled voice sounded far away. I didn't know if my mind were the one that had travelled or if his had. Perhaps both. Aspen and Lenore looked angry. Vanneck looked murderous and sorrowful, which in my experience, was the most lethal combination. He and Calan had been close. I staggered over to him and threaded my fingers through his, giving a bracing squeeze.

I'm sorry, I wanted to say. But now wasn't the time. He looked down at me, his mouth pressed to a grim line, and nodded his thanks.

Aspen and Lenore joined us, and I held Lenore's hand as well while Aspen stood towering behind me as Locke awaited the message.

"Port Azure will fall. You have two days to give up the Queen's Mark."

My very blood chilled. My breath stopped. The Queen herself had deduced where we were. Had killed two of the best fighters in Port Azure. And then sent them to us as a warning. She obviously didn't take us very seriously. She wasn't threatened by us. She was *toying* with us.

Wrath fueled me. Locke looked up and made eye contact. In his azure eyes, I saw the spirit of war reflected back at me. Fires of rage and hell danced in his eyes. I felt that rage bolster me, and I started to wonder if there were anything left to hold to. I looked around to see the fear around me in bounds. Scorpio's plan was working. Sowing fear and sorrow and despair.

I strode aside Locke. Using my Earth Magic, I raised myself up so all of Port Azure could see me as I addressed them. Locke looked at me from his place next to me, surprise and confusion written on his perfect face.

"No more," I started. My voice carried to every fae present. Every eye was on me, not one of them dry. "No more. No more death. No more sitting like ducks, waiting. Scorpio will not win. She will not get away with this." My voice was far smoother than it should've been. "We will not run scared. We will not back down. Not from this. We decide our fate, and we decide it together. Will we shatter before adversity? Or will we meet it head on in the fight of the century? Join me, Port Azure, my kinsmen, in avenging our fallen. Join me, kinsmen, in ridding Meridian of the scourge that is Scorpio. Join me, kinsmen," my voice raised to that of a cry, *"in war!"*

A resounding cry from everyone, fists filled the space as shouts filled the air. Locke's fist rested over his heart as he bowed his head to me, causing everyone else to follow suit.

"Queen Lark..." I heard, making my stomach flutter.

"...Queen of the Rebels..." No...

"Lark, Queen of the Court of Rebels..."

I knew. I knew in that moment I had been fighting my destiny. I was their Queen, at least in their eyes. A symbol of hope. Just as Locke was their King. Prince of the rebels no longer. Something shifted. Everything shifted. We entwined our hands. Together. We would do this together. Our clasped hands raised above our heads, our swords drawn in our opposing sides. Another cheer erupted from everyone around us.

"To war!" Locke cried, lifting his sword in the air. The crowd began chanting his words back at us, shouts and cheers deafening. A chill went down my spine. This was really happening. Come tomorrow, this would all be over. One way or another.

I looked around at my remaining friends. My chosen family. Who else of these fae that I loved so much would be gone before the end?

I knew the worst was yet to come.

Orders had come and gone. We had fae delivering messages to the Air Court to be ready to march in the morning. The forges had scarcely stopped since the battle in Port Azure, but now it ran full throttle, round the clock to ensure everyone was properly armed, their armor solid and defensible. Locke had called in favors from Goddess only knows where, and we stationed every single fae that wasn't fighting in the now very warded basement of the Citadel. In the event we perished and Scorpio came for them, even if she knocked the building down, she would still not have access to these fae.

Locke showed a group of fae that would be staying here how to access the tunnels at the very bottom of the Citadel. Like a basement I had no idea even existed. Old. Unused. A plume of dust rose up, making my cough.

"This tunnel leads to the edge of the Dead Forest. It'll put them on the road to Bleak. If Scorpio comes here, she may raze Port Azure to the ground, but its fae will be safe enough."

Looking out over the fae in question, their tear-streaked faces and red rimmed eyes, I saw the fear there, but I saw that same iron will to survive looking back at me too.

I had to believe that they'd survive tomorrow if we didn't.

Tomorrow felt like it was careening towards us and would be here far too soon. Our group sat one final time on the steps of the Citadel, overlooking the busy square. We had done everything we could do. Now that light was leaching its last for the day, it was time for us to prepare in our minds. But how does one get ready for such a thing as war? How does one ready for a death you know you can't possibly escape? Everyone's safety hinges on it? Was I allowed to be afraid? Would it hurt? Fear skulked around in the corner of my mind, waiting for me to be alone. Knowing full well that in my present company I was bolstered, but alone, alone I might crumble a bit.

I sat on the first step of the veranda, enjoying the warmth of the fire I'd started behind us. Locke sat to my right, his hand in mine. Lenore to my left, her head on my shoulder. Aspen sat, back resting against her knees on the step below her, and Vanneck at my own feet rested quietly. Nobody said a word. Nobody moved, just basking in being together. We knew. We all knew that this was the calm before the storm.

And the very real possibility any of us refused to acknowledge fully was this could be the last time any, or all, of us were together.

I looked at Aspen with a rue smile. I remember him bringing me here for the first time not so very long ago. How angry I was. How hateful. And now we were about to embark to Loc Valen to take down the most violent Queen our realm had ever seen. I looked at him now, a ghost of a smile on his lips. My own face lifted slightly. Words could never express how grateful I was for these fae in my life. I'd never lived before. Not before them. Not before Locke. I felt caught under the water's surface as I gazed at my friends and then over the sea of faces before us. It felt like my lungs were screaming for air, but I was caught in the tide. I was kicking my feet but didn't know which way was up. I didn't know who—if anyone—would make it through this.

"I love you all." I choked on the words. I squeezed Lenore and Locke's hands. "Thank you all for something I'd never had before. A family. I'd never had someone besides my father, and maybe Eldan. Now I look around and I see happiness. And beauty. Fun. Love. I see a life that I finally get to live with you all at my side, and I by yours." With a loaded look at Aspen and a secret smile, "I'm grateful you stopped me from leaving that night. Thank you for everything. For showing me how it can be okay. If I die, I can die knowing what all kinds of love feel like."

"Lark…" Lenore's words failed her, as they often did when emotions ran high. I smiled through the tears forming in my eyes and laid my cheek on her head where it remained on my shoulder.

"I'm so proud," Aspen started, "of everything you've become. I'm proud to be your friend. I'm even prouder for you to be my Queen. And yes Locke, you my King." He said at Locke's expression. "If this is all the time we have together, then so be it. The world beyond the veil is going to be an awful lot of fun when we get over there, whenever that may be."

Locke's stare levelled at us all. I felt the weight of it in particular.

"No. Nobody else dies. I will lose no one else," he said with gritty vehemence. "We have seen enough death. This ends tomorrow."

"For Lennox," Lenore whispered, fiddling with her dagger. I touched the point of my knife to hers. Her eyes followed my movement and lifted to my face with a grim smile.

"For my father," I answered. "For Poplar Hollow."

Locke's knife touched next. "For my family. For all those I couldn't save. And for Lark," he vowed, warming me straight through to my soul. I gave his hand a gentle squeeze, which he returned.

"For my sister. For everyone here," Aspen said, his voice rising an octave, his weapon joining ours.

Vanneck was the last to speak. "For Calan. For Wren. For the Water Court," he said bringing a lump to my throat, turning to add his own weapon. "For us all."

Chapter Forty-Six

Locke and I tried to settle into bed. Tried to get a solid night's rest before the coming day ahead. We'd dined on good food to fill our bellies, had a little wine for the nerves. There was also the creeping awareness of the curse, now filling my body with dread and desiccation. I knew my death wouldn't be long now—even if we weren't marching tomorrow, the curse would claim my life soon. The ticking clock inside me felt like mockery. I wondered if it was sentient. If it was aware. It felt like it in quiet moments like this. Locke lay unsettled next to me, his arms around me, holding me close. Our final night. This was it. All the time we'd ever have. It wasn't enough. It would never be enough. Even if we had forever, it would never be long enough.

"No matter what happens, you're worth all of it." Locke's soft voice reached me, gentle as the nighttime breeze.

"You can't sleep either?" I asked. He pulled me closer. In the limited lighting, I saw a frown etch his mouth. He pressed his lips to my forehead in lieu of a verbal response. I cupped his cheek, begging him to hear me. "We can't let her have tonight. She gets us tomorrow. For now, we have one another. That's all I've ever wanted in my life. You. My soulmate."

"Your place is here," Locke whispered. His head dipped low, eyes beseeching mine from under his brow and holding my gaze steady. "Beside me. Not..." His voice faltered. "Gone."

I cleared my throat, but nothing stopped the breath from catching in it, my lungs suddenly unwilling to cooperate.

"You should know that tomorrow I'm going to do everything within my power to come back to you. Even if I destroy the very veil itself, I'll make sure we're together again," I said. Not for the first time, I wondered if that were possible. To create a rift in the veil of death. But a sobering thought came almost right along with it—if it were possible, someone surely would have done it by now. I wondered if I would have my magic. If all my magic would be enough to do what no other to my knowledge had ever done. Because if the price of being with Locke again was my magic...

I'd give it up in a heartbeat.

"I'm sorry," Locke said, his jaw grinding. "This should never be happening. You shouldn't have to die."

"I'm sorry too. You shouldn't have to watch me die." I watched as my words landed. I watched the recoil of his body. The angry hurt flash in his eyes. Cold. Not hot, like his anger usually was.

"You have nothing to be sorry for," He said after a beat, his voice breaking. I broke with it. I swallowed the lump forming in my throat. Strong. I had to be strong. For both of us. "But I don't know how I'm supposed to let you go. How am I supposed to sit back and watch you die? Let Scorpio murder you?" He hung his head then, taking his fingers through his hair while loosing a long, shuddering breath. "How am I supposed to do that? How am I supposed to let that happen? When everything is raging within me to protect you!"

"You have to." I wanted to drop my gaze from his. But I found my eyes glued to the raging tempest that lay bare before me. I didn't need his gift to see his emotions. He wore them so clearly for me. And it gutted me. "Because the realm depends on it. Because I'm going to die regardless. I want my death to mean something, Locke. Because no matter how hard we've looked, there is no plan A."

Swallowing another lump starting in my throat, I tried to shove down the rising spike of fear before he could notice it. But I saw his eyes unfocus when he looked at me. A sure sign I'd noticed to him reading my emotions. He opened his mouth to speak but I beat him to it. "My death can save everyone. Make everything better for everyone. I don't want to be another helpless victim of Scorpio. Not when I can do something to free not just her, but you too. Before, we could've probably found another way. Before..." I couldn't say it. We both knew what I was trying to say. Before I fell in love with him. Before his curse became mine. When my dying wasn't a sure thing. When we could've captured Scorpio and tried to break her curse without the cruel mistress that was time. But a cruel mistress she was, and she had forsaken us. We were nearly out of time. I dropped my gaze then, tears in my eyes. I couldn't see his face with what I was about to say. "Your curse says you'll never love again. But once it's broken, maybe you can. If I don't come back..."

His eyes flashed and his face contorted into something I didn't recognize. His hands came up to firmly grasp my jawline, forcing my gaze to his as his thumb delicately stroked my cheek. The gentle gesture so at odds with the raging emotion he displayed. The skin around his eyes bunched, framing his pained stare. He was just a breath away. His blue and gold eyes were hard on mine under a deeply furrowed brow. And when he spoke, it was a cross between a restrained growl and an agonized whisper.

"Stop it, Lark." His eyes bored into mine. My heart leapt to my throat, my chest too tight to contain it. "Don't you dare say goodbye to me. I'm not going to lose you. I refuse. You're going to make it back to me. You're going to make it back." He lowered his face, his forehead resting against mine. I leaned into him. My hands came up to rest against his, giving his fingers a gentle squeeze. "You're going to make it back." I wasn't sure at this point if he were telling himself or me. But the fear had crept up on the edge of my awareness and I held to him, his words bolstering me just a little.

"I will make it back." I took a steadying breath. "I promise." His eyes registered the shock of my promise. I could tell he was shocked at my words. My oath. I pressed my lips to his before he could refute the promise as the magic of it settled over us.

"Why the promise?"

"You know," I shrugged awkwardly, "I need a little more motivation." The comment wrung a wry smile from his lips.

"I'm not enough motivation?" he whispered against my lips. Just a ghost of a touch. Just enough to make me want more. Need more. I tried to close the distance, but he leaned away, an eyebrow quirked up. "That's not an answer, love."

"That's because you don't want to hear the answer," I said, though I fought to keep a strictly straight face. He nipped my lip, sending a small shock of pain through me, doing nothing to dispel the want.

"I think you might be fibbing." His hands came around my waist, pulling me against him.

"I think you're just blind to the truth."

"How's this for truth?" he asked, readjusting me and growing serious once more. "No matter what happens tomorrow. No matter what we face. You were worth it. We were. I love you from now until our end. I wish we had more time. It's a crime that we don't have more, but if this is everything we get, I firmly believe we experienced more love in our time together than most see in entire centuries of living. And I'm honored to be by your side." His hand dipped under my chin to lift my face to his. I watched the intense sentiment settle there. Resolve. That iron will I loved so much darkened his features, as if steeped in shade. "I love you, Lark. This side of the veil, and the other." His lips lowered to mine once more. I felt his emotions. Every searing kiss was a promise. A promise to fight. A promise never to give up.

And a promise to return.

I woke from a nightmare, the details of which I couldn't recall, but the fear was fresh in my mind. I bolted upright with wide eyes assessing for the threat that felt just outside my door. My neck felt the chill in the air, despite the sweat that plastered my hair to my skin. My chest tight, my breath was leaving me in sputtering and incomplete puffs. I dragged my hands through my hair and reached for Locke next to me, hoping I hadn't disturbed his slumber, but when my eyes fell to his side of the bed, I found myself alone in it. His side of the bed was neatly made. I glanced out the window, fearing the sunrise.

The sun did not greet me. A dark blanket of clouds that covered the night did instead. No suggestion of daybreak hinted on the horizon. It was far too early to be up and about, especially when all of us needed as much rest as possible. I cringed at the curse within me, my insides feeling as dark as the night beyond me. It had started to ache too.

I settled back in bed. Locke was probably just relieving himself. But as I glanced to the washing room, it was dark and silent. My heart picked up for a reason I couldn't place. I told myself I was just nervous for tomorrow, which was true. But like a puzzle piece being forced into the wrong place, it didn't fit.

The night was silent, as it should be. There was no movement, nothing out of place. But worry's knife sluiced my chest regardless, and sleep, I knew, would never come. Not until I laid my eyes on Locke.

I crept out of bed, unsure of my next steps. Was I being foolish? I slipped my armed boots on, looking ridiculous when paired with my thin nightdress, but I didn't care. I had two concealed daggers. I decided my first place to find him was his offices downstairs. Perhaps Hell's Gate working off some stress. Perhaps Locke was just unable to sleep and took a walk. It made sense, but once again, the puzzle piece stubbornly refused to fit.

I walked through the door and paused to rub my arms together. My breath was visible on the air, but that wasn't what caught my notice. It was unfathomably, deeply dark. Not nighttime dark, where you could still see your way in places. This was darkness worthy of the term, swallowing all vestiges of light before turning on you with hungry eyes. Inky shadows thickened the air, threatening to choke me as realization came to me. Black magic. And there were two possibilities I could think of, and neither were good. Either Locke was using his black magic, which was unnerving enough, or Pisces and Scorpio knew where we were. Could this be a covert attack?

Slipping my knife from my boot, I wielded it in front of me. I'd hoped that the feel of the handle in my fingers would bring comfort, but all it did was cement the idea that something was wrong and I needed to find Locke. Now.

I listened for clues, anything that could direct me. But no sound came either. I was blind and deaf in the wake of these shadows and panic began to grip me.

No. Aspen had always preached keeping a clear head. I forced it down in much the same way I'd choked down bile in trying not to purge my stomach. The panic burned as it was sent back down, leaving the acidic feeling in my chest, but I began to think.

If shadow magic were employed, it would be very close by for them to be this enveloping. I glanced down the hallway that would lead me to the atrium. Was it me or were the shadows a bit... lighter? Turning my head the other way, towards the other bedrooms, I couldn't even make out large details. I couldn't see the painting that hung on the wall towards Locke's previous rooms. As I took my first few steps in that direction, the darkness seemed to hiss at me, blaring their unwelcome.

I gripped my knife, sure I was going in the right direction. I walked slowly, silently. I drew upon what Locke had done in the past, stepping lightly and landing toe first. Toe, step. Toe, step.

I'd only seen Locke use his shadows a limited number of times. I knew he tried to avoid them unless necessary. This looked like he'd all but bled the shadows with how swathed everything was. My unoccupied hand felt down the wall, going over the walls, the artwork, everything that told me where I was, until I now stood outside Locke's door. Even though I was in front of it, I couldn't see it. Even as my hand rested on the knob, I couldn't see it.

It was the voices that stopped me in my tracks—the first thing I'd heard this entire time. A voice like gravel against bone—unnatural and enough for the hair on the back of my neck to stand up.

"You have some nerve summoning me to your realm, Crowned Assassin. To what do I owe the displeasure?"

"Kill the curse," came Locke's voice, calm and deadly. "I don't care what curse you bestow upon me in return, but leave my soulmate alone."

A barking laugh boomed across the room then.

"Such desperation," the voice purred, sounding neither approving nor disapproving. "You didn't mind your curse so much when we last met. What exactly do you have to bargain with?" There was such glee in this voice now as it spoke. Such malicious amusement. And just like that, I knew what was happening. The shadows, the secrecy, the voice. Locke was bartering with the Grievling to un-curse me, at the detriment of his own curse. The exact same thing Scorpio had done for her brother.

And look how that turned out.

"What do you want?" I heard Locke ask.

My hand fisted around the doorknob and I threw the door open. Or I tried to. The door stubbornly refused to budge. I shouldered the door, but even more disturbing than the fact it still didn't budge, was the sound that had been swallowed up.

"Let's see what your little curse has to say about all of this," came the scratchy voice.

"Leave her the fuck alone," Locke snarled. "You deal with me. You bargain with me. Leave her alone."

The door swung open then, revealing me to Locke, whose eyes widened in a fix of fear and fury. Before I could blink, he was standing in front of me, keeping himself between me and the present danger and it was then I saw the Grievling for the first time.

When Locke first told me of its smile, far too wide and full of teeth to be real, he wasn't exaggerating. Its fang-filled grin ate up most of its face and spanned almost ear to ear. He was impossibly tall, closing in on the full height of the ceiling above him, his skin black and wraith like, like shadows come to life. Glowing, all-seeing red eyes were particularly panic inducing.

"Hello, little Curse," it purred, wringing its hands together, revealing elongated claws. "I've been wondering when you'd join us. I was wondering if I would have to," its gaze slid to Locke, "go looking for you."

"Lark," Locke's strained whisper reached me beseechingly. "Run. Please. Just run."

"Not without you," I whispered back, unable to look at anything but the monstrous shadowy creature that assured me that there was reason to fear the dark. "This side of the veil, and the other, remember?"

The Grievling appraised me the way one might appraise a prized sow. His movement reminded me of a blood wraith, crackling like kindling with every movement.

"I see your dreams, Little Curse," it whispered, gaze sliding to me over his shoulder. "I wonder what I could further give you, to curse you with. Imagine how much more powerful you'd be if you had my magic in your soul. Right now, you're just cursed with none of the benefits. Think of the victory the King of the Echo Isles could help you ensure tomorrow." The Grievling had the most unnatural purr in its voice—his large mouth of dagger-like incisors shouldn't have been able to make a sound like that, but alas it did. It was unnerving, leaving every muscle in my body standing rigid, ready to attack at the slightest provocation. His eyes raked me, reminding me of Locke's face every time he read my aura—like he wasn't seeing my body, but my essence. My very soul to the core of who I was. I'd never felt more exposed. "You would be unstoppable. You both would. The two of you could rule on high, taking out the Zodiac Guild, ruling over all of Meridian."

"You say you see my dreams." I met his disturbing stare, watching as it smiled every wider with glee. "Where in my dreams do you see me wanting to rule? Or Locke for that matter?"

"What happens if you don't? The fae either recruit the most powerful, or they kill them. Just ask your precious Prince Cancer about the rune trials. He emerged the strongest, but how many fae did he have to kill before emerging the victor?"

Locke's eyes narrowed in response, giving me the feeling the Grievling just shed some light on some of the ghosts that haunted Locke. The Grievling took at step towards us, a clawed hand outstretched. Locke growled, bringing his sword up between us, swathed in a frothing, frosted blue light. A silent demand to back off, that even the king of the shadow realm heeded, though his red eyes sparked with macabre delight. "The guild will annihilate you once Scorpio is gone. You're the weapon they need, but not forever. Don't you want the chance to be with your soulmate? You haven't had any time." He didn't sound sympathetic. He sounded manic. Fake empathy oozing from him, mocking us both, I couldn't answer him. I couldn't speak, couldn't breathe, beyond the idea of all of this being for nothing if the Guild turned on us. The Grievling took another step towards us.

This time. Locke didn't hesitate. His sword swept out in a flash quicker than lightning. There was a monstrous scream as the metal met with the Grievling's charcoal-like flesh, and the shadow king stepped back with a glare.

"Stay away from her. And get out of her head." Locke glared him down with malice. I'd seen fae turn and run after being on the receiving end of that look, but the Grieving just cocked his head. Locke's voice punctured the thick silence. "Release her from the curse, or I rip you apart by the seams. That's how we undo the curse, right? Kill the one who cursed us?"

The king of the Echo Isles only threw his head back and laughed. "I am the blackness and shadow eternal. You cannot kill me. Just as light can drive the darkness away temporarily, darkness always swallows it whole once again."

Locke smiled then, a dangerous, razor-sharp smile that left me scared. Not of him. For him.

"No, but you feast on the dreams of those in your kingdom. Those who have succumbed to your curses. That's what keeps you alive, is it not?" Locke's head tipped down, staring through his brow. "What happens when I rip apart your entire realm? When I dismantle it piece by fucking piece until you wish you'd never heard my name. Or Lark's."

Finally, the eerie smile on the Grievling faltered, but remained in place.

"You would destroy an entire realm for her?" the Grievling shrieked.

Locke's answering laugh was bereft of amusement. "Joyfully, without remorse or restraint," he answered without hesitation. His voice was so much more level than it should have been, given the gravity of what he was saying. "For her, I have no limitations. I would burn the entirety of the Echo Isles if it meant she lived."

"Locke..." I didn't even know what to say. Dread filled me at the thought of Locke destroying an entire realm of fae for me. I opened my mouth to speak, but no sound came. I had no idea what to say. What to even think.

"You cannot destroy the Echo Isles, as much as I admire your dedication. You cannot destroy a gateway realm to Hell." The Grievling laughed. Cold washed through my veins. Gateway realm to Hell?

"Then why is there fear in your aura? And your eyes?" Locke laughed, brandishing his sword, the only source of light in the room, washing everything in its blue glow. The shadow king's eyes darkened and his smile failed altogether now, but it laughed darkly.

"You cannot slay what you cannot reach. I reject your offer of a bargain and take my leave of you both. I look forward to your conjoined suffering before you ultimately rot in the realm you threatened to destroy. I assure you, I will be arranging special accommodations for you, Crowned Assassin." The Greivling's unholy, unnatural cackle filled the room and he began to turn transparent, like the wraith he so resembled.

Locke lunged at him, his sword deftly puncturing his shoulder in a final attack. The Grievling screamed, though no apparent wound was visible.

"I'll find you," Locke spat.

"You will not," the Grievling said. "I'll find you when death claims you at last. Until then, the door to my realm will be quite closed to you. Enjoy your suffering, Crowned Assassin. I know I will."

Locke swung his sword again, sluicing through the abdomen of the beast, but dealing no damage this time. With a final, withering look as us, he vanished, bringing all the shadows with him.

As if neither were ever there at all.

My hand swung out to turn Locke to me the moment the room returned to normal, though the word *normal* felt like a stretch. My heart still galloped in my chest, my ribs constricting my lungs. Had he really just tried to do what Scorpio did and exchange curses? Had he really threatened an entire realm for me?

"Locke..." Panic ebbed and flowed in waves, mixing with relief and returning as rage. I fisted his shirt, "What the fuck was your plan? You could've died!"

Locke's snarl of fury took me by surprise, his eyes boring into mine.

"Plan A!" he yelled. He stilled, eyes wide as if catching himself. The guilt, the disappointment, the vengeance, the emptiness mixed on his face, but what was noticeably absent was remorse. "I'm sorry, Lark. I'm one of the strongest fae in Meridian. But even I'm not strong enough to handle losing my family, losing Lennox, Calan, and Wren, and losing you in a matter of days. I found a shot and I took it. For you. I would happily take it if it meant sparing you all of this." Locke's eyes shone in the limited light with a quiet intensity under a furrowed brow, and a calm certainty I recognized all too well. He cupped my cheek so as to look deeply into me. "I'm not scared of dying with you." His voice low and gravelly, but never once wavered. "I'm scared of living without you. So I'll fight as close to that knife's edge as I have to because if I fall, I know you'll be there waiting for me. When you go to meet the Goddess, you'll have enough time to say hi you your loved ones while I avenge you, drag Scorpio and Pisces to the fringes of Hell itself, and I will happily meet the Goddess next to you. This side of the veil or the other." His voice dropped to a whisper. "I love you."

"Don't die for me, Locke. Live for me. If the curse is broken, it's more than possible you'll find happiness again. You have so much to do. You survived a broken heart once before. Do it again. Please. For me." Locke gave me a forlorn look. His chest expanded as he took a deep, contemplative breath.

"I'd see you in every sunset." His voice was heartachingly soft as he spoke. The voice of someone who'd been walking a knife's edge and had just realized their exhaustion. As full of despair as he was, there was also a grim acceptance that threatened to break me in half. "How you look when you're happy. I'd see it every time I went near the stables, let alone noticed the smell of horses. I'd see you in every swing of a sword, stab of a dagger, and every flicker of the fire." He brushed my hair out of my face while tears blurred my vision. "I'm not letting you go. I will either pry you from death, or I will join you in it. Either way, we will have the time we so rightfully deserve together. Our fates are joined and I wouldn't have it any other way."

"Kiss me." My whispered plea came before I ever made the decision to speak. "Kiss me enough so that we both forget. Kiss me so it's just you and me and nothing else."

His lips collided with mine so fast my final plea was cut off. His body pressed against me, his strong, corded arms melding me to him, inviting us both. My arms reached up to caress his cheek, his hair, anything I could grab in a desperate attempt to scorch his image perfectly into my mind. My very soul. Because maybe when that time came, when my death came, I could hold to it and I wouldn't feel afraid. He kissed me so that all I could think about was him. His hands roaming my skin, his lips tasting mine, nipping mine, walking that balance between sweet bliss and sharp pain. He barreled into each of my senses so there was no room for anything else. Only him.

And there would only ever be him.

Chapter Forty-Seven

S leep evaded us like the thief in the night.

The roof Locke had pitched us on was precariously steep and I found myself white knuckling the edge, just in case I slipped. In case the slats of the roof fell from under my weight. Locke's arm tightened around me as we sat facing the dimly moonlit water, listening to the sounds of our own racing heartbeats, our breath, and the waves. My own fire crawling over my skin drove away the worst of the cold.

"Is the night darker than usual?" I asked, tipping my head back to assess the steep, black sky. The moon didn't seem as bright, and the stars barely glittered overhead. I somehow felt simultaneously cradled and claustrophobic with how the night crept in around us.

"Dark is simply a matter of perception," came Locke's soft reply. "Going from light to darkness always makes the shadows seem steeper. And the same with the reverse, the light is brighter when we emerge from the darkness. You taught me that."

"You speak in riddles, Crowned Assassin."

"Do I?" He glanced sidelong at me, the corners of his lips teasing upwards. "It only seems darker because we can't see the light yet. But we will. And it'll be all the brighter when we do. When we make it out the other side tomorrow."

"When we win," I finished.

"Yes. Though admittedly, even if this night is long and dark, I'd be okay if it never ended and tomorrow never came."

"I wish we could pause too." As I rested my head on his shoulder, breathing him in, all I could think about was how much I would hate the breaking of the day ahead. How I didn't feel as ready as I thought I'd feel. And how this might be our last moment of peace.

Locke left to get our rebels ready to march. We would jumpstone as many of us as possible to our destination, a predetermined spot about an hour's trek from Loc Valen. Scouts wouldn't be that far out, leaving us concealed and close by to march on the city as one army.

I donned my dragon scale armor, putting more weapons on me than I ever had before, balking at the added weight. It shouldn't have made a difference, but my body wasn't used to having this much strapped to it. The two blades in my boots, two strapped to my thighs, one on either side of my ribs, and the sword at my back. I hoped I looked more formidable than I felt.

The square of Port Azure was almost impassable with the number of bodies. Fae flitting to and fro, saying emotional goodbyes and see you laters. The blacksmith's forge was as busy as ever, black smoke rising from it as it armed our masses. But I managed to make it through to the beach. To Hero Hill just behind Port Azure. A familiar hill covered in crosses and grave markers.

It had three more than the last time I was here.

I sat next to Lennox's gravesite, the morning damp and chill still clinging to the air. The sunrise was well underway now, much of the sky now blue, but my eyes were drawn to the remaining pink and orange of the daybreak. I placed my hand on Lennox's flower covered cross overlooking the sound.

"I never thought this day would come and you wouldn't be here. I miss you," I whispered. She should have been here. She deserved to be here. "I'll make it hurt. Just like I promised." After today, she'd either be avenged or I'd meet her beyond the veil too. The line up of fae to meet on the other side was quickly getting too long as I glanced with a heavy heart to Calan and Wren's crosses. "You both too," I told them. I had no idea if any of them could hear me. "Calan. Wow. You should both be marching with us today. I'm so sorry."

I didn't know what I expected. The wind to pick up, or maybe the flowers to rustle. But none of those things happened. Lennox was gone. Calan and Wren were gone. I turned and walked away from the Hill of Heroes and back to Port Azure with the sun's light at my back.

Eldan found me sitting on the steps of the Citadel and sat next to me, his knees crackling with age as he lowered himself being the only sounds. In his hand was a large cup of steaming liquid. I glanced up at him as he handed it to me.

"Child..." His throat was thicker than I ever heard before. I placed my hand on his after taking the cup from him. "You were the closest thing I ever had to a daughter. Ever since your father... I never wanted you to be without him. So I resolved to watching you flourish for him. I know that he can see you from wherever he is. And I know he's proud. As am I. I know better than most what you went through, and to see you finally have a chance to live..." He cut himself off, knowing I was marching to my death. "I've been tasked with making sure every fae here goes into the tunnels in the event..." In the event we weren't successful.

"I would trust few others with this, Eldan," I told him earnestly.

"This mug is an energy elixir. I know you didn't get much sleep last night. This will replace your energy in full. These," he pulled out a handful of pills and held them out, "Are regeneration pills. They regenerate your magic faster so you don't run out. I gave one to Locke already, and to Lenore. I've given as many away as I can. But I need to make sure you're going to be okay."

"I don't think you've ever spoken this much to me, Eldan," I said softly. "Thank you. For everything. I wouldn't have made it if not for you. You've saved my life more than anyone else. You're as much family to me as any of the knights here. If I don't make it back—"

His hand tightening on my knee interrupted me.

"No. You're not going to do that to an old fae like me. You will make it back. And when you do, I believe we have a marriage ceremony to complete, yes?" he asked, pointedly looking at the ring I'd attached to a necklace. It hurt wielding a sword with the ring on, but I'd be damned before leaving it behind. "I will see you when you return here, in one piece. You have survived so much, I believe it was the Goddess's way of preparing you for this. You are strong enough. So don't say *if*. *When*. When you return."

When I return.

But would I be on Hero Hill when I returned?

Chapter Forty-Eight

It was arduous. Locke and I spent careful time prepping for this. Locke had called in a few other favors—how he had so many others who owed him was uncanny, but I guessed that was the advantage of being immortal royalty—and obtained several more jumpstones. Enough for Locke, Aspen, Lenore, Vanneck, and myself to have one. Each of us would jumpstone as many fae as we could to the meeting point, charge the stone, and do it again. Eldan had supplied magic regeneration elixirs to ensure we'd be strong enough to fight. It took most of the remainder of the morning, the sun high in the sky by the time we'd finished. But I looked out at the force we had conjured and could only stare.

Others had come from surrounding areas. At my surprise, Locke raised a brow. "Did you think our only numbers were in Port Azure? We have numbers in most towns. We called for aid and whole towns have responded. Even those who hadn't heard of us previously but resent Scorpio's conscription order have turned up."

Our numbers had to rival Scorpio's. This wasn't just the Water Court versus a few rebels. This was two armies coming to clash. This was the Water Court fighting back. And the Air Court hadn't yet arrived with their numbers yet.

Did we actually stand a chance? Hope was such a dangerous crop to sow, I worried that nurturing it would be the death of far too many.

Smoke, fear, and resolve scented the air. I welcomed it; the sounds of sharpening steel, anxious chatter, and flapping leather could be heard everywhere, even the occasion *bing* of someone testing their armor or shield. Fae, like Vanneck and Lenore, and I, handed out additional weapons, providing support or encouragement where we could.

For so long now, this felt like a fantasy. A notion. A far-off concept. But here it was staring me in the face. For many of us, death waited patiently at the end of this road. I felt it grinning sickly at me, beckoning to me. I glowered into death and for the first time,

I was ready. Locke had asked me this morning and I wasn't. But looking around here, seeing the courage of everyone here, how could I not be?

I did my best to sear everyone's face into my mind, memorizing details as I went. Like how a fae in Aspen's charge—Brannon I think his name was--was avenging his father's life for the attack on Port Azure. He was my age, angry, and well-armed. I'd seen him train with Aspen before. His armor was mismatched, brown and black leather mixing. He grinned and told me some was his father's, and how he was proud to wear his armor. Like he was taking him into battle with him. I touched my own sword, knowing the feeling. Kirath showed off his new sword to his friends behind him. Kassik reclined against a tree, taking his whetstone to his blade until I didn't know which was sharper, his sword or his glare.

A boom sounded. I spun, my fingers finding my sword's hilt, thinking the plan was over, but instead I saw Queen Aquarius flying in on a griffin.

I had never seen such a creature up close. An eagle in the front, but feline in the back. It was astounding. A long, curving beak was menacingly sharp and I could absolutely see it picking the bones from my corpse. And despite everything, I couldn't stop myself from wanting to pet it, knowing those feathers would feel like satin under my fingers.

Aquarius looked very different than the last time I'd seen her. In Everwind, she'd been dressed in flowing dresses and finery that shimmered with every movement. She looked like gathering storm clouds and lightning strikes and all the beauty that came with it.

Today, she stood a warrior queen. Armored in glassy silver, so reflective I worried about her giving away our position despite our lack of proximity to Loc Valen. On her back, a bow but no quiver. Odd. She followed my gaze and smiled as if she knew something I didn't, which was likely the case, but turned her head to say something to her accompaniment.

Locke, who I hadn't heard creep up next to me, leaned in to speak in my ear, and nearly scared the daylights out of me. He chuckled and resumed speaking as if he hadn't nearly given me a heart attack.

"Her arrows are forged from lightning itself," he said. I gawked at him, somewhere between impressed and grateful that she would fight on our side. I had Air Magic, but never had I ever been able to spark lightning more than to conjure it. To control it was a whole other beast, as I'd come to know. Aquarius was truly a fearsome opponent. Even more impressively, lightning wasn't her main weapon. Fisted at her side was a large scythe the color of bone. It looked as if Death itself had handed her his weapon, but the glint of steel betrayed the look.

"Queen Aquarius," Locke bowed his head respectfully. "Queen suits you well. On behalf of myself and my company, welcome. You and your army."

"Spare me the flattery, Water Prince." Her tone wasn't nearly as harsh as her words. "When do we march?"

Locke smiled, genuinely. My gaze kept sliding between her and her griffin as she dismounted. The great beast gave a big shake and stretched, reminding me of all the times Haven or Valor did the same.

"As soon as we're all in formation. Within the hour in any case."

Aquarius's eyes flicked to me with amusement. "Lark, a pleasure to see you again. Now, if you want to pet the griffin, just do so already. Watching you eye it is exhausting."

"I can pet him?" I asked, unable to hide my giddy tone. Aquarius smiled. The first real smile I think I'd ever seen from her. She beckoned me over.

"This is Nimbus. And I think he'd be remiss if you didn't pet him." Its white-feathered head swung towards me, his eerily intelligent bird eyes watching me intently. That, combined with his beak, was a lot more nerve-wracking than dealing with horses. I offered my hand up slowly. I took a deep breath as Nimbus moved toward me, ready to dive backwards if I needed to. Though I seriously doubted I'd ever be fast enough. Even Locke looked tense as Nimbus sniffed me.

It made a strange rumbling sound in its chest before it nudged my hand and looked at me expectantly. I blinked. Was it... purring? Nimbus now looked annoyed as he nudged my hand again, harder this time. Smiling widely, I pressed my hand over his feathers, marveling at how delightfully soft they were. The rumbling deepened when I scratched his neck with both hands, and his eyes drifted closed.

How had I been nervous a moment ago? Nimbus was a sweetheart. If something happened to Nimbus, I'd pity the fool who hurt him.

"Of course. Lark befriends the Griffin." Locke made a sound like a chuckle and a sigh. I turned back and beamed at him.

"They're quite social creatures. They get a bad rep for the fierceness of their appearance and their ability in battle, but in reality, this is what they're like," Aquarius said, giving Nimbus a gentle pat.

"Hi, Nimbus," I crooned to him softly, loving how he leaned into my ministrations. Aquarius turned to go when Locke called to her once, turning her back around.

"Aquarius." Locke's voice wasn't a request for her attention but an insistent demand. A tone only a royal could use with another royal. "Don't forget your main role today." His glance slid towards me. "If you do nothing else today, do this for us."

"I gave you my word, Prince. Do not take me for someone like Pieces, or even Ignatius on his ruby throne in the Fire Court. My word means everything. You bargained for my help, and you shall have it. I haven't forgotten. Nor do I hope you've forgotten the favor you will owe me later."

Locke nodded, saying nothing. Her eyes sharpened.

"I will revive your beloved to the best of my ability. And the Air Court will get revenge on those who sought to take the lives of our fae, for Wren." At his name, my stomach soured and the moment of joy was eclipsed by a stab of grief. I was surprised at her mention of him, though perhaps I shouldn't be. Locke cared about each fae in his network. I thought of Calan, their easy camaraderie. Perhaps it was a similar relationship with Aquarius, which for a reason I couldn't explain made me like her all the more. Aquarius continued, "and our Zodiac Kinship. Myself included."

Chapter Forty-Nine

We marched within the hour as Locke said, all of our soldiers falling into lines of seven. Griffin riders walked alongside us to avoid early detection, much to the discomfort of many who walked alongside them. The riders seemed amused by the sideways glances they were given, but to their credit, they didn't encourage bullying tactics. Locke and I led the march, with Aspen, Lenore and Vanneck next to us.

The sound of oncoming war was a lonely, forlorn sound. If any sound could portray the calm before the storm, it was this. The rhythmic, uniformed steps ringing out, the clanging of metal, the quiet whispers between soldiers, destined for either the greatness of victory...

Or death.

I was the reason they would live or die. Win or lose. That thought sat heavy over my shoulders, weighing me down as I trudged forward, my own steps fueled by anticipation, anxiety, and quiet anger.

Locke stepped in time with me, his gaze never leaving the road ahead. We had an army prepped. We had done everything in our power to protect everyone back home. And suddenly, the certainty I'd felt earlier wavered. Locke's hand found mine, pulling me from the doom of my own mind.

"When this day is put to text, when future generations hear of this day, they will cite our courage and our bravery. We're on the right side of history. The Water Court is fighting for itself. This is the change we've been needing."

"Won't they see a selfish girl who refused to sacrifice herself?" I asked, needing to hear it one last time before I can put the final vestiges of doubt to rest. Forever. Locke shook his head, his hand offering mine a squeeze.

"They will see a girl who refused to die, yes. That's not selfish. They will see a girl who laughed at fate, and then forged her own for the good of everyone. They won't see selfish. They'll see a catalyst." There was so much pride in his voice, I thought I finally saw the situation the way he so clearly did. The burden lifted for a moment. A catalyst. I'd been a curse. I could shuck that identity, and become a catalyst. Locke's expression bored into mine now. "She will have defied death, and fate, and paved the way for Scorpio's demise. They will see a girl who ignited hope across the court. A Queen who fought and won against the threads of destiny itself. And I'm glad you're starting to believe it."

We trudged along with emotions running high, my nerves frayed from the anticipation, spiking when in the distance I spied the tallest part of Ari'inor through the trees. We're getting closer. My mind whirred with all types of scenarios, not knowing what to zero in on. We walked along the road now, not hiding our approach. I had no doubt now that they knew we were coming. Good. Maybe innocent civilians would be hiding and out of harm's way.

We could only hope.

"When we lay siege—"

Locke cut Aspen off with a sharp intake of breath as we broke through the tree line, gazing down at the land between us and the Jewel of the Water Court. Loc Valen. "Looks like there's been a change of plans."

I couldn't tell if I were surprised or not to see Scorpio's army waiting for us in the spot where Loc Valen forced the land to kneel before it. Part of me went numb looking at the sheer number of bodies clad in silver and blue armor, observing us with stoic stares. Kelpies in horse form had their own flank, adding to their numbers. Gnashing their teeth at us, eyes bright with violence. Water trolls and other assorted water monsters assembled as well.

There were hundreds, possibly in the thousands, of soldiers standing between me and Loc Valen. How did she know we'd be here? My guess was a seer, if the slaughter in Everwind were any indication, keeping Scorpio a step ahead. There went our surprise advantage. Upon approaching, I observed her troops, several of which I could see were hideously too young for battle. Her conscriptions were far too wide if she were bringing in fae who didn't even look to be my age. I seethed, wondering how someone could be so callous, so cruel, so wicked right down to their core. Movement snagged my attention as our army now filtered in off the road and formed a charging line at the crest of the hill behind me.

Red hair snagged my attention, breaking through her army towards the warzone. Bodies parted like a sea for Scorpio and Pisces, who fell into step behind her with a sinister expression and a charged gait. My nerves hummed, my adrenaline on overdrive. Who knew that the closer to death you were, the more alive you felt? They moved to stand at the front of their army staring us down intently as we approached. A parlay.

I glanced at Locke, looking for cues, eying his mouth set in a firm line of grim focus. In his eyes, I saw that iron will that always frustrated and enamored me. But I also saw something else—bloodlust.

He was every bit the nightmare Scorpio herself had forged: the Crowned Assassin, come home at long last. I saw in the furrow of his brow, the stiffness of his posture, and the white-knuckled grip he had on his sword. Today, he would exact his revenge for all the atrocities they'd dealt him, his Court, and the Rebels. Whenever I'd seen him fight, it had been to defend. Today, he was here for revenge. He was here to kill. I could feel anger roiling off him in waves. My own anger rose up to join his, especially when Pisces tossed an arrogant grin in our direction. Scorpio, on the other hand, just looked focused. Determined. And with each second, she showed exactly why her moniker was the Barbaric Queen. The destroyer of the Water Court. How much blood did she have on her hands now? And how much more by the time this was over? I quashed the thought. No more. *No more.*

Looking down the hill at the army awaiting us, the tension in my chest began to ache. Before us were fae that followed Scorpio, certainly. But I remembered all too well the day we went to Listwyne. The horror that lay there. Several of those fae now fought on our side, knowing a divide parted us. Down this hill were fae that were terrified of the Barbaric Queen.

Those that Scorpio had forced.

Those that Scorpios had threatened.

Those that Scorpio had forced their loyalty through fear and violence.

Never again.

Locke and I approached together, our steps matching synchronously. Aspen, behind us, rallied our warriors, bolstering them as he organized the front line. Aquarius's voice blended with his as she too rallied her soldiers and mounted Nimbus, who roared as he took to the air on massive feathered wings, joining the others of her air fleet.

As we approached, I saw Scorpio was wearing a crown, but not like one I'd ever seen. At first glance, I thought it entirely encrusted with rubies. As we got closer, I saw it for what it was. Sucking in a breath I realized it was blood. A crown dipped in blood.

"The war crown," Locke whispered. "Crafted from the blood and bones of her enemies." I didn't know whether to laugh or despair. It glinted in the sunlight, eerily as beautiful as it was macabre.

"If you had just taken my bargain, none of us would be here right now," Pisces taunted as we came to a stop only feet away, while making a show of inspecting his sword. Making sure I saw the glint and gleam that only came from meticulous care and sharpening. I didn't doubt that if a leaf fell over it, it would be sliced into two pieces cleanly. I'd be impressed if I didn't know that very sword would be turned on my soulmate. "How does it feel knowing that all the blood that's about to be spilled is your fault?"

The words would have landed home before, but now they washed over me, missing their mark. I glanced coldly at him. But it was Locke who beat me to the punch.

"Lark's death wouldn't have solved anything—"

Scorpio's eyes flared.

"It would have solved *everything*," she seethed, eyes flickering to me, looking far too much like the kelpies behind her. Her eyes were fully black now, no trace whatsoever of the green that used to be there. I wonder if that piece of her were truly dead and this was all that was left. I wondered if she cared at all. I used to think she must, to some degree. Even in Everwind, she said she didn't want to be alone. There was nothing but vengeance and violence in her now.

"You're wrong," Locke said. "You made your own bed, Scorpio. In trying to break the curse, you broke the realm. You broke the Water Court over and over again. These fae are the rebellion you're so rightfully afraid of, coming to make sure you can't hurt them or anyone else ever again. And Air Court," Locke glanced back with a knowing look at the Air Queen, who slashed the air before her with her halberd—a direct threat—"is here for retribution for Everwind. This will happen, and Lark's death is only a factor. You will die today. Both of you. And anyone who gets in our way."

"You can try. But you're not the only one with tricks up their sleeves." Scorpio said, far too calm for my liking. She glanced at me, poison in her gaze. "You can fight all you want, but when today is done, you will be brought to me. I'm going to have some fun. And I'll make him watch." She indicated Locke, who sneered openly at her. "Nothing you do today will save you. And you know it, don't you?" She cocked her head at me. "You feel death lurking."

My eyes narrowed on her. Does she know? Is this how the curse afflicted her? A puzzle piece I hadn't realized was missing fell into place, giving a small sense to a larger madness. It should have killed her. My eyes flashed to Locke glaring at Scorpio. But that would mean...

He knew.

The whole time I was hiding it from him.

"You'd know about death lurking, wouldn't you Scorpio?" Locke's eyes flashed. "It's your constant companion. That ends today."

"You think yourselves heroes, is that it? Pathetic." Scorpio laughed without amusement. Pisces scoffed behind her. She gestured to all those behind us waiting for our signal before bringing her gaze intently on me, speaking only to me. "You bring your friends, your so-called family, to fight your battles for you when you yourself could have faced me. You are a disgrace."

My temper flared, my lips curling back into a snarl.

"Bite your tongue!" Locke's jaw ground audibly before I could loose whatever nasty remark was about to fly from my lips. "Everyone will rejoice in your death. How does it feel to know that not one single fae here will mourn you after all you've done?"

Pisces growled, ready for a fight. Locke and Pisces were drawn and locked into a battle of their own right, staring one another down. Locke's magic held at the ready. It was then that I saw the hatred that Pisces held for Locke. The dead love that he held for Wisteria. How it festered under his skin and destroyed all that was maybe once good about him. Pisces wouldn't yield until Locke was dead.

"I hope you're ready, Little Curse," Pisces gloated, oozing smugness, his eyes dark and narrowing into slits. Shadows wound around his arms, coiling like living death to punctuate his point. "Today, your army of ragtag soldiers dies, and you will be dealt with. You've been lucky before. That luck runs out today. Go to your army, spout whatever bullshit speech you have, and send them down to their fate."

Pisces turned on his heel and left, back the way he had come. He would be fighting, of that there was little doubt. But he swaggered his way back inside the army and I had to wonder what it was that Prince Pisces had planned. Scorpio looked at me impassively.

"When I see you next, it'll be in the throne room. Where you'll bow before your Queen and your throat will be slit. Your death, as well as everyone else's on the top of that hill, awaits." With that, she turned on her heel and followed Pisces back. The throne room. That was where I had to fight to get to. I gazed at the high white stone walls, wondering when the right moment to bring them down would be.

Locke and I walked silently back to our army, feeling the weight of every eye on us with each step up the hill. It was too late to worry if our plan would work, but it didn't stop my mind from worrying nonetheless. Aquarius, as if reading my mind, offered me a sharp smile. Stopping before everyone, Locke turned to me.

"I love you. This side of the veil, or the other," he said in that voice that made my stomach flutter. "No matter what happens, you were worth everything. It's been an honor."

"This side of the veil, or the other," I echoed. "The honor is mine, Crowned Assassin. Be their fucking nightmare."

The shrill call of the wind sounded in the chasm like hill below us, with the army below awaiting us. The very air vibrated between both forces, charged and ready to explode.

Walking a few steps along the line, making eye contact with each fae: fear. They were all trained by Aspen, so I knew them all to be competent fighters. But there it was anyway. Fear. Doubt. Indecision.

"Kinsmen!" My voice rang out before I'd made the decision to speak, drawing all eyes to me as I paced the front line. I drew my sword from my back as I addressed the fae before me. "Today we make history. Today we become legends. You chose the Court of Rebels because the Barbaric Queen Scorpio destroyed your homes. Your families. Conscripted or killed your friends. She ripped you away from everyone you love. Today, she pays for those injustices. Today, she learns that she cannot take without consequence. Brothers and sisters, *we are* the consequence!" I raised my sword above my head, Locke's joining mine, followed by Aspen's. Lenore's axe too. "Rise and rage!" My scream disappeared into a chasm of voices, all cheering together as one.

"Rise and rage! Rise and rage!" they chanted back. Swords banged against shields in time with the rising war cry, those with spears hitting them loudly against the ground. They were ready. The cry became thunderous as it carried down the hill.

"Today we fight!" Locke bellowed, turning towards the waiting army below the hill. "Today we avenge. And today we are consequence. Today, we taste victory, and come out united as the Water Court once more!" A war horn sounded in the distance.

We would not fail.

He glanced over at me, that steely will proud on his features. In this moment, I refused the death that I knew was close. I couldn't—I would not die. Not while Locke fought next to me. Not while hope burned so brightly within me. I let that hope fuel me. That hope took a seat on a throne of wrath and ruination as a battle cry erupted from me.

And then we ran.

Locke joined my cry as we ran towards the army in silver. I tried not to notice the fear in their eyes, or how their own weapons were merciless. Many fell in the charge, the Water Court making the hill slick with ice. But the two armies met like two rival rivers, surging in power, and only one would be victorious and absorb the other.

Some went down right away, stabbed in the chest when the ice knocked them off their feet. For others it was slower, multiple thrusts from a sword before they fell silent. I blasted their front line with Air Magic as widely as I could, giving as many fae on our side the same advantage by knocking our adversaries off balance in turn. I tried not to notice how easily my sword dispatched them. Or the fear in their eyes as I did so. Several of these fae were dressed in armor but had no discernible combat training. And it showed. Scorpio's final smirk as she left made sense now. If we were going to fight, we were going to have to kill fae forced into battle against their will, as well as the full might of the Crownguard. That realization was a punch to the gut. Kill or be killed.

A blur of movement.

The hammer hit the chest of the fae in front of me. They didn't even scream. Instead, a short wheeze was all he managed before his chest caved in, his ribs no doubt shattered and splintered within. He dropped to the ground, dead. Mercifully quick, however brutal.

I reacted purely on the instinct my father and Aspen had instilled in me, and with my magic as Locke had taught me. My time in Port Azure meant I didn't even notice the first two that fell to me. My sword dispatched them quickly, only the spurt of blood alerting me to what I'd done. I didn't have time to think; there was only room to act. My blade clashed against metal, over and over, until that sound was all I heard. I focused on it, rather than the screams of the wounded as I carved my way into the mass of fae who wanted to see me dead. I had but one advantage; they themselves couldn't kill me. Injured was fine, so long as I was alive.

I had no such order.

Two more fae circled me in the limited room. I had almost no room to dodge. These two wore the vicious sneers of the Crownguard, their gore-smattered blades sharpened to perfection. One of them was massive. I didn't even know how to fight someone that big. He was easily the size of two or three regular sized fae. They both lumbered towards me with sickening grins under blood-smeared faces.

The huge one circled me as the other launched himself at me. I forced my magic out in the form of wind, knocking them both and everyone in the immediate area to the ground. Shouts of pain—many that were cut off—sounded around me. Giving the smaller of the two no time, I leapt, following him to the ground while everyone else got to their feet. He tried to defend himself, but with a another burst of air from me, I sent his sword flying. Now defenseless, he tried to reach out with magic, but it was too late. My dagger slit his throat before he even had a chance.

I turned to find the other one, the larger of the two, rising to his feet and grasping the handle of a new weapon on the ground. How resourceful. Anger seethed in his eyes as he grinned. He swung his new weapon—a giant hammer—to my face. I ducked just in time, not relishing the whooshing of the hammer as it just missed my face. He righted himself, recovered, and swung again in a downward arc this time. I shifted to the side, avoiding it. I knew I couldn't parry him; his hammer would destroy me in an instant. But it was taking him precious seconds to recover between blows. Seconds that might drag out longer as I wore him out. Fae fought around us but left us clearance. There was no leaving this fight until I was captured or he was dead. And if he fell, I spied several other Crownguards nearby with half an eye on me as they fought.

I kept my feet moving, narrowly dodging each attack. There were far too many swings of another hammer that I only just got away from. If I stopped moving, even for a second, I was dead. Or as good as. I couldn't keep this up for long. Sweat dampened both our brows and our breaths came heavy— his more so. It took him longer and longer to recover. An idea formed in my mind and I smiled, despite panting.

I knew what to do.

His next swing came in a slow arc from my left. I ducked, and before the movement had even finished with the follow through, I struck. I rushed him, using what remained of my speed as my asset. His eyes widened. I gripped my dagger in my other hand, and in the same movement, I plunged the knife into his neck, above his chest plate, fighting bile when I felt the tip of the blade strike bone.

The gurgle that was earned from him was the most disgusting sound, making me gag. But at last, his knees crumpled and he fell, reminding me very much of the clock tower in Port Azure—slow and tumbling and shaking the blood slicked-earth below.

Finally, I had a moment or two to appraise our situation before the bubble around me imploded. We were making good progress, slow and steady, our army carving away at enemy forces. Locke fought not far from me, the shadows, water Magic, and steel sluicing through all that approached him. Lightning from above me fried the enemy and the kelpies with ease. Griffons were just large enough to help with the fight, swooping down to grasp unsuspecting soldiers in their talons before swiftly climbing to high altitudes and dropping them to their demise.

I found Lenore by my side, swathing her way to me with her blood drenched axe. She pointed to the wall, words forming on her lips...

"Loose!"

That single word carried over the bloodied field a moment before a barrage of flaming arrows streaked through the sky, thick enough to resemble an actual cloud, though I suspected I'd like this kind of storm infinitely less. Their signal to arms was also my own call to magic, shoving outward with a sharp intake of breath for their arrows to hit, falling harmlessly to the ground.

Some arrows still broke through, if the screams were anything to go by. I pushed harder, relieved when the arrows hit my air shield and fell harmlessly to the ground. We were gaining ground. Steady, certain progress, carving our way closer to the battlements of Loc Valen.

"When do we attack the wall?" I asked. Lenore's axe dispatched another before she yanked it from between his eyes.

"We need to get Aspen a bit closer!" Lenore said, catching her breath. "The spell will break once he is in range and says the incantation." I glanced up at the wall looming ahead. I didn't think we'd have to be this close. We would be in range of the explosion at this rate. That wasn't something I'd factored in.

An explosion to my right made us both startle. Lightning rained down around us, opening a path forward. I glanced up to see Aquarius soaring overhead, as if she'd heard us. The enemy was beginning to thin. If a path were carved for us, we'd take down the wall in short minutes. Once the wall was breached, we run to Ari'inor. To Scorpio.

That was when the earth gave way.

The first rumble took the feet out from everyone on the battlefield, from the beach to the forest edge. The next sent a shockwave that shook everything. I bet Scorpio rattled in her throne. Was that the explosion?

Lenore and I both looked to the wall to see it still intact, another volley readying along the battlements. So what the hell was going on?

That was when the first scream sounded. Towards the beach along the far side of the battlefield.

Locke and I exchanged looks across what little distance separated us. His eyes were wide. Focused. But more than that, he looked afraid. His attention immediately went to the water as waves began to rise. Not enough to be dangerous, but enough to know that something was horrifically wrong. A screeching roar filled my ears as a monstrous dragon head erupted through the surface.

I thought dragons were extinct. How the fuck was I supposed to fight a dragon?

"That sound..." Locke said in fearful awe. "It's not possible..." A second slender, scaled head shot to the surface. Panic seized me. A third snarled its way to the surface, its gaze locked on the beach. Locke's response let me know exactly how much danger we were in. "Hydra. Scorpio found a hydra."

Chapter Fifty

"I thought hydras were supposed to be extinct, like the dragons!" I said as Lenore and I fought our way to Locke, who gave me a grim look as he blocked a sword with his own. Watching another head emerge, my jaw slackened in shock and awe. Lenore's face married surprise and horror as she too saw another head rise to the surface. She spared a look at me that had my stomach plummeting in fear. Lenore, the strongest, bravest fae I knew, was afraid. With how much rage she harbored, I was shocked she still had room for fear.

"I thought they were. One hasn't been seen in centuries." Locke looked at me, his mouth set in a grim line. "Scorpio can communicate with and control water beasts, so she must have somehow found one hydra that extinction forgot about." He turned to me with a thin-lipped expression. I pictured her walking into the sea and calling for aid. Demanding that the sea help and this creature somehow responded. This was what she'd meant earlier, I realized. When she said she had tricks up her sleeve. "What are the chances you don't engage with that thing and you run?" I gave him a flat look before I parried an attack from a sword that was aimed at my throat.

"About zero."

"I was afraid of that." Locke was about to say more, probably about me staying back while other fae fought the hydra, when Aspen cleaved his way through the thinning Crownguards to meet us.

"What do you suppose the chances are that thing has to stay in the water?" Aspen asked as fae from both sides fled the beach in terror when more heads arose with a shriek.

Aquarius was already overhead, sending lightning strike, after lightning strike into the water. Other corpses rose to the surface, fried and smoking, but the hydra barely seemed to notice. Its approach to land wasn't slowed remotely. One of the heads glanced up at her, fire spewing from its open maw. Nimbus was quick, thank the goddess, flying around the pillars of flame with an enraged cry. Water crashed and fell as the hydra took its first earth-shaking step onto the sandy beach, causing Aspen's face to crumble before muttering, "Of fucking course it walks on land."

I could scarcely look up at the dragon-like heads from the massive claws attached to its feet. They were each easily as long as I was tall, and sharper than any existing blade. This beast was meant to kill. Its hide would be as tough as any armor, though not as impregnable as dragon scales. This would no doubt be the fight of our lives.

Another roar rang out as each of the seven heads scanned the beach, appraising for the easiest meal. More horrifying, it didn't seem to separate sides. Both armies were sent scurrying away from the beach in fright. Scorpio sent this thing knowing it wouldn't discern ally from enemy. If she controlled it, would the curse be broken if it killed me? I didn't understand, why would she put her own army in danger? Just to ensure the hydra got to me?

Could it really be so simple? Could she honestly be that desperate? If she could wield the knife that would kill me, why would this be different? If she controlled the hydra, I had to assume she could kill me this way. I no longer had the advantage. And by the look Locke gave me, I could tell he had the same thought.

The scene unfolded before my eyes, as if in slow motion. One of the heads snaked down without warning, sweeping legs of fae, while other heads darted out to feast on those off balance like easy prey.

Fang met flesh.

Teeth shredded muscle and sinew and bone. Jaws wrenched horrible screams from those unlucky enough to be caught before cutting them short altogether. Interspersed were the sounds of steel hacking at the blue scales and flesh and the all too occasional roar of pain. Bile rose in my throat at the smell of blood soaking the beach.

And I actively ran towards it.

The hydra didn't discriminate as it attacked and made a meal of everyone who got too close. Some fell under the weight of its massive claws, crushed instantly. Unlucky ones were fried to a crisp or ripped into ribbons before our eyes. Rebel and Crownguard alike.

Scorpio raised this army to die, I realized with mounting fury. It didn't matter if everyone on this plain died today. As long as my death set free. If we actually started to win, this was her ace in the hole. She truly didn't care for the fae she ruled. She was damning us as well as her own subjects, something many of those around us seemed to realize as well. Several fae around me turned and fled from the beast, abandoning the fight altogether for the safety of the field behind us. I let them go. Crownguards scattered, not even seeing me through their panic as I surged forward. The bleakness of our situation became oppressive and apparent, and would no longer be ignored. It sneered at us with an ugly smile and taunting eyes as volleys of arrows and magical attacks came from the walls of Loc Valen. A war now on two terrifying fronts. The worry, the dread, and the inevitable impending doom was sharp and cold in my gut.

There was a shout from the beach, and more arrows, some flaming, were sent at the hydra. It shrieked as it reared up to an impossible height, and I caught a better glimpse of those horrible claws. I watched with my heart in my throat as Nimbus and the other griffins scratched and pecked and bombarded the heads, staying heart-joltingly just out of reach. Just long enough to distract the beast as a volley of flaming arrows lodged in its body, the flames immediately dousing from the spray of the sea. It roared, not with pain, but with fury as it walked fully onto dry land with seven sets of snapping jaws.

"Line up!" Aspen's voice rose above the chaos and fear. He showed no hesitation, surging forward in the crowd and raising his sword above his head, rallying his flank. "Hold your ground. Face front. Flaming volley on my command!"

I saw the raised point of Aspen's sword moving steadily away into the throng of soldiers as he bravely disappeared towards the front line. The hydra roared again, beginning with one head, each of the six other heads joining in individually. A war cry. One so distinct and terrifying, every soul on the field stopped in stunned silence for a single, blood-chilling moment. Locke and I moved through the crowd, most soldiers not paying us much mind, too focused on the hellish beast before us. Aspen called for a volley, reaching the archers, baying them to steady themselves.

"On my command," Aspen called to them as they startled in the wake of death and fangs, his voice anchoring even myself as I prepared for the start of this battle. The air was wrought with tension and the sound of bows aimed and ready. Locke and I readied too, Locke with shadowy ice projectiles, and I was ready with my flames. "Aim for their eyes. You have plenty of targets. Blind it!"

When the command rang out in the air, the hydra struck.

It didn't waste time with trying to stalk any of us. Three different heads lashed out, ripping limbs from bodies, screams flying out in their wake. The horrible sound of tearing filled my ears, turning my stomach turn to stone. At the same time, its huge, scaled tail ripped through the water creating a massive wave aimed straight for us. I summoned my air magic and rallied the Air Court soldiers to do the same. Aquarius, heeding my call to action, screamed her support. Our air shield crashed into the water, stopping its advance, sparking where the water touched it.

The middle head zeroed in on me, an eerie intelligence in its eyes. In that moment, I intrinsically knew Scorpio indeed controlled it, at least in part. The hatred that sparked in its eyes when it looked at me. The very same hatred I'd seen in Scorpio's eyes not minutes earlier.

Several of the heads flew out along the ground, wide hinged jaws snapping in their wake. Some fae were ended quickly. Others were left with torn limbs, but not the reprieve of death as they screamed in the wake of the legendary water beast. Others still were flung with the might of it, landing so far removed from the fight it was impossible to tell their fate.

One head oozed a foul-smelling black poison from its open maw, spewing it at the fae nearest it. The sounds of screaming and sizzling met my nose with each pass. Each hack from a blade bounced ineffectively off its scales.

"What the fuck are we supposed to do against that?" someone cried out fearfully.

"We kill it." Locke plunged his sword downward into the nearest part of the hydra—one of the necks. A pained scream pierced the blood covered beach as the head threw itself backward. Some luck at last, I thought, seeing its brackish blood. "Aim your blade between its scales!" Locke's voice hovered over the battlefield.

Locke and I found ourselves fighting back to back. At one point we were side to side, enough for our gazes to clash for a single, loaded moment. We threw ourselves into the fray, my blade ramming into the open maw of one head, while Locke fended off a second one coming for me. A barrage of ice and shadow, a scream of fury, and a well-placed blade strike from Locke sent one head shrieking back, but there didn't seem to be much damage to the hydra's face. Only anger. It seethed as it sized us up, its lips baring its hideous teeth before coming at us again.

"Pair up!" I cried, beseeching others around us who were still trying to take the beast on single handedly. "Cover each other's backs!" And I hoped they did. I was suddenly too busy to know. Gnashing teeth filled my vision and it was all I could do to keep myself out of reach, throwing my sword between me and certain death.

One reptilian head drove at me, not unlike a cat pouncing on a mouse, with incredible speed. A predator intent on its prey. I heard Locke scream in warning. I dove aside, its teeth grazing my armor with a horrible screech. Even more horrible was when one of the loops of my armor snagged on its massive fangs, adhering me to it. I screamed when the head rose skyward frighteningly fast, pulling me from the ground. My feet pedaled uselessly, nowhere to find purchase. My arm ached where the hydra's teeth had snagged my armor. I was pulled further upwards when the head rose to its full height, teeth lashing at me. I heard Locke's voice calling my name, but I couldn't focus on it. Before I could gag on the smell of rancid blood, I twisted, dropping my sword in favor of my dagger at my thigh, and put my weight behind me, using where my armor anchored me to the hydra for leverage to drive my blade into its eye.

It was the first thing that actually seemed to do some serious damage.

Its head catapulted backwards with a monstrous scream, sending me eye-level with the griffons, but my anchor still did not break. I bounced painfully, brutally, off the head once, twice, three times as it shook its head through the pain and roared its fury. Its one good eye settled on me and I felt real fear slither down my spine, stiffening my limbs, making me almost drop my weapon.

The hydra's head repeatedly swung me in front of his face, trying to bite me. I choked on a scream as its fangs grazed my hip, only a hairsbreadth out of reach. Far too close for comfort. The leather strap of my shoulder held fast, keeping me in place, on the edge of perpetual danger. The poisoned head Locke fended off a moment ago looked at me, and I swear to the Goddess it smirked in a very disturbing reptilian way before sending a wad of thick, purple poison sailing on the air towards me. The head that held me stilled to hold me in position of the oncoming miasma.

I reached deep into the well of magic within me. But as I looked up, I saw the black poison had turned to ice and was falling from the sky. Locke had frozen the poison so it couldn't hurt me. I turned back to my task at hand, freeing myself. Still stuck to a thrashing head, I hurried to unbind myself, watching as it hissed and its forked tongue tried to draw me into the line of its eager teeth.

A dark glow shone from below me, followed by a mighty cry. The head stopped moving only just long enough for me to realize I was falling from far too high a height. A scream left me as the ground rushed up to meet me.

Arms encircled me, plucking me out of the air. I craned my neck up, ready to fight, when I realized it wasn't arms that held me. They were talons. Talons that gently encircled my torso. Talons attached to bird feet and feathers.

Nimbus.

Looking down, I saw that Locke had gotten onto the back of the beast. He'd ripped off the scales and severed the head that held me captive. But he didn't look happy.

"You okay down there?" Aquarius asked from atop her mount as we approached the ground in a much more controlled manner than I was expecting only moments ago. I grinned, giving her the thumbs up and a whoop of victory.

That victory didn't last long.

The head fell limp to the beach below like a huge tree, fae scrambling to stay out of the way to avoid being crushed. But the bubbling sound from the base of the bloodied stump that Locke had just revealed dashed any hope I'd had. From the bubbling, writhing skin burst forth another head, identical to the first. Nimbus dropped me off on the beach, giving me lots of momentum to run to Locke.

Fangs became my entire field of view, stopping me altogether.

Chapter Fifty-One

I gagged and nearly lost my stomach contents from the smell, not that I had time to focus on that. I called my fire to me on a whim, wrapping my body in living flame. The head screamed, the mouth recoiling to the side, deterred for only a second.

It was enough.

Forming the sword of flames, I slashed out towards its throat. My blade of fire caught and melted through flesh, bone, and sinew before at last coming into contact with its spine, ending its thrashing. With a cry I surged forward, careful not to slip in the blood and saliva coating the ground below us. With one last push, it was over. The head fell still and silent.

The rest of the heads screamed in unison, rearing up towards the sky. We waited, all of us watching with bated breath.

The head did not regenerate.

A cheer erupted from us all. Fire. Fire was the key. The severed head had to be cauterized.

Unfortunately, I was the only one with Fire Magic. I was the only one who could lop off their heads. The heads all knew it as each one in turn swiveled to glower at me. One licked where it should have had lips, its forked tongue flecking out, unnerving me. Aspen and Locke appeared by my side while the hydra continued to thrash and scream.

"Are you alright?" Locke's eyes scanned every inch of me, grimacing at the gash on my arm from my near miss when my armor had stuck to the hydra's teeth.

"Dragon scale armor is only impenetrable if fangs don't get caught under the armor." My joke fell flat. Truthfully, with the adrenaline flying through my system, I scarcely felt my wounds. And looking around at those unfortunate enough to lie in pieces on the beach, I couldn't help but feel like I didn't have the right. "I'm okay, thanks to you," I said. His eyes softened.

"Set fire arrows at its eyes. Douse your arrows in poison and set them alight," Locke called instructions. "Rip the scales off! Your blade will be much more effective"

"If someone severs a head, call me. I'll cauterize it. We only have a few seconds before it regenerates," I said. Locke nodded. I didn't miss a hint of pride on his face that made my heart sing despite our setting.

Aspen turned to relay the plan to his warriors, calling for a volley of fire to be rained down on the monster. It hissed, all the heads in perfect synchronization.

An arrow whizzed by Locke, cutting his cheek. A red line formed as a result. My heart stopped. How lucky he'd gotten. In unison, our eyes followed the line, seeing several rebels and Windguard falling with arrows lodged in their backs, to the wall of Loc Valen where another volley of arrows was being readied. I tossed up another air shield, before Aquarius assigned several of her Windguard to take over, who seemed relieved to stay away from the hydra fight. Not that I could blame them. They could slow the attack from Loc Valen and buy us the time we needed to fight the hydra.

It took what felt like hours. And maybe it was. I had no grasp on the passage of time. Systematically, as a team we distracted and kept the heads busy with fire arrows, dealing damage, and I lopped off head after head with a sword of fire. Or Locke relieved one neck of its head and I blasted fire at it until the stump became still and fell to the beach with a thick, wet *thud*. Brackish blood polluted the water of the surf, turning it an unpleasant black color with a putrid stench. Lenore's axe made dents in the scales of the neck, leaving it exposed to attack. Locke and Aspen used their immense Water Magic of ice to bind and slow its response time. Aquarius would scream a warning to leave the water moments before she sent a maelstrom of lightening into the shallows where the beast stood. It screamed ear-piercingly loud, convulsing in the wake of the electricity in its weakened state. It bought me a second only, but that was all I needed to do the damage.

Until the final, middle head remained. Its stumps dragged wetly through the ground, so heavy it was nearly immobile. The cauterized tissues ripped and tore, leaving black blood bubbling, corrosive in its wake, dangerous even in death. But thankfully, no heads further sprouted from them. And we were down to the final one. My body felt heavy, exhausted. I wiped sweat and blood and fuck only knows what else from my brow as I sucked in air.

Our army, while down considerably in size, started to rally behind us with renewed hope and vigor. Sensing that this victory was close, at least on this front. But even I could see that our army was getting so much smaller. Far too few lines of fae separated the fight with the hydra from the fight with Loc Valen. I couldn't let myself contemplate who might have fallen in the charge, Monumental effort steeled my thoughts against it for now, knowing it would be acknowledged later. Just not now.

Time wasn't on our side. It was getting hard to move in the wake of all the bodies and shredded limbs discarded around the beach. Not to mention the sheer exhaustion.

I popped one of the magic regeneration pills Eldan had given me, choking it down dry. I gave the remaining two to Locke and Aspen, who did the same.

"Whoa! Who knew the old man's pills had such a kick?" Aspen flexed his fingers, magic springing from them with ease. A feeling I knew myself, feeling the magic surge within me. It was odd, feeling this drained of energy, but my magic roared within, begging for release as it coiled around my muscles.

The final head hissed, its tail waving erratically. Its shoulders hunched. Its eyes flashed with a sense of recognition. My eyes narrowed as I looked closer. Was it me, or were its eyes green?

The hydra roared as it moved towards me, quicker than it should have been able to, carrying the weight of all those severed trunks, claws, and fangs gnashing and goring as they went. The screams of the dying permeated my ears as it approached. I couldn't dodge fast enough. Weariness tugged at my bones, slowing my movements. Locke screamed my name as two rows of teeth ended up on either side of me.

The hot maw, blood, and gore dripped around me, and my stomach heaved.

With a scream wrenching from me like nothing else I'd ever experienced, I shoved my daggers upwards as the tongue began to guide me towards its foul-smelling throat, the steel penetrating the fleshy palate of its mouth. Its head shot skyward, knocking me off balance. I slithered perilously close towards the back of its throat. This was it. This was how I would die. In the mouth—or worse, the belly—of this goddess-awful beast. And there would be no way to bring me back from this. I would meet the Goddess like this.

But as I desperately rammed my blade upwards, finding resistance and pushing into it savagely. My dagger anchored me, lodged in the hydra's palate, my feet burning from the acid in its throat. The beast screamed, opening its jaw again, letting in enough light that I could see. I had gored a massive hole in the top of its mouth, my dagger deeply sitting in bone with blood pouring from the wound. I summoned fire, and with a brutality I wasn't sure I was previously capable of, I shoved my magic down its throat. Now instead of trying to get out, I held to the blade lodged in the roof of its mouth, desperately trying to hold on. I wrapped my flames around my body and pushed, my flames getting hotter and hotter until the scent of burning flesh and boiling blood overwhelmed me. Its screams were wild, manic. The scream of a dying monster. I sent my Fire Magic outward in a spiral. And the freefall began.

I'd never fallen inside a flaming severed head before. So, I really had to hand it to myself for the predicament I was in. The head was rotating on its axis in the air as it fell, the maw now slackened in death. I called off my flames, the air cooling immediately and making it easier to see. I half stumbled, half fell out of the hydra maw, the ground taking up my entire field of view. With a scream that was more terror than anything else, I pushed out with my Air Magic, praying to the goddess I didn't break something again.

The water met me head on, with no space for mercy.

I slammed into the surf with force rivalling the exploding violence around me, seizing the air from my lungs. My body couldn't move. I tried, but my head was so fuzzy.

Strong hands lifted me under my arms a moment before my face broke the surface of the water, the water quickly evacuating my lungs and burning its way through my throat in sputtering, painful coughs.

"For the love of the fucking veil." Locke sounded exasperated yet profoundly relieved. "That's what you call being careful?"

I was too exhausted to say anything. Locke and Lenore worked, hacked, and slashed opponents in the surf. Familiar green-tinged magic rushed up to conquer the wicked head spinning, bringing me much needed clarity. I was in the shallow surf. Knee deep at most. Locke must have swelled the water to catch me. He'd saved me once again.

The carcass of the hydra lay poking out of the water only a few feet away, the severed dragon-like heads swaying in the turbulent water around it. It was then that our situation became clear.

Several members of the Air Court had combined forces with Lenore, Vanneck, and Locke, and held off attacking Crownguards who'd stormed the beach now from the city, giving Aspen and another healer I didn't recognize time to heal me. Already I felt strength returning to my fingers, the ringing in my head receding. The Air Court's magic blocked volley after volley of arrows and projectiles. Those that did break through towards us were dealt with by Lenore, chopping them out of the air in an impressive maneuver.

"I swear to the Goddess if that thing grows another head, I'm going to lose it," I cracked, ignoring how my head hurt with each syllable. Aspen, who'd moved to kneel in front of me, shared a glance with the healer behind me.

"I'm going to focus on her concussion. Can you handle the rest?" he asked, returning his attention to me. "That was quite a fucking stunt. If we live through this, I'm killing you myself for that."

I grinned weakly at him. "Hey, we're alive, aren't we? When this is over, I'm not training for a whole month." Aspen's smile winked into existence, softening the stern expression, making me smile too. I sighed into his healing magic as he took the ringing pain in my head away.

"You freeloader." His voice said grumpy, but his face softened with pride. "If we live through this, you deserve the month after that display."

"Any chance you want to hurry the fuck up?" Lenore's shrill cry brought me back to the present moment. Glancing around Aspen, I could now clearly see what we were up against. "We don't have time for sentimentality!"

Either a large part of Scorpio's army deserted her, or had already been killed. Considering she'd unleashed a hydra on all of us, her army included, I couldn't say I was surprised. Locke asked her before if she were willing to rule over a court of corpses. She didn't answer at the time, but looking at the death and mayhem around us, it was clear to her that breaking her curse was worth any cost. Any number of lives. She would pay in any amount of blood, guilty or innocent. But still far too many Crownguards remained stubbornly between us and the city walls. We'd never breach the portcullis. Arrows, spears, swords, and magic guarded it like it was all that mattered in the world, and to them, it was. We needed to get so much closer to bring the wall down.

And then, my glower raised above the line of soldiers, above the line of the wall, to trace the highest peaks of Ari'inor, Scorpio.

Part of me knew that once I walked into that throne room, neither one of us would be walking back out.

Chapter Fifty-Two

The line of the remaining army advanced towards us like the certainty of death.

Armed with every weapon known to fae-kind, the remaining Crownguards advanced in a line, defending Loc Valen to their dying breaths. Their boots crunched in sync as they approached, sounding like quiet, rhythmic thunder. Griffins flew overhead, the occasional lightning in the backdrop foretelling Aquarius's presence.

Except we weren't after Loc Valen. Just Scorpio. I wanted to tell them we had no quarrel with innocents. That they were in greater danger by not helping us. But there were still hundreds of fae between us and the wall. The wall that stood between us and our objective. The wall that needed to come down. Volley after volley was still being sent from the wall, fae on our side falling silent if not close to air wielders.

"How much closer do we need to get to set off the time bombs?" I asked Aspen. His hands grasped mine, hauling me to my feet. I took my stance between him and a very relieved looking Locke.

"Welcome back," Locke said, looking at me despite the advancing line of Crownguards coming towards us. "Don't ever do that again. Fucking veil, Lark, I thought you were dead."

"Only because you asked so nicely," I said. His side-eye told me he wasn't as amused as I was. "What's the plan?"

"We need to get Aspen closer to that wall," Locke said. "So get ready to carve your way through as many fae as possible."

I smiled. Not because of what he said. Because I had an idea. I looked at Aspen.

"When see your chance," I said to him, readying myself, "run."

Aspen looked at me quizzically. "When will I know?" I smirked at his question.

I gathered my magic within me, readying it. Coiling it tightly within me. It was the last thing I was able to notice before the Crownguards fell on us like a pack of hungry beasts, hacking and slashing with everything they had. Locke made use of his magic, blue ice coating anyone unfortunate enough to be in his way. Ice projectiles pierced the heart of anyone too close to him.

I unleashed my magic, sending a torrent of wind straight through the heart of the enemy army towards the wall, like a tornado turned on its side. Crownguards were scattered, sent every direction, but one thing was truly important. The way was open for Aspen. I screamed at him to go. Get as close as he needed to, and he wasted no time.

We surged forward behind him, ready to defend as the force around us began to recover their equilibrium. In the resulting chaos, I lost sight of everyone. I could hear Lenore's cries of war and the screams of anguish that followed. I saw the shadows that had to be Locke. But I knew there were several others who wielded the shadows, thankfully not as well as the Crowned Assassin.

It was hard to move. Blood soaked the ground we stood upon, slickening it. But the sheer number of bodies began to stack up on both sides of this war. It was getting difficult to walk without stepping on the body of an enemy—or worse, that of an ally. A friend. I refused to look at the faces on the ground. It would shatter me if I saw someone there that I cared for and I needed my mind unfractured and focused.

I kept fighting. I was covered in blood, both my own and others'. Aquarius and I kept forcing our way to the back of their forces, me from below and her from above on Nimbus's back. I knew Scorpio just wanted to wear us down. To wear me down. To make it easier to kill me when the time was right. But she wasn't leaving this battle alive. I would personally see to that. My rage manifested itself into flames spiraling down my arm. I shot my flames into the nearest of the fae in the blue and silver armor ahead of me. I didn't relish the screams, but it was effective.

Something hammered into my abdomen with the force of a small cannon. A cry burst from my lips. I looked down to see an arrow on the ground. I fingered the area where I should have been stabbed. Dragon scale armor could not be pierced, Lenore had told me once. I was forever grateful to Locke for gifting it to me. It might have just saved my life again. But the pain and the bruise would be epic when all of this was over.

I fought alongside my friends, taking out as many of the army as I could. It wasn't long before fatigue began to pull at my limbs and slow my reflexes. I was too slow a few times. The cuts on my face, and anywhere my armor didn't reach was evidence of that. Grime, sweat, and blood mixed on my flesh, stinging the edge of my awareness as I fought. Wave after wave of enemies kept swarming us. It was endless. We needed to get to Scorpio. We needed to end this nightmare before more life was lost.

Only moments later did the blast come, knocking everyone to their knees and sending many to the veil. I thought there would be a moment of warning somehow. There was a tiny spark of white light that prefaced half a moment before the battlements exploded with a thunderous noise that sounded like the earth itself was being ripped apart. The earth trembled a long time in the aftermath. There was a split second after the explosion where I stood rooted to my spot on the battlefield knock-kneed and breathless in horror and disgust and absolution as fae were catapulted from their posts, some in pieces. The earth-shattering explosion was deafening. I shielded my face from flying debris after that, throwing up an air shield to protect myself and our allies in the immediate area. I felt bombardment of shrapnel and debris rampaging against my magic. Though I was too disoriented by the ringing in my ears, a parting gift from the explosion.

The sound of stone being reduced to rubble gave way to nothing at first. Just that endless ringing for a long time. Lenore called my name. I knew she was next to me, but she sounded so far away. Locke too shouted for me. I glanced at him stumbling forward, a bit shell-shocked.

All at once, my hearing came back, though the ringing took long minutes to fade away. Screams of the injured and dying began to echo in my mind. Even from my vantage point, I saw the death, dismemberment, and carnage. The blood and bodies—not all of them whole—sickened me, but I had no time to dwell on that. The fighting stopped momentarily as every soldier was disoriented. But it wasn't long before chaos reigned once again.

Denizens of Scorpio's army screamed their fury and were upon us once again with outraged vigor. I nearly didn't escape an attack headed straight for me. A volley of arrows hit and tore through my weakening air shield. A trickle of sweat beaded on my forehead as I reached for my daggers, laying haphazardly on the ground a few feet away from the explosion. I rolled away from my assailant. He followed me with a slow grin as he stalked me. Waiting. I scurried forward for a discarded sword. My fingers made contact with the bottom of the hilt, but only enough that it slid away frustratingly out of reach. I heard my name from too far away—Locke.

"What a pity," my opponent tsked as he raised his sword, poised for a death blow. But what he didn't realize was that I was not defenseless. I pushed out with my Fire Magic. It roared to life from within me, humming in my veins. And the last thing he saw were my flames devouring him. But I would remember his screams for however long I had left.

I gathered my weapons and rose on shaky legs to my feet as enemies closed in around me.

I fought like a wildcat with everything I had. There was no time to think in the thrall; just instinct. Flashes of my magic forcing fae back from me, my sword meetings theirs before meeting their flesh. I was winning. But I was tiring quickly. I knew I wouldn't be able to keep this up indefinitely.

"Behind you!" I heard someone yell. Vanneck, perhaps. I spun. Too late.

It was a well-placed blow. The moment the blade made contact with the small sliver of exposed flesh near my shoulder from where the armor straps failed, my assailant stiffened. Blood formed on his lip and dribbled down his chin before collapsing in a heap. Dead. Lenore nodded to me from where she was revealed behind him as she removed her blood-soaked axe from his still corpse, Vanneck immediately behind her.

"Thanks!" I called out above the noise as I engaged more oncoming assailants. I took stock of our position in the few glimpses I could manage. We were winning. The water soldiers were falling. We were pressing forward! Our plan was working.

With a sense of renewed resilience, I let out a resounding battle cry as I pushed my advantage on the two fae currently engaging me. I rounded on the one, a calculated sweep of my sword severing his neck and sending his head tumbling to the ground. I received a barrage of attacks designed to bludgeon and tear and injure, none of which I was able to counter. I could feel the welts forming, but my dragon scale armor held true, keeping me safe from his blade. His eyes widened when he realized I was about to retaliate. A massive flurry of magic projectiles followed my quick slashes of my blade put him in a panicked, sloppy defense. A low sweep with my leg was enough to knock him off balance and end him swiftly.

"We have to go!" Lenore grasped my forearm, tugging me into a run with her. We were quickly joined by Aspen, a very bloodied Vanneck, and Aquarius. I glanced around. Where was Locke? My head whipped around as we ran, looking for even glimpse he was with us. Fire and smoke and waving steel was all I saw, causing panic to creep up as Lenore tugged me after her. She turned to me, fire highlighting the violence in her eyes.

"He's coming! Nothing will stop him catching up to you," She said it like a curse. "Quit gawking, we have to run!"

My next steps felt like leaving a part of me behind.

Nothing will stop him catching up to you.

I held to those words with everything I had and threw myself into running. It was only when running at full speed towards the hole in the wall did I understand exactly how massive the damage was. Debris littered the battleground. Hunks of burnt white stone lay stranded over corpses of those who'd been unlucky in the explosion. As we got closer, more of the bodies were in pieces, and the devastation my idea caused lanced a hole in my chest.

We had just breached the wall when a volley of arrows greeted us. Aquarius raised an air shield faster than I did, blocking a few arrows. Not nearly enough. They were released too close to us; our Wind Magic did nothing to deter them. Aquarius's scream blended with mine. I looked down at my abdomen to see a bolt there. A bolt that had ripped through the dragon scale armor. My gut felt like it was on fire, and I fought to stay on my feet. I didn't understand. Until I pulled the arrow out. Harpoon would have been a better word for it. A massive, cruel looking bolt. My face fell, recognizing the unmistakable metallic sheen. It was coated with dragon scales.

None of us were protected from these arrows.

The one who shot me grinned as he reloaded. With a roar of fury and effort, my flames came up and destroyed the wood of his bow, in seconds reducing it to smithereens. I ignored the hot well of pain in my abdomen; one arm covered the wound, the other grasping the dragon scale arrow in my hand. He struck at me with another arrow from his quiver, his arrowhead close to my skin. But I was faster. He landed on the ground in a crumpled heap after my dagger deeply punctured his chest. I was missing three of the black daggers. I was down to so few weapons.

The other archers ran to take on easier prey as I readied my flames again, swirling the flames around me in a vortex, striking at anyone who dared move in our direction. That was the first time I felt the sucking on the well of my magic. The first sputter. I cursed, knowing I had no more regeneration tablets.

Aspen was next to me in an instant as Lenore began carving her way viscously through the fae around us, closing the wound.

"I can't do much, but I can stop the bleeding!" he called about the chaos.

Aquarius ripped the arrow from her torso as Lenore embedded her axe in someone who would have killed the Air Queen, giving her time to close her own wound. How was it that Locke and I seemed to be the only ones who couldn't heal?

"Duck, Lenore!" I hollered out, seeing a spear expertly thrown in her direction. She was fast. Lenore was small, fierce, and fast as she dropped to her hands and knees.

But not fast enough.

The spear grazed the top of her shoulder, opening a gushing wound. She fired her axe back, enjoying watching the death of the one who injured her. Three more took his place, surrounding her.

No one else. I would lose no one else. Lenore's cry of pain sent wrath flowing through my veins. I exploded in Earth Magic. Thorny vines, like the ones that ensnared Pisces, wrapped around them in a blink, rendering them useless. For the first time, I felt nothing as they screamed, my thorns digging cruelly beneath their skin and rendering them immobile. So close. They had been far too close to killing Lenore. Lenore gave a mighty war cry, shooting up from her knees and carving the first one up with her bloodied axe. He didn't even have time to scream. She turned to the other two twitching in vines with a viciousness I think only she was capable of and dispatched them with a voracious grin, coating herself in their blood.

I took my first steps into Loc Valen from through the massive crater in the wall. I tried not to cringe at the beautiful white stone now painted red with blood. Explosion marks had left singed black pieces, marring the stone forever. The resistance was significantly thinner here, as they didn't expect us to blow down their wall. Some fae engaged us; others ran from us in terror. I wished I could tell them we meant no harm to anyone who didn't attack us. For someone to look at me in fear...

It was not something I'd ever forget.

Where Scorpio saw that look and felt powerful, I never felt weaker. More powerless to help. I grit my teeth and ran on with Lenore, Aspen, Vanneck, and Aquarius next to me, desperately trying to ignore the horrid pain in my abdomen.

"Where is Locke?" I asked.

Aspen shoved me forward. "He'll be along. Keep going, Lark."

It was pure faith in both Aspen and Locke that I did as I was told. Aspen wouldn't leave Locke in trouble, and that was the only reason I wasn't clawing my way backwards for my soulmate. He could take care of himself. Still, I don't think my thoughts would quiet until I rested my eyes on him again.

I ran down now familiar blocks towards Castle Ari'inor, the only place Scorpio would be waiting. I ran, feeling the dirt and debris crunch unsavorily under my boots. I ran until my lungs threatened to burst, but I couldn't keep my eyes from seeing the barred windows, the debris jammed in front of doors. It reminded me painfully of the attack on Port Azure. To them, we were the same. That thought was like a nail driving itself into my chest. I wished I could tell them that they were safe from us. That we wouldn't hurt them. I wanted to laugh. This was the very square that I first fell in love with this city. I could only pray that Lorelei was safe. If I were to turn around, I'd see her inn. We pushed on through the cobblestone streets and I tried to ignore the fact that the city looked like a ghost town. To ignore the shouts of combat far behind us as we pressed on towards our goal.

Scorpio, I'm coming for you. With a violence, with a rage I never thought myself capable of, I thought, *I'm coming for you.*

Chapter Fifty-Three

An angry shout ensnared my attention as we walked into the empty square. Ari'inor loomed only a short distance away, perhaps a block now. My head swiveled, finding two Crownguards bellowing their hatred as they flew on fast feet towards us. I raised my daggers, ready to defend, when it was quickly rendered unnecessary. A flash of what could only be lightning took down two enemies bearing down on me up ahead. I turned my head to see Aquarius with a terrifying smile on her face, reminding me so much of Windermere castle, the engravings of her looking fierce and defiant. Here was that fae in the flesh.

The flash receded, granting us our eyesight back, but also revealing to us that we were surrounded. Crownguards drew their weapons and pushed in. Aspen, Lenore, Aquarius, and I all stood back to back with our weapons out, eying our new company sneering back at us as they pressed inward. I glanced around at our surroundings, looking for an escape. There were four exits, one on each side of the square. We had to fight to get to one of them and get out of here.

A horn sounded, loud and very close. The only warning we had for the squad that came around the corner, further barring our passage to Ari'inor. All the other Crownguards looked to them expectantly. Immediately, I felt nauseous. Their armor. I recognized it. My father had worn this specific armor. Like that of the Crownguards, but sleeker. More elegant in its design. I understood why the fae around us seemed to be waiting for something: orders.

These were the elite Crownguards. Stronger and far better trained than anyone besides the Kinship themselves. The Kinship's personal guard. As they drew their weapons, I saw that metallic sheen again.

Dragon scale.

My armor wouldn't hold against it. I didn't dare glance down, but I knew my armor was barely holding it together now as it was. I ground my jaw hard enough to make it click as I weighed my options.

Seconds went by seemingly in slow motion. And still my heartbeat seemed incredibly rapid as I took in the sheer size and number of the Crownguards; there had to be two dozen. And I didn't know who the leader was yet, but the rumors of his viciousness had reached me even in Poplar Hollow. My eyes scanned the faces of my taunting opponents as I sized them.

"Well, this is fun," Aspen's voice rose above the tension for just a moment. I bit back a grin as we all stood back to back in a circle. The only things between us and death were our weapons.

"You know, I'm having a hard time deciding if you're being sarcastic," I grunted, my dagger clashing blades with my opponent. Their attacks weren't even genuine right now. Just slow, lazy arcs. Mind games. They were playing mind games with me. Trying to scare me or break me down. I grit my teeth as I gave back what I got—a lazy but effective deflection of the blade. I made a show of how it took no effort and flashed them a dark look.

"What?" I could see him in my mind's eye grinning widely as the Crownguards closed in tighter around us. Aquarius snorted derisively as electricity ran up her arms, making the hair on my nape stand up. "This is bucket list worthy!"

"In what way is nearly dying a good thing to add to the bucket list?" came a third, very familiar voice from above. A voice that filled me with instant relief, bringing an odd sense of calm. I glanced up, as everyone did, to see Locke perched on the roof of the nearest building. His eyes flashed danger, betraying the smirk on his face, as he dropped down to the street. His head tipped down, his smile widening as the Crownguards murmured to one another and gave him some room with distrustful gazes and nervous stares.

Locke's hair was smattered with blood. He had a horrid-looking cut on his forehead that was still leaking. His armor was askew in places. And the blood. Goddess, he was covered in it. But he strode towards me confidently, without so much as a limp. My heart leapt in my chest and begged me to go to him, but my feet remained firmly planted with more than a few Crownguards in my way.

"Hello, love," he purred as if we were the only two in the square as he approached. But I didn't miss the way his eyes traced me, scanning for every injury and darkening further every time he saw one. He sniffed as if scenting the blood on the air. "Miss me?" One of the elite—the leader, I presumed—stepped between Locke and me, drawing his ire. "Warrick."

"Prince Cancer. How lovely of you to return," Warrick replied in a tone suggesting the opposite as he made a show of swirling his sword. "If you surrender now, your mate will be granted a simple, painless death from her majesty and we will let your friends live. If not," he pulled his sword slowly from its sheath at his side, "I'm afraid none of you will live. And the Queen's Mark will suffer. And you will watch."

"That's a lot of ands," Locke said, twirling a dagger with fluid, enviable ease. The kind that made it look like it was an extension of his own hand. "Traditionally, when you're listing things, it's ill advised to use the word 'and' until the last thing you mention. And I'll give you one more piece of advice." All humor dissolved from his face then as he glared at Warrick. "One you'd best not forget: stand between me and my soulmate, and I'll drive the darkness so far under your skin the light of the Goddess will never touch you again." Locke exploded in a way I'd never seen before. Shadows burst forth from him, blocking out some of the sunlight and casting us in dusk. Black spears were cast at the leader, blindingly fast.

How Warrick was faster, I'd never know.

Locke's attack on Warrick was a signal to everyone. The elite were unleashed.

"Bucket lists are supposed to be exciting!" Aspen grunted as his sword clanged against something steel. I heard a piercing male scream shortly after and I almost felt bad for him. Almost.

"You and this bucket list thing. If you fight as hard as you run your mouth, we'd have been out of this by now," I cracked before taking another hit with a steel metal arrow, paining my shoulder. I spun, relieving the offending party of their head, wincing as I did so. My breathing was rapid as my body tried to keep up with the demand for oxygen. My muscles were screaming for a break and my throat felt dry as I fought my way through the oncoming opponents. The dozens of attackers quickly decreased until we were standing in a pile of discarded bodies.

Two of the remaining elite Crownguards circled me, while another seven separated Aquarius, Locke, Aspen, and Lenore, and hunted them. Aquarius replied like a cornered animal. I saw the lightening grace her fingertips. It bounced over her body, the electricity in the air making my hair stand on end. I noticed the Crownguards' attention was snared away by Aquarius, a grim smile on her features as she toyed with her opponents. A true Queen among peasants.

Locke and the others were fairing similarly, despite being outnumbered, their weapons were drawing blood, while they bled little in return. The way I liked it.

Warrick's blade clashed with mine. I hadn't even seen him skirt away from Locke, but here he was blocking my attack with ease.

"Hello, Queen's Mark. At last, we meet."

"The pleasure is entirely yours," I said as I dove at him. He laughed as he spun away from my attacks easily. No matter how fast I was, how determined I was, he was faster. Each time he dodged, I received a new wound. Small. Shallow. He was toying with me.

"Do you know what this is?" he asked me, showing me his sword. It gleamed red with blood, silver steel winking underneath it. "It's steel infused with dragon scales. It can pierce your armor. But you suspected already, given that we've already blown a hole in it." He eyed my exposed abdomen underneath tattered armor.

I didn't have time to reply as he launched himself at me with a speed and a viciousness I couldn't quite negate. His sword nicked my neck, before I countered with my own blade and vaulted to the side, evading him. He'd tried to do the same to me that I'd done to his kinsman. I couldn't even say I blamed him.

We crossed blades, exhaustion seriously becoming a factor in my fighting. My reflexes were slowing again, the wound in my gut beginning to make itself known. There were far too many close calls in this fight. I wasn't trained enough to take on the leader of the Crownguards. He'd been around for decades, training daily. How was I supposed to win against an opponent so much more skilled?

But I had beat Pisces. Sort of. I remembered stabbing his flesh three times before being thrown over the cliff. I had to take him by surprise. My sword wasn't going to do it. His eyes were steely and clear, assessing my every move with cunning, and he delivered blows with lethal precision. It wouldn't be much longer before those strikes brought me down. No. I was going to have to do something completely unexpected. I backed up, giving myself some room. And I drove my magic into the earth, falling to my knees in the process. I winced, feeling the well of my magic wane. He froze, unsure what to do, eyes darting back and forth for signs of what I'd done. I kept pouring my magic into the earth, praying my plan would work. Even Aquarius shot me a questioning glance during her battle.

At first, nothing happened. A very real slither of fear came over me. My insides jumped into my throat. I poured the rest of my magic into the ground. *Please*, I begged, *work*. Whether I was begging the Goddess, my magic, the earth itself, I had no idea. Nothing happened again. The fae before me threw his head back in a taunting laugh as he approached me. I grasped my dagger in my other hand, ready for his attack. I gathered my legs under me, ready to attack or evade at a moment's notice. But as he stepped, the ground shook. For one single moment, the entire battle ceased, fae of both sides looking around for the source.

The ground opened up underneath my opponent, not a grave like what I'd done to Pisces, but a deep chasm—so deep and dark I couldn't see the bottom. He jumped out of the way, landing on solid ground, laughing at my attempt to trick him. I grinned weakly. With the last scrape of magic that hurt me to use, a vine grasped his boot and dragged him screaming under the surface of the earth, along with several of Scorpio's closest allies.

The screams were like nothing I'd ever heard. Locke created a wall of icy shadow—too long to dodge or outrun with the limited roomand sent the remaining elite screaming over the edge, the earth dragging them all to their deaths beneath its surface. And in that moment, I wondered if I were any better than the monarch we were fighting to dethrone.

I realized then that I was exhausted. The well of my magic was nearly empty. Aquarius at last won her battle and tossed the final fae into the chasm behind her, grimacing at his screams before taking her place beside Aspen, Lenore, and myself.

Locke came strutting up beside me, took my face in his hands, and kissed me fiercely.

"Let the flames fuel you, but don't let them consume you," he whispered to me, echoing back to all those weeks ago. The words rippled through me, igniting that hope in me once again.

"I am the fire. They can't consume me," I whispered back. He smiled.

"That's my girl."

Chapter Fifty-Four

Our group of six met very little resistance on our way to Ari'inor. I couldn't tell if it were because every single fae was behind us on that battlefield, or if this were another trap. I eyed every movement out of the corner of my eyes with suspicion. I kept a white knuckled grip on my black daggers, which twitched at any provocation. She wanted me in the throne room. She had said as much, so it made sense that the ease of our course was by design. The curse pulled at me now, almost coming to life within me in wicked anticipation. I imagined the same black runes carving themselves into my flesh the way Locke had described to me before. Only this was layer by layer from the inside out, at least for now. Enough to know that time was running out. Scorpio had to kill me. And fast.

I couldn't let any of this be for nothing.

I glanced at Aquarius, marveling at her strength. She prowled forward with intention, vengeance for her Court echoing in every step. I had to believe that this was possible. Because if it weren't, if this whole endeavor were doomed, I wasn't sure I could walk into that throne room ahead. I had only seen glimpses of the grounds of Ari'inor. Sprawling lawns that were probably lush and beautiful in the summer now lay under a blanket of slick ice and frost, each blade of grass shimmering green underneath and perfectly preserved. It was too perfect to step on. To the north, a wall of ivy cascaded down the far wall under a coat of crystalline ice. Towering ice sculptures, frozen fountains, ponds, even a frozen waterfall, majestic, and paused in time. The gardens were spectacular, glinting in the sunlight under a coating of icy frost. Colorful, crystalline flowers, roses, even my namesake, Larkspur, lay under the ice. It was the last thing I saw before we strode into the castle, hauling open the massive doors.

If I'd thought the castle were ornate on my last visit here, I was horrifically mistaken. The throne room was absolutely colossal, every inch steeped in gold decadence. Sapphire accented it in the most stunning and dizzying display of opulence. I wondered if it was done purposefully. The beauty and splendor serving to disarm you as you entered. A mouse into a snake pit. As before, all I could think about was how one gold trinket in this great hall would be enough to feed a single family for a year.

One familiar shape reclined easily upon her throne, not unlike a cat. Her once-green eyes watched every movement of ours on our approach. Scorpio's rage was apparent, her gaze sliding from each of us in turn before settling on me. The only thing that unsettled me, where was Pisces?

I scanned the perimeter of the room, searching every shadowed inch, but found nothing. The hair on the back of my neck rose, every sense sparking to life. Even casting my awareness beyond me only yielded the information I already knew. We were here with Scorpio. But she'd proven before she had some sort of enchantment that blocked my ability. I didn't believe we were alone. Even if I didn't feel the heaviness of Pisces's gaze, I wasn't stupid enough to think he was gone. He may have been a coward, but he was too prideful to leave. He was in the shadows, awaiting his moment. Of that I had little doubt. It was possible this was a trap. As my steps echoed through the hallowed hall, I found I didn't care. It didn't matter. This throne room would soon be my gravesite.

And hopefully my rebirth.

"Here I am," I said, striding closer and holding my arms out to the side in offering, my voice echoing in the hallowed hall around us. "You wanted me here so badly."

"And for all your confidence, you still think you have a chance. And with so many pets in tow." The words fell from her lips like a string of curses, every bit as black and malignant as the magic she had dominion over. Shadows, suffocating in their depths, surrounded us. For what I knew would be the final time, I found myself walking towards the Barbaric Queen, my soulmate and friends trailing beside me. My footfalls were heavy, but never wavered as they carried me towards the glassy throne.

Her face lit up with a grim smile, calculating and wretched and resentful. And a stare equally as reproachful, rife with unrelenting will. This was it. The beginning of the end. I took immense satisfaction knowing I might not be the one who would kill her, but as sure as the veil, I would be the reason she'd die. My eyes trailed to Aquarius, walking beside me with her chin haughtily inclined and a lethal glare focused on the enemy queen. It was all

I could do to hope for victory. To defy fate. Defy the very fabric of magic itself. My own fury, previously cold and frozen under my control, transformed then into something wild and hot and all-consuming.

I was boiling over at long last.

"Your army has fallen. Your hydra has fallen. It's your turn," Locke said. I'd always thought Locke's ghosts followed him everywhere he went. Haunted him. But it wasn't that. I saw it all at once with such clarity. It was more like his heart was a haunted house, carrying the ghosts of all he was forced to kill with him. He was chased and tormented every day. They weren't hunting him, as I'd long suspected. They'd caught him and he'd been at their mercy. But no longer.

I regarded Scorpio coldly as she glared at him from her icy throne on high, glittering icy steps all that separated us. I once wondered if I'd have been her had the circumstances been reversed, but as I watched her callous nature unfold, I found my pity waning. I had been traumatized. I'd been a victim. I'd also survived it. I'd been a friend. A lover. I'd become powerful despite my circumstances, and I never hurt anyone I didn't have to. That was the difference between her and me. However similar we may have been, however stark our circumstances, I resisted the choices that she herself made, and that alone was enough to fully destroy the pity I had left for her.

And today, I would exact justice. For myself. My father. For Locke. My friends. And my Court. The Water Court would fall no longer. It would be in tattered ruins no longer.

Today, I'd buy that freedom with my life. Locke's eyes flickered to me as if he felt my resolve harden, but I could scarcely remove my eyes from Scorpio.

"Queen Scorpio, if you're even worthy of such a title," Aquarius spat on the floor between them. The wood carving I'd seen before of Aquarius, the fight in her eyes, had nothing on the fear the real thing induced. The Queen of Air was terrifying in her own right. The wind made by her own magic moved around her, spraying her hair away from her face as she spoke. "The Goddess herself granted me her wrath and I bring with me the retribution of the Air Court. We will not be denied. Revenge will be had, and blood will out in payment of the lives you took in Everwind."

Scorpio chuckled dismissively. "I think not. You forget I'm immortal. You cannot kill me." Her arrogant tone eerily reminded me of the Grievling. I glanced around, half expecting to see his creepy eyes watching from the shadows, *I am the shadow and darkness eternal. You cannot kill me.* There was something proudly disturbing about that parallel I couldn't decipher. Slim fingers drummed the armrest of her icy throne before clenching the end of it as she watched us approach. I couldn't tell if it was fear I saw on her face or just the bitterness of anticipation. Her face didn't change. Her posture didn't either. Only a stop motion of her hands betrayed any emotion at all. Any fear of losing control.

She never actually thought we'd make it this far. I could see it in the incredulous look she gave us between her rage.

"Not yet. But what do you think will happen once you take Lark's life? Once the curse breaks?" Aquarius's smile widened into a sneer. "You're finished, Scorpio. Your reign ends now." The Barbaric Queen's gaze dropped down to me again as she rose to her feet, summoning weapons of black magic. Just black magic or were they black marked blades? Lennox came unbidden to my mind, her wounds, her blood stoking the fury within me.

"Yes, little curse. The time has come for you to do your service to your court. You die today." Scorpio ignored the Air Queen, her full attention rapt on me. Locke growled, his hand going back to his sword. "And as for the rest of you, good luck fighting me and living."

"I don't fear you. Nor do I fear death," I said, not bothering to hide the savage edge to my voice. A lie carefully concealed by my wrath. I wiped the blood and sweat from my face as I rose to meet Scorpio's challenge, my gaze barreling into hers. "Because when you throw me beyond the veil, I'll have a hand in dragging you with me. Your reign is over, Scorpio. This is your last chance to surrender. To be granted mercy."

"Mercy?" Her voice was barely more than a scratchy whisper steeped in ironic amusement. "Mercy? You'll give me no mercy, just as you'll receive none from me for dragging this out." Her voice broke, and for a moment, I saw a glimpse of the fractured faerie that lay beneath. The Scorpio before her soul shattered. The Scorpio before she became the cursed Barbaric Queen. But then her eyes narrowed on me, losing the glassiness of raw emotion. "I just want to be free," she growled, looking wildly at me, giving rise to the image of a feral, cornered beast. "This curse, this pain... I've suffered enough." Her voice dropped as she appraised me again, her tone moving to mock, "You really do think yourself a hero." Scorpio's bitter tone faded into a chuckle. "Don't make me laugh."

But she had the good sense to look a bit unnerved as she sized me up. Her eyes darted around her seeing, as if for the first time, how much the odds were currently stacked against her. Even from here you could hear the sounds of battle fading. There would be no help from them. Once the curse ended and she finally got what she was so desperate for, there was no chance of her escaping. Locke pressed close to me, his blade a casual warning between us and her; the line she was about to cross was one she couldn't come back from. She could either surrender and do this on our terms peacefully, where mercy would be granted, or she could fight it out and lose painfully.

She would likely not survive either. I saw the fight refuse to leave her, and I knew what that meant. It was a feral look I had worn so many times before. She would go down, but she would go down swinging and taking as many of my friends as she could. I narrowed my eyes. I would allow no such thing.

"Many would attest that you haven't suffered nearly enough for your sins," Locke hissed through his clenched jaw. "Present company included."

I knew what he was thinking. His family. Pisces may have been the one to do it, but she let him. She'd killed Lennox, the memory of that atrocity pumped hate and adrenaline through my veins. She and Pisces were the reason for my father's death. My imminent death. And so many others. So many fae were without their loved ones. Because of her. As many fae as Locke saved by bringing them to Port Azure, the Crowned Assassin had his hands tied in innocent blood far too many more times, leaving even more mental wounds on him. Wounds that may never heal. Indeed, her list of crimes was long.

"We can't have too much interference. Let me set the chessboard of your demise," Scorpio said, raising her right hand towards us, her Water Magic runes on her arms glowing blue under her armor. "A Queen and three knights!" A shriek that was far too swift, forced me to turn to see Aspen, Vanneck, and Lenore turning to ice before our eyes. I placed my hands on them, trying to wrench Scorpio's control over the magic, trying to stop the spread. It was no use. Locke and I tried, but Scorpio was Queen for a reason. She was the most powerful Zodiac in the Court. Her Water Magic would not be thwarted.

Aspen's stare was soft as he looked at me. I panicked, desperate to stop the ice from rising further up him. I remembered the statues in the highest tower, how they couldn't even breathe. Frozen in time. But Aspen looked calm, his eyes on mine. Just before his face froze, he said, "It's okay. I'm so proud of you, Little Bird. Go save us all."

Lenore dropped her axe before it froze with her, her gaze never leaving me. "In case you need it. Make it hurt," she said, echoing her twin sister's dying sentiment, bringing tears to my eyes.

"It's been... my honor." Vanneck's last breath turned visible in the air. In a blink, they were all frozen statues. Three of my best friends.

"Unfreeze them!" I cried, rounding on the now laughing water queen, daggers in hand. "Your fight is with me. Let them go!"

"Such treachery!" Aquarius snarled, shaking off the ice. "As if that would work on me. I am a Queen. You cannot thwart me so easily."

"I was hoping you'd say that. What I have in mind for you is so much more entertaining. You think, Air Queen, that you can waltz into my Court uninvited and lay siege to my armies? Bring death to my subjects? You won't be killed. Not yet. I have something much more exciting in store for you," Scorpio said in a tone that sent a shiver down my spine and forced me to peel my eyes from my frozen friends to look at her. "As for you, Curse, I don't want any interference. Consider it my way of hedging my bets. You've cheated me out of peace for far too long now. I will fight how I see fit."

Aquarius and Locke pressed closer to me.

Scorpio's eyes widened in contrast to mine, focusing on somewhere behind me and sparked with wicked glee. A glance between Locke and I showed me that he saw it too. It was the only warning before a familiar voice purred behind us all.

"It's rude to start the party before everyone arrives."

Chapter Fifty-Five

A snap of Scorpio's fingers sent a league of elite Crownguards pouring into the throne room, looking especially bloodthirsty. This many elite would be a challenge for any Zodiac. Aquarius ground her teeth and readied herself, swinging her bone scythe in preparation.

I knew better than to look behind me. Locke's turn was a blur with his Zodiac speed until we were both facing an adversary. He faced Pisces at my back, while I kept my gaze fixed solely on the Barbaric Queen in front of me. We stood side to side, watching each other's back. The way it'd always been with us, even if I were late to noticing.

"Why aren't you dead?" Locke's snarl echoed the room, blending seamlessly with Pisces's laughter. Locke's sword drifted protectively closer to me, a gesture that made my heart ache. His protection won't matter much longer. "I killed you earlier."

Pisces scoffed derisively. I shivered as I felt the black magic cool the air. I didn't have to turn to see that he'd summoned a weapon of his own. It was okay that Aquarius was busy at the moment. I had no doubt she could take care of herself. This fight was ours and ours alone. Scorpio rose to her feet and descended her throne of ice. I watched her every step on the glittering frosty stairs, gripping my daggers in a vice like, white knuckling grasp. This was it. The moment that had been haunting the edges of my nightmares for weeks.

"Did you?" Pisces noncommittal voice sounded behind me. I heard Locke gasp, and I forced my eyes to remain on the red-haired Queen before me as she descended the steps of her throne. "I guess I'm like a cat. Nine lives and all," Pisces retorted. I felt my face shift into a sneer at his tone. It wouldn't surprise me if Locke had killed a doppelgänger, if Pisces somehow found a way to mask the black wisps that escaped wounds.

"Pisces. I'd say it's good to see you, but I'm not much for lying," I spat, still not turning to look at him.

"Oh. Now that hurts, Lark. I always thought we had such fun together. You could lie a little bit, you know."

"Any last words?" Scorpio asked drawing her blade. The moment I'd been born for was upon me. The cold of her black magic couldn't touch me now, not with my anger, my flames fueling me.

Let the flames fuel you, but don't let them consume you.

This. This was what Locke had meant. *Don't be blinded by your hatred.* I saw it so clearly now, as clearly as I saw my own earlier response—I was the fire. I was the flames Scorpio stared down as they got closer to block her escape. And deep down, she knew that. That was why she didn't fight in the war. Why she'd used the hydra. That was why she didn't care how many lives were lost on either side of the battle. It was why she hesitates now, why she's stalling. On some level, she knew she was tied to the pyre and the stage was set to watch her burn in my flames.

I risked a glance up at Locke. And another at my friends. Every emotion I'd been holding off the edge of my mind hit me like a tidal wave then. Fear. Despair. Dread. A sorrow so profound my lungs stopped working under the crushing weight of it for a beat. Locke looked over at me, the same feelings echoing through his expression, now softer as he regarded me. Every ounce of love, of longing, of a life together we might not get to live, was written there in a perfect picture of devastation.

"I love you. This side and the other." His words echoed in my heart, settling there. A glimmer of hope amongst the madness. I fiercely wished I could hold him one more time. Kiss him one more time. I opened my mouth to return his promise. To tell him I loved him, here and on any other plane. In any lifetime.

I never got the chance.

Pisces laughed as he lunged at Locke in the next breath. an impossibly short time later steel clashed against steel next to my head, making me jump—an opening that was nothing more than a beckoning invitation for Scorpio and her daggers, her position twinning my own. I countered her first attack, the jagged looking dagger that made me swallow hard, and staggered to dodge her second oncoming blade.

Scorpio fought fluidly. If I'd thought Aspen or Locke looked like they were dancing when they fought, the held nothing on the grace of Scorpio's movements. She backed off a moment, assessing my abilities, looking so much like a predator toying with its prey. Previously, she looked cornered. Cornered no longer was this beast as she smirked at me.

"At long last," she whispered, eying me. "The curse will die with you. I'll be free."

"Fuck the veil, I get it. You want me dead. Do you have an original thought at all?"

Her glare deepened, her upper lip curling back into a snarl as my own smile appeared hand in hand with a dare. This was it. The moment the fabric of fate had woven for me. I clutched my blades loosely, relaxing into my epiphany with a strange sense of calm. The cold of the shadow magic she employed could no longer reach me. Not with my anger, my flames around me.

I was the fire.

"When you die, I'll be the reason for it, Scorpio. You can be certain of that."

Scorpio made a sound somewhere between a growl and a scream of fury as she lashed out with a speed and precision my training had barely prepared me for. I only just parried the blow in time. Aspen would be proud. I wasn't going to be able to counter her second dagger as it came for my open midsection. I reached out with my magic and pushed.

A massive influx of wind pushed her backwards enough the her dagger just caressed my open midsection rather than skewering it. I gasped at the fiery pain and choked on it. My hand fell away from my abdomen. It was stained red. Scorpio smiled widely.

There was something odd about fighting while knowing what the outcome would be. My instincts didn't know what my brain did, and they continued to fight for survival. But I knew. I knew what was about to happen. I just had to make sure my death was something I could be revived from. I had to disarm her. Exhaust her. I had to make it easier for Locke to take her down. I wasn't sure how the curse worked. If I wounded her mortally now, and the curse lifted, would she be healed or would she die alongside me? I grinned as I dodged her next attack and swiped at her with my own blade. Black magic coiled around her before swarming me. It was awful and cold, and choked the very air from my lungs. Not yet. I couldn't go yet.

I opened my mouth to scream but no sound came as I wrenched fire from deep within my soul and sent it at her, effectively breaking her hold on me. Air rushed into my lungs and a breathed deeply and gratefully. But I wasn't granted much of a reprieve. A barrage of tiny icy spears was flung at me, glinting their sharpness in the light. I shrieked as they hit me. I covered my head and open midsection as best as I could with what remained of my dragon scale armor, but its protection was minimal with my limited reach. Precious few were blocked, by the telltale sound of ice tinkling off my armor. I felt the impact of each one. Lacerations opened themselves along my head, where my armored arms couldn't cover. I saw her pounce towards me as the ice cleared from view.

I leapt back to give myself some time, bringing my blade between us but she stayed on me, a wild cat with a very feline grin savagely on her prey. I rattled the well of my magic, finding it almost empty. But each of her attacks opened a new wound. I couldn't overthink this. I blew her backwards again with air, the very last remnants of my magic. It bought me precious seconds to rebalance to face her head on. We traded blow or mighty blow. Even with my magic gone, magic reverberated off our clashing blades with each strike. I moved onto the offensive, hacking and slashing and forcing her to move her feet. In a moment I caught her off balance, I slashed my blade sending one of her curved blades flying and clattering far away.

"Now for the other one," I said as much to myself as to her, charging again. She pirouetted away gracefully avoiding my attack, and countered with a vicious one of her own. One I couldn't parry in time. I gasped as her blade slashed at my armor. Pain erupted as the blade dragged across my earlier wound, but the armor held. Not only did the armor hold; the dragon scale armor shattered her second blade. I couldn't believe my luck and sent up a silent prayer to the goddess. But I didn't miss the way blood welled and poured from my wound again, making my knees weak. I wasn't going to last too much longer.

In a blur of movement, she was on me, unarmed.

But it didn't matter.□

I shoved both of my blades in between her ribs, listening to her scream. I knew she wouldn't die. Not yet. But it felt good to make it hurt. No sooner had I skewered her, than she retreated with a haze of black mist pouring from her wounds. From a safe distance, she pulled them both out with a deeply disturbing smile.

"You won't be needing these. And neither will I." She tossed them, the metal clattering against the stone too far away for me to hope to regain them. Scorpio's smile grew and her palms twitched, as if she were already wringing my neck in her mind. "I like the idea of killing you with my bare hands. It's so much more personal, you see. And make no mistake, Curse, this is personal now."

Scorpio rushed me, her speed making her a blur. Her fist connected with my face, sending me back a step before I could even bring my hands up to defend myself. A few steps away one moment, on me in the next blink. I grinned, wiping blood from my face. Hand to hand combat. Aspen told me it was important, yet all I wanted was a sword. I ducked under her next punch, her fist glazed over with hard, frosty ice protruding from her knuckles. One hit from those and my face would look like ground meat. As her fist sailed over my head, I grasped her arm and used her momentum to throw her over my head, forcing her back hard into the ground. Before I could pin her there, she was up and on top of me.

I saw the hit before it landed on my cheek. A blow I could do nothing to escape. And when her icy, jagged knuckles ripped the flesh of my cheek open, the wound stung with a blazing fire. I didn't even have time to scream in pain before the next blow opened up my other cheek, blood pouring from the wounds. I gagged on the feeling of blood meeting the air. Scorpio mimicked the move I did to put her on her back, but this time I didn't get up. She smirked down at me, pausing her assault to admire her victory before kneeling over my broken body. Her hands were freezing cold as they dug into the tender flesh of my throat.

From somewhere I heard Locke screaming in agony. My name. He was screaming for me.

"Lark!" he shouted again between the sounds of clashing swords and the wet sound of blood hitting the marble floor. "Whatever you do, don't give up!"

Give up? My hands clawed weakly at Scorpio's of their own volition. Blackness was rimming my eyesight as it was, though my body remained desperate, relying purely on instinct. My hands clawed at hers, weakly protesting, to no avail. I searched for my magic on instinct and panic spiked as I felt the dull tug of where my magic had yet to regenerate, my body thrashing and bucking to try to get her off of me. She grinned at me.

"Long live the Queen," she murmured low in her throat to me as my heartbeat staggered.

Her hands were hard and unyielding as they wrenched the very life from me. My lungs screamed. And I knew this was it. It had to be. I could feel the rot of the curse pulsing through me as if in excitement and confirmation.

My vision blurred further as my thrashing heart began to slow. My limbs felt weighted as I struggled, not even to free myself for her vicious hold on me, but to see Locke. Teeth bared, he fought to reach me—abandoning Pisces, our plan, entirely, his sword swinging savagely at his opponent that stayed stubbornly between us. Not once did he even flinch as Pisces's blade scored his body, leaving bloody trails in its wake. Pisces laughed, an echo of a sound reaching my failing ears as he kept himself between us. I knew Aquarius was finishing the last few Crownguards. She would just need the right moment afforded to her.

I watched Locke in a haze, taking in his beauty for what I knew would be the last time. I no longer felt Scorpio's fingers pressing into the tender flesh of my throat, but instead I felt the softness of Locke's lips against mine, that spark that each kiss sent through me. I could feel the silkiness of his hair as I ran my fingers through those raven strands, even as my limbs were too weak now to move. I could feel the heat of his body against mine, wrapping me in his loving embrace.

My heart staggered, each beat weaker than the last. My lungs burned for air, but I could no longer draw breath even if I'd wanted to. Sweat and blood covered his face as he continued to fight to get to me, but we both knew it was too late. My lips opened I locked eyes with him.

This side or the other, I so desperately wanted to say. But my promise would go unspoken.

Time seemed to stand still as my heart finally faltered. As if he felt it too, Locke's eyes remained on mine—blue pools of raw emotion—as Pisces kept himself between Locke and me with a sneering laugh. Locke fought so hard—the picture of darkness and valiance. But he would get here too late. I smiled, or tried to. To let him know it was okay. I memorized every detail of him as my own vision turned black, forever painting his image on the inside of my eyelids, despite the growing darkness.

I felt myself grow lighter and lighter, fading away from the life I'd grown to love. Funny. It wasn't that long ago I'd tried to willingly leave this life, and here I was now, mourning my losing it.

Locke's voice was the last thing I heard, screaming my name with a heart wrenching agony that cleaved the very air in half.

And then there was nothing at all.

Chapter Fifty-Six

When I woke, I had the disorienting sensation of feeling weightless. I was every-where and nowhere. A blank void created by shadow itself. To my right, a shimmering waterfall of light lit the space, the most spectacular thing I've ever seen. Glimpsing into the water, I saw it. My throat closed on a sob as I stared into the water's reflection. Memories cascaded by me: me as a child, on my father's shoulders. Meeting Locke for the first time. Father, Eldan, and I playing cards well into the evening hour by the fire. Dinner with the Knights of Port Azure. I stopped seeing them then, the blurriness from my tears making it too hard to focus on any one memory now. A chasm opened in my chest where my heart should be.

I was dead.

Worse, I was caught between the life I was desperate to return to and the absolution and peace of death. There was no other explanation for what I was seeing. I could only hope that Aquarius could revive me still. I stayed next to the water, refusing to move further into the shadows. Where the Grievling may have been watching.

The hairs on the back of my neck stood on end. I wasn't alone.

I spun, my hands going for my daggers, my stomach dropping when they found nothing but air, but I was not greeted by the sight of the Grievling. Nor the Goddess. Instead, the woman before me was one I'd never met in person, but I'd seen her picture enough times to know her face. A woman buried outside of Poplar Hollow in the grove of Larkspur. A woman whose bright blonde hair I'd inherited.

My mother.

I didn't know whether to move and launch myself into her arms or remain aloof, but the decision was made for me when she rushed forward to embrace me. I could hear the sniffle of her tears, which furthered my own as her arms held me tightly.

The shimmering waterfall of memories lit up her form. Her green eyes sparkled with emotion as her hands cupped my face.

"Lark... my darling girl. You are every bit as beautiful as I imagined you'd be. And far stronger than I ever hoped. I couldn't be prouder of you."

"Mother... Is it really you?" My mother's face wore a sad, loving smile like an accessory; she somehow seemed more beautiful, more herself. The mother I'd never had a chance to know, the mother I'd always wondered what she'd think of me, now stood in front of me with tears in her eyes.

"Yes. We're within the veil itself, and if you'll forgive me, I couldn't wait to meet you. And there are two others who were anxious to see you as well." My mother glanced behind her. To where two familiar faces waited. Faces that had me sinking to my knees and tears falling down my face.

My father. And Lennox.

They all joined me there on the ground, our tears collecting between us.

"Father," I cried, "I'm so sorry. My last words to you. I didn't mean them. I'm so sorry. Please forgive me." His familiar soothing circles on my back began as he hushed me in that calm voice of his.

"Stop that line of thinking now," came his gentle admonishment. "You were right to be angry. Anyone would have been. There is nothing to forgive." I let myself just be small, be held by my father, and I embraced him in turn. All the rage, all the vengeance, disappeared. He even smelled the same way I remembered, and my sobs came harder. And I turned to look at Lennox, smiling at me.

"And you," I choked out. "You should never have given your life to defend me. What the hell were you thinking?" Lennox smiled, her hand reaching for mine.

"I was thinking that one of my best friends was in trouble. And she was doing her best to save us." She gave me a pointed look. "I love you. I don't regret it, Lark. Don't look at me like that."

"Like what?"

"Like you're heartbroken. I made my choice, and I stand by it. It helped get you to where you needed to be. It wasn't a choice I made solely for you. The hope of the Water Court rested on you surviving long enough to face Scorpio down. I wasn't just saving you. I was saving the Court. I'm proud of that."

"Lenore misses you," I told her. Her face fell.

"My one regret. I miss her too. Missing your twin is like missing half of your soul." The other half of my soul was still living too. Why wasn't I back on the other side of the veil yet? Locke...

It hit me then, hard enough it reminded me of the hydra attack. Locke and I were now separated by death. I glared now at the waterfall of memory with disdain. Rising to my feet, I walked over to it.

"What if we can come back?" I plunged my hands into the waterfall, withdrawing immediately as sparks ignited and pain exploded along the connection. I inspected my hands, surprised to see burn marks. Lennox's hand came to my right shoulder, my father's to my left.

"You can't break the veil, my girl," my mother said sadly. "Otherwise, don't you think we would have made it back to you by now?" It was much more melodic than I would have ever thought. And also sad. It was then that I realized that the wall—the veil itself—wasn't opaque. It was translucent. And like looking through murky water, looking passed the memories on the surface of the water, I saw Locke's face as he screamed my name. I called out his name, desperate for him to hear me. To know I was still with him.

On this side, or the other.

I damn well wanted it to be that side.

With a scream of rage, and desperation and longing I poured my magic into the veil. Fire, wind, water, and thorns attacked the veil in a brutality I'd never unleashed before. It sparked along where my magic collided with it, igniting a heat that made me wince and squint my eyes against. I turned my face away, my eyeballs feeling like they were melting. I continued to pour everything I had, my very essence, into the veil. *You will break,* I commanded. With one final surge, I screamed as I fought against my power draining. *Break!*

Blinding light filled the space, forcing me to shut my eyes against it. I backed up, my power failing.

When after what felt like an eternity, the light faded at last. I blinked at the veil, searching for any change. But there was nothing. No sign that the veil was disrupted. My desperation and hope gave way to the horrible truth. I was the most powerful faerie to walk Meridian. And not even I could break the veil that separated the living and the dead. All my hope now lie with Aquarius. I fell to my knees, unable to stop the sobbing. *Locke...*

We didn't have enough time. We were soulmates, Goddess damn it! We were soulmates... That had to count for something, didn't it? After everything—

My thoughts were cut off when a pair of arms wrapped around me. my mother smoothed my hair and ran her long nails slowly over my scalp.

"My darling, I'm so sorry," she whispered. "I wish we could meet under better circumstances. You can't destroy the veil. It was placed there by the Goddess herself. Even you aren't that powerful. Believe me, I tried. I tried every day, knowing you'd been born and I'd never even gotten to hold you. I clawed at the veil for days, weeks even, just for a glimpse of you. My hands were almost black from the burns, but I didn't care." Her grip tightened at those words, and it dawned on me. All those years I didn't have a mother and I had her here right now. For the first time, I had a complete family. Lennox may not have been my sister by blood, but she may as well have been. I looked at them, smiling through my tears, while simultaneously mourning the life I didn't want to leave behind.

"Lark, it's time," my father said to me. I felt my face contort at that, but my pulse spiked. That look on his face was nothing short of ominous.

"Time for what?"

"For us to go," my mother prodded gently.

"Do you have to go so soon? I'm still waiting." Everyone's face turned to that of quiet pity. And I knew. I knew deep in my soul that something was wrong.

"You're dead, my love." My mother said patiently. "You can't return to the land of the living. What's done is done."

I proceeded to tell them the plan, glancing at Lennox to back me up. But she remained stoically silent as the tears began forming and the sob built in my throat once more. The tears of a destroyed hope were worse than any other because it relied on so many ends of emotion—the uttermost end of sorrow and despair. Of soul-shattering heartbreak.

"We have a plan..." I choked out. I felt frozen. Locke...

If the plan had failed... If we had failed....

I fell to my knees, tears streaming down my face. I knew this was a possibility, but I truly never believed it. I never believed we'd get to this point.

The point where I was truly dead. And I had absolutely no way back.

We'd failed. □

My soul fractured in that exact moment. The moment where hope was lost. An agonized sob wrenched from my throat, but I would not be moved. Not yet.

Even though it was useless to stay here.

I couldn't leave him. Not yet.

Even for Lennox. Even for my family. I would not move, no matter how much they cast their pitying stares at me. No matter how much they cried for me.

I refused.

Chapter Fifty-Seven

Locke

She's dead.

Lark's heart stopped. I stopped with it. Movement. Understanding. Logic. The thought was more unbearable than the curse fracturing from within me, more than anything I'd suffered in my long life so far.

She's dead. She's dead. She's dead...

The thought sounded like an alarm reverberating off the very walls of my soul over and over and over again. The only sound, the only thought. It was desperate. It was agony. It was deafening.

My only solace came from watching Aquarius leap to Lark's side after dispatching the final Crownguard in her way. The tiniest spark of hope ignited. We all knew this part was coming, I tried to remind myself. But nothing could ever prepare me to see Lark's eyes, half lidded and dulled in death. Instead of the vibrant spring green so full of life and love, they looked almost a dull, colorless grey.

She's dead. She's dead. She's dead...

There was a clatter—a sound that echoed through the great hall. The sharp ring of metal meeting stone. A wide-eyed glance from me was all it took to confirm Scorpio falling to her knees in agony, my own knees buckling under the weight of the shattering curses, her blood crown falling to the floor along with her reign—shattered.

I was aware of Scorpio screaming. She doubled over near Lark's body, as I did, from the force of the curse breaking. I could feel it shatter within me. Funny, I always thought it would just evaporate like dew in a late summer morning. Not leave me feeling hollow as it scraped at my insides in a last-ditch effort to kill me. I glanced down, not surprised to see blood pooling underneath me from my injuries. On my arms, my runes born of shadow glowed, the black light visible under my arm gauntlets. The same was happening to Scorpio, her runes glowing black along her arms as she cried out in agony.

I screamed as the pain intensified and fought back retching, but I refused to take my eyes off Lark, Aquarius, and the scene before me. Even as I was forced to my knees, I watched numbly as the Air Queen placed her hand over Lark's heart with a cautious look to me. Pray, she mouthed to me. And I did. For the first time in so long, I prayed to the Goddess. *Anything*, I told her. *I'll do anything if you bring Lark back to me.*

Static filled the air, making my hair stand on end, the only precursor for the first jolt of lightning. Lark's body bowed upward from the force, her heart fluttering lighter than a butterfly's wings before ultimately falling silent. Aquarius primed herself to try again while I watched on helplessly pleading for Lark to wake up. A second strike entered Lark's body with a similar result, making my heart sink into my gut. Lark had given no response.

She's dead. She's dead. She's dead...

It wasn't supposed to happen this way. She was supposed to wake up. Why wasn't she waking up? Her biggest fear was dying alone. I had completely failed her.

I couldn't even bring myself to care as Pisces laughed at my obvious torment from his place on the ground behind me. I heard him choke on his own blood, stoking the fires of my vengeance.

"That's your play?" he snickered before snorting in derision, his laugh sounding far more wet than it should've, which under normal circumstances would've brought me immense satisfaction. He limped over to where I lay before falling to his own knees in ruin. But watching Lark with my heart wrapped up in chaotic emotion, I couldn't feel anything for him. It was all for her. Everything about me was for her. "Your plan had an awful lot of holes. I thought you were smarter than that. For example, why would you rely on someone else's magic when they could just... perish?"

I sensed the movement rather than seeing it. Pisces drained the room of shadows for a single moment, drawing them into himself, crudely knitting together his weeping wounds. He was horrific, shadow stitching his wounds together until he looked like a grotesque patchwork version of himself. He was using the shadows to hold his body together, though how he held to life, I had no idea. I wondered if the Grievling were fucking with me all over again. I growled at him. He just wouldn't stay down. I hauled myself to my feet, lacking all the coordination I'd had only moments ago. Gripping my sword, I turned to fight him, keeping my lurching body between Aquarius and Lark and him. Too late.

Pisces exploded in a way I didn't think his destroyed body could muster. With all his rage and pain, he sent cascades of black magic sickles in every direction. I launched myself in their path, desperate to keep them from finding purchase in their goal. Several lodged painfully in my abdomen, the force from their proximity obliterating what was left of my armor. But a gurgling semblance of a scream filled my ears, blocking everything else out. I turned, my eyes widening at the sickle lodged in the Air Queen's throat, the light dying in her eyes and her lightning dying from her hands. Lark's heart fluttered and went still once more.

"Remember how you failed Wisty? Live knowing you failed Lark too," Pisces spat. His words echoed off of me. For a moment, nobody and nothing moved. There was no sound. Time itself seemed to stop.

No. *No...*

It couldn't end this way.

Aquarius fell to the ground silently next to Lark, blood pooling under them both. I screamed then. I'd failed. I'd failed both of the fae I'd ever loved, the latter being my soulmate. I glanced down at my leaking wounds, the pain now failing to register in my hateful focus. My vision blurred and it took more concentration than it should have to bring Pisces back into frame. I glared at him as I rose to my feet. I wouldn't die yet. Not until I avenged her death. I would finish what I'd started.

And then I would join her on the other side of the veil.

I said I would love her on either plane, and I'd meant it. If that meant I had to join her on that one, then so be it.

I screamed a semblance of Lark's name as I detonated. There was only anger. Rage. Pain. Sorrow. All of them equally all consuming. All the magic, including shadow magic that had yet to leave me, burst out of me and centered on the faerie I hated most in that moment: Pisces. What remained of my black magic fused seamlessly with my Water Magic, creating an inescapable chasm. A deadly vortex, the likeness I'd never before seen. Something Pisces wouldn't be able to cheat his way out of. Not this time. My maelstrom of magic absorbed all the light in the room. It was impossible to see Pisces on the other side, whose growing fear I saw from where he stood, forced to watch as his fate approached him in violent swaths of black and blue. A horrid, feral smirk graced my features when I felt his presence meet my magic, widening when I heard the scream of anguish that followed. Yes, Pisces was at last going to get what he deserved. And when I was done, there would be nothing left but scraps. He wouldn't be able to stitch himself back together with shadows, because there wouldn't be enough of him left to try.

With the final notes of Pisces's scream drifting into nothingness, with the last of my magic fading from view, I turned around, taking in the scene before me. Aquarius's blood had soaked the ground next to where Lark lay motionless. Her heart far too quiet.

But what caught my attention was that Scorpio wasn't trying to escape. She was on her knees where she'd fallen. She'd turned in on herself, as if she might implode at any moment. She flickered her green eyes to me. They were actually green again, like they were when we'd first met. There was no more black ringing her eyes, clear of the shadow magic's influence for the first time in years.

And she was sobbing.

Fat tears rolled down her cheeks silently, though I could see the occasional sob wrack her body. I unfocused my vision to take in her emotions—guilt. Sorrow. Hot shame. Repulsion. Regret. Horror. All so strong it was a wonder she didn't collapse further under the weight of them.

As it stood, I approached where she knelt, my sword in hand, thirsty for her blood. For revenge. For years she forced me to play a part I didn't want to play. For years she forced me to kill. To threaten. To torture. She dangled my family in front of me and killed them. She'd turned me into a weapon. No. Worse than that. She'd turned me into a nightmare. I cruelly loved that I'd become her nightmare, come home to roost. And I was bringing the very wrath of the of those beyond the veil with me.

"Here we are at long last," I bit out through a clenched jaw, narrowing my gaze on her in a vicious sneer. She swallowed tightly but didn't otherwise respond. If she had any idea what was coming for her, she didn't show it. She scrambled to her feet in a flurry of movement.

"Cancer... Locke—"

I cut her off as she stumbled backwards, her foot catching on the icy steps to her throne. How fitting that this would be where she'd die.

"With all you have done. With all you've forced me to do. All the innocent blood you forced me to spill." I laughed without amusement as I took two languid steps forward, ignoring the pain in my bleeding abdomen, flourishing my blade. I made a show of it, as I bore into her from under my brow. Her blood would be the last blood I would spill in this war. And in this life. Her eyes tracked the movement. "The lives of my family. The life of my soulmate. And countless innocent lives snuffed out because of you. Is it not fitting that I end you here and now? Only nothing is forcing me. You chose this path. And I am only too happy to be the wings of consequence."

I felt the weight of those I'd been forced to kill on my shoulders every single day. I remembered names, faces, details I could never erase. But in this moment, instead of feeling weighed down by the heavy guilt, I felt each one propel me forward. As if the souls of everyone I'd been powerless to save fought alongside me with the same goal: revenge. Bring Scorpio down for good. Today, I made peace with those ghosts I couldn't save. I was done being haunted by them.

I had killed so many, the blood would never come clean from my hands. But as I looked over Scorpio, still far too close to Lark's crumpled frame for my liking, as I eyed the bruises forming over my soulmate's throat, as I remembered how I felt finding out that my parents had been dead for years, after they'd been dangled over me, I knew this death I would never regret. Not in this life or the next. This blood may not undo the bloodshed I was forced to do, but I would reap her payment nonetheless. Even better if it killed me to do it. I felt my smirk widen to expose my canines.

Let the rampage begin.

Chapter Fifty-Eight
Locke

I threw myself into the fight. Scorpio only barely leapt out of the way of my blade as it came crashing towards her head and embedded itself into the ice staircase. I wrenched my weapon, but it was stuck fast. As I thawed the ice around the steel, freeing it, I heard her scream my name, her voiced laced with fear and something else. Desperation. And regret. Good. She should regret what she'd done. But she wouldn't get out of paying. I fell on her like a rabid beast, with a blitz of blindingly fast strikes. She parried some but not all and fell away breathless, with a few gashes that dripped crimson. Funny how knowing I'd die here made the pain more bearable. I'd hardly been able to stand a few minutes ago, and now I was launching a one-fae war.

"Don't I get any last words?" she huffed, her tears still falling, mixing with the bloody cut on her cheek, giving her the garish appearance of crying blood on one side. Her red hair plastered to her forehead.

"I don't think anyone is interested in anything you have to say." Out of reflex more than conscious thought, I reached for my black magic. I felt a dry tug where it used to dwell. Shadows sluggishly came to answer my call, but not as powerful as they'd been. I'd forgotten the curse was broken. I was using what remained of the black magic. I eyed Scorpio's fading runes and knew her shadows would be much the same. What was entrenched in our souls would take longer to leave us. When that was gone, I'd be free of it forever. Or I would be, if I planned on being around that long. I cringed inwardly at the now gaping wound in my abdomen. I had to finish this fight quickly.

"Even if my last words could save your beloved?" she quipped. Time stopped. My hand stayed, mid strike.

"What did you say?" My voice was scarcely a whisper. She regarded me through her still spilling tears. The emotion in her aura was almost overwhelming. Crushing. Her guilt was tearing her to pieces.

"The last five years have been nothing but anguish. I'm not excusing what I did, so don't give me that look, Cancer. The other me, the shadow me... she did things. Horrible things. I always thought I'd get the chance to make up for it. I didn't always know what she'd done, but sometimes I'd wake up with blood on my hands. Sometimes literal. Sometimes figurative. Sometimes I'd just know something terrible happened even if I didn't remember. I buried my head in the sand, but now I remember everything. Everything!" She slowly got to her feet, throwing her weapons away. She released another sob before taking a slow, cleansing breath. "I want redemption. You want Lark back. I think I have a way to achieve both."

At my look of disbelief, she continued tearfully, "I have so much blood on my hands, Cancer. More than I ever wanted there to be. I can never take back or undo what I've done. And it's my fault. It's all my fault. I never wanted this. I just remember the pain... and the need to be free of it. Goddess, it never ended... But I know... I know I don't want to live like this either, with this crushing weight. It's somehow worse. I know what I deserve." She looked up at me then, tearfully and without fear. "I want Lark to take my place. To heal the land where I have scarred it. Let her be a better Scorpio than I was." Her words should have made me feel something. But all I felt was numb. On the other side of that dam was a host of anger that once it was gone, would destroy us both.

"Even if you did deserve redemption, how would you bring Lark back? You're no necromancer. That magic has been lost for eons."

"No, I'm not. But the Ari'inor library is home to books in more languages than you know. Many depicting spells that were outlawed for so long they've faded from almost all memory. Whole magic can be strong. And volatile. I only found them looking for a way to free myself of the curse."

"What are you about to do, Scorpio?"

She smiled. A real smile that against my better judgement made my heart ache for the friend she had once been.

"Go to her. And know that I'm sorry. I'm so sorry. And your friends will fully thaw the moment the spell is over."

I knelt down and cradled Lark's broken form in my lap. Tears prickled the backs of my eyes, stinging reminders not to hope for too much. But my heart and my head were completely at odds with one another as I observed Scorpio. She bent down to kiss Lark's forehead, and I fought not to draw my soulmate's body closer to me. I heard my own growl of warning before I even realized I was doing it. Ready to protect her, even in death.

Scorpio's voice rose over the relative, delicate silence. I watched, enraptured, as she began to speak in a language long forgotten. The old language. Magic flickered around us, making my fingertips tingle with static. This was old magic. Old, whole magic. Magic not bound to an element. Magic of the fae from millennia past, far before the times of the courts. I watched as the air around Scorpio glittered and misted, and for a moment, my heart sank. This wasn't a resurrection! It was an escape! I growled when her eyes slid to mine, and though her voice didn't reach my ears, I could read her lips. *Trust me.*

I wasn't sure how I could. I wasn't sure what force kept me holding Lark. Maybe because I knew I wanted to die beside her when Scorpio left. Maybe because I knew it was over.

The mist that enshrouded Scorpio glimmered and writhed like it was alive. Scorpio's voice, now stronger than ever, reverberated through the throne room, bouncing back and filling my ears with the ages-old, forgotten spell. And then she collapsed, her head thudding heavily on the stone and icy floor. Her eyes closed, a small smile gracing her lips. Not quite peace. But close. I felt for her emotions and found none. I blinked. I checked again. Nothing.

Scorpio, the Barbaric Queen, was dead.

The mist that enshrouded Scorpio moved gently on a nonexistent breeze, looking like a single cloud in the sky. It enshrouded Lark and wisps caught me as well.

"Let Lark's life heal the damage I've done." An echo of Scorpio's final wish sounded just as Lark's body began to glow. The glittering mist was absorbed by her, moment by moment, until nothing was left but my own ragged breathing ringing harshly in my ears.

I listened hard for any change, aside from the deep breaths of my friends as they thawed. I couldn't bring myself to care. I looked for any signs of life in my soulmate. I cupped her cheek, desperate for even the slightest change. Tears fell freely then, pouring down my cheeks as the long moments ticked by. She didn't move. I felt what little hope I'd accumulated turn to ash in my mouth. I pressed my forehead to hers as the realization came to crush me that she was, in fact, never coming home. My only solace was that I'd be there soon. I closed my eyes as I kissed her forehead, my tears running unchecked now.

Thump-thump.

My eyes shot open and I clutched Lark tighter to my chest. I dared a glance at Aspen, to shut down the hope before it sprung anew. But he also stared at Lark with hope blooming on his reddened face. And so did Lenore.

Thump-thump.

"Lark...?" I whispered her name, real fear clutching my heart with icy talons. I smoothed the hair out of her face and cupped her cheek. The mottled greyish purple bruises from the life being strangled from her were now gone. Her creamy skin was unblemished by death. Where her skin had been dulled by death, a rosy glow I'd come to love had graced her cheeks. Her heart faltered a moment—a moment mine also followed suit—before starting a regular, strong rhythm.

And then with a loud breath, her eyes slowly blinked open. And looked right at me. My own breath failed me, refusing to leave my lungs as I uttered her name.

Chapter Fifty-Nine

Lark

It was far too bright. I clenched my eyes shut against the intrusive light and the splitting headache it caused. I didn't understand. We'd failed. I was dead. I knew I was dead, but my surroundings didn't seem to agree with me. Especially not when I heard voices. Aspen, Lenore, Locke...

Locke...

I blinked against the harsh light. Time stretched, my eyes taking forever to adjust, but when they did, my heart sang. A pair of blue and golden eyes looked into mine from above in a potent mix of shock, trepidation, and disbelief, as if he couldn't quite believe what he saw. Blue eyes I knew too well. Blue eyes I'd sworn I'd never see again. Locke. I felt his arms cradling me against his chest. My momentary panic and confusion faded away into pure, unrestrained elation. Locke was here. Really here. He cried as he whispered my name. Leading me to wonder where we were.

"What side of the veil are we on?" I choked out, my voice raspy and odd feeling as I navigated how to use my previously ruined throat.

"You're alive, Lark." Locke's velvet voice rushed over me, stalling the panic trying to well up. It took only one glance up, but when my eyes focused and saw him above me, really saw him, and felt his arms cradling me as if I were as delicate as spun glass, I sobbed. "You're really back."

Sucking in a breath to pull myself together, I glanced around weakly. "Where is she? I brought her with me..." I cut off, the lump in my throat making speech impossible as I remembered. My fractured memory began filling in the blanks. Meeting my mother for the first time, reuniting with my father and Lennox. Introducing my first friend to my family. I had mourned being alive. I fought with everything I had to bring down the veil to get back here. What did it say about me if I now also mourned death?

I remembered fading, becoming transparent in mere seconds. There was no time for a goodbye to anybody. I remember grabbing her hands, unsure of what was happening. I glanced at my parents, unsure of what was going on, their faces as they called my name. I remembered calling for them before all fading to black.

"Who?" a voice asked from somewhere nearby. My heart picked up. Was I successful? Did Lennox come back with me? When Lenore's face slid into my view my gut plummeted. I tried not to show my heartbreak.

"Lennox," I rasped. "I saw her."

The stricken look on Lenore's face was enough to make me wish I hadn't mentioned her sister. Seeing the unmistakable sheen in her eyes, I reached out to her. Lenore's shoulders fell inward, her eyes downcast as she cringed away, unable to bear any contact in her misery.

"Is she okay?" She whispered the question, her composure as fragile as I'd ever seen it. I could only nod into the long seconds that passed. How could I tell Lenore her twin missed her desperately? That she mourned her life here with us?

"You—you died."

Locke's softer than shade voice reached me, with all the shattered pieces of him. My eyes misted over as I watched his soul cling to all its fragments. My hand drifted to his face, showing him wordlessly that I was here. Alive and tangible. His hand came up to clutch mine with a touch as gentle as a raven's wing, as if I might fall to pieces before him. He looked shell-shocked, like he thought I might be a ghost, ready to evaporate with his next breath. His grip on me was strong with fear.

"You were right." My whispered voice was small, frail as it thawed from death's clutches. "Apparently I'm so annoying, even death didn't want to keep me." Locke breathed out a relieved laugh and enveloped me in a crushing hug. I felt, rather than heard, the sob destroy his body as he crushed me close, which elicited another from me too. I was home. We'd made it. "This side or the other, I love you," I whispered. I felt Locke smile against my cheek.

"Let's try to keep both of us on this side a while, huh?"

"Can you help me up?" I flexed my muscles, evaluating my movement and control, testing each limb slowly. Each limb protested like old, rickety hinges, making me feel older than I was. But with each pass of each joint, my body warmed up and remembered its former self. Warmth returned to my skin, my fingers finally chasing away the last vestiges of the blue tinge that had overstayed its welcome. Aspen and Locke each took an arm and hoisted me to unsteady feet.

"Welcome back, little bird," Aspen's voice was little more than a croak. "Thought we lost you there."

"I'm here." My voice started to sound like me again, the last vestige of death to shake off. "We really won." "Fuck, you're okay. You're okay. Fucking Goddess, you're okay." He enveloped us both, smushing me between him and my soulmate. Aspen's and Locke's armor were horribly dinged, rough edges were biting into my flesh but I didn't care. I was alive. I was here to feel it. I hugged Aspen back fervently. Lenore and Vanneck rushed over, hurtling their arms around us too. At my grin, she glared at me.

"This is your freebie, Lark." Her relieved tone didn't line up with her usual snark. "I don't like hugs."

"Yeah, yeah. You'll kill me." A laugh tumbled out of me, "Newsflash, someone already tried that."

It was Vanneck that choked on a laugh at that. Locke silently tightened his hold on me. "That's poor taste." He admonished, his grin taking all credibility out of his tone.

"Where's Aquarius?" I swiveled my head around looking for her. The tension that immediately picked up, every face falling had me bracing myself. A stab of guilt struck me acutely in the chest.

We'd lost another one.

I was still surprised to follow the saddened gazes of my friends to see Aquarius's body behind Locke, a pool of blood beneath her. My hands flew to my mouth to keep from screaming. Or maybe crying. All that Aquarius had gone through, all she'd survived, just to die because of me?

Fuck this war. This wasn't fair.

I held her hand, now cool in death, and closed her eyes.

"Rest well, Queen Aquarius. May you meet the Goddess in kindness. Until we meet again." I almost couldn't force the final words out through my grief and guilt. "You were an exemplary Queen. One I don't think can ever be replaced, and for that I will carry this guilt with me forever. I'm so sorry, Aquarius, Queen of the Air Court. Rest knowing you avenged your kin and that you yourself have been avenged as well."

Chapter Sixty

That was how we were found by what remained of both armies; with the bodies of two Queens at our feet. Scorpio rested on a pillow of her vibrant red hair, her jaw slackened in death. It was the first time I saw her without her expression pinched by pain. She looked simply asleep, her eyes half lidded and the smallest fraction of a smile on her lips, leaving me deeply conflicted. The reasonable side of me was glad she was dead and gone, unable to hurt anyone else. One look at Locke, at all each of us had suffered at her behest, had me wanting to rip her back from wherever her wretched soul had ended up and kill her again. But it was hard not to notice the absence of black veining in her eyes. Even dimmed by the veil, her eyes were green once more. She died as herself. Whole once more.

Better than she deserved.

But still, the part of me that pitied her was grateful. She'd given herself to bring me back, leading to a confusion of emotion I wondered if I would ever entirely process. Anger held on like a petulant child, refusing to let go or be ignored. Always right there. Always in the foreground. But I couldn't deny that underneath that was gratitude. She saved me. As a way to help atone for what she'd done. As angry as I was, that couldn't be ignored.

That deed would be for others to judge individually.

My heart ached for Aquarius, the mighty lightning wielder of the Air Court. Fierce. Brave. Strong. Now gone. Her storm grey eyes would open no longer. Commotion from the massive doors snagged me from my reverie, drawing my gaze to our warriors pouring in with an excitement that was so potent you could taste it. One of our generals bowed before rushing to Aspen with a giant smile. He pointed outside, where I could hear a dull clamoring. "The war is won, my lord. The enemy awaits your retribution."

Scorpio's army had disintegrated. At the massive quaking that shook Loc Valen, they threw down their swords and spears in surrender, many following what an entire legion's worth of soldiers did after the hydra attack. Scorpio lost soldiers in more than one way with that stunt. Now they were forcibly filed into the courtyard of Castle Ari'inor, looking cold, exhausted, and bloodied. But most of all, afraid.

Of me.

They didn't know I wasn't here to hurt them. Goddess only knew what further propaganda the Kinship had fed them about the rebellion. About us. Locke and I approached the dais where each eye snapped to us with hostility and trepidation. That ends now.

"Queen Scorpio is dead," I hollered into the crowd, murmurs erupting from everywhere. Heads turned, lips moved, eyes stared with fraught anticipation. Some even elicited ghastly screams. Not that I could blame them. "The war is over. Water Court, esteemed Crownguards, your fight is over."

Locke's hand raised my own up, showing our united front. The last remaining Kinship member for the Water Court. Jurisdiction for what came next belonged solely to him for the moment.

"Peace is not designed through blood and death. Peace is forged in unity. And perseverance. And hope that springs eternal. That what's good can weather any storm," Locke's voice cut through the chatter, keeping my hand in his as he led me down the stairs to be level with every fae here, careful to take it slow as my body figured out the movements again. "Kinsmen, that storm has passed. I will never call myself your king, but you will accept Lark as your Queen."

My head had never spun faster. He kept his gaze steady on the crowd before us as a hush descended over everyone. I tried to not openly gawk, a task I found more difficult with each passing breath. What was he thinking?

"She hasn't done the rune trials!" Someone protested.

Locke's eyes flared, his head turning to the speaker. Though the shadows were now lost to him, his water magic was ever potent. The temperature decreased as he appraised him, appraised them all, reminding me of that moment with Tidas. With a voice sharp and unyielding and cold as a glacier he spoke again, "Lark fought in that battle. She killed the hydra. She died so the curses could be broken. She came back from the veil of death. She is why Scorpio is dead." He purposely danced around the details of what had transpired, I noticed. The details of Scorpio's demise. Was it out of spite? I couldn't say I blamed him entirely, but still Scorpio's last moments as herself shouldn't be only for us to know. She wanted redemption, something that required everyone knowing what happened in Ari'inor. "What Lark endured is far worse than any rune trial. I would know." I didn't miss the shadows that crossed his face. Nor did I miss the reverent tone his voice took before he continued speaking. "She is the most powerful fae in existence, and she has my every faith as Prince Cancer, the last remaining Water Kinship member left alive." He took a step back, not letting my hand go. "The queen we all deserve."

Taking my breath with him, he knelt before me, his head bowing. Murmurs passed beyond us to every fae in attendance as they decided whether or not to fall in line, or to fight again.

I thought I knew how long a second could last. I had felt my share of seconds masquerading as an eternity, but this was something else. I could only watch, my heart in my throat as every pair of eyes in the vicinity appraised me. Weighed me. Weighed my sins against those of my predecessor still lying dead in the throne room behind me. And then I watched as they all, fae by fae, row by row, took a knee before me.

"Hail Queen Scorpio," Locke said bringing his eyes up to me, my eyes widening when the response echoed thunderously across the court. I cringed inwardly. I wondered how long it would be before the name stopped evoking a defensive response. Locke's fingers squeezed mine, bringing me back to him silently. My eyes snapped back to his, looking for an answer in the madness. His eyes gazed up at me, unburdened for the first time. Reverent, worshipful love there plainly on his face as he gazed at me. "May she reign well."

Except it would never be that easy, would it?

Locke, being the only surviving anointed Zodiac Kinship member of the Court, ascended, however unwillingly, to the throne until the time I could be officially coronated. The Zodiac Guild showed up conveniently when all the mayhem had died down entirely. When the last of Scorpio's supporters, those who had refused and continued to oppose us, were taken to the dungeons to await their fate. By the look on Locke's face, it was exactly typical of them. Seven elders clad in black robes waded into the room, exuding power.

These fae were this powerful and still they did nothing. Nothing to help the fae that were dying. Nothing to turn the tides of fate. Nothing to stop Scorpio from destroying her court. Nothing.

I refused to hide my disdain as I approached the throne where Locke and the guild members stood with raised voices, especially as I remembered what the Grievling had said to us. That they either recruited great power to further their own ends, or they destroyed it.

"She doesn't need to complete the rune trials," Locke snarled at the one closest to us as I stepped up beside him. The tension crackling between them was electric. Palpable. Their impassive gazes gave nothing away, at least to me, but I had no doubt Locke could see through that impassivity with ease. Warmth in the room recoiled from Locke's anger, the potency of it. "She came back from death itself. We destroyed the previous Scorpio and Pisces. Lark brought about a new age. She's the most powerful fae to walk Meridian, possibly ever. If she's not in contention for the Kinship, then consider having her in your Guild," he said, sending fluttering concern around the room, the first real reaction anyone from the Guild had given him. He inclined his head in victory, knowing his words had landed.

"That won't be necessary," said a gravelly voice under the hood of his black robe. He held his hands out in appeasement to us both. "We took a council, and we have arrived at the same conclusion you have. We want no further discourse. We grant Lark the title of Queen Scorpio, and all that goes with it." At my surprised look, the one speaking—the leader with a face like sun-warped leather—smiled at me in the most unsettling way, bringing the Greivling's warning back to me, floating on a wisp of memory. "She will reign over the court she worked so hard to protect. But know this." He paused a moment to make sure we paid attention above the excitement. His tone was oddly grave, in direct opposition to the heart stopping news he'd just dropped. I barely heard his remaining warning through the ringing in my ears. Through my limbs feeling like they'd been strung too tight. I'd been processing the idea of being queen, of being Scorpio, but a part of me certainty never expected it to pass. "Immortality is as much a curse as black magic. You will eventually watch your loved ones die. You will have to put your crown above all others. Are you prepared to do so, Lark of Poplar Hollow?"

"I'm Lark of Port Azure," I said, standing tall, willing away the rushing in my ears. Willing away the shock. The fear. The indecision. I wasn't that person anymore. I couldn't afford to be. "And I am prepared."

I saw the uptick of his mouth even from within the recesses of his hood.

"A coronation will need to take place, before it's official, you understand." A sentence. Not a question. I nodded once again. "Then may we, the Zodiac Kinship, extend our congratulations, Scorpio, soon to be Queen. May she reign well," he finished. My stomach fluttered nervously at his words.

"May she reign well." Every voice of the Guild echoed before bowing their heads. All others, including Locke, lowered their heads in deference with one hand over their heart, before echoing the words as well.

May she reign well.

"Do you know what this means, love?" Locke asked me, the corners of his lips tilting up. His face showed relief like no other. The shadows that had followed him evaporated with his dark magic curse, leaving him looking lighter than I'd ever seen him.

"That sounds ominous. Dare I ask?"

"You'd better get used to parties. Because your coronation is going to be big."

Locke wasn't remotely kidding. After what had to be the largest pyre ceremony in recent memory, the city ran with sorrow and tears and flames and ashes. The dead were sent to the Goddess in kindness, regardless of which side they fought on. This was Locke's first decree as an acting King, as I wasn't coronated yet. A command I fully supported. The stacks of pyres were larger than I'd ever thought possible, reaching heights that rivalled the treetops. And far too many. My eyes streamed as Locke gave the final address, and all of us had a hand in lighting the pyres. Walls of fae holding torches sent our fallen to the Goddess in kindness.

United, we burn.

Once the fires died, taking with it the bodies of the brave souls we'd lost, the drinking began. Slowly at first, as they shared stories of their fallen. Memorialized them. Honored them. But it didn't take long for speeches to slur, and the drinking to descend into frivolous chaos. If I had thought Port Azure had been a big party, it had nothing on Loc Valen. A party for just being alive, for celebrating the end of such dark times, for just *being*, lasted an entire week. I was doubtful anyone remembered most of it aside from flowing ale, wine and spirits, and those spirits weren't the only ones flowing.

I sat on the steps of Ari'inor evading the winter chill by running flames over my skin. I chuckled, watching Vanneck and Aspen be overrun with more female attention than even Aspen could chew. Several inebriated fae cavorted for their attentions, though my heart ached when I saw Vanneck's eyes look sadly up toward the heavens.

Toward Lennox.

Lenore I'd spotted briefly. Wasted on fuck only knew what, throwing axes at targets. My guess is that Blue Dusk from before, or whatever it was called. Whatever it was, there was a sway in her step, and a fierceness in her eyes that became rather apparent when she drank. Most people release their inhibitions with drinking. Lenore fell into that category, but her predilection to violence meant that her inhibitions were drastically different than the average fae. I let her be, in order to avoid becoming the target myself. She'd come talk when she was ready.

"There you are. Fancy meeting you here." Locke's smooth voice met me, causing my head to tip back and a smile to grace my lips. He handed me a drink in a far too fancy cup that was far too gold, far too ostentatious for me, but I had to admit, for all Scorpio's faults, she had great taste in wine. I accepted the cup and drank it down as he settled next to me. His midnight hair shone in the fire light, giving him that ethereal affect that I'd once thought made him appear shrouded in mystery.

"If I'm using you as exhibit A, I'd come to the conclusion I only attract the best company." I batted my eyelashes at him in jest, breaking into a massive grin as he snorted a laugh.

"You make fun of my pick up lines and that's what you're going with?" His eyes sparked before settling into a knowing look. "Lark, you have to be able to do better than that."

"I come with the scenery, and we're a package deal?" I offered, earning myself a pained eyeroll.

"Is that a question or a line for me, your majesty?" He leaned over me to purr in my ear. I resisted the urge to swat him, but only just.

"Fuck the veil, Locke." I mimicked his overly colorful, newly favored expression that definitely seemed like in poor taste, a middle finger to death itself if you would. "Just call me Lark. For the love of the Goddess, I'm not even Queen yet."

"As my Queen commands." His roguish grin told me he didn't care if I was formally anointed. I was his. His soulmate. His Queen. Just his. And he brought his lips to mine before I could chastise him further about it. His Queen didn't have quite such a ridiculous ring to it. *Your majesty* sounded outright outlandish and *Queen Scorpio* still made me cringe inwardly for a half heartbeat before I remembered that was about to be my formal title. My coronation was in only a few weeks time. I had to remind myself that the red haired cursed Queen was gone, and I had my current life because of her. That was a mind bend I don't think I'll ever fully comprehend.

Since the curses shattered, Locke no longer wielded the shadows. No longer did the black runes score themselves into his flesh. It was odd seeing his skin without them, but the dark blue swirling runes of our court still adorned him and decorated his skin. But beyond that, I wondered if everything that happened had healed an integral part of him. Gone was the darkness that haunted his every waking thought. Disappeared were the ghosts of his past, the turmoil he relived day after day in the time I'd known him. He looked lighter, no longer weighed down by the burdens that trapped him for so long. It was wonderful to see the fae I love smile, those favorite dimples of mine peeking out so regularly, my own smile never failing to echo his. To see him actually happy, without the stress and tension of our doom waiting to upend it.

His ebony hair fell forward as he leaned down over me, just long enough to place us in our own world, under a canopy of him. I didn't get a chance to answer. His kiss collided with me in a way that entirely consumed every thought, every action, every single part of me, until I was entirely lost in him. The best kind of lost.

"This side of the veil and the other, you're mine. Even death won't be taking you," He pulled me closer even as he kissed me breathless. My hands wound around his neck, my fingers tangling in his hair, bringing him closer still. "Just as all that I am belongs to you."

I said forever, it was strange to think we actually had it. It felt like an almighty miracle, or an apology from the Goddess. Or perhaps I had to suffer in order to be worthy of such a fate as this. A down payment for the best of things to come. I kissed Locke again, our forever solid between us, unshakable and perfect.

We had won. And we earned forever. He'd said he wanted the time we deserved together. I'd said we had a small, solitary chance at this future. Looking onward together I finally let myself realize it, fully embrace the fact that we had done it. We'd lived it. And that I would do all of it again, every last moment, endure every agony, if it meant I could be on these steps with Locke. In every lifetime, in every age, and in any life beyond this, that would remain true. The darkness and shadows actually being behind us was so odd, but Locke's words from before the war came back to me in an echo of memory.

The light is brighter when we emerge from the darkness.

Epilogue One
A Few Weeks Later...

S tanding in the hallway to the throne room in a resplendent gown of teal and gold, with my hair up in a style that took one of my lady's maids an hour to rake and tease my hair into, and not without more than a few flinches from the comb digging into my scalp. She flinched each time I did, certain that a stern scolding—or worse—was in store, but of course, none came. She made me look lovelier than I ever had before, even for my vows ceremony. And I was sweating my ass off.

Why was it so *hot*? Even with my Water Magic, I couldn't seem to cool off. Everyone had attended. Everyone in Loc Valen, the courtyard filled to the brim of fae elbow to elbow in attempt to get a glimpse of the festivities within the castle Ari'inor. Fae from every corner of the Water Court were reported to be in attendance. Emissaries from other courts couldn't be missed in the throne room. From here, I could see the flickering red and gold finery of the Fire Court. Their bronze skin tones contrasted the red, making it appear more vivid and vibrant and indeed part of flame. Ignatius, I believe their king was named. The number of names I had to remember now was nearly enough for me to shuck Locke on the throne and wash my hands of this entire business.

The Earth Court, in their green finery, looked stoic and unfeeling as they cast judgmental eyes around the room. My gaze fell with hesitation on the Air Court. My heart twisted in my chest knowing I wouldn't recognize anyone. Certainly not friends who should have been here today.

Wren... Aquarius... In my mind's eye, I saw the Air Court fae whose absence was noticed like a stain. Standing and elevating her chin at me. A silent nod of approval. Wren stood in a shadow, avoiding attention but giving an awkward wave. Even a figment of my imagination, he was endearing, making my chest constrict so breathing impossible for a moment. I missed them fiercely. They both deserved to be here. Instead, the current Aquarius who bore the symbol, a tall, curvaceous woman with dark hair to her waist gave me friendly smile. A smile I returned out of politeness. I wasn't ready to see her, or anyone else, in my Aquarius's place.

Unbidden, my eyes travelled to the site where only weeks ago her body lay next to mine. I shook my head in an effort to dispel the thoughts before they ran away with me, looking for anything else to think of. Without hesitation, as if his soul called to mine, my gaze drifted to the one from whom death could not part me. The one whose body was entirely free from black magic. My heart. My soul. Locke. He stood resplendent in blue at the front of the hall, awaiting my arrival. I'd still never understand how being a prince and an assassin wasn't somehow a conflict of interest, but I'd digress. He was stunning standing before his own smaller throne next to the one I would be walking to shortly.

And he's mine. Our white vows rune on my collarbone above my heart, and his matching one I knew was under his shirt, saw to that. Not the clean, almost sterile white of the Air Court. This one was soft. Warm. Almsot pearlescent, with a slight shimmer that reminded me of a diamond catching the sun's rays for itself. After a previous ocnversation that felt like a lifetime ago, I was just glad it wasn't pink.

I'd never forget how Aspen bawled during the ceremony. Something Lenore never let him live down either, the memory drawing a very sincere smile, one I needed in that moment. He mouthed the single word to me, and despite everything, I felt my face heat slightly and a smile dawn on my lips.

Beautiful.

"Are you ready, Little Bird?" Aspen asked from my left before readying himself to meet Locke and the end of the aisleway. My head fluttered in a nod.

"You can't call me that anymore," I chided him.

He grinned wolfishly down at me, not remotely remiss. "Agreed. Calling you your majesty is going to be so much more annoying for you."

"I hate you." I tried so hard to keep my face straight. I fought valiantly, but ultimately the war was lost.

"No, you don't." He winked before turning away from me to take his place. I shook my head. He had me there.

The time had almost come. The Zodiac Guild had filed into the throne room, their black cloaks looking like ink spills in the foray of stunning gowns, glittering jewels, and an entire list of courtly titles. All to see me officially crowned. I thought it would feel like descending into the viper's nest. Instead, with Locke and our chosen family awaiting at the end of that aisle, it felt like a homecoming.

The walk down the aisle wasn't too bad. I kept my gaze on Locke, where he now stood next to my destination: the throne. The moment I took my seat, everything felt so real. So official. I sat where she sat, and the power of that wasn't lost to me. This was much harder than the walk down the aisle. Sitting here, I could do nothing but stare out to the sea of unfamiliar faces, the familiar ones all too few buoys amongst the strangers before me. That was when the heaviness of the moment cascaded around me, and I had to fight not to let it show in my shoulders. Locke's hand caressed my bare shoulder, a silent comfort. Movement to my right snagged my attention, drawing many an eye to see the Zodiac Guild stepping up the dais to the throne, despite my deadpanned expression. Frankly, deadpanned was probably the kindest I could manage them.

They exuded power. I could feel it from here. So why they did nothing to help anyone before The Fall was absolutely beyond me. They opened their mouths, speaking about honor and glory and righteousness. All things they themselves turned their backs on. I bit my cheek against my dislike of the Guild and the Greivling's whispered warnings about them. That they may come for us.

I'd like to see them try. If they couldn't thwart Scorpio, they certainly wouldn't thwart me.

"This coronation day is a bit unique," the shadowed guild leader said in a voice like stone. He crept his way across the dais to stand on the opposite side of the throne from Locke, directly next to me. I watched as his second in command, an unnamed member of the Guild, carried something forward. Something that solidified this moment in my head more than walking the aisle or sitting on the throne—the crown, resting gently on blue filigree, the gold and sapphire headdress shimmering and sparkling dazzlingly enough to mesmerize even the wealthiest of fae. A crown that was fated for my head. "This coronation comes without rune trials. But it did not come without strength. It did not come without sacrifice. It did not come without death. The trials prove one is capable of putting the crown above all else. Lark's own experience freeing the Water Court from the Brutal Queen was in itself a trial, and the Guild declares her worthy of the Scorpio title."

A flash of whole magic that descended upon us like a blanket of energy, flickering along my skin. I turned my gaze up at Locke, who flashed a quick smile.

"Lark of Poplar Hollow." The leader spoke again, turning to me as the fae with the crown padded up the steps towards me, my breathing growing more erratic with each step. The flickering of magic along my limbs, my spine, didn't leave. If magic were in some way sentient, I pictured it watching me, assessing me with ancient patience. "Do you swear to uphold the ideals of Scorpio in all things?"

"I swear, my lords, so to do," came my practiced response. My voice was stronger, less breathy than I expected.

"Do you swear to serve the fae in your charge so long as you hold the power of Scorpio?"

Were they always this grave and intense, or was it just the gravity of the ceremony? Of the moment?

"I swear, my lords, so to do."

"Prepare the swear spell, Lark of Poplar Hollow."

I stood once more. Once there was a time where I would have stood here trembling. Terrified. No more. Today I stood, my knees straight and still as I addressed the Court.

"I am Lark, not of Poplar Hollow," I began, watching with pride as Aspen, Vanneck, and Lenore lit up from their places before me in the front row. "I am Lark of Port Azure. I solemnly swear on my beloved husband, Prince Cancer, the Crowned Assassin, that I will act in the best interest of the realm. That I will hear the fae I serve and never let their concerns fall to my own interests. That today is the dawn of a new age. An age of healing and prosperity. An age of peace for everyone but those who threaten it."

I glanced at Locke through the corner of my eye, my chest lightening to see his proud smile on his face. The magic of the promise settled over me, forever binding me to my words.

"Sit once more, Lark of Port Azure."

Was it my imagination or did his voice warm slightly? Tepid water instead of the glacial tone that was there previously. I retook my seat on the throne, energy humming along every nerve. In that moment, I knew I was wrong before. Killing the curses wasn't my only destiny. *This* was.

"Rise as her majesty, Queen Scorpio of the Water Realm."

The moment I took to my feet, I felt that crackling magic along my skin sing and disappear, the magic spent. Cheers and applause erupted thunderously around the hall, deafening me.

<h1 style="text-align:center">Epilogue Two</h1>

The days following the coronation were a blur, after which I all but collapsed into a heap into bed and was unconscious before my head even hit the pillow. I saw so many faces, some new, some not. But Locke and I both felt the absence of one beloved fae—Lenore.

When I asked Locke about it, he thought she might have gone back to Port Azure, to seek comfort and process everything by her sister's grave, a sentiment Aspen also verbalized.

"She lost more than any of us," Locke said, his brows pinching in the way they did when he was concerned. "Give her time."

I remember what it felt like when I lost my father. When I'd lost everything. Revenge was, for a time, the only thing that kept me going. Lenore got her revenge, though I doubted her need for bloodshed was genuinely slaked. In the wake of that, knowing her, she'd feel like a buoy lost at sea, but would in no way ask for help. We would be her lifelines, as they all were for me.

Now Locke had jumpstoned to Port Azure to look for her, and I found myself at the door to her rooms in Ari'inor, feeling both concern enough for me to want to run inside and look for her, and a sense of trepidation at invading her privacy and getting something sharp thrown at my face.

My knuckles rapped three times against her door. "Lenore? Are you there?"

Silence.

I knocked again, louder this time.

Silence mocked me back.

I couldn't say why, but intuition begged—no, screamed—at me to go inside. The feeling that something wasn't right slithered under my skin until the hair on the back of my neck stood erect. Twisting the knob, I peeked inside, pausing and shielding myself with the door against potential projectiles. I almost hoped there would be one pinging off the door because I'd at least know she was here. My gut felt heavy as I padded into the room.

"Lenore?" I called out again, louder this time. "Where are you?" She was here. I could smell her in the room, the earthy, almost floral scent that I associated with both twins was sharp enough to tell she wasn't far. So not in Port Azure then. Dying embers in the hearth told a story too. A jacket lay draped over a chair, forgotten. I moved forward, peeking my head around the door to the bathing chamber and all I saw was black everywhere. The walls, the sink basin, the floor. There was hair on the ground, and the smell of blood tinting the air.

"Lenore!"

I rushed forward, hearing her gentle sobs from her place on the floor. I rushed forward, nearly slipping on the black, oily substance all over the place to get to her. As I held her to me, running my hands through her hair, I saw my nails turning black before my eyes. "Lenore, what have you done?"

Through her hiccups and sobs she told me in a voice more agonized, more vulnerable than I'd ever seen her, "I couldn't look in the mirror anymore."

I understood, realization hitting me like a battering ram. The oily substance everywhere was dye. Lenore had chopped her once blonde hair to her collarbone and dyed it black. But that didn't explain one last thing.

"Lenore, where are you bleeding?" Mutely, she showed me her hands, the knuckles sliced in a dozen or so small cuts. Then she pointed behind me to the mirrors, which lay smashed on the floor. How I didn't descend into a pool of razor glass when I ran towards her was beyond me. "We have to get you to Eldan. Please." She began to pull away from me, tears still rolling down her cheeks.

"Don't. I will not be seen like this. You cannot force me."

"Will you at least let me bandage them then?"

It was a long moment of her appraising me, looking so much like the first time we met before she gave me a single nod. I didn't hesitate. I was up gathering what I needed, some gauze, some tape, and with my knowledge of Lenore, it didn't take me long to find some alcohol to clean the wounds, though I was a little concerned with how little was left in the bottle.

She flinched but didn't utter a sound as I tweezed glass out of her cuts and sterilized her wounds in front of the hearth. I'd hoped the fire would drive some warmth into her frosty skin, but she remained cold as ice. She sat motionless and rigid as I bandaged her, all the while giving me nothing. I tried not to look at her, but the task proved impossible. Her hair had been sheared unevenly, black as pitch now, with dye all over her forehead and hands up to her forearms.

"Talk to me, Lenore." It wasn't a command, not exactly, but my tone told her I wasn't leaving until she complied. She was one of the reasons I stayed in Port Azure. I would be one of her reasons to stay, whether that was here in Loc Valen, or here on this plane. That hopelessness in her eye was something I recognized all too well.

That was when she finally looked me in the eye and told me the heartbreaking truth. "I couldn't look in the mirror. I can't." Her anguished sobs began anew. "Not without seeing Lennox. Every time I look in the mirror, all I see is my sister and I can't fucking stand it. I've destroyed every mirror in my rooms."

I watched Lenore shatter every bit as much as those mirrors. The strongest, most terrifying fae I knew, tumbled into a fit of loss and grief and despair, and I didn't blame her one bit. I held her through it, the same way she once did when I was falling apart and ready to leave Port Azure. My tears joined hers, knowing Lennox missed her sister just as much. Knowing Lennox could get glimpses of this, but she couldn't let us know she was here. And what let me know the depth of Lenore's pain was that Lenore, the same Lenore who pushed others away and held us all at arm's length, who didn't like hugs unless they were on her terms, clung to me as she sobbed, the fingers fisting on my sleeves. That might have broken my heart more than anything else.

I told Locke that I found Lenore, spiraling. I told Locke of my concern, not that he couldn't see it already. But his demeanor was confounding.

"What could you possibly be smiling about?" I deadpanned.

His assured smile widened, and with confidence in his voice he replied, "Because I think I have something that will snap her out of her depression. A project of sorts."

His project of sorts led the three of us to the dungeons, the torture rooms where Locke and I found out about his family. I dared not peek inside to see if that fae from before, the guard, was still there. The smell alone would be an offense to the senses, let alone the sight. It was odd not having to sneak around Ari'inor, much less Loc Valen. I kept eying every nook and shadowed cranny for someone to attack, but of course nobody did. Those loyal to the previous Scorpio or Pisces were long removed. Locke delivered us to a room just like the one we were in, and as I suspected, they were outfitted exactly the same. Lenore gasped, disbelief evident in the wide eyes, taking everything in. A large fae rattled his chains when his head lifted. I knew exactly who it was without anyone having to tell me. The same curve of the nose, the same deadly expression, the same eyes. This was Lennox and Lenore's father.

Indeed, Locke had been correct. Lenore's eyes brightened almost immediately with the fire of bloodlust, helping her to feel something other than despair and grief. She looked at us, and in a voice sweeter than molasses, she said, "Thank you for this gift. if you don't mind, I have a few sharp words for my father." She punctuated her point by glancing at the wall of sharp weapons. I didn't see which she chose to start with. Locke and I walked out just as the screams began, silenced by the door closing in a way most unnerving.

"How's she feeling?" I asked Locke on our way back up the stairs. "Is her aura looking any better?"

"Well, It's not instant!" Locke's dark throaty chuckle sounded his amusement, before his face sobered, concern creasing his brow. "She looks--" He paused, chewing over the words at his disposal, trying to grasp the right one-- "Satisfied, perhaps." He shook his head as he finally landed on the right word. "Focused. She seems focused, something I think will help her find some direction. She feels robbed of vengeance for Lennox because she wanted to see Scorpio suffer. But she's always wanted revenge against her father, so my guess is she'll be down there a long time. And when she's done, we remind her that she's never alone."

I couldn't have said it better myself.

Epilogue Three

I basked in the sunshine of summer, the thin material of my dress allowing me to soak in the rays like a cat, a brief bit of respite amidst my duty as Queen. Before me, I watched Aspen sending a small legion of soldiers through sparring drills, and I *almost* missed the days I would do it. The day was fast approaching that I trained again, but I was thoroughly enjoying my break for now. I smiled wistfully but remained more than content to relax and assess our army's potential. It was still odd to see training happen under the warmth of the sun after doing so underground in Port Azure for so long.

"Everyone looks good, *Commander*," I quipped, just to watch Aspen turn around to face me with a wide smile at his new title.

"Why do you sound so surprised? Unless you'd like to take a turn and show them how it's done, *your majesty*." His tone held the same teasing quality mine had, amusement flaring between us. I held my arms up in appeasement, a smile breaking my face.

"Those days are absolutely over for right now. If you think for one second you can make me do another sit up, you're set for the asylum." I grinned at soldiers sneaking looks at us. "My commendations to you all. I understand Aspen isn't always as likable on sparring mats as he is elsewhere," I glanced up at him before finishing, "but we sweat in here so we don't bleed out there. If you listen to nobody else ever, do listen to him." I gestured beyond the walls.

I thought Aspen was about to fall over. How many times I had rolled my eyes at that saying, and now I said it on his behalf. I couldn't tell if he wanted to laugh or throw me in a headlock.

"Who told you that?" he smirked. "Whoever it was, he sounds super smart."

"One of the smartest fae I know," I admitted to his widely grinning face. It was a rare moment, me feeding his ego like this. He was a lot like Locke that way; a single compliment went straight to his head and then there was no suffering him.

"In case you lug heads didn't know," he turned to walk back towards them after tossing a waggling eyebrow at me, "she's talking about me. I'm one of the smartest fae the Queen knows. So no more bullshit, get back to sparring."

A familiar face caught my eye in the corner of the training grounds. A small face, one much too young to be here. And yet, my own father taught me when I wasn't much older than him.

Elias watched diligently from the corner of the grounds, a wooden sword in hand. The youngest survivor of Poplar Hollow's massacre observed each drill with astute perception, mimicking each movement. His adoptive family had told me he wanted to join the Guard. That the second he was of age, he'd cast his sword in the fray for me. Which made it all the sweeter and more endearing to see the moment he noticed me watching him, turn beet red and run back the way he'd come.

I pressed my lips together in amusement.

Baby steps, I supposed.

Epilogue Four
Six Months Later

I walked the brand new cobblestone streets of Loc Valen, my footsteps fading into the throng of thousands of other footsteps around me. It was amazing how in six months the fae here were able to restore this city after The Fall—that's what we called the demise of the Brutal Queen's reign of terror.□

But it wasn't without scars. Or sacrifice. I insisted that the wall of Loc Valen, my first decree as Queen Scorpio after Locke insisted he was happiest in his role of Prince Cancer, was to be fixed in marble and gold. Complementing the pure elegance of the white from before while highlighting the memory of The Fall in a beautiful way. Some fae wanted to put the past behind us and forget about it. I refused. My father was adamant that was how history repeated itself, and that was not something I ever wanted to see happen again. Instead, reminders were everywhere in the newly renamed square—the very one I came to on my first journey here. Lennox Square.□

From here you could see the monument built into the marble section of the wall, seamlessly added in an impressive feat of magic, architecture, and incredible hard work. Every name of every fae we lost that day was scribed in gold with pride and tears into it. A memorial that all of us could visit and pay homage to. And in the center of Lennox Square was a statue of marble of my lost best friend. They even got the flowers in her hair to look delicate and beautiful despite being carved from stone.

On the wide and impossibly tall square rock she stood upon, were names of the rest of the fae lost to Scorpio and Pisces. I myself had scribed my father's name with tears running down my cheeks and Locke by my side as he carved his own family's names. Lenore stoically wrote Lennox's name, her breath leaving her in a sound somewhere between a shudder and a sob, the only vulnerability she'd dare show around this many others. But I was just glad to see her getting better. Becoming herself again. Fae huddled in groups with baskets of flower petals at the monument, adding their beloved family members' names and weeping with Lennox shining brightly above them, as she would have in life. Seeing her so lifelike in the stone before me both broke my heart and forged it together again.

"It really turned out perfect." A familiar voice, soft as a raven's wing, had me turning around. Raven back hair and sea-colored eyes met me, looking more relaxed now than I'd seen him, possibly ever. Though I didn't miss the sadness that shadowed Locke's face as he beheld Lennox's statue in her honor.□

"She'd love it." I smiled through the pang of sadness as I turned back towards the beautiful depiction of our friend. He nodded his agreement, quietly gazing at the statue as if he were searching for a way to speak directly to Lennox. Perhaps his soul was trying.

"Queen Scorpio!" Someone to my left brought my mind back to the present. I didn't miss the almost instinctive hiss, the collective flinch the entire square did before setting eyes on me in collective relief. It was just me. "Hail you, my Queen."□

Something that in my heart I knew I'd never be totally happy to hear that. Every time the words *Queen Scorpio*, my newly ordained official title, graced anyone's lips, it was everything I could do not to cringe. Though Locke reminded me every day that it was my duty now to cleanse the title of Scorpio from its reputation.□I waved with a smile before turning back to Locke.

I may not ever be the Queen they deserved. One who knew politics and the ins and outs of war. But I swore to these fae and the Zodiac Guild at my anointing when I ascended that I would heal the wounds of the past. And as my gaze flickered to a small mural of the former Scorpio, the Scorpio as she was before the curse, that was exactly what I intended to do.

A message from H. L. Hamilton

HOW IS THE CURSES DUET OVER?

I hope you enjoyed it! The only story I ever imagined myself telling. When I first started writing this, It was supposed to be a standalone, and as I wrote, I knew the story was too big for that. And now here I am trying to figure out how to say goodbye to these characters who have been the main focus of my life (sorry Justin!) for the last three years. I began writing only planning on telling this story, but I promise this isn't the last you will hear from me!

Follow me on socials to keep up with my next projects!

Special thank you to my friends Tess Watters, Bee Delcan, my favorite chaos fiend Kayla, my best friend for several years Nikole (who **you** may know as Aquarius), and M. L. Burns. I cannot thank you enough for supporting me through this entire book because I couldn't have finished it without you. Truly. Booktok is magic, because it has connected me with some of my favorite folks that I couldn't imagine my life without.

To Rachael Bindas, my writing coach for book one, my editor for book two. This duet wouldn't be nearly as impressive without you and I'm so grateful to have you. You were a stroke of luck I'd never anticipated but am so glad I have. You're a gem of a human being.

And then, darling reader, there is *you*.

Without you, there is no story.

Without you, Locke and Lark would only exist for me. To know that you love them too is a kindness and a thrill I can only begin to describe. Thank you. Thank you. *Thank you*. I'm so grateful to you for taking a chance on a baby author like me. If you enjoyed this, please consider leaving a review or taking about it on social media. I can't tell you how much this helps!

I adore and appreciate each and every one of you. And remember, when you're going through something, the flames don't need to fuel you. YOU are the fire. Watch your problems burn.

All my love,

H. L. Hamilton

Locke, Lark, Aspen, Lennox, Lenore, Vanneck

(Lenore signed for Lennox because she loved you too)